MODERN GREEK WRITERS

CROSSROADS

NIKOS BAKOLAS

CROSSROADS

Translation
CAROLINE HARBOURI

THE GREEK EXPERIENCE
Books, Music, Video, Art
www.**GreeceInPrint**.com
262 Rivervale Rd, River Vale, N.J. 07675
Tel 201-664-3494 Email info@GreeceInPrint.com

KEDROS

The translation costs of this book have been covered
by the Organisation for the Cultural Capital of Europe
"Thessaloniki 1997".

Typeset in Greece
by Photokyttaro Ltd.
14, Armodiou St., Athens 105 52
Tel. 32.44.111
and printed by
M. Monteverdis & P. Alexopoulos
Metamorphosis, Athens
For
Kedros Publishers, S.A.,
3, G. Gennadiou St., Athens 106 78,
Tel. 38.09.712 – Fax 38.31.981
July 1997

Title in Greek: Η μεγάλη πλατεία
Cover design by
Dimitris Kalokyris

© *1997 by Kedros Publishers, S.A.*
Athens, Greece

ISBN 960-04-1368-1

PART ONE

Fotis

No one ever knew, no one could, no one heard whether Fotis remembered his mother as he struggled in the high seas of the English Channel in '74. At the beginning he was clinging doggedly to a hawser on the deck, battered by the raging tempest, then later cursing in the dark, swallowing water and oil and tar, no companion beside him in the dark waves, not a voice to be heard; the sea took hold of him and he found himself tossed upwards, stunned, then lost in the depths, struggling agonizingly back up into the foam in a world that was nothing but salt and blackness, but then down once more, again and again, time after time, hour after hour, till in the end he was no longer able even to think whether he remembered how right his mother had been. For tell him she did, fifty years earlier, at home on the island, that "you can't swallow the whole sea but the sea can swallow you" – and it was happening right now, the waters gaped like a mouth beneath him, sucked him down.

His mother had told him, she'd foreseen it from the very first time he realised he could walk, could step over the threshold and wander off, when he seized the neighbour's two horses (one was enormous, a veritable wild beast) and rode them away towards the sea while his father foamed at the mouth and yelled, "Grab that pirate." Later on they lost him again one evening and set out to search on the mountains, calling "Fotis, Fotis, you little bastard", and only his mother took the lane leading in the other direction which came out onto the mole, and there she found him with the tide lapping against him, having fallen asleep as he babbled to the waves. The next day they hung him up in the olive tree, just like a criminal, and his father said, "you can stay there till the vultures find you and rip you to shreds so that we get some peace." But his grandad set him free – it was late noon by then, the others were all in the fields or in the village – and gave him a small coin: "here," he said, "lift Sultana's skirts for me" so that the old man could get a glimpse of her white thighs, this was what he longed for, to see them and groan; she wouldn't stand still for him and anyway neither could he lift her skirts himself – for years he hadn't been able to do anything except just feast on her with his eyes, a widow, fortyish, dark and wild.

However this might be, Fotis couldn't turn his back on the sea, its lure held him in thrall; come daybreak, come dusk, he was always to be found down on the shore, even during school hours – whereupon the neighbours would go running to his father laughing and tell their friend, "Fotis takes his book-learning measured in spoonfuls, here, take his exercise books, his pencils" which they had found by chance, the baker behind his loaves, the greengrocer amidst his melons, nothing but blank pages, crumpled and sopping wet.* Never once did Fotis hate or fear the sea, not even that evening when it rose and threw the whole household into confusion, his mother weeping, the neighbours lamenting that "now you will all be poor starving orphans", eight mouths to be fed – no, he didn't hate the sea, not even the night when they found his father butchered and drowned on the seashore and everyone said, "the Turks", for in truth this soul now departed had been reckless and his blows had fallen heavy on anyone in range, Christian and Turk alike – though on the latter more frequently. Fotis stood beside his brothers (together with their sisters they were seven in all), he stood in silence in a dark corner and gazed sullenly at the stocky corpse which they'd laid out on the kitchen table covered

---

* Fotis Katakouzinos or Evangelou or Psarelis (or even Sirtsis when the need arose, but Dimitrios not Fotis in this case) was born in Mytilini in the year of grace 1907 and perished, as is assumed, in the shipwreck of a freighter in the middle of the English Channel in 1974. His body was never found. In 1976 the police were looking for him in Thessaloniki, supposedly as the member of a smuggling gang. In the end no trace of him was found and his file was then declared closed forever. Some of the remaining members of his family wondered, compared and calculated. In vain.

only by a clean white sheet: wet patches revealed the form of his father's body and the soles of his feet were uncovered, huge, dripping.

He did not hate the sea, he did not cry, not even when they took the boat, his mother all in black with six of her children beside her (for her little Fotis had wandered off), her gaze blank and lost as if on purpose, as if to avoid seeing as first the coast and then the dark mauve-coloured hill with the tower of the fairy tale princess and the trees on it faded from view, as even the smell of the house faded and the scent of the olive grove which belonged to the landowner, yet they loved it. Fotis didn't hate the sea, he just looked at it in puzzlement, a little way off from the others as he hung from the gunwales, though by now the ship was under way and the waves were getting bigger, sometimes lead-coloured, sometimes foaming, so that you felt a chill down your spine and said, "if I could only snuggle down at her feet and get warm" – well, this was the sort of thing his sisters said, not he: for he was always seduced or spurred on by the sea so that in the end everyone said, "the sea got him" but didn't grieve since they'd lost him years ago anyway and used to laugh at his exploits, his adventures, as if it all came out of a book or was something that they'd seen at the cinema.

In '57 he wrote his last letter to her, to his mother, and this not because he had a guilty conscience or forgot but because their sensitive and forever complaining Myrsine left them. And his last letter to her was yet one more promise, "I'll come home" – and everyone was afraid that he really would. By now he'd lost everything he possessed, all he had left was a mouth for swilling whisky and eating, for telling stories; he'd offer the moon and stars and sign himself "your loving prodigal son" as if he was joking or laughing at her, and above this signature he'd draw a bird and a wreath, eternally blossoming May, and a bleeding heart, at which they either cried or burst out laughing. In '38 he'd come back just like some prince of Araby, in a silk suit, with a claret-coloured foulard and a solid gold watch on his wrist, with an utterly magical lamp whose flame sparkled like diamonds. His sisters and brothers and brothers-in-law all gathered round the table; like a magician he drew them closer, burnt black as black by the sun of Beirut, with a Douglas Fairbanks moustache, then, unscrewing the bottom of the lamp in a single movement, spilled out diamonds and jewels onto the table, a veritable treasure: though actually it wasn't Aladdin's but Eleni's. For no matter how much his sisters hoped and licked their lips and envied, a few months later they were obliged to recognise that the blood-sucking witch had swallowed up everything, their own Fotis included, who proved to be in love to the point of simple-mindedness.* And Christoforos, who'd known him at the Garden of Princes, said, "myself, I'd never wash her feet" – who told him about that? – but subsequently she lost all her fortune, a certain Antypas ran through it, a notorious pimp; he left her starving in one room, her looks gone, her titivations a thing of the past, and she well nigh gave up in despair but in the end made the best of things (a fine sieve, this old art of compromise) and got together two or three of the local females and set up her own "house". This was in '42. She managed to keep body and soul together: various doddering old devotees took care of this, as well as black marketeers and a captain from Dangoulas's security forces. From time to time Myrsine visited her – always in the morning – and they'd weep together over Fotis whom they both still loved, and when his mother left it was always with her nosebag full.

He meantime was a seaman once more, fighting on the high seas with the Allies, in the Libyan sea, then off Malta, until they shut him up behind a wire fence and he got a bit of peace and quiet. Later on, after the war, he was told the whole story; he went and found Eleni, and they both wept and made plans for

---

* The police officer N.M. knew all there was to know about Fotis Psarelis or Dimitrios Sirtsis. A long time before he became world famous as a result of his handling of the Polk affair, he had helped Fotis and Eleni bring their diamonds and sovereigns from Beirut to Thessaloniki. There was a rumour that the two men were old friends; however, this was either a deliberate distortion or a lie, for "the pirate" had set off to sea and to exotic lands in 1924, as soon as he was fully fledged, and had remained almost permanently far from Greece, whereas during the same period the other man was still living in his village. The most likely thing is that the policeman – who liked presents – either mislaid or forgot (the difference is small) some customs report. All this took place during the summer of 1938 while the country was staggering under the burden of the costs of rearmament and Alekos Kanellopoulos, Metaxas's right-hand man, was organizing repeated collections to raise money for the air force.

future enterprises. Except that this time Fotis didn't wash her feet – he'd come to his senses – but tricked her and left her and they both went their separate ways. It was said of Eleni that she'd settled down in some hovel in Alexandria, people forgot about her, she withered away and died. And he stayed true to the sea, until that night when he struggled in the Channel with the storm and finally the waves won, only then Myrsine wasn't there to tell him, to remind him, "don't stay out late, son, I'm scared of the cut-throats, the Italians with their razor blades." Because it was then, in '17, in Salonica, that Fotis jumped off the ship and said this is the place I've been looking for (even if he did abandon it later, fickle as he was, and preferred the sea, then later the desert, Beirut, adventure) – stories, so many stories ...

Anyway, that day when the ship arrived in Salonica the sun was setting deep crimson and everything was bathed in violet and rose pink – the seafront stretching out in a line, caiques and fishing boats everywhere, the houses a white wall with windows and balconies, sharp minarets here and there piercing the heavens like needles embroidering a picture. Gradually the crowds of people coming and going acquired feet and hats, some were in khaki but most in dark clothes and among them women like white butterflies, their skirts billowing in the breeze, and in a while you could make out their little hats, yellow and blue and bright green or whatever colour their heart desired: his own heart was already leaning from the ship in longing, ready to drink in whatever was offered, whatever it could find – eyes and lips and hair as it was to be before long, and in the end laughter and flirtations and a shawl thrown into the air. And Fotis said, "what fine people," no matter that they were arriving as strangers among strangers, as foreigners and orphans.

But by '74 the whole family was scattered. One fragrant rootstock remained in Salonica but all the others had left for Athens – indeed one of the girls, with a husband and children of her own, had crossed the ocean and lived in Sao Paolo, while another girl had travelled even further, to the other world, her family all in black with bitter mouths and tear-stained eyes. And in the depths of the Channel the lost, failed pirate battled in desperation with the waves with no one to hear his pleading and cursing and tears, nor any survivor to bear witness to his end or to tell whether it was as prodigal as his life – he who used to sign himself in tearful affection as "your prodigal son" yet always forgot to enclose among the sheets of paper with their hearts and birds the ten pounds that he had set aside or promised (of his own accord) and which he remembered after he had posted the letter and was certain that there was no way of getting it back – not even if he begged; he'd put his hand into his pocket and to his surprise find the ten pounds, all forgotten and crumpled, and he vowed they were for his mother, he swore that whatever he won at dice from that fellow would be for Myrsine and for the dowry of Niki, his youngest sister who was still unmarried (goodness knows, after far too long). But no one was ever aware of his vow if he won or for whom he grieved if he lost.

And once, in the days of his affluence, with the diamonds and the canaries and the exotic garden, his mother told him "you're heartless" – for all he ever sent them was postcards of luscious oriental girls or bedouins, or else tearful letters saying that two drunken Frenchmen had broken his ribs, that he was in pain, with no Myrsine beside him to soothe him as he lay feverish in his opulent bed and all his singing birds struck dumb. This word "heartless" stuck to him: Myrsine's daughters adopted it and it was then chanted by nephews and grandchildren – no matter how much pain Fotis had suffered from his ribs for two months and more. And Eleni it was who acted as his nurse and guardian angel; as they were beating him up she strode right into the middle in her shimmering satin dress with a glittering pistol in her hand and she shouted to them in French, just like Marlene Dietrich in a film, "hands up or I'll blow your brains out" – and that's how Fotis got off with only a couple of broken ribs – only two.

And this wasn't his last adventure by any means, nor his first, nor his greatest. In the end people called him "the adventurer", both strangers and his own family, and they made up their minds never to be surprised at anything, not even if they were told that an aristocratic lady and an expensive whore (who just happened to be called Aspasia) had come to blows over his favours in a courtyard and had torn each other's hair out like fishwives. For this too happened before he drowned, before he was in peril, long before, just when the battle of Athens was reaching its climax, in

December, the time of darkness and hunger and merciless killings, when Fotis had already forgotten El Daba, telling himself that it was one of his mistakes and erasing it from his memory. But all this was lost in '74 that night when the sea raged and the waves devoured him. And when five days later a calm had fallen and they were continuing to search, nothing of the passions of prodigal Fotis was recorded or betrayed or preserved in the papers that they found, nothing in the foam of the sea, in the roaring of the ocean, nothing of his life and of his city, nothing of the tales from Baghdad, of his wealth and poverty, of his loves or of his final agony at death.

For Fotis was gone forever, the admirer of Douglas Fairbanks, the actor and lover of pantomime, player of every part there was to be played – even that of the callow bridegroom in the Jewish ghetto at Ramona. And perhaps it all began when he said "this is how my life will be." And Myrsine and his sisters had wept for him, as if he were setting out on a journey to the angels.

Christos

Christos declared, "in that case I shit on it," and you might have said that he already had a philosophy, that of taking his work lightly. However, this judgement wouldn't have been quite fair, since the young man who was running furiously down the stairs at the "Independent" had already penetrated into the secrets of murder and all the jobbery that lay hidden behind it: how the Levantine banker had not been butchered by gypsy woodcutters but by some others – or maybe some other – who had wanted to learn his secret or the ins and outs of his bedroom, about the young man in the white shirt with plump haunches and curly fair hair. Except that the victim – and perhaps the perpetrator – had well-known names and it so chanced (?) that they were promptly forgotten, laid away in the drawers of the editor's desk, who once upon a time had worked as a teacher and who had learnt his lesson thoroughly. It was nighttime, past midnight, when Christos burst out "in that case ...", for earlier on, in the afternoon, he had gone to the Turkish baths in Egnatia Street – following information received – and had seen that two gendarmes really were taking the beaten up gypsies out by the back door (the younger one was on his own two feet, even if in poor shape, while the other was being carried on a café chair by two boys); and he thought of asking, of ferreting out who was treating the gypsies now, erasing their traces, so that they'd be forgotten and only their confession would be remembered: "yes, we killed him in order to rob him." And everything worked out neatly, just like the dice that Christos played with at Christmas, and his father would say, "watch out, they cost a fortune" for he was making a coloured painting of the Eiffel Tower, with the flower beds round it and the river and high above it the clouds. But the young man said, "it's no light matter" and doggedly went on shaking the dice – or the gypsies and the gendarmes.

All was in vain, however, because the former teacher amazed him; he buried the tell-tale papers and scared him by announcing that the case was closed – and with it all the questions and the doubts. "In that case..." said Christos in outrage, and he cursed all bankers and safes and all the corruption of the wealthy who were allowed to play with death, to buy it and sell it, to dress it as love and tart it up, a flashy perversion – and he cursed their mothers and their fathers and their riches and their sins. All the same, it was still all in vain, no matter that he felt like crying, like sobbing out his last stifled breath in a wave of tempestuous tears that could surge as the scalding water might rise – in a nightmare – to swamp his loins, his cock, his pale chest, then his tits, then further. And he said once more, "I shit on it"; the road was deserted, in places wet and dirty, and he could find no other way of relieving his feelings but to shout, "I shit on it, you bastards." Then, like a thirst, the idea came to him that what he needed now was a bit of dancing and some wine and Victoria with her plaintive songs and her white body.

The lampposts were out and Egnatia Street plunged into darkness like a dry furrow in the deserted countryside, except that lost in the depths (the depths of what?) two red lights were struggling not to commit suicide. And Christos hoped that they'd still be awake at Victoria's place, and they were, except that she herself had already left. But her devotees were there, her dispossessed and her remnants, scraps of paper or feathers that blew about in the wind and she the woman who swept them up, and a little way off from her place was a group of revellers – someone rather full of himself who fancied that he was sought after at the opera, and a dwarf who pushed his way in everywhere and gossiped and said, "there's a job lined up for you," and two other nameless people shrieking with laughter. Behind the lights was a tree, an unruly fig tree, and beyond it thick darkness, autumn, faceless sounds and voices, unjustified terror. And, like moths or mosquitoes, everyone stayed within the comfort of the lamps, within the narrow haloes of light that weren't large enough even to contain their song, let alone second it. Their voices rang out like clarinets wailing in the wilderness, they said, "in the time it takes for the night to end, we'll part."

And the next day Christos remembered the dwarf, that flotsam of the night, was reminded of how he'd said, "there's a job lined up for you"; for his boss sent him back to the police where, as they'd heard, Greeks and Jews had come to blows and were shouting, "there's maybe going to be blood spilt" or whatever they had been told to say. And he was obliged to push and shove and be jostled and battle in an underhand way with strangers' bodies in order to open up a path to the police officer's door, and there once more he was jostled and had an argument with the Cretan who was blocking the view but not the voices, and in the end he managed to squeeze in through a crack, to be squashed and humiliated but nevertheless to get in, and to stand in a corner where he could recover and get his breath back. From his corner he could hear the policeman telling a dark-skinned young layabout with a moustache and sideburns à la Zalamor, "you can't even undo the drawstring on your own knickers" while the boy was insisting that yes, "I can support a wife and children" – God alone knows on what his hopes were based, what he imagined. Only his mother said nothing but wept in despair; she seemed unable to bear the other mother, the Jewess, who was shrieking and chattering quite incomprehensibly. And the Greek mother, with all the bitterness that she'd swallowed down over the years, said, "ever since he was a baby he's brought us nothing but trouble and grief," as soon as the boat had reached Salonica he'd jumped from the gunwale onto the jetty and they'd lost him, they'd searched high and low until they'd run him to earth in the darkness at a cinema and had hauled him out by the ear – for he was only just over ten, nothing but a kid. And the gendarmes roared with laughter, perhaps asking themselves, what kind of a bird have we got here? while he stood in front of them, his eyes darkening as if he was on the verge of springing at them.* However, the policeman – whose face

---

* In October 1924 the case was heard in Thessaloniki of the abduction of the Jewish café chantant artiste Matoula E. by the unemployed Christian Fotis P. The offence had been committed in Larissa but because the two young people (he was 17, she not even 14) were both – albeit temporarily –

was so bright red that you'd have thought he was about to burst, either from laughter or from obesity – said, "get him out of my sight, I can't take any more," and the adventure thus ended in hilarity.

Christos couldn't help remembering that at the baths the gendarmes weren't laughing at all (perhaps they were looking sour on purpose), in spite of the fact that the gypsies were crying, "what can we do, Squire?"; maybe they were reckoning if we're going to be beaten to death we might just as well say yes, we killed him – better be finished off by a single rifle shot or give up the ghost in jail, for who knows when that would be? Although what seemed most likely was that they'd rot away in the Turkish baths where they'd just received such a thorough cleansing, or that they'd suffocate in the vapours of scorching steam or fear. Well, worse things happen, reflected Christos, they could throw you out of the window from up there, thirty feet above the ground, and then say he went crazy and jumped, or his brain was eaten away by syphilis, after all he had the nerve to kill the king. And this one here must really have lost his mind, for at the age of seventeen he'd had the nerve to abduct the girl and then marry her and was betting on a son: the policeman discovered this in the midst of all the hilarity, he discovered it with tears of laughter in his eyes and thus noticed neither the abductor's eyes nor the hatred in them nor the tears that he wouldn't allow to flow, which in any case nobody could have heard because the mothers were crying so loud, the Christian woman's sobs more wrenching, the other's more hysterical.

When the performance finally ended Christos went out into the broad street, into the freshness of the trees and the fragrance of the neighbourhood; in his pocket among his notes he had their names and addresses and discovered that the abductor and his sweetheart were both from Victoria's theatre, that the carnival pantomime troupe sheltered the beardless boy and his plump dark

residents of Thessaloniki, they were brought back to this city. The culprit, in the presence of his lamenting or tight-lipped family, admitted his guilt and declared that he was ready and able to make amends. Indeed, five days later Matoula was baptised Christian and they were married. A newspaper report of the time stated that the relatives cried all through the ceremony. Her name from henceforth was Marika.

little Jewess who had quailed in front of the policeman and tried to hide behind her bold lover – he who had led her astray and intoxicated her. And Christos felt they're like my own people, Victoria's children, who all got drunk together; as far as the newspaper was concerned he'd forget all about them, their names, where they lived. And this indeed is what he did, whereupon the editor blew him up and asked where they'd taken him for dinner and what they'd given him to drink that had made him lose his memory. Then Christos got drunk too and remembered the gypsies and the king's madman, he said, "I'll leave you the note with his name" and he meant the good-looking young man in white who slept (so they said) in the murdered banker's bed – and there wasn't anything in the least secret about this, not at the "Independent" anyway. Meanwhile out in the world it was twilight once more; the birds were hastening away to roost like feathers in the wind, and the taverns and cafés had switched on their lights, as he could make out in the distance from his window – somewhere out there shone the far reaches of Egnatia Street, the populous Vardari area with its little theatres and its low-life characters in the narrow lanes by the Barrier, the peasants who would be going to bed early and waking at dawn, setting off in the dew of daybreak for the climb back up to their villages. A breath of fresh air as Christos recalled childhood excursions: once they'd had a dip in the river and the teacher had thrashed them – but at this point the young man heaved a deep sigh as he bent over his notes and said, "poor gypsies" just as if they'd died and were being hustled into the grave unmourned*.

However nothing remains unpunished in life – and least of all at the "Independent" where the former schoolteacher was an expert both in punishment and in how to apply it. So they hissed at Christos, "we're taking you off crime" since he was too incom-

---

* In 1952, outside a small café in the Depot area, an old gypsy was to be seen who sat there permanently. They knew that he was paralysed and unable to work and they took pity on him and fed him. And he, half-crying, constantly stammered, "we didn't kill him, Squire" and he was referring to the murder of Arigoni which shocked Thessaloniki just before the war. The old man was alone and abandoned – his companion had died in the Occupation. Sometimes he plucked up enough courage to ask, "can you spare a fag, Squire?" And later on he too died and was forgotten.

petent or dangerous, and on the third evening of his unemployment (for such it was since they gave him nothing to work on but left him to his misery) he was sent to the merchants' club to waste time watching a song contest – girls who cherished the fond hope that they'll notice me, they'll listen to me, I'll be heard somewhere further afield than the kitchen and my own neighbourhood – and it's true that some of the businessmen were noticing them, all ears and eyes, while others were smiling and making signs, ready lovingly to help them achieve their ambitions in much the same way as they fed their canaries and their chicks of all kinds. And Christos's verdict was all these girls are a tragedy. He longed for the hurry across town and the patrols and the murderers and the harried two-bit thieves who'd stand in front of the policeman like so many saints and virgins, who when the officer said, "what, not you again, you ugly mug?" would shrug their shoulders as if to say yes, me again, how can I help it? However, round here everything was clean and shining, the dominant note being patent leather and black clothes, gold chains and carefully styled hair. Christos suspected that it was all a fake, both the singing and the hospitable atmosphere. He wandered around, feeling bored, thinking what have I let myself in for? In the end his ear was caught by a blue-eyed girl who stood out from the rest; they'd reached the third round and were insisting on continuing, and he thought, "she's got something." Beside him a bald man stood, smiling and beating time to "Since those days are past" which is what the girl was singing. She meanwhile was casting agonizing looks at everyone, although most of the patrons were busy eating or downing their drinks; their hardheadedness was having a day off in pursuit of worn-out bedroom visions, daring adulteries perhaps and kinky fun: some of them seemed to be making signs at her.

In the end the blue-eyed girl won the prize, her cheeks aflame, laughing and crying at the same time as everyone crowded round her and kissed her. Christos pushed his way in too and came up to her. On her jaw she had a mole – which transformed her into a young lady of mystery – and she blushed even more as they filled her arms with flowers and handed her the scroll containing the prize, and a violin was heard to make sounds of longing – he was a crafty one, its player – and someone else sighed ostentatiously for all to hear, and she received a flood of laughter and applause.

However, Christos thought, "that's quite enough of the performance" and went up to her and said "Amalia" – which is what he had heard people call her as they acclaimed her; she looked at him in amazement with a touch of panic in her eyes, she was wondering where've I met him? In spite of this, though, and with a great deal of trouble he managed in the end to take a photograph of her, in order to promote her. And the girl (soon to be the epicentre of everything) couldn't explain quite how it was that later that night they came to be walking together in the deserted streets, he telling her all about the various goings-on of the evening, both of them laughing. At one point he asked her, "are you on your own? Do you live alone?" "No," she said blushing. "In that case whoever it is has forgotten you or let you down," and she blushed again. And a little bit further on she confessed, "I live at the black tree" just as one might say at the White Tower or at the palace, and they both laughed. Christos thought, maybe she's a bit simple – but she wasn't, for in fact she did live at the "Black Tree", an old tavern, her house was somewhere beside it. And in she went, said "goodnight" and bolted the door. And he just stood there transfixed, the sound of the bolt being shot home imprinted for a second on his mind, and then he heard a woman crying in the bolted house, crying or laughing. However just at that moment two drops fell in his eyes and then on his forehead and on his outstretched palm: the black cloud must have been right overhead, above the black tree. So he set off back in case a storm was on the way, as usually happened; the crying in the house had stopped – maybe he'd just imagined it – and now heavy drops of rain were falling and he thought my suit'll be ruined. The following day he studied her photograph where her eyes weren't blue but where the mole showed like an erotic adornment on her chin, upon which Pervatas came up next to him and commented, "that's a nice little piece" and laughed at him, saying that women were his speciality (one evening he'd come in all beaten up with his clothes torn and had crowed, "the husband"), he bore upon him some trace of their fragrance. And Christos reflected, I'm twenty-five already and I've never seen a woman without any clothes on, a naked woman, he thought, then sighing took his notes and the photograph to the editor in chief, whereupon the teacher smiled meaningfully and said, "reduce it by half" which made him swear inwardly. It was a feeling of despondence, edginess, disappointment which he drained to the dregs like bitter coffee. He said to himself, "maybe if I went back to the black tree ..." He watched Pervatas sprucing himself up, combing his hair enthusiastically, getting ready perhaps for another assault – and he bent down and started writing and cursed.

Yannis

"The devil really is a many-legged beast," said the neighbours, who all the same couldn't have sworn that the devil wasn't called Yannis or that he wasn't a well-nourished young man dressed in white (mostly), since it was in summer that they'd made his acquaintance. And the gossip multiplied and spread that this scion of the upper classes who lived on his own, who had suddenly turned up amongst them, had a liking – a great liking – for strange company which didn't always consist of women or people of his own age. Yannis suspected all this – or imagined it – as he noted the looks the neighbours gave him or read their ironic smiles; it was mostly the girls who smiled, but one day it was the old bachelor. They happened across each other at dusk in the street and the old man looked as if he was laughing at him, as if he knew him, then entered a garden gate which he locked behind him and disappeared into his great house. He lived alone in the upper town and had a garden full of roses, honeysuckle over the gate, red curtains at the windows; in the narrow lanes of the Turkish quarter the legend was that his house was fitted out like a palace, full of expensive lamps and other precious objects. And Yannis said to himself, "one day I'll get in there" (this was when he had just learned of the old man's existence), for there must be comfortable low tables with strange new drinks and sweetmeats – just like some paradise lost and gone, secured behind lock and key yet not uninhabited.

And the devil indeed walked on his many legs. Except that in this case these legs wandered and wove their way, getting lost and discovering little alleys, new fragrances beneath wind-tossed baleful trees, they wove their way around in the twilight all alone, as if the neighbourhood had become strangely deserted, as if everyone had shut themselves up inside on purpose and said, "let him go to perdition"; maybe they were afraid of him because he was an outsider who didn't fit in, his sweat had no smell to it, only a whiff of lavender emanated from his curly hair or his half-open lips – lips that never spoke to them, for he never wished them good morning or goodnight, just as if he were soft in the head or mute, the handsome lad – which was something that didn't fit in at all with their street or their lives. And he wandered as though lost, except that in the end (by chance?) he came upon the great gate, all wrought iron and cast iron and impregnability, behind which were locked away the flower garden and the oriental sweetmeats and the secrets. He grasped the iron bars, the latch, the chain and muttered stubbornly, "goddamn you". And then he saw the doorbell, bright red, and he thought I could press it and scare them, they'd think I was the angel of Death – in spite of the fact that his shirt was as white as snow, open-collared, and a gold cross round his neck.

Then he thought better of it and moved away, set off on his wandering once more, enjoying the sound of his heels ringing on the cobbles in the lane and the redolent fragrances of unseen meals cooking, while above his head other fragrances proclaimed the blossoming of a world of trees. It was night, he was alone, he could have sung or danced in abandon, he felt a great thirst for it: this was what his wandering was in search of. At one point, like a whisper, he heard someone singing quietly but with deep longing – through walls and shutters the song came, perhaps through a white curtain embroidered with flowers and urns, impregnating them. And his solitude weighed heavy on him, he felt, I'm walking in search of someone, some company of the kind that suits me – for the banker was already dead and buried by then, lying beneath a great weight of earth and above him the impenetrable barrier of a gravestone whose coolness you could only feel against your cheek as you wet it with your tears: nothing but emptiness and pain.

And he walked without fatigue, he wove his way through alleys and unexpected little narrow passages, he suspected that he must be passing through the same places or by plants with the same scents, and then all of a sudden in this empty world a woman was approaching, or rather a pale blue dress, a flowing mid-calf length skirt, a handkerchief in her hand which she brought coyly to her face as if she wanted to conceal it. Yet her eyes as he came near her were burning with light, they fixed startled upon his with a spark of youth then were veiled once more beneath her eyelids, and she and her skirts flitted away, leaving only the scent of soap behind them. Yannis stopped short with a strange premonition; his wandering forgotten, he turned and watched her fade into the darkness and in his heart was the longing to see her again – maybe his diabolical powers would prove true. And he followed the sound of her footsteps, getting faster now as though she was anxious to disappear or was scared – and Yannis said there, that's just what I imagined, for the girl had reached the garden gate and grasped hold of its iron railings, she must be trying to open it, in vain though, and the next minute Yannis saw the handkerchief and the hand raised, he felt a sense of triumph, he'd guessed it, she was going to ring the bell. He stood silent, quite still, then regretted it: I've frightened her, and he wanted to tell her so, to reassure her, to confess that the only thing he cared about was proving his powers of prophecy or premonition; however, all he could see was her back, her short hair, two shapely legs, in front of her the familiar garden gate, beyond it dense bushes and the pure white honeysuckle, a garden without any scent – or at any rate whose scent Yannis had not noticed. For he was occupied solely in wondering what this gate and this beautiful stranger could conceal, yet the only thing he could perceive was her expression, some idea of her panic.

She muttered something to him, go away, and all his manners were forgotten, everything his mother had taught him before she died and he was left with his sisters and his father – and they indeed would have told him to go away, to leave, since they wouldn't have considered her to be the right sort of girl for Yannis who was the baby of the family and whose two sisters played with him like a doll, putting ribbons in his hair and round his wrists, covering him with kisses; they wouldn't have considered even this girl suitable, specially not this girl who was unknown, a woman with a secret maybe, her white handkerchief like a decoy, who was pressing the bell once more, this time with greater insistence perhaps. His feet remained rooted to the spot as if they had a will of their own, a doubtful will that was on the look out, watching, perhaps blaming him for so much curiosity which would disturb the pale blue dress and the floating handkerchief. He stayed there as if transfixed, said to himself, now she's got the wrong idea, felt himself blush; and perhaps they would both have remained there frozen in indecision or bewitched – but something was stirring at the gate, a picture was framed behind the bars, something that was taking a thousand precautions. And Yannis made out the mysterious old man who was approaching and looking at her – and who surely could see him too: a white presence in the dark, as if he'd worn these clothes on purpose in order to stand out in the darkness like an open wound, a bleached ulcer, a threat. The old man seemed to stand there in two minds, Yannis felt even more undecided; his ear caught a whisper though, and the girl asked, "when?" and then a word was hissed which frightened her so that she said out loud "excuse me".

And the indiscreet scene ended, the old man disappeared into the darkness or the bushes and the girl moved off, just as if she'd got the wrong address or person – which would have explained her apologies. And Yannis reflected that everything is possible, it's possible to get strangely involved with someone, to appreciate his charm, to see him secretly at night, to be tender with him, to lie in the midst of all the comforts that old age possesses, then one night to find him with his skull split open, a scarlet horror, and to leave by the back door even though you're not the murderer – for whichever way one looks at it you're a suspect. So nothing should seem odd, not even the fact that a girl comes at night to the locked garden gate or leaves as if she's hunted, tamed, obedient – or as if she's waiting for him, indiscreet youth, to move off before she comes back to ring the bell again. "I could have set an ambush for them," said Yannis out loud, and the sound of his own voice frightened him.

"You don't love animals, you heedless boy," he remembered the murdered man saying. This was when his mother had died and he had no one else to comfort him, to give him shelter for the night, to caress him. "I do love them," he'd said as if defending himself, "I do love them but they're tiring." For his father had a dog and had ordered him to feed it and take it out for walks, and it was terrifying to see the way it jumped up and barked so that strangers screamed in panic. "I don't like dogs either," his tender friend admitted, who was always cuddling his cats and hysterically holding them close to his breast. And when word went about that he'd been found murdered his cats had disappeared, and they searched for them in the gypsy quarter; however, it was a lie or a rumour, like so many of the other allegations which he feverishly read about in the newspapers, until they said, "the gypsies" and everything stopped short as if sliced through with a knife. And it was then that Yannis came and rented a room, he left home as if he was on the run, he said to his family, "I've got to be alone" and they all understood it or found it natural; and his father declared, "better that he should be away from us, so that we can cleanse ourselves of his prodigalities." He found a perfectly clean room and a woman not given to chatter, who, you'd think, neither saw nor questioned a thing: you'd say that she didn't breathe or that she flew even. The room had a narrow iron bedstead, a table and two rush-bottomed chairs, and on the opposite wall an old cupboard with a meagre mirror – and she promised him, "I'll clean it, it'll be like a palace," since she saw that he was gently nurtured and wore silk shirts. And she never asked what he was doing in their poor neighbourhood, she was always silent, her expression blank.

He could have set an ambush for them, he thought again. And without the slightest sense of shame or hesitation he found a corner in the shadows – where they wouldn't see him – and thought, I'll catch them. But there are sins and sins, he reflected, his own wouldn't pass through the needle's eye and perhaps not through the garden gate either, his father couldn't forgive them, and it was no consolation in a little while to see once more – as he'd expected – the pale blue girl coming back, casting a suspicious eye around, then taking hold of the iron gate once more. And he regretted having played games with her, said to himself, "she must be in need" probably of money or of something else, and he didn't think of revealing himself but instead held his breath, although he saw the old man come back, the gate open, the blue dress slip inside and then the darkness swallow up both of them in the nocturnal garden; and the young man was sick of it, there's no savour in it, he thought.

Everything within stayed dark, as if there was no one at home or as if they lived an odd kind of life, without laughter, without speech, the windows dark and no light shining under the doors. And Yannis wondered to himself, does he have cats which he holds close in his arms? But there were no signs of any living thing anywhere around. High above in the sky the stars were suspended, playing their lonely game as if threatening, "we might go out," except that Yannis wasn't taken in by this, he thought things are strange and without savour, and he stayed there in the shadows undecided; in the end he ran to the iron gate, searched for the lock, saw it was fastened and pressed insistently on the bell – it rang for a long time with a wild insolence. Yet no one answered it, no one even stuck his head out of a window or shouted; "just imagine if they'd put a doorbell on a tomb," he said to himself. All this was madness, however, the deafness of the house, his own behaviour or their secret which they kept so well hidden: perhaps this secret was a pale blue dress on a coat hanger or flung carelessly down, perhaps the handkerchief was left on a chair and the old man was in disguise like the sort of thing you saw at the cinema, scaring the women so that they said, "we're never going again," and the chief vampire emerged, or maybe it was just an old man with weaknesses. And he promised himself that the next day he'd go to the cemetery, he supposed that it must be the season for chrysanthemums by now, and he said, "if only I had someone to come to my room," and perhaps if he did they too would turn off the lights and not answer the door, no matter how much people knocked.

Then suddenly a voice said, "come on, Mitsos, play us a serviko" and the unseen person called Mitsos filled the nocturnal street with the wail of a harmonica. And he remembered once again how on the day they'd had him in for questioning about the murder he'd got muddled up without meaning to, "they might have been musicians or clarinet players," he'd said – but "or maybe gypsies" was what the investigating officer preferred to suggest. Now, closing his eyes as if the serviko was boring into his being, he pondered what might have been the cause of all this evil, and he remembered the split skull, blood everywhere, some of it missing, carried off by the murderer on his clothes, so that he must have groaned and cursed and washed it off. The investigating officer found evidence up there; "we can rule him out," he said of the boy whose clothes were white as white and who wore a glittering cross round his neck – and that's how he got off.

Nevertheless the crisis went deep, his family was badly shaken and his father said, "I disinherit him"; this didn't necessarily mean that Yannis was about to die, so he went off and took refuge in the upper city, in a poor room and in his walks. "It's as if he'd hidden himself or buried himself alive," said his sisters who loved him; they wept and beseeched their father and kept their pocket money for him – maybe he'd need it for he'd never learnt how to manage. Yannis was stubborn though, and acted as if he were punishing himself, so much so that his sisters' tears became ever more copious, they searched for their brother and couldn't find him, they were afraid that he "might do something crazy", something to which the naughty boy – or, as his father exploded, "the little tramp" – was not unaccustomed. Everyone had good cause to say that the front door of their family house was never opened again; except that no one cared to find out whether Yannis ever knocked on it, whether he accepted the way things were.*

His grudge evaporated in front of the iron gate; the house remained deaf, the garden dark and the entire pale blue story plunged in obscurity. The lament of the harmonica dragged on, it seemed to have settled somewhere at his back, to be whispering in his ear "go away from here"; they were words spoken with love, and in the humble house people were clapping their hands and a rasping voice said, "unfaithful women should die," and maybe these women were hiding in the darkness. But this was pure imagination, linking things that didn't belong together; now of his own accord he said to himself, "you'd better go." The night's adventure was over, he could go and lie on his bed and enjoy the fragrance of his cool pillow, and there in the uninterrupted dark-

---

* A great many different things have been said about Yannis's life during this period. One rumour maintains that he was taken care of by a part-time gravedigger who used to take him home from time to time or helped him in other ways. Others meanwhile claim that a woman, a certain A., was the person who gave him shelter and maybe fed him. Nothing has been established with any certainty, however, and perhaps these various versions were reinforced by the fact that for the rest of his life, until the day he died, Yannis remained close to these two people.

ness he could dare to set out the problem, he could open the exercise book of fantasy, could caress the pressed leaf which would mean the end of the fairy tale or the beginning of the dream: the dream that his good friend was still alive, caressing him, speaking to him in a tender murmur about his mother, about animals, about the blue dress which was confusing the problem in his mind – and he said the solution to be shown on the screen next Monday at the "Modern", in the last dark rows of seats where he had once seen two men unbuttoning their trousers and pulling their cocks out. "How disgusting," he said in front of the iron gate; and what he really meant was himself who was leaning and sliding towards grossness – "like a pig wallowing in the muck" would have been his father's harsh comment.

At this point, as he turned to leave, he saw in a window opposite the silhouette of a woman, dressed all in black, silent. His steps became more rapid as if in terror, he remembered the day when they had buried his mother, the women all in black, he increased his speed, started to run, realised that his lonely heart was beating hard. And the last thing he remembered was the sound of the harmonica fading away.

Angela

If people asked Angela, "where did you once hang up your hat?" meaning, "where do you come from?" she would answer, "the lost city" where they spoke an orientalised dialect, a bastardised version of the language, and she called it "lost" not because the Turks had swallowed it up but because it was lost somewhere in eastern parts and didn't even appear on maps – so it wasn't even a city. In any case, she wasn't from Smyrna nor from Constantinople or Bursa or Iconium. And her first hat had been a little pale blue cap that her mother had knitted for her: "put it on now, it's snowing," she'd called after her as Angela ran out into the plain like a fawn. That was in the time before the Agamemnons came, before the savage hatred. Because in the end everything turned to tragedy, the family was scattered; when she arrived (it was dawn as she disembarked from the ship) she couldn't even say any longer who was alive and who was burnt to death – or butchered – and all this took place at Smyrna. For they had longed anxiously to get to Smyrna, people used to say, "it's our homeland there, our own sea." Nevertheless it was there that she lost her mother, her father was drowned and her grandad couldn't take any more, and she sobbed in agony, "I'm all on my own in the world now," just like the lost daughter in the fairy tale who's surrounded by misery and terror though in the end everything works out all right.

However, in order to get through to the end of the fairy tale she had to live, she had to sleep, she had to dream. Eugenios used to accuse her: "you spend your time lost in fantasies and lies," he said, Mr. Eugenios who only desired company, all he wanted was for them to fall asleep in each other's arms under the bedclothes – nothing else. It could be that he was afraid of being alone, "there are so many gypsies out there in the alleys," he would say; and Angela thought about the murder and one night said laughing, "don't hide your gold under the mattress," it was a chance remark spoken at hazard, but he looked intently into her eyes, scrutinising her meaning. "Who do you go around with?" he asked her, and it was as if they'd entered some different house and he'd put her in an antechamber and had locked his soul out of her reach. Afterwards she laughed at him and caressed him and kissed him, but he remained dry-eyed and stiff, like a dead body no longer sentient. It might have been his solitude that made him nervous, yet maybe he wouldn't have taken just anyone for company; one day he said, "I trust you, you can have charge of the house and the keys of the cellar" which was always empty, pitch dark and full of cobwebs – thus Angela laughed, "you haven't got anything to make me envious," she murmured, then felt sorry for him, the night that they went to bed she laid herself bare before him, "I'm not a virgin any more," she stammered, but he seemed terrified and sighed, "why, Angela, why?" he whispered and began to caress her.

The master's hand, raised in benediction, the first three fingers together, the last two crooked, reminded Angela of their little church with its stand of candles; "you must light them," they told her, when everyone else was about their business, with the animals or out in the woods. The image came back into her mind, somehow it was connected with the night that she'd first gone to Eugenios, when he had put out the lights and left her only with a candle: "this way everyone will think there's no one at home," he reassured her. But Angela couldn't understand why they had to hide, she'd been recommended to him to work for him, nor did she come to understand it afterwards, not even when she started staying there at night – anyway it was too late by then to worry about it and she trusted him. But Eugenios had his own world, his own rules, and thus told her, "come after dark" so that the neighbours wouldn't see and envy him or perhaps gossip about him. And it was all a signal: her white handkerchief, the doorbell – except that everything became a bit more serious when the girl said, "someone was watching me." "I hope to God it wasn't a gypsy," said

Eugenios in terror, but "no," she reassured him, "he was like an angel, all in white." And the old man teased her, "the angel and Angela", he said but neither of them laughed.

"I'm afraid to get mixed up with boys," she confided, remembering the ship and the evening when they'd surrounded her – there must have been five of them – and she ran like a hunted animal; but the corridor and stairs were dark, she ran, gasping, and remembered their village, her father saying, "I'll slaughter it" and a young goat running, whereupon little Angela had stolen the knives, hidden them, thrown them into the stream, so that the following day they all went hungry and the girl hid in the tree, a huge mulberry tree, its canopy of spreading leaves full of sweet scents and insects. So maybe the young man in white was one of the men from the ship, he might have cut one of the sails from the rigging to make his clothes – and she said to herself, "I'd better cross myself to exorcise him" and out there someone was ringing the bell, knocking twice, three times, then fell silent. Eugenios ordered her, "don't move, don't go and open the door" and extinguished the candle. "I'm afraid of the dark," she confessed, and he held her close, her face against his chest so that their words wouldn't be heard (this was what he thought), wouldn't even reach the threshold – and his body smelt of lavender which made her feel dizzy. I'm afraid, thought Angela, for when they were pursuing her on the ship everyone else had been asleep, she remembered, she'd heard their snores, asleep as if drugged or under a spell, and her pursuers the only living beings left.

On the outskirts of the village was Omar's hut, everyone knew him, he used to sing for them. Well, one day as she walked by his place Angela got scared stiff; he was lying stark naked smoking, lost in a dream (he didn't even notice her) and the whole place smelled as if someone was burning incense and from time to time he laughed at the trees. He might be drunk, she'd thought, but then one day her father got angry and hit the singer again and again, shouting at him, "you're stoned, you good-for-nothing" – and the phrase stayed in her mind like a question, and she said to herself, "it must mean something like 'you've stripped naked'", he had round breasts covered with a black fuzz, and hair on his belly growing downwards, and ... On the ship one of them had taken his trousers off, "hold the bitch still," she heard him cursing, and she felt his nakedness against her nakedness, the others had her by the hair, pinning her arms, like a slave-girl, and she felt (it wasn't even a thought) that all she could do was kick and she heard a howl of pain, "the bitch", then a door slammed, the lights went on, then nothing else. Later two old women took her under their care; they wrapped her in their black kerchiefs, whispered, "she's fainted," they gave her food and water and never once left her on her own.

But later everything went wrong. And there in the dark, in the lavender emanating from Eugenios, she said as if in invitation, as if weeping, "I'm not a virgin any more." But all he did was hold her close, "hush," he said – in case anyone was listening at the door. Someone was playing a harmonica somewhere, maybe someone was clapping, Angela fell silent and reflected, it's a wounded sick house, and she meant Eugenios's. Only she could find no healing in her torments, he was afraid to go out into the street even at midday, which was quite inexplicable. And once when she complained to her elderly friend he said to her, tight-lipped, "you can't say that you've been hungry or hurt, if that's what you think you'd better go," for he might have considered her ungrateful, only he called it "ingrate" and confused her; the following day she cleaned the whole house for him and washed the curtains and sang for him. Nevertheless she saw that he was pensive, and when she asked him he answered, "I'm thinking of what will happen to you when I die," and he meant in whose arms she would seek protection and food and love. But she embraced him and petted him, "I can't stand young men," she assured him, their naked skin and their black hairiness, the way they look at you as if they're hungry, like hounds with flaring nostrils scenting their prey or like that pack on the ship who hunt you down and catch you and bite, then scream in pain when you kick them, and go off leaving the sound of their crying in your ears.

The night had advanced, everything was quiet, the darkness remained impenetrable, and Eugenios was sitting perfectly still, as if he was afraid of his own footsteps, afraid lest someone should pick up his scent or ring the bell again. At last Angela said, "it must be midnight" and nature was calm, surely the neighbourhood must be too, and in the nether world as Eugenios used to call it, playing with words (when he was in a good mood – he

meant the lower city that spread beneath their feet), the only
people still about would be the outcasts: actors, night watchmen,
pimps, a few journalists, women with no family. He said nothing
though, only she felt him give her a slight push and then get up
and go to the window. From somewhere a faint light reached
them – it must have been from the stars. She got up cautiously
too, the creaking floorboards scared her, and said, if only I could
slip out and fly, and she meant out of the window and out over the
trees, above the lost neighbourhood which she now felt was held
at bay by the iron gate, out over the tangle of little lanes where
people might be shouting and laughing. And after a bit Eugenios
whispered, "you'd better leave alone," he considered it wiser, for
himself (as she thought), for his reputation, for his own safety
he'd open the gate, let her out, then lock up behind her in silence;
it never occurred to him that the streets would be deserted, that
pitiless darkness would reign, that Angela would find no succour
but would be pursued, running downhill like a woman deranged
until she was out of the network of narrow lanes and had come to
the main thoroughfare, with lights and people singing. And as she
emerged from the garden she heard a boy's voice singing tipsily,
"you don't want me once, I don't want you twice," while all above
was a confusion of stars, and at the side of the footpath on the little
ledges in front of the houses, were old tin cans planted with
flowers and all manner of aromatic herbs, so that her fear was
quieted and she thought, if I follow the scent of my own footsteps
I'll find my way, and into her mind came all the householders and
respectable workers who might be saying, make up a bed for her
to sleep in, give her food to eat – just as the old women had taken
care of her on the ship, and they had brought her to where the
paved streets began, back onto firm ground, where there were
dozens of large houses and people coming and going and chatting
to one another, and in the end they caught sight of her ragged
clothes and wondered a bit, drew back, but didn't laugh.

And she ran and ran downhill along the alley that snaked its
way through houses and fragrant courtyards, until she came out
at the square with the plane tree and said, "now I know which
way to go" because she had once lived in a hovel in this quarter –
she ached as she remembered it, for it was here that they had
robbed her of her last treasures. But that was another story... And

when she had finally got up enough courage with Eugenios to tell him of all her trials and tribulations he had sat silent as if being punished, then had whispered, "I'm sick of all these fairy tales" and then even more quietly, "if you hadn't wanted to ..." as if she'd put herself in pawn to him, as if she owed it to him, when six months ago she hadn't even met him, hadn't climbed the path to his house or to his double bed – "I like having space to stretch out in," said the man, so she lay right at the edge just like some poor rag or a pet animal that is loved and brought in on rainy nights and fed on left-overs. "Don't tell anyone about it," he begged her, for fear that his good name be sullied – he who had lived a lifetime of politeness.

"And a lifetime of shame," Angela might have confessed, who felt something rending her insides and her speech as she hastened down the hill. Only a little bit further, she thought, then I'll reach the tramlines where a different sort of people are about, the cafés still open, cars, groups of upper class people coming back from parties, singing and laughing. Only she said to herself, "some people sing in the poor alleys too" and then was startled by three men in dark clothes who were leaning on a lamppost, its pale light illuminating their shoulders, their necks, their large, strong hands in which were held guitars that they were tormenting, just as if everything happened on purpose. They were singing a strange ditty as they stood in front of a two-storey house

> *... your last hour*
> *has struck, Saporta,*
> *I'll stab you over and over again*
> *as soon as you show yourself at your door...*

and she reflected that she'd never heard it before, but of course it was a large city, how could you manage to hear everything.* And

---

* This was another of the exploits of F. and his companions, someone called Kokonas and a certain Douflias. Saporta worked as a clerk in the Belgian electricity company where F. also "worked" for a short season between his more risky undertakings. The Jew was either peace-loving or timid, married with two daughters. He must have trembled for nights on end before he finally confided his trouble to Christoforos and asked him to intervene with F. who was a relation of his. However, even if he escaped

hypochondriac Eugenios came to mind again, with his gramophone kept closed and silent – "the neighbours might hear," he said, at which Angela got angry and snapped, "it's not as if we're swearing at each other or having a row" and the old man went off and shut himself up in his best room and stayed there in silence – until they both repented.

And as she was passing the three men and saying to herself, only a little bit further now, she heard one of them sigh – the others both laughing – "come and heal my wounds, sweetheart," mocking her, and he started to follow her. And the other two were amused and called to him, "Zalamor, that isn't what we came for," but by now he had caught up with her, he wore a curious cap and had long sideburns, a little moustache and predatory eyes; "I'd take you back to my room," he said, "except that my wife and child are there waiting for me." Oh God, what an incomprehensible man, for now he simpered as if dancing or making a bow and they all burst into laughter, "I don't do it up against a wall," he said and clutched his privy parts. And then just as suddenly he left her, the other two were waiting for him by the lamppost roaring with laughter – and Angela was near tears, she'd been frozen to the spot but now her steps were hurried and behind her she heard the verses again

> ... *my stiletto is well honed,*
> *I'll draw it fast,*
> *I'll rip your heart open*
> *and I'll ....*

but she didn't hear what would happen in the little lane in front of the two-storey house that night.

from F., mainly because the latter fled from town, he did not manage a similar escape from the Germans, in spite of the fact that in '43 Christoforos helped him once more. He and his family disappeared in the camps in Poland. The two-storey house went on standing until 1952. At the end of the Occupation and for a little while longer it was lived in by people who'd been made homeless by the guerrillas, then by a family who flitted by night in exactly the same way as they had arrived. For a while it stood empty, as if haunted, then one night it was burned down – by whom or why was never known. Perhaps it was simply carelessness.

For she had already reached the main road, and her heart was leaping like a bird that's been frightened. In her soul she was crying, curse all the Agamemnons and their army. But in front of her she spotted an officer walking briskly; he was dark and slender, something like Omar back in their old home, of which her godmother had said quite incomprehensibly, "wherever there's land there's a homeland" and she'd never understood what this meant. For a moment she considered running up behind him and asking him, "can I walk beside you" for she was scared of the ditties and the knives and the darkness; however, she changed her mind again and thought, Eugenios will have got undressed, he will have hung his jacket on the chair, and his trousers with his waistcoat on top and his uncreased shirt, maybe he was dreaming of perfect peace where no one would ring the doorbell and scare him or wake him. But she herself was wide awake and alone in the street which was steadily becoming emptier, she saw her reflection in a shop window like a pale blue ghost, her arms almost bare, her little heart jumping as if in a fit of ague. And she remembered her first hat which was also (by coincidence) pale blue and which her mother had knitted for her. And she gave a single sob which stuck like a lump in her throat. And it was a long way to her little shack and to her longings and her stubborn tears.

Fotis

"Abducting people seems to run in the family," joked the policeman, and another added, "same old characters, same old comedy." Only the two mothers were not laughing, they were looking grim and pleading yet one more time, and by the end were shedding bitter tears. The toddler stood doubtfully in the middle, the Christian woman pulling him one way, then the other woman the opposite way, so that in the end the policeman ordered the child to be brought to him. Who had abducted the little boy and to whom he should be given was a matter for the policeman to decide – except that the Christian woman's daughter leapt forward and said, "we're not going to have him made into a Jew," but the other side fought back and insisted that he was their child, their daughter Matoula's child, who had been baptised Marika and abducted for a second time. "But where have they gone?" asked the policeman who was getting confused – and he meant the parents – their bold Fotis and the little Jewess whom he'd actually married. "They've run off to Egypt," wept his mother, "and they hid the child from us." And when they'd found out about it (she didn't say how) the women set off on the lonely road and the whole business between the Christians and the Jews started up again, for the women asked and asked and discovered; and there in the unfenced courtyard in the Jewish quarter of Ramona they found the child, urine-sodden and snivelling without cease; the other family had left him bare-arsed and barefoot, and he was eating with a puppy. And lucky it was for them that they came upon him alone and abandoned in his own filth, beside a wall that curved away without end, and they took him by the hand and caressed him and said, "come with us, angel," but he answered them in Hebrew, he cried "tsinika" and "tsinika" and the women were horrified that he'd become an infidel. However in the end they understood when he pointed to the plate ("he was famished, officer") so they took it along with them to make him stop crying, afraid lest the whole quarter should rise up against them – but all the same a little way further on they threw it onto a rubbish dump just as if it was poisoned bait, and no matter if he cried his heart out now; for they were out of the danger zone, and were even safer when they found a cab, they crossed themselves and sank back under its black hood and the horse's shoes flashed.

But running away and Egypt were not any kind of solution and Fotis and Marika came back just at the crucial moment, they rushed in and said, "our child" just in case anyone was about to butcher it for them in a fit of pique. And everyone was now present at the police station, shouting and bewailing their plight, except for the girl who was merely crying. And just at the most difficult moment the Jews pulled out their ace, "he's a murderer," they said, every night he went and sang threats outside their houses, and the next day at the Works that no-good Fotis skived off from work, it was a crying scandal, every so often they'd see him walking off whistling, pretending to limp, farting at them, saying provocatively, "I'm off to have some fun," as if implying, "you poor fools". And they had words with Saporta who went easy on him and let him be idle – they went running to the director, they told him the whole story but Saporta answered, "what can I do?" and he was trembling, it was if he was saying he'll kill me, and true it was that Fotis had a stiletto which he displayed to the terrified Saporta, the others didn't see, nor did they hear how Fotis muttered, his back to them, how he hissed between his teeth, "a ten inch blade", then "you'll be hearing me in the darkness" – and he meant the threats that he used to sing to him in his own neighbourhood, below his windows.

"Where did you learn these skills?" the policeman asked him in surprise, for he was something more than a petty thief or a gypsy woman only capable of pinching the odd loaf of bread or at most some washing from the line, or at worst the Virgin Mary's eyes. But when it came to arts he was a master, he used to act in the pantomime and danced a hasapiko for them, leaping over a chair, he used to sing at night in the streets round various neighbourhoods, he'd carve the handles of pistols and knives with hearts and birds and little leaves. And everyone laughed when they heard him except the two mothers who had both found rifles under their beds and pulled a long face in despair – each for a different reason.

"A whole lifetime on the run," Myrsine would have said, and Fotis would have agreed that in the great fire – they had only just arrived in Thessaloniki then and were living like rats in a basement – they ran to steal what they could and were pursued by the Englishmen with their lashes; and when she asked him, "how come they didn't catch you?" he replied that if they managed to run as swiftly as deer it was because the cobblestones were scorching their bare soles so that they ran in great leaps in order to find some relief or to get away.* "And the lashes, the Englishmen, the blacks?" – they were a whole different world like something exotic out of a fairy tale, which Fotis knew, perhaps he'd been in search of them, dreaming of them since the old days back in the island, the time when he'd made off with someone else's horses and all the women in the neighbourhood ran out and tried to scare him with "you'll kill yourself" – but he survived. "A lifetime on the run," sobbed Myrsine when the Jews caught him and beat him up, "he's a foul-mouthed thief," they said, "lock him up" – and it's true that he had abducted Matoula, and it's true that he had cursed the pentangle, and in the end turned everything topsy-turvy by marrying her. And the baker and the grocer were after him too for the bills he'd run up, he was aware of this and came home at dawn or slipped away like a shadow at night, and in the end he upped and offed and didn't come back – and his sisters paid his debts, his sisters who embroidered and laughed and at

---

* Among the many things that took place during the fire in August 1917, Stratis and Fotis Psarelis and a gang of children from various neighbourhoods went to the burnt quarters in the hope of benefitting from the looting that their elders had begun. The police force of the Allies and the Cretan gendarmes were trying to maintain order and were hitting out with their lashes at anything or anyone in range. Thus the two children returned empty-handed or with trifles of no value. And they complained that they'd burnt their feet on the hot cobbles, that they'd been on the receiving end of the lashes and that the smoke made them vomit.

last said, "our pirate's run away" and remembered their drowned father and all the exploits and the departure from the island.

Myrsine in her desperation said, "we've baptised him and his name is Angel," and the policeman seized on this, "fuck religion – make the sign of the cross, you little bastard," he laughed, and the child looked at him without moving and in the end burst into tears. However, the officer happened to have a couple of sweets in his pocket and he gave them to the child to cajole him; he gave a searching look at the adults, one by one, then bawled, "right, get out of my sight, you animals." Myrsine imagined that he winked at her so she picked up the child and said, "let's go" – and off they all went, except for Matoula's mother whom the policeman ordered, "stay here, I want to talk to you," and no matter how much she protested he held her back. So the others left, the mother in front with Angel, beside her the sister and behind them Fotis and Marika looking as bitter as if she'd swallowed poison; they walked home, went down the steps, and everyone was there sitting round the table waiting for them. And they decided and insisted on it, they'd clear out one of the rooms and the couple could sleep there with Angel, they'd feed them with what little they had – and "it may be little but it's honestly come by," as Myrsine used to stress, who was a familiar figure at all the churches in town and known to many well-to-do ladies; she washed for them and ironed for them and left late in the evening, then back home to her own housework, to look after her own children who – as was amply demonstrated – were of marrigeable age, now that the English had left and had taken with them the niggers and the Chinamen, and the Italians and Serbs and all the other foreigners had gone too.

"But you two aren't afraid of the blacks," Myrsine probed, and her son laughed and replied, "Marika's terrified of them," who vanished one day as if by magic and they searched the whole neighbourhood asking for her; until in the end they reached her mother's house – it was dark by then and they saw lights, so they said, let's spy on them and eavesdrop, and all they saw was the girl weeping and her mother standing there without speaking to her or listening to her, just standing there like a rock. And Myrsine took her son's hand in warning, lest he dare some further exploits, she held on to him and only just managed to bite back the cry, "see what you've done, you accursed man." And they didn't go in, neither did they make their presence known, but by hook and by crook she managed to get him back home; "she's a mother," she insisted to him, wanting to say that she herself was too, she'd have done the same if she'd been insulted. And thus Fotis and Angel slept alone that night, and when they awoke in the morning they found Marika on the steps; his sisters brought her in and kissed her and gave her something to eat and drink and they gave her a red dress – it was the end of summer and the leaves were turning gold, falling in the courtyard and decorating it.

So they lived like the holy family and three months later Fotis said, as if enjoying it, "any minute now I'll be off to sea," for they'd called him up to do his military service, he'd reached the age for it. And the crying started up again, mostly from Marika this time, she hugged Angel and said, "how can you leave us?", but there was nothing to be done about it, the sea was calling him and off he went as a sailor dressed all in white, only now he seemed to them dark-skinned, just as if he were playing yet another role. And when they got their first letter from him they couldn't make out a word of it but they could understand the drawings which told a story in hearts and flowers, where "I love you" was woven into a wreath of unknown plants and the signature "Fotis" looked like hooks and other shapes, and they laughed in the midst of their tears, and that evening Marika hugged Angel even tighter and was afraid lest the flesh of her flesh should be lost; she didn't understand these people or feel for them, she wanted her mother.* And when she received her own letter, then it was that she couldn't make out a word because neither would she have been able to read it – no one had ever taught her to read – nor did he, who knew her, bother to write. He'd worked out his own way with the inventiveness of the first-born; there was a

---

* Until then Marika seemed all right. This is borne out by a photograph of her and her baby, taken at an expensive photographer's shop and printed on good quality paper. Both of them are looking straight at the camera. She is lively, with sparkling eyes, and the boy is plump and clean. Later they both lost weight – the mother as a result of all she went through during the Occupation, in the famine, and A. because he suffered from liver disease.

heart as large as the sheet of paper, and in the heart were masses and masses of flowers and beneath he'd stuck a photograph of them both, taken when they were acting in the little theatres, with her as Genovefa and him as the knight – but now times were different, she couldn't dance now or play the tambourine, they couldn't take their clothes off in the tiny dressing room and kiss and cuddle, and then laugh at his stories – about how they'd go to Baghdad and find diamonds, a friend of his had done so whom she never met (maybe no one else ever met him either), it was all exploits and stories. "What's he called?" she asked him one night and he simply answered, "Takis" and nothing else.

In the end, one afternoon someone knocked on the door and when they opened a window to look out they saw her mother. She was wearing her best clothes, she'd done her hair and they didn't recognise her at first; Marika went and kissed her hand and her mother said not a word to her. And when they'd taken her in and sat her down in their best room the girls left and the two old women remained alone, and Myrsine stroked her hand, but no response from the other, you might have thought she was injured and forbidden to move, except she relaxed her lips which had been tightly clenched. After a bit Marika came in, bringing the coffee and the water and the sweetmeats, the Jewish mother drank a few sips then rose, searched in the depths of her pocket and got out a knotted kerchief full of something and put it on the table. She said something to Marika in their own language and the girl shook her head as if to say "no", but she was tearful and trembling. And the kerchief stayed where it was and Marika's mother left in silence; and in the evening Myrsine and her daughters said, "we'd better open it, in case it's a magic spell" and they heard Marika choking with sobs. And she came and undid the knots for them, and they saw a pair of earrings, a little chain and a fair amount of money – "she'll never come back," Marika told them, crying without cease.

And the next evening someone came and told them that she'd died. And Myrsine, Marika and the elder daughter went to do what was necessary for her – since the dead woman had no brother or relative or any other support except two neighbours, two impoverished old women clad all in ragged black. And a dry wind arose, blowing great clouds of dust into their eyes. It was night by the time they got back home and not one of them spoke a word. They just put the water on to heat and washed and went to bed and slept like the dead, and the next morning Angel woke them with his laughter.

The Middle Ages – I

And now that everything is over, I should tell you about who Christoforos was, what his story, what his end. The last time we saw him was when they were taking him away on the caique, and he was as white as a sheet, silent and calm. We were standing on the edge of the shore, and someone called to him, "where are you off to, dear heart?", he seemed not to have heard, two or three women knelt down, then it was all over. The next day, and the day after that we searched through the gazettes in agony. In vain though. Nothing was ever written about it. It would be better to forget all about him, we were warned secretly. It would be better. And everyone thought that the affair of Christoforos and Irene would end here. I remember how he'd said to us one night, "we mustn't think only of ourselves or we'll be defeated." Yet he did think of himself. Further down from our house, right at the edge of the sea, was the hut where all his secrets were hidden, we used to think of it as a place of mystery, he would hide down there for days and nights on end, he'd say that everything he planned was well thought out, "we must act together and be united," he used to say. Beyond the hut lay the thick reed beds, then a row of iron railings which ended half way up the garden, a old door lying discarded among the weeds, buried in the brushwood and chamomile and thorn bushes, and above lay the great house, uninhabited, behind oleanders that had run wild and thrived and flowered by themselves. Foreigners live in the house now, Englishmen; in the morning they awake ready to drink their tea, and chase the children away, and receive the visits of girls. Christoforos had foreseen all this, he told us we had to fight to keep foreigners from walking all over us. At that point cunning Apokavkos got up and shouted, "you traitor, what you're doing is pushing the humble folk into misery and starvation," and then the voice of the sea responded that everyone fights for his own bread. Well, the strongest hull was called Christoforos, they launched it on the beach, by the wall, where we used to go and swim when we were children. One day Christoforos said, "I'm not lacking in lovers, but come and I'll show you something." He regretted it afterwards, he went to court and said, "at times like this you should remember all those things you used to preach at us at school, or else you should have taught us that it's the rogues and whores who have the upper hand in life." They wanted to expel him, foremost among them Metohitis and Kavasilas who shouted, "who is he that he thinks he can tell us what to do?" And they ran to the bishop to ask his opinion. And he, according to what people say, answered that although the Church was two thousand years old, the fathers of Christianity would not die. They were trying to overthrow the regime, to say that it was all the fault of the villeins, all that rabble who had no respect for the proper order of things. And then word was spread about that these people were murdering their mothers and raping their sisters, the womenfolk of respectable householders. Once they jeered at Christoforos, "tell us about peace, big mouth," about Irene. She had been killed during the uprising, they carried her home on a wooden door. And it is said that Christoforos was half crazed and kept on howling "murderers", you could no longer hear the gunfire, just that great cry, no one knew at whom they had been aiming, who was meant to fall, "we know what plans the police have," shouted some tramdriver and everyone made up their minds to finish with them once and for all, that night no one went to bed except only the children; "we've got to hold on to what we've paid for in blood," they said and remembered Irene. Then they set off to seek out Christoforos and ask him, "tell us, what do you command?" And down at the house in the reed beds, in the dark garden with the discarded door and the oleanders Argyris was waiting, "all this has to come to an end," he said without looking at us or listening to us. Everyone respected his age and Irene's struggles and they let him speak, let him tell of the old warriors, those he'd met in Asia Minor, about the man whom they killed in front of his children's eyes; it was in another place, other times, we used to sit on the banks of the river and sing, and from time to time the nobles would come and admire us, "what pretty girls, what lovely voices" – but those times are gone now, never to return. And then suddenly Christoforos appeared at the door of his hut, "I can't get any sleep," he complained, "my thoughts go round and round in circles," we'll have to go back to the beginning, to the time when we played barefoot in the streets, when the Allies' armies fed us and the old people used to say, "all this is paid for in blood," in Asia Minor they left us in the lurch. And he raised his hand to his ear, to his scar. "Hard times may come, they'll be descending from the villages, we shall be entangled with horses and sheep and goats, it is thus necessary to put things in some sort of order, to establish what is paining us, who cares about us." I can still hear him today. His mother ran out and counselled him, "don't go beyond our road," and he answered that they will abandon us at some crossroads, we shall search to find the best way. One day they surrounded us in the Turkish village, our eyes smarted from the smoke and the dust, the captain arose and said, "I want two brave lads to go across the bridge and throw the flares there, then to come back and join forces with us"; the other man was a shepherd, "I can see in the dark," he used to say, anyway I set out with him, and when we reached the bridge I heard a scream, "they're slaughtering us," so we ran to the nearest bush and burrowed under it, and then the horses were pouring over our heads, "the irregular troops," the shepherd hissed to me, we stayed roosting there all night, we buried the flares in the earth, and at dawn we heard the children crying, the soldiers had been killed, so all we could do was find a place to hide in the vineyards and to make our way westwards at night; I never did learn what happened to the captain. His mother listened to him in silence, "I don't understand your story," she murmured. "I didn't tell it to make any point," he answered. We never understood the senselessness of it (he continued), they said advance and we advanced, fight and we fought, only when we'd left them far behind did we reflect that it was time for us to think for ourselves about our own affairs. "Now that you're one of the leaders, what are you thinking?" they asked him. "I have not yet understood how to bear the office," he said to them, "you have to be trained to it in order to spread awe and disaster far and wide," so that people say, "he is a true leader." "Listen, captain," some field-hand interrupted him, "now they've decided to put everything upon your shoulders, you can take it as certain that your life's going to be a hard one, and full of perplexity." All night long I reflected, he complained, but I could not find the beginning. We have to sort responsibilities into some kind of order, to take hold of the end of the thread, "to discover the wild beast's lair". I know very well that my mouth will never again taste any sweet morsel, that for me the sweetness of bread is a thing of the past. And he sighed all the while in deep thought. And people say that they showed him then a picture of a young man with a white naked body, pierced by lances, and somewhere in the background was a male figure on horseback, a remnant of the Renaissance, a white horse from a forgotten world, and up in the corner was the sly bishop, dark featured, with lustful black eyes. Then he remembered in an instant the ill-fated child whom they pursued from the baker's shop, whom they fell upon in a frenzy and beat with branches until the blood ran, until she fell to the ground and everything became a mud made of tears, broken flesh and hair all drenched in sweat. He remembers that he took her lifeless hand by the wrist, tried to turn her onto her face, her dress was pulled up above her knees, sodden with mud and water, and from somewhere trickled a ribbon of blood, of sweat and blood combined, which congealed on her spine, "this should not have happened," he raved like a lost soul, "we should have been more careful and not overstepped our power." And he caressed her flesh one more time, "this may be the last time," he whispered to her, then felt that the door no longer hid them, and the curtains with the amphora embroidered on them, and the walls, that they had fallen into the middle of the road and that round them dozens of people were bending, muttering, breathing, smelling, "go away," he shouted, "keep away from us, this is a moment that belongs to us alone." And he felt a thousand hands taking hold of him, wanting to remove him, leaving her body at their mercy, her bare legs in full view, her back, her neck, the flesh which he had stolen and guarded at all costs, each knew the other even simply by his or her scent. And he struggled and heard words tormenting him, words that wished to deceive him, so that her body would be left there without embroideries, without songs, and he fought to remain alone and then once more felt seaweed and tentacles, and he was once more the child that they used to take to the sea and hold him, and he was racked with tears and all around him a thousand feet were passing, passing and leaving and they again enveloped him suffocatingly and he cried, "leave me alone, she's mine." And then five workers appeared, he knew one of them, he had climbed up a lamppost and had been throwing stones, they stood around the body, they stretched out their hands and covered it, they took their jackets off and threw them over her then stepped back, and other people brought an old door, they laid her on it and raised it, they bore it on their shoulders and shouted, "murderers", you'll pay for this, and Christoforos got caught up in their feet as if he was begging them to take him too, and four of them set off with their burden and the fifth remained as if guarding the spot, there where they had kissed the earth. And he was drowned in the crowd which surged like a sea, whose waves were breaking somewhere further off and whose roar could be heard as far as here. And as the sea comes and goes and he lies hidden in the reedbed watching it, he is dizzy and adrift, his eyes empty, his feelings knotted around a bitter kernel, which he chews and licks and swallows, in order that an even more bitter one will emerge and torment him.

Christos

All that remained after the drama was over were three photographs; he put them in his drawer but kept on getting them out and scanning them, specially the one that showed the crowd, the demonstration and the fallen worker, his face a mask of lost hopelessness, while above him reared a tram-driver in a torn shirt and beside him a girl running to get away, to find safety. But in this picture too, right in the corner, in the midst of the crowd, he suspected he could make out his own self, a little dot with a grey trilby which nobody else would have been able to recognise.

He remembered how he'd plunged into the crowd, then at one point the river of people had swept him away, he had heard them shouting and panting and thought, I'm with them all the way, in spite of the fact that he wasn't one of them, that they didn't suit him or he them – from the night that they'd come up the stairs at the "Independent" and screamed, "we'll burn you out like rats, you traitors, you've sold out to them," which was something that didn't apply to Christos, for it was something he neither could nor would have done. However the teacher, the editor, had locked himself in, he wasn't so young any more, had lost a brother from heart disease and was struggling to keep the paper going, all the responsibility his alone. And there on the stairs, when he saw their sweating faces and enraged eyes, he was terrified that they might tear him to pieces, might throw him down and trample on him; "you've sold out," they screamed at him, "you've sold out," and they surged upstairs like a wave breaking above the shoreline which makes people leap back in terror. His sole thought was I'd better not turn my back in case they stab me, he tried to walk backwards, feeling for the stairs with his feet. For a moment he thought, "what's the point," if they stretched out their hands they could strangle him, and he shouted, "I'm not one of them" – but who was listening to him? And when he was pushed and stumbled, when he felt them passing him, cursing him, when he felt someone hitting him in the belly, he made up his mind that it was all up with him and he remembered Amalia and his children: what a sin to leave them orphaned like that. And he let himself fall, roll downstairs, to slip away ignored like some tattered scrap, like some useless, forgotten torn sheet of newspaper; except that it wasn't so easy, because the river had swollen and overflowed by now, it bore him up again, he felt immense weakness and from somewhere heard windows breaking, doors being beaten down – "you've sold out."

After a bit he fell into the maelstrom, he saw nothingness in front of him, he lost his footing on the stairs and thought, "oh God, I'm falling, I'm going to be killed." And this was really happening, he fell and was crushed, the crowd faded and the lights went out, only a sort of buzzing seemed to be going on around him, he came to and saw that he was among a sea of boots, he smelled khaki and heard someone say, "get hold of that bastard," and two hands pulled him up and dragged him along and hit him until he croaked soundlessly, "I'm on the side of the law, I'm a victim" but the blows did not cease, and he was losing consciousness once more. He heard a pistol shot, then a second one – then nothing more.

Later his family would laugh at him – he was the only person who was in danger and was beaten up "by both sides" as the teacher was to mock. "But tell me, whose side were you on?" she asked him at dawn, when he came to in his own bed and reflected that, thank God, I'm still alive. He wasn't on the side of the demonstrators, they didn't suit him. "All the same, you kill yourself earning our bread," Amalia said to him. "I wouldn't beat people up, I wouldn't threaten people to earn it," he answered. There's a kind of order, a hierarchy, he added, which states that some people give the orders and others carry them out, that you have to climb one step at a time and think about things, otherwise the world would be turned upside down, just as he himself had been, quite unjustly. That same evening as he went up the stairs (and his ribs and guts were hurting), he wondered how come the staircase hadn't broken, hadn't collapsed, for it was made of wood, a twisting staircase that always creaked: between the street, Egnatia Street, and the offices it made two or three turns, and it was a wonder that it had withstood the onslaught.

And Amalia would have said, "human beings can withstand anything," her two children, the fact that she was pregnant again, and most of all the fact that she had a husband whom she didn't enjoy in bed; he was always dreaming and used to say, "the black tree was my greatest dream," back in the days when she had lost her grandmother and been left all alone and Christos ran round helping her to sort things out and make an honest living and in the end they agreed, "let's make it together." And everything ended in church or began there – in the middle of nowhere – and Christos said, "I want to be worthy of the wedding wreath and your suffering," and he said it beautifully, like a voice singing in the midst of chaos, because it's true that the girl was full of bitterness. And everything led to a little lonely church in the middle of nowhere, which Amalia and a friend from work had chosen, and they walked there separately through the fields, through the freshly ploughed wet earth, like Adam and Eve, the girl in her white dress and he approaching from the other direction as if they were conspirators (but against whom?), when three gypsies appeared unexpectedly, with them they had rugs which they were going to sell or perhaps spread out and sit on them and start playing the clarinet and making merry. Her white dress became embroidered with little brown stitches of mud and water, and then in a little while it began to drizzle and the bride and the groom and the gypsies started to run and the best man, all inexperienced, was left standing there, wondering, "now what?"

Except that nothing ever remains secret and just as the priest was reading the service over them a cart was heard and neighing – it was Christos's father and mother and brother from the village, and following them came the teacher who had learnt of it and told the others about it and was now smiling at them, happy at their surprise. But his family had forgotten to smile, their minds were preoccupied with thoughts and questions because they had dreamed and planned other things for their son, and his mother grumbled, "she doesn't have anything except the knickers she's standing up in," and it was true that her entire fortune began and ended with her beauty, worth more than any amount of fine clothes. However the wedding service was about to end, his father came up to him with tears in his eyes and stuffed two hundred-drachma notes into his pocket surreptitiously, "it's all I've got," he murmured, something he'd kept secret from his wife and felt apologetic about. And they left in silence as if tired, it had been an utterly odd wedding, original: only his brother hung back and spoke to them, rather like a puppy who can't manage to say anything except, "I'll come again," just as if this would cure all their troubles and woes. And when they were alone once more they said, "we can't possibly go on foot now" because the whole place was sodden with rain, they might drown in the mud or put down roots and start growing in the field. Then for the second time they felt the mystery of surprise, for the teacher, like a fairy godmother, had arranged for a car to be waiting outside for them – "just call it my little gift," he said and laughed. They got in and nestled together in the back seat, they saw the leaden sky and an angry vivid green tree dripping. The teacher sat in front with the best man next to him, also a poor man and silent, and they took the road back to the city. The car left them at their own door, in their own little corner which really was just the corner of a single room, with his old bed and a chair, a basin of water to one side and the small old mirror.

"No matter how much you look you'll never find that person," the teacher told him, and he meant the photograph, he'd understood what it was that Christos was searching for in the picture, "I should have kept you close to me," said the editor, with a tone that seemed to imply he believed that Christos needed or deserved some support, in order to find his way on some faint path or discover some solution to his problems. Which weren't merely the search for a person or any vague consolation, any justification that "I've behaved properly towards them" but were more Amalias's terrible anxiety; "Dimitris will ask," Dimitris being his eldest son. Christos recalled that two days earlier he'd been wondering, "who is behind it?", when the tobacco workers surged forward with their banners, then the gendarmes on horseback – and the women had been wailing, frightened.* For heads were split open, the mean streets resounded with curses, one or two people sang their anthems and called on the others not to retreat, and they saw a woman leap forward as if possessed, she overtook the men, she was running, grabbed the leg of one of the riders and pulled him off, and all everyone could see was a confusion of horse and humans, the sound of sword blows on the paving stones made your blood run cold, then they saw the woman up again and running, stones raining down all around her, she was like a jet black standard flying in the breeze, and then was heard the rifle shot which, as Christos said, seemed to come from some other world, like fire from heaven, and the woman made a great leap as if someone had lashed her legs, then fell forward, dragged herself along, started up like a foal being slaughtered, then collapsed like a skein of wool, like a small black stain on the grey stones. And some people said, "they've hit her in the legs" which were white and sturdy; it was not from her legs that the blood came, though, but from somewhere in her belly or her side, like a red ribbon decorating her thighs or her black-clad breast (for afterwards who could remember clearly enough to be able to say?). And everyone froze then, you might have supposed they'd all been hit by the rifle shot, a circle formed with the black mark at its centre; but only for a moment, then the crowd drew determinedly together again and swallowed up the fallen body as if drinking it in, eating it – so that from then on it was hidden from sight. And the next minute Christos heard the horseshoes dancing on the paving stones as if the horses were hesitant, he saw the gendarmes looking around suspiciously in case they were in any danger, then an arm was raised as if calling them back, they fell into line one behind the other and left.

"You're as white as a sheet," Amalia scolded him when he came back up their road, and he saw mothers and children waiting (who had let them know?) and he said in terror, "get inside,

---

* May '36 was not the first time that the gendarmerie and strikers – tram-drivers, railwaymen, tobacco workers and others – came to blows in Thessaloniki. However, it was the last time, at least until the years of the Metaxas dictatorship. Dakos, the head of the gendarmerie, received orders to make a general assault on the striking workers. Policemen in civilian clothes, concealed on the balconies of the hotels, fired at random. Nine people were killed, among them a girl whose surname was Karanikola.

the whole lot of you" and he took them in his arms, Amalia, Dimitris, Alcmene, he enfolded them with his wings and gathered them all into the room. "Don't ask," he said to her and wouldn't go on, not wanting to scare her by telling her of the woman who'd been killed, the maddened crowd, "things got out of control, order just dissolved" was all he whispered to her and lapsed into thought. It was May, the garden full of fragrance, they should have been opening the windows to be flooded by springtime and singing. Somewhere in the distance they heard a sound like thunder, "it might rain," his wife was saying to him and kissing him. But the only thing to be heard was the twittering of a bird, it must have been hidden somewhere in the acacia, joyful among the sweetly scented leaves. At this point Christos fell asleep, and it was like dying, as he himself said later – maybe he was dreaming: of being snuffed out, his heart blamelessly stopping – so that when he awoke he was struggling to draw breath, to get his pulse back to normal and his reason working once more, "my time hasn't come yet," he said to himself and was once more calm.

That very same evening it was that the editor called him in, "get out there fast"; her name was Irene he said, and they were late, the other papers would scoop them, "you're sitting an examination every day," the teacher used to say, and it was a damnable profession, no sweetness, just the bitterness of the downtrodden, deprivation. It was already six o'clock, dusk was drawing in and the sky was quite clear – "did it thunder at all?" Christos asked reflectively but the teacher laughed at him, "I don't understand you one bit," he said, "and I'm not going to pay any attention to you." But he called the cashier discreetly and said something to him and Christos felt he'd be off the hook, maybe for two days, maybe a little longer. "Damned profession," he muttered and got on the Vardari tram. The little house he sought was somewhere outside the castle, among the shanties that crept up the hill, among the wasteland, but the roads and footpaths were dark by now, not a single lamppost to offer comfort or security. Thus he followed the sound of weeping, the muted voices, like a hound he scented them in the air as they came through the little houses, the narrow lanes, and in the end he came upon grieving and murmurs enfolding the black-clad body, which now lay on a pure white bed, and around it all the old women of the neighbourhood – so that

Christos thought, maybe her dwelling is an unblemished sheet and the blood has slipped away like quicksilver and disappeared. The room was full of incense and the smoke of the gas lamps which decorated the walls with shadows; but in the world outside, in the courtyard, in the open space that it offered, the men stood deep in talk – afterwards he was to remember only one of them, a man constantly holding his ear as if it ached or as if he wanted to hide it. There were trees and stars, like in the holy garden of Gethsemane, and people were saying, "perhaps they'll crucify us," for the gendarmes had their blood up now, the bosses too, the heartless and selfish of the world. And perhaps Christos was one of this tribe – when they saw him they fell silent in mistrust and muttered, "informer" – but he had seen what he had seen and thought, "I'd better go," for the darkness scared him, and the idea that he was an outsider, all on his own here, and on top of this a girl came up to him – as if she was his good fairy – and said, "go" while the going was still good.

And as he slipped through a narrow gap in the castle walls he saw below him a multitude of little oil lamps. And he started to run downhill, leaping like a goat, afraid lest he stumble in the labyrinth of narrow lanes and spoil the configuration of the lights. It was already nearly ten when he went up the stairs, took a couple of deep breaths and started writing the story of Irene and the killing.

Angela

"Maybe it's all the fault of my unlucky star," whispered Angela, who had decided that "things won't get anywhere with Eugenios", specially when the fever epidemic broke out and mothers wept and hurried off to church to make endless vows. Except that she couldn't say or foresee where this star would lead, whether it would turn out to be lucky or unlucky for her – but however this might be, she was scared, and now that he had managed to get in here she reflected, I ought to be afraid of him. Even if he did have the shape of an angel, now that she was gradually beginning to look at him more closely; he was an upper-class boy, one of the masters, his clothes were redolent of good breeding, his flesh too, you'd say he was radiant, his rosy colour conquered you. And she thought to herself, he's like a painting, a wonderful bird with a rich mane of hair, his lips that breathed in everything about him, whatever scant air sly Eugenios left to be breathed in the room. And they discovered that he was called Yannis, that he'd left home and was living alone in the neighbourhood just below.

Well, and what did all this mean? As time passed he showed them that he had become bolder; he must have been a tender-hearted creature, for before long he was embracing them with a warmth which bothered Eugenios. "I'm longing for the feel of a human breath," he confided to them, but Angela thought of small children whom you take into your arms and hug and then they bite you. "You'll always be unfair," Eugenios chided her one evening, because on the first nights the girl would depart before midnight, she'd leave them drinking and talking, though she never discovered about what. And both of them were puzzled when once Yannis said, "this is how I imagined it" – the choice drinks, the boxes of chocolates, the divan. He was certainly alarming, like water which might flow in through the smallest cracks and drown you, feared the girl.

"There's something abnormal about him," Eugenios said one day, without reason; this was at the beginning, when he and Angela used to remain by themselves and talk about things, weigh up what he'd said to them, examine it. The girl put her hand on his shoulder though, "you are protected by your own goodness," she told him, and wrapped a blanket round his knees, warmed him. Winter was drawing in, the city was plunging into its old stagnation, threads of rain and mist hung in the air; and her elderly friend reiterated, "he's keeping quiet about whatever it was that drove him from home." So his doubts were tormenting him, then; but that same evening the three of them met once again in the same decor, the curtains ever drawn close in front of the windows, and Yannis said, "I don't understand what it is that we're hiding." And without them asking, without any invitation, he told them about his life from the days when for years he had slept in his mother's room, when they let his hair grow long ("like a girl") and bathed him with sweet scents and colognes. "I was their pampered darling," he confessed, as if it was his own fault that Ergini and Euthalia, his elder sisters, had played with him like a little doll.

And they felt less comfortable when he began telling them about his friendship, about the close relationship he used to have with the man who'd been killed, about his agony that they might have been going to pin the murder on him. Eugenios asked him repeatedly, "just what exactly were your relations with him?" and Angela stared at him with amazement, what did he mean and what was he trying to find out, for he seemed to her to be wrapping himself ever more closely in his clothes, as if huddling into his dressing gown and his armchair, specially when no clear answer to his question seemed to be forthcoming. "He was a man who was open towards everything," replied the young man – maybe that's why he got murdered, thought Eugenios in the back of his mind. But even Angela couldn't be fooled, she said, "I wouldn't go to sleep on the grass in the dark, with the river smelling beside me," and this river might swell in your sleep and rise up and drown you.

"All the same, it was with an axe that he was killed" was the idea that came into Eugenios's head, in other words something that meant strong arms – and he kept observing the boy's arms which couldn't be disregarded, no matter how gentle his fingers were as they touched and seduced and played with the senses, as the nights passed they became bolder, they promised, see how beautiful and sweet, as the palm of his hand lay like a snowflake, ever cool and light. It must surely have been the gypsies, with all their hunger and savage instincts – and the tale of passion unfolded, Yannis whispering, "I'm the boy who was lost" and wary Angela felt sorry for him, even though she was terrified of any man who didn't come from her own village, whom she didn't know; back there at home people were good, at least while daylight lasted, when the sun shone and beasts and men were awake, at night they watched over her yet frightened her, they used to say, "the Turks will come" although they never did come, the only one was Omar who seemed obedient and lazy and a bit of a coward, and only in his own hut did he become bolder and do crazy things – Angela would pass by at a distance and look at him, bare from the waist up, like the goat that someone stole from them. Who though could steal Yannis or fool him?

"I suppose you are as heedless and naive as ever," Eugenios rebuked her, and he meant that they had missed an unexpected opportunity to find out for sure, to learn all his secrets, to hold him, so that they would no longer be frightened by his knocking on the door, by his past. And she did indeed prove herself to be heedless, for at a certain moment she felt sorry for him and stopped him, "you don't have to remember all that any more," she comforted him, as if her senses had unexpectedly ripened and she felt that he was bleeding, that she should put him to bed and wash his wounds and then lull him to sleep – at which point her friend was sarcastic and said, "you remind me of penny romances." And Angela was a little suspicious of him, it could be that he intended to tell the boy such things himself, she reflected, that he was jealous of the tenderness which was so dangerously spreading. But her heart was large enough, it held them all, felt compassion for them, she thought, one day I might leave both of them, for they would have much to speak of and to do. She couldn't remember when or why she'd first thought of it, only that everything she had so far lived through made her feel that men remain little boys to whom you must give advice or comfort, though you have to watch out for their bites.

And at one point she felt, I knew it; for she was surrounded by suspicion, which she could smell even if she couldn't see it – she had said, "I mustn't grow old in here," nor was it possible, yet time passed, Yannis arrived and all the things that happened, and then came their last meeting at which Eugenios whispered to her "courage", and then "I feel for you, sweetheart" and his eyes misted over – it must have been broken, his heart, as they were soon to find out, so broken that he didn't manage to promise her the most important thing, he simply stuffed a thousand-drachma note into her pocket, the last one, and she told him, "I'll return it to you one day," at which he smiled in utter sadness and the girl left as if hunted. And she would have sworn that she meant to return it to him or to go and see him again, though in hopes of what is unknown, perhaps that willfulness would have faded, dark images, words that came creeping through doors, into the corridor, the boy's laughter, who would say to her, "let's play in the dark, let's hide" and caress her alone in the kitchen, then in a little while she'd find him back at Eugenios's feet, scowling at her.

Perhaps it was the end, or a beginning, when in a few days' time they heard that he had fallen ill, that the house had been locked up (so he did have relatives after all) and then that they'd taken him to hospital, and afterwards that he had died, all in three evenings. Angela was bitter and felt, I want to see him again, his calm of old age, his transparent hands – and they opened the iron gate just once for people to go in and pay their last respects, and a great many people said, "we never really knew him" for he didn't go out or speak to anyone; then the gate remained closed for a long time, tendrils and weeds grew rampant and bound it fast. However, before she left for the last time, Angela picked flowers from the honeysuckle, from the garden, and strewed them on the coffin, on the steps, a great many people said she was deranged, and some bent and whispered, eyed her, choking and lost in tears – "but what was she to him?" the younger girls asked, though they knew perfectly well and didn't require an answer. Only from out among them stepped a man, he must have been about fifty or a bit older, he went up to her and said, "you've made a laughing stock of us," but Angela looked at him as if demented, then stopped, stood in a corner and no longer saw them. And the whole neighbourhood talked of it, told of it in the evenings, of Angela's tears and of the dead man, of how when the moment came to lift the coffin a young lad hurried in, he seemed dishevelled and distraught, searched round the room for a moment then found the girl, went and took her by the hand, finally they wrapped their arms around one another and he comforted her. And at this point the neighbourhood became confused, for Mitsos revealed that "he used to lie in wait for her in the evenings when she came", at which the women all crossed themselves; and finally the coffin passed the flower beds, passed through the gate and was gone, and after a little while everything was silence once more and everything forgotten, all that remained being the mystery. And the neighbours said, "let them sort it out by themselves," because that was the only way, and they meant the boy and the girl.

Nobody cared what became of Yannis and Angela, they were soon forgotten. Eugenios's house remained there for people to see, at the beginning it was locked up and the fence repaired, but one day two children from the quarter got into the garden in search of their dog, which they found, but then forgot about it and started playing; in a couple of weeks there were a lot of children and dust, they poured in over the wall, they burrowed into the bushes and the long grass and played, their mothers shouted for them in vain and cursed, then one day it was all tears, a girl emerged from the garden torn and bleeding, they went in pursuit of the bastard who'd offended their honour and he was from a different neighbourhood. For a while the garden seemed deserted once more, then later they saw two broken windows and the curtain blowing in the breeze, catching on the thorns of a rosebush – one night there was a candle on the steps, someone was going up furtively, it was as if Eugenios had come back; in the morning they saw a petticoat hung up, a child's knickers and a home-made blanket. And they said, "maybe she's come back" and they meant Angela and goodness only knows what else; but they were wrong again, the children told them this, it was some unknown woman and her baby who pulled their rags about them in there and said, "whatever be God's will." But their prayers were not heard at all, for three days later a man all in black arrived, with a moustache and knitted brows; he'd received information and he turned up with the gendarmes and they threw the poor woman out into the street – more tears and more pain – and the women from the neighbourhood came running and gave her whatever bread they could spare, whatever food they had, and said, "what kind of antichrist could have done this?" – one of their own people – and then they told her, "go to the church" for not one of them would let her into their own poor dwellings, all of which were all tiny and uncomfortable, their families were large, old men and children, wretchedness.

But no one saw Angela or Yannis come, and they began to criticise them saying, "they've shaken the dust off their shoes" and maybe this was true, if by dust they meant grief of heart – though one night their grief was sore and they stole in like thieves – the neighbourhood was plunged in sleep – stepping lightly, slipping like shadows in the shadow of the wall. And they said, "what a pity that it's all abandoned" as they saw it ruined and dumb, and their hands were closely entwined and they remembered Eugenios, all his precautions, and she said, "there wasn't even any need for them." And the young man asked her if they could go inside, what he meant was, do you want to? – but the girl answered with a shake of her head, no, she was afraid of ghosts, the images held in her memory. "I would go in if he had married me," she whispered to him, and this was her first and last confession – but in any case Yannis laughed at her and stroked her hair, "I'll help you forget," he murmured to her. And he was full of assurance and tenderness.

A time was to come when he would be powerful, able to pay, to give orders, to wear his best clothes and his best mood. But they had been through difficult days before then, Angela knew that she would lose him – then in a while he would come back, would disappear again, the room had not space enough to hold him, neither her room nor his room, and she feared the worst; he's proud and accustomed to the best, she thought, he always wants to give, to show you that he's got enough and to spare. And then the next night the same thing happened, and Angela ran (though at one point she said to herself, as if reflecting, "but why am I running, what do I care about him?") and asked his old landlady if she had any news of him – but the woman was dumb, her eyes full of tears, as if some illness was making her cry, as if maggots were coming out of her two eyes, as if they were rotten and disintegrating.

And on the third evening she didn't need to go out looking, didn't get time to go out, for he was knocking weakly on her door, and when she opened it he was standing there drained of courage, he was smiling his bad smile, his jacket was crumpled and his trousers even more so, and he smiled as if down to his last reserves of smiling. But she said, "come in"; the boy cast a look behind him in case people should gossip (in case he was being followed, she suspected) and then came in, sat down without speaking. Angela took her worn blanket and hung it in front of her sole window, said, "we'd better turn off the light" just as if Eugenios was there with his mysterious way of doing things. And Yannis confided, "all I want is a corner to sleep in" without explaining to her who had given him shelter, why he had disappeared, without the girl asking him. And in a little while everything was ready, water for him to wash and a face towel, a plate of broth, a warm bed, and above all she who was smiling at him, and he said nothing but sat in a corner, as if it was all agreed between them. Some time later, he admitted, "I fell into perdition," and he neither smiled at her nor wept, perhaps forgetting that he was not alone. At one point Angela thought, I'd better rouse him, for he looked to her lost to the world like Omar when he staggered and fell and rolled on the ground. So she took him by the shoulders and said, "take your jacket off" and he obeyed and then Angela knelt before him and undid his shoes which were covered with dust and suggested that he'd been out wandering. But as she knelt there a thought came into her mind which flooded her with strange sweetness, she might be his mother, she thought, and look after him and lull him to sleep in her arms, if only there could be some mother in the room so that he would not feel so parched, so lonely. She was wholly mistaken though, for she felt a hand creeping uncertainly down her back, slipping under her armpit and making itself comfortable on her breast – and she heard the voice of an angel say, "you were chosen for your warm heart" and she felt as if Eugenios was receiving her; his hand was warm, suddenly full of longing and trembling, then she sought his embrace, found she liked this position, blew on his breast, "I don't feel cold, I'm young," the angel spoke again, and maybe he was finding a chance to free himself of his sorrow, of the weary wilfulness, the old men's embraces, which smelled.

And the girl said, "I've known worse things" and made as if she didn't understand where he was touching her. And when she was quiet and they lay together and the poor girl said, "all I have for us to share is poverty," he held her close, like a completely different person, and sobbed, "let us unite our poverties," although that night they lacked nothing. And at dawn when Angela awoke she found she was alone once more – he has flown, she thought wildly – and she ran to all his old haunts asking for him and the woman told her, "he's not here." And on the fifth day, by which time she was in despair and had lost her courage, she found him waiting for her by the little church; he was leaning against the closed doors like some ancient figure on a painted panel. "I've got some good news to tell you," he announced. And she remembered her mother, who had taught her to light the candles and set the church to order. It was a honey-sweet afternoon – time to confess, to take Communion.

Yannis

People had once accused him of killing his father, though that was thirty years ago. And perhaps what they said wasn't untrue – or not entirely. For, in spite of the fact that his sisters kept quiet about it, the industrialist's health had certainly been shaken, maybe by his own past sins, aches of the heart and tyrannies of the flesh, maybe also because of Yannis's exploits. And it was Euthalia who revealed everything: how one day their father was called to the Public Prosecutor's office, how they gave him a letter, how he shut himself up in his study till late at night and the next day they found him fast asleep in an armchair. And then he summoned a notary and told his two daughters, "you are all that I have now" and that he was disinheriting his son. And a week later he fell down in a fit of apoplexy, he lost his speech and the use of his whole right side. In spite of this though he gave the letter to Euthalia and it was as if he'd made a second testament or pronounced a sentence.

But Euthalia hid the envelope, saying, "I'm not going to open it lest it poison me" and she meant her own soul or the love she bore her brother; for she more or less knew what she'd find in it – and then there was the matter of what it had done to her father, who lingered on for another fifty days or so and then passed away. Thus the envelope remained hidden, Yannis cried like a baby in church at the funeral, and that very night his whole body came out in spots so that he looked as if he'd caught some dreaded infection; the spots spread up his neck and to his mouth, they made his cheeks swell, and finally one broke out just above his eyebrow and slowly caused his eye to close. It was a fearful sight, quite terrible, and his sisters were half-crazed with worry, "this is the second disaster to strike us," they said. They called in a pious aunt of theirs from Hortiatis, who made the sign of the cross over him and washed him with an infusion of wild herbs and then read some mumbo-jumbo over him. Nevertheless he remained blind and disfigured, "bowed down with the weight of his sins" as their aunt grumbled, so they decided to call the doctor, Dr. Tzamaloukas, who'd just come back from Paris and who said, "wash him in the waters of Siloam" – whereupon their aunt crossed herself. But he prescribed bran baths and Euthalia undressed him, she delighted in his body which was gradually becoming pacified, said to him, "don't be ashamed," that he was having a bad time of it and that sin didn't matter.

Then one day they lost him again, he'd got his strength back, his clothes were clean once more but above all he had an urge to escape from the bonds of kindness in which they were binding him; for he felt like a stranger, as if he'd abdicated from all ties of blood and family. It may be that running off, disappearing, being searched for had become a habit for Yannis. But they couldn't find him, not even at Angela's, and Angela was maddened by him, "I can't stand that weird boy any more," she swore, she'd lost sight of him (and hadn't even heard about his illness, nor would she in any case have dared to knock on the door of his family home). And she was desperately trying to find a good job, she got taken on as waitress at "Michalis's", a café not far from the Harilaou quarter, where by day people played billiards and cards but at night there was dancing and singing. She liked the fact that the customers were cheerful, that she got her food, her bread, her nice dress, and it suited her that Michalis was so busy screwing Domna, a sweet girl from Constantinople, that he didn't have the energy even to talk to her but merely looked at her with a puzzled expression as if to say, how come I'm not getting you on your back. This fact alone brought Yannis to accept her job (though that was later); at the beginning he sulked, wouldn't eat, went to bed and fell asleep in a thoroughly bad mood. "What are you to me?" she screamed at him, but all the same she was patient and couldn't help feeling tender towards him: "I can't tell you to go away," she confessed to him one day, "but neither can I keep you" and she meant forever. And she felt like crying, as if she'd failed without ever having been given the chance to put up a fight.

However, worse things were to come. One noon when she was alone someone knocked in irritation on her door: short, sharp knocks as if a machine was drilling into it. Later she was to say, "it made me think of the single night that we spent at Smyrna, when we were all gathered in a cellar waiting and we heard the gunshots and my mother cried, get out, they'll burn us to death in here like rats, and then when we were out on the waterfront waiting for the dawn to come, men on horseback came galloping up and yelled at us, 'get back inside or you'll be hit by stray bullets,'" and these knocks on the door were like gunfire. And when she opened the door anxiously she saw a lady looking at her, examining her from head to toe, who said, "you are Angela" – stating, not asking – and entered her humble abode without hesitating or waiting for an invitation. Later, though, sensitive Euthalia was to depart in tears and Angela was left there with her lonely heart; Yannis was not there, nor did he reappear – it was as if he'd been watching everything from a distance and had decided that it would be better not to make the women angrier.

But "you wasted your trouble" as Angela could have told him. For it was all in the letter which had passed from the father to the perplexed daughter and from her into Angela's hands, though Angela, suddenly lost, said, "I can't read it" – not that she didn't want to or was ashamed to, simply that no one had ever taught her to read and write. So there the letter's perambulations came to a halt, for a few months anyway, until one evening Yannis burnt it, heaving a sigh of relief and saying, "there, that incubus is laid to rest" – in vain though. Because his sister would know it forever, for as long as she lived, for as long as she went on seeing him, he would detect the passion in her eyes, her chagrin that they had betrayed her, that her rival was a refugee, a cheap little tart – for the old women, implacable and conservative, confused the two ideas as they saw their neighbourhoods surrounded by newcomers, their nights pierced by the sound of oriental songs and musical instruments and sin.

"In vain" as Euthalia could have mocked him, for from some murky cavern deep within her entrails an idea had stolen into her mind – a clever idea, but diabolical all the same – to copy that evil letter and to secrete it in some dark corner of the cellar, whither she went from time to time to check that it was still there and occasionally to read it; it was as if this flooded her whole being with pleasure, a naked craving to bite into his fresh young flesh. For the things the letter said were like wounds, making him bleed, hurting him, tearing him: indeed what really seemed to give the knife one final twist was the fact that on the top corner of the first page was pasted a photograph of him, a youth sprawled stark naked on a pure white bed, lying there as if unconscious. And Angela blurted out, "just like Omar" and burst into tears as if someone had cursed her. Euthalia didn't understand, she was perplexed, yet wept even more for she was able to read what the letter revealed, to read it again and again till in the end she knew it by heart, it gave her pain, but then also pleasure, to read the sentences aloud, to fondle the sheet of paper in a curious way and to think, I can rip him to pieces whenever I want to. And she used to enjoy reading the letter from the beginning. What it said was as follows:

My dear Sir,

It so happens that your son, Ioannis, pictured above, is of criminal and perverted character. The photograph, which indeed speaks for itself and of which, let it be noted, I have preserved the negative lest the picture should suffer destruction at your hands, was taken by the writer at a moment when the young man was in a state of befuddlement. I hasten to make it clear to you that I had no wish to take advantage of his youth or, at the very least, that I was not the first person with whom he developed an intimate relationship. I believe that you can be in no doubt whatsoever as to the role played by Ioannis in the murder of a distinguished fellow-citizen of ours which occurred during the past year, or at least of his thoroughly suspicious relations with the debauched but ultimately unfortunate banker.

I hasten to inform you that I owe my acquaintance with your son to an initiative entirely his own, which indeed discomfited me and, I will not conceal it from you, provoked in me great fear by reason not only of the unusual mode of his attempt but also of the previously occurring murder, which of course should serve as a lesson to all of us. Moreover, the fact that I reside alone played no small part in my fear (a young woman comes to carry out the housework for a few hours only), as well as the fact that my place of residence is situated in an area of town far removed from the well-frequented centre. In any case, your son, experienced and bold as he is, finally managed to make his way into my home, having previously attempted various contrivances which even the creator of Rocambole would envy, and (I must admit that the young man exercises great charm, well taught, as I believe, by his experiences to date) succeeded in winning my friendship and interest.

I consider it of relevance to inform you that until this time I lived a life of monastic virtuousness, mainly as a result of an illness which, from my earliest youth on, forbade me all indulgence in any kind of enjoyments, and even more so in abuses and pleasures. In evidence of this, were such a thing necessary, I could provide you with the testimony of various persons, including that of the young woman who takes care of my household matters. I am not, however, in any hurry to supply you with their names for the simple reason that I do not require their testimony, given that the purpose of the present letter is not to justify myself or to prove anything whatsoever about my own character, which indeed stands high in the estimate of my acquaintances, but rather to bring to your attention any of the actions of Ioannis of which you may have remained in ignorance. I should add moreover that I did everything that lay within my power as a friend to restrain your son from further descent down the slippery slope, a descent which it is highly probable will involve him very shortly in disagreeable circumstances or even fatal adventures.

My anxieties on this point stem mainly from the fact that the demonic young man has a tendency towards acquaintances and relations which at the very least could be considered dangerous. The murder of the banker and your son's involvement therein should afford you dramatic proof of this. I do not, of course, in the least believe that your son had any hand in the actual act of murder, for the shedding of light on which the most proper authority is the police force. Nevertheless I am plagued by various questions regarding your son's affluence during the long periods of time in which he neither resided in your home nor received any financial support from you. Of this latter fact I am fully cognizant, since he himself repeatedly complained of it, although simultaneously refusing to accept any assistance from my part – for a long time at least. Indeed, in the early days of our acquaintance he was in the habit of bringing with him various gifts such as sweets, drinks and on one occasion a silk scarf for the girl who looks after me. I do not wish to imply anything in particular, yet I recall reading in the press that there was some mystery as regards the disappearance of bonds from the desk of the ill-advised banker. Since the gypsies who were arrested were destitute individuals, it may of course be taken as certain that they committed the crime with a view to theft. Nevertheless, anyone possessing some small power of reflection may wonder how it was possible for these gypsies to know anything about bonds or about their probable value, given that they are accustomed to transacting their own business in coins of minimal value. Well, so be it. I fear that I am digressing and straying from the point, in the manner of an unworthy pupil who attempts an essay without any knowledge of where a well-founded thesis begins and ends.

I consider that what it most behoves me to tell you is the fact that at a certain period your son showed signs of penury. I suspected this when, to begin with, I observed that his generosity was no longer unlimited and that he was wearing the same shirt for several days in succession, he who had always been a model of elegance and cleanliness. However, what finally dispersed any shadow of doubt was the greed with which, from a certain day onwards, he used to consume sweetmeats and fruit, indeed even the humble repast of bread and onions whenever the girl whom I had in my house offered such things to him. For previously he had touched almost nothing; indeed, I might say that he used merely to cast a glance of contempt at the delicacies which the young woman offered him, and moreover with such ostentation that it would put her into a state of high dudgeon so that she referred to him sarcastically as "the young gentleman" – I have, I should add, no wish either to offend you or to approve the young woman's attitude (which, in any case, she was later to change for reasons that I shall explain subsequently), nor do I wish to condemn his behaviour. On the con-

trary, I should say that the obstinacy with which he clung to some at any rate of the marks of his breeding was pleasing to me.

I will confess to you that I was astonished – anyone would have felt the same – when I suddenly observed in him a new and unexpected affluence which I originally attributed to some support emanating from you or from some other relative, perhaps from one of Ioannis's sisters, about whom he always speaks with devotion though also with some guilt. However, from the converse that I had with him I succeeded in eliciting that your son had no contact whatsoever either with you or with your daughters. I felt great uncertainty, as well as (I shall not hide it from you) anxiety, principally because I had my doubts as to the strength of Ioannis's character. I was obliged to undergo an evening most painful, I assure you, during which I began by questioning and gradually found myself interrogating your son, now slipping towards the very brink; he armed himself with a fixed disarming smile and either mocked at my anxieties or took refuge in confessions manifestly designed to lead me astray, such as "I knocked off an old woman and pinched her savings" and other such crude vulgarities, as if acting the part of some hero of Dostoyevsky or some figure from the Parisian underworld transported to Thessaloniki. In spite of this, my instinct warned me to continue in the disagreeable role of interrogator, even when your treacherous and wretched son changed tactics and, jumping up from his seat, came and sat on the floor – luckily upon it was spread a fine, thick rug – and, suddenly embracing my legs, said almost sobbing, "I love you like a father, but I've never been able to extract even a single sigh from you" – and he was, I must admit, a faultless actor. For a moment I thought of abandoning the "interrogation" as fruitless; I realised, however, that this was precisely the outcome which Ioannis wished to achieve, whereupon I reacted in what might be called a homeopathic manner: I stroked his rich mane of hair and assured him of my sentiments, my friendly sentiments, while he clung ever more closely to my legs and rested his beautiful head on my thighs. I must confess that my position was extraordinarily difficult, and was made even more so by the sudden arrival of young Angela (for this is the name of my home help, an unfortunate girl who is alone in the world having lost her parents and all other relatives in the Asia Minor tragedy), who, entering the room, was dumbfounded by the sight before her eyes, which it is to be admitted would have startled anyone, even someone as naive as this young girl.

I fear that I am digressing and entering into details that – for you at least – are insignificant, without so far having told you that which is of essential importance. It may very well be that some unconscious sympathy is leading me to postpone the painful revelation which, I make no doubt, will cause you as a father to feel much bitterness. Nevertheless, I consider that it is preferable and indeed a duty absolutely laid upon me to make this revelation. Your son, then, having reached a state of financial and subsequently mental desperation, has been transformed into a robber and a thief, whose victim has been you yourself. I am calmer now that I have said it. That fateful evening Ioannis, after sending Angela out upon a pretext, charging her to go and buy drinks and sweets, confessed to me, wretch that he is, that together with a "friend" of his, experienced in such matters, he had burgled your factory in Aphrodite Street, that narrow lane of shame, and had removed from thence a piece of electrical machinery of some value, a small generator I believe, which his accomplice transported by car to Serres on the following day and there sold it. Are you aware to what depths Ioannis has descended and with what sort of people he consorts? I may reveal to you (since I have already offered you the bitter chalice and it makes no matter whether you merely taste the contents or drain it to the dregs) that the accomplice, so to speak, of your son is an individual of dubious morals, well known in the houses of ill repute in Irene Street, regular patron of the notorious coffee houses of the Vardari quarter, admitted repeatedly to the hospital for venereal diseases in the parish of the Resurrection, found guilty – and this is the worst and most worrying aspect – of pederasty and of living off immoral earnings. What more can I say to you? You drove your son from your home, in justifiable anger as I believe, yet you did not consider or foresee the terrible outcome consequent on this act. You may perhaps be wondering in what manner I have amassed all this information, as to the accuracy of which there is no doubt whatsoever. You may rest easy: I have not resorted to the police or to any other authority. Almost all this information was given to me by Ioannis himself in a momentary outburst of honesty, contrition and remorse (for, as we should recognise, he still retains the remnants of noble feelings as well as the sensitivity of the devil himself) but, in addition to this and quite unexpectedly, by information which the much put-upon Angela confided in me.

This young girl is a noble creature, in spite of her humble origins, who is also in peril through the corrupting influence of your son. I do not know whether, finally, that which compels me to write and send to you this letter is not in fact my anxiety about this young girl's future, for I must admit that I feel a great degree of love for her and fear lest she should be corrupted (if this has not already happened) by your perverted son. I am indeed extremely anxious when I consider into what dark byways this all too experienced and unscrupulous young man may lead the innocent Angela to stray. I have already learned that she takes him to her humble room, that she supports him and, poor naive girl that she is, takes him round to churches and chapels. Yet how does the unhappy girl find the money for this, in what manner does she come by it? I call to mind the "friend" and accomplice of your son, his relations with prostitutes, and I tremble. It is criminal, I am overcome with panic and great pain as I consider the corrupting methods and influences of Ioannis and his kind. I shall reveal to you one last matter and then I shall have done, for I cannot conceal from you the fact that the writing of this letter causes me unimaginable mental anguish. I shall tell you the most important aspect of all this. Angela is no longer a virgin (who could have hoped as much in a creature so attractive and at the same time all alone in this cruel and immoral world of ours?), nevertheless she retains an amazing purity of spirit. Appreciating this purity and having dwelt with the girl for some time, I had made up my mind to propose marriage to her – a marriage in form alone, naturally – and to make her my sole heir. However, the appearance on the scene of your son blew my plans and all my good intentions to pieces.

I am addressing this to you in order to ask you to intervene.

I beg you to do so, for otherwise I fear that I shall not be able to control myself and shall finish by making myself ridiculous (I could reach the point of begging Ioannis on my knees to remove himself from her life and from our lives) or by lowering myself, as, for example, by giving your son up to the police, or even by resorting to some act of violence. Do not underestimate my despair. For, finally, I shall not spare your son, nor do I care how far he falls. I repeat, do something, I beg you on behalf of the orphaned girl. I even fear that in a short while I shall forget my mature years and shall start running after Angela's skirts like a crazed old dotard thus making a laughing stock of myself. Do something. I beseech you this for your own good as well.

The letter ended here, and bore no signature or address. Everyone wondered why it wasn't sent to the unhappy father, how come it ended up with the Public Prosecutor. Moreover this wasn't the only thing that his family wondered, nor the last thing, nor the biggest thing either. Euthalia searched and searched for a long time to find the letter writer and the other characters in the drama, but the only one she succeeded in finding was Angela; she explained the letter to the girl and it was just as if she'd given her Communion, for Angela burst into tears and confirmed everything. However, she knew nothing about accomplices, about them she could give no evidence. And neither did Yannis have anything to say about them when she handed him the letter; for a while they remained without speaking, then after a little while he wondered aloud, "I'm puzzled why he gave it to you" and he meant their father, the letter, why it hadn't been given to Ergini who was the elder of the sisters. Both brother and sister thought about it, and maybe it was the same suspicion that was causing both of them pain. In the end the boy said, "I wish my mother were alive, and my father" and there were tears in his eyes. And the following day he awoke like a new person, regenerate.

Fotis

Somewhere round about the middle of '28 Fotis said, "I'm done with adventures at sea," although he was inconsistent, as the future was to show. But it might have been at that moment, in Skopelos, that his long affair with foreign lands, the desert, the *felaheen* women began. And his plans dated back a long way, maybe even back to his childhood, and now the time had come for them to blossom, to throw out leaves and shoots. It didn't seem difficult at all, there'd be no pain involved, he wouldn't drown, when he saw the mountain looming in the night and someone told him, "that's Skopelos," he simply skulked in a corner till both his superiors and his friends had forgotten about him, then jumped into the sea and was lost to sight. The roar of the engines was loud and the waves ceaselessly breaking (which Fotis had allowed for); he said to himself, I'll swim slowly and calmly. And in a little while the ship had disappeared into the night, with no one thinking to search for him, and before the day even broke he was being bruised on the rocks, roundly cursing this goddamn place, until in the end he found a strip of sandy beach and collapsed on it. Youth, stubbornness and his island upbringing all burned strong within him, so that after a couple of hours' sleep he was up and searching for a hiding place. And all the while he was seeing himself as another Robinson Crusoe, whom he'd always envied at the cinema, and then made his way deep into an ancient olive grove, thinking, "they mustn't find my clothes." He could see a whole string of difficulties before him but was determined to overcome them.

And his mother and his brothers and sisters wept when the letter arrived saying that he'd disappeared, they all thought he'd drowned with the exception of Marika, who neither went running off to church nor genuflected but simply hugged her Angel and dreamed of her lost happiness – or of her lost husband – sure that he had set out on his wanderings, maybe even deeper into the desert, beyond the point where they had stood one day in great thirst and he had said to her, all woebegone and sulky, "let's go back home to our own country, so we don't die here."

As it happened, though, he was not so very far off, he was not being roasted by the sun, not yet anyway; a tree offered him protection, before him lay a beach whose name was The Vineyard, all about him nothing but red earth and pine trees and beyond them a strip of sand which the sea lapped calmly, like the placid waters of a lake. And this wilfully shipwrecked mariner was constantly on the lookout, keeping an eye out all round him: everything was progressing tranquilly, the sun rose higher and the sea turned a deep blue, then almost white like a desert. Then voices and laughter, at least three people, all of them young. Fotis calculated, "let them have fun" or take their clothes off, so that his plan could be set in motion. And everything worked out exactly as he'd planned, like a sailor's knot to be tied or untied whenever you feel like it. Two men, a woman and a little girl came into sight making their way down between the bushes on the rudimentary path that led down to the beach, then walked along the shore towards the rocks where the loneliness of the place was even greater. Fotis watched them from his tree, bit his lips, concentrated his gaze on them; he saw them undress, their bodies as white as paper, the woman well-built and plump. And they hung their clothes on the branches and at the foot of the pine tree left a basket – and Fotis said to himself, "they've thought of everything," that he would be naked and hungry. And he bided his time patiently until they'd plunged into the sea, shouting, "it's cold, it's cold" and laughing to warm themselves up; "what would you have said if you'd been with me in the night, in the deep water," muttered the shipwrecked sailor, and kept on biting his lips because they were beginners as far as the sea was concerned and didn't go in any deeper, they were merely splashing around in the shallows and spoiling his plan.

In the end both the sun and fortune smiled on him, the swimmers came out of the water and lay on the sand; then, when they felt the time had come, they set off for regions unknown, round the corner behind the rocks, maybe looking for a cave or in search of grapes. Fotis couldn't see which, in any case he had eyes only for their clothes and the basket. And as soon as the place was deserted Robinson Crusoe said, "this is the chance to act" and, leaping like a goat, arrived at the tree, helped himself to a pair of trousers and a white overshirt, not forgetting the basket, and in a few seconds all of them had disappeared with him into the woods, as far away as possible. And Fotis congratulated himself, "it wasn't for nothing that I watched so many films," and that night, walking along alone in the darkness, he saw the pale little lights of the village which spread around the harbour and then climbed obstinately up the hill. Then, feeling his way and groping, he came to the place where they left their boats, where they caulked them and painted them, he found a can of red paint, returned to his "lair" in a lonely spot and spent all night painting the white trousers red, red as a flame or a rose, so that no one would recognise them. Like a wary cowboy, he didn't light a fire though, no one was to notice even a single spark, and anyway it wasn't necessary in summer, in peaceful Skopelos, where just as his eyelids began to droop he heard two dogs howling.

The following day at noon he mingled with the crowd down by the harbour, the boatmen, the porters, the captains. And no one asked who the porter with the red trousers was, his face hidden as he bent beneath the heavy sack, going nimbly up the gang-plank and then down into the hold to unload his burden. Nor did anyone attempt to find him again, specially since he didn't try to find them or ask to be paid. The sun was burning and the heat induced drowsiness and the activity was feverish; for the schooner was due to leave in an hour's time and the agent was still cursing, the harbour master was cursing too because the paperwork was enough to reduce anyone to tears, and the cargo dangerously large.

Fotis couldn't hear them, however, because he was plunged in darkness behind some sacks, and he said to himself, the only thing I can do is go to sleep, as if he might possibly dream of happiness. And he cast his mind back over his whole plan, the sailor's cap and collar that he'd buried high up on the mountain, the swimmers who would have been obliged to go home stark naked, the longing or the laughter of the woman. And as he thought of Marika he was struggling with fatigue, and a nagging idea came into his mind which said, they'll all be wearing black, they'll have gone crazy, and he fell asleep. And he no longer saw the daylight or the starlight either, which in its turn faded and was extinguished as another day arrived, at which they opened up the hatches of the hold and he was startled by the blue sunlight and the voices cursing and swearing. But he was telling himself, don't wake up in case you move, even though pangs of hunger had him in their grip and he said, "if only I had a drop of water to drink."

The captain said savagely, "I'll throw you into the sea and then you can drink your fill." It proved impossible to escape from them, so he had to come out of his hole like a rat in search of a bit of cheese or even just a morsel of dry bread. They gathered round him, the crew, and laughed, "we've never seen a rat in bright red trousers before," and the captain asked, "so where were you hoping to make for?" to which the stowaway answered, "I was thinking of getting off at Tunis?" "We're not going that way, get off now," and they all roared with laughter once more, they'd already reached Volos, were on their way to Piraeus, then Crete, then back again. And Fotis said, "well, anyway" just as if he was doing them a favour. But the captain became serious again – he was an ugly, squat man of about sixty – and said, "what's your name? Let's see your papers," but the other man replied quite simply, "Mitsos" and nothing further, as if butter wouldn't melt in his mouth. The sea was lively, with a brisk wind blowing his hair into his eyes so that he kept bending forwards. "Hey, you're from Mytilini aren't you?" cried the captain who was trying to get to the bottom of things, and the young man answered "no" and shook his head. And when the interrogation was over the captain said, "give him something to eat, we don't want him dying of starvation on us and bringing us bad luck," and in the afternoon they set him to washing down the decks to earn his bread honestly. The sunset was a heaven-sent joy, everything bathed in an orange glow; the sailors came and stood around and started telling tall stories and tales. And when they'd finished "Mitsos" told his own tale, how he'd idled his way along at the Works and gone out singing at Saporta, "and one evening," he continued, "a girl came by and begged us to take her with us, for her husband was an old man and her tits ached, I can see her now in her blue dress, just like a little night bird who wanted to sing for us" – and he winked at the sailors. But by now darkness had fallen and the sea was black, and the captain was heard commenting from his corner, "just like a flower bud, aren't you, little spiv" and he was being sarcastic.

At Piraeus where they left him he sensed that he was among people who didn't love flowers, didn't water them or feed them. However, the cook of the schooner had foreseen this and just before they put him ashore had slipped into his pocket two ship's biscuits and some olives in a screw of paper: a farewell present which staved off his pangs of hunger until the following morning. For Fotis had his plan all worked out – tried and tested – and passed himself off once more as a graceless porter, he heaved a sack onto his shoulder, clung to it – two days and nights in the hold without any more food or anything – then heaved it off staggering from hunger, deposited it in the warehouse and stood there incapable of any further effort, moaned, "where are you, mother?" and collapsed on the foreign soil with the sun burning his dry face. And he lay as if dead in a world without sound or colour, until he felt something like dew on his cheeks, then in his mouth, on his tongue, his throat, and voices began to be heard, maybe they were birds or fish, for he couldn't see them and they didn't caress him. And the first thing he saw in this lost world was the black foot of a barefoot angel which after a bit was lifted, came closer, kicked his insentient pale hand, and then the birds were chattering once more, till in the end they were driven off (he saw them flying away like black rags in the air) by a woman wearing a black robe who seemed to be burnt dark by sun and sand, her face a dry mask apart from her eyes which burned feverishly. And it was her earthenware cup which was being carried to his mouth, his nose and was watering him, refreshing his lips, sending little rivulets running down his neck, his chest – it was ambrosia and nectar to him.

And as she was hanging out her washing one day, drops of water running down her legs, Myrsine saw the postman approaching, grinning like the bearer of good news, and he gave her the envelope. Except she couldn't read it and had to call her daughters, one of whom managed to make out the words – a true feat, spelling out the syllables, one by one. For a moment the girls were puzzled, who could this Dimitris Sirtsis be that was sending them a letter, but in the end Myrsine said, "it's his scrawl," and she meant her Fotis's who'd been lost at sea, and she was proved right. And they laughed and cried, that their boy was alive, that he hadn't been swallowed up by the sea, not this time, even if the navy had written to them that he was "missing" in the waters off Skopelos. He was alive and told them all about it, all higgledy-piggledy:

Respected Mother,

I am in good health, and hope the same for you. I am writing to you from the desert, the Arab lands at the world's end. I'm working in the oil fields, at construction, fate and my own pig-headedness cast me up here. Our bosses are English and they lash out with their whips if you take things easy and don't work. We're digging and laying pipes which will go all the way to the sea. I act as both cook and electrician when needed – better not ask how. For months now the only thing I see is the sky and the sand. They pay us well, in English money, except that there's nothing to spend it on here. They give us rations to eat with sand in them, tea with bacon and meat that stinks by the time it gets here, what I wouldn't give for your cooking, Mum. Don't ask how I ended up here, it's a long story. I would have been locked up in Beirut if it hadn't been for an Arab woman, bless her heart for taking pity on me and looking after me. She sent us here to work in the desert, me and her son, hoping we'd do well out of it, but mostly to get her Ismail away from the bad habits he was picking up round the port, quite a job looking after him. Mum, Fatima is like you, only she's darker, she sent us here to live like monks, tell Marika so she knows. I think of all of you, and specially my little yid of a son. They don't take money for abroad, so I can't help you out for the moment. As soon as we get back down to Beirut or some other port, you can be sure, I'll pay you back in a lump sum. Love to all my sisters and Stratis, to the crowd at the Works, my respects to Kokonas and Tzamalis and anyone else who remembers me.

I kiss your hand, your prodigal son, Fotis.

But at the end, as if he'd had second thoughts and had wanted to erase the names and the greetings there was another scrawl which begged:

I mustn't forget. Don't tell anyone that I've written to you or that I'm alive. Not Kokkonas, and not Tzamalis. And don't write to me at all, the address I've put on this letter is false, like the name I've used.

And they grumbled, "when did he ever say anything true?" And they caressed Angel who was a great big boy by now, they were thinking of sending him to school, but all he did was play, he was obstinate and naughty and pulled up all his granny's flowers – and got walloped. And they thought of Marika who had said a few days ago, "I'm a widow now" but instead of wearing black had returned to her old ways, the cafés' chantant and billiard halls, but as Myrsine said, "don't blame her, it's our boy's fault." So his sisters kept silent, but they picked up Angel and cuddled him, they'd started him off on the right path, they thought, every Saturday stripped naked in the washtub and every Sunday off to church, where Myrsine was a regular and devout member of the congregation. And that same autumn they took the child to a teacher, an old and feeble woman who gathered all the infants in her courtyard and taught them their ABC and counting on their fingers and songs. And Myrsine said, "let him not grow up like his father, like his mother, with all their wheelings and dealings."

Months passed before another letter from Fotis arrived, it was in spring, at Easter time, that he sent them a postcard of Christ on the cross with only a couple of words on it, "I'm still being tortured like this" which made them cry and fear the worst.* But his brother Stratis said, "just wait till you see him resurrected and

---

* All that remains of this legendary period of Fotis's life, known from now on as Dimitrios Sirtsis, jack-of-all-trades for a petroleum company somewhere in Mesopotamia, is a single photograph showing the deserter dressed as a "commando" with high English puttees, a beret, and his everlasting moustache à la Gilbert, plus a few postcards of harem women or the gardens of the Orient, or bedouin women with jars on their shoulders. On the back of these cards a lot of spidery scrawling full of indescribable spelling mistakes attempts to make jokes and to conceal torments.

we'll be having a good laugh" and started telling them about the time when they used to be up at dawn, going to grab the morning papers and hawking them round the neighbourhoods.* And Myrsine felt nostalgic, "those were the days," as if it had been a paradise now lost, in spite of the fact that her boys would be up before daybreak and would be loafing around in unfamiliar streets where trams passed at speed, where there were Jews and Arabs, and life was one long struggle of deprivation, down in the basements, but where all the same they used to get together and sing, and the sisters would dance and the mother relax, deceived by it. Now they'd got another house, a bit bigger, just above the church of the Resurrection. They had their own garden with a lofty mulberry tree and their own livestock. And one of the daughters was married, was a lady now and had a son of her own, whom Angel used to play with or to pinch, so that his grandmother had to go after him, and she remembered Fotis, what a disgrace he'd been, the whole island had known of it. And she'd sigh and think of him, the frights he'd given them, the times they'd had to go running after him to the police station, and within her heart she had the secret hope, "maybe he'll make money and be all right." And she waited for the next letter in the hope that it might be more cheerful. And she spent hours in front of the icons, in beseeching prayer.

---

* When Anastasopoulos set up the first rudimentary news agent in Thessaloniki, Fotis and Stratis, hungry little barefoot paupers, were just what he needed for the group of paperboys he started, who needed the few pence they could earn and would go around from Vardari to the grand villas and gardens, crying their wares. This was before 1920. And the business did well (though in the end he had to pay for it, when his son ran through everything and they went broke), and they did well. Later on the two orphan boys went to work in the "Company", as everyone called the Belgian firm that installed and received the proceeds of the trams and the municipal lighting. Stratis used to hand over every last penny to his mother and she'd give him some back as pocket money. Fotis always had expenses of his own, and before too long he had family obligations, Marika and his son.

Christos

Major Euripides jumped onto the moving train and disappeared, but Christos ran to the "Independent" like a madman, closed the door of the editor's office behind him, then in a little while re-emerged looking as if he was crying. "They won't ever let me get ahead," he was thinking, maybe right now this minute the coup was breaking, ministers would be in danger, newspapers too, and afterwards everyone would say, "whoever would have expected it?" All the same, everyone knew whom the major believed in and what he loved – in '23 he was saying that heads would roll, then later they sent him to Paris, a good safe distance so that everyone would get some peace. Christos had read of all this, but his father had also told him about it, "he was my platoon commander in the Balkan Wars," he said and remembered how the man would hold his machine-gun close in his arms and run on ahead of the soldiers like one possessed; on one occasion they lost sight of him and didn't have a clue where they were meant to be going.

They'll lose him again now, reflected Christos and bit his nails with impatience that they wouldn't let him do anything or make a name for himself. In the office across the corridor he could see Manatoglou dozing off, he was responsible for labour issues and people said he only wrote what he was paid to write, once three men from the village of Epanomi lay in wait for him and beat him black and blue, claiming that he'd sold out on the tram-drivers. "I can't manage to get off to sleep so easily," grumbled Christos, sure that he'd be fidgeting all night long. "You're touchy and selfish," his father scolded him one day, because a cousin from the village had been sent to visit him and he'd been annoyed that they'd given him the burden of looking after her, that he'd had to take her on the tram with him – she was wearing her village clothes and a kerchief on her head and every time the tram swayed she almost fell over. And he'd seen one or two people casting scornful looks at her, what an animal she is, he thought, and stood as far away from her as possible, for he was wearing his trilby and his black gloves. It was a trial, he saw her eyes filling with tears but said to himself, well I never asked her to come; and when they got out at the main road leading to the market he'd hurried along three paces ahead of her, never saying a word to her, acting as if he didn't know her. When she returned offended to her village he got his reward, his father wrote, "you don't care a scrap for us any more."

In '33 Euripides took his lost brigade and entrenched it in Rentina, it was May and they were hidden by the foliage, and everyone was singing the praises of Democracy and Venizelos; one evening two soldiers came to his tent, declaring, "we are the committee," the people's will must be done, they said, time to dismantle conservatism and join forces with the workers. But Euripides said, "first come discipline and knowledge," which is what he'd been taught in Paris, at the General Staff College. Later he was to tell (and to write) that it was the soldiers who were right – "but who are they fighting for?" he'd ask, because he had seen their leaflets, which showed workers and soldiers and peasants, all bursting their chains against a brilliant red background. Christos knew about all this, the soldiers had told him about it, they said, "he'll make another coup and it'll be a popular one," they placed their hopes in Euripides in spite of the fact that he'd meted out punishment fatigues and they'd cursed him in their barracks. So Christos went and confided all this to the editor, "don't imagine that they give a damn for Venizelos," people said he was old now and had become conservative, populists and royalists, it was all one.

"They're destroying law and order," lamented his father, who had his field to think about and his work, continuity. "But what good has it ever done you, killing yourself all these years?" complained his mother – who was up at dawn to work, yet when evening fell her son's work was never finished. "Let's see what you've achieved," his father would add, who prided himself on the fact that "I for one don't lack my daily bread," and what he meant was that in Thessaloniki people were taking to the streets and shouting, "we want jobs, we want bread" and raising their clenched fists. "Much better stay on the vegetable patch," his father advised Christos who had abandoned them, turned his back on the earth and the world of green growth, handed down through the generations, a wisdom which bore abundant fruits, the cellar full, the wine strong and dry and the flowers not so numerous. But the lad replied, "you're buried alive here." And he preferred the city.

And the paper was also a sort of tomb, specially for a boy arriving from the village, scared of the trams and the women. And when he got a job at the "Independent" (at the beginning he used to sleep on the desks and worked as night watchman, then he was put in charge of the inkwells or the stove, and in the end one day they told him, "you can write the funeral notices"), he decided to change his whole person, and for two months went without an evening meal, then appeared in a suit, a panama hat and a cane; everyone roared with laughter, for they couldn't forget how one day he'd stood in front of the editor like some neglected cur and said, "I'm hungry," and it was a pitiable sight. However, those were other times, the war was raging and the English had left, who gave away their possessions quite casually or left them lying around to be stolen. Then one day he was clad in uniform too, they were trained in a rough and ready sort of way to go and conquer Asia Minor – and that was how he met Euripides, who held the reins while Christos pulled or ran around, until they were back again and everything seemed hopeless; there was hunger, there were refugees, and on the other hand various pretentious types who might not have had much to eat but spent their whole time at dance halls, adorned their lapels with a flower and wore dark glasses even on cloudy days. But his father wrote to him, "leave off all these vanities, start putting something aside for a rainy day, in case you have to tighten your belt again," for they weren't rich themselves and he wasn't going to unloose their own purse strings, which anyway Christos's mother kept tightly fastened. And it was his mother who grumbled; "what did you want to go and get married for," she wailed, she'd heard stories about the crazy Thessaloniki girls, "they paint their faces just like actresses" – this was their crime – and his own girl, Amalia, had actually stood on a stage and sung, though this they kept secret since in any case the only people she sung for nowadays were her own children.

People said that Euripides would never marry, that he was passionately devoted to his career, and moreover had a mother and two sisters and two nieces who adored him. Except that one day Christos said, "that's a pack of lies," for he had gone to get a breath of air in the lonely parts of Votsi and in among the trees, in the old pine wood, he'd seen a man in uniform embracing a woman in a bright green coat, whose black hat hid her face. It had rained that morning and the ground was steaming with mist, yet Christos could see and make out quite well that the man was angry and that the woman, when she left, took the narrow road towards Ay Yannis, lonely and muddy, where a car was waiting; she got in as if hunted and in a little while was out of sight. Christos stayed where he was in the field, breathing in the damp air, then realised that the officer was walking right up to him, in a minute he'd be looking him in the eyes from beneath his cap and would be saying nothing (maybe he'd be remembering some detail that needed going into), however instead the man set off towards the main road and was soon hidden by the mist, becoming one with the earth and the trees. Christos managed to recognise him though, "it must have been Euripides and his secret love" of whom he'd heard something, how she was a foreigner and a married woman. And he thought, the major has his weak spots too, his hopeless love.

It was just getting dark and the telephone rang and Christos hoped, "this will be about the coup," but it was the police saying that a factory had been burgled. And in a little while he'd set off to find out more about it, the editor advising him to "be careful" since it was a positively satanic coincidence, he remembered the name perfectly well – and the death of the banker. "How the devil does shuffle the pack sometimes," for someone had burgled a factory, and they'd thought him mixed up in matters in the past, they'd hushed the names up, a young man who kept strange company – "I don't believe he'll prove to be a thief," the suspicion was a bold one. But when he got there they presented everything as rather trivial, all that had been stolen was a small generator, maybe out of order, which could easily have been thrown out as rubbish.* And Christos said to himself, "then why did he send me out here at night," for it was out beyond Vardari in the disreputable alleys. But on his way back, in Egnatia Street, he froze for a minute in terror against a wall, for horsemen were galloping by, their equipment on their backs, their rifles slung over their shoulders. Something's up, he thought, he remembered Euripides's disappearance and hurried towards the tram stop. From the cafés came the clatter of backgammon and the buzz of conversation – he liked the carefree atmosphere, remembered his father who, before he'd left, had said, "steer clear of gambling" and always used to boast, "I don't even know how many cards there are to a pack." The only people in the tram were two working-class women with their shopping baskets full, chattering away and laughing.

All the little theatres had gone now, who knew where Victoria and her suitors had found a niche, all those people who abducted young Jewish girls and got dragged off to police stations and interrogations. He couldn't forget the great awning with its red lights that flashed on and off, the bell that was always ringing to attract customers; it all seemed just a memory though, on the site of the theatre now stood the hotel called "Vienna", with its hundred rooms, all luxury, the doorman in uniform at the entrance, the grandeur. The two women were giggling away again in the front seats, the tram had now reached the "Alcazar", the market-

---

* This little lane remained quite unchanged, both as to its buildings and as to the professions that used to flourish there, until the roads leading to Vardari were widened, blocks of flats and hotels were put up and the inns were lost forever. In 1942, during the great famine, Christos sent his own son to this alley to collect a sack of wheat which had been promised to him. But the boy couldn't find the right address so he knocked on the half-open door of a low building and saw a woman naked from the waist down, with everything she'd got on show. She rose and invited the boy to come in, a customer. But he was terrified, even though he was almost adolescent – and he explained to her what he'd come for, the address he was looking for, the wheat. The woman seemed to wilt before his eyes: she must have been about his mother's age. All the same she pointed out the door that he wanted. That evening his father questioned him closely about the address, said something to his mother, then chuckled – to himself.

place, and the lights were becoming brighter, people were making their way up the hill, going home, to the upper town and to the St. Dimitris quarter, where the gardens began, high walls and latticed windows. But Christos said, "maybe we'll be making a night of it" and he felt an inexplicable anxiety pressing in on him, as if he were going to get ill or lose his job and his security, in spite of the fact that Amalia caressed him and promised, "I'll work as a washerwoman or laundress," but he knew all the same that "the responsibility for everything lies on my own shoulders."

And at the "Independent" the editor gave him a talking to and said he should start shouldering his responsibilities. But Christos thought, "they don't need to talk about rope to hanged men in this damn place" and he remembered how they always used to stop him short, "don't write it, you'll get us all put in jail," so instead they wrote, "everything is wonderful," and "the poppy dance" was a great success, and so-and-so had made such and such a donation, philanthropic sentiments, and side by side were the advertisements for novelties, Floka chocolate, Zenith watches – "that's what brings in our daily bread," the teacher said to him cynically one day, and it was the bitter truth, things were not easy for him and he was struggling to keep the newspaper afloat. "Don't tell me that you want to do your editorial?" he'd ask him sarcastically, and Christos knew that he'd never write it. He admired Mr. Aristos who would come into the office in the early afternoon, pick up his pen and paper and fire off broadsides at Tsaldaris and Metaxas, then put on his hat with dignity and leave. In winter time one or two of the humble hacks would run forward to help him on with his coat, and Aristos would smile as if thanking them and say goodnight, then as soon as his back was turned they'd start denigrating him, for, as they'd discovered, in the mornings he used to go to the "National" where with fanatic passion he'd extol the royalists and consign the others to outer darkness. Probably he had people there as well to help him on with his coat and praise him and Aristos would smile at them.* "That's

* When Aristos got old it was during the time of the Civil War, and the hatred between the royalists and the supporters of Venizelos had been buried, all the middle classes having united to combat the reds. He ceased to write his articles, which were out of fashion and dangerous. And in a few years things became even more difficult. And Aristos was set to cor-

what the art of journalism consists of," the editor said in tones of compromise, and he meant that Christos didn't possess this art, so he sent him to report on burglaries and dances, but even then he rewrote Christos's pieces, "because you're too long-winded and dangerous," he shouted. And the young man remembered how his father used to drill into him, "if you've got nothing to say for yourself people will walk over you," even though he himself was always rather timid and pushed by Christos's mother.

"You've got to start taking some responsibility," the teacher scolded him, the editor. And he threw a sheet of paper down in front of him, "there's your Euripides," he complained – that he'd sneaked off to Kavalla like a thief in the night, that he'd roused the guard and set his own terms. And Christos said, "I told you so" but the other man wasn't listening, he was the boss who had a right to get angry and to order, "be quiet." And just at that moment the telephone rang and the teacher grabbed it in a fury, then got up from his chair and said, "yes, speaking, General ... of course ... certainly... yes, I understand that ... we shall be behind you ... yes ... yes ... yes, don't worry" and then hung up thoughtfully. "Things look rather black," he said to himself and drove Christos away, "hurry to the telegraph office and wait there," he ordered, but the young man thought, I wish they'd send me to Kavalla, which he knew from his days in the army, and in his mind's eye he could see the row of tobacco workshops, where the others used to hang around in the afternoons waiting for the girls who worked there in order to flirt with them; and a little way further off were the grand mansions with their decorative arabesques in plasterwork, and then climbing up the hill were the little alleys that reminded him of Thessaloniki and below the sea was shining and on the horizon the shadow of an island, like a vision. Now Euripides would be in command there, maybe he might have taken the Ay Silas heights with the pine trees and

---

recting the spelling mistakes and grammatical errors of younger journalists – for he had graduated from the Evangelios School at Smyrna. Someone told people about the way it used to be in the past when people had run and held his coat for him, and they mocked him. In the end they said he was going gaga and retired him. And all his articles and feuilletons and boozing sessions were forgotten. Only his name was remembered.

beeches and would be threatening, "whoever comes up here will pay the price."

He spent the whole night at the telegraph office, but it was a waste of time, for the lines had been cut and with them all information, and it was as if the other city had fallen asleep. At one point Christos saw fat Aristos sticking his head in at the door, he had an air of brooking no objections, but in the end he called Christos and told him, "I'll be at the Grapevine," in case he needed any help; Christos was flattered, it's a collaboration, he thought. But would the article writer remember it? Day was breaking when Christos left the telegraph office and he shivered in the dawn, he turned the collar of his jacket up a bit and waited for the tram. The first souls he encountered were five carts making their way slowly to the market, then after a bit three workmen with their elevenses tied up in handkerchiefs – they were having a lively conversation, and when they saw Christos said loud enough for him to hear it, "it's all right for some who can go out partying at night," for they saw that he was wearing his brown suit and a tie, with a handkerchief in his breast pocket. When the first tram arrived, Christos jumped onto it with agility and enthroned himself on a seat – the window was misted up and he could only make out trees and the closed up houses and the grey road, all of them blurred and uncertain. When he got off in his own neighbourhood, he shivered once again in the early morning chill and muttered to himself. Above Hortiatis the clouds had parted to reveal a milky sky. As he opened the door he said, "it's dark in here" and switched on the light in the bedroom; "whatever happened to you?" cried Amalia who'd stayed up all night waiting for him. And he begged her, "just let me sleep" and both of them made up their minds that this was how their life would always be – little did they know.

Angela

The story of the lost uncle who was found again might have changed her fate; however, it was all lies, even though in the end her life took quite another turn in the direction that she least expected. And Angela was puzzled when she suddenly acquired relatives who'd been looking for her and found her and then in the end turned into a mystery. "This sort of muddle always seems to happen to me," she confessed to Michalis, who had unexpectedly promoted her and put her up on the stage to sing to them, and she now had two showy dresses, a red one with spangles and a white ankle-length one, and her wages had gone up as well. "Always muddles like this," she said to herself; and she remembered the tragedy of Eugenios or the adventure with Yannis, which was still continuing – he teased her, "now we're both on the up and up," he said mockingly.

However her voice was wounded when she whispered to him, "I don't recognise you," for he was in a pitiable state, and he revealed to her that they were after him; "but why?" she asked suspiciously and he replied in the tones of a saint and martyr that he was fighting on behalf of the poor. He must have been about forty, dark-skinned, his hair thinning in front, almost bald, his eyes burning feverishly. He was wearing worn overalls and his hands were engrained with grease, yet when he got his wallet out Angela said to herself, he's not doing too badly.

She asked him how he'd found her; and he told a tale full of skipped bits: how he'd grown up in Smyrna, how during the last night of the massacre her mother had searched him out, how they'd met and she'd recounted their whole dramatic story and "she made me swear to stand by you" – but the girl complained, "where were you when I was starving and cleaning other people's houses?" And he showed his remorse, "I was out having fun," he whispered, "or I was preoccupied with foreign matters." Outside it was raining cats and dogs and you could hear the music of the drainpipes streaming with water. Thus she decided, "I can't turn you out tonight" and his eyes shone, he smiled and promised, "I'll owe you for this," but Angela thought, everyone smiles at me like that, all men anyway, but there's no love in it.

"I feel tender towards you," Yannis used to say, but never "I love you," and the girl reflected, the only thing you love is your own skin and having a good time. One day she chanced to cry in front of him, it was the only time this ever happened, and he enfolded her in his arms and begged her, "don't ever cry again, because there is nothing that is worth even a single one of your tears." Whereupon lakes of tears flowed, she almost drowned in her own sobs, then afterwards confessed, "I cried for all the things I've been through but you'll never see me cry again" – and she kept this promise. Until '80 when they brought him home dead in a sack and it was a miserable sight and her eyes filled with tears, only then he couldn't see them or tell her, you didn't keep your word.

And her uncle told her that he was called Elias,* "I prophesy that one day you'll rise to great heights" – and Angela didn't sense how much he was mocking her; and as they talked late into the night they heard a lonely bird singing, "how odd," said Angela but her uncle looked at her strangely, as if the unusual voice in the darkness stirred in him some remorse. And the man told her, "the night of the killings I was in your neighbourhood, searching and asking for you, even outside town." How it was on the afternoon when the working girl was killed, by coincidence that very same afternoon, that he'd been told where Angela lived, "and I passed outside the house and I saw you laying her out with the old women" – "I was fond of Irene," said the girl as if lost – "yes, it was there that I learnt it, and I saw you from a distance, and people assured me that it was really you" – "but who'd be able to do that," she wondered, since in the shanties she was a stranger

---

* Translator's note: Elias = the prophet Elijah.

among strangers as far as her family and her roots were concerned. He said, "I don't remember" and the conversation stopped; after a bit the girl said, "stay here and I'll treat you, tonight we'll share whatever I've got, but at dawn you leave." It was a small place, eyes everywhere and tongues ready to wag – and the other nodded and whispered, "that's plenty for me." And when they'd eaten he got out his tobacco, "I don't suppose," said he, "that you mind" – maybe he knew that she sang in a tavern where the atmosphere was always thick with the smoke of the customers' cigarettes; "no", she whispered to him and they both smiled.

And he stretched as if in satisfaction; everything was going just fine. "You know, we have common friends," her uncle suddenly said, and Angela wondered how this could be. "I saw you talking to a young man outside that house," he said, "the night you were holding a wake for the dead girl"; she was still puzzled, "no," she said, "I didn't know anyone there" – "all the same, you advised him to leave," he was on foreign territory, a young man in a brown suit, and she remembered, "I didn't know him," but he was in danger of being beaten up, the way he was sticking his nose in and asking questions. "I know him," said Elias, "he's a friend of mine, a journalist" and he gave a meaningful little laugh, "he's married though," and the girl said, "I didn't ask" – now I know all your little ways, she was thinking, having lived them and studied them at Michalis's, she could have told them off on her fingers, or maybe her toes come to that, for one night an afficionado had bent down and cried, "I kiss your dainty little shoe," and the next day she'd received a pair of pure silk stockings and protested, "what does he think I am?" but Domna scoffed and scolded her, "watch out you don't offend him," and she kept the stockings, for he was a good customer and a gentleman, every evening he and his companions set to and spent money and drank and danced and distributed a whole fortune on flowers.

In the morning when they awoke she looked out of the window at the little garden with its humble flowers, the sun embroidering the drops of dew left by the night; Elias said, "I'll never forget last night" and, turning up the collar of his overalls, was off and out of sight with such speed that Angela wondered, was he perhaps only a dream? But a moment later she changed her mind, "dreams don't leave little notes behind them," she muttered, and all it said was, "thank you, your uncle," without anything further. Don't tell anyone about it, her heart advised her, for she was always afraid of mischances, and as she turned it over in her mind she came to the conclusion, he was making a fool of me, uncle Elias whom she didn't even know where to find again – "and who needs him anyway?" she laughed. And she kept thinking that the whole thing was perhaps a fairy tale, for she didn't believe that he'd arrived at the poor neighbourhood outside the castle walls in search of her traces. And there was something else that was suspicious; when she asked him where he lived, where his house was, he stammered, "it's a mansion" without giving the address – it could have been dipping its toes in the sea, or perhaps somewhere near the market or the White Tower, at any rate all this was left vague, as if he'd been wandering in a strange city, late at night.

And Angela was constantly trying to find a way of moving to another neighbourhood, somewhere closer to where she worked, for that quarter seemed quieter to her, and the people calmer, though even there misdeeds and poverty were not lacking. And she remembered the gentleman who bought all the flowers, who, as people said, came from Bulgaria; his father had made him leave in order to escape (he used to say "from the military" but everyone else would laugh and say "from trouble"), he bought a house and a great many vineyards and lived off the wine and eau de vie they produced. However, gossip spread round the neighbourhood about various matters, supposedly he made a habit of having many women over to his house and of living it up all night long – and within three years he sold his vineyard at Inglis, saying it wasn't worth his while. "Come round to my house one evening," he invited Angela politely; he almost kissed her hand – and Domna said, "shall we go?" for she was on the lookout for this sort of chance, and Michalis threatened, "I'll flay you alive." In the early hours one morning the whole neighbourhood was disturbed and angered by the groans of a woman; later word went round that Michalis's girlfriend had fallen down stairs and had broken two of her ribs. However, this wasn't the way the street boys told it, who fancied her but never had her.

And it was on the third day that the revelation was made and Angela exclaimed, "I knew it." And the revelations came thick and fast, first the diary of a barber who was found hanged in his shop, "I had the suffering of two innocent men on my conscience," as he confessed. And he recounted in detail how he knew the layout of the house, how he was obliged to exploit the relationship that the banker had with a young man, how it suited him that the gypsies had been cutting wood all day. And he took their axe which they'd left lying in a corner (they were going to continue cutting wood the following day), he hid it among the bushes in the courtyard, he shut up his shop as usual and went to the coffee house

when it began to get late I said that I was going home to bed, because I'd have to be up early the next morning to clean up my barber's shop. I followed the stream bed until I arrived behind the banker's villa. I climbed over the wall and jumped down into the courtyard, I took the axe from where I had hidden it and I knocked on the door. I knew the house well, for he'd often called me in to shave him in his drawing room on Sundays. He opened the door and he asked me what I wanted at that time of night. I said I wanted a favour, to ask him if he could let me have a loan from the bank, supposedly to buy myself a little house. He let me in. I kept the axe as well concealed as I could. Luckily he went first and I followed him. He smelt of eau de cologne just like my barber's shop. I didn't wait any longer because I was afraid I might not get a better chance. I raised the axe and brought it down right in the middle of the top of his head. He died quickly. I confess that I killed him because I needed money. He was old and used to throw his money away on worthless boys. I only found 3,250 drachmas which he had in his trouser pocket. I didn't find anything in his study, nor anywhere else. I took his gold watch and his cufflinks. His ring was too tight, I couldn't get it off his finger so I left it. However, I thought that even the watch and the cufflinks that I'd taken would give me away at once. I dug a hole in the shop under one of the cabinets, the right-hand one, and I buried them there after wrapping them in gold paper. The police can find them there. I don't regret having killed him because I'd been thinking of it for a long time before I did it. But I'm sorry about the two poor wretched gypsies that I dragged into it without mean-

ing to. I don't ask anyone to forgive me because anyway they're not going to. Life is just a mockery, it's a sentence that we have to come and serve and then die.

The newspapers wrote all about it, they had photographs of the murderer and the victim, and that night Angela couldn't sleep, she kept hearing the door creak and something like footsteps pacing to and fro in the yard outside. Before dawn came she got up and went to ask a woman next door to let her in, but the woman looked sour and suspicious so she went away again. And she wished that Yannis was there – he too must be breathing more freely again – and she thought about Eugenios and all the passions and the bitter conversations. And then, right on top of all this came the next revelation, the biggest one; it was a Saturday, never to be forgotten, and Angela was with Domna on their way to the tavern, but suddenly the singer froze for there in front of her was Elias, who also seemed to her to have frozen at the unexpected meeting. And he was well dressed now, in a grey suit and a tie and a trilby, but his eyes glittered – maybe out of pleasure or out of agony – for he put his finger to his lips as if beseeching her, keep quiet; twilight was drawing in and the sky was full of colours and in the trees birds were twittering, in a dishevelled pine tree and in the acacias. And she was even more surprised that Domna smiled at him and said "good evening", nothing more, for the girls walked on and Elias said nothing. But Angela couldn't stop herself, she turned her head, but it was already too late – all she managed to see was half of him disappearing round the corner. And it really was a great surprise to hear what Domna disclosed, who had a small scar on her lip these days which made Michalis say, "now you look more roguish," whereupon they both laughed.

"Elias is what people call a character," the roguish girl told her that same evening. He'd come, people said, from Smyrna though other people said he was a Cretan (because his name was Kaounakis) and he claimed to be an engineer; he put up shacks for the patriots from Asia Minor (some people said he sold them dear), he was always on the various committees that handed out food and clothes to the refugees. One night two cut-throats from Smyrna had got him up against a wall and told him, "you thief, you'll die" but the next morning they were caught; he went along and stated, "it's not them" and they were set free. Then word got about that he was a red and everyone smiled. And in '25 the bombshell exploded: the man from Smyrna, their red, made an arranged marriage with an upper-class girl, a sensitive and beautiful and polite island girl, but unapproachable. And in three years Elias had built a three-storey mansion, the tallest in the neighbourhood – and during the same period Dorothea (for this is what she was called) gave him his three sons, of whom the third was named Vladimir (after quite a few rows with the Church and with her family), and everyone was puzzled as to where he'd got this name from; but he must really have been a red and have been honouring Lenin who was called Vladimir, and also Ilyich as those with some education said.

So the mysterious uncle was married with children. But Angela said nothing, she kept his visit to her humble dwelling a secret, and Domna, who liked having people listen to her, went on talking, so much so that Michalis said, "you've gone crazy." And she really seemed to be devouring him alive, the way she was ferreting about in his secret life. But Domna corrected this, saying that there was nothing secret about it, or at any rate not for the police, who had gone to his house one day and asked for him; but his good luck or else his devilish cleverness came to his aid, for the engineer was in the middle of doing odd jobs when the police arrived and they took him for a workman, what with his overalls and his grease stains, "do you know someone called Kaounakis, mate?" they asked, and he said that he knew him, "third floor on the left", and made off fast.*

---

* In 1937 E. came to the end of his first phase of illegal activities. Maniadakis's gendarmes arrested him and sent him straight to the island of Anaphi. From there his family received short, dry letters and some yellow flowers which were called everlasting since they lasted for decades. Later it was found out that the Party had expelled him because this engineer of many skills had been passing himself off as a doctor. The village women protested that all he ever did was caress them verbally and nothing else. No one knew any details, not even whether everything that was said was true. The only sure thing was that one day Dorothea received an embittered letter from him, the single letter in which he allowed some sentiment to slip out, saying that he was having a hard time in Anaphi, alone and despised by all the ungrateful people who'd forgotten his struggles for them. However, later on everything was to change once more.

And at this point Angela came wide awake, "was it perhaps the day of the strikes and the killing?" and the other girl calculated for a minute and then answered, "yes, it might have been," though she wasn't quite sure of it. Then the lonely girl understood, fitted the jigsaw pieces together in her mind – he must have been running in desperation and had reached the other end of town, outside the castle walls, and there, by asking and enquiring, the "workman" had ascertained that she was from Asia Minor and all alone in the world. He had found the best hiding place possible and everything else was pure fabrication, Smyrna, his meeting with her mother, his search for her – and Angela said to herself, "he was in need, what else could he have done?" just as if the uncle had been a penurious incapacitated wretch. All the same, something didn't quite fit, some doubts remained and she felt sympathy for him; what did he mean, poor man, by getting mixed up in all that, what was he in search of when he played at being an uncle or a red? Maybe it was the adventure of it all that held charms for him, being on the run and escaping them, with Dorothea in agonies of anxiety and the children bewildered, for they were still young and couldn't understand.

All the same, "what a mystery men are," Angela said with a smile, full of bitterness – for not one of them had ever offered her any security. And she made up her mind to it, "I'll just have to manage for as long as I live." But she lived long and grew old, her eyes saw much, in the end even wealth. When she was an old woman and was taken to hospital, in '84, they asked her, "what did you enjoy?" And she murmured, "I remember Michalis and how we used to stay up all night having a good time." And everyone was puzzled and said, "she's lost her wits" because they didn't know about Michalis or about anything. All the people from the old days, all those who could have borne witness, were long gone.

Fotis

He'd remember that a friend had told him, "you're indescribable" and they'd laughed about it in the tavern. His life could have been the subject of a novel: a comedy perhaps, as he himself considered. He had second thoughts about this later, though, when he was suffering in a tent in the desert and you couldn't get up to any shenanigans because Johnny would be standing there with his whip, tapping it constantly against his breeches, and the Arabs would run around like crazy for fear of getting a taste of it, and in the end the pipes were laid, one after the other, and they'd nearly reached the sea. And Fotis swore to them all that when they got there, "I'll get my pants off and have a good soak" for the sand had got right up their noses, into their ears, "into all our orifices," he joked, and added, "into the pores of our hides," which were tanned and toughened like a camel's hide. However, Ismail came up to him that night and said, "I'll be there beside you" and he meant beside Fotis on the beach, but Fotis didn't understand his Arab logic, the other man's eyes clouded over and he said, "so that no one steals our gold sovereigns"; for Fotis had charge of them, both his own and Ismail's, and he'd sewn them into the waistband of his trousers which he never took off, not even when he slept, not even when he relieved himself. And Fotis roared with laughter but then reassured him, saying, "don't worry," and they agreed that they'd take turns swimming. And Ismail calmed down.

One night though they leapt up from their mattresses, for gunfire was all around them and everyone yelling, they saw the Englishman in his underpants, with his pistol, firing into the darkness which was full of the dancing shadows of horses and riders. They were desert bandits, they'd heard of them before, how they took whatever they could find and then burned and wrecked what they left behind. And Fotis said to himself, they'll steal the very sweat off our brows, and he wriggled along in the sand like a scorpion, the dust whipped up by the horses' and camels' hooves getting into his eyes and blinding him, and when with immense difficulty he'd managed to get out of the circle he thought, I'll dig a burrow to get into, but bullets were whistling past his ears and he saw that they'd surrounded him again, he was lost amidst their robes, they got their hands under his armpits and hauled him upright, then dragged him along and threw him down on the heap where all the others were, the whole miserable workforce – the Englishman was lying face down a little bit further off, a dark foot trod on his neck, his pistol gone. And Fotis crossed himself, "they're going to butcher us," he sobbed, but a hand reached out as if to advise him, "hang on" and it was Ismail's; he vowed, if I get out of here I'll make a pilgrimage, and all the while the bandits were howling around them. In the end, however, they took all their rations, their fuel oil, their food and disappeared into the night like demons. And everyone began to laugh with relief that they'd survived and that the bandits had left them their water, and Fotis said, "and our sovereigns," so that Ismail laughed too even though he was terrified – "we were within an inch of being killed," he told Fotis later. But the only one who was dead was the Englishman, staring out over the boundless sands with his frozen gaze – and they buried him. For five days they remained there all on their own, with nothing but water and hope to keep them going. And as the sixth day dawned three camels appeared in the distance, and it was their new bosses, and after them, in the evening, arrived a truck carrying bread and dry beans and pasta and water, and along with everything else the whisky which was for the bosses. And Fotis said, "three more weeks to go in the sand and the scorpions" which, if they stung you, you'd had it.

Anyway, Fotis and Ismail survived and said, "time for Beirut," time to make life sweet for their mothers and sisters. Only before they set out the Arab took a sharp stiletto and hid it in his belt, and Fotis found a pistol going begging and a bag of bullets and secreted them in his bosom, because they'd heard of the terrible attacks of the desert irregulars, who might be fighting the English or the French but who certainly didn't despise money – even if it was Arab money. However, their fears were unfounded as it turned out, for the two friends reached Beirut in one piece and decided that they needed a drink before immuring themselves at home. In front of them was the entrance of the cabaret, the first lights were coming on and the photographs outside were driving them crazy, blonde dancers and a Turkish woman with all her belly and her legs on show. And Fotis pronounced, "just one drink," for he knew Ismail and his past exploits – and they agreed on this. But there were people there, men and women, some in khaki and some wearing their white suits, so that the two friends felt ashamed and said, "they'll take us for gypsies," and they hid behind the staircase and admired what they saw.

The following morning they were once more at the foot of the outside staircase and Ismail was lying staring at the heavens with his chest bare right down to his belly and his ears buzzing quite inexplicably; it was dawn and chilly and this is what had woken him, he curled up like a little child trying to find some warmth, and then thought in wonder that it was daylight again. He couldn't get up though, his head was as heavy as a stone and he was dizzy. So he said, "I'll lie here and listen to the birds" but all he heard was footsteps and cars and in the end smothered laughter. And opening his eyes he saw two young girls of his own race staring at him curiously and clinging close to one another, perhaps because they were cold; when they met his dull gaze, though, they ran off flying like little birds, they were black and red and like decorations against the pale blue dawn. And the next image he saw was a man with an ash-coloured beret and an old khaki shirt and he wondered, where do I know him from? and the man spoke to him in Fotis's voice but he couldn't make head nor tail of what he said. However, in a little while his friend disappeared and Ismail was later to search for him in vain.

And it didn't occur to him to ask the women from the cabaret or the servants, who would have seen him slink up the great staircase like a cat and go into her room. Everything happened just like in some exotic film and later Fotis was to boast about it, saying, "I was expecting it" just as if it had been his destiny that Eleni should meet him in her fine premises one night and mur-

mur to him, as if drugged, "where've you been hiding yourself away?" However, when they had been to bed and made love she told him, "you're the sweetest I've ever known" and she meant sweeter than anything in the life that she'd lived so far – about which she later told him, and it was all just like some tale from Bukhara. And as the daylight began creeping through the shutters she whispered to him, "time to sleep now" and he caressed the nape of her neck and massaged her shoulders (something that he remembered from Victoria) and she said, "bless you, sweetheart" – and then just as her eyelids were closing added, "you needn't bother to search, I never keep a penny in my room," for life had toughened her with all its tricks and deceptions. But Fotis felt himself to be in a pitiable state and said, "I haven't got a sou left, not even if I sell myself into slavery" and the memory of how everything that he'd saved up working in the desert with Ismail had been lost in a single hour at dice pierced him to the heart.*
"And even if I sold myself it wouldn't pay off my debts," he said to himself, then, since day was just beginning to break, left the nightclub like a sleep-walker and found Ismail lying sprawled in the street, dreaming maybe – he went up to him and spoke to him, said, "I've lost it all, I'm ruined," but his companion's blank eyes laughed and Fotis understood that he hadn't heard a word. He thought to himself that he'd better lie low so they wouldn't find him, and the only hiding place that he liked the idea of was her warm bedroom, his hope that she might keep him there. So he went back up the stairs (the light was now shining through the glass doors) and he slipped in through the crack, neither opening nor closing the door in case the hinges squeaked, and the lady woke up: she can't have been very old for her legs could still

---

* Later on much money and riches were to pass through Fotis's hands. Nevertheless, he always managed to end up penniless. After he lost Eleni and her coffer he always worked hard to survive, jack-of-all-trades and permanent good-for-nothing, lover of cards and women and poverty. In 1970 his family – what remained of it – received a letter informing them that he had been locked up in jail in Holland. He'd gambled at cards (and lost – which is how he was found out) with forged dollars. They made a collection and somehow or other sent him the money he owed and thus got him off. After this he went back to sea again; he got taken on as cook on an old rust bucket of a freighter and set off on his last voyage.

grip and her embrace was pincer-like as he came.

And when they finally got round to having another look at one another it must have been midday, Fotis had fallen asleep in an armchair and felt a hand prodding him: it was the Arab servant who was giving him a nasty look and the deserter was scared – they're going to throw me into some dungeon – but the bedclothes stirred, a sweet scent caressed him, and he heard her voice drawl, "so you haven't flown" and she meant from her cage – and she smiled at him. Then she gave some order to the slave, who instantly slipped out like a shadow, and stretched out her hand to him, "come," said she, "and massage me again" and she undressed him. "Where did you spring from?" she asked when they had finished and he replied, "from the desert," but she was asking about his homeland so he told her which island he came from, "hey," she crowed, "olive oil men or arse fuckers?" and she turned her little arse towards him. And as he was wrestling with her and hurting her his grandad seemed to emerge from out of the bedclothes and offered him a coin if he'd lift her skirts so that the old man could see her thighs or her bottom. And he heard her groaning, "you're a devil" and he kissed her.

So the devil stayed on at her house, for he had tastes she liked. One day he whispered to her, "but who taught you?" as if he was the only one with such privileged knowledge; and she told him her story, like a fairy tale, how she'd been in Hamid's harem, in his palace – "they kidnapped me from my mother's arms when I was thirteen" and Fotis began to do sums in his head, she can't be fifty yet, he reflected; into his mind came Victoria's life, the little theatre behind Egnatia Street, her tiny dressing room and Matoula weeping, "I'd scratch your eyes out if it wasn't for the fact that I love them." And just for a second he saw a baby under its mosquito net and thought, "my angel" or Angel who was being looked after by Myrsine and his sisters.* But a fragrant palm

---

* Myrsine and the family learned about Fotis's wealth and "his" fortune fairly late, after 1935, and this was when he sent a postcard of the beach at Beirut with a fine white building above it which he'd marked with an X and the words "my house, my mansion". And it was decided to ask him to take Angel at long last to live with him, so that he would be brought up as a young gentleman and they would be spared all the expense and trouble. His mother wrote to Fotis about it. Eight months later he sent them

passed in front of his eyes, his lips, and he heard her voice say, "don't leave me, my husband." And he stayed.

That same evening he was dressed like Valentino and his eyes were shining, and within a few days he was ordering everyone around, for Eleni instructed them, "he's your master" even though in the dawn she used to cry, "you bastard, you're killing me." And Fotis shone like a star, within a month he'd forgotten everything except the torments of the desert. And in order to combat the bad memories he went and had a glass-house built, which he filled with birds and plants, and in the middle was a ceaselessly flowing fountain – and Eleni laughed, "I'll give you whatever takes your fancy," she said. And in it he put the craziest things he could think of, plants with white leaves and bright green chairs, and he dressed her like Marlene Dietrich in white men's suits and little white hats from beneath which just a sketchy idea of her dark eyes and her red lips could be glimpsed, lips which told him, "lover, I feel that our very roots are becoming one, our blood itself" whereupon he corrected her, "I'm from the island with the olive oil men" and they both giggled.

Then one day he conceived the idea that they should do a good deed, like in the films. And it was afternoon when they set out to look for Fatima; they found the Arab woman sitting on her doorstep and she saw a black car shining in the sun and a woman all dressed in white coming towards her, who said in Arabic, "I'm from Ismail" and put a bag of gold coins into her hand – but Fatima burst into tears and said, "he can hardly send them to me from heaven," for they had found him drowned among the lonely rocks. And that night Fotis cried like a baby and remembered about his pilgrimage and told Eleni of it. And she said, "you can't go off and become pious now," and she meant now that she'd found him and was enjoying him. So she gave him an expensive watch as a present to try and help him forget the river Jordan and all his crazy ideas – and he kissed her and murmured, "one day you might betray me" and was then made gloomy by this prophecy.

another card in which he bewailed the fact that he was bedridden, his ribs broken, and that his wife was wearing herself out looking after him and bearing all the cares of the business on her shoulders. However, they wrote him another letter when he'd recovered until in the end they got what they wanted – for a little while.

The Middle Ages – 2

For he could contain within himself an ocean of love which it was not possible to divide into shares, it was for everyone and for her, he couldn't measure it out, he couldn't deny the other people, those from the yard, his companions who came on foot from Pipilista to tell him, "leave your musical instruments now and the theatre and all your doubts, the day has come for us to return to our posts"; they were his old comrades, he remembered how they had hidden him, given him meat and drink, brought him messages and gazettes, "only a little while longer," they used to say, "and we'll have you out for a walk," as if he'd had a broken leg and they were waiting for it to heal. Often he would go down to the sea, he loved to look at ships, "you who are from the mountains," they'd say, "what do you want with boats?" – "I'm not some kind of savage mountain man, my grandfather was born up on those heights there, the Albanians killed him, because he refused to realise that if you leave the slopes and the forests and caves the bastards will be lying in wait for you, hidden behind the trees." But his own way of seeing things was different, the men who were hunting them he considered to be his own people, they used to work together in the workshop, at the meeting they had told him, "we are brothers" and once when he invited them home his mother said, "don't pay too much heed to the fact that they embrace you and kiss you, for you don't know what might lie hidden in their hearts," and one night the youngest came and told him, "they have betrayed us, and are coming to arrest you," but who? Why? And it was then that he went into hiding, this is called putting yourself beyond the law, it's wrong and the gendarmes come in pursuit of you; anyway, two days earlier as he stood before the soldiers, they shouted, "haven't you ever gone into hiding?" and the man with the ring laughed, they still couldn't believe that the city was in control, they thought they might fall into the hands of some gang and were getting their ransoms ready, for they were afraid lest their own people together with the ruling class might not be in time, lest a gang should come one night and knife them all or throw them on to the beach in sacks – "this is why I believe it would be better to bring in the judges." And she took his hands once again, "I lose you a little bit more each day," she said, "wait and see," he told her but she wept and asked him over and over what was left for her to wait for, and he often remained silent in his weariness. "I know that your love is not bounded by me," she told him, "and that if I died you'd be ashamed to weep," and in her mind's eye arose a green hope, a meadow that she loved and longed to be crossing once more, to find the place at the end of rainbow which they had left behind them, the treasure. "I never gave my whole self to anything" – she understood this and spoke to him as if she was expecting the end, "we shall never finish this fairy tale which so much enchants me" – "but I love this love of ours, the fact that we're together and weep together, you may leave tomorrow but our love will remain, the secret of the passion we felt, the certainty that it is something that exists and will come once more," and then she kissed him only, as if it was not possible to change his ideas and she had come to terms with this. One day she would tell him, "I remember...", it would be the beginning of another epoch, where memory would stand in front of love and would hide it from him, "I can manage without you, not seeing you any more, not hearing you, no longer waiting for you." Perhaps he did not give himself to anything: this is a sort of poverty which you do not understand, you feel that you are not living or that you are living in a time where the moment you dreamed of has already been and gone. "You have a way of adapting which alarms me, one day we might lose you from our side, we'd find you on the steps of the palace, you up there standing on the top step and us down below on the ground, and we would not dare raise our eyes to look at you, we would be unable to, you can move easily from hot to cold, I suppose it's your male nature that is to blame, it would never be possible for a woman, a woman is bound by feelings, she takes them onto her and warms them like rejected children"; but he still remained silent, he was thinking of weights, "I have hung you all around my neck like talismans," he told her, but he was thinking of other moments, the whispering moments: "I want to feel your weight on top of me," she'd say, "to feel how much you are my lord and master," and then he'd raise his hand and "hit me," she would murmur to him and close her eyes, "I cannot tell what mountain awaits us, what sea, what lake," in this world here below repentance is possible, you can say, "I have forgotten you," the day before yesterday she held his hand and whispered, "we are not always the same, there are moments when I hate you and wish you were dead," this too is one of your ways of adapting, he suspects her in the same way that he frequently feels he is being watched and turns round abruptly only to catch a shadow slipping away, then once again acts unsuspecting and once again turns in an instant to see the ghost of a face; one day he began to run like a madman, he rounded the corner and came upon an old blind woman crying to herself quietly and saying, "where have they abandoned me?" and he struck a match in front of her eyes and again she said, "where have they abandoned me?" so he took her by the arm and started to lead her, saying, "take me to your own people," but she was weeping, "I lost them in the fire," she lamented. Then another time he was startled, he was waiting at the edge of the beach and suddenly feared that they would come and push him into the water and start stoning him and he cannot run and hide, these were like bad dreams, "I'll go and see a neurologist," he said, "all these things are a sign of other, terrible things" and once someone called to him from the crowd that he was unhinged, these worries gnawed at him because he had all of them hanging round his neck, they had hung themselves there, he begged them to leave him alone with his children, "but it is you who will bring Christ and the Resurrection," they insisted. He didn't know what they thought in the guild, he remembered the Jews who used to stand apart at the side, "once upon a time your race used to produce fire-eaters," he told them, but now they were thinking twice about it, "they might arrive and pillage our homes, come up into the mountains," but they wouldn't listen. In the end the rebels promised them that they'd be well treated, the crowd gathered below, women and children at the front, feeble old women and boys who'd abandoned their trade and now dragged sheep and dogs along with them. They opened an iron gate, then another and in the distance the first man appeared to be advancing. He was middle-aged, with dirty, threadbare clothes, when he reached the light they could make out his pallor, he stood for a minute without knowing whom he could trust, whether it was the women and children who would judge him – and then he advanced. For a single instant the sun seemed too bright to him, he half closed his weary eyes, licked his lips and walked on. This ash-green crowd no longer spoke, moved closer to one another and then bit by bit drew back, allowing the boy with the bloodied face to be seen, half his clothes torn off by branches, his sides pierced and crushed, he would breathe his last before his mother and his sister could get there. And then the women gathered together, huddled in a corner and the workmen could be seen to arrive. "Do not forget that you gave us your word, you must keep him and behave nobly." They continued to advance like automata, the man made as if to turn back, "what you are doing is not manly; you promised you would behave well to us" – and then sobs could be heard, the mother and the sister were running to dress their boy, to wash him, and behind them the workers followed, "you'll pay for what you are doing, I never harmed anyone, I never harmed any of you, I never harmed these women, I don't even know them" and the women are weeping and lamenting and dressing the inanimate body and caressing his wounds as if seeking thus to heal them. And then people thought they should have remembered Christoforos, "he always preaches justice and right," he could make all the keening women tell what happened, bring the boy's body across the river, say that Irene is following them to the church service. But all of a sudden Theologos burst from the crowd, "he gave me orders to speak to you on his behalf," he shouted to them, and the women huddled even closer together as if they were a wound which was closing and he was hitting their temples, "we mustn't miss any of it," not one of the women should leave or should weep, wait and see what he's going to say and then. On the seventh day they started from the beginning, for nobody could agree that they had already begun it, one of them claimed that the uprising had been attempted by others earlier, years ago, and then those who followed Theologos cried, "we hold that to be an insult and an offense," and got ready to draw their swords, but "put your knives back in their sheaths," Christoforos ordered, and when they reached the nearby village the landowners came out to receive them, "we will give you from our own livelihood," they wept, "if you will only go back to the city, you have never worked in the fields, you have never tilled the earth, you have no knowledge of what tempests and starvation mean" – and then a small child came out from among them, "I demand my mother who was killed in your parts," he accused them, "these people here took me in and fed me." "Listen," Christoforos then said to the villagers, "at the point we have now reached nothing is yours and nothing ours, the traitors and the enemy will burn everything, gather your possessions and your families and come back to the city where we can barricade ourselves within its fortresses," but the villagers were saying that they preferred to fight on their own land which they loved. And they left without touching anyone, still as hungry as when they came. On the road they found the child waiting for them, "I'm coming with you," he said, they set off without speaking and he followed along behind them. And as they climbed the uppermost steps they felt that they were alone, that this house had been abandoned, and that the doors had been left unlocked because there was nothing left worth stealing. In the last bedroom they chose the barest corner, where a child's cot had been forgotten, its frame dressing the empty place by the window, as if leading them out onto an unknown balcony, it was as if they had dried chrysanthemums and daisies and leaves from unknown plants and lain down upon them, saying this is a dream that can only be dreamed by lovers, and below them spread a child's game full of little streets and dark corners and empty fireplaces, and their memories were suspended, setting off down the paths into fairy tale, the day they had disappeared into the vineyard and there lived as man and wife, they tasted her apples and then ran to find the well and at its lip they laughed, above the water, perched on the rim, only her hand was less timid, wandered over his cheek, explored his ribs, and from the window a voice is heard singing, "I want us to leave the city, to go and lie together in some other place, to say now we are embarking upon our love," but what followed was silence as if he was lamenting that she would never be able to enjoy her wish, "since I was a small child I knew that I would never have a husband, and never travel," and once more he said nothing to her, and she then turned and looked at him as if seeing all the dark world which was descending from the heavens and slipping into this house, and it was good and it was bad and it was entirely their own, as silent and lonely as self-deception, as a dream, as oblivion. "Which is the heaviest sin?" she asked him again. "Every time I have embraced you I have remembered how I used to have a slight pain beneath my breastbone, I was always singing and embroidering and people used to say to me that I was weaving my own longings into the cloth in order not to fear them. Now there is nothing left for me to ask, only that I should be there where you walk, there where you lie down to sleep, I like to feel you unprotected, to know that I could hurt you, many times I have wished that you would die so that I could remain beside you secure in the knowledge that you would not wake up and leave again." And then from within the cracks in the stone came a voice, "I am happy," behind closed eyes and hollow cheeks, the dry branches and the wall, which was impregnated by the nocturnal dew. And again she dreamed that from behind the leaves of the tree came shining, stabbing rays which blinded the walkers so that they bent double and ran groaning in the sand, on the cobbles, in the snow, fell and prostrated themselves before the queen then ran to be lost from her sight, as if the dreaming time were over and it all must come to an end. The following night they left in silence; the dry riverbed would remain unforgotten, along with the solitary tree and the mud, the low-growing scrub, the brightly lit windows of unknown houses, of unknown people who would say "goodnight" – "tomorrow at midday we'll be going to the doctor" – "I wish you a speedy recovery" – "we shall see" – "goodnight to you" – "goodnight".

Yannis

The next day was Wednesday; Yannis decided, "time to put an end to wanderings and prodigalities" and disappeared from his usual haunts, the poor neighbourhoods and Angela. For he got up at crack of dawn and chose his best clothes, Euthalia had them all ready for him, she dressed him and adorned him and counselled him, "don't make a fool of yourself and back down," and what she meant was that he should give orders and maintain his dignity and the high ground. And later on Yannis was to say that if he'd fallen he would have been killed, for he did indeed rise up unto the heights, they had hung a red banner from his chimney stack, as if to welcome him. And he vowed, "I'll rip it to shreds," forgetting his decision, forgetting Euthalia, he pulled off his tie, flung down his jacket and up he climbed – for they'd left a ladder lying there as if on purpose, as if to challenge him, "if you've got the guts, go up." But later they declared that it was pure coincidence, they hadn't expected he'd feel so strongly about it; and the doorkeeper Pavlakis* (he was an old man now, small and slight)

---

* Pavlakis had known his moments of greatness during the years of Turkish rule, when he served as a secret policeman and detective with great success. Known as "Pavlaki effendi" he had elucidated (as he himself told it) the mystery of the theft of some diamonds from the house of the all-powerful bey, discovering that the culprit was the Turk's own son, smitten by an Italian cabaret singer – and Pavlakis had been promoted and had risen to high office. Except that Venizelos and Constantine who arrived and took Thessaloniki didn't agree with this, so that he got thrown out into the street. In 1917 he was found to be acting as a forest guard at Hortiatis, he'd introduced himself somewhere as an agronomist, until he was thought that they ought to have them rounded up and thrown in the cells, there were ways he knew, he'd tried and tested them during the Turkish rule. But Yannis said, "leave the police out of it, I can fight them myself" and threw himself into the job wholeheartedly.

And afterwards word went around that Yannis had got together to work for him a couple of useless good-for-nothings, you couldn't tell where they'd sprung from or who they were, they were constantly under the workers' feet, chatting and forgetting themselves. And one day the workers said, "they're his pimps," and they meant Yannis's, and in order to punish him they threw one of them into a vat of dye and rolled him naked in the street as if printing a transfer. That same evening Pavlakis went running to the master's mansion, he drank the wine that Euthalia offered him and told her all about the strange goings on; that Yannis had taken his soaking wet friend and had given him new clothes to put on, had given him food and told him to come back in three days' time. "People say that he's a gravedigger who used to feed your brother," the guard risked venturing.

But people had got things muddled, for the gravedigger was someone else, as Yannis confirmed when his sister asked him about it, sniffing, "you really are quite incorrigible" and telling him off. But Yannis then revealed that he had a plan of his own, the business would have to be expanded, and he could rely on his two faithful followers. His sister didn't understand, though, "what have those good-for-nothings got to offer?", and spoke of their father's policy – "those were other times," replied the young man, "and even then we didn't lack debts and problems," he reminded her. She kissed him and calmed him down, "stop blaspheming," she told him, Pavlakis was there, "your pimp" as her brother muttered. And she blushed at that word and wondered

---

found out and sacked. He must have gone through hard times; he used to frequent Nicolas's grocery and live on olives, onions and ouzo, recounting his past feats with nostalgia. In the end he was recommended to Yannis's father and was hired by him. Pavlakis donned his boots and a cap and threw himself zealously into the job of watchman and his master's spy. He was found dead in his garret in '43, alone, starved, having perhaps been ill for days. He was over eighty by then and, like so many others, could not withstand the hunger and the cold.

about the company he kept, the things they did, the evil influences.

And then Yannis said, "I'll tell you the story of the man who got dyed, and perhaps you'll understand"; one day he'd been travelling on a tram and in front of him was a little man, unshaven, wrapped in his overcoat with the collar turned up, singing without cease to the passengers. "They were all unknown songs about a heartless woman. He kept on singing oriental amané laments and the passengers were all laughing at him, but he didn't care, went on singing about the woman and about a prison and his pain." They had got off at the same stop, Yannis felt sorry for him – "here, have twenty drachmas" – but the other man refused the money, "I'm looking for a job," he murmured, "I thought you liked singing," commented Yannis, to which the other replied, "I sing about my own pain in my own way." They were his own songs, then; Yannis said, "I'd like to buy one of your laments" and offered him the coin again, but the man went on smiling his sad smile and wouldn't budge an inch, "they're not for sale, I'm looking for work, to earn my bread." And Yannis took him to the factory and told him, "put a chair and sit here outside my office" thinking that he might hear one of the man's amanés. Nothing, though.

And Euthalia said, "I don't believe you, your mind is like an underground chamber full of secret corners," and she remembered how he'd promised that he would change. "But I haven't finished the story," her brother whispered, one day the singer was missing from his place and he'd found him down among the vats and the dyes, the chemicals. At the beginning he would sit there on one side, then he began fetching and carrying the buckets and water and wood, and the others let him because it lightened their load, and when they stopped for their break he sat at the side again and stared at them. One day the heartache and the longing laments broke out again, he sang, "faithless woman, you'll put me in prison, the bitterness will stifle me, I shall be buried there"; the others were eating their bread and their olives and herrings, while he sang, "they'll bury me in the graveyard, they'll swallow up my land," they chewed as they listened, "I'm betrayed, half-dead already," at which they stopped, and one man said, "do you mind, mate, we're trying to eat our food" and the other was going on about graveyards and death, quite hopeless.

"I still don't believe you," laughed Euthalia, remembering the information that Pavlakis had supplied, and she stroked his hand as if to seduce him. Then Yannis opened his palm, as if invitation, and her hand rested on his, his fingers closed around it like tentacles and he squeezed it; "don't say again that I'm lying," he requested, and it was like a velvet threat, like a carnivorous flower. But the next day the singer was harping on the same string again, a lament at their meal break, sour faces, mouthfuls chewed with difficulty that just wouldn't go down, and in the end someone couldn't stand it any more, "goddamn you, you're his pimp," and they grabbed hold of the hapless man saying, "time for you to dance now" and threw him into the vat and dyed him, then rolled him wet and naked in the dust, before he even had time to speak or to spit out the dirty water and the dye.

"I don't understand what you see in them," remarked Euthalia, and she meant in all this riff-raff, and she remembered his past, the time of the wanderings, of the murder. But Yannis answered that the moment had come for redeeming pledges, and he had a mysterious air about him, which might have been a pose or a mask, though it could be that he was putting into action some plan, concealed in murky corridors, a whole chain of cunning, of the kind that had fooled his father so that one day he had burst out in outrage, "I'm frightened of his mind because it is corrupted, it's as if from his mouth comes shit," whereupon the sisters had blushed and wept and lamented that their mother had left them and one by one they had gone astray. But now things weren't like that, they'd got their brother back home again, he came in every day clean and calm, he seemed to have set his mind in order, set his life in order, "I've got a plan," he would answer them, as if these words were a refuge or his slogan; "like a joke" his elder sister would say, for she never gave him an inch even though she loved him. Except that one day it proved to be no joke at all, so that the workers said, "that's what plutocrats are always like" and even Pavlakis was scared. "I'll be back on the streets again," he wept to Euthalia, and she remained silent.

For Yannis had sacked three men from the Works, all of them people who had tormented the singer. And this singer he now set up in charge of all the others with the retired gravedigger at his side. Everyone said, "he'll be digging the grave of this business," and they meant Yannis, who was putting people of no expertise in charge. But one day a fleet of lorries arrived unexpectedly, bringing vast numbers of crates and with them a cringing man, whom they discovered had been brought all the way from Austria, he had a funny little hat and a round head and a briefcase full of documents and plans. And when they opened the crates they found them to be full of black machinery, shining black with some kind of foreign writing on it in red. And in a few days the cringing man had got the machinery set up, he never spoke except to give commands or to order his coffee, and beside him were the gravedigger and the singer, whom the engineer used to take aside to explain how the machines would work. And the old skilled workers complained, saying that "all proper order has gone out of the window", and they threatened to walk out and bring the factory and everything else to a standstill. These things came to Yannis's ears and he laughed. One day he said, "we'll talk about it tomorrow"; and he had a table set up outside in the yard, he brought roast lamb and wine and ham and cheese and told them all, "we'll have fun," and a couple of players with a santouri and a violin and an outi, their crazy troupe, and everyone muttered, "how does he know about such things?" and decided that it was just a whim, while others congratulated themselves that he was scared of them and trying to sweeten them. The singer started off on his amané songs, the wine flowed, everyone ate, and as a finale Yannis took off his jacket and led the dance, with his two followers beside him leaping and bending, after a while people started clapping, carried away by the high spirits, forgetting themselves, the gypsy children gathered round and they were laughing too, till the lamps were lit and everyone felt heavy and fell back on their chairs burping.

In the morning they collected up all the greaseproof paper and bones, hordes of dogs turned up to lick them, Pavlakis took an airgun and aimed. The first of the bosses to arrive was the engineer, he was the only person who had neither drunk nor danced, he'd spent the whole time sitting in a corner and watching them with a mocking expression, "in Austria we don't do things like this," forgetting his native village beyond Kozani (as they were to discover), his father with the bagpipes and drum. Later the singer and the gravedigger rolled up, took their overalls, put them on and waited for the others to come so that they could tell them what to do. And Pavlakis muttered to himself, "that's the plan and there's the danger"; and the three men stood beside the new machines and the "Austrian" instructed them, the gravedigger was to be in charge of the buttons, the singer would be noting down the hours they worked and the amount produced – and to the others was left the job of fetching and carrying. The skilled workers were furious, "he can't just suck us dry and spit out the pips," they shouted; and they demanded to see Yannis, to reel off their complaints, but he wasn't there, "he's travelling in Europe," they were told. Euthalia was away, Pavlakis was feeling the chill, the workforce cringed, for whichever way you looked at it the autumn rains would be beginning, the feast of St. Dimitrios was approaching, they'd have to start lighting their charcoal braziers and their stoves and mending their old clothes. And the engineer from Austria said, "you can have your full wages even if you didn't work," for it was Yannis's kind heart that had left the instruction to "pay them" while he was away and the engineer in charge. Except that before long it was all found to be a lie, and someone saw the boy down on the shore one evening, sitting in an armchair at a café; he had a new suit on and a red flower over his heart, and at his side, it was said, stood the gravedigger serving him and laughing with him; beyond the road the sea was getting dark and the fishing boats were rocking their weary fishermen gently, and the world was strolling back and forth, enjoying the scents of the gulf before the rains and the north winds set in.

It was all lies, that talk of trips to Europe, and the skilled workers were enraged, "white dog, black dog," they muttered, "they're all from the same litter." However, they were bound hand and foot and they knew it, no easy matter to find another job, and – here they became even more enraged – Yannis also knew this full well and was exploiting the fact. Thus they bowed their heads, found comfort in thinking "our time will come", and hated the gravedigger, the singer and the engineer who had been their undoing with a hatred greater than words could say. Everything was done on the sly and there were no more festive meals or songs or dancing. One evening, though, Yannis told his sisters, "put on your best clothes and we'll go out and celebrate," and he took them by carriage, they went along the shore with the bright lights of all the cafés reflected in the sea, then on past the Tower, in front of the villas ornamented with their gardens and fountains. Yannis said, "one day I'll install you both in a palace" and the sisters laughed, it wasn't something they particularly thought of or hoped for, their sole wish was "let him do well and get on in life" for they loved him.

And he finally put them down in a garden; there were trees, there were shrubs and at the back a fountain of some kind and in the middle a large nightclub – bright lights within and the sound of voices and singing. And in a little while they were sitting at a table with Yannis ordering, laughing and promising them, "we'll have a good time." But something was bothering Euthalia, she was gazing about her and not speaking, all round them were people of all kinds, various men decked out in fine clothes like dandies, and others more workmanlike, women of every variety, all dressed in their best, all of them looking, admiring, vying with each other. And then the violins started, and the wine and the fun. Euthalia forgot that she'd been thinking, but why here? and the two sisters laughed and unwound a bit, they said, "no one's looking at us, no one knows us," and tomorrow would be another day, the girls would be back in their decent, silent house and all these people would be in their own houses, in their courtyards, back with their longings which would belong to a hopeless, lower world. Except that things didn't end smoothly, people didn't let that happen, and when they went to sleep that night they had nightmares about all the strange events, all jumbled together.

And Euthalia wondered where the misshapen man had sprung from who suddenly appeared in front of her, laughing and bowing, just like an actor. When the music started she lost sight of him for a while, she was watching a woman all in red come up on to the stage, her hair as blonde as blonde, her eyes blue, who seemed to remind Euthalia of something, some piercing memory – and she began to sing with passion, she sang, "I have forgotten the colour of your eyes" and everyone applauded, it was like the swell of the sea, then she began "Loneliness", a song of great melancholy, and Euthalia's slender hand reached out, sought her brother's hand, found it, squeezed it discreetly. But just then, as if someone had caught them at it and wanted to spoil the moment of tenderness, the violin embarked on a wild song, as if they'd been transported to the East all of a sudden, a tambourine was heard, the singer sparkled and launched into "Coachman, get going, we're off to Tatavla" and the atmosphere was merry, people began to clap, the women's figures relaxed once more, wine was remembered, glasses were raised and laughter rippled; and just as everyone's blood was coursing through the veins more warmly, faces perspiring and the whole place drowned in a sea of good humour, the funny-looking man was suddenly in the middle of things, just like some kind of hobgoblin sprung from nowhere, and was swaying beside the girl, who was startled at first but then amused as he sang a second part to her song. And actually it was amusing and the hobgoblin sang, "let me take her in my arms" then began singing his laments in a high voice; the girl smiled and he became bolder, he began to dance and sing, every inch of him a performance. But in a little while the boss arrived – the well-known Michalis – and took him by the arm, whispered something in his ear, but the other man acted amazed and looked at him with an increasingly clouded gaze, shook off his arm in anger, "am I annoying anyone?" he asked, and he was already right by Angela, the girl in the red dress, and was bowing just like Karaghiozis.

The singing had stopped, the room froze, some of the patrons were muttering in annoyance. And Michalis said, "pay and get out" and took him by the arm once more, the atmosphere in the room was thick with smoke and wine fumes and the funny man was stubborn, he shouted, "I'm paying" and searched his pockets, finally they saw hundred-drachma notes float in the air and the man saying something to the musicians and the girl singer. And there was a hubbub of voices and laughter, everyone wanting to express their own opinion, only Michalis wasn't in the least interested in hearing it, he picked the bank notes up off the floor and stuffed them into the man's pockets as if they were rags, then gave him a powerful shove, squeals were heard as they saw the singer stagger, lose his footing and fall down, then get up as if he'd twisted his ankle, covered in dust, ready perhaps to burst into tears or to curse. And Michalis gave him another push, said "layabouts like you aren't needed in this joint," except that as it turned out he didn't know and hadn't calculated right.

Because at that moment a gentleman stood up in front of him, young and handsome and blushing, his eyes darting sparks, and he said to Michalis, "get back" and then they saw him turn towards the girl singer and, as Euthalia swore, he winked at her rakishly and the orchestra began rather stumblingly to play, the violin seemed to be keening, and Yannis was saying again, "get out of the way and we'll pay our bill." And everyone wondered why he was speaking in the plural, just as they wondered when they saw Yannis picking up the hobgoblin, setting him on his feet, dusting down his jacket and saying, "you must beg the gentleman's pardon." But Michalis had already walked off swearing, and a moment later all the lights in the place were turned off, a woman screeched, "they're going to kill us" at which point a general hubbub arose. And when the lights went on again Yannis saw his sisters getting up and hurrying to the door and he said to the singer, "wait here" and ran to catch up with the girls. Everything was topsy-turvy, men and women alike were shouting, someone moved in front of Yannis as if he intended to hold him back, and it was then made clear that the boy was not joking, for the man found himself on the floor beside the stage, with the young man hurrying off into the darkness.

The cool fresh air was like a whiplash, he searched round desperately and just at that moment – before he had time to take it in, before he could catch up – a carriage passed in front of him at speed and he heard Euthalia say, "go back to your swine and your little chanteuse," he heard her say it quite clearly, and then the carriage was moving away, he was determined, I'll catch up with it, to plead maybe or to take his revenge, but then another carriage passed in front of him, "get out of the way, you stupid bugger," cried the coachman, who was holding his whip raised like a flag. And as Yannis ran he was thinking, which of the two should I go after?, but in the end he seemed to be panting and stopped running in pursuit, which was pointless anyway, he could sense it, he said to himself, "maybe I'm going to be sick," told himself to go back, to pay, to give the man a row; then next to him he saw the singer, which was another inexplicable thing, "I'm sorry, boss," he muttered, his whole stance reminiscent of old songs, nothing but sadness. Except that Yannis was suspicious and flashed out, "you did it on purpose, you scoundrel," for he could find no explanation of how the singer had come to be at the nightclub on the same evening as his sisters, how the man had known about it and from whence he had sprung, what he meant by capering about beside Angela; "who put you up to it?" he asked. But the other acted as if he didn't understand, and they walked along side by side as if reflecting, as if there was no time left for speaking. In the end, Yannis gave him two five hundred-drachma notes, "go and pay," he ordered; and the other made off, and the young man thought, tomorrow I'll give him a good talking to.

But the night didn't end there. Because when Yannis arrived back at his family house it was pitch dark, silent as the grave, and no matter how he knocked and banged on the door no one came to let him in. So he sat down on the steps, it was cool, he thought, it was assuaging, and a light rain began to fall; after a bit though Angela came down from the tree and took his clothes off and said we'll bury you stark naked and her face was moist as if she were wearing a waxen mask she threw the shining blade at him and he crouched to avoid it and heard people screaming and he shouted and hoped they'll hear me and come to save me. And when he opened his eyes he was feeling himself carefully, he was glad that they'd thrown a blanket over him which smelt sweet like his sister, just like the soap she used in the bath.

Christos

Christos persuaded a reluctant Amalia, "it's a Christian act," he said and she recalled Elias saying, "your Christ was the first Marxist" for he it was who said if you have two jackets give one to your neighbour; however, Amalia grumbled, "I haven't noticed him giving us a room in his palace" – his three-storey mansion. Whereupon Christos was irritated, "but it belongs to his wife and children," he pointed out and the following evening brought Elias to the house, even though it was pouring with rain; spring was coming and the scent of trees and fresh foliage was everywhere. They closed the windows and secured the shutters, though, and told the children, "you'll be sleeping with us tonight" – for there were already three children, well able to understand what was going on around them; Christos and Amalia told them, "don't go into the closed room and don't say anything to anyone" – this was directed specially at Dimitris, who was a boy scout already, he seemed a restless and intelligent boy, he kept company with children older than himself and at night, said his mother, muttered in his sleep, "he's dreaming, that's all," Christos reassured her, remembering his own agonies, how one night he had soiled his pyjamas and had been terrified.

"You've got nothing to fear," said the editor to Christos, "as long as you're on the side of law and order," but the young man remembered the books about Lenin and Mussolini which the "Independent" had serialised – "it's to educate people," boasted the teacher, the editor. All the same, other papers chose to serialise romances like "Les Trois Mousquetaires" or "La Dame aux Camélias". And Pavlakis – who was a neighbour – told him one day, "you're all commies in there"; his own job was keeping everything in order at the factory, and in the afternoons he passed himself off as an agronomist or a gardener. From time to time he used to have a drink with Christos; "in '12 your father and I barricaded ourselves into the barn, it was about two cigarettes' worth of walking away from Salonica, through gardens, we were praying that the Greeks would arrive so that we'd live to see better times." He drank down his raki with passion: "they wronged me, supposedly believed I'd been working for the Turks, whereas in fact all along I was protecting their property from being looted and their lives from ending with a knife in the back" – but who was ever going to recognise this? One evening they met at a performance of Karaghiozis* and Christos said without thinking, "you were rather like Hadziavatis," which put an end to all conversation between them, at least until about the time of the war.

Meanwhile Elias made himself at home in their house, which consisted of two rooms only, with a kitchen barely wide enough to get into and the lavatory across the yard that Elias could only visit at night, whether or not he wanted to. All the same, Elias seemed to have made himself at home; in the afternoons he devoted himself to the children, made toys for them out of wire, carved little figures out of wood, tied them all together and made them dance, and Dimitris said, "I know all about tying knots." But Elias outdid him every time, in the end the lights were flashing on and off without a switch. For he had made them a house out of wood and cardboard, with red paper covering the windows, and when a lamp was lit inside it was pure magic, like a fairy tale palace or, as Alcmene said, "the palace of my dreams" which was something that she'd got out of one of her books. Antigone, the youngest, went to light it, put her hand in the wrong place, the wires gave her a shock and she cried, and her mother said, "he's upsetting us all."

And it is true that they were upset one day when Christos came home unexpectedly, it was only eleven at night and he

---

* Translator's note: Karaghiozis is the eponymous hero of the popular Greek shadow-puppet performances, the little man surviving by his wits in a Greece under Turkish domination. Hatziavatis, his friend, is something of a collaborator with the Turkish authorities.

should have been out and about scurrying around or writing, but he saw a light switched on in the kitchen and he was worried, "they'll get wind of us," he said to himself, thinking of the gendarmes. And he burst in at the door, then froze, Amalia was sitting there in her dressing gown and Elias was kneeling in front of her whimpering – and for a moment all of them remained frozen like statues, motionless and pale. Only for a moment though, then "don't get the wrong idea," she whispered to him, trembling. And Christos took her and they went into their room and shut the door, without a word spoken since the children were there and might be listening. But they lay down with their backs to one another and Christos thought, shall I turn him out, and at that very moment they heard their front door open and close, light footsteps in the dark and lonely street, full of foliage and scents now for it was almost summer. Where's he intending to go and snivel now? wondered Christos and felt irritated, thinking, "he's got the devil's own luck and will always land on his feet"; he listened stealthily to the sound of the others breathing, thought to himself, "Amalia isn't asleep," and whispered to her, "it's better that things have worked out this way," just as if he was continuing some earlier conversation they'd been having, but there came no answer, she might have been dead or asleep, so Christos got up and went out and sat on the steps, all around him were plants in pots and at the bottom of the garden an apricot tree, Pavlakis was right about the commies, he reflected, then thought, we were better off on our own, and he meant his wife and children, yet once more the vision of Amalia in her dressing gown came into mind, could it be? – a tingling of suspicion made his spine burn – but no, he didn't believe it, she was always complaining about Elias, about his tricks and the danger involved, "yet you leave her alone in the evenings," whose voice was it that pointed this out? And he remembered how one day at work a colleague had said, "I never go home earlier than usual, just in case I catch the other man there" and had laughed.

One day the teacher had told him how "over there they've abolished the family" and he meant in Russia – however, Christos replied easily, the book on Lenin didn't say anything about this; "why do you bother going through them?" groused the teacher, as if admitting this is what newspapers are like. But Amalia herself used to grumble, "he doesn't even miss his wife and children," she would say disapprovingly of Elias. He heard someone cough next door, everyone had their windows open now, you could hear everything, "they'll hear a strange voice," Amalia warned him – what could they two have been talking about at midnight then? For an instant a slight breeze seemed to blow, their apricot tree swayed, something caressed his spine, but then ceased again, like sleep for a moment restless then once more sinking back into deep slumber. It must be past two now, he reckoned, at the paper they'd be gathering their notes together, saying something about Spain, going to be a war there maybe, in Athens the body had been found, people were saying that his mother-in-law killed him with Foula's lover, "but what on earth made her bring him to the house?" wondered all the respectable householders. And he kept thinking of their own story, the murder of Agamemnon, the boy who killed his mother. They are all examples, he concluded, "but anyway, it's over now, I shan't be so foolhardy another time" letting her have strange men in the house, the danger from Elias being a double one.

However, things didn't turn out quite the way he expected, for the danger came into view again: Elias, in other words, standing against the wall opposite, like a white rag hung out in front of the humble ochre-coloured building. But Christos didn't move, I'll pretend I haven't seen him, and he remained stock-still on the steps as if turned to stone, while in front of him the garden was also turned to stone, drained of all colour or light, and above him a firmament of stars; Elias revealed how desperate he was then, for he came away from the wall, came and grasped hold of the railings and said, "I've nowhere left to go," and he seemed humbled or repentant (or "shitting himself" thought Christos) because all doors were closed to him. Whereupon the paterfamilias said, "come back in till we work something else out" and that was the end of the episode. And the next day Christos hurried to Dorothea and told her about her husband and the danger, but said not a word about the nocturnal converse with Amalia, all he said was "have some pity," and he didn't so much mean for Elias as for his own family. Dorothea was polite – "she must be feeling hurt and having second thoughts," Christos confided to his wife – but apologetic, "what can I do?" she said and her face powder and hair gave off a fragrant scent. Amalia muttered, "he's a liar" and her husband gave her a searching look, for she gave the impression that she'd been made a fool of and was stubborn, and Christos decided once more, I'll certainly have to get rid of him, only it was getting late and he had to leave in a hurry for work, telephone calls, constant running around.

The following night an end was put to it, though Christos despised himself for the excuse he used, he said, "I've seen secret agents prowling around outside" and the other man, the jack-of-all-trades, smiled and promised that he'd be off. And he couldn't have slept a wink that last night, for in the morning on the table they found a little sailing ship made of wood, painted blue and red, with the name "Irene" on it in white letters. And this is where the story ended for Christos, a long time was to pass before he set eyes on Elias again, although he heard about his exploits, about how he rose to great heights and then sank, so that in the end people said, "it was like a fairy tale, like the stories we read in the press," but Christos thought to himself, "the stories are all exaggerated, I remember him when he was in hiding, when he was begging and weeping." And Amalia rebuked him, "none of that proves anything" and remained pensive. One day he took her and the children to meet Dorothea; Christos had calmed down by now and said, "I would have let him stay, but people were fixing a label on us." The lady, however, was unmoved: "I think of our sons," she confided, who were the same age as their own children, their Dimitris and her Haris, her Alekos and their Alcmene, their youngest and Vladimir. "Let the children come and play in the garden," said Dorothea, and they all became friends and played with the iron boat in the big garden and they remembered his "Irene".

One drawer remained closed, however, and this was the drawer called Amalia, in which lay powders and perfumes, a few photographs of her when young taken with a girlfriend on the flat rock in the sea by the White Tower, a postcard from Athens (mysterious, this), her father's old watch that didn't work, a whole collection of expensive embroidery threads and various curious buttons and brooches, and right at the bottom some letters. Thought Christos, she never opens her drawer, and what he meant was she has things she keeps secret from me, and maybe the most recent of these things was named Elias; he felt as if a sharp knife had shaved him close, terrifying and painful, but in the end he told himself, "let byegones be byegones," we all have our secrets. His own was that his mother had come to see him, she'd preferred to come to the newspaper offices one evening, "I'm in a hurry to get back to your father" was her excuse, she didn't wish to see her daughter-in-law or her grandchildren, but "bring the children," she said, "and come and see us in the village" – and Christos was to remember that she'd stressed "bring the children," in other words only the children was what she meant. Father is different, he thought, and in his mind – curiously – remained the image of his mother's hand: a hand immobile, a hand dried out, its juices gone. "That is what my mother is like," he whispered, as if he must try to absorb this knowledge, and he never dared tell Amalia about the visit because then he would have been obliged to speak about other things, about the invitation, about how much they two had grown apart.

"We ought to become closer," Amalia said, for she could see not only Dorothea's loneliness but also the sort of life she longed to get to know, to feel was hers: all fine embroideries and sweet scents and porcelain, tranquillity behind closed curtains through which the sun was gently filtered, where conversation was in hushed, polite tones, like the old violin she remembered from her childhood that they used to hear from the neighbour's house, the Armenian girl's. "Our children ought to become closer," she added in explanation. Dorothea's kingdom for children was full of trains and dice and books; one day they lost Dimitris and found him shut up in the little storeroom all by himself reading about how they went to the moon. Christos smiled inwardly and murmured, "his ambition is awakening," yet he couldn't forget Elias of the feverish eyes, lips moist as if he was constantly licking them. However, neither could he raise any objections, Amalia's plans were sensible and when she said, "people with full bellies make better company," he agreed. He couldn't even remind her that Dorothea was attractive – and desperately lonely.

The end of autumn had arrived when they next spoke of Elias. For such a long time they'd been strangely silent about him; although devoured by questions ("regrets" said Amalia one night) they didn't dare bring up the subject. However, they could sense from the atmosphere that Dorothea knew, that in some way she was receiving messages, perhaps sending him money or clothes, she seemed tranquil, which was something that they'd neither expected nor hoped for, something in fact that scared them. And she said, "let me show you a photograph" and went and brought it: it depicted a circle of women dancing in a meadow, with the musicians on one side, and Amalia and Christos were puzzled, not understanding anything. And the lady said, "look at the swarthy man with the drum again" and it really was his eyes and his lips, and she turned the photograph over and they read "always close to the people" and laughed, only Dorothea said with bitterness or sarcasm, "always close to the women," and fixed her hungry gaze on Amalia in case anything else might come to light. But there was nothing else written on the picture, no date or place or signature; "it's his writing, though," she confirmed.

And Amalia recognised his writing too, for she had a sample of it in her drawer, "forgive me" and some other words, written the day after, when he was about to leave, and pressed into her hand by a silent, almost wounded, Elias. Later, one night during the Occupation when they were talking about things, Amalia was to reveal the secret and Christos was to say that he'd understood it, that Elias really had made an attempt but that Amalia had brought him to his senses even if she did feel sorry for him when he said, full of bitterness, "my wife doesn't understand me," that his life consisted of solitary wanderings, searching and begging for what he needed. And Amalia had told him, "I wouldn't want to give anything out of pity" and she meant not even a single caress. That was when he had fallen on his knees, crushed, – "perhaps that was also part of the performance" – and Amalia sighed; "you can't always have everything you want," she'd whispered to him and neither of them knew whether she was speaking of herself or of him. And at that moment Christos had come in. "All right," he said, "I believe you," for since that day they'd lost sight of the "beggar" and only heard news of him from other people.

And one day at noon when they had just eaten and Christos had said, "I'll go and lie down," for he worked every night until dawn almost, there was a loud knock on the door. A soldier stood there, suntanned, hair cropped, smiling, and Christos put his arms round him and hugged him, for it was his brother, and he kissed Amalia too. "I'm on my way to Verria," he told them, and had come by to see them, he'd missed them, and it was quite by chance that he was also penniless and hungry. Amalia gave him some of their soup, and bread, cheese and fruit which they also had in the house, and he told them about the army where they half-killed you with long marches and sentry duty at night – and in the end he asked Christos, "you wouldn't have a cigarette by any chance, would you?" but his elder brother didn't even smoke, and Amalia ran to her sideboard where she still had five or six cigarettes left over from Christmas which they'd bought to offer to their friends, and the soldier took them gratefully in spite of the fact that "they're stale", as he with his experience was able to declare. Luckily he was leaving at five and Christos took him into the other room and gave him a hundred-drachma note "for cigarettes", and he embraced them both warmly and called, "I'll be back." And Amalia remembered the afternoon of their wedding, her parents-in-law, "he's always managed alone without any help," she thought with a tenderness for him, for his work was crushing, the children were getting older and needed things, and Amalia helped as much as possible, knitting and sewing, and singing so that no one should notice her suffering. And Christos said, "I'll have to change myself," for he had remained proud and never went cap in hand. And the editor was tight-fisted and always grumbling, "we're struggling to keep our heads above water," he'd say, "what you ought to be praying for is that we don't have to close down."

And one evening Christos said to his wife, "I'll have to have my suit turned the other side out, so that it'll last a bit longer," and Amalia said nothing in response but went out into the courtyard and weeded her pots; all he could see was her back, her hair in a plait, her white hands. "I might lie down for a bit," he said and fell asleep; however, always incorrigible, he was late getting up and then had to run – what a tyranny...

Angela

"All of them just exploit me," she wailed and was scared by the sound of her own voice in the lonely room, as if the furniture or the bedclothes had suddenly spoken. It was dawn and the grey light was beginning to pierce the shutters, making her think of clouds, a world without sunlight; and as it happened she wasn't wrong, for in a little while she heard a whispering among the leaves, as if trees and rain were speaking to one another, and the next moment the drainpipe was singing its familiar tune. Well, if she'd waited the steps would have been washed clean, God was sending his torrents to cleanse nature and the greyish leaves of the trees, the walls that changed colour, but above all those steps which Angela had cursed, remembering orphanhood and refugee-dom, her stupid fate, the fact that she'd said, "what harm can it do me?" and had hastened to join the fun. Except that Domna had said, "the moment came for you to exploit, but you threw it away" – everything boiled down to an idea or a way of looking at men, sizing them up.

And she thought of poor Eugenios, whose whole life had just been caressing hands, romanticism, "the only thing you must think of is feelings," preached he, by which he meant a courteous gesture, a regard, a word, maybe a gift with nothing expected in return. But this wasn't what the world is like, nor what Michalis and Domna said when they gave her advice, so one evening she decided, "I'll go and have fun" when that great fun-lover from Bulgaria had invited her, who'd begged her so often to come and had made promises. Maybe it had something to do with all the bitterness caused by Yannis, left over from that evening with his sisters when the whole nightclub had been thrown into disarray and her friend had gone running out into the streets, leaving her with nothing more than a brief wink, like a promise with nothing behind it, like all his other promises in the past, his deathly tears and complaints, the nights when he'd confided, "if it wasn't for you I'd be rolling in the dirt" – sleeping out in the fields perhaps, or on a bench in the big park, or something even worse which she didn't like to think about or allow her imagination to picture. "I can't enjoy what you give with only half your heart," she had sobbed, and Yannis had said, "maybe there isn't any trace of anything" and he'd meant feelings, but, thought Angela, such poverty couldn't exist.

But "it's all done on borrowed money," he said:* the furniture, the food, the high spirits; they were sitting in the back room and from the room next door could hear the singing, a girl who'd been given too much to drink and who was bawling, "I play them like dice" with her knickers off, "I like it here," whispered Vlachos, the fun-lover from Bulgaria, whose fine wines and whose money it was that spoke and who unbuttoned himself boldly. At this moment tempers rose and Vlachos found himself with his head wet, for Angela had been manhandled and had taken offence, telling him, "you can have your wine as a present" and he was swearing and cursing her, "well what did you think you came here for then?" he shouted. And Domna jumped up (she'd disappeared from sight for ages and Angela had been trying to find her) and had a lot of trouble calming him down, and in the doorway appeared a whole crowd of heated faces, a woman with her hair all

---

* One day, in '32, the court bailiffs went and stuck a notice on the house and ten days later went back to take possession. Then Vlachos woke up and began to run round and beg, swearing, "I can't read." Among his neighbours was Christoforos, who gave him all his savings and thus saved him. The following year the same thing happened with his vineyard, and once again Christoforos saved him. In '52 things had changed, Christoforos was building a house and was short of money, water was coming in through the ceiling. He went and knocked on Vlachos's door, who by then had got on his feet again and had made a packet. However, Vlachos had a little note-book in which he entered all his outgoings. Shoes for the children 500, teacher 850, electricity 150 and so on. Below was the total: 13,000. Christoforos was not entered into this little book, he told him, "I can't spare anything" and almost shut the door in his face.

tousled, an old man with his collar undone, two girls who were giggling away as if they hadn't a clue what was going on, and standing above them a man in uniform (he must have been an officer of the gendarmerie, he had peculiar hair which looked as if it had been combed from the back forwards) and Angela felt as if she was burning, she wished the earth would open and swallow her up, but the man got up, made his way to the door and left them, it was as if they were all acting in a play, and they lost sight of him for a while. Some woman started to sing, they saw the girl wearing a trilby, and the gramophone started up, playing "Hard hearted", people were taking partners and dancing as if thinking we came to have a good time – and Angela remained sitting on the divan as if she were all by herself, cut off from everyone, and she watched them as if through a window.

Then she thought, why don't I leave, just slip away and disappear, for no one was paying attention to her, and she got up as if benumbed, but Domna was standing in the corridor and said, "Michalis will find out and he'll kill me" but why should Angela care about this, and the other woman spoke again, "come on, let's go and sweet talk him" and she didn't mean Michalis but their host, whom they found in the kitchen with a towel bound round his head, complaining, "it's splitting." And Angela couldn't help bursting out laughing, we all look like something out of the carnival, she thought; he though was puffing and blowing, he'd gone bright red and was looking at them – "come back into the other room," Domna persuaded, her eyes and lips sparkling, and the girls linked arms with him and led him into the salon, where now everyone was sitting in a circle clapping their hands while in the middle a girl was bending and swaying. She'd taken her shoes off and her stockings were falling down but she didn't give a damn. Someone said that the pitchers of wine were empty, but they soon came back full again and everyone kissed Vlachos for his open-handedness and shouted, "long live your daddy" and burst into fits of laughter.

And the shoeless girl said, "I wet myself laughing" and it's true there was a puddle on the floor, so she knelt down and wiped it up with her skirt and her garter fell down, showing one plump red leg; and Vlachos sighed, took Angela in his arms and whimpered, "I live as lonely as a cloud" and he meant in his great house, which was overshadowed by two big old pine trees and in front of which was a flowery garden full of roses and honeysuckle, right up to the gate which was of lacy wrought iron with the tips painted gold. It must have been well past midnight, maybe getting near dawn, for one by one the partygoers were drifting away, but the girls stayed as if they were lost, as if no one was waiting for them anywhere, so they stayed; somewhere behind a door was the girl who'd peed, trying desperately to get herself together, "she's crying," Domna said, and Angela was later to remember that she never saw the girl again, when she remained alone with Vlachos and she caught him handing out hundred-drachma notes to all the females, who then disappeared as if on wings, and she alone remained, afraid, sorrowful, and he took her hand and begged her, "I can't bear to be left all by myself," and the girl said, "I won't leave you," and in a way she was reminded of Eugenios, his great house now empty and languishing perhaps, the mummified world with the red curtains and the iron gate to the garden, "I will always be constrained by a garden gate, by a wall, by a man who doesn't suit me."

And one morning she had got lost wandering around the cobbled lanes which don't lead anywhere, in spite of the fact that they were familiar to her, till in the end she said, there's the tavern, and went on down the steps that led to a courtyard which resembled a village square paved underfoot with a drystone wall and a few bushes and there in the middle in front of a marble table swaggered Eugenios, swaggering but pale so that she said, I thought you were ill – "I can't bear to be left all on my own," she heard again, and she saw that he was embittered, like a different person, nothing now to recall his assurance and that rich purple laugh of his, lascivious, spoilt. Of course she wouldn't leave him, even if she did declare that "everyone exploits me", even her red "uncle" of whom, now that he'd become a neighbour, she'd lost sight, she comforted him, "I won't leave you" – luckily as it happened. Because as she got undressed and lay down she saw that he was watching her thoughtfully, he was now bright red once more and perspiring and he fell onto her in an unnatural way as if he didn't want to and someone else had pushed him, and he stayed thus without moving, except that "he was making a noise like a machine" as she was to say later, and she wondered, she rolled him onto his back and was scared stiff by his expression, from which all the light seemed to have drained, she leapt up like a madwoman and got some water which she sprinkled on him, she caressed him and unbuttoned his clothes, but the rattling sound from his chest continued unabated, maybe it was the death rattle, she threw the doors and windows wide open and at one point was on the verge of screaming for help. But then he sat up, looked at her as if dazed, got to his feet, "but I'm an animal," she muttered in panic, for she remembered the cinema, Frankenstein, as he walked with a heavy tread towards the kitchen, tall and monstrous. The sound of running water relieved her, and his sighs mixed up with it, after a bit she heard cupboards and drawers being opened and closed, and Angela seemed to wake up and said to herself, I'd better go and see how he is. And he was sitting as if turned to stone on a chair, with a multi-coloured towel bound round his head on which she could make out leaves and greenery, and down his trouser leg flowed shit.

When Angela came to tell Domna all about it she grumbled, "the other girls got all his gold and the only thing left for me was shit." But she took him and got him undressed and brought a basin of water and washed him like a baby, she said, "come and lie down and you'll soon be better," and he obeyed, he reminded her of a powerless child scared of the state he'd got himself into, and very soon he fell asleep. And Angela reflected on her ill fortune, "anyone would think I'd had a curse put on me," she moaned, but all the same it didn't even cross her mind to go off and leave him. So she sat in a corner, the armchair was deep and for a while she was lost to the world, though the light was on and she could hear his breathing. From time to time she opened her eyes again, then again: it was as if she was making repeated dives into the ocean waves, her ears were buzzing, she came up to the light once more, then suddenly she saw the square again full of people now with the marble table nowhere in sight and Eugenios lost in the crowd in front of him two girls who were chattering and laughing and then three wild horses which they said belonged to the gendarmes then poor Eugenios again one of his eyes oozing pus he put up his hand and drew out a piece of cotton wool and gave it to her saying it is death or maybe some kind of discharge from the eye – and at that point Vlachos groaned, the girl woke up and wondered, "is there any meaning in dreams?"

Outside it was still night, she heard a car go past at speed and then a light came on in a window; a curtain decorated it, a white embroidered curtain, a sort of comfort; she wondered, "why am I sitting up with him?" and remembered how through that window a girl used to look out at the afternoons, she had a baby in her arms, every day in the same position as if painted, "maybe he's going to wake now and cry," but the light went out and in the window pane was reflected nothing but chaos. Beneath the window slept a humble little garden with pansies and mallow, it belonged to a lame old man, he had a dozen sons and daughters, the oldest boy was in the navy, one of the daughters had consumption and they lost her, they dressed her like a bride and wept for her, for a couple of months the little garden was abandoned but then in the end the old hands got to work and brought it to life again.

He sighed once more now and opened his eyes, he looked at her fixedly, and his eyes glistened as if he was crying, but then they laughed at her and he said in a tone barely audible, "you poor wretch, why did you stay?" and she went and put her hand on his forehead which was cool and boundless and she discovered that he was a handsome man, just a little spoilt and abrupt.

And Vlachos said, "if only I had a girl like you to look after me"; outside the sky was getting light; I could keep him in order, she thought, and took him in her arms, "are you feeling better?" she asked him, and somewhere Yannis and Eugenios laughed ironically, but why should she care? "I'll stay as long as you want," she promised – and she'd hardly slept a wink, a little breeze began to stir the curtain, a white flag which unfurled and she lay down beside him, "just to keep each other warm," she reassured him, he could easily have faded out in the night, the leaves were rustling outside and into the room came their scent, acacias and fig trees, "you could have been my wife," his voice murmured and they held each other even closer. And later on she was to tell Domna, "it might have come about if only everything wasn't always such a mess," if only everyone didn't always exploit her. Because at noon she left in a happy mood, he had got up, he put himself under the tap once more, she heard him singing, "what a lovely night, the moon is shining bright" and they laughed and arranged to meet that evening; and that evening it was that she waited in vain and complained, "people exploit me." But Domna undertook to find out what was going on, or to find Vlachos and give him a talking to, for he'd disappeared in the days that followed which was something that puzzled Michalis who imagined other reasons for it.

In the end, on a starlit night, they said, "let's go and sit in the garden" beside the nightclub inside which Michalis was struggling to get things ready before the customers descended on them; and Domna revealed to her that the Bulgarian was up to his ears in debt, that he owed money to everyone in the neighbourhood, specially to his guests, an officer of the gendarmerie and the other old man and a tram-driver, and he invited them to his parties as a way of paying them back, but it was in vain, what they wanted was to have it all, their cash and their wives and a good time into the bargain with the girls he got together. It was all folly, Domna assured her, "you were wrong to believe him" – but she'd felt sorry for him, that was all. And she did indeed feel dreadfully sorry when they came and told her, "he's getting married," for it really was a matter of sorrow, the fact that they'd found for him a woman not in the first flush of youth, people said she had two houses in Kamara, she played serenades on the piano and they said, "she dyes her hair to make herself more palatable."* She was even more sorry for him when the wedding took place and all the relatives were gathered there who, as was quite clear, held their heads high, there were two doctors with goatees and monocles, and people had got out their tail coats and bow ties, the women in their evening dresses and gold jewelry, it was all like some grand performance at the theatre, and Vlachos was breath-

---

* This history will make no further mention of it, but the truth was somewhat different. The bride's property consisted of nothing more than a ruined house above Kamara, in a little cul de sac. It was sold a few months after their marriage to pay off debts – a few at any rate – which were not hers. And thus it became clear that he had not married her for her "dowry", but rather because he'd had his fill of debauchery and was in search of some tranquillity, or at least wanted to avoid going under once and for all. And this is the way it worked out. She gave him every possible support, she bore him two children and in the end made him rich. In '46, however, a father was after him with a knife, because (he said) Vlachos had attempted to rape his twelve-year-old daughter.

ing heavily and sweating, and in a corner the violins were playing – no one was clapping or dancing wildly, only the table was set with fine crystal and silver and the guests sat around it and ate with their knives and forks: all the things that the Bulgarian had mocked and laughed over, Greek pretensions and Greek poverty.

She really did feel sorry for him when she and Domna left the nightclub, left it stealthily and stealthily climbed onto the wall and parted the rosebushes and saw him all buttoned up in his black clothes, "his shoes must be pinching him," laughed Domna, and Angela thought, I didn't fit, I couldn't, and remembered her room and her necklace that was fake and their plebeian merrymaking at Michalis's. Just then a few drops fell on her, then they became steadier, and from within someone said, "it's raining" and people ran to secure the windows, "let's go, they'll see us," she heard Domna say, they got down, pricking themselves on the rosebushes, and from up there they saw Vlachos as he closed the windows; he must have recognised their figures as they passed near the door, he might have called "come in," but they weren't fit for a wedding party, neither from the point of view of clothes nor from that of mood, specially Angela whose shoulders and hair were soaking wet, and specially her cheeks which were dripping.

Fotis

And when they were dry again they got out of the bathtub and Eleni said, "maybe Angel is his devil"; he was hugging her tightly and kissing her, he'd arrived five days earlier and she was determined, "he'll be like my own baby to me," however he was already more than twelve years old, his eyes always straying just like his father, he'd be talking to you and at the same time his eyes would be searching beyond you as if he was looking for something and not finding it, "maybe he got that from the yids," she thought ironically, but at the same time she felt warmth for him and cuddled him and had dressed him just like a little prince, like the French children, and she washed him and combed his hair, "until he's squeaky clean," as she and Fotis agreed. But the difficulty didn't lie here, as was later made clear; she was going to have greater trouble keeping him in order, getting him out of his bad habits, his little ways – they used to find him with his bed soiled and the Arab maids would grumble, they'd say, "why don't we throw him into the sea and get some peace." But this was not something that he was afraid of, he too battled with the waves and his father took him out in his boat, they went out into the open waters and fished, looking across at the city in the distance, their own place, Eleni's, the casino, then further on other grand houses, a white wall of buildings, as if they set a boundary on the sea, and they collected the fish, his father strung them on a string and they returned in triumph; "now you have a fishy stink," laughed Eleni, herself redolent of perfumes and warmth.

His own room smelled of paint and whitewash and outside the windows bougainvilleas, purple and white, which meant nothing to him, and he remembered his grandmother's garden; she used to yell at him, "don't play there" in case he wrecked it for her, for she had it all arranged nicely and was in agony about it; out there was the pure blue heat, nothing but a monotony of sky which at night took on the hue of ink, only the stars shining, and he hid himself under the sheets afraid lest these stars should see him, for one night a woman was being beaten and was screaming and he thought that there weren't enough bedclothes and he lifted one corner of the sheet to look and he saw a camel's head coming into the room and licking him, whereupon he felt his bowels turn to water (and who'd pay any attention to the Arab woman who would have to clean him up?) and he got up in terror, perhaps things would be better on the stairs, he thought, and it really is better for he sees a girl taking her clothes off, all lipstick smears and laughter as if startled, and meanwhile people were coming up the stairs, a door slamming somewhere as if by the wind, and without understanding how he is amidst her young girl's flesh which smells like the Turkish baths and then in a little while they are in his bed and she's kissing him, she's saying something into his ear, she makes him remember the crying and her fingers grip him, but the bedclothes really are too few, they lie there as if in a daze, warm, scented, her legs are plump, her hands, which are slowly twining round him, and her lips are on his neck, on his ear, they are whispering to him, but it is all incomprehensible and disturbing.

And right then the lights go on and the sheets are pulled off them, Eleni has fallen from the heavens, she appears to be flashing with anger, the girl is like a poor rag which they toss here and there without a word spoken, just like in silent films, but Angel is suffocating, a voice seems to come from his stomach saying, "I can't, I'm going to throw up" and he starts screaming as if he's being beaten, he's howling and crying and the household is in tumult, and his father is there in front of him, apparently startled and distressed, he grasps hold of Eleni and yells "that's enough," the rag emerges as if blown by the wind and crawls along the floor, and Eleni says to him, "and where might you have been that you got here so fast?", something violent is afoot and Fotis tells her "I'm sick of you," but she insists, "how did you manage to get here?" but his father doesn't answer, just grabs her hand, "let's go," he mutters, "the boy is listening"; she, though, apparently can't take any more, "let him listen then and let's make an end of it," she screams, "let him learn all about it and admire his father," they are both red in the face and sweating and they're shouting at each other in a different language, Arabic maybe or French, but the child cries in his own language, for a moment he imagines that he can see the Arab maid, but she then disappears again as if terrified, Fotis storms out like a madman and in a minute the only one left is the beautiful lady, what she's wearing doesn't seem to be shimmering any more but looks crumpled, and she comes and enfolds him and says, "hush, it's not your fault," it is a garment that feels slippery in his hands, "when you're older you'll find out," she confides in him, as if she were his own age, as if they played together and she's covering him up, she strokes his hair and sponges him, "you're not to blame, poor boy," she whispers and then kisses him; it is a paradise of scents and all her jewellery is flashing, she covers him up again, "all right," she says, "it's over now" and the only thing left is a sob which gradually fades, it's like a sigh then in the end like the breathing of a sleeping child, but a strange person says wake up someone who is tall like a stork and has a tiny little head it's like one of those cloth balls and he chases him into his grandmother's cellar but it's a dead end in there no way out and Angel finds his sword raises it and strikes the cloth man laughs though he can't be cut and he chases Angel through the dark rooms the boy grabs him by the throat but he slips through his hands a threat who can't be killed he won't go away and in the end he dissolves in sweat and desperate struggle and he screams and the lights go on, the cellar is gone, the sword and the cloth man no longer there, and the perfumes and precious stones are once more bending over him and saying, "you've wet the bed again" and the Arab woman will then come in and mutter, "what a horrid habit."

And the next day Eleni and Fotis are like lovebirds, as if none of the night had been true, and they decide "to get his brain working" and they lead him by the hand to the school run by the priests, it doesn't in the least remind him of the old woman who used to teach him in the open air in her courtyard; this is a garden with trees that reach to heaven and a high stone wall, a place apart, quite cut off from the world, in the morning there was church followed by hard lessons until the sun was low in the sky and they said, "you can continue at home" with lots of books and exercise books, whereupon Angel said in despair, "they don't leave you in peace." And the second week found him climbing up into the branches of the pine tree and from there over the wall and jumping down onto a dirt track, saying to himself, I'll take this path wherever it leads to, for it was an opening, in fact it really does lead to an open space, and on the far side, in the shade of a fig tree, are some Arab children shouting and playing at knuckle bones and laughing, they give Angel a funny look, maybe thinking that he's fallen from heaven, and they begin to stroke his clothes, his best belt and his shiny cap, and they show him the knuckle bones, there are five of them and all of them younger than him, and they show them to him again, the knuckle bones, but he's suspicious of them, so the little Arabs take them and start throwing them, paying their forfeits in dates and pistachio nuts, they're all black and pass from hand to hand, but the chatter and laughter go on, at one point a fat black boy stretches out his bare hand and offers Angel a date, but Angel is wary, it isn't that he's afraid because it's dirty or because they might have stolen it, he remembers all the exploits back in his homeland, the unripe plums and being chased, stomach aches, vomiting and his grandmother's cane into the bargain.

He is wary more than anything else, he believes that if a foreigner gives you something it must be the bait in the trap, however by the time he's thought all this out the hand has been withdrawn and offered to another mouth; a woman then emerges from the house a little way off, she's a voice asking for something, a hand, and the knuckle bones disappear, into their rags maybe or up into the leafy branches of the tree, and Angel is alone once more, walking along in a place that's nothing but earth, nothing but sun, weary, sweaty rags, he goes on walking and then finds himself in a cobbled alley, various brightly coloured awnings spread overhead and at the end blinding light; the boy says to himself I'll stop here and cool down a bit, but he advances like a cat constantly licking himself and in the end gets his centimes out of his pocket, he sees a bedouin with a tin pitcher slung round his neck, "drink something cold," his dry mouth tells him and so he goes forward. Except he thinks, "where should I go?" for Eleni and his father will be looking for him, and as he rounds a corner a new view comes into sight, beyond is the familiar sea and in front of it houses, as if the open ground and the openings had ceased to exist, now he says to himself, I'll go downhill then I won't get lost, a ship is floating as if suspended in the air, in the distance the white sea. And he goes down between the houses, finding carriages now, pedestrians dressed in suits, women with flowery dresses, their faces painted like Eleni's, whose face must now be in a thoroughly bad mood.

Behind the closed white door their lights can be seen shining, then Angel sits on the steps, it is deep twilight, his legs are exhausted, his mind searching for a lie which turns out not to be needed; the doorman comes out and stares at him in amazement and instantly the steps are full of people, Eleni gathers him up without a word and Fotis follows, and Angel hears someone saying, "leave the whip out of it," then he feels his breath taken away, a stabbing pain rising to his brain, and Eleni says once more, "leave him to me," however his father insists and gives him half a dozen slaps, Eleni catches one too, "you brute," she screams at him, "don't you remember your own misdoings?" and his legs are hurting but Angel is stubborn and won't shed a single tear and so the lights go out, Eleni takes his father away and Angel hears the key turn in the lock – who does the woman want to secure? Now only darkness remains, moonlight through the window, and the five Arab boys who give him the dates, their shabby clothes and their world of beaten earth, the voice from the hut and then nothing.

But the next day back once again into the garden of the school with the Frères standing on the steps gazing at him all serious and expressionless, and in the end one of them takes the boy and leads him into an empty room, two others hold him down, they undo his trousers and Eleni is nowhere around, they beat his bottom black and blue with their cane and in the end lock him in the empty room, and it's in this room that all the tears which have been growing within him finally flow, and he thinks, I'll open the window and go, not towards the sea this time though, but he finds the window barred with iron like a jail and behind it is another wall, a grey barrier without any trees. So then he says to himself, I'll sit here and I'll curse them, and he gets his prick out, now I'll show you, thinks he, and he wets all their little tiles for them. From somewhere he hears voices and laughter, it is the children playing, then silence once more, then laughter again, "I'll keep track of the breaks," and he's hungry, they've condemned him to hunger and thirst, this is why he pisses on their wall, "it's midday now," he says to himself and feels comforted, four o'clock will come, he won't leave any of the walls unsullied, and he thinks of the three Frères: the one who wielded the cane is short with tiny spectacles and a nose like a turd.

And at four o'clock they let him out, he takes his heavy satchel and goes down the steps, somewhere in the garden he can see the priest with his little spectacles who smiles at him as if they're friends and then goes back inside, letting byegones be byegones, and at Eleni's place everything is as usual, he doesn't complain that they beat him and made him go hungry, he knows quite well that they're watching him on the quiet and exchanging meaningful glances but he acts as if he didn't understand anything, like an idiot, and Eleni brings him a sweet cake, says, "we bought it specially for you" and gives him lemonade, then in a little while they turn on the lamp for him, its shade is green with yellow flowers on it and it transforms the room, the music from the nightclub can be heard from his room. It's a prohibited area, all he knows of it is the sound of the trumpets and the laughter, one night he thought he heard pistol shots but his own room is on the other side of the building and high up, and during the night he feels warmth, he is lying between two plump thighs, a mouth is tickling his neck, his cheeks, giggling and talking, saying as if introducing itself, "Marie", somewhere in that courtyard now gone he hears "Marika", who is a woman who hugs him and sometimes cries and makes him sopping wet and in the end fades away; now he feels great sweetness, it is a soft hand creeping into his pyjamas, caressing his legs that lie as if bound together and his belly, then behind, where they'd beaten him, and all the time Marie is kissing him, kissing so much that the boy wants her and holds her close.

In the morning he wakes up alone, but the melancholy is of a different kind, as he eats his breakfast he feels all the while that some other flesh is beside him, somewhere a lily-white neck awaits him, a neck that descends into breasts, his own breasts or her girlish ones, they caress him until it's time for school whereupon everything fades and his breast tightens, he thinks let the hours just pass so that he can be back in his bed again, in the warmth, outside the classroom windows there is a bush with bright red flowers, it must have been planted today already in blossom, he repents of what he did to his grandmother's pot plants, on the first of May they used to go to the little wood, his uncles and aunts would be singing and two carts would be waiting, they'd say, "what's that naughty boy getting up to" but he hears a thwack, it is the Frère's cane for he's noticed Angel daydreaming, seen his mind wandering, "Angel," he calls to him, "votre leçon," but it's all in the satchel, only there, like things dead or unknown, and at that point he remains mute, looking at his teacher, the Frère seems to be measuring him up and to be wondering, the boy remains without moving or speaking, what's he going to do, he thinks, is he going to beat me? for he sees him moving his cane and somewhere he hears someone laughing at him, it's a boy so blond that he's almost white, just as if they'd plucked out his eyelashes. There isn't even any breeze, thinks Angel, and the Frère is standing over him in his black habit, his hempen girdle, bending over him, and the boy is uncomfortable, he sees a plump red hand, "Angel," he hears, "votre livre" and his satchel is taken from him, now they'll find it all he thinks, for in it he has his glass marbles, a boy scout badge, a note-book with the "Black Eagle" on the front, the little chain with the bead on it, the box of matches, the blank exercise books, all of them now thrown onto the table, a moment of triumph for the Frère and the other children all laughing, maybe they're whispering, "the Greek boy's gone too far"; and he really does go too far, for he leaps up from his place with the speed of a bullet, reaches the Frère and falls on him in a frenzy, the cane is now in his hands and he's hitting him wherever he can, some child comes between them, but the cane is raining down blows quite heedlessly and the child is screaming and holding his head, Angel whirls round in despair and one minute bites his teacher's ear then the next minute grabs him by the habit and the cane is beating the air like a sword, terrorising all and sundry, and the door opens and they all fly out like birds with Angel howling in pursuit, one child's glasses have fallen off and in his frenzy he stamps on them, he is like a small animal screeching and snarling, everyone frightened lest he bite them, until the gaoler Frères arrive in panic with their rods and nets, maybe they'd already had to restrain other people who'd gone berserk – and his final despairing action was to hurl the cane through the window, breaking the glass so that a little gust of wind came through and Angel runs towards it, wanting perhaps to fly or to jump out ...*

When September came Fotis said, "better do it before winter and rough seas set in" and they put him on a boat going to Piraeus; he'd sent a letter to Myrsine, "go down and pick him up," he wrote, "the little devil will destroy us." And his sisters were thoughtful, "it's his woman's fault" that the boy's visit was ending before its time, with Myrsine weeping, "he came back emptyhanded," with new clothes only and two pairs of shoes. However, they were used to it, "poor little Arab boy," they said, for he came back to them just as naughty, his expression sullen, bringing only a packet of dates, nothing more. And they laughed at this little gift.

---

* The truth is even worse. Every so often A. used to beat the little French boys who refused to play with him. One day, when the Frère came to intervene his spectacles fell off in the struggle and A. broke them obstinately. Fotis paid for the spectacles, but the boy was expelled from the school. And all Eleni's money, in this particular case at least, was of no avail. All this as well as various other things he did led them to have rows. So they sent him back to Greece in order not to quarrel irrevocably.

Christos

It all must have begun that night, when Christos returned from work as dawn was nearing, he was oppressed by a feeling of despondence that was painful and longed "just to lie down and rest", for it had been an evening full of tension, piles of paper mounting up beside him, the telephone that kept ringing but he couldn't hear what the people at the other end were trying to say to him, a writer protesting and shouting (you've ruined my article) and the teacher complaining, about his creditors, the workers, his nephew who was leading him a merry dance. But now it was all over, for a few hours anyway, and he arrived back in his neighbourhood and at his own house thinking, "I'm like a dog taken out for a walk at midnight," except that he had neither the strength nor the inclination to run. And in the midst of his weariness he saw a light glowing somewhere to the south, maybe in Kalamaria, among the shanties, it seemed as if trees and houses were lit up and after a moment the air thickened and was full of smoke and soot, shadows and the whole city dancing wildly. And Christos said, "I'd better run," but the effort seemed too much for him, maybe he was worrying about nothing; what could it be, he wondered, and he meant what evil? but then he saw the glow seem to spread, he stood where there was an opening between the buildings, saw a mulberry tree, leant against it thinking how he was always robbed of sleep; he closed his eyes to trick himself for a moment and remembered his mother who'd scolded him when he slept outside, telling him that he might perhaps lose himself in melancholy dreams that would pin him to the ground. And at that point he began to walk quite unconsciously, mesmerised by the glow, it was certainly a fire, something was burning somewhere and the sky was full of the smell, not like the straw they used to set fire to in the days when he was a child in the village.

Then he heard a vehicle approaching fast, it was like one of the lorries in the war, laden with crouching men, and in a moment it passed him, metal and wood creaking and groaning, then turned the corner and came to a halt, the exhausted engine was boiling and he heard it stop, then his ear seemed to catch the sound of talking, as if the people who'd got out of the lorry were saying something hurried, maybe agreeing, maybe not, and after a little while they stopped speaking and he heard the growl of the engine once more, iron and wood once again jolting together, then everything was lost in the darkness as if sucked down by a well or into chaos. It was still night, yet the glow was everywhere, it had become stronger now and Christos thought, something stinks, and he didn't only mean the breeze which was bringing a stench to his nostrils like that of burning rags and fouled wood, or so he thought. He was still alone, standing now on the ledge in front of a garden fence which refreshed him, and behind it lay a humble house, he thought of hurrying and felt that he was dallying inexplicably, then heard footsteps and saw someone coming towards him. It was a man who was fat and tired, after a minute he came up with Christos, his head bent and silent, passed him rapidly, as if annoyed by his presence, and then was swallowed up by the darkness – and Christos thought to himself, "what's he doing out and about at this time of the night?" for he recognised him. Then he set off in the opposite direction, reflecting, I don't like these goings on, and he meant the lorry and then also this neighbour, and he said to himself once more, "something really stinks." And in a little while he was out in the main street with the tramlines, the pine trees shadowing him overhead, but it was still dark and in the distance the light glowed: perhaps it was at the very end of the road, past the depot and the gardens and the cursed, haunted house. And he found himself walking in that direction, his steps increasingly rapid.

And in a little while he saw someone else, then another person, then a car which passed them at speed, so that he thought, I'm not alone and it really was something serious, and finally he came upon five or six gendarmes, all of them apparently hurrying, who said, "something terrible has happened, they've set fire to the Jews in the Campbell quarter," and Christos's heart turned over, he thought he'd been expecting it, there'd been whispers, it had been brewing. And he remembered the E.E.E., it all kept weaving in and out of his mind like a well-known film, so that he started running himself, breathless, he thought he heard voices, people had come hurrying out into the streets by now, but the houses were becoming fewer and more and more lowly – refugee houses – and the trees were becoming more and more numerous, trees and open spaces, gardens, neglected allotments, and all the while the stink was becoming thicker, the wind hotter. Then finally he saw the rows of shanties but most of all the flames, a world of flames and a world of shadows struggling in despair or frenzied or as if possessed, and voices, weeping, curses; he approached nearer, feeling that he was becoming one with the smoke, almost fainting with the stench, something seemed to be gripping his skull as if threatening I'm going to suffocate you. He thought, who can tell which are the victims and which the perpetrators? whereupon, without knowing how, he found himself among the former, running with a tin can of water, jumping in among the hovels and battling with the flames and the smoke. But everything had been perfectly planned, because there was only one tap and this gave nothing but a mere trickle, so that the men grabbed their old blankets and flung them onto the fire, as if they wanted to catch it, lest the evil should get away from them and grow, and the women were ululating and Christos prayed for it to rain, but it was a dry and starry night, and his own voice and his breath turned to vapour, like in bad dreams where you scream for help but no one can hear you, and he ran back to the tap, who forced me to do it, he was to wonder – but this was later, at midday when they'd fallen exhausted to the ground, choking on ashes and outrage, watching the fire brigade run to and fro who'd only arrived once the sun was up, the women and children gathered on one side and struggling to overcome their terror.*

---

* The burning of the Campbell quarter took place one night in 1931 and Salonica was shocked. Everyone said that it was the work of the "E.E.E." who used to copy the exploits of the Hitler Youth. The dreadful thing is that the whole business had received support and some fanatic journalists,

But the woman who was really almost out of her mind was Amalia. When she saw him coming back pale and exhausted she said, "I might have known you'd go running off to help them"; word had got about that the cause of it all was a Christian child who had been found dead near there, and some people whispered that it was in the depot, in the pit, while others said he'd been discovered among the shanties where they always hid the barrel and the nails and the blood. Christos made no reply and only murmured, "poor people" as he remembered how they'd been screaming and running, how they weren't given any water with which to put out fires or to wash, "poor people," he said once more. And Amalia muttered, she heated water in the copper and undressed him and shoved him naked into the bathtub and gave him a row, and she boiled his clothes, boiled them again, she seemed to have entered into a sort of battle as she hung them out, dried them, made them smell sweet, and when it was almost dusk she watched Christos put on his other clothes and leave in a hurry: all she got time to yell at him was "don't let the fact they've got rich relatives bother you," and what she meant was the large villas of the merchants on the wide avenue, where they had five servants, a gardener and a coachman – all these villas belonged to Jews, none of whom were starving.

But he had a good think about it, he got things into some kind of order in his mind, and he told the editor with great heat, "it was the lorry and the fat man in the night," he'd seen them, the E.E.E., and the other man said, "be a bit more careful with what you write," always the same old refrain, as his pen ran on he'd feel a sharp stab in the lower part of his back – "it's because you're killing yourself," Amalia said who ached for all his trouble and effort, she told him fondly one night, "you're too honest, that's why people rob you" and she meant they exploited him, for the children were growing older and needed things, they never had enough money for shoes, hardly even enough for bread and sugar. But Christos insisted, "they set fire to the poor people," the Godforsaken Campbell quarter where the children showed their little arses through the holes in their ragged breeches, and the vil-

anti-Semites and other trouble-making elements, had said that Jews are reds and had reminded their readers of Benaroya and other socialists.

las were just fine and unattainable, and the coachmen in the carriages were just fine – "don't make a melodrama out of it," said the teacher, and at that point Mr. Aristos came up behind him and Christos thought, he's reading the lines I've written and he felt that he was being robbed, that Amalia was right. But things turned out to be even worse, for they took what he'd written and read it and got in a huddle over it, they said, "this matter requires great care" and Christos recalled the affair of the banker and all of a sudden he had a flash of memory, "wait," he said, "I've just remembered the people at Michalis's, the young man and Angela, I've just thought of the Bulgarian" whom he'd seen in that loft where the E.E.E. met, on a day when they had put on their short trousers and paraded and the whole neighbourhood had laughed, and as quick as a cat he grabbed back his notes, "I'm not letting you have them," he said to Aristos, but they looked at him as if thunderstruck, and in his anger this sight remained in his mind as he went and ran down the stairs in a fury and then stood in Egnatia Street, it was completely dark by now and he saw a group of people laughing and joking with each other and singing, they were wearing their best clothes, handerchiefs in their breast pockets, trilbies, for certain they were on their way to a party, and Christos hurried by, thinking of how he'd flabbergasted them at the newspaper, "there's no going back now," he said to himself and someone turned to look at him, I must be talking to myself aloud, and without noticing it he'd reached the Fountain and he could smell grilled meat and ouzo, "perhaps I should go in and have a good time," but he continued walking, slipping along, because such things were not for him.

And at home when his family saw him they said, "he's ill," for he'd got back before midnight, but he reassured them, "I came to get a bit of rest," he told them and smiled. And they supposed that he'd been given time off, for he'd worked himself to the bone the previous night; but Amalia muttered that "I don't like all this," the fact that they'd eaten their meal and hadn't exchanged a single word, Christos plunged deep in thought. In the end he said, "make up the bed and I'll go and get some sleep" and he went to bed, he had a sharp pain like a knife in the right side of his back, and Amalia came in, she too lay down, worried, "I heard you groaning" in his sleep or in his peturbation, and thus they spent the night, she was scolding, "you're not cut out for getting into the hurly-burly" and only when the day was dawning did he apparently fall asleep; at one point he seemed to shake in a sudden spasm as if someone had prodded him in his sleep, and then there came a little sound like whispering, rather as if the trees were speaking, and it was a shower which after a while turned into heavier drops of rain splashing down, "why couldn't it have happened yesterday?" he asked her and Amalia replied, "don't think about it," for she could sense his pain, his anguish, and she laid the palm of her hand upon his burning brow, "don't go on fighting any more, my brave lad," she begged as the rain came drumming down bringing them the scent of the earth, just like it had been in his father's fields, one May Day when he had spoilt everything ...

"How can I help it hurting?" he answered her, for the wreckage had been smoking and smelling, and he just standing there as if under a spell, watching as wretchedness gathered its rags together in the drizzle, searching maybe for something that the flames hadn't reached, while all around stood the gendarmes, silent and uncomfortable, "in a single night they were transformed into tattered bundles of rags," Christos sobbed, before him he kept seeing people bowed and stooped as if condemned, as if wounded, and then he could take no more and set off walking along the street, and after a bit he heard behind him the creaking of a cart and horseshoes rapid on the paved road, "come on, mate, I'm going as far as the depot," someone called to him, it was a carter aged about fifty, smiling at him, inviting him, maybe feeling sorry for him as he walked along as if struck by death, but Christos said, "leave me to walk and get some air" and the other man replied, "as you like," and he heard the whip cracked and the horse's hooves quickening once more as the cart was borne off leaving behind it the smell of vegetables, and Christos remembered their own vegetable garden, his father in his straw hat working the rich earth, sometimes its master but also its slave, and he longed to find a water fountain so that he could drink a bit and maybe refresh his face, he could feel that the skin on it was roughened, taut, and his cheeks hurt.

Some time I'll have to speak out, he thought, about what he'd seen and suspected, so that the teacher wouldn't complain and accuse him, "you're secretive," just as he might have said you're one-armed or hard of hearing. And he heard the sound of running water, it was a large public fountain in the middle of the road, quite deserted, and he bent down and drank, then refreshed himself, put his head under the flowing water, let it run down over his eyes his throat, he felt his ears buzzing and a slim cold blade running down his breast, to his navel maybe or further, and then he stepped back, "I'm still a village boy at heart," he reflected and said to himself, "I suddenly feel like going barefoot," but all the same he got out his handkerchief and dried his face. And the teacher says, "that's enough" but Christos disagrees and grabs him by the collar, "there," he hears the man say, "you've turned into a revolutionary," he lets go of him and returns to his desk, "I'm not letting them get away with anything," he mutters; what got into the poor boy? the others later said. A few sheets of paper with writing on them, an envelope of photographs, a set of blurred images: soldiers waiting in a queue for their rations, Christos and Kostoulas in a tent, the hut, the wireless, Christos, Euripides seated, a single star on his uniform, Christos with Amalia beneath the White Tower, the Salikourtzides gang before the firing squad, their caps flying off as they fell, a group of friends dressed as Romans and knights, with "February 25" written at the bottom, the opening of the Fair with everyone wearing panama hats, Dimitris standing at a tree with his legs apart and in front of him the mark where he'd pissed, a woman lying on the cobbles, and beyond her the workers in their best clothes with their banner, a circle marked in pencil, Christos just a felt trilby, Polychronis wearing a panama hat and gaiters sitting in a cane chair with his long cane beside him, May Day by the young plane trees, everyone lying on the grass and the tablecloth white in the middle, plates and empty bottles, three photographs attached together with a paper clip, a body lying on the carpet, two gypsies and a gendarme, a house in the upper town with its iron gate closed, and at the bottom the yellowed conduct report "excellent", five ten out of tens and the rest nines, a girl's head with curly hair and earrings, Michalis's shack with its signs and Manos in the middle talking, at Kamara with Euripides in civilian dress, postcards from Athens, Brigitta Helm in passionate mode, and Valentino with Wilma Banky, a row of girls all dressed in white, the display at the

Schina school, then press cuttings, two poems and a proclamation, the autograph of Delios and a card of his, and finally an invitation to an evening party, a postcard of roses; and Christos wondered, "what are all these things doing here?"

When he got home he stayed out in the garden, humble low-growing plants at his feet, mallow and pansies, the rose whose flowers wouldn't open, and he sighed, "my blood hurts inside me," no matter if people told him that there wasn't any such malady. It was past noon when he finally went inside, smiling, but Amalia looked at his eyes and asked, "why have you been crying?" and he wondered if he really had been crying, but was sure that he hadn't, and Dimitris and Alcmene and Antigone came home, all three of them were tall and slender, "when did they grow so good looking?" thought Christos – but now things were going to be difficult.

And the next day he started going the rounds, to the doors of newspapers, offices, then shops, to find a job he could do and which would feed them. But he couldn't find anything then and there, he had to wait, they had to know hunger, Amalia had to tell him, "if only you didn't strain at a gnat ..." and she meant he was fine in other respects. And at the beginning they managed all right, the pot was boiling on the stove and there was bread, but for how long? And lucky it was that two friends came to his help and recommended him at the market, he went to work for a shopkeeper who sold salt fish in Egypt Street, he sat in a little room like a nest and kept the accounts and the books and on Saturdays he paid the wages – it was a tragicomedy, for one day they were short of hands and Vassilis the boss said, "please, just so that we can unload," for the cart was waiting and blocking the road and curses were making themselves heard, and that's how Christos found himself with a can of fish on his shoulder, then another, and then another, and he learnt what it is to be a porter. And in the evening Amalia complained, "the stink has got right into your skin," and it really was in his hair, on his shoes, right into his vest, his armpits, even if he did say "there's no shame in work" and thus found consolation. But in the nighttime both of them cried and begged, "just let all this end," if they could only escape from the fish stink and the humiliation. And sixteen days later their prayers were heard, Christos suddenly found himself dressed in khaki once more, there had been a coup and he was sent off to a military camp. It was Kondylis again, perhaps Euripides, ambitions, discord, one night they closed down the "Independent", people said that they smashed its windows. But Christos had already gone to Kavalla, who knows whether he was glad when he heard this news, letters were not getting through; Amalia was weeping and scurrying around, "things couldn't be worse," she wailed, she was at her wits' end, wrote to her father-in-law telling him of their dire straits. She received a cheque for three hundred drachmas and the next day a letter written in spidery writing, "we can't manage anything more, bring the children and come to the village" but she didn't pay any attention, they'd be starting school any day now. One night the doorbell rang, it was a strange man, swimming in his light-coloured suit, his face waxen, "I wanted Christos," he said, they were looking for him at "Esperini" and he was sorry not to find him, "he'll be back though," he assured her, the coup was over and they were discharging all the people who'd been called up. He came in and sat for a while and smoked, then told her again, "don't worry, we'll help him" and pressed her hand and left. And Amalia lay awake at night, feeling at her side the warmth of Dimitris who had fallen asleep all curled up, from time to time he kicked her in his deep sleep. For a moment the flame of the little lamp in front of the icon flickered and shadows danced and in the end it all turned into a dream, while outside the cock departed from his normal timetable and crowed.

Angela

Maybe it was just a coincidence or perhaps it had something to do with them having the same name, but Angela made up her mind, "this is going to be my last disappointment" and she meant that it had been yet one more failure or one more dubious game set up for her. Except that she was wrong, as it later proved, since the other Yannis actually reached the point of making an attempt, and it could easily have been the end of him if he'd paid more attention to the rope, if it hadn't let him down, or if he hadn't finished by breaking both his legs when he fell onto the tiled floor of the kitchen – and Angela said, "just imagine if the bridegroom was lame," and half-cried. It wasn't out of pity that she cried though, more from a sense of the cussedness of everything, as if she'd been invited somewhere and then had the door slammed in her face. "You shouldn't be so proud," poor Eugenios had advised, but that was years ago, years of ill luck and bitterness, so that Angela complained, "all my sins will have to come to an end one day," sins of the future and sins of the past. And Domna used to say, "you're like the Virgin Mary, everyone burdens you with their sorrows."

And really it was a matter of sorrow that she met the other Yannis, that she saw him one noon in the restaurant, that he stood in front of her and asked, "may I sit at your table?" for all the other tables were taken, and she said yes; he seemed as gentle as a lamb, he ate his food carefully and didn't speak, their eyes met by chance for a minute, then he said "thank you" and left. Only, as he was going out, the light apparently shining through his body, he turned round and looked at her and smiled, and made a little movement with his hand as if it was wounded, "he must be a poor timid wretch," she said to herself, but a moment later had reverted once again to her own thoughts, that summer was drawing to a close and she'd be back shut up again in Michalis's little place, whose very mood and smell were familiar to her, where the beams and the curtains and the benches all spoke to her; and Michalis himself used to say, "it all gives me a sense of security," by which he meant that he knew his way about and could find the mains switch for the electricity.

A few days later the two of them met again, this time in a familiar narrow lane, he was walking along with no security and seemed disturbed when he saw her, he made as if to stop and said "good morning," the phrase left hanging though, as if he wanted to go on and say something further, but Angela continued past him, thought again what a poor wretch he looked, and a moment later had reached the main road, she heard a tram coming and someone calling "Angela" and it was the married Bulgarian, who smiled at her and put out his hand, whereupon she pretended she hadn't noticed, stood there indifferent, without moving, "when it boils down to it," said the man, "you've got right on your side" and he walked on. And she proceeded down the road with the gardens, oleanders and roses, now in their full glory, their leaves making a play of shadows against the blue like an embroidered curtain whose end dipped into the sea. And Angela felt a great longing to stop at the water's edge and take her shoes off, along the shore were small taverns and a little further off the courtyard of the "Luxembourg" where the rich people went, and in the shallows little boys fishing who looked as if they'd been born in the water and played there day and night, equally at home with the clattering and hammering of the shipyard and the music of the violins in the evening, one with the salty tang of the sea, voices crying "Cyclops is coming", Arapis's song, the one man being their father who'd had lost one eye in the disaster and the other their uncle, an ace at dancing, smuggling and bragging.

They were a familiar tribe to her, they'd sprung from the same Asia Minor soil, apart from the fact that this family spent their whole life on the sea, they knew nothing of the Turkish villages in the hinterland, but nevertheless would say, "we've all been through the same troubles," for they too remembered homelessness and knife blades, the burning of Smyrna and refugeedom, a couple of years in tents where the water seeped into your clothes, or sleeping huddled together ten to a room, everybody hearing everything, everyone afraid. "You're like us," they told her; and one night they came into Michalis's place as if in fancy dress, they'd put on their best dark suits and ties and patent leather shoes, but their ugly snouts shone under the lamps, and they ordered drink after drink, sobering up a little when Angela asked, "where are your wives?" to which they answered, "at home with their babies" without adding anything further. But in any case the girl had her own work to do and forgot about them once up on the stage, where they started off with love songs and by the end were into all the old songs from Smyrna, "Dawn" in a minor key, and then the Bournovalia song, plates were being smashed and people were murmuring, "they're troublemakers," for they were drunk, and just at the height of the uproar Arapis held up a flare, laughing, so that the whole room glowed in its light, and he shouted, "now I'll blow you all up like fish," whereupon people started squealing and a few men ran for the doors, and what remained were the guffaws of the two brothers, their flare extinguished now, saying, "we've got out the dynamite," but after a little while three gendarmes came in, followed by five or six of the customers. And Arapis said, "they called them in to give us a row" and explained that nothing was the matter, they'd simply been slandered by some shitters, at which the other customers blushed, but the gendarmes didn't leave and Cyclops was explaining things to them, and they heard him say, "the girl over there will tell you," meaning Angela, who raised her hands and cried, "I don't know anything about it, don't get me mixed up with the police." And when the episode was over the fishermen left without saying goodnight.

"I don't care," confessed the girl when Domna told her that the other Yannis was from a good family, "except that from time to time," added Michalis maliciously, "he gets so plastered that they have to carry him home." And Angela said once more, "what's that to me?" and her friends smiled, they had discovered that he was following her around, invisible, at a distance, that in the evenings he waited for her on the pavement opposite. But she could have told them that she'd seen him in the tavern, three or four times it must have been, smiling at her and waving to her almost imperceptibly, as if he imagined that he was annoying her and didn't want to. And Domna pressed her, "don't let opportunities slip," she said meaningfully, but "what opportunities?" asked the other girl, into whose mind came the unforgettable Eugenios, and Yannis with his sisters, or even the lost uncle who'd disappeared once again, miserable stories all of them, and she thought of her own loneliness, with no one to support her, no one on whose shoulder she could lean and cry without fear, as she could in the old days when her father and mother were alive, when she had been able to wonder whose embrace was the sweeter and had a choice. And maybe the other Yannis would turn out to be an opportunity, for she felt no fear or suspicion of his ways. And one day at noon she met him in the tram, his hat in his hand, he looked her in the eyes, outside shop windows and houses and trees were rushing past in a play of colour, and he murmured, "well, there, I've found you again" as if he'd been searching for her and puzzling how to find her. And they both smiled and were silent, Angela felt he wasn't like the others, he was more restrained, she thought, which might be no bad thing.

"However, no one is without sin," she remembered Eugenios saying, even if he himself had been no more than a limp hand or an innocent embrace, a few words which made the blood run faint, and she felt, I'd like to kiss him, but I'm afraid he might shy away. Only when they got off at the stop, he put out his hand to help her get down, the way people assist great ladies although they don't blush like Angela did, and she felt that he was without guile, no ulterior motives in the palm of his hand, which then was returned to his pocket to lurk there. They'd advanced a few steps, she thought, is he coming with me or is he scared?, and he could have been scared for he was pale and distracted and at one point stumbled, upon which they both laughed; and she heard him say, "I can't manage very well," perhaps this was a confession that escaped from within him, and the girl said, "do you have a mother?" though she knew quite well he didn't since they used to meet at restaurants, "no," he replied readily enough, "I don't even remember her face any more" for she had died and left them orphans, "I've got a brother," he explained. And Angela consoled him, "I'm on my own too and all alone in the world," and the other Yannis said, "I know" which meant that he'd been asking, that he was interested.

"You like asking questions," Eugenios reproved her, "but there are so many things that can't be told," and she might have confided the same to him about all the things she longed to forget; but in the end when three hours had passed – or maybe more – and she saw that they were the last customers left in the restaurant, she realised that she'd told him all her secrets, that she was naked and defenceless, however the other Yannis assured her once again, "I feel for you" and he touched the tips of her fingers with the tips of his fingers, just the fingernails, as if to touch was painful, burning him, and they both smiled uncomfortably, outside it had begun to blow and the windows were rattling, rousing them so that they paid the bill and went out, "I'll leave you now," she said and gave him her hand (what had got into her?) and he warmed it, which proved that he was on fire, each went his own way as if fearful, and a light rain began, playing tricks on them, sometimes getting heavier, sometimes stopping, so that Angela hurried and thought, he may be the worst of all of them, she feared him because he was tearful and made people lay themselves bare. She had learned to tremble in front of weak men.

And Michalis grumbled, "you don't seem to value proper men like us" and he didn't only mean Domna but Angela too, in whom he confided one night, "you and I could hit it off together" and took her in his arms, it didn't go any further than that though, because Angela threatened, "I'll tell Domna" and he swore; afterwards he begged, "forgive me" like someone who has received a whipping, and she stroked his face and his hair, "it's late now," she reminded him. Outside the other Yannis was standing waiting, a shadow among the shadows of the trees, like a bird that has lost its foliage and is casting round to find some familiar point of reference, her blue dress shining like a beacon, her footsteps or her scent, the breath of her armpits. And Angela thought, I'd better not make him unhappy, no matter that she was terrified at the way he was slipping in, had opened her door just a crack, just a tiny bit, then a little more, then more, until the crack was wide enough for him to pass through, to whisper to her, "I can't do without you," so that she felt her eyes were being flooded by a swelling tide of blood which is perhaps what was making her cheeks burn, her neck maybe, her ribs and her precarious heart. For weak people are indeed terrifying, you fear lest they might cease breathing or lose their reason, and she felt sorrowful about it.

And they walked together to her door, at one point she murmured, "what a sultry day" but he made no response, he seemed to be sleepwalking, his arms hanging down like useless wings, his white shirt a wide expanse as if the evening breeze passed through it, his footsteps soundless. Somewhere someone was hammering nails and they said, "he must have gone crazy," both said it at the same time and laughed; then she plucked up her courage and told him, "we said all there was to say in the morning," the other Yannis disagreed though, "I could talk to you for days on end," he whispered as if it was an effort to say it, then leant against the wall of her house and seemed to fade out, white against white, now he's going to faint, I'll lose him, she thought, and an image blew through her mind, Omar, a world which had faded, where everything had foundered, and she heard his voice saying from the wall, "we'll have to part now," and it was like a sob or a complaint, and she saw his wings open and say, "I'm going," it was as if he was acting in the theatre, and he said once more, "I'm going, I'll leave you now," a whole drama that she lacked the courage to put a stop to. And as he walked off his footsteps were so unbelievably light that he was like a sheet of paper blown by the wind, might he perhaps be a dream, she wondered, as she saw him turn round and look at her, then open his two arms once more, they must surely be saying, "I'm going," as if he was announcing the Second Coming, a significant secret from another world which she heard yet remained unmoved, while above her hair a world of leaves and stars complemented the magic and the revelation.

The Middle Ages – 3

"That was the night I was telling you about, at the edge of the dry riverbed, when we were left speechless and bitter, and each one of us departed by a different path and I came and knocked on your door in the middle of the night; if you had not opened it to me I would have fallen, would have been killed or would have lain wherever it chanced." And a gaping wound opens inside her, "it's not the dreaded sickness," she assures him, "I bleed on the slightest provocation and become faint," in the underworld princes and wizards are waiting, a pure blue fairy and the river, the river that went up to the bare solitary tree, with the shepherd in the night, the sheep of silence and the voice that said, "one day we shall be drowned in oblivion, you will forget the feel of my skin, my scent that you say overwhelms you, the only thing that will remain to tell of our nights together will be the memories held in other people's minds." They said that love slipped in stealthily, that in some corner of that night of the majors she stood in thought and, taking his hands, said to herself, "does he know how ceaselessly I have loved him all these years?" She forever hears his tender words, his breath coming faster, and then "beloved soul, dear heart" as a sweet scent of roses spreads round them, for he never liked the scent of carnations. She remembers once more the greenery, unadorned by any flower, "I like the dense foliage and the tall grass, and in the midst of everything the orange fruit, girded by the embalmed serpents of the Deluge; come and let us speak of wild beasts, of lost treasures which people say were forgotten in oceans and desert islands, come and let me recount to you the story they told me about your grandfather's love." Outside the wind had been blowing since morning, the whole of creation was enclosed in a valley, we should take this road, the horses may get their legs wet, their knees, but the men will surely stay dry, provided only that they hold on fast, we shall arrive at Pipilista at evenfall, there their cousins awaited them, their wives, their daughters and sons, unarmed, uncircumspect. They dismounted and went into the great chamber, all around were divans covered in sheepskins, above them the massive roof beams, impregnated with smoke and a history of hanged men, of difficult years spent lost at the foot of the mountain opposite, with the oak woods untrodden, the vines never ripening, the bandits' mill and the burnt chapel. And she said, "I suspect that they had laid the trap for us right from the beginning." Beyond the bare field stood a man with his body bent, as if his task was to study the ground around him, he asked her, "have you left one of your brooches behind? They could be incriminating evidence," at which she laughed sadly, "who would have thought that our love could be suspected?" and told him the story of foolish Argyris, "I'm afraid that you have not clarified your inner feelings," and she bent once more, "I don't want you to think that I came to you because I was unhappy," she said, and he did not want to think this either, "when that man who is sitting and watching us leaves, we shall go to the uninhabited chamber, I have kept it for you alone," he does not want to believe that she knew this field in the past, that the chamber was not always uninhabited. And then from the other direction two youths seemed to be coming downhill, one smoking, the other talking, "don't be afraid," he tells her and takes her in his arms, the young men approached and stopped short in front of them, "so, one day when I was young, we went down to the shore and stole a boat, we were just wild children, looking for ways to have fun and grow up, regardless of whether we caused other people pain" – and then the two youths set off again, one of them in his shirtsleeves, the other seeming to be enveloped in his clothes, they noticed them, passed them, stopped short, and then Irene said, "we'd better go," he held her hand by force, "let me go," she said, "they will have it in for us," somewhere they heard swearing, he held her close against him, "here," he said, "before we go" – "you think you are still a wild child," she tells him but does not smile at him, she considered his white hairs, yet how to tell him, "I have grown old now," the other man who was bending has made as if to move and breathe more freely, she seemed to be letting herself go, oh God, to be pressed against him like this, so old and yet her body firmer and sweeter than a girl's; then it seemed that the three men knew each other, they were speaking in low voices, they might have been perverts or be planning some dirty business which required a lonely spot, "we'd better leave," he heard her say, but what does it matter if there are three of them, he reckoned, I can handle them, from the road came the sound of singing, the three men turned round and looked at them, maybe they themselves were what the dirty business was aimed at, and he feels her trembling mount in him, communicated hand to hand, he would never believe it of Irene, "do they perhaps know you?" – "I am afraid," and this was the first time. For the last few nights he has been woken from sleep by the same dream, in the days when they first went to the house with the acacias, sleep would not come to him till dawn, he was afraid lest someone should open his window, should pass into the great chamber where Areti and Eugenia were sleeping, now he dreams of it all, "it's a strange figure, something between an animal and a monster, he reaches the window, jumps in before I have time to defend myself and we chase each other through the hall, along the passage, in front of the door which the girls lock, and there I grab him by the neck, he has a tiny head which keeps getting smaller and slipping out of my grasp, and at that point I scream and the others wake up, we have to get hold of him from all sides, lest he escape us this time and come back the following night." Well, things were better when they were children and got up to all sorts of craziness and mischief; he remembers the time they went to Egnatia Street, there was a garden with kind-hearted girls at Vardari, "in the evening we'll perform for you," they told them, one of them was a Jewish girl aged twelve, "do you want to come along with us?" she asked him one night, he caressed her hand, "leave this evening and come back another day," she was abducted and the police came running and kept asking, "which of you saw her last?" and someone said, "the man who abducted her," one day when he was with Theano in the park he told her this story, "I'd like to see all those people," she said, "but I cannot with you, I am afraid of you" and afterwards she died, Aegisthus and the captain were lost too, "the dreams betray your disturbed soul," Irene said to him the following night – "you who knew the captain, can you tell me what that man hid within himself" – "I have forgotten, do not ask me about things which happened before I met you," and then he embraced her, "I think my sins vanish when I am with you", – "what sins?" she asked, "I would like us to walk together one day on the beach, with not a soul around, and you would undress me, I don't know what else I have left to live for"; he told her, "I'd like to kiss you all over, to be drenched in your scent," the most terrible dream was when he stood one night and gazed at the beach for hours and the darkness remained immutable, a darkness which foundered in the sea, darkening it too – he would never forget the river and the wall, those indicators of an unending world, the house with the beautiful garden, the stony places, the silence and her, the whole story is like a green velvet tablecloth, faded. He remembers how he adorned her and comforted her in her poverty and knows now that there is nothing he can bear. "I could bear everything, your lies, and Irene too, if only you did not make me feel humiliated" and her eyes reddened, the voice that was speaking to him choked, then she said, "I ought never again to ask anything" and looked at her hands, her wheaten skin, "this flesh that has been born is your work and mine, only do not show me that everything starts from desire, many times I wish to walk by myself, I begin to believe that I cannot rely on words, I open my chest, I take my old clothes into my hands, I hug them to me, the apron I had when I was a girl and the photographs, at Edessa with Antonis and Roula, in our castles with the girls, alone at the White Tower, taken in those days when my world consisted only of the word wait, the carriage that they'd send you secretly, with not a passenger in it, the days when you said they are awaiting me at the end of the beach, he might be handsome, well-built, and somewhere there you appear, you take me by the hand, you enfold me, there are times when I have not been longing for you, when I think of other things, but you come and take me, you enfold me, everything else fades from before my eyes and I float like a ship in the mist, only lulled, in a lethargy, so that I forget him and am afraid, and I say where is he for me to lean on him, for us to walk together, to ply the oceans together." And once more he felt that

165

rain was falling within him, the water flowing into his heart, freezing him, so he thought, I should curl up at her feet and say, "this is the last time that I shall make you grieve" and then to be united with her and to find some corner where he may hide in her embrace, to be warmed and to love her forever. There is a voice from heaven which insists that he erred, that perhaps it was necessary for him to err, but as he passes through stream and water and mud he sees her always awaiting him, stretching out her warm hand to him, her heart, and he falls at her feet in humility. The memories have been festering for three years now, like the uniforms on the dead as they lie on the field of battle, past which no one wishes to walk, where generations of birds have been buried in trees and in foliage and where proud voices founder and are lost, they say, "these two corpses which your sheet has cast up" which are a man, a woman, their burnt photographs, and they call in despair, "it is you" and "you."

Angela

But she didn't feel any of the magic and the revelation reminded her of the sky when all of a sudden lightning flashes and terrifies you, your blood and bile surge and warn you that this may be the end. And it really was. For as Angela and the other Yannis were walking together and it was already midnight and they were saying, "it's getting late" and feeling sad about it, as they stood in front of her door on yet one more evening and she was expecting him to announce, "I'm going, I'll leave you now" and fly off, they suddenly realised that they were not alone but that a man was watching them who wasn't concealing himself, he seemed to be saying to them, I can see you and I came here to see you – at which the other Yannis was upset and said to Angela as if asking for support, "my brother", who came up to them and stood there and looked at her, particularly and searchingly at her, then remembered and said "good evening", followed by "I was waiting for you," and Angela kept trying to think where do I know him from? However, she was not to remain in torment for long, he had a way of speaking that was both clear and angry and he addressed himself to the other Yannis, he said, "say goodnight to the young lady and come home," it was like the lash of a whip, but the other man found his voice, "I can't, I'm talking to her," he stammered, his brother caught hold of his hand though, "you've talked enough and to spare," he spat, "and the young lady understands what I mean," he could have stood beside her, the other Yannis, he could have said don't be scared, I'm beside you, I understand it all, but it's your garden that I prefer.

On the night of all the trouble, when his sisters had taken

offence and left, and Yannis had run after them, Angela had disappeared into a dark corner where the singer came and found her, he looked as if he was about to faint and he took her hands, very overwrought, and begged her, "give me your forgiveness" and got stuck at that point, saying the same phrase over and over again as he saw her with tears in her eyes and bereft of speech, trying imperceptibly to draw her hands back, to liberate them, to breathe, as if he was stealing her very air and causing her to suffocate, in the end he fell on his knees ("such actors," she was to say later, with contempt) and there he revealed to her that "he's longing for you and asking for you," and he meant his master, "but there are other reasons which don't allow him," whereupon Angela jumped up as if on springs, she knew the reasons and was lamenting, "don't be discouraged," he told her, still on his knees, "he sent me" (which was a lie), "he told me to come and assure you of it," and he was embracing her legs, she felt as if she had strayed into some marsh full of dangerous plants and lies, which grapple you and may suck you down, it had happened to her one noon back in her homeland, the sun was shining in the sky above and the water got ever deeper and the plants ever taller and she said to herself, "no one will find me" and screamed for help, a gypsy passing by with his cart heard her, he came and grasped hold of her hand, in the end they sat beneath a fig tree until she had no more tears left to cry, all panic and shame; and she said to the singer, "aren't you ashamed of yourself?" and she meant a man of your age, but he kept on holding her and pleading; and in the end she kicked him.

But what actors they are, my God, and she meant all of them, all men, for someone's shutters were opened a crack and light shone through, and she saw that the other Yannis's brother was one of Vlachos's acquaintances, one of the crowd from the parties with all the girls, that unforgettable night when she'd been afraid he was about to die in her arms, and she thought that everything has its own part to play in life, its own time. And she whispered to the other Yannis, "I'm going, I'm leaving you now," this was not said in sarcasm or mockery though, it was more that she felt sorry for him, but the young man said, "no, stay," and maybe he wanted to gain confidence from her or to show her that she was doing him an injustice, for he had read the expression in her eyes and felt pain, "I told you that I'm going to stay and finish our conversation," he said to his brother, at which the other man smiled, his teeth glinting between his lips, "so be it," he said, showing himself to be understanding. But as he turned to leave he fired a parting shot, "if you need any help, whistle," and at that point the door was hastily opened and closed, Angela was inside, furious, while outside remained the two brothers, then only one of them, beside himself, shouting, "I'll not forgive you for this, Christoforos," and after a moment tapping on the door, calling "Angela" and telling her, "I'm alone now," and finally leaning on the door in despair, crying and pale perhaps, his shadow visible through the cheap glass pane, and she could hear his harsh breathing, then nothing more.

Because Angela remained speechless, the revelation was unexpected, and she felt, I can't cope with any more letters, for she remembered all that Eugenios had written, and his wounded desire, and thus she left the envelope unopened, let it lie like a dead thing on her chest of drawers, a white reminder which inexplicably seemed to pierce her somewhere a bit below her heart, on the right side of her chest, as if she had some festering boil there which started throbbing only when she looked at the envelope. And Domna said, "either tear it up or read it," which was the voice of common sense, except that it would hurt Angela to do either. However, the revelation was inevitable, he was someone who wouldn't just leave her to turn pious or be resurrected, and he came back in the form of the other Yannis's brother, who knocked on her door (it was early afternoon and she was sitting dreaming, having just finished her coffee), he stood there as if waiting for an invitation and in the end said, "I'm still waiting for an answer." She could have thrown him out and slammed her door on him in anger, but instead said weakly, "I don't understand what you're talking about," using the second person singular on purpose; the man then asked, "may I come in?" which he seemed to consider natural and was insisting on, and she stepped back without a yes and without a no. And when he entered the room he looked around him as if interrogating her, and stood there uncomfortably as if his plan wasn't working, but they both sat down and he caught sight of the letter, "is it from you," she asked and he was startled, "I can't read," she explained, holding the lifeless letter in her hand, then put it down on the table, "you're a crafty one," he said, smiling at her as he said it and thinking hard.

He looked like a cat that has had the cream, at a first glance he was a bit like Yannis (like the colour of ivory, as Eugenios had said that first evening), but he rapidly showed that he had claws, he had hands that took her own hand (well really, thought Angela in outrage) and he assured her, "I'm only interested in your own good," then proceeded without stopping, "do you know what sort of person you're getting involved with? What's in store for you? He's a sick boy, when he was a child he got ill, the doctor was trying to give him an injection, he leapt up in terror and the needle snapped off in his leg, the old man had to go running round from hospital to hospital, don't even ask, once when he went to the doctor, Dr. Dakos, for his teeth, he fainted when he saw the instruments and they had to throw water on him to bring him round"; at that point the door opened and the other Yannis was standing there, all pale, and he told her, "every word of it is true." But Angela screamed, "what's the point of so much hatred?" and felt a flood of faintness rising through her body, blocking her ears and closing her eyes, she heard a buzz that sounded as if it was in the yard outside saying, "don't cry" and felt two hands supporting her, trying desperately to calm her, then the door opened and closed and they were alone, the cat had slipped silently out and she heard the other Yannis say, "maybe it's all done from pain and love," and he was explaining his brother's temerity; "I realise it now, he must have been hurt," insisted the boy.

Yannis, though, had suffered real wounds, he had turned up one night, torn and bleeding, at her old hovel up by the castle and told her, "one of these days they'll knife me," whereupon Angela had trembled, young and innocent as she was, she'd found something that suited her with Eugenios, for with him everything was calm and secure, his house was like an old wooden chest, albeit decorated with carpets and red curtains, whose key remained safely in his pocket. "But, dear God, what are you casting me into now?" she wondered aloud, and heard no answer, only a hand speaking to the right side of her back, counselling, "calm down," but why did he have to be so inexperienced? She felt sorry, turned and regarded him, "I must look terrible," she murmured to him, then kissed his hand, "listen," she said, "it would be better if you went home now," blood is thicker than water, she thought, "it would be better if you listened to him," and there might be others, sisters or brothers, maybe sisters-in-law, and a father; "better that you should listen to them," but the other Yannis said, "who?" He didn't have anyone else, their only sister was dead, "Christoforos ran round and spent money on doctors," but it had been in vain; "our father is paralysed," he told her, "I cook for him, I wash him and get him dressed." He looked as if he had tears in his eyes, full of grief, and Angela thought, well, there you are, I'm not the only one, but that way lay melancholy, the feeling that unhappiness loomed over all mankind, like a sort of epidemic as she imagined it, like a fatal illness which strikes and leaves people incapacitated and useless.

"I could get a job, I could struggle," said the other Yannis to himself, his father had sent him to the commercial college, "Noukas was one of my teachers," he continued, as he recounted it to her, but his strength had been sapped by malaria, his family wept over him, and in the end all that remained were the books and the dreams, people said that his brother had beaten up two of the teachers, and then finally he left for Asia Minor; when peace came and things got back to normal, they put the other Yannis to work in a chemist's shop, for he knew a little French and could read the prescriptions, and the family said, "all right, so he's never going to be a merchant" but it wasn't the end of the world. "So why didn't you stay there?" Angela asked him, trying hard to find some place where her anxieties could be laid to rest, "I'm a ne'er-do-well, haven't you understood?" – "but then you'll die," she teased, and caressed him as if to say I don't believe it, he was blushing and smiling, "it's your fault for being so tender," she cooed to him, and outside they could hear two boys quarrelling, stamping and swearing, "you wanker," shouted one of them and the other sounded as if he was crying, "do you know what it means, what you're saying?" he complained, and Angela wondered, then laughed, "I haven't got a clue either," but the other Yannis said nothing, remained pale and sad, he might even have been deaf perhaps. Maybe he was thinking, I could get a job, I could make a struggle.

And Angela said, "a final attempt", but no one (not even herself) understood what she meant, and the other Yannis took her hand – a week had passed since that afternoon in her room – and said, "let's go and see my father." People could have told her that he'd been drinking again, and it's true he smelt of alcohol, but he seemed desperate and afraid, scared of setting off for battle, maybe he was engaged in some inner dialogue and had settled in his mind, "it's now or never." And as they walked in the twilight Angela suddenly froze; in front of them was a coffee house, and inside the door in the half-dark an old man in a white smock was sitting and looking at them, he had close-cropped grey hair and a fat face, and Angela gasped to herself, "oh God, it's Father," and in the half-light he raised his heavy white arm as if he was calling her or asking for something, and Angela went straight in as if hypnotized, though she heard someone saying, "it can't, it can't, Father," she hastened to the old man and the white figure was getting up, standing on his feet, he looked her in the eyes and asked, "take my arm and help me walk, I want to go outside and get a breath of air" and he began to cough, "where are you from?" the mad girl asked him, and he answered, "from far away, from Vourla" – and she took his arm and led him out and he thanked her, "bless you," he said when she had settled him under the acacia tree where a perfectly good breath of air was stirring.

And the other Yannis seemed pleased, "you're kind to old people," he whispered to her, whereupon the girl answered, "he was the spitting image of my father," who had died on eastern shores, and that was more than twelve years ago. By now night had fallen and lights were coming on, somewhere a gramophone was playing "But even so, but even so" and the other Yannis stopped in front of a two-storey house, "we're here," he said, and it was as if he was trembling, "don't forget to kiss his hand" and he meant his father's, and Angela was to say later, "the man couldn't even feel it, it was his paralysed hand." The old man was calm and well set, sitting quietly on a divan with his jacket over his shoulders (he couldn't take it off or put it on by himself) and in his left hand was his stick, of shiny black wood, a most faithful friend to him and perhaps also a means of expression or of power. And the other Yannis said, "this is Angela that I told you about," and the old man gave her a very thorough looking over, she bent and kissed his hand, and you might have thought it made a faint movement, then he looked at her again with moist eyes, his jaw seemed to quiver, and the other Yannis asked him, "do you like her?" but the old man lowered his gaze, as if reflecting that he'd been sizing her up; what am I doing here with all these invalids? thought Angela. And she felt she could detect a whiff of old age and medicines, they were new people whom she didn't know, whom perhaps she couldn't love, she looked once more at the old man who sat silent and a voice within her said, so what are we waiting for?

And at that point the brother came in unexpectedly, though he didn't appear to be at all surprised, as if he'd known whom he was going to find there and already had his first words ready, he said, "don't upset father with foolishness," then the old man raised his stick like a sceptre and Angela was terrified, thinking whose head is he going to break? And the other Yannis said, "I have decided to get engaged," his voice sounded somehow altered by his determination, and then Christoforos's hand came down like lightning on the other Yannis's cheek, whose eyes flashed, but he neither said nor did a thing, even though Angela jumped back in horror and cried, "you didn't ask me," she ran in terror to the door and opened it, paused in thought for a couple of seconds, went back, knelt in front of the old man, "forgive me," she whispered, then recollected once again the other two and her own terror, went out into the yard and breathed a bit more freely, from upstairs she heard a woman's voice begging, "don't get upset, Christoforos," she raised her eyes and saw a woman in flowing white clothes, and in the end she found herself in the road, under a pale streetlight. And as she began to walk away, along an endless line of fences with ivy and flowers, she heard someone running up behind her, said to herself, "pray God it's not him" – but in vain. However, luckily he didn't say anything, just walked beside her for a bit, then took her hand and squeezed it feverishly, Angela turned to him, she was afraid to look at him, afraid lest her pity should choke her, but his eyes were without expression, he seemed to be thinking of things long gone, maybe some image from his childhood. And in the end he disappeared; she felt an emptiness beside her, as if her ears were being blocked or the air she breathed was being stolen, by his scent, his voice, the way he'd caressed her.

And the following night she heard his echo resound once more, when Domna came shouting to her, "they've killed him" and Angela asked "who?" – the other Yannis had committed suicide, the whole neighbourhood was in tears, and Michalis advised her, "you'd better lie low," people would be cursing her, maybe would be after her, for Christoforos was hasty-tempered, but Angela wept, "what fault was it of mine?" and she couldn't help thinking that death seemed to stalk her, "anyone would think I was cursed," she sobbed in Domna's arms, but who could have put a curse on her, she would never have harmed a fly, "they always exploit me," she moaned and her eyes overflowed with tears, which might perhaps never stop. But after a while Michalis arrived and "don't cry," he said, it was like the raising of the dead, for he told her that the other Yannis was still alive, "although he's got two broken legs," he explained – apparently because the rope had been old and rotten and had broken, and the boy had thus escaped from the jaws of death, and Michalis said, "maybe he chose it on purpose," meaning the rope; and Angela was comforted, "that's that then," although he might be lame for the rest of his life, "you'd better disappear," said Michalis once more, for he was sick of all the rows – "since she turned up the rows have been coming thick and fast," and Domna agreed. Maybe it would be better if she left, but they talked about it secretly, the two of them, as if trouble was looming over the business, one night someone smashed two of their windows, and Michalis muttered again, "I don't have any enemies," and he sat with Domna in a corner and they watched Angela and tightened their lips.

And when the other Yannis reappeared (he had crutches and was in pain) they informed him that Angela had gone, they didn't know where – he had a melancholy smile, his voice came out hoarse like an old front door creaking, all worm-eaten wood, and he complained, "I can't run round any more." It was time for work, Michalis and Domna went inside and began getting things ready, and thus they had no idea how long he stayed, when he set off again on his crutches, how long it would be before they saw him again. And winter was coming, the endless drizzle was setting in, and walks and romances were fewer now.

Fotis

One day at noon Fotis confessed, "my kith and kin are drawing me back"; they all lived in Thessaloniki and were struggling and suffering under the blows of life, he received despairing letters about his son, about one of his sisters still unmarried, whom he ought to help, about his mother, growing old now and weeping, "maybe I'll never set eyes on my child again," and this child of hers was forever mixed up with troubles and the police, was forever prodigal and heartless. And Eleni spoke of her own woes, "our kingdom's beginning to creak a bit," for the gendarmerie was after them, and all the people who were losing at dice or who were ever more frequently casting hungrier and hungrier eyes on the chanteuses; "one of these days they'll make it all come tumbling down on us" and she meant the French and the locals, no matter that they sent little presents wherever necessary, whenever they were demanded or schemed for. And Fotis persuaded her, "after all, at bottom you're a Greek too," they could start all over again in their homeland, "it's a port full of cosmopolitan people," the man added, "only it's not going to be easy."

And it was perfectly true that they would be up to their necks in problems (which in fact proved to be more numerous and more frightening than expected), there were his old scores with the navy to be settled, his forged papers, and – even more important – the question of how they were going to smuggle in their fortune, the diamonds, their life style of ease.

And Eleni said, "there's nothing that can't be bought and sold" and explained that she had her own well-tested method. And he agreed, "go and have a try, it's easier for you" since she had a genuine passport, she didn't owe the Greeks anything, except perhaps a man whom she'd been keeping shut up in her cage and enjoying. And thus she made her first trip, travelling first class on the ship, surrounded by a host of cabin stewards and an equal number of lady-killers, she laughed at them, she talked and drove them crazy, her perfumes intoxicating, her eyes an abyss. And most of them were gallants just showing off their French and their good manners and their smart suits – only one turned out to be trouble and he was one of the crew (the engineer or something) and one night he came to her cabin, he said, "solitude is hard to bear" and he pushed open her door, however a tigress growled at him, "go back to your mother before she gets good cause to grieve" but he asked, "what's the tariff?", thinking of what it cost in the place he knew, but he felt the lash of a whip and saw something that looked like a toy gleaming in the half-light, and the tigress spoke once more, said, "I swear your family will be bereaved and grieving, because I don't fancy you" and another door was heard opening somewhere, and the man said, "I'll leave so as not to damage your reputation" – what gall he had to use the second person singular – but the next day they arrived at Piraeus and she didn't set eyes on him again.

And when they saw her (she was dressed all in white, with a hat that concealed her face, revealing only two lips and a shapely chin and a hint of sunglasses), his sisters said, "it's obvious why she bewitched him," for ever since he'd been a child he'd always worshipped stars and adventure, and Eleni came among them like a vision, the whole neighbourhood was open-mouthed in wonder at the lovely woman who generously spread around her perfumes, her expensive peignoirs, so that they all dressed up as femmes fatales, and Eleni said, "I can bring you lots more" that she no longer wore, and in the pocket of each one she put some little bit of jewellery, in one a medallion, in another a brooch or a necklace, and everyone said, "what open-handedness," but "it's from our brother," they added, and Eleni smiled to herself, she'd got it all worked out right and knew that Myrsine was the only one who'd be grateful to have three thousand drachmas slipped into her pocket accompanied by the whisper, "it's for food, so you can go out shopping and think of your son." Thus it was a happy time for everyone, all day spent talking as she recounted Fotis's exploits, every second evening spent out in the large restaurants, at the "Luxembourg" which was near where they lived, or beside the White Tower, and the chanteuse prided herself, thinking my own business is better though, and Thessaloniki lacks something like mine, it's a good place here with the sea in front, smelling fresh, and when it comes down to it there are people here who like luxury, flashing lights and birds of paradise; "maybe I could put down some roots in this city," she wrote to Fotis, "everyone sends their love, take care of your stomach and look after the shop, don't forget yourself at cards and don't drink too much, on Wednesday go to the policeman and give him the packet that I left you, Marie has to go to the doctor every Thursday for treatment, lock up carefully at night, leave a light on in the main room, keep a note of what you spend and what you receive, your family are crazy about me what with the robes and the presents, tomorrow we're going to meet someone from the police, he's a friend of your brother-in-law, I'll let you know all the details, I embrace you, take care, sleep well at night and mind you eat properly, your Eleni who hasn't forgotten you."

And the following day she really did go with Christoforos, "he's my man," he told her, "we'd best ask him," and in a few days another missive from Eleni arrived, "I miss you and I'll be coming back, we have to start selling things off, find that agent who was asking about the business, tell him I'm sick and I'm going to be leaving and we'll see what his answer is," beside these words was a lipstick print of her mouth, "I've missed you, you dirty lout, and I send you my love." But there was a second sheet of paper on which was written, "maybe you'll manage to get off without punishment, you'd only have to serve six months and they'd fix it so that you'd be with the Port Authorities at Thessaloniki, that way we'd be together, find a gold watch in Beirut, the policeman says he likes them, Christoforos is astute, what a man, he boasts that he's a Vlach, but he's tight-fisted with everything, don't buy anything for him" and then once more the print of her lips, "your son is just the same as ever, only he's got a bit skinnier and even more sneaky, his granny bathes him now with green soap to teach him not to swagger too much, and if he so much as moves she clouts him on the head with the bar of soap and shuts him up, but your Angel gets his revenge on her by pulling up her flowers; anyway, when you come maybe we'll knock some sense into him, only we have to think carefully about how to bring the money and the diamonds in, Christoforos has his own money-changers who'll help us, that Vlach has his finger in every pie, so much so that I'm beginning to be a bit suspicious, your sister is a saint, it seems she's a victim and knows it, yet she doesn't complain to anyone, but I gave her two peignoirs, the Chinese silk one for summer and the other which is reversible, red and black capitonné, and she looks like a queen in it," then once again a bright red lip print ("the whore, nothing escapes her," muttered Fotis) and the writing ended there, but beneath was an arrow so Fotis turned the sheet over, "under the roulette table there's a secret drawer, I've left a pistol in it for emergencies, only don't get into quarrels over nothing, we don't want to be closed down before we're ready" – and here the letter really did end, without so much as a signature or another lip print, and Fotis said to himself, "she'll manage it all," which was something he'd never doubted.

And he gave orders for the carriage to be brought round and in the meantime wondered: will she be there, though? He took a bundle of clothes, two wicker baskets of fruit and sweetmeats, and set off for Fatima's neighbourhood, he didn't have any cash to spare and thought, "it's not that I'm about to become a saint, but it's the last chance," and in front of him he saw a blind old woman and wondered, have so many years passed? Then a girl came out and mumbled, "she's not here," that the blind woman was Fatima's sister, and Fotis asked, "where can I find her?" to which the girl answered, "she's gone back to the village," and before him stretched the road, nothing but aridity and bare earth and dry grasses, he set out on foot, perhaps cursing or perhaps weeping, a prickly pear was growing at the side, white with the dust, and he murmured, "I'm sorry" to the blind old woman, got out two clusters of cool fresh grapes and placed them in her hands, "it's a present from Ismail," he smiled sadly, then got into his carriage again and departed; he had left the baskets and the bundle of clothes and, as the carriage moved away, he turned and saw them, the blind old woman in this earthen landscape and the girl turning over the clothes, and he called, "they're for you and for Fatima" and lashed the little horse which got going and trotted along fast, beyond lay the refreshing sea, through its waves a caique was ploughing a foaming wake with a yellow flag like a decoration on its mast, he could just make out two or three small heads like little dots, how cool they must be, he thought, and then as if talking to them said, "I'm like one of the damned" for there was no tree anywhere in sight, no shade to shelter him, no breath of wind, and he gave another stroke of the lash to the horse, who was not to blame, who didn't cry, who didn't even protest.

Eleni arrived three days later and they discussed everything more thoroughly, "you didn't look after a thing," she scolded him, she was always the active one. And the next day at noon she came home and announced, "I've sold everything," for everything was in fact hers to sell, it was all in her name, and Fotis thought, so I've lost it all, the paradise-like garden and the canaries, the seventeen dancing girls, but above all security; all the same, he accepted that it had been his decision to start off over again in Thessaloniki, the city of his old haunts and his own people, he'd have certain advantages in the game and would at least escape all the kicks of drunken Frenchmen and starving Arabs, he'd be free of all the noises in the night, which might prove hostile, like the nightmare where his arms hung paralysed at his sides and they hit him and stabbed him and he was powerless and strange apaches sprang up from somewhere their eyes were red and black their mouths dripping and they were spitting they took his clothes and in the end he was surrounded by people hidden behind black veils and like a hunting dog a woman came with her golden lance pierced him just below his thing and she said, "it's the middle of the night and you're screaming," Eleni kissed him and smiled at him in the half-light and caressed him, "do you know," said she, "how much I missed you?" and he could feel that she was wearing only her silk nightdress and beneath it all the perfume of cedar trees and then it was only the naked fragrance, like morning in the forest before the mist has evaporated, and he enjoyed kissing the coolness of her arm and her cheek which reminded him of a fruit – then everything became a dream once more.

Until there came a moment when he reflected, she may just be lulling me, because apart from the times when they were making love Eleni went her own mysterious way, she might have been selling or buying things, laying plots with her unknown business partners or cheating the money-changers in order to slip away.

However, on their last morning they awoke, they were due to take the boat that afternoon, they'd already dismissed the band and the dancers, the waiters and croupiers had all left, and the watchmen remained sitting in a corner, the chambermaids and the cooks also remained, and Eleni told them, "look after the household and the shop, mind you're careful" for Fotis was to come back, this was what had been agreed, they were going to hand over the business later, they'd take care of the staff so that they wouldn't lose their jobs. And thus it was that they took their trunks and their suitcases, whatever was of greatest value, and she called Fotis into their bedroom, said to him, "here's the ring, the watch, the locket, the cross" all flashing with brilliants and diamonds, they used to have a whole fortune tucked away, a house, maybe a cabaret's worth, and she catechised him, "you won't leave the cabin" in case they were robbed, in spite of the fact that both of them were armed as they set off on their great adventure.

And when they were on board ship Fotis declared that he was ill, shut himself up in the dark in their cabin and didn't poke his nose out once, he complained, "it seems I'm fated never to enjoy voyages" as he remembered all his exploits, being a deserter, playing hide-and-seek down in the holds, and all the hunger and thirst, whereupon he ordered the cabin steward, "bring me some chicken and rice," then later some chilled champagne, which seemed like a pretty odd kind of diet, so that people wondered about the patient and his beautiful wife, but on the third evening they said, "we're arriving at Salonica," and they meant the following morning. The couple then locked themselves in their cabin to guard against the most difficult moment of all, during the night they concealed an entire treasure, some of it in a lamp, some in a couple of belts, some in the hems of her skirts. And the September morning dawned with a calm sea, the whitest of skies and on the horizon a strip of dark-coloured land, then the city began to appear browner and whiter, on the right its highest mountain, in shadow at first, then blackish green, behind them the milky sea, an ocean almost totally becalmed, and to the left more mountains, and Fotis said, "there's snow on the peak of Mount Olympus." And a little while more and they were within the bay's embrace, it was as if the land was stretching out her arm, telling them now you are mine, and indeed now they began to be able to distinguish houses, two caiques crossed the water lazily, and further off two skiffs flashed in the morning light, they could see the oarsmen strain, then they said, "there's the White Tower" and Fotis felt a wave of longing, a faintness, a sort of pain above his belt, on the left side, and he thought, it feels as if something is squeezing my heart, and relaxed.

Someone banged on the door, called, "we're arriving," Eleni put on her showiest dress, it was red with white sprigs, and her wide-brimmed red hat, and said, "now comes the most difficult bit of all," she put on her sunglasses which concealed all trace of her feelings, her fears, the adventure was about to begin, the agonising moment, because they were arriving on the quay which already seemed to be baking in the sun, porters were running here and there, and all among the crowds were the snow white uniforms, Fotis reflected, I know them and they know me, and as he went down the gangway carrying their most expensive suitcases he felt her hand caress him, she was saying, courage, it'll soon be over, for a second he felt like loosening his tie but his hands were full. And in the end he set foot on the paving stones, then onto the cobbled road, he thought, I could leap over the railings, beyond them was a square and behind that a marble mansion, some things he remembered and others not, it's all become unrecognisable he thought, and just then he saw a curly-haired man come and embrace him, laughing, murmuring "welcome", and he wondered to himself, is this Christoforos? And Christoforos indeed it was, a bit fuller in the figure, a bit darker skinned, but with the same moustache and intelligent eyes which were gazing and laughing at Eleni, maybe protesting what a woman, then his eyes were lowered once more as if fatigued and they heard a voice from deep within him say, "it's all fixed." And the customs officers really had been spoken to, all except one who looked offended or annoyed, and a friend in a grey suit turned up, a man with a round face, and he seemed to be speaking in sign language, he must be a Vlach, thought Fotis, his fair hair was thinning and he was sweating constantly, but then after a moment two porters appeared (who had summoned them?), they picked up the closed suitcases, for two hadn't even been opened, and left; the taxi was at the gate waiting for them, and the man in the grey suit was standing there smiling at them all and Christoforos said "thanks" and the other, "I'll be expecting you in the office for a coffee" and left, leaving only a trace of the sweat from his hand on their hands, and they thought, right, that's over, and Christoforos said later, "he's one of our tenants and a good friend," all parties and dinners, yet those words "I'll be seeing you" hung in the air like a threat. But then the car turned into the street with the acacias and Eleni remembered how they'd gone out and about in the evenings and she told him about it, on the corner the house stood out, it was almost noon and everything bathed in sunlight, and there on the three steps they saw Myrsine, as always dressed in black and somehow withered (so that Fotis thought, she has grown old), her prodigal son smiled at her and they both stood there, for a split second he was racking his brains, what ought I to do? and then he fell on his knees before her and kissed her belly and her hands and smelt the green soap and all the past came flooding back to his nostrils, the whole family had gathered round, his sisters with their children, Stratis laughing at him, and behind him Eleni in her red dress and her perfumes, soon to be in everyone's embrace, and Myrsine said, "you've got the most beautiful wife" – "and the best" – "a good one, a good one," muttered his mother but she was thoughtful.

And one of his sisters wondered, "but where's Angel?" upon which Myrsine laughed and confided, "he's climbed up high in the trees," for all about them lay a copse of elms, sturdy deep green trees, and in the midst a ruined two-storey house lived in by mad Chrysoula and Matina ("the bawd" as they used to call her) and it was the permitted paradise, full of birds and ivy and lizards, a whole strange world which might grab you, trap you by the legs, suck you down. This is why Angel preferred to stay high above it, he would walk along the top of the high wall, from there to a well-known branch, into the fork of the tree, into an embrace which would never betray him, where he would never be beaten or scolded, where father and mother seemed like distant visions, maybe imaginary shapes conjured up in the clouds which were mostly hidden from sight by the dense foliage.* And when he

It was an old enclosure, it must have dated from the time of Turkish rule, for it was surrounded by high, impassable walls, and the trees must have heard them calling "Angel", he saw that there was an even higher branch above him, and the web of a small spider which now you could see and now you couldn't, rather like a dream image. And he grasped on to the higher branch, got hold of it, felt his chin and lips tickled by the spider, but he grasped the branch more firmly and climbed up; now what he could see was the grandeur of the green carpet below, woven from clover and wild flowers and stinging nettles, full of reptiles and insects, all of them small and harmless. And he heard them calling again, "Angel", Myrsine had come out onto the verandah outside the kitchen at the back, she was gazing upwards and calling him, she could see nothing but leaves, a green world of shadows and exhalations and birdsong, maybe a brief flash of white, his good shirt, maybe not. But she got tired of calling him and went back inside, she wanted to see her son and enjoy his presence; after a while, though, she went into the little room and saw Angel asleep there and wondered how he'd got in, but the window was wide open, he'd come in, tucked himself up, thinking that by morning all the anger and annoyance would have evaporated. And Myrsine whispered, "when they go I'll bring you something to eat" and for a moment thought she saw a smile, more in his eyelashes than on his lips.

And it must have been almost midnight when Angel's sense of smell spoke to him of a familiar fragrance, and she trusted him, saying, "I'll wait till morning for you to give me a kiss" and she caressed him all over. And the boy said to himself, I'd better go to sleep now, so that I can wake up at the right time; his eyes were already shut and all he could see was deep darkness against which

been hundreds of years old to judge from their height and the girth of their trunks. This forgotten paradise, which they said had once belonged to some bey, lived on until after the war of '40, until after the Occupation, until construction contractors decided that it was time for the luxury of family houses with gardens to come to an end, and for a new epoch to begin, a profitable one, with blocks of flats and asphalted roads and paved pavements, where, that is to say, there was no space left over for courtyards and gardens, nor for hiding places to bury secrets in. Angel and his generation were the last children privileged to know the little neighbourhoods, the open spaces, the trees or the reed beds. In 1970 this very same place had become a paved park, with new trees, swings for the children, with a lot of sun and light and almost no shade except that cast by the blocks of flats, and this only after midday.

little worms of light seemed to wriggle, electric blue and green, twisting and crossing the darkness again until in the end they disappeared into his sleep, where dwelt a naked woman washing herself her body all shining and then a pale blue sheet was spread and she lay down and advised him to go to sleep now, and all the candles and the shining light were extinguished.

Christos

The last frontier of his resistance was at about quarter to six, when he would mutter, "I've a short time left to sleep, then I must run and see what is happening" and at that point he thought his father was speaking to him, telling him that the marriage had been arranged for the following Saturday, and he smelled the familiar fragrance of her hair on the pillow, he was afraid lest the spell be broken and everything shattered to smithereens, for he thought all breakages will be blamed on me – and then nothing more. Except that when he woke he remembered that he was the victim of ill luck, and into his mind came the proclamation, the king, Metaxas, the way people's eyes had clouded over at the newspaper as they said, "now they'll muzzle us," the day was already getting hot and the sheets unbearable, he heard children's voices calling in the street, across the road they'd all be converging on the bicycle shop, drinking lemonade and quarrelling, only Alcmene and Antigone, his own two girls would be hidden in the shade of the tree, reading. For Christos had told them, "now that Dimitris has gone off to camp, it's an opportunity for you to read his books" which were all some nameless fairy tale, a king with his kingdom falling apart, a prince suffering and fighting.

And everyone at the newspaper muttered that the king had betrayed them, that he'd brought in the general, the tyranny of the mounted gendarmes. And at one point Christos heard singing and cheering, he got up and opened the shutters, so that the blazing light poured into the house, it must have been nearly noon, and he looked over at the garden next door, but there wasn't a soul about; he heard singing again though, people singing "Son of an Eagle" and laughing, and at that moment the door opened and in came Amalia, "they've gone crazy," she said, "who?" asked Christos, and his wife pointed. It was the tram-driver's little house at the back, "I don't understand," he said again, for he knew this neighbour, people said of him that he had a liking for the reds, that during the great strike he'd been throwing stones, they'd caught him and he came home hobbling and cursing. However Amalia laughed, "run and admire the sight," she recommended, and it was indeed a surprise, for he'd covered all the walls, doors and windows with photographs of King George, with two Greek flags arranged crosswise above, like they have in the parade at the town hall and on national holidays. And Christos closed the window once more, "now I understand, he's nothing but a shitter," he shouted, but Amalia signalled him to hush with her finger on her lips, just like when she scolded their Antigone.

And after a bit the afternoon arrived when Christos said, "I'd better be going," you'd think he was trying to summon up the courage or was hoping someone would say don't go, for "Esperini" was in a narrow little lane, a street full of shadows, specially in the evenings. However, he had no choice and he understood it as soon as he crossed the threshold; usually he'd see Vassilis in front of him, watchman by day, general dogsbody in the evening, porter at dawn with his face dark, strained, uncomfortable; now though he was nowhere to be seen, or maybe just a shadow somewhere in the background, a change in the crates and the shelves, and in his place stood a gendarme who looked him over from head to foot, asked, "do you work here?" and when Christos said "yes" let him pass. But before he even sat down at his desk they were calling him, a voice coming from the editor's office, the little glassed-in room at the back with the worn furniture, the smell of old paper, the tall cupboards with the volumes of the "Pyrsos" encyclopaedia and all the old editions, where the two Enzoloras brothers sat, whom everyone used to mock, and the elder of the two said to him, "these are difficult times and you'd better watch what you write," for they knew that he didn't put a bridle on his tongue, they knew how he'd left the "Independent" and maybe even knew of his acquaintance with Euripides. Christos answered, "I know" and in the evening, when he got home, lit the fire in the kitchen and burnt Lenin and Mussolini, two of the tobacco workers' proclamations and the red calendar, which for a moment flared up so that Amalia said, "you'll burn the house down" and threw the burning paper into the brazier. But maybe they'd over-reacted and they remembered the neighbour who in the space of two days had found a framed picture of Metaxas and hung that up as well, and he felt safe, for Christos said, "I don't suppose they'll search our mattresses" even if for good or for bad he had burnt his books.

The Enzoloras brothers said, "you can put all the easy living behind you" in spite of the fact that the paper was on the populist side – and on the third evening two schoolteachers and a sergeant of the gendarmerie appeared, they fell to it and read all the reports and the news articles, constantly deleting things, they had a red rubber stamp which made the paper seem to bleed, and the journalists and compositors swore when they had to do everything all over again. "You'll get used to it," the teachers said and looked at the sergeant, who muttered, "you'll just have to learn," and he meant learn what was prohibited and what would be passed. But the Enzoloras brothers said various inanities about toeing the line, and in the end the journalists declared, "we'll have to do it the crazy way" which wouldn't be so very hard for them as they'd all composed satiric verses, had written various humorous pieces or comedies for the theatre. Only Christos got angry – for he had never written anything of this sort – he was cursing all by himself as he left, calling them worms, though always when he was alone and always in a hiss, and that night he moaned to Amalia, "all this misery and fear will choke us to death," but she consoled him, "we can't save the world," she said as she remembered how they'd gone hungry or how her father-in-law used to say, "no political party ever gave me any bread," simplifying things.

And in a few days the teachers and the sergeant of the gendarmerie disappeared, which, whatever you might say, was a relief, "not having them breathing down our necks" as people said, but it was all a trick for the control still existed, red rubber stamps had become a permanent feature of life, and the Enzoloras brothers warned, "it's more dangerous now" in case anything should slip by them, in spite of the fact that they took their reports once or even twice to be vetted – and Vassilis cursed at having this extra torment on top of everything else, running up and down the stairs, coming and going in the small hours of the morning. But Christos offered him a cigarette, maybe even a glass of ouzo, for they'd become friends and the other man respected him; "we're all being tormented," he assured him, so they were all in the same boat, one of them in his office and the other at the door, and the doorman smiled, "well, if you put it like that ..." he agreed in a spirit of compromise. And one day the great news arrived, that the Great Helmsman was leaving the press to those whose job it was, and they said, let's go out and celebrate, but it very soon turned out that censorship wasn't being abolished, it was simply being put into their own hands, some of the journalists would have to undertake it and would be paid a separate salary for it, rather like being a civil servant. And all of them were wondering who would be chosen, who would agree to do it, and Amalia was eaten up by the feeling that "it's an opportunity", but Christos said nothing, for he knew in his own heart that they wouldn't propose him, that they wouldn't approve him. It was the season of the Fair, all round the White Tower everything was illuminated, and one evening they took the children, Dimitris was beside himself with excitement, he wanted to see the human cannonball but the girls were terrified and preferred the swings, and in the end they all collapsed exhausted into chairs and the grown-ups had beer while the children had lemonade, their youngest slumped sideways and fell asleep, and Amalia said, "right, time for home" and they all started grumbling, and Christos seemed almost to have regretted coming, "we would have done better not to stir from home," for his salary left nothing to spare.

And his salary didn't receive any increase either, for "they chose their own people" as he told her one evening, and Amalia consoled him, "well, your heart will be all the lighter for it" – she would have said your pocket, but she thought, I don't want to upset him, he struggles all by himself. And when winter came they said "luckily", for Dimitris came home one day in a terrible state, stammered, "they took our teacher away," he was a good man, Amalia knew him, she'd gone to the school to collect her child's report, and the next day they saw the newspaper and were horrified and the woman said, "but that can't be him,"* tight lipped, with his tie undone and his hair dishevelled, and Christos said they wouldn't bother about making him look pretty at the Security Police, and Dimitris heard them talking about prison and beatings, exile maybe, and was outraged, "we'll get the whole school to rise up in protest," he said, and Amalia screamed that they'd drive her out of her wits, now that there were two of them equally lacking in common sense. Her husband understood her though, and took Dimitris into the kitchen and had a long talk with him, the girls had shut themselves in the bedroom, maybe they understood, maybe not, at one point she heard them singing, and Amalia thought, she's inherited my voice, something special that Alcmene had; and her youth rose up again in her mind, the ambitions, the dreams dead and gone, and she was puzzled to hear a voice saying, "it isn't possible" then recognised that it was her own voice, "I'm raving," she murmured, as if she meant I've grown old now and lost it all. That night, though, there was more trouble, they were woken up by screams and saw their Dimitris hurrying to the lavatory, "what could you have eaten?" asked his mother, but Christos understood better, "it's because he's sensitive," he whispered to her. And the next day they kept him home from school.

But they still hadn't seen the worst, no matter that Christos was scared, no matter how much they learned at "Esperini", where his employers told him, "you're quite safe just as long as you're careful," and he felt that they had their contacts, followed their politics and were in no danger, for the Enzoloras brothers used to say, "we are the guardians of the nation," and they meant order and family and religion. And Christos remembered the editor of the "Independent" who used to preach more or less the same things, in spite of the fact that now they were making prob-

---

* Ladas, along with others, was taken in the spring of '38. I remember when we used to meet on the steps of the Lyceum, he was short and fat with baggy trousers. Later, in 1963, I was remembering the story to my teacher Yannis Kalantzis, may he rest in peace. They had both worked together at the Practical Lyceum, Y.M.C.A., both of them philologists. "They destroyed him quite unjustly," he told me. He looked pensive, far away; maybe he was remembering his own past, how they had exiled him in 1949.

lems for him, as Christos had heard, because he supposedly was attacking the king. But they're all cut from the same cloth, thought Christos, and he recognised that he himself was no different, for he couldn't understand the reds, "they're a breed apart, another world," he would agree with Pavlakis, who used to come and prune their trees, then sit and drink a dram of ouzo with him and they'd have a chat. And Christos remembered that one day the younger Enzoloras had told him, "our people need someone standing over them with a whip," according to him the Greeks are a nation of braggarts (into Christos's mind came the picture of the tram-driver's little house, with the framed portrait of King George and the laurel leaves and the musical accompaniment), and they both smiled awkwardly, but Christos most of all who was thinking that he couldn't go on balancing on the tightrope forever, that maybe a time might come when there wouldn't even be a rope, and he would fall and be crushed beyond repair. All the same he despised himself for everything that was happening, specially that he himself was part of the game, he was inevitably supporting it, and he wasn't even Elias; "but they won't be going hungry," Amalia corrected him, and she meant Elias's children or their mother, always just as polite and bitter, who welcomed them into her sweet-smelling little drawing room.

And finally, one midday, Dimitris said, "they're knocking on our door," and two men were standing there, one a fat man without a hat and the other shorter and thinner, his hair cropped right down to the roots, with them they brought sorrow, they said, "from the Security Police" and had already stepped inside, they asked Christos his name, where he worked, whether he knew Elias, Elias Kaounakis they added, and "yes" he answered, "I know him and everyone in his household" as if trying to remind them that it was a family friendship. Whereupon the first man asked, "did he leave his papers with you maybe?" – "I don't understand," stammered Christos – "I mean that time when he was staying with you," and the other man smiled because he had the upper hand, he knew everything and could play with Christos, knowing all the cards in advance and catching him out, he smiled and displayed a row of gold teeth, a chilling sight. However, quick as a flash Christos said, "he came one evening and played with the children" and Dimitris was scowling, he understood what was going on and was angry, maybe thinking of his teacher, that unforgettable photograph with the battered face, the tie that they had knotted any old how, and then the short fat man decided, "we'd like to see for ourselves" and Christos asked "what?" and the one with the gold teeth answered, "we're going to search you," at which Amalia began to cry, "why is this happening to us?" she whispered as they began to open the drawers, mixing up all the clothes and all the papers, and then a clumsy cry was heard, Christos was shouting, "I will not allow you to do it, I won't tolerate it" and he started closing all the drawers, he stood in front of them and said again, "I won't allow it," then the thin one put on a sour face and said as if his mouth was dry, "get into the corner and shut up," but his order was not obeyed, instead Christos shouted, "I'll report you" and stretched his arms wide in front of them, at which point they showed that they were not joking, they grabbed him and hustled him outside, everyone froze as if they'd fainted, a dreadful silence fell as if it was thundering, then Dimitris leapt up and screamed, "you're barbarians" and started kicking them in a frenzy, and got two slaps so hard that they made him stagger, Amalia was weeping and she said to the girls, "get out, go" as if she meant that she'd manage by herself.

But at that point they saw the fat man straightening up, he'd been bending down searching among the bedclothes, he smiled triumphantly and asked, "this book, who does it belong to?" and he showed it to her, on it was written Plechanov, this was all she had time to notice, and she replied, "I don't know, we don't collect books" but the other man insisted, "it was under the mattress" and he flicked through it, then once more triumphed, "there you are," he said, "your husband's name." And she could have told them that he'd burned his books, but she held her tongue and just looked at the other man, as if searching his eyes, his open lips, his sweat, as if she had to understand what makes this sort of machine tick; but they called Christos in and threatened him, "do you know where a book like this can send you?" and he was indignant, "what book? I don't know" and the other two laughed, all assurance, "here it is," they said "it's got your name in it," but he gave it a good look, amazed, said, "it's nothing like my writing" and he wondered whose writing it was, it wasn't Elias's nor

Dimitris's;* he wasn't able to recognise whose handwriting it was since in fact it resembled that of the man who was speaking. "That's enough," said the fat man, "we'll take it with us and examine it" and he appeared to be threatening them, but as they were leaving – and they suddenly seemed to be in a hurry – they advised him to be careful, because they'd have their eyes on him, they might come again perhaps. And as they opened the courtyard gate and hurried away Christos saw his neighbour on the pavement, the tram-driver was standing there watching as if he was searching for something; when he felt them looking at him doubtfully he went into the bicycle shop next door.

And that same night – it was Amalia's advice – Christos plucked up his courage and told everything to the younger Enzoloras, who listened to him frowning and at the end produced the verdict, "someone has denounced you, take care" and after a minute, "the book is the usual trick they use for catching you, right now they'll be looking for it in someone else's mattress, in some other neighbourhood," they bring it with them and slip it into a chest or people's beds or their kitchens; and Christos said, "I realised that," as if this was the problem. In the end Enzoloras said, "you'll have to be very careful they don't put you inside"; and that night when he got back to his own neighbourhood he was constantly turning round and glancing behind him, the faces of everyone who happened to look at him seemed strange to him, as if he didn't know them, until he put his hand on the door knob and opened their own door and saw Amalia sitting under the lamp embroidering and pondering.

---

* One night in '42, Leopoulos, a colleague of my father's who had been through exiles and prison cells, told how, during the Metaxas dictatorship, the secret policemen themselves had planted two communist books in the chest where they were collecting together his daughter's dowry. And when his wife, Maria, said, "that's one of your well-known tricks," they had grabbed her by the hair. She had wept then, and wept again as her husband recounted it. What hurt her most of all was the insult.

Yannis

One evening Euthalia waited, full of anguish, thinking, "when it's raining the tears don't show," and Yannis thought, all this is quite incomprehensible, for he saw her unhappy and lost in her own thoughts, from time to time her knitted brows seemed to bear witness to great suffering; and the only solution he could think of was to talk to his eldest sister, except that she was always withdrawn, as if she had private areas in her mind, in her heart, which she maintained ever inviolate, for she said, "it's girlish melancholies" and slipped away from him, in spite of the fact that the difference in age between them didn't justify this view. But in any case they sat up talking till past midnight, Euthalia being asleep, and they had all the time in the world, and deep armchairs, two glasses of cherry brandy and sweet biscuits to eat, the familiar house breathing quietly all around them, and some kind of relief emerged; "maybe it's my fault," he said and his sister looked at him in silence, perhaps waiting for something more, perhaps searching his face, thinking that it was bound to happen and it was his fault, and he was something of a liar, a hypocrite, for he continued, "I've been absorbed in work, in my own affairs" – and this was quite true and no secret – "and I haven't been taking you out, we haven't been having much fun." And he stopped there, for the scorching memory of that night at Michalis's came into his mind, the fact that he knew none of them had forgotten it; but his sister revealed something that terrified him, "she locks herself up in her room and smokes," and Yannis looked at her as if lost, as if confessing it's incomprehensible.

This wasn't the only secret, nor the most disturbing one, and the young man thought to himself, I'm wrong to suppose myself so clever, for everyone flattered him that nothing escaped him, the industrialists used to accost him and say, "we ought to propose you for president," while others simply preferred to invite him to their houses and introduce their daughters to him. And he wondered, have they forgotten it all, his abnormal life style, the relationships, and he wanted to ask them, did their daughters smoke too, but he was quite sure that they did, for people had told him about what went on at their club-houses, at the nightclubs by the sea, in the half-darkness of the little parks. However, he had other worries on his mind and the following evening announced, "we need to get away from it all," he was talking to Euthalia and searching in the depths of her lost eyes; and in a little while the two of them were getting into a taxi (Ergini had a headaché) and Yannis casually reached out, touched her shoulder, her arm, which might have been made of marble, and said, "close the window so you don't catch cold" for it was windy and her hair was being blown about, caressing him. March had just begun and was playing tricks on them, cheating the trees into coming into leaf and then terrifying them with a sudden cold spell, and Yannis commented, "all the basements have flooded," for it was an endless downpour, and he heard her voice say, "you ought to be more careful," he mused either she cares about me or she's betraying me, but he preferred the first interpretation and drew her to him warmly, Euthalia leant towards him and was now in his arms; he was relieved that she didn't move away and they felt a lost, wasted tenderness, wasted especially, since it was something that Yannis squandered without always feeling love.

They ended up at the "Oasis", right on the sea, and they sat inside the glass-fronted room looking out over the darkness of the Thermaic gulf, somewhere out there in infinity a light was fading then shining again. Yannis was attentive, it was as if he was begging her to smile, and he took her hand and whispered, "now everything is more beautiful" and saw the girl enslaved by his lips, which, he thought are crimson and moist, for he knew himself and his own weaknesses (he used to say, and feel proud of it, "I'm a weak man of great strength"), and at one point he offered her a cigarette, which Euthalia refused, "I'm not going to smoke outside our own home," she decided, as if they were playing at complicity, as if they had spoken of her passion; "I saw our mother smoking once," she added like an excuse, and Yannis remembered a scent in his mother's clothes, a scent that lost itself in all the others, which he connected with his father's smell when he was a tiny child and was danced on his knee.

Above them wafted the fragrance of violets and Yannis said, "I've been longing for them," took a bunch from the old woman's basket and laid them before her, it was as if he was telling her, I'm different tonight, he knew quite well what would captivate her, knew what game he was playing, what he was losing or what he might win, and when the orchestra came in and struck up a waltz, he invited her to dance, like the old days perhaps when they used to confess, "we love each other," when they ignored all the curious looks, and now too they disregarded them and he was perhaps priding himself that they were the most handsome couple, for a moment he felt her leaning close against his breast, heard her admit, "I feel as if you are my own skin" and he whispered in answer, "it excites me that we share the same blood," which they would not dare to intermingle.

And when they sat down again she sighed, "we've reached the end now," she said softly, and Yannis felt that she cared about not hurting him, he drew his hands together to guard them and as she was speaking thought, I've done the right thing for he has betrayed me, and he was to remember later that all the while he could hear a singer who liked to show off her high notes, after a bit he recognised her, it was Corinna, the Jewish girl, but dominating everything was Euthalia's voice, her confession, "I'm leaving because I can no longer stay," she said, "before our love turns to poison," and her voice might have been dripping blood as it told how Euthalia had already decided to leave for abroad, she'd get married there, and there she would live her life. And Yannis asked her, "where, though?" but she remained silent, only she turned her head away, maybe she's crying thought her brother, and Euthalia was looking at the whole scene reflected in the glass of the windows, and everything was indeed becoming blurred, the lamps acquired coloured haloes, and the music was insistent in the background, but Yannis's voice was a dissonance, "tell me where you're going," he begged as if this was the only thing left that mattered, thought the girl, and she turned round to look at him, and he felt that her beauty was wild and strange. Their hands entwined automatically, as if each was feeling for the pulse of the other, the heartbeat of pain, and they smiled at each other sadly and he asked again, "where?" it was as if they had lain down and he was caressing her, then she struck unexpectedly, she said like the lash of a whip "to Vienna", so sharply that it hurt him and he bowed his head, he almost cried don't, but "I can't understand" was what he managed to get out, he couldn't comprehend girls who smoked, who seemed in despair, like birds gone mad in the cage, whose song was weeping and who begged, "don't be hurt, don't despair," as Euthalia was saying out of her great solicitude to spare him.

Then Yannis asked, "who will look after you?", for it was a place unknown, its people perhaps hard-hearted and supercilious – and she answered, "I shan't be alone" and the young man felt that the lights were dimming, the darkness becoming deep red, then after a moment a spotlight came on and Corinna was standing there smiling, she was dressed in a Spanish costume and sung Argentinian songs to them and Yannis said, "why don't you go to hell," for he'd lost his self-control completely, he couldn't manage either sarcasm or laughter. And when he said, "you've all betrayed me" it sounded like a snarl, for he had learnt the whole story, the exploits of the engineer who might have been cringing and unlikeable but who offered a convenient solution for Euthalia; they had met for the first time at the factory and the man from Kozani had been struck dumb, then he blushed and a week later a bunch of roses arrived, which had been handed not to Euthalia but to the other girl, the elder sister, and Yannis cried, "why didn't she tell me about it?", it was indeed strange, and on the next day the visit took place, the man from Kozani was all dressed up and the sisters received him, they talked a lot about Austria and the outside world, only Yannis didn't hear a word about this either, it was a real plot he thought, and felt weak, hopelessly alone, her hand became icy and was withdrawn.

And the same night he had the yellow dream again, that Angela was wandering somewhere disappearing into a doorway that was a trap and he hurried to reach her in time but it was hard to walk and after a bit he fell to his knees and over there a broad yellow tube was crawling which seemed to curve a bit then a door opened just wide enough for it to pass through still crawling only then it was on the ceiling of the room and he was searching for some kind of ladder but could find none and Angela was sitting there strangely dark-skinned so he begged her get me a ladder but she didn't even look at him and he thought my only hope is to go back out but the yellow tube had him in its clutches the only hope was to drag himself upside down but the walls were agonisingly slippery and he was choking with panic it seemed he was doomed to die by suffocation – but he heard a window being opened, the shutters being pushed back and then the window closed again, out there the sun must be up bringing him relief, he sensed that there was someone in the room and was bothered by it, thought he would have to return to the suffocating grip of the tube, then sat up suddenly. And indeed his elder sister was there, sitting by his feet, he heard her say, "you were the only one to get any sleep" as if accusing him, for she'd been sitting up all night with Euthalia who was shaking and crying, "like a wounded animal" as her sister said, but then preferred not to go on for Yannis had jumped up and was preparing to hurry out, "stop," she called to him, "she's just gone to sleep," anyway it was better to forget it all, to concentrate on his work and the factory, but he disagreed, "you hide everything from me and lull me," he accused, to which Ergini replied, "if you knew all that I know," and he felt that she was trying to frighten him.

And he was taken by surprise that night as he was sitting in his room in the dark and pondering, when the door opened silently and she appeared, wearing her white nightdress, behind her came a little light from the drawing room and everything glimmered, he saw her long legs as shadows and at the same moment switched on the lamp thinking I want to see her eyes better, her face, but in it he saw a strange weakness, she said, "if you don't hold me I shall fall" and indeed crumpled at his feet, "I'm utterly lost," she recognised, and he helped her rise as if her arms were broken and he had to be careful with her, to weigh up every single thing she said, everything she revealed, "nothing is beyond remedy," he comforted her and he folded her against his breast, against his smell, lest she slip away from him – or he slip away from her – and his clothes echoed "beyond remedy", the whole thing was like a corrosive torment burning his skin, as if it had been drenched with some poison, or with alcohol. His sister was staggering, as if unbalanced he thought, for she was once more another person telling him, "everything is over," and he was watching out for a fainting fit , perhaps she might do something crazy, thought Yannis, for at one point she was moaning as if breathing was painful to her, and he wondered, what is over? and she said again, "only beyond the end shall we be able to live" and he hoped that these were only words.

But her actions proved him wrong, for when he returned the following evening he saw his eldest sister waiting for him, standing upright on the threshold, and she looked at him with sadness and in the end said, "she's gone," as if incapable of further speech, and they stood there like marble, neither of them could have said for how long, and in the end Yannis turned round, it was something beyond his control, and ran off, knowing neither where he was heading nor which way he went, he was mumbling deliriously, heard a car coming up behind him, its lights were hurting him, he jumped automatically to the side and in the end smelt the sea, felt that what he needed was the silence of its depths, where no answer would be found.

And the next day he insisted to Pavlakis that he didn't want to hear anything about it, that his memory and mood alike had died, he had stayed among the trees until dawn, listening to the waves, a little beyond Salamis, thinking all the time I shall have to bury it all deep within me, and especially the questions, who would be waiting for her (though he could sense the truth), how much she would suffer, how many tears she would shed. And he remained dry-eyed, ordered the other man to be silent, not to confirm what he suspected, for then it would all become definite and irrevocable, he would be obliged to bury his hopes. However, this cure proved to be mere charlatanry, his anguish went on throbbing like some dreadful boil, so that he thought, I must lance it before it kills me; and thus he called for Pavlakis and told him, "go ahead and speak" as if shooting at him, he saw the old man's expression and thought probably the idea is crossing his mind that it's his turn now and decided "all three of them are to blame", most of all his two sisters though who had plotted it all, "and the other man? Who is the other man?" snarled Yannis, and "your engineer" came the answer, which he was sure of anyway, however little he wanted to believe it, "but when though, when?" he asked again.

She had left by the midday train (that's why Pavlakis was absent, calculated Yannis), it was the elder of the two sisters who'd been in the greatest hurry, who agreed, who played the main part in it ("but why was she so frenzied?" wondered Yannis) and right at the most critical moment – Euthalia stood on the step of the railway carriage, it was only for a second, she made as if to fall back and you might have thought she was howling – the other sister, almost out of her mind, gave her a push, looking as if she was seeing all her plans collapse, pushed her in and shut the door, and Pavlakis was afraid in case she had a fever, yet stood at the side unable to do anything – scared maybe, struck dumb. And the last picture, the one that stayed in his mind longest, was Euthalia behind the glass pane of the window, a wooden mask with two black holes staring at them motionless, then the train began to move and the window pane was filled with other images, reflections, a little yellow house, then trees, and then only the blinding sun.

"Your sister didn't see me," the old man ended; the older sister was crying without cease, then deciding, I must go, and hurrying towards the exit, Pavlakis following her in terror, he saw her bundle herself into a taxi, her head bowed, and all that remained was dust, leaves and rubbish dancing in the wind. And Yannis made up his mind, "they did it all on purpose, to punish me, to humiliate me." But Ergini told him, "it was the only way out," a month had passed by now, "it was the only way to save both of you," so there clearly had been a plan, perhaps made only by the elder sister who it seemed had been afraid (or maybe jealous) and had decided to step in before the worst happened – "but what did you imagine?" her brother cried, whereupon she remained silent, probably because she didn't know where to begin, what year or what event to start with. And the two of them lived isolated in almost complete silence until one day a postcard came, it showed a park in Austria and on the back was written "I always think of you, I send my love" and beneath only the initial E, and Yannis murmured, "there might be a war" which was something that the whole marketplace was discussing, saying how Germany had prepared itself, which it wouldn't have done if there wasn't a reason.

And he gave his sister a look full of meaning, accusing her perhaps, perhaps mocking her – but afterwards he regretted it, fell into her arms and sobbed, for hard times had come upon them and they saw death with their own eyes.

The Middle Ages – 4

In the night he got up to go to the river, he found the door guarded by his mother, "don't go to that lair," she begged him, "there's only one entrance, if they trap you there they'll destroy you instantly." Beneath the bare branches of the trees the two of them felt entwined, it was a mad hiding place, a brilliant discovery, whose keys had fallen into the river. As he unfastened her bodice the branches gave off their fragrance, the grasses whispered, "I'll wait till dawn, then people will think I've got up to go to work" and she burrowed beneath his clothes, "I want to know what you hide within yourself" and she caressed his chest, his neck, "for otherwise I feel that you are a stranger," she kissed his ribs, where his armpits began, "this is the Christoforos that I know," she said. Except that you cannot tell what is within myself, he thought with pain, for even I have never been able to see it clearly, I walk along a thread stretched taut, I feel fear lest it should bend under my weight and snap, many times I myself have wondered, what am I, what is it that I want, and when he saw Theologos roaring like a wild beast in the streets, fanatical, feared lest he should be found wanting and unsuitable, yet "you all made me do it" he was to say, and he bent once more and embraced her, bent and kissed her hair, feeling that the branches had become one with them, her hands and the branches and their breathing and a voice saying, "I am happy," he remembers voices at sea, then voices in some street, this world is full of voices, each one seeking to find its own justice, and "you," they say, "are the person who must get it for us," but sometime I must tell you who Christoforos was, people used to say it was Irene who had given him almost everything, "she taught me how to give orders, how to feel my heart bleed," he told them one night. There came a time when people said he had met his end in Asia Minor, he was forgotten, "the neighbourhood," they whispered "is tranquil once again," and when he came back one of his ears was missing, "well, that's war"; his mother was half-sobbing but he spoke to her thoughtfully, "you haven't seen anything, you don't know the half of it," they made them run swift as horses on the plain, on the wild mountains, "who are we pursuing?" he wondered aloud, he remembered the general whose coat had been pierced by the bullets, "but people said he was not brave, only deaf" and he shouted to them to go on, in the end, he recounted, they had run out of bullets, run out of bread, "what was left to keep us going?" – "so is that what war is like?" asked his mother every so often, but her mind was fixed on one of his two ears, "other people left their legs there, or their lives," said Christoforos. On Sundays he would go and find his friends, but they bored him, "they have got nothing to talk about," he complained to her, he got up in the morning to go to his work, returned in the late afternoon, the evening found him silent, one day a lame man came looking for him, "we served in the same company," he said, and for a while Christoforos seemed to come to life again, they offered the man wine and fruit, treated him, the next day he was going back to his village, "but what work can I do now?" he asked. One day when we were sitting with Christoforos and talking, he recalled that man's voice, "I've often wondered what we wanted to go running off to Asia Minor for," when we worked in the workshop he was always talking of exchanges, "how much is a leg worth?" he would ask, someone told them that Christoforos was the best dancer, the wildest merry-maker, "but when?" they all asked dubiously, "before the war". And behind it all, they said, lay the secret, an abandoned garden, his friends kept a watch on him for three days and nights on end and said that unless Aegisthus helped they would never be able to make head or tail of it. But behind it all was his mother, and she begged them, "she begged me too," said Aegisthus, he remembered the time of the pantomime, but those days were now long gone and seemed as if polluted, "never speak to me about any of it," he warned them, for he held on to old enmities, "his oddness, his obstinacy, his tenacity are enough to make you wonder," until in the end it came to murder. And his mother was always running to find him and to advise Christoforos not to get mixed up with those people, and afterwards they spoke to her about some grasping woman who would suck him dry, the black-clad women huddled together and wailed, but the woman kept herself apart from them, it was said that she would go down to the garden at night and curse all by herself, "she doesn't get on with her mother," many people murmured about some kind of madness, there are cases that drive you out of your mind, and Christoforos's mother ran then, beside herself, "they've stolen his reason away," she lamented, and one night when her son had disappeared they found the mother out in the streets at dawn and counselled her that the best road for her to take was that which led to the garden and the locked house, with its enchanted portal and its black-clad temptress. The following day when they saw Christoforos they saw how the blood had been sucked from his neck, two little red marks bore witness to this, but he laughed, said, "there are no witches, only women" and the next night disappeared again, and the one after that. Well, this is a malady for which there is no cure, after a while he found himself running in the streets, blows raining down on all sides, "so, whose side are you on?" thundered Theologos, "I am on the side whose blows are backed by justice," he answered. Only the judges can decide such matters, with our poor brains I fear we shall wrong them, "but they wrong us every day," they replied, remembering the boy who died wounded and screaming, and they say that the only time he ever suffered was that first nightmare, then when his mother was beseeching them, "let me advise him" and they cried, "this is a holy place, go outside and settle your scores there," and behind the wall dogs were howling, "it is no longer the time or the place for playing games," I remember the mulberry tree, the pomegranates, the gypsy, one night we stoned him, "don't expect me to come to your wedding, I won't be singing for you," now in the night no voice is heard, but only that dream which seems to plunge into a pit of murky water where the weed grows monstrously large and where huge toads lie in wait for you like primaeval creatures, it reminds you of the malady for which there is no cure, and they advise his mother to wrap him in swaddling clothes and lay him at the crossroads, "if the first person who passes is a young man, he'll be cured, if it is an old man or an old woman, then you will have to mourn for him." And then they discovered her name, Electra, she was not even twenty years old. And they ran and found her and fell at her feet, "I remember your father and your mother," said they, "but we are of lower station in this world and lowly we shall remain and we shall worship you like a princess," at which she laughed with a sound like a dog barking, "don't tell your son he was born lowly," she said, "because he comes to me and boasts that he will prove who is a prince and who is not, he is full of pride," then she looks at them ironically and says, "don't ask me to send him away, for I fear he would drown in the sea and you would be weeping for him," and as she closes her door they are left pensive, for only witches and antichrists speak like this to mothers, so then they decided to bring the wise woman secretly and get him released from the spell, but he was off again the next evening and they lost him, and for as long as the incense was burning they hoped, but, they said, it is God's will that he should be tormented. And as night unfolded and the stars began to take their places and shed their light on sea and on land, on trees and on roofs, they scented the sweet fragrance of the May leaves, the hour when birds and animals go to roost, and Christoforos sets off on the track of the lost bear, he tells them then, "do not try to prevent me, I have taken a vow to carry all these things around my neck," now I should tell you what happened to his ear, over there in Asia Minor they were abandoned and left to run like lost sheep, and one night when they encountered the irregular Turkish troops there was nothing left to do but draw their swords and strike, with their hands all too quickly bloodied, and suddenly he felt his head pierced as if they had hit him at the base of his neck, "one day I'll have to tell you about it in detail," he promised us, how he was saved and how he suffered, then he begged once more, "don't prevent me, the woman you mean, Electra, is not like other women, I like to talk to her, we speak of her pain and her loneliness, she has never taken me into her house, to her room, I like to spend the nights in the garden, she may get angry or be afraid, I would like it if she would let me see the house, the room where all the trouble happened, but you know the room, she whispered to me one day, however I denied it, the policemen would not let me in I assured her, and she spoke once more of all the lost years, they are not over yet she said to me thoughtfully; don't ask me not to see her again, don't go to that woman" – and then they started visiting all the churches, kneeling, weeping. One day they learnt that he had received a beating in the garden of the princes, he had tried to save her brother and smuggle him away, and they fell on him yet once again and begged him, "don't get mixed up with murderers, they will get you killed," the knives are locked up in a garden, Irene told me this one night, we shall have to decide whether we are going to resort to violence or whether we shall abide by the law, "but they made the law to fit themselves, they can bring false witnesses to claim that we were plotting a crime." Christoforos preferred the judges yet once again, he went down there alone and unarmed, "I saw them kill the boy, they were chasing him to put him on a spit and roast him," and then he requested the first man to get up from his place, "was it me? do you recognise me?", but it had been dark when they hit him, he did not have time to see their faces, they had been crouching in the shadows, "let's get out of here because they've got it in for us," Irene muttered to him, but he strode up to them, and they hit him on his head, in his stomach, and he doubled up and fell to his knees and they kicked him. "Bastards," he screamed but they remained silent, their orders were to beat him up, not to curse him, "was it me? do you recognise me?" – but he could only drag himself along the floor, could only recognise their shoes, their hose or their cross-gartering. And the judges bowed their heads in silence, "what you say has nothing to do with this trial, you must tell us who you saw holding the sword, who ran and followed them," but Christoforos stopped, "I saw nothing, only the boy that they were kicking" then stopped again, got up as if benumbed and asked them if they would let him go. In the evening he went once again and rang the bell, "I wanted to visit Iatrides," he said, but it was late and it was not permitted, memories exist, the tortures, I remember how we lost the courier, they let him run into the night and there in one of the narrow alleys he was lost, "he was killed by the darkness and the labyrinth and sometimes I visit him in my sleep, I remember the church and the shade where we used to lie, I think of him as always young, as he was when he arrived distraught from the village and shouted, 'they are slaughtering us like goats,' and from then on he never closed his eyes." And Christoforos was bitter and told how he had warned them, "I saw them kill the boy, they were chasing him and he was running like a lost soul, afterwards his mother and his sister came, they washed him and begged him to speak." He had told them that difficult times were approaching, that sacrifices would be required, "I feel that all the past, all the comrades, are beckoning to me, there are moments when I think of raising my arms to show them how much I am crucified, to tell them we must walk on the water, for if we fail we shall be obliterated forever." As far as Electra is concerned, everything came to an end, she disappeared from the city like a witch, he was abed early every night like a baby, arose in the morning without speaking, then withdrew into himself once more at night; and his mother gave thanks to all the old women and the magic herbs and hastened to light all the candles that she had vowed.

Angela

    She cast in her mind for a way to disappear, and smiling in sadness reflected, maybe I'm starting off on a new life, where her friends would look for her and not find her, like the time when she had hidden in the forest in her lost homeland; and it probably would be best to leave, maybe go to another town, maybe to another country – one evening a woman had come in with her husband, they'd applauded her enthusiastically and then proposed a job in Arab lands, "we'll make you the queen of the cabaret." Perhaps she'd find what she was searching for, forget all the misfortunes, the men who'd tormented her or made a fool of her or forgotten her, who, to be exact, was one man, the most dangerous of all, he had begun as a nocturnal vision in white in the upper town, then pursued her from neighbourhood to neighbourhood, without making up his mind which bit of him hurt, who would be able to heal his wound, and he wept, "I can find no cure" far from her side, as if he was moonstruck or the prisoner in some story full of elves and fairies.

    Her new house – in the little cul de sac – might perhaps be a hiding place for her, it was like an old dovecote in Acheiropoieto in which all kinds of birds had found shelter, an eternal drunkard with two little daughters that he beat, foolish Marika with her husband who'd left her and her irritating cough, an old Russian whom people called the philosopher, he had long hair and a long beard, he sang psalms and children came and kissed his hand, and opposite was Beauty's garden, with glass of many colours in the windows, a reminder of Eugenios, the iron gate obstinately locked and flourishing fruit trees within. Angela lived right at the top of the building, she felt fairly unapproachable, unassailable, for the stairs were labyrinthine and her door hard to find, she hung thick curtains at her windows and liked to stand behind them unseen, to watch and listen to everything going on, to consider that she was safe, isolated and maybe undisturbed, even if the house was noisy, which was something that she'd got used to, the way its every timber and every stone creaked, its breathing as she called it.

However, all this didn't seem enough; and she went looking for a nightclub in a different quarter, and in the end took a job at the "Faliro", which was always plunged in semi-darkness and frequented by a whole unknown world of people; and she remembered how the boss, Petros, had been puzzled when she said, "I want you to re-baptise me," and they laughed, then with a sudden inspiration he asked which was her favourite flower, whereupon she answered white roses and violets, and he said, "I don't think I'd call you Rose" and thus they decided on "Violetta". But even this wasn't enough for her, she'd fixed her mind on change with a vengeance, and so she went and had her hair dyed red, and Petros said, "I like you even better like that," and that very same evening they were at his house, he had a strange air, seemed to be ordering and begging at the same time, he told her, "come on, let's go to bed" but Angela wept, "I'm sick," she whispered – she had prepared this excuse – that she had a wound right there where it mattered, and he drew back as if afraid of being stabbed, he looked cold and dangerous, "if I'd known," he said, "I wouldn't have hired you" – and the girl was apologetic, "you don't understand, I've never had anything to do with the bad sicknesses," at which he gave her a very searching look. In the end he came to his own decision, "you've got five days to get well."

And in two days' time her name was outside the club, Violetta, and a recent photograph of her, fiery-haired angel, and she thought to herself who'd recognise me now? When she sang the lighting was dim and she wore a black net veil in front of her eyes, for Petros said the patrons would like a bit of mystery, the woman with the incurable wound, one evening though he said, "I want to see it" whereupon she decided, "I'll show it once and that'll be the end of it," and Petros sighed, "never have I felt a sweeter pain," nevertheless at dawn he was alone and all his pleas and promises got him nowhere. For Angela locked herself into her dovecote and began to cry hysterically, below she could hear the two little girls singing and wondered curiously what they could be so happy about, outside her curtains were clouds and a bird singing in Beauty's garden. And she thought that there was always a trap or a well-appointed cage, perhaps the wisest thing would be to let herself be exploited, to put an end to the wounds and all the rest of it and say, well, that's my fate, my golden torment, which might be called Petros or might have no name at all, no traces, no memory, no scent perhaps.

Except that one evening she sensed a fragrance around her, someone recognised her and called her Angela and said, "we've been searching for you everywhere," and there in front of her stood Yannis and his follower the singer, better dressed now and certainly sober, they called her over to their table in the corner but she refused to come, "I've got my own work to do," they wouldn't let her sit with the customers though, so that Petros shouted and got angry, "you're working for me," he insisted, they had a specific agreement – and all evening she could see them watching her, clapping her, Yannis with a permanent smile on his face, for a moment she thought his forehead is broader, but his eyes were as full of light as ever, and his lips full, surely moist, maybe with a touch of bitterness at the corners of his mouth, he seemed to be far away, a man in dark clothes with his collar buttoned up and a tie, so that no one could see his breast or whether he still wore his cross.

And Petros said to her, "keep your mind on your work" because his clientele was select and noticed and commented on everything, woe betide her if her dress was creased, a black evening dress with a single line of silver that flowed from her neck to her fine décolleté, and from there continued down over her hips where it swayed slightly and then on till it reached the tips of her high-heeled black shoes, and she felt sure that Yannis must be wondering, where is Eugenios's poor little girl? And maybe he needed to think about it a bit more, for at one point she saw him get up, open a door somewhere and go out, it was the back door leading to the garden, shrubs and trees and roses, and at the bottom the shallow sea which most of the time had a fragrant smell and where couples would walk barefoot, usually at night, like lost angels. And the other man remained alone, constantly inspecting his hands, or sometimes the tables nearby, but never looking at the orchestra, and Angela thought maybe he's ashamed, until she saw him get up too and also prefer the garden, in spite of the fact that it must be full of mist, then in a little while both of them returned, they seemed to have perked up, like a bunch of flowers left outside the house all night, and they sat back more comfortably in their armchairs and then after a while ordered another bottle of champagne, someone said, "it's midnight already" but Yannis seemed quite fresh. Violetta went into her dressing room to change, put on a dress of bright scarlet, with a flashing tiara in her hair and earrings that hung down to her shoulders, of which Petros had said, "how much would they cost if they were real?" Then the drum began to beat which was the signal for them to begin, the lights were dimmed, on the tables red candles were lit, and on the front of the dance floor a circle of crimson light which was Petros's inspiration, and here Violetta stood and sang until their eyes were smarting.

And when they left they found that outside a grey world awaited them, the day was dawning before their eyes and the lamps getting weaker, and they hunched their shoulders in the piercing cold, the last customers to leave were the singer and Yannis who stopped and stood outside, then the musicians appeared with their instruments, and after them Angela with Petros, who wished them "good morning" and left. And the young man said, "leave me to walk" and he meant by himself, his house was not far off, he liked the trees and the old houses in the park, one of them was supposed to have something suspicious about it, but now it looked closed up and deserted, suddenly there was the sound of wings, a bird weaving through the branches as if in play, then a weary carriage passed, all that he could see was a white shawl and two dull faces, and finally he arrived at the White Tower, thought for a moment of having a coffee by the shore, but then set off through the lanes that led upwards, past the Hippodrome, he saw two workmen coming downhill and a woman standing shaking at a window, she must have insomnia he thought, then in a little while he was standing in front of their own door, "we're all like lonely clouds," he said out loud, as if he needed to hear a human voice.

Angela was to complain, "I'm suffocating in loneliness" as she sat at home and thought about Yannis, about the evening at the nightclub; and she asked herself, "why am I hiding?" because indeed there was no longer much point in it, specially when one afternoon she thought she caught sight of that singer of his strolling in the little lanes near where she lived, "it might be just a coincidence," thought she, "or again perhaps it isn't." And this second interpretation was confirmed when someone came knocking on her door – it was late afternoon and she was washing her hair – and she said, "I can't open the door right now," whereupon someone was turning the doorknob, apparently very sure of himself, though the bolt prevented him from opening it, and she asked, frozen with fear, "who is it?" And then she heard the voice that she'd been hoping for, of which she felt no fear although she shivered; but Yannis smiled at her as if embarrassed, he appeared to be carefully dressed, grey clothes, well combed hair, shaved, scented as always with eau de cologne. She didn't invite him to come in, yet stood back from the doorway in a kind of mute acceptance, he said, "I know I'm bothering you, but I came anyway," as if it had been something too strong for his own powers or his good manners or her will – she did not deny it – to resist, and he came in and sat in one of her old armchairs. And it was soon clear that he hadn't changed very much, except that a certain bitterness was perceptible at the corners of his mouth, specially when he said, "we've lost Euthalia" and told her the whole story and how perhaps his sister might be regretting it and suffering now that Hitler had installed himself in their home, and Angela responded, "I don't understand what it is you're telling me," she was probably expecting to see him look pleased. And Yannis thought, it's lucky that suspicions aren't catching, lucky his elder sister hadn't said anything, hadn't mocked this girl.

She, though, thought let's tease him, and revealed laughing, "I'm getting ready to travel too," at which the young man started in spite of his apparent coolness, "I've been asked to go to Beirut," she added, which wasn't exactly a lie of course since Eleni and Fotis had been back twice and had spoken of contracts, of a high-class club, of a big community of Greeks over there who were all well-heeled and enjoyed having a good time – he looked her in the eyes, searching for some small sparkle to assure him that it was only a matter of caprice or wounded vanity, but the heartless girl continued, "they've asked me to go off to the land of the Arabs," and not even Petros knew about it, it would be too much for his self-confidence, his belief in his own power. Outside the twilight had fallen, birds flying past in flocks, Angela had learnt to recognise the weight of them on the roof tiles until they all flew off to Beauty's garden and from thence to the tall pine tree that grew in solitary splendour just like a painting; "I'll have to leave you," she announced, they'd be expecting her at the nightclub, and he got up as if benumbed and stood there pensively, "come again if you want to," the girl said, as if in answer to some unspoken plea. And she watched him as he took her hand, said "thank you" and kissed it, maybe he was thinking she reads me like a book – which was the truth.

And she predicted, he'll come back in the morning, she'd cleaned her room and put on the table an ornament which Petros had bought for her, a beautiful dancer made out of porcelain with one arm outstretched, when suddenly she heard heart-rending weeping and someone asking, "is he dead?", which is just not what we need, thought Angela, specially not right now, and she opened her door to listen; up through the building, into the very roof tiles, came the sound, penetrating every single corner and hiding place, and among the tumult of voices she distinguished one saying, "if the doctor doesn't come soon, you'll lose him," and she heard the stairs creak and there was Yannis coming up, he told her, "they've just carried a man in drunk and unconscious," and Angela thought of his two little girls* and wondered, "how

---

* The final dying adventure of Alcibiades P. took place in 1951, by which time his family had been through countless longings and shames. They were always having to pick him up off the streets for he got so drunk he passed out. Most times, though, before collapsing unconscious he'd pick a quarrel and get beaten up – or rather he'd beat people up and smash things, for ever since his youth he'd been a man of great physical strength. He was the son of a priest, a loafer and lover of all the back alleys, the performer of unforgettable exploits, as when he got into a fight with a crowd of Jews, stole their hats, punched holes in them and strung them on his arm like a trophy. In the end he took refuge in the house of Thomas T. until the priest agreed to forgive him. And his "legend" lived on, and later people were to go on telling stories of him.

did he manage to get drunk so early?" for it wasn't yet eleven in the morning, "he spent the night sleeping in an alley," explained Yannis, and everyone thought he was dead with his ashen face and arms spread wide, as if he was struggling in vain to breathe.

And Angela said, "it chokes me" for she couldn't bear misery, specially she couldn't bear to see his youngest daughter always pale and terrified, and Yannis tried to reassure her, "do you want me to help them?" he asked, and it wasn't said simply to win her over, but she thought I don't want to lose him now, and thus said, "leave it for the time being, we'll see later" since the tumult had died down and all that could be heard now was someone crying quietly, "it was for something else that you came," she told him meaningfully. And they both smiled as if embarrassed, dear Christ, what has become of us, reflected Angela whose memory was good and who recalled every single detail of their times together, when they had wept, when they had been happy, their lovemaking and his body, a fallen plane tree that now in her attic had lost nothing of its sweet scent as the sun played on the curtain, and she thought how lovely a carriage ride would be, in the lonely places out beyond Harilaou or Votsi.

Then he began to speak, and his words were like rain in May refreshing her soul with its fragrant drops, like fresh young grass and trees, and suddenly he terrified her when he said out of the blue, "let's get married" then stopped, knowing he had to let her get her breath back for she had become silent and blushing, and she seized his hand, maybe wanting to stop him while there was still time, maybe wanting to check that his pulse was still beating for he seemed to her almost to have dematerialised, to be nothing but a pair of burning eyes. Yannis had not changed his mind though, he insisted, "there aren't any obstacles now," at which Angela thought, what are you confessing? But Yannis cared only to be sure that "there aren't any obstacles for you either" since he remembered Petros and how they had left together that night when he walked in the park in great pain, but Angela said, "you are driving me crazy for no reason, because you have another sister" with the result that they both felt pain.

And it looked as if they were fated not to agree, despite the fact that he said, "let's go to a church and make our vows" for he knew she believed in such things, "let's go so that you'll believe in it," he begged, but Angela told him, "I don't want to tie you down," meaning perhaps I don't accept your proposal, and then they both fell silent, as if they were ill or as if someone was forbidding them (but who?), and the last words said were "goodbye", and she heard the stairs creak as he went down, there was a moment of silence and then once more his slow steps. And she wondered, "what's the matter with me?" for she felt the tears streaming from her eyes and the sobs in her chest making it hard to breathe. She heard someone say, "it can't all end here" but there was no other soul in her attic, no other tongue, no other lips, his bitterness and suffering somewhere else now. And she thought, let me ask the icons, which gazed at her, sad and pensive, from their silent corner.

Fotis

Fotis decided hastily to set out on his final voyage, the fatal one as it proved to be, though this was something unexpected, so much so that he shouted in exasperation, "they're all whores" and he was speaking of the female sex, how faithless and slippery they were. But all this was to happen later, not then when they were embracing him and kissing him goodbye at the station; he was taking the train down to Piraeus and from there would take the boat to Beirut where their last possessions, perhaps the least valuable ones, remained. A year had passed since they'd first arrived and everything had worked out perfectly, Fotis had gone and done six months' naval service, though he spent every night between Eleni's legs – all of them somehow crammed into Myrsine's house, though they spent generously – and in the end he got his discharge papers and they breathed a sigh of relief, thank goodness they had a friend in the police whom they saw often and took out and treated, they were always talking about Nikos this and Nikos that, at which Christoforos would smile and say, "I like to be of service," which in fact was rather strange since he never asked any favours in return; one night Fotis asked Eleni, "what do you think of him?" and the woman pondered for a minute and then replied ambiguously, "I don't think of him."

Fotis sat and smoked in the train and looked out of the window, trees and fields were unfolding before his eyes, then in a little while a river, whereupon he said to himself, I remember that river, and felt depressed when they arrived in Larissa, where might Matoula be dragging out her existence now, he wondered, in poverty and adventures no doubt, somewhere over there must be the Jewish quarter, or maybe it no longer existed for even then it had been in ruins, but the train was leaving over the plain and soon reached the mountains and precipices. And once he was on board ship and at sea, Fotis reflected that here at least there were no memories or sore places, and he was lying on deck on a comfortable chaise-longue, enjoying the breeze and the smell of the sea, the little ports where the ship put in, and in the end the picture presented by the shore at Beirut, all the white houses and behind them the low hills. It was a magic city, one of his pasts, and Fotis said, "I'll be leaving again in three days," though in fact it didn't prove quite so easy, because there were all sorts of unsettled accounts, everything had been sold and scattered to the four winds, and on top of this there was a mass of debts and a mass of servants waiting for him, who may or may not have been hungry but who were certainly hopeful. And Fotis assured them that he did not possess as many francs as that and hurried off to the bank, where everyone was most polite but informed him that their deposit box was empty and had now been leased to other customers, and Fotis felt himself becoming anxious, he began to search through the house, searched for a whole night and the following morning too, but he found neither a single sou nor any gold jewellery, and said to himself, I might have known it. The only solution was a telegram, "I haven't got enough money, send more" with "Fotis" below, which he sent anxiously on a Thursday and hoped that by Saturday she might have forwarded some money, he wandered round the closed up house as if lost, one night he made a tour of the seaside boulevards or as far as the telegraph office – but in vain. And when the following Monday arrived and he had received neither money nor even a brief message he decided that things were getting dangerous, for the staff had become angry and were muttering, "you're stringing us along."

And he was scared, "maybe they've cheated me," and felt like a lonely hunted bird, maybe not such a clever one either, for when he made up his mind, "I'll sell off everything and leave" and made overtures in the market, two gendarmes arrived at the house accompanied by a stranger wearing a fez and ordered him, "get out." And Fotis was taken by surprise, "I don't understand," he said, to which the man in the fez snapped, "ask Madame," Eleni, who had sold everything to him (and he stressed the word "everything") and they'd signed the documents, so that Fotis wondered to himself, then why did she send me here? However, he didn't have enough money left for another telegram; he suddenly felt a pain in his ribs, breathlessness, and whispered, "what about our clothes and our birds?"; the other man thought for a minute then said, "take them," as if he felt sorry for Fotis or was giving him charity. And it really was like charity, for when he opened the two trunks he found the dancers' rags and his own clothes from the desert, a whole collection of beads and feathers which no one would ever want to buy, so he gave them to the Arab women who wrapped them up and laughed, the sly bitches. And there was not a thing to be done about his canaries – it was fated that he should part with them, perhaps they were to die of thirst or of a decline.

And the only way left was for him to hide out in a little hovel down by the harbour so that they'd say we've lost him, to hide yet one more time and wait for the ship that would take him back to Piraeus; and he said, "praise be to the Almighty that I already had my ticket" – but he was once more thinking like a fugitive, like a deserter once more, and he had to wait for thirty hours without food or fresh air, all he had to eat was bread and fruit and he drank water that was brackish. And in the end (on the day he'd been waiting for) he hurried up the gangway, stepped on the deck and breathed freely once more, on the other side though, the side facing out to sea, since in any case he didn't have anyone to see him off or wave their handkerchief at him, and he waited in fretful impatience for the anchor to be weighed, for him to feel that they were leaving. Only in the late afternoon did he finally feel relieved; he went over to the other side of the ship and saw the city receding into the distance, getting smaller. And when finally the houses had sunk into the sea and only a rose-coloured suspicion of the hills remained, Fotis thought, I'll not see this place again, though this proved to be a rather hasty conclusion, for he wasn't able to foresee all that lay in the future.

And he lurched from one surprise to another, when three days and three nights later his mother told him, "she's left us," and of course she was speaking of Eleni, she seemed frightened, offended perhaps and anxious, she begged him, "stay here a bit and recover" for he looked weak and haggard, his clothes hanging off him in a way that was sad to see, and a spot of grease on his trousers which once he could never have forgiven. So he sat down as he was, with his black suitcase at his feet as if it too would rest for a bit and then be off, and he demanded that they tell him what had happened. But it turned out to be a muddled and awkward sort of story, and Fotis jumped up, "this has got to be sorted out," said he and started running down the road, and his mother called after him, "watch out for them, don't let them trap you inside and then knife you" – and Fotis thought about this plural pronoun and after a minute turned round and went back, "tell me again what happened," he asked, "and where I'll find them," which was the main thing.

And they called Angel who was sullen and said, "yes, she was sleeping with another man," faithless Eleni in other words, who, as soon as Fotis had left on his trip to Beirut, had announced that "we don't all fit in this house", which puzzled Myrsine since she'd given them her own bed, her own bedroom, and was herself sleeping on the floor uncomplainingly, "you're my son's wife," she said, and maybe she meant her own property, no matter how much Eleni smiled and dragged voluptuously on her cigarette. And in the end she said, "I've rented a house" and they gave her Angel in the hope that he would keep an eye on her; except that everything only lasted five days and as many nights again, and then the boy came home again – he was a grown lad by now – and recounted all the shameful things, how Eleni had another man in and they laughed and made merry and in the end went off to bed. "But what does the law have to say about it?" wept Myrsine, then thought that Fotis had the law on his side whichever way you looked at it, for on the one hand he'd been betrayed and on the other hand they had Christoforos's friend, the policeman, who'd risen to great heights and was busy beheading people, gypsies and others. However, Fotis didn't deign to seek any help, said, "it's for men and blows to sort out now" which scared them, and he set off fast along the street once more – Angel went with him, "show me the way," he ordered.

However, what they found was a deserted courtyard and a house with tightly closed door and shutters, a house unbreathing, and for a moment the two of them stood there in uncertainty – suddenly Angel rushed forward and searched in some secret hole by the doorstep, underneath the pot of basil, and found a key which unlocked the door for them, whereupon an aroma of woman enveloped them. As they stepped over the threshold they saw two eyes examining them, from the house next door, and a woman called, "Angel, don't go into the house," she seemed to be old and decrepit, "don't open the door, Eleni will beat you." But Fotis cried, "I'm not afraid of ghosts" and a moment later had flung open the windows, letting in the sun and the fresh air, and they settled down to wait, no matter that Angel was bored and was silently praying for them to leave, so he could escape the rows and get back to his games. But soon what he feared and longed to avert happened, and Eleni appeared with the man (he must have been around fifty, with a weary face and a cringing calmness) and the woman said, "you've arrived" just as if she'd been eagerly expecting him for a chat, but Fotis asked, "what is this gentleman to you?" – "a friend," she answered and didn't laugh, upon which Fotis ordered, "let him go about his own business then because I want to talk to you," he could feel the other man watching him, not speaking, maybe not even breathing, and Fotis said again decisively, "I don't like his ugly mug" and was praying that anger would kindle within him, for that was the only way he could come to blows with someone, only if he was beside himself with anger, otherwise it was all like some broken down machine that wouldn't function, and everything he said was deliberately aimed at putting them into a fury, except that the other man was some kind of reptile, he turned and looked at Eleni then said to her as if hissing, "I'll leave you to sort it out between yourselves" and walked off without saying goodbye. At which point Eleni laughed, "you see?" she said to him as if he'd misunderstood everything, then she sent Angel away, "I don't want him under my feet," said the woman, supposedly he was the cause of the trouble between them, "I can't stand his skirt-chasing and his lies" – and they sat down to talk about things, "to have a few explanations and get things straight," she warned him. And as she spoke and explained, Fotis felt infinitely impoverished, one by one all his suspicions and fears were shown to be true, he said to himself, "it was all planned beforehand, but how long beforehand?", the voyage, her inability to stay in his mother's house and her flight from it, a whole series of humiliations, but Eleni laughed to calm him down, "nothing has changed," she assured him, so she was still in charge and he the servant, not a penny to his name, nothing that belonged to him except the pleasure of her in bed, and, said Fotis, "even there I'm serving you."

And indeed he couldn't change anything now, he couldn't have her in the house with his mother, maybe he couldn't even have her to himself – and he remembered, "and that other man?" She didn't answer immediately and Fotis yelled at her, "the other man?" – "a friend," said the woman and seemed to tense; then he saw red, reached out and caught hold of her, heard her voice cry "you're hurting me," and he pushed her as if she was his prey, there was a wooden divan and she fell onto it, yet instantly had slipped out of his grip like a cat, "stop playing the macho man," she warned him, and he said, "I'll show you" and in a flash had his belt off, thrashed the air once or twice and then was beating her, somewhere on her back or arms, "you bastard," she screamed and fell on him, and they became a tangled mass rolling on the floor, a confusion of skirts, trousers and flesh which in an instant was panting and sweating and bleeding, until other hands got mixed up in it, a pandemonium of voices, pulling them apart, saying things to them, and in a little while separating them; Fotis found himself out in the yard, lying on his back on the earth, with the woman standing at the door like an evil spirit, and between them a barrier which billowed and stiffened, agitated men and women who had heard her howl, "you're finished, you layabout, you lout," and he got up and shook himself, he felt that everyone was against him, he stood still, shook the dust off himself again, he could feel earth on him, her bites, her claw marks, and as he turned to leave he saw his mother standing there as if rooted to the spot, he saw his Angel silent and scowling and a moment later heard the sound of windows being smashed, like pistol shots.

And it was midnight by the time he had washed and lain down, the whole house was silent, at one point it seemed to creak, and he closed his eyes and saw everything brightly lit getting whiter and whiter as if from somewhere an unseen light was shining a light which got stronger and so intense that he felt the heavens would break would fall apart and nature too and the big lamp that they'd had in Eleni's salon in Beirut which two men came and stole but the white light was getting brighter and they heard a groan – it was Angel who had fallen out of bed and was holding his belly and disturbing them all. Through the shutters they could see darkness, a feeble lamppost in the street, and Myrsine said, "it's not dawn yet," she made chamomile tea and calmed Angel, she saw the tip of his cigarette glowing and fading and thought it is burning him, endless hours.

And then was set in motion a business of which they'd never reach the end, Fotis going the rounds of either lawyers or coffee houses, Myrsine permanently embittered, willing to serve or to listen to fairy stories about how one day the wealth* would return, and Eleni had established herself in a larger house with a high wall and a well-secured chain on the gate. And his sisters said, "sometime he'll have to work, to believe it," for they were convinced now, and other people told them so too, that there was no alternative nor any other hope, Fotis didn't even have a piece of paper saying he was married to her or was the master, and thus all the complaints and curses and black forebodings grew and grew. And the only person who smiled ironically was Christoforos, he said, "I scented it brewing" and they hated him, maybe he'd heard about it from the policeman who helped them once more (for the last time) when they were being dragged into trouble about the row, Eleni accused them of having broken down her door and robbed her, Myrsine wept, "what can you expect of a woman like that?" and she placed her hopes in Christoforos, in his contacts, but he proved to be the shrewdest of them all, with money salted away and control over his own household.

And so the winter months passed, they prayed for summer to come for it was always a more economical season and had its own charms, walks down by the sea or in the orchards and gardens, which Fotis prowled round and got to know quite well; he had realised by now that he would lose, that if you play with women

---

* In effect there was never a trial. The lawyer whom F. employed rapidly realised that he couldn't win anything since there wasn't even a marriage certificate. Thus F., all through the autumn of '39 and even a bit longer, could do nothing except tell his mother how much he stood to gain if... And he was still saying it even when he had reached a state of desperation, effectively the others were supporting him and he was planning to leave again. Myrsine, however, was always willing to listen to him and to smile with pleasure at the thought of what her son stood to gain if...

you need to keep an ace up your sleeve, or at least keep your savings well hidden – and he thought in exasperation, I'm just like a male whore who's been cheated on, and he no longer had the courage for new loves, or for new disappointments and cheatings. Only one day he dressed himself up in his best, he was wearing his gold watch and his ring, and he reflected that he still had all his old acquaintances who continued to work for the "Company", at the old factory. The staircase was familiar, except that it had been painted white, and at the end of the corridor lay the door, with the hatch beside it, just as it used to be, and he bent down and asked for Mr. Saporta, there was an unknown young man though, who gave him a good looking over and then pointed to the door opposite, as if he spoke in sign language, and Fotis made a gesture as if to thank him in the same lingo, and went and opened the door and he saw nothing but a desk and a man without any hair, who looked at him without speaking, no matter how much the deceived Zalamor smiled and begged, "might you have a job for me?" but the man was puzzled, "what are you doing here?" he asked in the end, and he saw standing over him the gold watch and the massive ring and a flashing stiletto which made him quake; whereupon the other man roared with laughter and assured him, "I won't come and sing to you at midnight," then opened the door and was gone.

Angel

On the day that the row took place, Angel set off through the streets feeling lost, feeling as if he wanted to cry or to smash something, for breaking Eleni's windows had not been enough, had not relieved his frustration; he walked along the main street till he reached a quarter that was unfamiliar to him, a place of small humble houses, alleys all earth and mud, no little Arabs or gypsy children but instead a gang of barefoot children shouting and running about after a cloth ball; they were all small and clumsy, and he ran into their midst and kicked and snatched the ball away from them then ran off to a distance, upon which the smallest child started crying, screaming, "my ball, my ball", and Angel sent it back to them with a hefty kick so that their protests stopped, though they yelled at him, "I fuck your mother," whereupon Angel smiled at them, said, "someone else got in first" and his thoughts returned to Eleni, to the row with his father, he had run and told his grandmother all about it, how they'd been defeated, then had lapsed into sullen silence.

And all this while he was thinking, I'm not going to go home, he couldn't bear to face his father brushing the earth off himself; thus he preferred to wander, perhaps he could climb his tree, up to his favourite branch, where in a natural cranny he had hidden a little chain and three marbles, as if needing to feel that he possessed a treasure all of his own. And he continued to wander, at one point he heard a tram coming, clattering along fast on the tramlines, from time to time its bell was ringing, and he thought to himself, I'll see if I can catch up with it and jump up and hang on at the back, for this was an art of his, grabbing the bar and pulling himself up, or jumping off if necessary when the conductor was after him; once in a fit of mulishness he'd farted at the man then somersaulted off, for the tram-driver was old and only shook his fist. And now he perched on the bar at the back, keeping down so that they couldn't see him from inside, and he watched the tramlines speeding away behind him, and a whole world rushing past, and he felt remote from all of it, a woman with her dog, the mean little shops, a few trees thick with dust and the ice cream man, the pictures outside the cinema. Gradually, though, it all became more familiar, he thought in a moment I'll be by Eleni's place, the house where the row happened. Then he jumped off the tramcar, saying to himself I'm at the "scissors", in other words the shunting point where the trams manoeuvred and turned round, and he gazed round the open ground, recognised the red building – I could have a game of ping-pong or beat them at dominoes.

And up the steps he went – it was the EON offices where they gathered boys together and made speeches and got them all singing, Angel was quite indifferent to all this though, and used to say, "I like the games," what he enjoyed was winning and then leaving in a good mood, or being given free passes to the cinema – at one point they promised him a uniform but he said, "I don't like fancy dress," at which they banished him for a few days, until the battalion leader, who had the barber's shop a little further down the street, advised him, "you ought to work for the organisation," for they had checked his family out and they were all right. Angel smiled craftily and answered, "I'm too young to work," no matter that he already had down on his cheeks and upper lip.

They were all gathered there and the barber was speaking, Angel wondered, how come he doesn't get sick of it, for he always went on and on about the same things and the boys used to get bored as they waited for the barber to finish so that they could begin playing – but this time Angel went out into the yard and said to himself, "I chose the wrong time to turn up," so he continued his wandering, set off once more down the narrow alleys, among lush green courtyards, beneath verdant trees, and he felt a longing for his own little forest, for his own branch, ever faithful and inviolate, a hiding place up in the sky. He came out now into stony open ground, at one end of it a thicket of reeds into which one day he had heedlessly penetrated only to be chased off by a woman with a double-barrelled shotgun (people said that she'd been a captain in the war against the Turks, though she was half-crazy), thus this time he turned to the left in order not to run into her again. Then he heard boys' voices and the thwack of a ball and said to himself, "it's the boy scouts' playing field" and he pushed open the gate as if he knew them, there were about ten boys there, and a net, and they had organised themselves into teams and were playing volley ball. Angel stood in a corner and watched them, they were boys of a different sort, well-behaved, neatly dressed, and he thought to himself their day is over, EON has the upper hand now with its leader the barber; however the ball rolled to his feet, so he picked it up and threw it back, and one of the boys suddenly called to him, "we already have full teams" as if in excuse, but Angel shrugged his shoulders, as if saying I enjoy watching you, although in his heart he was raging.

In the end he joined in their game even though he didn't really know how to play, but they laughed and said, "it's not as if we're going in for a tournament" and later they all sat on the grass in the shade and one of them, the eldest, told them stories about the jungle, said that Robinson Crusoe was a good boy scout and Man Friday his wolf cub; Angel listened and mocked, thought to himself, just a whole load of theory again, and when they suddenly asked him, "but what do you read?" answered, "stories in 'The Mask', which the other boy, who was called Dimitris, dismissed as "utter claptrap", "well, what's your Robinson Crusoe then if not bullshit," Angel snapped back and they all were silent for a moment, as if they didn't understand his language or didn't want to speak it themselves. And then they started singing, at which point Angel fell about laughing, how naive, he thought, and Dimitris asked him, "do you know any songs?" so Angel launched into "Hardhearted" and then "Even though, even though" and they asked him, "where d'you learn them?" and he answered, "from my aunt's gramophone" which was kept in a corner, lovingly decorated, and they used to tell him, "don't touch it or you'll get a wallop"; and in the end the boys asked him, "sing us another" for they thought he sung well, and he didn't hesitate, laughed slyly and began, "Why are there smiles and joy on the faces of men, Father?", at which he saw the boys around him freeze, "for the sun now shines and the day rejoices" – and they all rose up against him and said, "get out of here," but he wouldn't stop, he'd always had a taste for trouble-making and obnoxiousness, he went on "because, my boy, this golden day" and felt the sunlight blotted out as their bodies fell on him – "this day hails ..." and their hands were on his mouth, his throat, his eyes, and he felt his jaw hurting, and his nose, and he kicked out like a cockerel being slaughtered, he lost all sense of smell, all sense of touch, lay motionless and taut in their grip, till they were scared and let go of him and he heard Dimitris ask, "are you out of your minds?" then felt him take his arms, open and close them, give him a couple of slaps; and then once more he saw the sunshine, it was rosy, he rolled onto his side, gasping and stubborn, lying on the grass to one side he could see the enormous ball, noticed its seams, its laces. And he sat up and spat and his spit was pinkish, they've made my mouth bleed he thought, and he saw Dimitris kneeling down beside him, watching him, "how are you feeling?" he asked and Angel muttered, "OK" then got to his feet, went to the gate, stopped a minute, for he had to pay them back, shouted, "Communists", noticed that none of them moved, thought they must be afraid of him, "Bolsheviks, I'll deal with you," he shouted at them, and closed the gate, leaving them standing there stupefied.

He was startled for a moment as he realised that the sun had already set, at home they'd be worrying about him, maybe out searching for him in the streets, which were now cool and bathed in grey light, yet he set off in the opposite direction towards the shunting yard and the red house, to report the incident to his battalion leader, to bear witness against them, have them punished. The electric lights had been turned on by now and the only people there were adult men, he watched them through the window as they discussed whatever they were discussing, on the wall were the king and Metaxas, he went in and saluted with his arm straight out in front of him, the barber noticed him, asked, "what do you want?" He felt numb and the words stuck in his throat so that in the end he said, "I want to buy some battalion stamps" which people used to stick on their identity cards, but the barber didn't have any, "we'll be getting some more in a few days' time," he assured him, then remembered, "you walked out this afternoon," he said in reproof, and Angel realised that everyone was looking at him, someone said, "what he really likes best is coupons for the cinema" at which they all laughed, and he felt himself blush and thought fuck you – "is there anything else you want?" enquired the barber and he muttered no, but as he reached the door stopped, saw them looking at him and waiting, in the end it was the barber who asked, "who ripped your clothes?" and pointed to his trousers which were torn open at the side so that you could see his underpants, all covered with earth and grass stains, and he was obliged to say, "the Bolsheviks".

By the time he approached his home it was already quite late at night and he thought that another beating would be awaiting him, which could maybe be avoided if he slipped in unnoticed, however as soon as he turned the corner he saw a patch of darkness detach itself and Myrsine was standing in front of him saying, "so there you are, you devil" and she grabbed him by the hand and when they reached the steps stopped, "your father has shut himself up in the back room and isn't saying a word to anyone" and Angel could smell her tears, the fact that they're all worn out from being upset will be my salvation, he said to himself, and at this thought some of his courage returned, and in a little while he was tucked up in bed, sweating and praying just let me fall asleep, let me sink into such deep sleep that I'll be incapable of feeling when they discover my torn trousers. Somewhere from the kitchen at the back he could hear voices which were becoming fainter and fainter until in the end they faded out, and then he felt a hand creeping into his belly and squeezing and it hurt and he thought of crying out, but then had second thoughts, except that the hand was coming back again and gripping him like pincers squeezing even harder, it was as if it was twisting his insides, his guts, threatening to rip them out, but he still preferred not to cry out, only he tried to stretch and to turn over in case he could escape it this way, but he felt himself flying and in a minute he'd fall he'd come crashing down, and all the lights went on and he was clutching his belly again lest he lost control and shat himself. And they hurried him off to the lavatory, he saw the white tiles shining, and his grandmother in her nightgown with her hair down, and Fotis blaspheming somewhere in the background, because perhaps his son was the mirror image of himself. At some point they put him to bed again, and he huddled up and his grandmother said, "drink this," it was the chamomile which he himself picked for her on the open ground, and then he lay down and didn't speak in case he shat from his open mouth; and he fell asleep.

It was midday by the time he awoke, the house was empty and the shutters closed, was it raining, he wondered, but then saw that the sun was shining, maybe he might meet up with some friends and play, maybe he might climb high up into the tree, checking on his property and the world around him, all the same, I'll have to be careful, he said to himself, and he remembered his grandmother's chamomile and his father swearing, and he told himself again that he'd have to be careful, he took a hunk of bread and ate it, then heard footsteps outside in the yard, it was Myrsine and Niki, his youngest aunt, and his grandmother told him, "here, come and drink this and it will heal you," she had brought holy water from the church of the Ascension, "drink it," she said, giving him the little bottle, and Angel obeyed, except that he then said, "it's only water" and his grandmother scolded him and said, "don't blaspheme" because it was holy water and would cure him, although Angel thought to himself, bullshit. He got dressed without speaking and watched them, Myrsine crossing herself in devotion in front of the icons with Niki at her side copying everything her mother did – and he made the most of this opportunity and slipped out. However, he set off in the opposite direction, not towards the scene of yesterday's adventures, but towards the sea, and in a little while saw the high wall that he knew so well, the large garden with the lunatic asylum at the bottom of it, bars on all the windows, and at one of them a clean white handkerchief spread out as if someone wanted to dry it, but then a head appeared, a man with curly hair, who stared at him insistently and in the end said, "are you my George?", whereupon Angel made off fast even though he could see that the bars at the windows were solid and the windows themselves high up and the wall insurmountable. But "George, George" he heard, and until he'd rounded the corner he kept on hearing this cry.

Now he was in a street bordered by acacias along which he often ran, and at the end the main avenue, cars and numerous trams and occasionally buses. And that led into the other street which ended in rocks and sea, the "smokestack" of Pendzikis, where they went stealthily to bathe and were chased by the wealthy owners, beyond lay the shipyards, a magical world full of caiques and boats, smelling of paint and tar, and then further on a flower bedecked garden, a little wooden house like something out of a picture, and over the fence the branches of the pear tree hanging where one day they'd chased Angel and he'd dropped all the unripe pears and cursed – he hadn't cried. Yet now he stopped for a minute in indecision, he saw two eyes watching him, which then became four, then six, and he mused, I know them from somewhere, and indeed they got nearer and it was Dimitris, the boy scout, smiling and saying "hallo", to which Angel replied though in a serious tone, offended that the other three were eyeing him as if examining him – one of them asked innocently, "what's your name?" and he said "Angel" and they looked at him pleasantly enough, their names were Andreas and Armandos, and a voice within himself pronounced: soft little middle-class kids, who bore no marks of beatings, whose clothes were clean and ironed, whose hands were white as white.

And they were indeed quite another race of beings, for they said, "it's midday and they'll be expecting us home," the table would be laid, their mother, their father, the appointed hour, so that you couldn't miss lunch, maybe even grace; in the end only Dimitris and Angel were left, and Angel asked, "do you cross yourself?" and the other boy answered, "of course" and seemed surprised, but reds don't say prayers, Angel remembered the battalion leader, and Dimitris was informing him "my mother's religious" – "so's my grandmother" and they both laughed. They were getting near their homes now, Dimitris stopped for a moment and then whispered, "you got us wrong," as if they'd been having an interminable discussion, a difference which they needed to resolve, he could go and play with him, borrow his books, and Angel said "all right", that he'd like to do both; and there they parted.

And when Angel was alone once more, I know that house, he thought to himself, for he frequently passed that way and paused there, beneath the tree always sat a girl, one noon she stood at the door and looked at him, but from behind the railings though, she was dark and beautiful, he begged her, "don't be afraid" but she ran off like a wild thing, opened the front door and vanished. Now the garden was empty, Dimitris had gone in through the same door, maybe they were all sitting round the table together, and Angel wondered, what's it like? He set off home, from where he was he could see the wall and the trees, the sun was blazing overhead, the end of summer, and he thought that his arms and legs, his thin face, were burnt really dark, Myrsine used to say "gypsy boy" and put him in the washtub on Saturdays and scrub him. And when he entered the kitchen, scowling as ever, he saw his grandmother dishing up the food, looking at him in amazement (what on earth has happened to make him turn up at the proper time? thought she), ordering him to take some soap and wash. From somewhere in another room he could hear whistling, maybe Fotis's bad mood was abating, and in a little while they were all sitting round the table and Myrsine was making the sign of the cross, and Niki copying her as ever, and Angel did the same; whereupon his father laughed and muttered, "Angel's getting ruined, he's mocking us," but Myrsine gave him a black look and after a moment all of them had taken their spoons and were drinking their soup without speaking. And the boy felt a kind of deathliness, as if his powers of hearing and sight had been sealed and he was in an incomprehensible world.

Antigone

She opened her secret exercise book and wrote, "I don't understand, I am afraid of him," then put it away again in the hiding place behind the wardrobe where no one was likely to slip his hand; she had another place too, which nobody knew about, where she kept a little tin with two drachmas in it, and a scrap of silk ribbon, some sweets and a piece of chocolate, a little drop – and this place was on top of the shelf with their books. And outside in the garden she had yet another secret little hole, a cranny in the garden wall where a brick was missing, with their rosebush in front of it, and from this hiding place she would retrieve and admire her carvings, her buttons, a teeny weeny doll and other wonderful things, which she could never have borne to share with anyone else. And Alcmene used to tell her, "don't bother trying to hide things from me, for I can read you like a book," but she was a completely different sort of person, constantly had her nose deep in a novel, old dead stories thought Antigone, she took endless pains with her schoolwork, always kept her satchel and her exercise books in order, her blue school overall always without a crease, her hair always neat and tidy. Antigone was a jarring note compared to Alcmene, never cared a whit for her beauty, her plaits, threw herself wholeheartedly into games with the boys, would not cry, was stronger than their brother Dimitris when they all three slept in the same room and would fight over nothing in their beds.

And she felt, "I'm afraid" when she saw Dimitris's new friend, who wasn't in any way a stranger since he used to stand at the gate and watch her, until one day there he was in their living room with Dimitris saying, "this is Angel," an Angel however who had a curious way of shutting his eyes when he spoke, who always seemed uncomfortable when he laughed and who convinced Antigone that he was a mysterious boy, maybe something to be afraid of, whose hands stuck out from his sleeves, rough and dark-skinned, with badly torn fingernails which might prove dangerous if they touched you. And she recalled Andreas, with his white shirt and his good manners, who used to bring her little butterflies and flowers and ladybirds, would say, "how are you getting on with your lessons?", though in fact she always came top, like Dimitris and Andreas. And that evening she wrote down her fear, as if by so doing she could shut him up safely, secure him, secure herself, but Dimitris teased her, "you're acting like a baby," he scolded as he noticed her withdraw and disappear every time Angel was supposed to come.

However he wasn't someone you could avoid, for one midday she saw that he had climbed on a fence and from there onto one of the gateposts, about three metres high, and was attempting to stand upright, a high-flying statue, which terrified Antigone so that she cried, "come down, you'll kill yourself" and he obeyed, and in a moment was standing before her, once more the dark-skinned lad who had asked, "is Dimitris in?" as if this was the burning problem. So they walked a few steps together, then Antigone said, "Mummy will be expecting me," by which she meant that her mother knew her timetable, and he stood there speechless. And the girl thought about it, she was sorry she'd left him, had second thoughts and turned back, saw that he had climbed onto the wall and was walking up and down on top of it, balancing with his arms outstretched like wings; yet she was incapable of turning round and begging, and she thought he's incorrigible.

She might have written it in her secret exercise book, yet she reflected and came to the conclusion that the best hiding place of all is one's own mind, no matter how much Alcmene accused her, "you're secretive and you don't tell me anything." However Antigone too might have made the same complaint about Alcmene, when one night her sister woke up in tears with her sheets blood-stained and her insides aching, and their mother came hurrying into the room in a state, and their father alarmed, and Dimitris, but Amalia sent them all away, they took Antigone too, her father held her in his arms and kept saying, "go to sleep, it's nothing serious," and Amalia stayed with Alcmene all night, and in the end her sobs were quieted and the light turned off, as if it was something that had happened by mistake and everyone simply needed to calm down. And they kept it secret from her, no matter how much Antigone asked, "I'll tell you later," promised her sister, who was calm the next morning though with circles under her eyes as if she was tired. And the younger girl complained, with reason, that they kept things secret from her, even though her mother promised, "I'll tell you about it all in good time," for she felt that they were weaving a conspiracy all around her, and she confided the feeling to the exercise book in her hiding place behind the wardrobe, as if this would solve the problem.

It was towards the end of October, the little garden beside their house was fresh and cool, so that Antigone huddled into her school overall, sought out the sunny spots against the wall, where she read or pondered, she caught herself watching Dimitris to see when he'd come home and with whom, but usually it was Armandos and/or Andreas, who bounced their large ball on the paving and pitched it high into the air, then threw it from one to the other; they were strong, well-built boys, they smiled at her from a distance as they left, and she suspected they thought she was too young. And so one day she stood in front of the mirror, she saw a skinny sweet-faced girl, examining herself carefully, with thin shoulders and lean arms, however, she took a pure white ribbon and tied it in her straight hair, put on her mother's high-heeled shoes, then the only hat she possessed which had a bow at the side, and finally found the lipstick and painted her lips; now her eyes sparkled as they looked back at her from the mirror, smiled at her, until suddenly she heard the front door opening and took everything off at once, crammed it all back in the cupboard, scrubbing at her lips in panic as she heard her mother's footsteps approaching.

One day it occurred to her that she never heard Angel as he came up to her, it was almost as if he wanted to startle her, "he's a funny boy" was Dimitris's verdict, and Antigone remembered his acrobatics or his skill when one afternoon he'd taken Armandos's ball and bounced it off his head while Antigone counted "five ... six ..." and he continued the feat, then bounced the ball onto his shoe, kicked it upwards, hit it, said, "it's not going to touch the ground" and in the end brought it back up to his head, "twelve, thirteen ..." then bounced it hard in the girl's direction, who caught it, laughing. And Dimitris applauded him, "you're an ace," he admitted, but didn't get more than a single glance from the boy in return; he seemed to be only interested in what she would say, and when Antigone sensed this she said, "I've got to get back to my maths homework" and left them. Except that she didn't lose them from view because she went to her mother's bedroom from where she could see them through the shutters, a thin slice of Angel's face, a small portion of Armandos's head or her brother's lips which were speaking though she couldn't hear what they were saying; she opened the window out of curiosity but the hinges squeaked and she saw them turn round, perhaps they'll see me, she thought in terror and froze, blushing bright red maybe, but then she realised that they'd gone, heard their footsteps and then the garden gate, now all she could see were the paving stones and the flower beds, if only what I could see was their hair or their feet she thought – then in the end went back to her own room.

But she was to see them again on Sunday, which was the day after the feast of St. Dimitrios, and the mother said to her son, "tell your friends to come round and you can offer them something to celebrate your name-day"; once more Armandos came, and Andreas, and a younger blond boy who was constantly blushing, and finally, when they'd stopped expecting him, Angel knocked at the door. He'd put on his best clothes and combed his hair and looked all polished and shining, he sat in a corner and listened as Alcmene and Andreas talked, they were disagreeing all the time and the others were listening to their argument and laughing, for the girl was being the "soul of objection" and disagreeing on purpose in order to attract attention. The youngest person present was Antigone, and in fact there'd been a battle for her to be there at all, for Alcmene had said, "it'll just be the older ones" with a tone that brooked no dissent – in the end Antigone had gone crying to her mother who had worked out a compromise, "you can stay just till eight o'clock," she'd said, and made her put on her green dress, and the girl had gone running to her secret place and got out her best ribbon and put it in her hair, and then sat silent against the wall of the room, as if fearing that her world would fall to pieces, that she'd give them some excuse for getting rid of her. But after a bit she found herself near Angel, or rather he came and stood near her and murmured, "how are the books going?" and she answered him, "fine" and couldn't think of another word to say and felt that she must be blushing to the roots of her hair, but then her mother came in with the tray and Alcmene said, "I'll hand it round," acting the older sister in other words, and the boys laughed and took the sweetmeats offered and chatted away, Andreas was telling them the story of Captain Blood which was playing at the cinema, and Alcmene said, "don't begin yet, I want to hear it" for she was coming and going from the room, bringing things to offer them, but Angel at that point said, "I know the story" and started singing the praises of Tarzan which he'd gone to see with his whole school at the "Elysia" and they'd been whistling and drumming their feet, and then the elephants stampeded and trampled the natives to a pulp, and everyone was quiet listening when suddenly a glass smashed, it had been dropped by the boy who was blushing, and Angel swore and said "fuck" at being interrupted, whereupon the girls blushed and that was the end of the story telling.

For the door opened and the children's father came in, whose hair had gone grey by now – like my own father's, thought Angel. He said, "I'll sit with you for a bit" and started talking to them, but mostly to Armandos and Andreas whom he'd met before. First they talked about school and how they were doing, and the boys answered his questions, measuring their replies carefully and enunciating them as if they'd given each word a good lick first. At one point Andreas asked about "the situation in general" which they'd been reading about in the papers, and Alcmene started something like a song, since she couldn't stand being serious, but they were talking of the war in Poland, about which side had more weapons, and their father seemed to sigh and said, "the Poles have been fighting with nothing but their cavalry," while on the other side Hitler had aeroplanes and tanks, for a moment he paused and got his watch out of his pocket, at which Antigone trembled and prayed that it wasn't yet eight, and luckily it wasn't, but her father said, "time for me to go," they'd be expecting him at the newspaper, but he asked, as if he'd just remembered, "how's the scout group doing?" to which Andreas answered "hopelessly", for the scouts were now helping EON and attracting all the boys with outings and free cinema tickets, whereupon Christos sighed and concluded, "they've destroyed everything," at which point Antigone saw Dimitris making signs at him, but Angel got in first and said, "that's an utter lie" and everyone turned and looked at him doubtfully, specially Christos, and Angel said, "the youth movement is just fine" – silencing everyone.

Outside darkness had fallen, their father left the room, then reappeared with his coat and hat on, his lips were tightly pressed together though, and Antigone could read their message, "it would be better for you all to go home now," he advised, but Antigone begged, "just a little bit longer," and her brother scolded her, "Father knows best," and all their friends got up with the exception of Angel, who was watching them from his corner like a little wild animal which might be thinking I'll bite them, but Dimitris went up to him without any fear and almost ordered him, "you'd better leave," Angel blushed to the whites of his eyes and promised, "I won't betray anything," at which Antigone thought "well done", but her father stood there in hesitation, apparently bewildered, and in the end asked, "what could you betray?" The small animal made no answer though, whereupon the unexpected happened, Christos reached out and grabbed Angel by the ear, "get out of my house," he said in a curt voice, and Antigone felt that she was about to faint as she watched her father drag the boy out of the room, resisting, without a word being spoken, without anyone daring to move, except that she heard her sister ask her angrily, "what are you crying for?" and realised that her cheeks were wet, that her tears had run down as far as her jawbone, yet said stubbornly, "I'm not crying," until she heard the outside gate slammed shut; the other boys then left one by one, the last being the boy who'd spilt the water and who was now white as a sheet. Their mother came in, followed by Dimitris who was looking gloomy, "what on earth did you want to bring him here for?" she asked, but her brother remained silent.

They ate in silence and went to bed, with Antigone wondering what Angel could betray and where. It might harm him, people would say "stool pigeon, stool pigeon" and he would cringe like a whipped cur, he'd want to be swallowed up by the earth or to climb onto the gatepost so that people couldn't get hold of him by the ear again and so that she wouldn't feel sorry for his humiliation. She put her ribbons and things away in their hiding place and contemplated what she would write in the exercise book; in the end she couldn't decide because the world around her faded into an eerie light and silence, which was suddenly rudely shattered when someone said, "wake up, we're at war" and she remained dumb, maybe they were mocking her in her sleep, but then she saw her father and he said again, "wake up" and she heard her mother saying, "I can't believe they'll put you into uniform?" – since he was almost forty. It was a sweet mild autumn day, with the sun playing in the branches of the acacia, it might have been a day like any other; yet they were sent home from school, the headmaster said, "the die is cast" which Antigone didn't really understand,* and they set off home chattering and laughing, at one point a lorry roared by them, laden with young men who were shouting and waving, until they disappeared round the corner of the avenue. A man came out of his shop carrying the flag, which he hoisted on a pole and all the children clapped, a woman was crying excitedly, "they've taken my man" and her voice was like an old forgotten bugle. In the end Antigone found herself alone once more in their little garden, beside her secret hiding place, amongst the flowers, and she wondered how things would be now. The sun had come out properly and she felt it caress her, it might have been like any other day; except that after a bit she saw her father coming along looking gloomy, but when her mother came to the door he laughed and said, "they've called me up too" – and they saw no more of him till the evening, when everything was hushed and the streets were dark and deserted.

---

* The headmaster was called Schinas, he had straight hair which was constantly falling forwards on both sides of his face, like little curtains, and he kept on pushing it back. This was one of his characteristics; another was his hoarse voice. He had a very young and beautiful wife and everyone made envious comments. That day, Monday, 28th October 1940, he spoke in thundering tones and said, "we shall win." The children never saw him again at the school during the Occupation. Later it became known that he was in the resistance and had all sorts of adventures, unbelievable both to himself and to others.

The Middle Ages – 5

In the end they decided to find out about Kali Meria, to search and discover what was hidden in the pit. They set out at dusk and walked all night. As they passed the hovels and the tents they could feel the miasma closing in on them, suffocating them, "it is not possible for any human being to live here," he would be eaten away by malaria and loneliness, yet so many people have been here before us and stayed and struggled here; and Christoforos then gave the order, "we will stay until dawn, and anyone who doesn't agree can leave, only don't lie down lest you be frozen there forever, pierced by the chill and the dawn dew; when we were children and used to come here in summer, we used to stumble on the couples hidden in the reed beds," it is no longer the season for love (he remembered Irene getting cross with him, "you are my dead time," she would say), and snakes might be lurking here. From far off they could hear whistling, was it our own men changing guard, or could it be others who had advanced to set an ambush for us? One day at the cinema we saw Tim MacKoy, who lit a fire in one place and then went off to sleep in the icy cold somewhere else, so that the conspirators stabbed his blankets through and through and then left – how many blankets must the lad have had? – the film director knows that sort of thing and buys them for him, said someone, closing the conversation. And without being aware of it they gradually fell silent and waited, in the distance the sea glimmered with a faint phosphorescence as if it had swallowed up the day and was lulling it to sleep; after a while Christoforos decided that they should not light a fire, "we'll put look-outs all round to make sure we are not taken by surprise," no one had any thoughts of sleep, and when they had finished their preparations they all drew close, huddled together and gazed out silently into the night. And then Christoforos said, "if we are going to get through till morning we shall have to talk," they shared out their raisins and dry bread, warmed themselves with a couple of mouthfuls of grape spirit, and their leader started the story. "My strongest memory is of the time when they killed Veroglou; I remember how I had got up early and was watering the garden, at the back, where we sowed vegetables when we had to contend with hunger. It was early and everyone was going off to his work, and as I was picking some roses for my mother three volleys rang out and I came out of the little garden gate, it was still quiet and empty and from the other direction two young men were coming, deep in talk, they passed me slowly, one was fair-haired and pink-skinned, I can see him now, a tall village boy, the other was the same height but as dark as could be, they were talking as they passed me, but as soon as they reached the corner they began to run and disappeared from sight, and just then I heard screams, they have killed Veroglou, people were calling, and it was as if the whole neighbourhood came awake, you could hear the women running and wailing, and I felt myself running with them, dry-eyed, and there at the side by a wall we saw the dreadful sight, Veroglou lying all white and bloodied, his eyes wide open and wild, and the women stood there and clawed their cheeks." Christoforos stopped there, pensive, then seemed to sigh and said, "a whole heap of things of that kind happened during those middle years, the summer of '43, '44." All around him everyone was frozen, yet no one said a word, on the fringes of the darkness they could make out two trees and beneath them some animal, which puzzled them as they wondered who had left it there and what it might mean. For a moment their leader was disturbed and stretched out his hand towards the west, they could see his ring shining on his finger as he pointed but were bewildered and could see nothing, even though he told them, "it is as if there was a window hanging in the sky, with light shining through it and a curtain red like blood." But still they could see nothing but his hand; until the sky began to lighten and they began to hope that they would be returning to the city, to their own tranquil corners. And then they could make out two ships floating somewhere over in the direction where the sea was, they seemed to be flying along with their red and white sails, those ships are not bringing any of our own people, they reflected, since all the roads were blockaded, the world was becoming narrower and rumours were swelling, people talked of traitors and cheats who wormed their way stealthily into the city by night through the secret doors, and always found a nest awaiting them, to protect them, to feed their strength until they were needed. In the end Christoforos gave the order, "time for us to move," but he seemed incomprehensible and remote, as if he could no longer raise his bowed shoulders or his eyes, as if he was walking towards no destination. And someone said, "he resembles the tree that bears no fruit" and neither was Irene there to belie him, nor was any word spoken to call him a liar, something which would have come as a relief, like the fresh-scented breeze from the sea.

PART II

Antigone

When the day begins everything seems washed clean, the light dances like a breeze, trees bring a breath of fresh air and houses seem renewed; this means, she thought, that night is a dark pit in which empty space might be choked by gigantic insects, all of them greenish black or deep purplish red, which smell of stagnant sea water trapped in the reed beds, in among the rushes, a miasma that offends the nostrils so that you think a great quicksand might be gaping open to suck you down, down to the underworld, like one night when they took refuge in the cellar, bombs were falling outside or artillery shells, and Andreas urged her, "let's go further in" and they seemed to be passing through doorways, into catacombs, lost chambers, till they reached a pitch dark corner and she felt that each of them was locked into the very entrails of the other, and their breath came short and anxious. But someone called, "Antigone, Antigone" and she answered as if crying, "I can't see, I don't know the way out," for she and Andreas were reluctant to re-emerge.

Thus tranquillity gradually flooded her as the tops of the trees caught the morning light and a green scent rose from the garden, from the garden wall even, whose every cranny she knew so well, every crack, every ants' nest, every join between stone and brick and tile; the garden is a world where exploration is without danger, where flowers and fruits are without taint, into which the girl would go at dawn and feel that the foliage enfolding her gave off a breath of rebirth. Occasionally she felt that she resembled Angel, that they both liked the same things or maybe that he had bequeathed to her his refuges, for he himself was gone now from their haunts, their house, their company. One afternoon Andreas told her, "write him off," because he had seen him working for the Germans, at the shipyards which lay opposite his house, indeed people said that he got drunk and swore and did a whole lot of nasty things, all of which scared Antigone and she reflected, he always looked like someone who'd take risks. And her brother assured her that Angel really was "risking his own skin", a skin that was now adolescent, a barely visible beard on his face, around his eyes the first imperceptible wrinkles, unnatural all the same at his age. She had only run into him once by chance, he was wearing his long trousers, his thick pullover with a tie knotted at his neck (the knot was all she could see of it) and he said, "Hallo" and immediately got out the packet, took a cigarette and lit it like a grown-up, dextrously, at which Antigone teased him, "so angels smoke now, do they..." and his eyes smiled.

Months had passed since then and the girl thought summer is better, for the garden is more accessible then, more lovable either with the morning dew on it or when night embraces it and it breathes imperceptibly, as if the trees were relaxing their sinews or as if their leaves were whispering – all the same, she preferred the mornings, that summer of '43. And Alcmene used to tell her, "you have magic in your heart," which might not be something so very praiseworthy (this was highly probable), or which might have been something that Alcmene had heard somewhere or read in a book, not something that had sprung spontaneously to her mind. They were both older now and were listening for different sounds, they had learnt how to read eyes, hair, to know the feel of his skin, his breath. Except that the elder girl had taken a different path ("a mysterious one", as Antigone ventured to think) which might lead through doors that didn't show, which the younger sister didn't see, whose existence she didn't even suspect, even though she did go through Alcmene's clothes one afternoon and searched her drawers and her books, and found Errol Flynn on his galleon, two romantic novels with coloured covers, pages cut out of a book whose title stood out, "Abortion in the Communist Paradise", and Antigone thought, I remember: they'd gone to the "Astoria" and had been shown terrible things about Russia and the Bolsheviks, and at night she'd heard Alcmene groaning and found it quite inexplicable.

And there probably existed other, even more secret doors, enigmatic ones perhaps, that Antigone could only sense led to an utterly incomprehensible place, which would smell of fears and suspicions, as one night when they were pursued and ran, a little way outside the town, and she had felt them falling into water which gradually became deeper, invisible, yet she could hear it and feel it, licking up to their knees and then their thighs – suddenly – and they retreated as if instinctively and grabbed onto the tufts of grass or the muddy earth and came to rest there; it was winter of '42, in one of their hopeless sorties, searching at dusk for wild greens to stay their pangs of hunger, and night fell early then, so much so that they almost died from terror there in the stream. Now Antigone said to herself, I am terrified by incomprehensible things, things to do with Alcmene once again, who might have a pale blue sheet of paper, folded with unnecessary care as if it were a present, and when you unfolded it you could see beautiful handwriting, small rounded letters, which all the same concealed a secret, so that Antigone wondered what "I have invented a way to weep" could mean, who could dare to confess this – to whom? – but she judged that Andreas couldn't be the sender, nor Alcmene the person who would be able to understand it. And thus dawn was the best time, when the colours awoke once more and all the sounds distracted your attention, imaginings and thoughts could be put aside, suspicions that slipped into your sheets in the darkness, which consisted of heavy breathing and inexplicable moans as if invisible hopes were exerting their power, or repugnant reptiles or insects. Dawn was best, when she liked to walk in the garden and to whisper, "but I assure you I have invented a way to weep" – it seemed like playing with a conundrum or implying one.

And the whole conundrum ran thus: "I have invented a way to weep, an invention that suits me, just as statues stand as if in terror, their empty eyes motionless, whose death moves you, and doors open and close behind which lies nothing, which lead to nowhere and to nothing, I have invented a way to weep which suits me in company or in solitude, it is as if a tap were turned on, and the other world gushes forth, the water, and nightmares and visions are expunged, some shame too perhaps, some lack of daring, the locked room with the hidden skeleton, but I assure you I have invented a way to weep, it represents yet one more flight, some pretext or alibi, so that it is encompassed by a globe of security, an impassable vacuum, wherein sight travels in one single direction, from the centre outwards, like the rays of the sun which blind yet fill with joy, I have invented a way to weep, a way of living that is without peril, as when one walks with confidence on the pavement or on the waterfront at a distance from the sea, somewhere in this world here below yet somewhere clearly remote, it is a way."

How beautiful, thought Antigone, who could have written it? For the handwriting was like embroidery on the paper, decorating it, so that you felt you had to take care and fold it delicately as if it was a pale blue piece of handmade work entrusted to you. The garden was now full of light, her mother had opened the windows and could be glimpsed from time to time as she prepared something for them; her father had left at crack of dawn with a friend to go to the vineyards where they worked as day labourers, over towards Thermi, beyond the foundries, where they were paid in kind, wheat and peas for winter, and grapes and figs now. Alcmene was asleep, Dimitris reading perhaps, the garden was hers alone, full of a fragrance that concealed no doubts, particular well-known scents, rose and honeysuckle, the old wall which no longer served as a hiding place but which continued to provide security, on the other side of it lurked the Tsimonis family, "thieves" as her mother called them, who (so they were accused) went into other people's houses and stole copper pans and clothes, they were mixed up in various kinds of dirty business and contraband with the Germans and neither their behaviour nor their dress was decent. But Antigone was sitting on a low child's stool and the wall loomed solid and high, and if she raised her eyes all that could be seen was leaves and sky – deep blue now, with the brilliance of the sunny day that was to come.

After a bit, though, she sensed that she was no longer alone, and indeed two figures were standing outside the gate talking; the girl said to herself they're strangers, and at one point they turned round and she saw their faces – one of them was a tall fair-haired man, he reminded her of a boy from Kamptzida, and his companion was shorter and swarthy, they seemed to be waiting for someone and were exchanging brief phrases that she couldn't catch.

They're from somewhere else, some other neighbourhood, thought Antigone; but at that moment she saw them move, as if they had some job to do and had to get it over with – I'll read it one more time, she thought, in case I can make more sense of it, the beautiful handwriting on the blue paper, from which emanated an air of mystery, probably with an ulterior motive, something cunning, from a person who was in hiding or who was scared. And then the morning was rent asunder by the noise, like a huge rattle being shaken, and Antigone said, "my God", maybe the Germans were carrying out some exercise and firing their machine-guns, but then nothing followed, only quiet, and the girl went to their gate and opened it and stepped outside, and just then saw the two young men coming back, walking along and talking, they reached her and gave her a good look and the fair one said "hallo" and smiled, but it was a false smile which had come and gone before she had time to answer, and she saw them quicken their pace, above his eyebrow she thought was a mole, and just as they reached the corner of the street they walked slap into the mother of the Tsimonis family and for a second looked lost, terrified, but she advised them, "run, so they don't catch you" and Antigone wondered, but what have they done? However, as they rounded the corner they seemed ready to run.

And soon what had happened was beyond all doubt, for in a while they heard wailing and a voice crying, "they've killed Veroglou," impossible to tell whether it was a man's, a woman's or a child's voice, and Amalia came hurrying out in alarm as if someone had pushed her from the house out into the street, and you could hear the neighbours running, their voices, their footsteps, and Antigone followed them, hearing as they approached the sound of weeping which was guiding them, drawing them towards it, and when they came to the next street, it must have been Gravias Street, they saw women wailing and tearing their hair, all of them neighbours, and at the edge of the pavement the man in white lay awkwardly on his back, his suit soaked with blood, his head twisted at an ungainly angle as if his neck was broken, his eyes staring at some indefinite point, perhaps the door of the house across the road. And Antigone was horrified, she didn't cry though, but found her mother's apron and buried her face in it, on the familiar bosom whose harsh breathing she could feel and from whence a voice came crying, "they'll wipe us all out," she heard it like a jolt against her cheek, like a beloved shudder, and her ears were assailed by other voices and cries, and suddenly someone said "Yvonne" and the lamentations swelled and grew and turned into panic, at which point Antigone detached herself from her mother's embrace and saw a woman approaching, distraught, a woman whom she'd seen in their neighbourhood and knew, a lady both slender and aloof, who now was running in her silk dressing gown with her hair uncombed and her eyes seeming to be questioning them all; and when her gaze fell on the dead man she stopped dead as if struck by lightning, motionless, but the other women drew her forward, and there was blood on every breast and hand as if the evil was an infection transmitted as each woman touched the other, and Antigone in her terror caught sight of Dimitris standing in silence a little way off, he became aware of her and came and took her hand, his own was hard as if angry, "they riddled him with bullets from top to toe," he murmured to her, as if these were things that he knew and could speak of, and at last two gendarmes came running up, and Antigone couldn't tell what happened next because her brother pulled her by the sleeve and said, "let's go, my stomach is turning over" and she too felt as if her guts were rising to her throat, like a lump that stuck there and wouldn't be swallowed, and there was an unpleasant smell, perhaps coming from the dead man.

After a while they were all gathered in the kitchen, Dimitris was saying, "they may send the battalions" who would go at night and haul people out of their beds and butcher them, and Amalia was panicking, "where is all this going to lead to?" she was sobbing, "we've reached the point of killing each other," and Antigone saw before her eyes a window display in the market, perhaps it was at Lambropoulos's, where they had put a large painting of two men with their heads severed and in the background the village burning, labelled "the crimes of the red mob", Alcmene who was with her declared "propaganda" but Antigone was upset; and now her sister had got out of bed, the voices hadn't woken her nor the morning's events, she seemed still half asleep, but was instantly awake when she heard the horror of what the others were recounting, "things are getting savage," she muttered, and ran back to her room, which seemed strange to

Antigone and to their mother, only Dimitris appeared to be unsurprised by anything and murmured, "we'll have reprisals," he was now a grown lad about to finish high school. Then they heard Amalia say, "we'll have to tell your father," and what she meant was send him a message, for by now he must be digging and pruning; "you'll have to go," she told her son, "tell him to stay where he is, in case they come at night and round up all the men," but in Antigone's mind as she watched him put on his shoes and leave was the thought, "our Dimitris has grown up."*

And before too long someone knocked on the door and it was an officer of the gendarmerie whom they knew, one of Pavlakis's cronies, he had a sly peasant's face, in the old days he barely fitted into his clothes but now he had lost weight noticeably and his trousers hung baggy on him; "good morning, Madame," he said, but Amalia didn't bother to answer his greeting, "we are searching for the murderers," he announced with the weighty tones of authority (he must be Koulouris, thought Antigone, who had heard her father mention his name, maybe he knew him through Pavlakis) – "I never got a glimpse of him," said her mother, meaning the murderer, "there were two of them" – the other man had his information – "I didn't see them," said Amalia again and Antigone examined her hands, has he realised anything? she was wondering, for the man was as crafty as a fox and his clothes gave off a whiff of the barracks, "they'll burn us to death," said he, "the bastards," and the mother and daughter did not understand who was to be burnt; he said goodbye and left as if annoyed, except that he warned them, "watch out" and perhaps he meant that he knew they knew something and wouldn't speak.

They didn't even have time to say we had a lucky escape before they heard other footsteps coming up the steps, the shuffle of slippers in a hurry – and Amalia said, "don't open the door," she

---

* After I had walked for two hours, beyond the great ditch and the foundry, I began to see the vines green on the low hills. My father was there digging, bathed in sweat. When he saw me he was alarmed. I told him about the murder, but he decided, "wait and we'll go back together" because he couldn't bear to think of us by ourselves, whatever happened. Nothing further happened, and at some point, late at night, we went to sleep. But he kept on talking to himself, "Tasos," he said, "you pig-headed fool." He went on repeating it, again and again.

needed to be alone to get her mind back in order, her pulse back to normal which perhaps she felt was bounding beyond its normal rate, making the blood rise to her head, and she put out her arm as she heard knocking on the door, made as if to prevent the girl from opening it (which was unnecessary, since her daughter was obedient), but the person knocked again more insistently, and the two of them stood where they were without stirring, whereupon a whisper came through the door, "it's me, your neighbour, don't be frightened" and as they were slow to make up their minds, "I know you're in there," said the wooden door – so they let her in. She seemed terrified but all the same ready to deal with any problem, and asked them, "what did you tell him?" at which Amalia got angry and answered shortly, "we didn't see them, we don't know anything," and she seemed to be saying "go away," but the other woman was approving, "that's what I said too," as if this was some feat, and she cast a sly glance at Antigone, then put out her hand and stroked her, but the girl drew back, she felt that the Tsimonis woman's hand was unclean, "be careful, pet," she said, "we neither saw nor know a thing" and Amalia was annoyed that she seemed to be making a deal with the "thieves"; thus the other woman left, probably feeling that she'd gone too far. The sun was fully out now, it looked as if it would be another baking day, and Antigone saw once more the white-clad man covered in blood, then the hands and embraces dipped in blood, the fingerprints and other strange marks, and in the end she said, "I've got to tell you something" to Amalia who stood in front of her waiting, "I saw the men who killed him," she whispered and felt her mother freeze; "don't say anything," the terrified mother advised, "say nothing or we'll be lost," for she had heard appalling and terrible things about interrogations and torture, and the girl said, as if to get it all off her chest, "the Tsimonis woman got a better look at them, they ran into her and she helped them escape" – then Amalia came to life, that's why she visited us then, she thought, and it was some relief to know that the other woman must be even more scared, "don't say a thing to Alcmene, nor to your brother," and they were plotting without realising it, as if they could dig a deep pit and bury the danger.*

---

* The only eye-witness to the murder was Costas Hal., a youth with the

Then Alcmene arrived, stopped short at the door, seemed to be looking out for something or waiting, and indeed she was, just as Antigone suspected, for when their mother turned her back for a minute she saw her elder sister make a sign to her, meaning come into the room, I want to tell you something, then disappeared into the room herself, and when in the end the younger girl went and joined her Alcmene said, "I'm missing a pale blue letter," she didn't even ask, she knew, for she stretched out her hand and waited. Antigone gave it to her and whispered, "I couldn't understand it" and the other gave her a slap and snarled, "that'll teach you not to go through my things" and hid the letter in her bodice, against her flesh, which was by now well and truly curvaceous, "I didn't understand it," Antigone said again – to which her sister replied, "it's written like that on purpose" which maybe hid a threat or a danger, but she didn't dare ask anything, in case some door should open and she should find herself in the darkness surrounded by incomprehensible voices. And her elder sister commanded, "don't breathe a word, people's lives are at risk," which indicated that it was indeed a suspicious business – and she shook her head, agreeing that no she wouldn't. And that night when her father got home with Dimitris behind him ("you're both mad," Amalia scolded them), Antigone cuddled in his arms until the sound of their talking had soothed her and she heard the darkness say, "you're a grown woman now yet you still want to be hugged" – and she really was a grown woman, for Alcmene had explained things to her; they were in a friendly mood and laughed together secretly.

mind of a child, who raised his arms in the air, without anyone having told him to, and remained thus until the murderers had left, indeed until the first women arrived wailing. But he didn't open his mouth, no matter how much people questioned him. And when he opened it (later, to the police), they were neither enlightened by him nor believed him.

Angel

If people could see us from outside they'd say the shutters have eyes, thought Angel, for the whole family was glued to the two windows, whose glass panes were open (it was the end of summer) and you could have faintly made out Myrsine's mouth, her thin lips and the ring on the finger raised in front of these lips as she ordered them not to speak. Outside the glimmer of dawn was growing, it might have been a day like any other day except for the fact that now they were frozen in terror, because through the cracks they could see men from Dangoulas's security battalion gathered just below; there were more than ten of them, all carrying rifles and hand grenades, and in the middle two boys – one appeared to be barefoot, in his vest and shorts, aged about eighteen, and the other the same age but fully dressed and wearing shoes, and the men had their gun barrels trained on them, no one spoke as if awaiting some command, and for days Angel was to remember the hunched shoulders of one of them, the boy in the vest who was shivering. In the end someone said, "let's get it over with," it was like a thunderbolt, and Angel could feel himself being drawn as if they wanted to protect him, yet he remained glued to the window as if mesmerised, while all the time the strips of the picture seen through the shutters were becoming better and better illuminated, so much so that he could see quite clearly how one of the boys, not the barefoot one, the other one, pushed aside three of the men guarding him like one possessed and was off down the road like an arrow; except that seen through the slats of the shutters he looked like a white shape sprinting further and further away, by now he must have reached the place where in the old days they used to play marbles, now he must be under the windows with the lunatics, someone snarled, "kill the sod, fuck it," and they heard the men arm their weapons and the same moment a rifle shot rang out, then another, and another which sounded as if it was exploding right in the room, and another, and one more, and oaths and the smell of the fumes of gunpowder and they all leapt back in terror and Myrsine and her daughter fell to the floor. Angel suddenly felt his back against the wall, he thought we're safe here, but all the same as he closed his eyes and pressed his palms against the whitewashed surface, he heard a sharp sound from far off in some other quarter like another bullet and a voice screamed, then all the gunmen who were beneath their windows ran off, and the place breathed once more.

Daylight was now entering the room and he heard his uncle from next door, opened the door and let him in, white faced, his hair tousled, and his uncle said, "they killed him" for he had watched to the end, the gaps between the slats in his shutters were wider, then "get up," he told Myrsine and his sister who were still crouching on the floor as if paralysed, like two old, useless garments flung down and abandoned. And in a little while the place was tranquil again, even if only on the surface, for the armed men disappeared as if by magic and the road was once more empty, the sunlight at last touching it now so that it looked as if a new carpet had been laid, on which a man's bare feet then trod, trod and jumped and said, "they got the boy," and then came other feet, the comments multiplied, someone said, "those are his brains," and Angel's uncle then got up his courage and opened the two shutters and they saw that a whole crowd had gathered by now, in spite of the fact that everyone was frightened and the smell of the gunpowder lingered in the air. Someone put out his arm and pointed to the place where the road ended at a stone wall of great height, always moist, and the man said, "he's still there" – and before long his uncle went out wearing only his trousers and a vest, and Angel hurried after him. And quite unconsciously they walked down the road to the place where the hand had pointed, and Myrsine suddenly called out from the house, "why have you left us on our own?" which sounded absurd right then for they had reached the wall and saw a scarlet mass lying there,* "they blew his head to pieces," someone said and Angel felt faint, his mouth filled with sour liquid and he spat, but it filled again, and again – and someone grabbed him by the arm and pulled him away, "if you can't stand it, go home," and then in a little while he was back in his room and they were bathing his forehead to bring him round. He said, "I'm not going to work."

Because people were saying other things that frightened them, that the boys had lived a little way further down, in a ruined house (which Angel remembered, that's where I used to hide and piss) yet were unknown to the neighbours, and his uncle pronounced, "maybe they were members of the Communist Youth Organization" – and everyone stared at him dubiously – they'd caught the boys while they slept, all unsuspecting. Angel felt that he was trembling, but no one was paying any attention to him, they couldn't know who he met or what they talked about, and suddenly another rumour reached them, that supposedly they hadn't hit the boy when they fired and were cursing that he'd get away, and that just as he was nearing safety he ran into Maria, she who wore a German uniform and kit, and that she drew her pistol and fired, hit the boy in the body, and then as he crumpled and fell to his knees put the barrel behind his ear and fired once more. And everyone said that she was well-named "the bitch's whelp" since she had a German mother and a Greek father, a hot-tempered man, swarthy as a gypsy, and before the war they'd gone hungry. And Angel remembered how he and Maria had had a roll in the long grass one day – the Germans had just entered the city – how they'd hit each other and wrestled with each other and in the end had fallen onto their backs and burst out laughing, and she had said, "I can't westle with you," for she couldn't pronounce the letter 'r' so that all the children teased her and called her "Mawia", and her eyes sparkled; now, however, they took care

---

* Much later I learned that the EPON boy was not unknown in the quarter. A. knew him, and was mixed up with the boy's sister. She is still alive, one of her arms withered as a result of all she went through during the Civil War. I remember that morning, the morning of the killing, when we didn't dare go near the wall. In the end I went past with a friend. What was to be seen there was a red mass, blood and flesh, maybe spilled brains: who could find the courage to look too closely? Afterwards we used to avoid going by that spot. As for playing there, out of the question.

not to meet her or to happen across her path, for she now wore a military uniform with a belt and a pistol and a green kerchief round her neck, and she slept (so they said) at the barracks, she'd taken on something of the look of a she-wolf, her mouth always half-open and moist, ready to bite you or lick you – and thus Angel avoided her, even though they did both work for the Germans, the boy at the shipyards as an interpreter (since when?) and one day he'd seen Maria most indecently up against the wall in an arcade with a sergeant.

I'll have to take precautions, he thought, and his mind was not on Maria or her brother, a vivacious child called Rudi who had been nothing but naughtiness, beaten by most of the others, and now he'd become a slim blond boy with an ironic smile who spent most of his time shut up at home and didn't speak, then one day he was no longer to be seen in his old haunts and word got round that he'd left for Germany, to go to his grandmother who, they said, was rich and all alone. As Angel reckoned it, the danger from these people was negligible and he could probably sort it out with his captain who had a soft spot for him and with whom he used to drink ouzo and punch; it was something quite different that made him afraid and nagged at him, now that he'd actually seen the battalion taking someone out right in front of his eyes, now that people were whispering terrible stories, about how they were finding people killed in the streams of the Toumba and further down, in the orchards, and everyone kept saying, "each new day dawns on a mass of corpses," from their own side or the other side, and he decided the best thing would be just to keep his mouth shut. And what this meant was that he had been seeing Dimitris secretly (some nights in a narrow little alley in Harilaou, where they didn't know anybody and nobody knew them) and giving him scraps of paper, saying which caiques or patrol boats were going to be repaired, what freight they were being loaded with, where they would be going. And he thought, I may be putting my head on the line – or my brains – for he could not get the bottom of that high wall out of his mind, behind it you could hear children's voices, little girls who seemed always to be joking – I could be putting my head on the line, he thought in terror, as if his head were a ball that could be kicked about, for fun or in a frenzy.

Not even his father could help him, he was nowhere at hand

(in fact they didn't have a clue where he might be hanging out or even if he was alive), for he had left at the beginning of the Occupation, since he had been the last to leave for the Albanian front – from the navy he was sent off to be a mule driver – and had been the first to come back when they withdrew, dark and unshaven and terrified, with chapped lips and a determination to disappear again; which he did. So Myrsine was once more in charge of the boy, whenever she saw him, for as long as he was around; she smiled when he brought her bread and potatoes from the Germans and one day went almost mad for joy because a cart appeared, drawn by two stout, strong horses with a German peasant holding the reins, and filled her yard with a mound of manure for her little garden, where now as well as the flowers, of which there were fewer these days, she grew tomatoes and lettuces and other salad herbs. No one else cared, no one had any idea where Angel found his pleasures or where his pain, what he confided to Dimitris, or, the most mysterious thing of all, what his friend did with the scraps of paper and what they were used for, and it might well have proved true that he was "laying his head on the line". Inside himself, deep inside, he felt a burning pain, perhaps he had got mixed up in all this flippantly, in pursuit of adventures or of an image, something like Zorro's black cape, the espionage and swashbuckling – and all he had inherited from his father was a roguish glance, ironic, you're laying your head on the line he might have told his son.

Because they were indeed dangerous times, when every day you felt anxiety boring into your heart or your entrails, like once one afternoon when he went to visit his aunt, in Mitropoleos Street, who lived in an attic and the view was panoramic, on one side you could see the great expanse of the sea, and on the other side the old town with the little houses climbing up the hill, the Kafé-Koulé as it was called, and next door there was a similar attic in which lived two little girls, who always seemed to be on their own and scared, as if they were orphans. And, hearing shouting in the street, Angel jumped across the railings and went out on the other side where he found everything quite deserted, and advanced as far as the wall which was broad, with grass growing on it as if no one took care of it; from up there Angel saw that there was a crowd gathered in the square, most of them wearing open-necked shirts, a few men in suits, and all round them soldiers holding alsatians on the leash, and he could hear German voices giving commands. In one corner were five men – one of them with white hair, one of them bald – and a soldier was making them do gymnastics, one minute press-ups, the next minute jumping on the spot, then arms out, up, forward, down, and the bald man tottered and fell, and the German's voice screamed out, then in the end he took his dog and moved away, a little further off a man wearing a jacket was standing, the German shouted at him as if in fury, and the other man got some papers out of his pocket, gave them to him, then an order rang out again and the man began to jump up and down on the spot and the German to do the same, laughing as if in great satisfaction that he had achieved precisely what he desired, especially when the man began to stumble while he himself jumped even higher and his alsation copied him. In the end general orders were called out, everyone was to stand in line, and at the front tables were set up at which, one by one, each name was noted. And the loudspeakers were now blaring out military marches, the sun was going down in the sky, and Angel heard footsteps behind him, though when he turned round and looked there was no one there. But as he jumped back over the railings he heard the sound of a key being turned in a lock, the sound of strange metal in a strange place.

And on his way back he thought perhaps among the crowd, the herd, Bettina's father might have been, who lived in the house opposite and had another younger daughter to whom fate had not been kind, she was always to be seen sitting behind a closed window, always wearing a beret (people said that she'd been born without any hair)* and listening to gramophone records, crying

---

* I went one evening to the house where the girl with the permanent beret lived; her cousin and I were at school together and we both collected stamps. The girl's father had a wonderful collection and my friend asked him if he would let us see it. And thus we met: the father was a Jew from Larissa and spoke like a Greek peasant – the girl sat in a corner and laughed non-stop, I avoided looking at her. At one point when her cousin came near her she pinched him and burst into fits of laughter and everyone else laughed too as if she'd made the cleverest of jokes. Then she was taken out of the room, and from somewhere we could hear a tap gushing water, and her father showed us his stamp collection without expression.

out from time to time, either out of madness or for comfort; however, Bettina was quite different, a beautiful, tall and slim girl with a mane of long hair, who used to sit deep in thought on their steps, she would look at Angel without speaking, as if she was part of the white steps, a detail, he'd say "hallo" but never received an answer – her father must be among the people in the square, he worked as cashier at the bank, and in the summers, before the war, the family would disappear from sight, people said that they went to a spa, that the mother's whole body ached (and some people said in mockery that you don't grow hair by going to Edipsos), sometimes at night could be heard something that sounded like a baby crying, at which the neighbours felt sorry and repented of their jokes, for the crying and sobbing went on and on, and Myrsine crossed herself and prayed, "Lord, have mercy," and Bettina was always completely silent as if ashamed when late at night the cries and rending sobs were heard.

All this happened during the previous summer, which in the end came to seem an innocent time, for in spring followed the terrible events, painful to the memory of Christians, painful to remember everything they had denied, or everything they had seen or heard, which they had hoped would all prove lies or imaginings, a nightmare that might come to an end, like one of those terrifying films seen at the cinema which go on keeping you awake at night. And Angel was to say, "we have forgotten so much," and he meant what happened in the summer of '41, a little before Fotis disappeared; they had all been gathered round the table in the large room one noon, they'd just finished eating, it was hot and they had the door wide open to let a little air in, then suddenly the doorway was darkened and when they turned to look they saw a slender woman standing there, dark, her hair dishevelled, she gazed at them without speaking, and Fotis asked, "what do you want?", but they saw Myrsine going pale and getting to her feet, on her face an anxious smile, for a second she stood in front of the woman, she must have been examining her intently, then she took her in her arms, "we weren't expecting you, Marika," she

When it was time for us to leave, late at night by then, her mother gave us sweets, biscuits made with sesame and raisins. I never went to their house again.

whispered, as if apologising (but for what?) and at the same moment Fotis got up, as white as if he'd seen the apocalypse before his very eyes, unable to get a word out. But the wizened woman asked as if in a whisper, "how are you, Fotis?" and Angel then felt her eyes fixed on him, running over him; and this seemed to have been a sign, for he heard Myrsine groan, "ah, my child" and immediately Niki started sobbing. And Angel heard himself being called, "come my angel, come and let me see you," the unknown woman was begging him, but he made no move, felt uncomfortable; then he felt Niki give him a push, "she's your mother," she whispered in his ear, and he felt an icy chill within himself, freezing his arms and his legs, and his will too, but she asked again, "don't you recognise me?" and he stared at her, frowning, mainly because he had no idea what to do with everyone crying all around him, specially when he noticed that his father was going out onto the verandah and shaking inexplicably. And Angel felt ashamed, I'm the only person not crying, as if this was a fault in him, to be ashamed of; in the end, without understanding how (they must have pushed him) he found himself in Marika's embrace, rivers of tears flowing down her face as she squeezed him like a mad woman, while he stood with his arms hanging down at his sides. And for days afterwards his nostrils still felt the smell of cooking that impregnated her clothes, her teeth had become fewer and crooked, he remembered how she had two little earrings in her ears, showing through her dishevelled hair.

They sat her down and gave her food and began questioning her about where and how she lived; their tears were dried now and they chatted away like friends and laughed. And Angel now managed to take flight, later when Marika was leaving and Fotis was hugging her without speaking, he watched from a hidden corner on the steps and did not come out, even though he could feel his mother's glance searching around for him. He always remembered how Myrsine used to say "the Jewess" when she was angry with him and beat him. And this was the last time that Angel and Marika ever saw each other, he forgot about her afterwards and was to remember her only when the ordeal began for the Jews, and he thought of her then not so much out of pain – but out of curiosity.

Angela

"Mountains don't mix with mountains," the man told her, surely thinking of himself, for he was tall and fat, with a sort of undigested looking face, probably always reddened, short cropped blond hair and two eyes like blue holes which could look at you slyly and laugh – but they're all just tramps and hypocrites, Vassilis advised her. They had reached the third winter with the Germans, some people had formed friendships with officers or soldiers, some others looked askance at them or avoided them, but all the same no one said no to their bread or their saccharine, and Angela thought that she had known young ladies whose hearts melted at the sight of the blond lads, specially if they had stars on their tunics and a short sword hanging at their hips – she remembered an evening when everyone at the "Faliro" had been disgusted at a girl, who couldn't have been from anywhere round there, and who was out for a good time with two foreign officers, she must have been well and truly drunk by then for she was kissing one of them quite openly; he seemed embarrassed, trying to pull away from her, but she was determined and started giving him little nips, her eyes glassy and her hair dishevelled, in the end they took her and left, and she was crying.

However, it wasn't that sort of place here, no German would ever set foot in here, only Greeks; "except that some of them aren't all that clean," said Vassilis. He had a popular orchestra, with bouzoukis and sandouris, and all the riff-raff would gather in his place: shady-looking faces, black marketeers, who got lit up on ouzo and danced with élan. It's true, mountains don't mix, thought Angela whom necessity had obliged to change clubs, and the only thing she could find was this popular tavern tucked away in the back lanes by the Hippodrome, whose customers included few women except the lively sort or the despairing. And at the beginning Vassilis was constantly objecting to everything, looked at her as if she was a plate of food that he didn't like, and finally told her, "forget the shimmering dresses and all the frou-frou" because what was needed here was a black skirt and a little blouse open at the front; anyway in the end they managed to see eye to eye, for she was from Asia Minor and her lamenting amané songs were sung from the depths of her being. Except that he himself was not from over there like the others – some were from Smyrna and others not – but came from some village in Thessaly. "What unites us are the singing and poverty," he comforted her one evening, when he saw that his manner had made her lose her bearings, and he took her in his arms and smiled at her, and she remembered Michalis and Domna (they'd disappeared from sight, had they separated?) and she smiled bitterly at the fact that everything was once more becoming difficult, that she had to face everything all on her own.

And no one was at hand when the fat man stood in front of her and talked as if they knew each other, he said, "I remember you from Michalis's when you used to live round there" and she searched her memory, in vain though, "I never used to come in or join in the fun" because (and he said it as if he was proud of it) the most he could have done would have been to glue his face to the window and lick his lips; and he explained laughingly – again as if boasting – "I couldn't dance, I would have been afraid that everyone would step on my toes, barefoot as I was" and Angela felt that he must probably be wounded, deeply wounded, inside himself, yet there was no room in her for pity, she felt a kind of loathing for him as if he had just arisen from filth and stank. All the same, she asked, "what's your name?" and he said "Eratos" and, when she looked at him in bewilderment, added as if in mockery "Eratosthenis", for which name his damn godfather was to blame, who had been a judge living in their neighbourhood and since the family could find no one else willing to pay for the christening (and he was already seven years old so that he walked to his christening on his own two feet and all the riff-raff gathered round the font and laughed at him because his little prick was showing a will of its own), so his mother had begged and pleaded – as a favour – and the judge had consented, on condition though that he gave the child his dead brother's name; and they agreed, but they brought him up as "Eratos" and everyone who didn't know the story was puzzled by the name. And Angela murmured, "I've never heard of you" – "you will now," replied the fat man with confidence.

And the next evening he brought along two Germans, "they're friends, they're all right," he reassured them, for it was something unheard of, and they sat and drank for hours until Eratos suddenly got up and said to Vassilis, "play the Minore," now that he was wearing shoes. And Angela felt repelled by his plump hand with which he was fanning himself, and he wore a red ring, suddenly she saw that he was holding a bundle of thousand-drachma notes, then in a flash they were birds winging their way through the tavern and at the side the Germans were guffawing and clapping, then Vassilis whispered, "they're trouble, watch out" and the fat man danced, showing off, as if he thought he was doing something special, but the foreigners didn't understand this at all, as was proved when one of them got up and barged into the middle of the floor and started jumping up and down indecently, and Eratos stopped as if counting but the soldier yelled "tanz" and went on making tasteless leaps until his companion came and dragged him off and the company breathed a sigh of relief. But it didn't end there, "it's one of those evenings," complained Vassilis as he tuned his instrument, tried it out, and told Angela, "you'd best be going now, little one" as if like a hunting dog he could scent something in the air – and she put her coat on, but it was already too late.

For just at that moment two gendarmes appeared and pushed her back inside, as if she was in their way, and Angela felt that invisible currents might now be revealed, maybe mysteries would be solved – or maybe confused even further; for out of the corner of her eye she saw Eratos getting up, turning his back, seeking a way out, but there was only one door and that was blocked, now I'll see your true colours my lad, the singer thought, for all the élan and the wind had gone out of Eratos's sails. And things got worse when a captain of the gendarmerie appeared in the doorway, he was plump and red-faced with sparse fair hair, and he cast an icy look around, then, each word falling like a blow, announced, "we'll check identity cards" – whereupon Eratos sat down again at the table with the Germans. He must certainly have papers, thought Angela, noticing the change in his demeanor, how he was sitting back on his chair, crossing his legs, as if everything was in order now – and he started talking away to the soldiers (in what language though, thought the girl sarcastically), the conversation embellished by gestures and grimaces, all of them on his part, of course, for the Germans merely nodded their heads as if agreeing with what the fat man was saying. And then the captain was standing in front of him, ordering the Greek man, "your papers" seeming not to notice the company he was with; and Eratos hesitated, gave an embarrassed smile, and pulled from his pocket a green paper (and Angela heard it called ausweis), whereupon the other man handed it back and said, "your Greek identity card", and Eratos shrugged his shoulders, for a moment glances were exchanged, and then the captain called – loud enough for everyone to hear – "one day we'll be running into each other again," but the other man smiled idiotically, knowing that this time he was going to get off, and picked up his glass and drank, which was from embarrassment.

Yet even now the trouble wasn't over, for as soon as the gendarmes and their captain had left, Eratos was up again, called to Vassilis, "play us a serviko" so that he could dance, and now he was behaving wildly, just as if he was celebrating some kind of victory, and a couple of people were clapping their hands which got him even more worked up so that he danced in abandon, arms and legs flying, and Angela thought, I can't take any more, I'm dizzy, and opened the door and went out to get some air; the wind outside did indeed restore her, lashing her cheeks and blurring her eyes with coloured circles of light, I must have tears in my eyes, she thought. At that point a broad shadow detached itself from the darkness, stood before her as if saying, look at me, and she heard him ask, "do you know the fat man?" and recognised from the smell of his uniform that it was the captain who was standing in front of her, his face expressionless, almost invisible. "No," she answered faintly, then amended it, "I don't know, we may have lived in the same street once," and she told him what the man had said about the past, about the time when she used to sing at Michalis's; "I don't even know his other name, though," she added, and the captain said, "Tsimonis" and then remained silent as though considering, he must have been calculating and making connections. And it was his last question that worried her, "what was the neighbourhood you lived in?", as if he was delving into her past, "which of all of them?" she attempted to escape, "the one you lived in when the fat man knew you" and Angela felt relief, "by the Depot," she replied with a tremulous smile – and the man turned as if his mission was accomplished and it was time to withdraw, but stood for a second as if in two minds about something, then asked quietly, "what direction are you going in?" – "a little bit beyond Egnatia" – "come along with me," said he, "for these are evil times." And they walked together.

"So now he knows where you live and who you are," Vassilis snapped the following evening when she told him about it, but the girl thought he could have found out anyway, there were much easier ways for him to learn it, however Vassilis had suspicions of his own and gave her a meaningful look, but received the answer, "he didn't even take my hand" – upon which they both fell silent. But as she went up onto the stage the fat man came in, Eratos, waved to her from a distance and then sat down, but he looks as though someone has beaten him up thought Angela, and in a little while they'd begun their first song, "Let's walk on the Acropolis" and acted as if they'd forgotten all about him, at which he sat sullenly brooding over his own worries and ordered retsina – "our pal's lonesome tonight," Vassilis hissed at her through his chords, and launched into wild riffles with the plectrum, "to warm us up," he said, for outside it was bitter, with a dry icy wind that made shoe nails ring out like iron on the cobblestones. Over in the corner someone laughed, like a cock crowing, with other laughs sounding in accompaniment, most of them smothered, then once more the cock, who seemed to be enjoying his own screams of laughter, though they rapidly became irritating; and Vassilis stopped playing his bouzouki in the middle of a song and suddenly everything in the tavern seemed out of tune, and Angela said, "you can give your anger free rein," for there were five of them and miserable specimens at that, though on the other hand you wouldn't have admired Vassilis so much for the strength of his arm as for the skill of his fingers on the plectrum. The laughter had stopped and they started the song again from the beginning, a ballad of yearning from Bournovalia. Eratos had stayed silent throughout, as if drifting among his own preoccupations, which must certainly have been endless and weighty, for he drained his first bottle and then a second one, he seemed even redder in the face now and they noticed him unbutton his collar, from time to time he was casting glances at Angela who thought he seemed to be begging her for something – or expecting something from her – but there's not a scrap of good faith in his whole carcase, she reflected with certainty, no matter how sad he's acting now. Suddenly they heard the cock laughing again, and Vassilis and Angela looked at each other, but before they had time to react the door opened and in came the Germans, Eratos's friends, except that now they were sober and well-clothed, wearing oilskins; and the girl was puzzled since it wasn't raining. They went over to Eratos, said something to him as if accusing him, and he got up, drank one more mouthful of retsina, and followed them out – only just as he was crossing the threshold he turned and looked searchingly at Angela and waved his hand as if in farewell. Beside her Vassilis was complaining on the strings of his bouzouki, Angela teased him, "don't torment it"; the door had closed behind them and not even their footsteps could be heard.

However, there was a lot to be heard the following night. The tavern was abuzz, since bad news travels as fast as lightning, people telling how Eratos had been confined since daybreak in the German dungeons and his friends the soldiers with him, "they were pirates who robbed the poor," said the musicians, this was what they had heard and it might not be the whole truth since they'd heard it from two black marketeers who said, "we've got papers from the Kommandatur" and were despicable creatures. In the end, mixing and matching all the snippets of information and gossip and exaggeration, they discovered that Eratos, along with another man (who had a small boat with an outboard motor), with the two Germans at their side, had been stopping every passing vessel and seizing either their merchandise or their money – it was said that Eratos had been armed and had roughed people up, he'd become the terror of the seas, the bastard; and the victims decided that it was intolerable the way he was snatching the very morsel from their mouths (or their gold sovereigns) and thus went running to the Kommandatur* – or at least those of them who constantly had comings and goings there and had greased the palms of the dragomans at the door – whereupon, it was said, the general was enraged and roared that "the German army are not pirates" and that very same night had sent a patrol boat with five or six heavies armed with machine-guns. People said that they caught the gang just as they were stripping a ketch full of cans of olive oil and that they kicked Eratos till he could no longer stand, the owner of the boat jumped into the sea and disappeared, maybe he had drowned or maybe dived deep and escaped.

"Now they're looking for his friends," said Vassilis, giving Angela a sideways glance, but she said, "I neither know him nor have anything in common with him" though at the same time she was reflecting, I'm always getting mixed up in pitfalls, and she remembered the gendarmerie captain who wouldn't have swallowed the insult, perhaps now he was bursting with spite, because – and this was something they'd heard about too – he would make trouble for people, whether or not they'd done anything, and then you were lucky if you got off. And Angela said, "my stomach aches," and she really was looking as white as a sheet – so they let her leave since they felt sorry for her. She put on her coat hastily and went out of the door frantically, which might have looked strange or suspicious. And as she hurried out, she walked straight into a man wrapped in a dark mackintosh, with a hat whose brim was just above his eyes, who cried to her almost happily, "you're not escaping me this time." And it was Yannis's voice, a little hoarser now but more sure of himself.

---

* I can still see the fat man: he used to have binoculars slung over his shoulder and would go to the theatre, by the White Tower, and ogle the actresses through them. Later, as people said, he would scan the sea through the same binoculars, surveying it like the commanders of warships that he used to see in films. He did other unpalatable things: he'd bring Germans to his house and his sister would dance with them, then withdraw with them into some dark corner. The fat man would come out and stand in the doorway whistling.

Christos

Christos decided then, there is no other way, I'll just have to beg, for things had become unbearably tight, and there were patrols a block further up which five journalists from the Association's offices had happened to run into, they'd sealed off the streets, set up a blockade, from somewhere the growl of a motorcycle was heard, and someone came running and announced, "they're putting them into a black Maria" – but who? – Rodinos didn't wait to find out though, he got a package out of the drawer, "we'll either have to hide it or eat it," he said, as though it was all a joke they were having. And Christos wanted to know, "what are you hiding from us?", because it could have been a transmitter or ammunition, but Rodinos gave him a searching look (perhaps he was thinking, how far can I trust you?) and then said "proclamations" and Christos grabbed them and left; this was in the spring of '44, and he was thinking I was better off at the vineyard, even if he'd had to dig and struggle with the weeds; but anyway, he went down the road fast, thinking, ten more houses and I"ll be there, this was his sudden plan, he'd made the decision and wouldn't go back on it.

Suddenly he remembered the first summer, when the Germans had just entered the city and everyone was saying, "come winter, we'll die," and he thought if I can't count on my mother and my father, what shall I do? And thus he took Dimitris and they set off early in the morning – they took the tram as far as Vardari, "but now," he said "we'll be going on foot," to see what they taught them at the Boy Scouts, and Dimitris asked, "how long will it take?" And it wasn't going to be one hour, nor two either, and they trudged along beside endless orchards, and at about midday Christos said, "time for a rest" and Dimitris was the first to lie down on the grass in the deep shade of an oak tree, by a little stream bed, dry now though; and they opened the bundle tied in a handkerchief that Amalia had prepared for them and found half a loaf of bread and some cheese, two pieces of pie and several small pears – "but what did she keep for the girls?" worried Christos. But they ate and were filled and the father pronounced, "in one hour's time we'll get going again," all around them the earth was gently steaming and from the clearing could be heard conversation, not of humans though, more of birds and cicadas, to which in a short while Christos's snores added a bass note. And Dimitris stayed quite still lest he alarm him or wake him, for he had learnt years ago that his father slept in the daytime so that they all had to walk on tiptoe, speak in low voices, be careful not to slam doors – for he wore himself out at night working; and looking at his father as he slept, dark and thinner, his hair completely white by now, his nose a bit longer than it used to be, Dimitris remembered how he had seen him all of a sudden when he had come back after the retreat, his head bare, his buttons missing, but laughing, and he'd asked, "where's your mother?" and they'd let him sleep for three days and two nights, for he'd been walking for eighteen days on end, coming from Thebes to Thessaloniki, and he said, "praise the Lord" they hadn't been killed by the stukas, but also that they hadn't been taken prisoner, for the Germans were moving south as if hell-bent. One night, when they'd all been gathered together and Pavlakis had come round and they were having a drink or two, his father had roared, "they sold us out" and the other man had said, "our mother country, our mother country" and Christos had exploded, "what are you jabbering on about?" he said, "from the moment when they put us aboard ship in the harbour, they knew full well that everything was lost" – "you can't know that," Pavlakis dared to say, "man, I'm telling you, from the moment they weighed anchor they were dumping the cooking cauldrons into the sea," and he'd wanted to jump into the sea too, he revealed to them, "only I felt bad about the uniform," he added. And Pavlakis had taken on an air of forebearance, as if saying, if you knew the things that I know, higher secrets, he implied, things confided only to a few – and Christos swore again, "bloody freemasons", but the other man only laughed somewhere in his throat, as if giving a dry cough.

And now he arrived at the door and felt out of breath, for a moment he was aware of a pain in his left arm, he was holding the package under his right arm; he went in and closed the door carefully behind him, waiting till he heard the click of the lock. It was on the first floor, outside was a sign saying "New Europe", the place was deserted at this time of day, this he knew since from time to time he used to come here, he went through the main room with the portrait of Adolf in profile as a Field Marshal on the wall, next door was the office of the editor, Papastratigakis, and Christos said, "good morning" and stood there. The other man raised his head from his papers and looked at him through his spectacles, the problem with his eyesight must be getting worse, reflected Christos, because his lenses were getting thicker and thicker so that by now they almost seemed to deform him, "what's new?" asked the editor, and they started the usual sort of exchange, at one moment the man frowned as if remembering something, "they were cursing me from London again yesterday," to which Christos made no reply, "did you hear it?" asked the other and took off his glasses, rubbing his eyes as if they were itching, "they don't let us have a wireless," stammered Christos, but the other man smiled as if saying, tell me another. Christos remained without expression, though what he was thinking and then added was "don't pay any attention to them," at which point the other man said, "sit down, don't keep standing there." Outside the sun was shining and behind the window panes the tallest branch of the acacia was green, but within the atmosphere was foul, tobacco smoke and old furniture creating an unbearable stench, maybe he never lets anyone in, thought Christos, but he sat down in the armchair and listened, "they attacked the security battalions and the result will be a disaster," Papastratigakis said, without specifying who, as if they both knew and it was superfluous, and Christos felt worried, he ought to say something, "they'll get us all burnt, the bastards," he broke out, as convincingly as he could, and the old man only nodded his head, quite white now and going thin on top, he rubbed his eyes once more and showed signs that he wished to be left on his own, for he took up his pen and dipped it in the inkwell, and Christos finally plucked up his courage, "could you look after this package for me?" he asked, "it's some of my savings," and the other man reached out his hand, took the package and buried it in his drawer, "don't worry about it" was all he said.

When they reached the dry riverbed, just outside the village, "we're among our own people," he told Dimitris; but he himself (as he remembered) had a private fear of his own about how meanly the old man would be obliged to behave under his mother's disapproval. Thus it was a relief when they found only his father, he hasn't aged, he thought as he saw him, dark and rosy-cheeked – before his mother and brother had time to arrive he told his father that he'd come to buy wheat, "people will be dying when winter arrives" and his father said, "don't worry" and hugged Dimitris and called him "Mitsos" and "well, Mitsos" and Christos and his son exchanged glances and the smiles in their eyes were false. The sun had set and the sky in the west was aflame by the time his mother and brother arrived and kissed them and set out food for them to eat, and the younger brother said, "they've remembered us in the city" for people were now coming from Salonika to buy provisions – "but what good are all your papers to you now?" grumbled his mother who could smell that money was a thing of the past. At one point she asked Dimitris, "how is your mother?" and Christos replied, "fighting" which was no lie, "that is the duty of all good women," his mother pronounced, whereupon they fell silent as if there was nothing left to say. And after a while the old man harnessed the horse to the cart, "I was just saying that I'd have to go down to the city," he said, and explained, "we need some tools"; and he loaded two sacks of wheat onto the cart, and at the last minute Christos's mother brought her own sack as well, "I've filled it with beans," and then she kissed her son, and Dimitris, "kiss the girls for me," she said, then called, "take care" as they moved away, and looking back they could see his brother standing in the background, his hands tensed in his pockets, until they passed the bend in the dirt track and could see them no longer.

But Christos was always in agony, and even more so when he saw the Germans coming in, there were three of them, all well-built, and they stood at attention and saluted, with the interpreter behind them, Papastratigakis, however, said, "leave us, if you please," since he spoke their language like a German, and in a little while they were talking, then smiling, at one point one of them looked at Christos, but Papastratigakis got out a packet of cigarettes and offered them, only one of the men took a cigarette, but didn't light it, instead he got out his own packet and held it out to Christos, "bitte," he said without smiling, and Christos took a cigarette but also refrained from lighting it, "danke schön", he murmured; and then they saluted, said "Heil Hitler" and left, and it was over. Papastratigakis said nothing for a while, he seemed to be thinking of something in the past, and in the end asked, "where are you now?" and Christos said, "I'm not working for any paper" – "I don't have a position either," said the other, and it was as if he'd said: for you. Christos bowed his head and an uncomfortable silence fell, then "do you want to take your package?" the old man asked suddenly, he had got it out and was weighing it in his hand, "take it," he said "but don't do it again." Christos thanked him and left as if ashamed, you can't fool him he was thinking, it was noon by now and hot, the sun was burning, and he walked uphill without hurrying, after a little he passed Ermou Street and went to the offices, but everyone had already left and had locked up, one more problem said Christos to himself, and then "fuck it" in irritation, and he reflected, they'll need these, I could leave them on the doorstep, but he didn't have the heart to do it; have I made so much effort all in vain? he wondered and felt angered.

"Difficult times for all of us," his father said. He was sitting with Christos up at the front of the cart, they'd put the boy in the back beside the sacks, but night had already fallen and the old man said, "better take precautions" for he had a certain cunning of his own, embroidered over the years by past episodes and experiences, and thus he stopped the horse, got down, jumped into the adjacent vineyard and started cutting – "people do the same to me," he said in excuse, bringing several bunches of grapes and even more branches and leaves and piling them on until the sacks didn't show at all, "it's better this way," he said once more, and neither of them offered any objection, he was on his own territory, peasant ways. And thus they set off on the road again, bouncing up and down, trees and stars dancing, a little way further on lay the highway and they could hear the foreigners' cars, "I know of another track," said the old man, which proved to be full of potholes, pitch dark, neither man nor beast to be seen, "it's a lonely road but safer," he reassured them, at one point he laughed, "are you awake, Mitsos?" and he looked back at Dimitris, who replied, "I'm not asleep" at which they all laughed, they passed over a bridge beneath which the frogs were raising their jubilant cacophony, then turned onto another dirt track, "when we reach the curve we'll be able to see your lights" and he meant the lights of Thessaloniki, however for the moment they were still going along in the dark, with only the stars to provide comfort in these lonely parts. And thus they were all startled when they heard voices and the creak of wheels and after a moment saw two large carts loaded to the brim coming through the fields, whereupon the old man slowed down, said, "let them pass us" and the two carts pulled in front of them, bouncing along in a hurry with their loads shaking up and down. "Time for a cigarette break," said his father, stopping the cart, he seemed to be preoccupied and assessing something, "do you know them?" asked Christos – "no," replied his father, "they're not from anywhere round here"; and he explained that in summer the area swarmed with merchants and petty tradesmen – "they'll strip us all bare, both you and us," he muttered. And it was better to wait and smoke their cigarettes, "better keep a distance from them," he declared, for he knew nothing about them or where they came from – and in the end they threw away their butts and the cart set off again, "right, Mitsos," said the old man as if he felt he had to say something to the boy since they were all three of them together; in front of them in the darkness they could hear the carts groaning, for "they've overloaded them," as the old man said. And just as he said, "we're arriving at the curve," and the sky did indeed seem lighter in that direction, they had a new encounter, they saw a shadow emerge from the vines by the road and call "halt" and they halted, and when the man had come up to the cart he asked, "where are you going?" and Christos's father answered, "to Thessaloniki, I've got my son and my grandson with me," and at that point the man put on a uniform cap which it seems he had been concealing, and Christos said to himself, but why? However, it wasn't his business to ask questions but the other man's, who examined them and asked, "what have you got in the cart?" and

Christos felt his father's hand restraining him, as if saying let me handle this, "some grapes and a little sack of beans," he said humbly, and as the man was examining them they saw a star, and another, shining on his shoulders in the dark. But the policeman was suspicious and started searching the cart, and said "damnation" when he pricked his hand on something, but in the end he found the wheat and triumphed, "black market," he hissed at them, and ordered them "straight to the police station", and Christos was outraged and asked, "what about the two carts in front, didn't you see them?" and the other man looked at him spitefully, he appeared to be short and thin, aged about thirty or thirty-five, and he ordered "to the police station" and felt for something in his back pocket, if only I'd had you in Asia Minor, you bastard, thought Christos and rose, but he felt his father holding him down again. And they had no choice but to follow the man and in an hour they arrived at the police station.

It pained him to think of these things, even though they now seemed far distant, in those days they knew terrors like those you might feel if pushed and jostled in some dark unknown forest, especially that year, when so much blood was spilt for nothing, when people were being killed in the streets, security gangs and members of EPON, and you never knew what each dawn would bring. It all pained him as he stood at the top of the stairs, outside the Association's door, holding the bundle, "I go fetching it just as if it was a packet of sweets," he said to himself out loud, and instantly decided it was time to have done with it, so he made his way silently down the stairs, stood at the door to the basement; in the past there had been a heap of coal here and now all was pitch darkness, he caught a slight stink of piss, felt his way in and came to the wall, high up was a crevice and he left the package here, only he was disgusted when he felt cobwebs brush against his face, and his back started to itch, and he stumbled out and shook himself, for he was covered with dust, his sleeves, his trousers.

They kept them at the police station till past midnight and a gendarme got up from his bed so that Dimitris could lie down; Christos and his father stood in a corner and waited, at their feet the sacks which seemed to be becoming heavier and heavier as each hour passed, in spite of the fact that the sergeant asked at one point, "who do these little sacks belong to?" and the captain gave them a dirty look. The man was just plain twisted, and in a little while they got proof that no good could be expected from him, for a taxi passed full of drunken passengers singing and laughing, and the policeman got into a fury and ordered the taxi to stop, whereupon from within it a voice said, "fuck off"; after which the policeman and the gendarmes fell on its occupants and arrested them,* dragged them into the police station and started hitting them wherever they could get their blows in – Dimitris woke up in alarm, saw two of them holding a man by his arms (and he like an untamed beast and drunk) while the policeman punched him repeatedly in the stomach, and was sickened. In the end the drunks were all lying on the floor groaning, which seemed to satisfy the policeman who had reduced them to it, after a bit they called Christos and asked him whether he was a farmer, to which he replied "a journalist" – well, they could take their sacks and leave. But of course they had to wait till dawn, since at night there was a curfew and everything was forbidden (what about drunkenness and beatings up, wondered Dimitris), and indeed they set off the minute dawn came, feeling the dew chilly on their spines, because "they might change their minds," as the old man said. And as they turned the corner into their own street they saw Amalia in her night clothes, weeping, "I thought you'd all been killed or arrested," she said, but the old man put his finger to his lips and advised, "let's go inside."

This was their first and last trip to the village and Christos said, "we've got something to live on for a while," not only wheat but hope too, though during the following three years more things were to happen, much worse things. Now Christos dusted himself down again as he got near home, he didn't want Amalia to learn anything about his exploits; he would keep them all to himself, lest she became frightened and angry. However, just as he turned the corner he seemed to hear screaming and crying, and he won-

---

* One day with my father we met the sergeant of the gendarmerie who had helped us; it was just before the Liberation and he said, "bad news, we're destroying each other," and as we parted had a sudden thought, "do you remember the man who arrested you?" – "the thin one, the policeman?" asked my father, and yes, said the other, "the guerrillas killed him somewhere in the villages of Grevena." And it was as if he was saying that he'd expected it, the man was pig-headed and had it coming to him.

dered, who have they killed now? And he saw all the neighbouring women coming and going to the house next door to his own, and he heard crying again, at their door Alcmene was standing alone and impassive, "what's happened?" he asked her – "the Germans have executed Eratos," she murmured, not showing what she felt, whether she was grieving at the fact that they'd taken thirty men from the Eftapyrgo prison and put them up against the wall, because a German had been found murdered. And Christos said, "the Tsimonis family were expecting it from another quarter," for they had long had unsettled accounts with the police. And all afternoon the crying continued, and late into the night, and the women ran to comfort the family as best they could, for they hadn't even been given the dead man's body – all had been buried in a common grave.

Yannis

This was what he always believed, that nothing escaped him, nothing that he'd set his heart on, or his mind, or his stubborn determination, with the passing years experience had ripened within him, and confidence, and the hoarse voice in which he drawled like a spiv, someone of the streets, all prejudices left behind in the past. And Angela said, "quite the contrary", in other words that she was not intending to escape, maybe she had been seeking him without knowing it, although in fact she could always find him – at that point a sudden gust of wind blew and she felt its chill, "let's go and hide somewhere," he whispered to her and unbuttoned the front of his mackintosh to shelter her, "come inside, like in the old days," and Angela might have said like when? For in those days he had never been so tender, nor so quick to reach the point either, but all the same she burrowed against his body and smelt his scent, his tobacco. And thus they walked along awkwardly, their legs and their very breath seeming entangled, and they both burst out laughing, and Angela said, "you've made me forget everything," meaning maybe Tsimonis or the policeman, or maybe their own past history, "God must have sent you," to which Yannis suggested "or the devil" – more laughter.

And suddenly he felt something like kisses on his forehead, something inexplicable touching him, but then a moment later he felt it on his cheek and then in the corner of his eye, blurring his vision, and he said, "it's beginning to rain" and Angela burrowed deeper for protection, but when he looked up he saw that the night was inundated with white butterflies which were settling even on his eyelashes, and "it's snowing," he announced to her, in case she might burrow even deeper. She, though, jumped out of his shelter as if someone had given her a toy, cried, "oh, how lovely," so that Yannis told her, "you're still my little Angela" because everyone now called her Violetta, and she was not afraid of the snowflakes but stretched out her hand to catch them, it was deep darkness, the worn-out asphalt of the road dry, and Yannis's conclusion was "it will settle", just beyond them stood three trees, bare of leaves now and arid, like eerie remnants of nature, but they walked on through this landscape without fear, at one point they encountered some foreign soldiers, yet neither side paid any heed to the other. The snowflakes were falling thicker by now, a world of whiteness, but he begged her, "come on, let's not get cold" and he opened his coat once more, and Angela burrowed in again and said, "it's so beautiful," and Yannis felt that what was beautiful was the way she was snuggling in to his armpit in search of warmth. And he asked her, "do you still live in the same house?", meaning the attic behind Acheiropoieto in the little cul de sac, but she answered, "it's freezing" and at that moment a sharp demon gust of wind blew, making him gasp and filling his eyes with snow and Angela said, "look how it's decorating you" – and they came even closer.

In the end they walked on past the Tower and the park seemed wild in the darkness, they felt the wind lashing them, sending the snow down thick and fast, stinging their eyes, covering their lapels and shoulders, and Angela asked him, "where are you taking me?" for his own house didn't lie in this direction either, they'd left it behind them, its sole occupant tonight being his eldest sister who had become rather odd, so that Yannis used to wonder, when will I find someone to take her off my hands, for his own shoulders, his own patience, could no longer bear the burden, regardless of how sorry for her he felt. And when they had both become thoroughly white, specially him – his hat, his chest – he announced to her, "we've arrived," they were in a little street unknown to Angela, small, humble houses all around, and Yannis told her, "this is my hiding place" because he always lived in two places, but Angela amended, "it must be your little nest," probably well known to birds of a female variety. Except that she was wrong, for as they pushed open the gate they entered a large courtyard with the house standing at the back, and she couldn't exactly have called it a one-storey house nor even a tall two-storey house, for it seemed to have sunk so that half of it was plunged in the ground with the other half rearing above, it had a curious little staircase leading upwards, everything hidden in a tangle of honeysuckle now strangely white. Below the door downstairs light showed, and voices could be heard, so that Angela concluded, "the little nest must be upstairs" – and they both laughed.

However they didn't manage to get upstairs, for the door on the ground floor opened and a little man was standing before them, asking, "is it you, Yannis?" He stood there and said in tones of complaint "you don't deign to come and see us these days," whereupon Yannis whispered to her, "we'll just go in for a minute or two, then we'll leave," and a moment later they were inside the downstairs room which smelled of cooking and tobacco smoke. And six people were gathered there, the little man who'd come out to receive them and his wife, a short bald man, a little girl and two other men, of the popular class, who smiled at them and said "good evening", and Angela thought, now they'll be mocking us in their own minds, but they made room for them on a low divan and said, "make yourselves comfortable," the woman was smiling ceaselessly, her hair was coming undone, she showed them her hands greasy from cooking, in explanation of why she wasn't doing her hair, pinning it back up. And they sat down just as they were, in their coats, as if to say we'll only stay a short while for we have other things to do, and Angela was tormenting herself with the question where've I met this man here, the little man, but in the end he made a small skip which gave him away, and she said, "I remember you singing" and that whole dreadful performance, one night at Michalis's, with Yannis and his sisters – "I remember you," she said again, except that now he had shrunk, he looked like half his former self, his trousers kept slipping down and he was constantly pulling them up. And very soon hors d'oeuvres and glasses were placed before them, and the little man said, "pot luck", their meagre rations which in fact weren't meagre at all but consisted of meat and fish and good wine, and Yannis whispered, "we mustn't give offence" so they set to and ate and drank – and the woman of the house said, "you'll get too hot," for the stove was crammed with planks and brushwood, and thus they took off their coats and felt more comfortable. And then it was time to put the gramophone on, and they played popular rebetika songs, and the man of the house got up and danced, and plates came and went and Angela thought what liberality, and at that point people started clapping their hands, then someone knocked on the door and a woman came in, about forty but fresh and lively, and they all cried, "well, Andriana, welcome" and moved up to make room for her, and she grabbed a glass at once.

And as the time went by both the fun and the faces blazed and Andriana's dress had come open at the front revealing her opulent white breasts, and the fat man exclaimed, "if only I could just lie down and drift off" and everyone burst into fits of laughter, and they said to Yannis, "forgive our vulgar ways" at which he raised his glass, just like a lordling and said, "it makes me glad that you are enjoying yourselves," but the bottles and the demijohns were empty and they sent the girl next door, "these ones are finished," they said, "fill them up again" for next door was a tavern, but she said, "it will be shut by now" and they looked at the clock and it was almost midnight, and Yannis and Angela looked at each other as if saying it's our time now, then one of the men took hold of the bottles and disappeared, and when he came back they saw that he was white all over but that the bottles had been refilled and everyone cheered, and suddenly the fat man got up his courage and said, "will you sing for us, sister" and they clapped as if saying to her come on, and Yannis made a sign which meant yes, and she began singing "Yelekaki" and the little man got up and said, "I'll sing an accompaniment" and they were making merry, and Angela saw that Andriana was leaning towards the fat man and that he had undone his flies and was scratching himself, at which Yannis called to him, "the lice drive you mad" – and what he said was no lie.*

---

* During that tragic winter of 1941-42, when the grip of hunger was being felt, the upper classes mingled with the poor, especially if the latter were risking their necks and bringing food from their villages or islands. This made Mitsos T. bold, so that he would undo the flies of his trousers and scratch himself ostentatiously in front of ladies – whether he had lice or not. However, it seems this became a bad habit of his. In 1952 he was arrested for flashing in the street, by which time the black market, and all its great moments, had become a thing of the past and order had been restored.

As soon as the second song was over she said, "that's enough, we don't want to wake up the whole neighbourhood," and she wondered about the company – or the gang – since putting two and two together she realised that they were not doing so badly out of trade, that they were sailing south in their caiques, bringing olive oil back, and transporting people's wheat out in return, and the fat man was a butcher who would slaughter whatever people brought him. But on their last trip they'd had trouble with the stormy seas, had come ashore at some lonely spot where they'd hidden but had been devoured by lice – at this point Angela thought we'd better leave, she felt an itch somewhere on her side and said to herself that would be a joke, however she could see Andriana roaring with laughter and constantly rubbing up against the fat man, who was now scratching himself shamelessly, he'd unbuttoned his shirt and his hand was delving deep inside it voluptuously, his eyes closed as if in a dream – their little girl had slumped over and was smiling in her sleep.

However, they confessed that she wasn't their own (and it's true her hair was pure blonde and they were dark), that they'd found her starving in the street somewhere and had taken her with them, for they didn't have any child of their own, and she wasn't from this city but from the villages of Karatzova. "One afternoon we were on our way back from the fields," the singer recounted, "and we saw her running up behind us, she said she'd lost her mother, that she'd left for the city, we told her she ought to go back to whoever she lived with, however she lived, and she stopped following us for a while, but just as it was getting dark we saw her running up behind us again, take me to find my mother she begged, and in the end we felt sorry for her," she had a corner to sleep in here, and a plate of food, and Angela reflected, maybe she'll be preserved from all the Eugenioses of the world, and she turned, looked at Yannis. And she asked him, "who puts up the money?", then again as his eyes scrutinised her, "who gives the money for trading?", and he said, "we are a company" which the girl had realised, and Yannis added, "with a view to profit" quietly. But Andriana was pulling her by the arm, "let's dance," she proposed, and the gramophone was playing a tune that they knew, but Angela didn't budge, by now the fat man had jumped up and began to dance opposite Andriana, both of them swaying, their eyes flashing as they gazed at each other, and the butcher burst out excitedly, "let's set the place on fire" and people said, "we've run out of wine" whereupon the woman ran off and fetched a bottle, "grape spirit from the village", she said, and it caught in their throats and everyone began coughing; nothing could stop Andriana though ...

It must have been almost dawn when Yannis and Angela came out and stumbled up the outside staircase; in the pure white night a greyish light fell on them from somewhere. Behind them came the singer bearing a brazier of glowing charcoal, "you'll freeze to death up there, Mr. Yannis," he murmured, but Yannis said, "bring it here," took it from him, hurried up the stairs with it and unlocked the door – a little oil lamp was burning somewhere and casting its light on the sole room, which was neat and orderly, with heavy curtains and rugs, thick blankets on the bed – and Angela said to herself they look after him, and she could smell lavender, his very own scent; in the end they put the brazier near them and lay down. "I'm not going to ask you anything," he declared, and she had already fitted herself into his embrace, "nor me you," she agreed, unable to see him now but only to smell him, for she was deep and snug beneath the bedclothes, and she felt the palms of his hands on her spine, he has claws that can hurt, she thought, and thus burrowed even deeper into his flesh, as if we inhabit the same skin she thought, and she grasped the back of his neck, "I am yearning for you inside me," she moaned, but just then footsteps came running up the stairs and in the yard someone was calling and crying, "come back down, Andriana," the fat man must have been drunk, and Angela was scared, "do you think they're going to come up here?" but Yannis was already plunged deep, and she heard his voice crying wildly, "take a knife, kill me" and the very sheets seemed to be weeping, and she pulled him to her with force, "we are one forever," she cried. In the end they heard the steps going back down, Yannis was lying on his back and the oil lamp illuminated the whiteness of his chest and on it a tiny shining point, his cross, thought Angela.

And it was midday when they came down the stairs, they saw the fat man stripped half-naked in the courtyard, washing; the snow lay deep and everything was still, "they've all been devoured by the lice," said Yannis, and Angela remembered their own lice, when they'd been refugees living in huts, in '23 and later, how they used to boil their clothes in the copper and drench their hair with petrol, all the hairy parts of their bodies in fact, and the old women used to tell them not to be ashamed, that it was something that had to be done. But the butcher was washing in the snow, as if punishing his body, by now bright red; as Yannis and Angela approached he said, "now everything has been sorted out," but they didn't understand what he meant, and they stood at the door as if waiting, whereupon the little girl came out and wailed, "they couldn't find her" – and Yannis got a million drachmas out of his pocket and gave them to the child, "here," he said, "get whatever you like" and the girl ran back into the house, shouting and laughing, a moment later the singer came out and said, "she doesn't lack anything, boss" but Angela said, "except her mother", at which the man admitted, "she's dead, only we don't tell the child," and then Yannis embraced him and took him a little further off and they began to talk, that is to say Yannis began to speak, and the other man listened with his head bowed, or nodded from time to time. And Angela thought he's their leader, and didn't know whether to admire him or feel sorry for him, as she looked at him with his mackintosh tightly belted and his hat pulled down over his brow she wondered what is it that he's seeking here, since he doesn't lack the means to live. And when they came out into the street – they'd reached the edge of the park and three boys were throwing snowballs at them – she asked him about the factory, but he replied, as if evasively, "I've set up another business now" without adding anything further, and Angela thought maybe black market or worse, for word had got about that various rich people were doing well, had got permits from the Kommandatur or had taken over whole fortunes from the Jews, whose cellars, as people said, were treasure houses, who were all gone now, for whom many were grieving.

And in the end sparse flakes began to float in the air and he said to her, "we are starting over from the beginning again" – "what do you mean?" she asked, and his eyes smiled at her from beneath his trilby but he said not a word, only took her in his arms, and they stood there like two dark figures in a white landscape, then set off again, each one to his own separate house – to face another day. However, their separation lasted only until that evening, when the door opened and in came Yannis and he didn't leave; and Vassilis said, "he's another character, he is" and Angela tormented herself puzzling where Vassilis could have known him from, maybe she'd noticed that he was breathing as if scornfully, as if jealous, and his feelings found their outlet on his instrument.

The Middle Ages – 6

So Christoforos was not the man of the sword, of killings, burnings. The next day at dawn, running and leaping, panting and almost sobbing, he climbed from the seashore to the colonel's house, and stopped at the door, beneath the ivy, and saw Clytemnestra there, lost in her thoughts, with a carafe of ouzo beside her, her hair dishevelled, unrecognisable, strange, and the women of the neighbourhood said, "someone was screaming in the night," and then a crowd gathered and amongst them was a lad in a white shirt who, they said, had run up the steps like a madman, and then leaped down them again and disappeared, shouting "follow me." And at that point they turned and looked at Christoforos, "he was about your age, about your height" and they gave him another searching look but said nothing more, they withdrew into the corner and watched him steadily, whereupon he asked, "did you notice whether he had one ear or two?", but the old women remained silent, "I haven't got any other sins around my neck," he said, and he was meaning his lost ear and how he had requited it. And the man who was the first to step out of rank, shouting, "you gave us your word that you would deal with us honourably and nobly," demanded that Christoforos be his judge, for "you are praised as a just and good man," he told him, and then they were assured that Christoforos had not given the order to break them up, and the first man took the ring from his finger and said, "take it, you are worthy of it," it was a heavy silver ring with simple, sure patterns on it, "it is my seal," said he, "with it I buy and sell, with it I marry and put asunder," and Christoforos turned and said, "to whom should I give it?", it would have to be a man, though, with thick fingers and a hand as weighty as iron, and he turned round once more and gave it back, "it does not," he said, "fit any of us" – and he tightened his lips, "we would do better to go to the judges." And the man smiled as if ironically, this is your shortcoming, he was saying to himself, the fact that you do not have a hand of iron, no matter that you are just, you fear lest it should be said that you were high-handed and behaved like a leader. And then they summoned the man of whom it was said that he only knew sad songs, they requested him to set out and come to them, to see who it was that had first taken the decision to torture his boy, but he sent back the message, "I cannot remember, I have exhausted myself trying to forget, at night I pace up and down in the yard, it is only two or three steps wide, it is where we brought him up, once he climbed out through the fence and disappeared, people told me if you want to find him go and ask the Jews, for it is they who steal Christian children, grandmother crossed herself and said we should not even speak of such things, because the weight of our sins will smother us, when we went to war I had a little Jew marching alongside me, one day he put down his weapon and his knapsack and climbed a tree, come down, the others shouted at him, but he laughed and started pelting them with damsons, but then they fired off a volley from over on the other side, the bullets caught him in the chest, he fell to the ground and suffered and clutched himself and then died, I cannot remember these things without pain." And then he made them all come out of the room and stand in a line, "tell us who it was that killed your son," and they were all standing there looking white round the gills, was it perhaps me? each man was thinking, "it was all of them," he cried – "but sometime we must put an end to all this, perhaps when all of us are dead and gone new people will arise who will not remember any of these things, perhaps then the killings will stop." So they let the man leave, mumbling to himself, and Christoforos ordered, "better lock them up in the back cellar and call the judges." The next day, as he entered the church, he felt himself enveloped in porphyry and gold, a world of candles and icons, a sea of hair and shoulders, and there in the midst of all the icons the bishop in his simple attire stood out, "it is not the proper time now," said he "for ornate decoration" and the humble bowed their heads and wondered whether all his gold and his valuables had been stolen from him, and then Christoforos remembered how when he was a child he had loved the chanting, the hymns, and there was a moment of silence, then from the back of the women's part of the church came a triumphant "in the name of the All-Holy Virgin, the Victorious General, the Ransomer from all terrors", at the Good Friday procession two years ago he had stood with his friends, in the middle of the road, and the choir boys carrying the poles bearing images of the cherubim are standing there, and the people like a river of lighted candles and Christoforos comes forward to speak to them at which the priests rise up in fury, "you are disturbing the order of things," they cry, but the boys think the opposite is true, as the "Bride unwedded" comes to an end, the whole congregation kneels and the only people still standing are the bishop and Christoforos, who is lost in his thoughts, and everyone stares at him disapprovingly, he leaves then as if offended, says to himself that is the last time I go to church, and makes his way up the lane towards Irene's house, "I need some peace," he complains to her, at which the woman turns back the sheets and "lie down," she says, "and I'll sing you a lullaby," and when he next remembers to turn over in bed the gold and the porphyry are lower in the sky, from far off comes the chanting, and people are suffocating in the smoke of the candles and the incense, then they all fade, as if creation had been emptied of its beings, no sound or colour left, as if mankind had cast away his weapons, his instruments, to float on a fair wind over chaos, there where dreams appear and speak, it tells him I am the dream and I was born in Padua my noble blood is in peril at this very moment through having become involved in a game that will be to my detriment it resembles a huge kite made of pale blue and deep red and green paper and you cannot tell who is holding it or who guiding it only it becomes entangled round my body as if strangling me and then I say if only I could get up to find where the end of the string is but the kite seems enormous it fills the courtyard the statues the gardens and I have lost hold of the string once more and we are travelling on a mediaeval ship, those were times full of charm and once our teacher told us that Greek ships used to bring silk and glass and silver, that they carried with them ideas of democracy, but then the ship too disappears and my mouth is flooded with a strange taste, in my mouth

I hold a rose and somewhere torrents of rain are inexplicably falling, it is strange to stand holding flowers in your mouth, but who is it that is saying all this? All around me the world is deserted a single person plays and a strange sound is heard in this place but at the same time there is nothing but boundless emptiness only one person is playing and in his mouth a rose and he stands motionless and says perhaps eternity is like this the man turned to stone the flower motionless and everlasting and a kite hanging waiting in readiness like a threat from a game that must not be spoiled and thus the years pass without nights without suns, and at some point, in an unsuspecting moment, his eyes open and Irene's mouth, open and deep porphyry in colour, is kissing him and caressing him with her lips, "what tales," she says "you have been telling me," and among the hairs on her head are five or ten white threads, and he thinks they come from experience and suffering, and then the noble from Padua imagines that he is walking in his garden in which the shrubs and climbing plants might have been left over from some fairy tale, princes bewitched in punishment and princesses and the day may come when their humanity will be restored and then they will confess that it would have been better to go on living in the fairy tale for all eternity and never be parted and he is at the foot of the rosebush kissing her in veneration where no words or oaths are needed and the noble says to himself how much I would like to lie here and have the garden creep over me and obliterate me but I do not recall ever having seen such a picture gardens everywhere are orderly and geometric, and at that moment the electric light goes on and Irene's mouth is against his eyelids, "my boy, you are wandering and talking wildly," she says and he thinks of getting up and raises his head, but Irene strokes his hair and tells him, "stay, it is not yet dawn" – "did night fall while I was here?" he asks in terror, and then she reveals to him that two days and nights have passed while he lay plunged in his own world and talking wildly, "there are a thousand things that bind me to this world which I can in no way deny," he complained, "we should have let the matter be finished by the judges," he now thought, Theologos the fanatical would be reaping his harvest, "if I had a horse, I would go to the prison," he said, up there in the upper town where he had left his home behind him, had forgotten his wife and children, and "once, when I went to see them, they offered me figs and bread and served me, my sons had grown tall like willows, I asked them what they would like me to bring them, but they withdrew into the corner and only stared at me." And he felt now that he was unimaginably poor, with no work, no ship, and he thought he should search for and get out the clothes that he wore on high days and holy days, "I am not with anyone or on anyone's side." He waited until the day dawned, then put on his clothes, his bandolier, and set off on his way.

Angel

But it was still dark and the house was silent. Thus when they heard the thundering they were startled, disturbed by the sharp and imperious raps on the door, reluctant though to open it, and Angel thought it's the army and a cold sweat broke out on him, it's all up, he thought, they've found out about us, and he jumped up and ran to the kitchen, he remembered the tree, his secret hiding place, which he might have abandoned years ago but which all the same he always kept in mind (specially when he was frightened), and he said to himself I've got a last refuge. But he bumped into his grandmother, a pale vision in the darkness, who cried to him in puzzled uncertainty, "they're knocking on our door," and this was indeed something inexplicable to her, who crossed herself regularly, and then they heard army boots running backwards and forwards in their yard and Angel felt that they were being surrounded – maybe their end was at hand. And the knocking was heard once more on the door, even louder, and a voice ordered, "open up," so Stratis went in his pyjamas and pulled back the bolt and unlocked it, and there stood the captain of the gendarmerie with his men behind him; there must have been a lot of them, for coughing and talking could be heard at the outside gate. "We are searching," he said, "for Efstratios Psarelis," and Stratis said, "that's me – what's up?" The other man had entered the living room and was looking all around it, in a moment three of his men followed him in and suddenly the room was full of pistols and belts, "you'll have to get dressed and come with us," ordered the captain, at which the whole family was bewildered (and his sister had stood up and was trembling in her nightdress), but he bowed his head and said, "all right" and went towards his room to get dressed – it must have been about three in the morning. And two gendarmes went with him who, as Angel saw when he bent down to look, started searching through the clothes, the drawers; he thought, I don't understand, for he'd been afraid about his own affairs, he had been almost sure that Dimitris or Alcmene had grassed on him. However, things were turning out differently, some murky business seemed to be afoot, for he had always thought of his uncle as a peaceful fun-loving man never involved in any illegalities or trouble – and Angel once more thought to himself it's odd, as he saw his uncle putting on his shoes and leaving the house white-faced, with Myrsine crying by then, begging, "don't take him from me" and other such foolishness, for she hadn't grasped that when gendarmes come knocking on your door at that hour of the night they are not about to do you any favours or let you off. And the captain shouted, "we've had enough, old woman, shut up that snivelling" and only then did her son speak, hissing, "you ought to show some respect for a mother's agony" but the other man didn't bother to answer, only one of the gendarmes said, "you can thank your lucky stars that it's us."

And they were indeed lucky for, as they learnt the next day at noon, that very same night the Kalamaria quarter had good cause to groan, for the battalions had descended on them, pulled people out of their houses and killed them; and among the dead were a couple whose children, four of them, were now orphaned, and the next day Angel said, "it was the mother and father of Mavrochliatis" who once upon a time used to go with him to EON and who was always asking, "when are they going to give us a uniform?" since his trousers were always full of holes and darns. And the neighbours told them that they really had been lucky, but Myrsine wept and couldn't be consoled and said, "why did they take him?" and asked, "what does EAM mean?", are its members robbers or guerrillas, for word went about that along with Stratis they had picked up five other men from the Works, and the mother broke out again, "they've all of them spent time on the islands," in exile – while her own son used to stay out till dawn at clubs and dance halls – and one of her sons-in-law answered, "just be thankful that the battalions had work elsewhere" whereupon Myrsine got in a temper and accused him of always saying nasty things to her, "I'm speaking the truth," he said, so he must have known something which he'd been keeping silent about.

And Angel thought, yes, I was lucky, for what he'd been fearing was something different; when the gendarmes had left with his uncle he went to the lavatory to have a piss, but he felt as if his cock had been cut off, it felt burning, shrinking, and the piss wouldn't flow – luckily no one cared too much right then, for he came out and, just when he wasn't expecting it, when he'd come into the living room and was standing there, he felt wet, realised he was wetting himself, and Niki screamed, "you dirty pig" and his grandmother cried and looked at him. But he was consoled by the sweet relief that it wasn't him the gendarmes had dragged off – something he had feared and still feared, for Alcmene had threatened, "mad dogs have to be drowned," and Angel wondered, "why did I get mixed up in it?" For he was meeting Dimitris constantly and one night – unexpectedly – Alcmene had turned up and they reassured him, "we're in this together," meaning we're all on the same side, and Angel pretended to be glad even though he was afraid of getting into a mess, for he thought, the more people know about it, the worse it is, since they might bring trouble. However, he smiled and asked, "how come you didn't bring Antigone?" but Alcmene answered, "leave her out of it," as if being with them would be dangerous for her.

And it really did lead to trouble, for awkward Alcmene was always getting in his way, regardless of who was present she'd make fun of him and ask, "how are you doing, little Angel?" and after a bit she got bolder and challenged him, "little Angel, you don't condescend to us" – and it was indeed true that he was avoiding her – but he saw that all the others were mocking him, Armandos and another friend whom he didn't know, he suspected that they'd planned it in advance, maybe she'd said, I'll show you something that will amuse you, and he remembered the little animal that dwelt within him, that could become enraged and growl – or bite. And two days before the blockade he said to himself I'll have to teach her not to play around with me, and when they were all together and laughing he felt his cheeks burn, which could have been the result of temptation, and he heard his own voice as if it was a stranger's saying, "I want to give you something, close your eyes," and she didn't hesitate, she closed her eyes and smiled and stretched out her hand and waited, and there in front of everyone he bent down and kissed her inside her mouth, her flesh was like a stolen fruit, its flavour something he couldn't identify though, for she screamed at him in fury, "get out of here, you bastard" and he saw that a deep red stain had spread over her, as if every single pore had filled with blood and her eyes with tears. Everyone had frozen and Alcmene said again, "you always were an animal" and kicked him, said "Dimitris will deal with you" and then "I'll tell everything" whereupon he himself froze – what would she bear witness about and to whom? – but he wouldn't give up, "did you like it?" he asked stingingly. And he felt them pushing him and as he turned round saw Armandos shouting, "you're not a man" and threatening, "get out of here before I beat you to a pulp," at which the little wild animal awoke, a humiliated animal that cursed, "soft little spoilt kids," hurled himself in a frenzy onto Armandos, hit out blindly without thought. And they were stifling in a tangle of earth and clothing, when he heard voices round him and found that he was on top with the other boy lying on his back beneath him, he had blood on his cheeks and in his eyes, Angel noticed, and was crying, "I can't see" – then hands grabbed him, hauled him off, gave him a shove, and he staggered away tasting salt on his saliva. But he could hear Alcmene crying, shouting, "I'll tell everything" and he ran off and disappeared, he said to himself the sea is all I've got left, he went and fell face down on the little wall at the water's edge and thrust his face into the saltiness. He kept his eyes open and saw tin cans and broken glass shining and sand, and he felt how lovely, how peaceful, so that even the stinging of his eyes became a pleasant sensation.

All the same for two days he lived in fear and trembling, remembering Alcmene and her threat – and he was ashamed to meet Dimitris. He took other routes where, he hoped, he wouldn't run into him, he stayed as long as possible at the shipyard, the German who had a soft spot for him would, he thought, protect him – but what to do about the evenings? Thus when they were battering on the door he had thought of the courtyard at the back, thought of climbing the wall and into the trees; and lucky for him that he hadn't done so because – as was later discovered – they had surrounded the whole block and his flight would have looked suspicious. And his grandmother cried all night, no one slept at all, and early in the morning she called her daughters and sons-in-law round, though they asked, "what do you expect us to do?" for everything was dangerous, "evil days" as Christoforos said, and Myrsine thought I'll manage alone again, and remembered the first years, '17 when they disembarked from the ship, herself all alone with her five girls and her two boys, that time when Fotis had disappeared and they'd been searching for him, and dusk fell and they stayed alone on the seashore.

And two days later, as soon as they'd finished eating, she set out alone with Angel, and didn't tell anyone – not even her grandson – where they were going, though he was puzzled and kept asking until she ordered, "not a word", and they went on climbing higher and higher, above Karagatsia and Hirsh, into a neighbourhood that he wasn't at all familiar with, though she suddenly asked, "don't you remember how I brought you here when you were little to take Communion?" She had made a vow to St. Barbara, it had been a morning of wind and rain, nipping the child's thighs, but – he remembered – his grandmother had hauled him along, wrapped in her black kerchief, all resignation and faith. And he asked her, "where are we going now?" as she walked along like a dry stick, thinner now and dark, "you'll see," she promised, "only mind you behave," and they turned into a little lane which you wouldn't think could possibly lead back to the city but only to a world of trees and bushes and flowers, and Myrsine said, "we've arrived" and looked him over from top to toe and warned, "be careful what you say." In front of them was a little house of a sort of reddish-yellow colour and a door that looked varnished – a completely discordant note – and Myrsine rang the doorbell which they could hear sounding in the depths of the house (they must have it in the kitchen, thought Angel) and the door immediately opened, and there stood a beautiful girl who asked, "what do you want?" – "is your mistress in?" said Myrsine, and the door was automatically opened wide and Eleni was coming down the steps, and embracing the other woman as if there was deep love between them, "oh mother," she stammered, "mother," and in a minute they had all gone inside, with a reluctant Angel bringing up the rear, thinking to himself I don't understand – because it really did seem incredible. And as they sat down next to each other, Myrsine and Eleni, he was thinking, it's not possible, they must have been meeting, how could Granny have known the address, how can they bear to embrace each other? – "goodness, how you've grown, Angel," the woman said to him, and he noticed that her cheeks and neck were puffy, and just above her ears her hair was going white, and he thought, where's all her past glory now? But his gaze strayed to her eyes, which alone still held some velvet charm, at one point she sat with her knees apart and the boy saw how the flesh led upwards, plump at the furthest depths, so that he lost himself among the mysteries; and he lowered his eyes lest she should catch him looking, since he was no longer the child whom she had enfolded close against her flesh, in her shimmering dresses, in her palace, in Beirut.

And his grandmother recounted the bad news, that Stratis had been arrested and that they might be losing him forever; the other woman was alarmed and asked, "where have they got him?" – "they said at the Security Police or in a camp" and Eleni fell into thought, she seemed to be casting in her mind, sizing up her acquaintances, maybe which strings could be pulled, but Myrsine had her own solution (she's thought of everything, admired Angel) and jogged the other woman's memory, "do you remember the man who helped you back then?" she asked, and she meant the man who'd helped them get through customs and they'd become friends, gone out eating and drinking together and having fun, and she'd given him some fine presents, the gold watch, the cufflinks – and Eleni said, "yes, Nikos" – "he'll have become much more important by now," said Myrsine with certainty; and they arranged that Eleni would send them a message the following morning, she meanwhile was looking insistently at Angel again, "the more you grow, the more you look like your father," she murmured (and through Angel's mind flashed the answer, that's why Myrsine had brought him along, to make Eleni feel sentimental), and he thought, "where's he knocking about now, I wonder" and he looked at his grandmother, who shrugged her old shoulders, and the two women hugged each other, "oh mother", lamented Eleni, and Myrsine said, "he'll be back, you'll see him again." And in a little while the grandmother and grandson were leaving, and Eleni gave them a bag which she'd filled with fruit and sweetmeats, and as they were going out through the door she embraced him and kissed him; and he felt that her breasts were larger now and slacker.

The afternoon was fading and as they took the road back down the hill they saw that the sky in the west was crimson, "it'll be windy tomorrow," pronounced Myrsine, and Angel thought, I wish it would blow a bit now, for he felt his face burning, his cheeks and his chin. And his grandmother said as if thinking aloud, "just as well we left when we did, because they'll be starting to arrive" and as Angel looked at her in bewilderment, "she's gone back to her old art, the slut," and her face shone strangely, all red and black, and her eyes seemed like glowing points of light. "Don't let slip where we've been," she cautioned him. And when they arrived at the little bridge, at the dry riverbed, she threw the bag into the dark grass, and Angel said, "that's sinful" – "I don't eat food that's tainted," she snarled, and was no longer in the least pious or compassionate. At last they arrived home, it was dark by now and she reminded him, "not a word", and Angel spoke not a word but thought of the sea again, and in a little while he was back on the shore and dipped his head once more, oh God, he thought, if I could drink you, for it was lonely and dark with only two stars shining in the sky above – yes and no.

And two days later they set off once again, Myrsine, two of her sons-in-law and Angel, but this time they had further to go, outside town, for they had heard (perhaps from Eleni) that their relative was being held behind barbed wire at the "Pavlos Melas" camp, they set out at midday, and arrived at about three, but they were ordered, "stand here" on a little hill, with below them a deep ditch, beyond it the barbed wire fence and in the background the low buildings of barracks. And they stood and waited, a long time passed, there was a whole crowd of relatives waiting, and then at last the doors of the huts were opened and Angel heard a sigh from everyone round him, for one by one the prisoners were coming out and lining up against the walls so that their families could distinguish them from a distance, you could hear names and cries and weeping, and Angel was the first of them to call, "there he is, there he is" and to point, and then the men saw him too, but Myrsine was sobbing, "I can't see him" for her eyesight was dim and it was too far away. And the two sons-in-law muttered, "so much the better" for Stratos was deathly pale, his trousers hanging off him and his shirt open – for a moment he waved at them and then, he alone, went back into the hut and did not re-emerge. And Angel felt that he was choking, he took hold of his grandmother's hand and kept pointing to where the prisoners were now a massed crowd as they were herded back inside. And Myrsine said, "we'll see him again, we'll come back," however the old bus they found and got into jolted them terribly – and the same night Angel became ill, they said, "it must be his liver again" and his grandmother spent hours and hours in front of the icons, whether or not there was light in her room.

Christos

And people lamented, "they didn't even leave a single one" and everyone had frozen, standing rigid, like still photographs, at their windows when they saw the procession dragging its way down the road, pity that knew no end, and Amalia was crying as she said, "where are they taking them?", for surely among their number would be friends – but on the men and women walked, laden with bundles, some with toddlers on their shoulders, and in their midst prams and little handcarts were being dragged in which the old people were buried under clothes and heavy blankets. And Christos ran out, he felt that he ought not to absent himself, and in a few minutes he was near the avenue where the head of the procession had already arrived, with the Germans in front, silent and fully armed; for a moment he leant on a door and sensed that within it voices were struggling with tears, turning his head he saw a withered wreath hanging, mostly twigs and a few leaves, and he remembered, I know this house, it was a Jewish house, inaccessible, the door always closed, the curtains covering the windows, but as he leant against it he felt the door give behind him, and he went up a dark red polished staircase with a greyish stair carpet, spotlessly clean. Now he could hear quiet weeping, sounding like some incomprehensible chanting of psalms, and as he went further up saw, in the semi-darkness, three men and women standing who were making not a sound, so that Christos wondered who was grieving, then suddenly he heard someone say, "at least wait until we have left," he seemed to be an old man, beseeching; and as he mounted the last stairs Christos found himself with the other people, all of them looking at an open three-leafed door, with large glass panes on which was painted a strange composition of something like lilies or long-necked birds, and in the middle of the drawing room was sitting an old woman who was crying (except that now you couldn't even hear her) and above her, straight-backed stood a tall old gentleman with his black hat, his gold-rimmed spectacles, his overcoat and a walking stick like a brown cane which he raised as if it were a child's toy and begged, "wait until we are gone" and then "have some pity for my wife," who was getting up, with the old man supporting her, and Christos bent sideways, it was as if he was stretching out his hand, pulling the glass doors even wider open, and he felt the back of his skull burning, his scalp, and then his throat which had a choking lump in it that impeded both speech and breathing, but his heart was shouting no, and he stretched out his hand.

For already the drawers in their secret cupboard hidden in the wall were being pulled open, and two women were getting out white sheets and blankets and linen and throwing them down into two heaps, as if they were sharing them out; then the old man and his wife began to move, he walking ramrod straight, looking ahead, with his wife on his arm, and as they reached the top of the staircase the people waiting there surged forward into the drawing room, the sound of breaking glass was heard and footsteps running back and forth (they had poured into the bedrooms), and Christos went down the stairs, he stopped for a moment behind the old couple, the light from the street outside could be seen now, as if it was waiting to meet them. But the old lady stopped, seemed to want to lie down on the steps, and Christos put his hands under her armpits and whispered to her, "courage", and just then curses were heard upstairs – "you thieves, you ravening beasts," shrilled a woman, and someone answered her, "bitch" – they were on the bottom step now and Christos was thinking that's it, when the old man turned and looked at him, raised his black hat and said, "I am Alberto Matalon," as if it meant something, and Christos thought what good would my name do him? For it was his hands alone that were able to help, supporting the old lady and assisting her to step down from the pavement onto the road, the shiny cobblestones along which were now passing myriads of people of their own race, most of them poor, from the hovels of the ghetto known by the number "six", and the old couple stood there as if wondering, how can we step into this river of people, but a soldier came along and barked out an order at them, his voice had the hoarseness of someone who has risen too early, and at that moment broken glass fell in smithereens on the pavement, at which the German ran into the house with his machine-gun. However the river was flowing past, the woman and Matalon had been swept into it, and Christos followed for a little until he realised that there was nothing he could do, so he stood and watched the slender old man for as long as he could make out his black hat, they had come out into the avenue, by the tramlines, for a moment he thought he saw Dimitris, but he felt his stomach rising into his throat and he collapsed onto a low wall, behind him he could feel railings, he opened his hands and grasped them and thought what coolness – and the river kept flowing on.

And he was afraid that he would choke, his neck felt as if a tight band was squeezing it, and it was a relief when he saw a hand in front of his eyes and recognised the voice that was saying, "Dad, what's the matter?", and felt more confident, it really is Dimitris he thought, and said, "nothing, I'm just tired" and got up automatically, took his son by the shoulder and spoke more calmly, "let's go, there's nothing more we can do to help." And they turned up the first street they came to, along which wound a wall, all stone and dampness, its upper part lost in thick foliage, but he remembered Jews lived here too, they were called Malach and never spoke to anyone, such pride, and across the street from them was the white three-storey house, this belonged to Jews as well, he reflected, people said they used to spend six months of the year in Paris and the rest in this palatial mansion, and everyone whispered that the lady was having an affair with a Christian engineer, that they were always running off to lonely places, by carriage or by car. And without noticing – so deeply was he plunged in memories – he realised they had reached the lunatic asylum, and suddenly Dimitris gripped his arm, said "there's Angel," and indeed a young man dressed in white was standing there as if in thought or grief, and when they asked him his voice was cracked, and he simply said, "look what they've done to them," for all around lay paper, books that had been ripped up, broken black gramophone records, "that's the end of Bettina and her sister," grieved Angel, at which the others stood for a moment as if bewildered, till Dimitris said, "we didn't know them" in excuse, but his friend gave no explanations, maybe thinking it no longer mattered, "what have they done to those poor people," said Christos, and he reached out his hand and patted Angel, "there's nothing you can do," he comforted him, but "we could have done something," said the boy, and his voice was full of stubborn bitterness.

It would have been a wasted effort though, sobbed his voice and he couldn't explain it to them, nor would they have listened, because Christos moved off quite inexplicably and Dimitris promised, "we'll meet this evening," for the unpleasant events had not yet taken place. However, as the father walked feverishly along he suddenly asked, "where do I know him from?" and he meant the boy in white, and Dimitris explained, but "he's all right," he said in conclusion, Christos though remained silent and full of reservations but continued to hurry along, after a moment he recognised his own haste and excused it, "your mother will be anxious." All the same, when they pushed open the garden gate they found her sitting there deep in thought, she looked wounded, horrified, and she was speaking as if to herself, "I once had a friend called Rachel, we grew up together and played together, where are they taking her now?" And Dimitris said, "they could have taken refuge in the mountains," but Christos gave him an angry look, "Korech sold them out," once they used to know his son, a blond boy with an expensive bicycle, they'd come from Austria and the children used to say, "Hey Bubi, let us have a ride" but this he found impossible – "the Chief Rabbi sold them out," everyone had gone and he was the only one left, he shut himself up in his two-storey house and they never saw him these days, nor Bubi's bicycle either, the blond boy's, who had a lock of fair hair that fell forward over his eyes, just like the Germans.

And as they were discussing things on their little balcony, they saw the Tsimonis woman going into her house, she was carrying a bundle of clothes, all white, and a little while later her fat son appeared bearing two chairs; they went in, then came out again in a hurry, and Christos said, "the bastards are stealing," for they were plundering the Jewish homes and grabbing whatever they could find, whatever other people hadn't already taken, and

Amalia said, "this is their second trip" and it wasn't their last either, for till nightfall they were coming and going and had taken the two younger brothers with them as well, running backwards and forwards with their loads, like ants provisioning their nest, and there was no end to it; and Amalia said, "it's all of it stolen and will bring them bad luck" – and indeed they lost the fat man the following year.

And the next day they were to be even more upset, and Christos burst out in outrage, "that boy brings nothing but trouble," for as the boy sat with his own children, Dimitris, Alcmene and little Antigone, he'd told them, "it makes me choke," because two days before the deportation Bettina's mother had come to his grandmother, whereupon she'd ordered him to leave the room, they had serious things to discuss that weren't "for children's ears", to which Angel said, "fuck it, I already know everything," he knew what Niki's sanitary towels were for and why they got bloody, at night he used to imagine his aunt naked, sweaty invitations and embraces that flooded him with sweet wetness, however his grandmother ordered him, "get out from under our feet"; he thus nodded, "all right" and left the kitchen, but climbed back in by a window and hid in the empty bedroom with his ear glued to the door, so that he heard Myrsine saying, "it would be death to us" and the other woman pleaded, "you're a mother, you understand my agony" – "but where could we hide her, we haven't got anywhere," not any secure hiding place, and Angel thought that their cellar was labyrinthine and dark, but Myrsine insisted, "I can't risk my family's lives,"* the other woman was weeping and begging, at which point Myrsine heard the thud, opened the door and saw her grandson writhing on the floor, let out a wail, "ah woman, what have you done to us?" she moaned, and the other woman had gone white as a sheet, she fell to her knees and stroked the boy and spoke almost deliriously, "oh Bettina", she

---

* It must have been a sunny afternoon; Rachel came with her son Sammy. Grandmother, though, told her, "don't beg, it can't be done." All the same, in the evening a family council was held and Stratis said, "are you out of your minds?" – if the Germans caught them with a Jewish child in the house it would be certain death. After that we never saw the mother again, or her son. My mother had grown up next door to Rachel and they were close friends. But when Stratis spoke, no one ever gainsaid him.

sobbed, "Bettina", and Angel opened his eyes, heard Myrsine promising, "I'll ask my children," but the other woman left as if half-crazed.

And as Angel was telling them about it and crying, Amalia said, "I hope to goodness he's not going to pass out on us" for the boy was as white as a sheet, and Dimitris ran to the window to open it, for the boy's eyes had closed, and they all said, "let him have some air," and it was a smiling day of breezes, the sun playing with the white clouds, and Antigone ran to bring some water, but Angel had opened his eyes again and was looking at them, "we all got together that same evening, my grandmother, my uncle, my aunts' husbands, just as they'd said we would" and Myrsine decided they couldn't risk it, "because we've got children of our own" and she meant her grandchildren Angel, Nikos and Constantine. And the boy stopped there, and Christos consoled him, "we would have done the same," but Dimitris and Alcmene stared at him in disapproval – Antigone was talking to Angel, "so Bettina was lost," she concluded, but the boy made no answer, only looked into her eyes (one of the few times he did so) and whispered, "poor little thing", and Antigone asked, "is she our age?" to which he replied, "she's older than us, she's taller." In the end Christos declared, "we simply have to make up our minds to accept it," dusk had fallen by now, and he begged, "let's eat" and they kept Angel with them because they were sorry for him, they gave him a plate of macaroni and everyone sat round the table, eating in silence.

Later that night they heard Antigone screaming in her sleep and Christos said, "he disturbed us," but "all this has upset us," amended Amalia and they looked at one another, and her husband felt her hand as it reached out and came to rest on his forehead, like cool dew on his hair, "we're grieving for them," she whispered but he didn't speak, I prefer her caress, he was thinking, which brings me peace, which consoles me, and in a little while he is alone in an unfamiliar room which smells unpleasantly of diesel oil and a dog comes in who cries what have you brought us to then stands up on its back legs and says I remember you in your torn tent was a charred stone the whole world there remembers you you are colonel Euripides but the other man bent his head look, he complained, how my hair has fallen out which always used to be thick and fair and cannon fire is heard somewhere nearby perhaps it is a thunderbolt and their stone is rent in two and all falls into chaos and he hears people screaming save us, "it's your own screams that have woken us now," and it's Amalia speaking, she presses the switch and the bedroom is brightly lit, the sheet is twisted in a knot, his pillow damp, "ah what nightmares", she is saying, and once more her hand reaches out and wipes the sweat from his brow, "it's dawn," she tells him and he seeks refuge in her arms, he can hear her breathing, then he touches her hips and caresses her, then her thighs which he can feel have grown plumper, he caresses her more and more boldly, but Amalia whispers, "we can't today" – "since when?" he asks – "it's the third day," and he feels that she's blaming him, what's happened to us? he wonders, once he would have been able to read it in her eyes from the very first minute, the dark circles under them, but what's happened to us? he worries, afraid that he's betrayed himself to her, that she is silently accusing him, and thus he locks himself tightly in her embrace, kisses her, assures her, "I love you" as if denying all guilt; and outside the shutters the dawn is coming to offer them relief, like a small green plant emerging from the earth, which you know has only a single root, white like a thread, which will not break and which will grow stronger.

Yannis

When they told him, "get over there fast, they're wrecking it for you" it was already late morning, in their securely closed house, for his sister was frightened and used to say, "everything makes me tremble," and she didn't mean only the bombings. For other terrors were about too, malcontents roamed the streets, shouting, "we'll burn everything down," the previous night the last of the soldiers had left and they'd blown up the port and the fuel depots, and everything had been brilliantly lit up, for the Germans would arrive any minute now – and people were weeping – who knows whose lives would be lost. And Yannis jumped up, as if stung by a lash, his heart anxious about their property, the closed factory, and he found himself out in the streets, where there were not many passers-by to be seen since people were venturing no further than their front doors, looking up and down in case the enemy had arrived, in case a knife blade awaited them. And Yannis searched for a taxi, in vain though, he reached the Fountain and couldn't see a single tram, so he said to himself I'll run there, for there wasn't any choice, and he did indeed set off walking rapidly as if pursued, and after a bit his chest felt tight and he realised that he was breathing hard, however he only loosened his tie and went on even faster, since there was a long way still to go, he had to go out beyond Vardari, to the disreputable little alleys. He suddenly felt sweltering, the sun was playing through the gaps in the clouds, he felt a hand unbuttoning his collar, and it was his own hand, and he went on running a bit further, then stopped; he had reached the beginning of Egnatia Street where the square opened out, and said to himself, "here are people," for he could indeed see people hurrying about, some laden with burdens, some who appeared to be waving, maybe shouting, but he couldn't hear them. He said to himself in determination, come on, one more effort, and at last arrived at the little lane, Aphrodite Street, and relaxed.

Because it all turned out to be untrue, even if not an outright lie; the factory was closed up and the lock was still in the door, and somewhere behind the bars was the elderly head of Pavlakis, who emerged as soon as he saw him, and Yannis said, "I was worried" – except that it was not quite for nothing, because men and women were running down the lane with their arms full, panting. And Pavlakis enlightened him, "they've broken into the warehouses" which were round at the back – they belonged to the army – and were taking whatever they could find or smashing things, and Yannis said, lucky you came, whereupon the other man displayed his pride and joy, his breech-loading firearm, which might look ancient "but it does its job," he assured his master. And the two of them stood there like guards in front of the door – they looked quite comic – and at one point they saw a man staggering along carrying two big tin cans, one in each hand, he was panting, and some devil stirred in Yannis, so that he said to himself, "let's see" and went up to the man, "do you need some help?" he asked, putting out his hand, "want me to take one?", and the man said "yes" out of necessity, whereupon Yannis grabbed the can and turned away, "this way", called the man, meaning his own home, but Yannis laughed, "I live in the other direction," and the man became furious, "you thief", he spat, "my can" – "how much did you pay for it?" mocked Yannis, and Pavlakis was standing behind him with his gun, "you bastards, you sods", howled the man, but began to run, his load lighter now, for fear they should take the other can too. And Yannis roared with laughter, "might is right," he said, and gave the can to the watchman, "take it," he told him, "it might come in handy."

But before they'd even finished speaking they heard the heavens split asunder, the sky was blue now and the sun had come out, and they saw five aeroplanes diving low over the houses, "they're stukas," yelled Yannis and they took shelter under an open-fronted shed – the can abandoned in the middle of the yard – and after a moment the planes seemed to have disappeared,

Pavlakis ran to grab the booty, but again the sky was rent and they heard the rattle of gunfire, the can remained where it was, the street was full of crying and screaming, people were running and flying with whatever they possessed, bundles and sacks, a baby's pram full of containers, and then the street was empty once more; they stayed huddled there under the roof of the shed, time passed and after a bit Yannis said, "they've stopped," they emerged and everything was deserted, no one to be seen, except that the door of a small house standing a little way off opened – two girls lived there who provided comfort to the workers – and he saw a half-naked woman in the doorway, but she went back in at once for she had certainly seen him. Let me go and help her, thought Yannis, so he picked up two of the abandoned sacks and took them to her doorstep, he didn't knock on the door for they would have been aware of his breathing, they would have heard him, and the door thus opened and she was almost completely naked, "come in," she murmured to him in sweet tones, but he laughed, only as far as this, and he hurried off and brought a tin can, deposited this too at her doorstep and listened – she'd put on an ankle-length dressing gown now and was hugging it around her, "what times these are," she whispered, and arranged the things he'd brought in a corner of the room, then "go and fetch the watchman," she said.

And after a little while Yannis left them, he thought perhaps they know each other – Pavlakis and the woman – and he chuckled to himself, how I would have liked to be standing at the side and watching, however he thought of his sister, who must be dying of fear; and he increased his pace. He was walking down the lane with the inns, which was now deserted, only he could hear conversations in the inner courtyards, and neighing, and from somewhere above a voice warned him, "get under cover" (at which he looked up and saw a girl at the window, for years to come he was to remember the white kerchief on her hair), and at that moment he heard the roar of a motorcycle, then it was coming up behind him, covered in mud, and on it a helmet, a pair of thick goggles, glistening oilskins, the machine-gun slung crosswise, a headlamp – and the roar. It was the first German, who passed by at speed, expressionless, and Yannis stayed glued to the wall, by the closed trapdoors, and breathed again; however it occurred to him that he was exposed there, a man standing in the middle of an unknown street, which in a little while would be inundated with motorcycles and cars, he looked up again at the inn, and all he could see was a woman's white arm, she must be sitting by the window and have leant her arm on its sill to rest, perhaps her companions were inside, talking, waiting – or maybe they were trapped there. And he hurried onwards; before he reached the square he heard another roar, he slipped into a door that he found open and saw the motorcycle again, an identical driver, perhaps he was a different one or perhaps the first one, and then a third, and he thought, they've arrived.

And when he stepped over the threshold he felt strange, something hurt, it felt like a shooting pain, and his sister said, "you're very pale," and she went and brought the eau de cologne and moistened his brow and then his throat and his breast, and he saw the picture once again, the square being invaded by tanks, they looked like something at the cinema, newsreels, and as he'd been hurrying to get away he'd almost walked into a car, with an officer in it and two civilians, it was the mayor he remembered, hastening to the square as if desperate to arrive in time. And in a few days he was to say, "look what a reception they gave them," for they saw the picture in the papers, with the professor leaning forwards, stretching out his hand to shake the hand of a German from the tanks, and he looked cheerful and pleased, but all that was later however; now he was at home and his sister was sitting in the drawing room looking as if she was waiting for him, except that suddenly Yannis thought that he remembered this spot, his father had been pale and dry, he said, "get out of my sight" as if snarling, and even the furniture was fixed in his memory, the rectangular table of reddish wood with chairs to match, the glass-fronted cabinet with crystal ware in it, the luxurious chandelier above, which was lit only on special days, and on the wall a greenish picture of scantily clad nymphs bathing in a lake. And Yannis whispered, "I'm thirsty," but she didn't move, hadn't heard him, she only wrapped her shawl closer about her shoulders, he advised her, "open up the shutters, the sun is burning outside" but knew that he'd get no response, thus he went into the kitchen and found the place deserted, he thought that they couldn't not eat, and a little while later pulled the black-out curtains back from the window and saw two men standing and talking in the street, what are they saying? he wondered, in the background was a dull rumble as if of cars constantly passing – and the sun was indeed shining and the tree across the road was full of leaves.

Then for no reason he reflected, I'm nearly forty and what have I achieved? He had filled out and had more colour in his face, above his ears the white hairs were becoming increasingly numerous; and his next thought was of Ergini, she was forty-five and without a husband. That's where we've failed, he thought, and it was like crying when he said aloud, "where is she now?" and heard himself say it, and she heard it too, he thought, but she was lost somewhere, and the formal letters they received from her were few and far between, from Vienna and then later from Graz, "we are well," she wrote to them, always the two of them, without offspring, as if they lived together like brother and sister sharing a house. I'm almost forty, and it was like panic, yet he could see the two men talking, the sun was shining more brightly now and one of them put his hand to his brow to shade his eyes, he went into the lobby and looked in the mirror, he seemed to be inspecting or examining himself, and he said there, I've got a mark on my temple, half of it under my hair, half on the exposed skin, and he wondered, did I always have it?

Then someone was ringing the doorbell and he saw a silhouette behind the glass panes, he opened the door in curiosity, but saw Pavlakis standing there waiting to be asked in, and he said – which puzzled the other man – "we haven't prepared any food today," but all the same stood back as if inviting him to pass, and the old man entered hesitantly, then after a bit asked, "what are your orders?", he was holding a whole bunch of keys, "are we going to open it up again or not?" and Yannis answered, "how old are you?", whereupon the other man looked at him as if he was drunk, "I don't understand," he stammered, "how old are you, lover boy?" they had teased him, but he replied, "sixty-five" and added immediately, "the girl sends you her thanks," and at this they both laughed – at last they'd understood one another. "What's going to happen with the factory?" he asked again, and Yannis said, "let's wait and see," that it would indeed have to remain closed until things settled down a bit, until they could see what the Germans were going to do, until the workers got back from the front. And thus the keys were left on the table.

And as it turned out they were not doomed to get rusty or be put away in some corner, for Yannis was to decide one day – and it was not such a distant day – that their life would have to go on, that the workers had to eat, who were back and had been coming knocking on his door seeking work; it was almost summer by now, and the Germans hadn't taken a single man prisoner but had said instead, "get off back to your jobs and your homes," and the roads were full of soldiers, capless, weaponless, beltless, who were making their way back to their homes, some on their way to Crete, some to the Peloponnese – and people took them into empty houses and courtyards, and fed them and gave them water to wash and then sent them on their way, crying and thinking of their own loved ones and wondering where they might be trudging or dragging themselves along. But Yannis wasn't awaiting anyone, all his workers had returned (one, they said, had lost his voice for two days and they'd had to take him to church) and one day at noon he took Pavlakis and they went and unlocked the iron gate; for a minute it seemed to him that the yard was overgrown with grass, but of course spring was well and truly here, he saw a window broken, yet they found the doors still locked, just as they'd left them, and all the machinery was in order. He smelled the familiar odour of gas and engine oil and felt as if he was entering his own home; except that a thick layer of dust had settled and everything looked white, and thus they picked up wads of cotton waste, master and man, and began to wipe and to enjoy once more the black machines, the letters on them spelling out the trademark, their steel fittings. And they worked on until they could barely see each other, and Yannis said, "what got into us?" for dusk had fallen by now, and as they tried the switches they found that there was no electricity, but luckily they laughed and Yannis said, "everything will be repaired," no matter that Pavlakis looked like a corpse, his cheeks sucked in, breathing hard, so they took a couple of chairs out into the yard and sat there to recover – "all we need to resurrect us is an ouzo," pronounced Yannis, but the street was pitch dark and the old man suggested, "shall we go and ask the women over there for one?" and grinned like a satyr. He hobbled out of the yard, and as he was disappearing up the road Yannis called, "watch out you don't exhaust yourself," but he didn't have long to wait, two women came (were they the same ones?) and said to him, "come on in, we've put him to lie down," and Yannis asked them, "what are you offering us?" at which one of them laughed and answered, "anything you care to name."

The next morning found him lying under the shelter of an outhouse in an unknown courtyard, bathed in grey light, with a woman standing over him and prodding him, "get up, someone's looking for you," she announced, there was a woman at the factory door who seemed to be searching, she was calling "Yannaki" – and Yannis leapt up, he said, "oh Christ, my sister", who must have been out of her mind with worry, for he'd left her on her own all night; he put on his clothes like a whirlwind and started to run, only to ask at the last minute, "how do I get out of here?", at which the woman laughed and pushed him into a room, "this way, Yannaki," she teased, "this way takes you out at the back" and she guided him, "only you'll have to go round the block" – it was like a plot, a trick they'd worked out together. And Yannis assured her, "I'll be back" and she seemed puzzled, and as they were going down a sort of corridor he saw a half-open door, through which could be seen a struggle, a woman crouched half-naked, and beneath her a man moaning faintly – he managed to get a glimpse of his curly hair as the woman moved back and forth, and for a minute he stood there, "well done, old fellow," he muttered, but his girl gave him a shove, "get on with you," she said, "the peepshow's over," and at that point the other woman turned round and smiled at them, made as if to stretch out her arm, but Yannis was being pushed, "you've forgotten about your sister," she said mockingly.

In the end he slipped out through the secret little door, he had to stoop, creep along the wall, then hurry through the little lanes till he came out at the end of his own street, where he saw his sister in her brown dress, and she ran towards him, "what happened to you?" she was complaining, and he saw that she was without makeup, drawn, he thought she can't have slept, "where did you sleep?" she asked him, and he answered, "we spent all night at the factory," they'd lost track of time as they worked and had got caught by the curfew, "I was just having a stroll now to get my blood flowing again," she was examining him though, as if searching for something, and her eyes kept going back to his neck, to the right side of his neck, and in the end she put out her hand and touched the place, "someone's been sucking your blood," she scolded, then "I'll be waiting for you to get home," she said and left. And there were two little marks on his neck, one of which looked as if it was bleeding – he found a mirror and examined his own reflection thoroughly. In the end, he put the blame on Pavlakis, who turned up at midday and was useless; he told him, "get out of my sight, I don't want to set eyes on you," and it was a week before they next saw each other.

Angela

From then on they were to see each other more often; as the springtime burgeoned, like a great feast, they would hide in her room and look through the curtains at the sunny day, the tops of the trees and the sky with its white summery clouds, they would lie for hours on end enchanted in each other's arms, and Yannis said, "when I say I love you, it's as if I am walking in the rain wearing only a shirt, and I feel the raindrops piercing me – but very gently – and I think that they are stealthily permeating me, and that maybe I will regret it when I've been hurt" and she wondered, what book did he get all that out of? for they couldn't have been his own words, yet she was consoled by the thought, he learnt it all by heart for my sake. And when they went out, to Panorama or even further, the whispering voices of the earth gave them ease, they lay on the grass and smelt the spring, and she heard a voice saying, "when you caress me it is like a spell; I want to speak to your hair, to burrow into the very depths of your skin" which had become more familiar now, the fingers recognised it, just as the lips or the cheek did, and would have confessed this is our world, the feel of him known to us, and she thought, I caress the birthmark on your chest, or the parts where your skin is darker or creased, or seems to be tired or faded, for he is forty now, reflected Angela – and she too was almost the same age.

And she was constantly fretting that time was running out for her, "at my age my mother looked like an old woman," she admitted, and examined herself naked in the mirror, where she saw a white-skinned woman, her hips broadening a bit but her breasts still firm and her shoulders still glossy, to remind her of the girl who used to wash in Eugenios's kitchen, with the bolts drawn and the windows shut, "but that was fifteen years ago," she said to herself in surprise. And her deepest thought, perhaps the one that pained her most, was I must have a baby if I can, for she feared lest she might be losing the capacity for motherhood and was approaching the time when she'd have to confess that she was useless, her insides no longer functioning, something that she'd heard of happening to other women – and some of them younger than herself – their juices dried up and they withered. But she couldn't be certain even now, for she was living with Yannis as man and wife and at the moment of ecstasy he would cry to her, "you are my wife," yet always withdrew in time and spilled his dew on her belly, it had the scent of a strange flower, and Angela was left thrashing, until one day in the wildness of their great passion she locked her legs around his waist and begged, "inside, I want your dew inside" – and so it was. And when they lay back as if wounded, their eyelids closed, she sang to him, "thank you", she felt an indescribable sweetness, her arms and legs limp, but Yannis stayed silent, and the woman told him, "don't worry, it's not the right time of the month" and stroked his curls with the back of her hand, then he smiled – still with his eyes shut – and whispered, "but you are my wife."

And she looked at herself in the mirror once again without any clothes on, I have matured, she said to herself, and felt a pain as if the fruit within her was continuously expanding, as if it wanted to burst free of its shell, it was like an image which tormented her in her sleep, that she was drowning in the mud and saying all the time my belly will open, and she did indeed look at her skin, it was full of lines, at the beginning fine and invisible, but then turning into ever broader furrows, like melons out in the field in whose rind you can feel the scars and her mother was standing beside her saying to her in a little while you'll be free at which she cried out in agony and the shutters were grey, outside lay a world where you couldn't tell whether it was cloudy or sunny, for a moment she smiled sadly, "it's growing," she said as if talking to someone, "or else it's shrinking and shrivelling more and more." And she remembered that the days passed (she had been counting them in hope – though in expectation of what she couldn't have said) and it turned out that the "attempt" had been in vain and thus she complained to him that "I've grown old", at which he pretended to laugh, but his laughter was false, thought Angela, and wondered, what is it that he wants? – one night he carried her off from the tavern where she worked, said, "put on your best clothes" and took her arm, they went to a grand house by the seaside, and without any hesitation he introduced her as "my fiancée", there were only men there, apart from one old lady who gave her a thorough scrutiny, as if to say how did you get in here? Because it was indeed a foreign world to her, they didn't speak the same language, but Yannis must have known it, for he was in heated conversation with an elderly gentleman who was bending forward to listen to him, as if this was the only position in which he could hear; after a while the doorbell rang and the elderly man asked, "who is there left to come?" and as the door was opened Angela saw the policeman she knew, the stout one who had come to the bar, I keep tripping over him wherever I go, she thought, but here he seemed to be a person well-loved, it was "Nikos" here and "Nikos" there, until suddenly he was standing in front of her and saying, "how are you, Violetta?", apparently oozing with honey, then he took Yannis into a corner and talked for ages, looking at her from time to time and smiling at her – and she thought mockingly, goodness, what a love affair!

And at that point the elderly lady came and spoke to her, said, "it's just us," meaning they were the only two women present, and she took her off to the kitchen to prepare something for the men to drink, and everything in the room was white and shining, she could see her pink dress reflected in all the little tiles and glass, and she thought, I suppose we could be said to live too, in her old attic; and they got the hors d'oeuvres and the wine ready, which in fact the lady had already almost prepared, so that Angela thought, what did she want me for? And when they went back into the drawing room everyone was sitting round and talking, laughter forgotten now for they seemed to be speaking of serious matters, a short fat man without any hair was talking and the others were listening, he was saying, "anything may happen, we simply have to be careful," and when the two women came in they stopped talking, but the old man said, "we all know each other here," and Angela could feel the short fat man looking at her and wondering, then the others too, whereupon Yannis said again, "she is my fiancée" – the second time – and the curtains stirred, you could smell the sea, and the lady said as if proud of the fact, "at this time of the evening we get a wonderfully refreshing breeze" and thus took Angela out onto the verandah and they both breathed in deeply, back in the drawing room the discussion had started up again and she was to remember hearing the phrase "the reds", they must have been worrying and making their plans, only once did her ear catch the sound of Yannis's voice, saying, "the question can be solved with money," regardless of whether the others agreed, anyway she couldn't hear because they were whispering, and she suspected that they'd taken her out onto the verandah so that she wouldn't follow what they were talking about, although "but what's it to me?" she said when later they left, for it was nearly time for the curfew and they ended up in her attic – any further away would have been dangerous.

And summer came, time was going by fast, and Angela said to herself I can't be mistaken, days went by and she still felt doubtful: perhaps on Monday, but once again no, and she touched her waist searchingly and her breasts, and felt that they had grown harder, and more nights passed and one evening she said to Vassilis, "I'm choking," she ran to the lavatory and begged, let me just throw up, and in the end went back into the room looking green, and he felt sorry for her, "go outside a bit," he advised, "get a bit of air" and she nodded, she thought I'm not wrong about it, and didn't know whether to be glad, or what Yannis would say; he introduces me as his fiancée – this was some comfort. And outside the tavern there was a tree, an ancient acacia which gave them its shade, she stood and rested her back against it and prayed if only there was a breath of air, and indeed the leaves rustled slightly, two foreign soldiers went by, talking about something and laughing, she could tell them that everything was over, that she was in a delicate condition – she'd managed it, and wouldn't take any risks. But Yannis didn't agree and surprised her, "we'll have to think carefully about what to do," he assured her, but first he took her in his arms, kissed her and said, "I'm very moved," there was a shadow in his eye though, some whiff of anxiety which robbed him of a fraction of his pleasure, he hid it and laughed and said again, "we'll have to think carefully"; and there were indeed a whole host of questions, which exhausted her in both body and mind – even though she felt a kind of security in the fact that she was still capable of it – the biggest question being how not to lose an atom of the sudden happiness, that everything had worked out perfectly, or at least the most important things. And Yannis laughed as he read her mind, he stroked her hand and said, "I'm glad for you," – "for both of us," she pleaded – "yes, for both of us," he amended, and his hand was trembling even if imperceptibly, he brushed her cheek like a leaf, bearing witness to the fact that everything was hanging by a single thread, which they could both half-see, both of them taking care to make no clumsy movement which would snap it.

And the thread held for only two evenings, they were sitting at a tavern in Karabournaki, with the dusk drawing near, and the sea lead-coloured, plashing and fragrant, then Angela saw the shadow in his eyes again, told him, "just say it and get it over with," and he did not even deny it, made no excuses, but instead simply spoke as if continuing an interrupted conversation, "logically we ought to get married" – "and then have a child," she completed, following closely on the heels of his artfulness, so much so that he gave her a good look, searching her, "and we can hasten the marriage," he replied, and she felt that her insides were angered, he seemed to be the cleverer of the two, obliging her to say the words that he wanted spoken, yet when she spoke them it was like a sob, "I'd better get rid of it," she suggested. And Yannis remained impassive, for "I couldn't ask you to do that," he murmured, "we might come up with a better solution," and within herself she said, you're a liar, you know you don't want any other solution, nor are you going to come up with one, within her a mother howled, nevertheless she preferred to smile, until she felt the tears flowing, "I'm absurd," she admitted, upon which his hand was raised, a pure white wing, and placed very slowly on her hair and she heard him confess, "I love you," and her tears flowed faster, she got up automatically from her chair and realised that she was leaving the courtyard, that the road was made of crushed stone and that all around was a landscape of dry thorn bushes, and in the background two large houses with lots of windows, and she thought irrelevantly that she hadn't noticed them when they arrived. And now she lost her grip once more, for he was taking her hand, and in the twilight his voice was saying, "wait, where are you going?", then spoke again and said, "you left your bag behind," as if this was the most important thing, and they walked on together in silence, each afraid to be the first to begin, and on they went without leaving the shore, beneath their feet plants, stone, sand, pebbles all unobserved, for the only thing she could feel was the power of her blood flaming within her, obliterating all common sense, making her balk at I'll have to get rid of it. After a bit she heard Yannis, who was holding her up, say, "we'll decide together," and surely he could see her sad smile.

She arrived at work out of breath, Vassilis was sitting on his chair singing, he gave her a curious look and said, "get your breath back," for as he was to tell her later, "I was afraid you were going to collapse," and all evening long they sang together, as he could sense that her voice was strangled and dull; at one point she reached out her hand to him, "I know you care about me," she whispered, and he spoke to his instrument, the evening seemed endless, until finally they left and walked together, then stood in her little cul de sac, reluctant to part, especially when she confessed, "I'm scared if you leave me on my own," somewhere round the back they could hear a man's voice singing, "he will have got drunk tonight," said Angela, and the whole neighbourhood seemed to be listening, as if it were a vast empty hall in which a single cry was echoing like a bell. And Vassilis said, "it would be better if I came with you up the stairs" for there were no lights on the staircase and the wood creaked frighteningly – and when they opened her door the room smelt like a garden, and she explained, "it's the breath of my basil plants," and she felt his arm round her shoulders and did not have the energy to pull away from him, "what's wrong, little one?" his hoarse voice was asking, and she sat down on the edge of her bed, in search of a nest in which to find comfort, to feel that she was not alone with her tenacity – her misery – Vassilis might be the right person, for he cared about her, was fond of her, maybe wanted to sleep with her. And he did indeed show that he was thinking of her, for he advised, "don't do anything which you'll regret," maybe he himself was afraid of getting hurt; and he asked her once again, "what's wrong?"

So then, she ought to make up her mind to it, count on Vassilis to help her find a good doctor and have done with the whole business; and the musician said, "I can't understand what your friend is afraid of," men should shoulder their responsibilities, at which Angela begged, "don't humiliate him," though she realised that Vassilis was weighing things up, maybe making comparisons, complaining, "if you're reluctant, leave me to cope alone," she said and trembled, it was almost noon by then, voices from the street rose all around them, and the sound of cars, "he may have his own reasons," she murmured, even though in her heart she'd written him off and was weeping, maybe thinking of some swear word too, which she regretted instantly, for she couldn't bear to sully his pure white image. Which in a little while appeared before her, and she thought luckily, at least at the beginning, when he told her, "I care for you and you care for me" and they embraced as if they'd been parted for years, and stayed silent locked in each other's arms and his breast smelt of flowers; for a moment he complained, "you've shown once more how little faith you have," he said, – for she had sought some other support – Vassilis had still been there when he had knocked on her door, though he'd left immediately in some constraint, as if declaring I understand, that they had much to talk about, to explore and find some way out. And Yannis did indeed seem to have been in anguish, to have been exercising his mind and boldness, and he set out his conclusions in one brief speech, just as if they were establishing a business.

There are two ways (he said), the first is that I marry you and we go to some church, most people know about us, they won't wonder too much, and my sister will be obliged to swallow it; the second, which is not something that I want and which is what I'm asking you about, is that you get rid of it and we put everything off till next year, I don't like this and it hurts me – specially for you – but all the same we have to come to some decision and make an end to all this, because otherwise the feeling that we have for each other will be poisoned. And as he spoke, and Angela searched him with her eyes and ears, she felt that he had condemned the fruit of her womb, that it was all just play-acting, and that what she was supposed to say was "do you know a doctor?", and at this she felt Yannis breathe easy again, his face clearing like the sky after clouds, in spite of the fact that he insisted, "it's not such an easy matter to decide." And thus the performance continued for a while (he was to deny it later though, to say, "you do me wrong" and weep), and in the end, with great difficulty, he was persuaded to reveal his plan – and Angela laughed within herself and mourned: but there you are, he had everything worked out – a friend of his was involved in the plan, that old singer of his, together with the man's wife who would go with her and look after her for him; except that Angela couldn't take any more, "you got everything sorted out just fine in your own mind," and she wept and wept and longed to be alone, if she hadn't been in her own home she would have walked out, specially when she saw that he didn't answer, didn't protest, but only went over to the window and stood and looked at the world outside, as if there was something of interest there or some duty which he must not neglect. Thus silence fell between them, from time to time they heard the house creak, from the road came a child's voice calling, "Niobe, come back, don't go to the car," and the man selling grapes from a barrow crying his wares, for a moment the sound of a woman singing, then their stairs creaked again, until she couldn't bear it and said, "please leave," and thus he turned and looked at her long and hard, though she remained with her head bowed gazing at her apron and her hands, even though everything was blurred, and then she heard his footsteps echoing slow and reluctant, they stopped, then set off again and finally began going down the stairs. And she howled at him, "you are murdering your own child," a great jarring cry that made him halt, and Angela repented of it and was relieved when his steps continued downwards and then were heard no more. And that same night she caught hold of Vassilis and said to him, "let's go now this minute," but he calmed her, "they don't work at this hour of the evening – and anyway, there's the tavern" where they played and sung in a frenzy, and Angela belted out, "You men are all a bunch of whores," and the other people laughed and clapped their hands, and said, "she's lively tonight."

Antigone

The story of the unruly boy who disappeared and who was being searched for was something the family talked of on many evenings, and although Dimitris assured him, "they haven't caught him," his father kept getting things confused and speaking about "the man who was arrested", but again Dimitris was better informed, "that was the boy's uncle," he said, "they've taken him off for forced labour, to Stavros" where they set them to dig trenches – "they're frightened of the landing," interpreted Christos, for it was nearly the end of August and the messages they were receiving bore good news. One night Alcmene said, "personally I'd call him the lost devil," but Antigone was hurt and remembered Angel and his kiss, his hopeless approach, "he's not the sort of person you can trust any more" was how the elder sister summed it up, better that he had disappeared. And yet one night when they had decided to get together and dance (it was in Armandos's garden, down by the sea) she imagined that she caught sight of him for an instant between the trees, she couldn't see his body or his hair, only his eyes with their usual expression, which made you feel he's mocking me, he's devaluing me, and then nothing, as if he had simply been a figment of her imagination, however she thought to herself I'm grown up now, I shouldn't be afraid of shadows, of which this garden possessed a great many, mostly in pairs; and then suddenly Alcmene was cross with her, "don't hang around under our feet," she hissed.

Only she felt that she wasn't taken in at all, knew perfectly well what they were up to, when they introduced her to Haris and she told him, "I already know you," he was the slender boy she used to play with when she was small, when they went to the grand house and he used to take her out onto the back balcony and say, "look down and see what it's like," where a sea of leaves spread below them, and in between they could see children playing – his perfumed mother would cry, "don't lean over," but it was hard to fall. "I know you," and she meant I remember everything, how when they used to get back to their own garden in the evening Christos would say to Amalia, "she's bringing up her children all on her own," but Amalia would remind him, "she doesn't lack money" – "I'm talking about the responsibility, how to bring them up right," and Haris had indeed grown up to be a man now, he seemed to her to be tall and thin, with his hair well-combed, but hesitant though, most of the time he answered her with a smile, but Antigone thought that it was only his mouth that smiled, his eyes remained sad or thoughtful. He was wearing a pair of white trousers of which he was taking great care, and his shirt hung loose on him; afterwards she was to learn that people teased him and called him "the dandy", he was preparing for university and he spoke to her in a low voice and slowly. But over his shoulder Antigone noticed two shadows talking together and thought with surprise that she knew them – he had dropped from sight long ago and she seemed to look like her sister, and she reflected that she was looking at some incomprehensible tangle, but it dissolved instantly, became once more just leaves and darkness, with the accompaniment of an accordion, and Haris said to her, "come on, let's dance" and she measured the beat in her mind and found that it seemed to be a tango, he took her in his arms as gently as could be and they started pacing, she could feel all the while his breath on her hair and the perspiration on his hands – and Alcmene was standing opposite, she wasn't in the place where Antigone had imagined her to be, she was talking to Armandos and Antigone kept observing her and her eyes were saying, but where did she spring from, and she felt her breast pressed against his boy's breast and unconsciously curved her body, to draw everything into herself, to drink deep.

When they sat down she was given orangeade, but somewhere in the background she saw a tiny point of light glowing and fading, she thought they're smoking, but who? Armandos and Haris were standing near her, Andreas was talking to Dimitris, who was making irritable movements with his hands, at one point a breeze blew from the sea bringing the smell of seaweed and paint from the caiques, and tears came into her eyes, she felt that they were stinging, some little bit of grit or tiny fly must have got caught in her eyelashes or be drowning in her pupil, then she saw once more a little glow of red light, then another, they must be smoking cigarettes, she shook her two plaits back, as if afraid that they'd bother her, and heard Haris say, "you're like a little fawn gambolling," but this wasn't the first time she'd been bothered (one afternoon as she was walking along a boy on a bicycle passed her, "if only I could caress your little tits," he called, then pedalled off like a whirlwind), and she felt the breeze again, thought it was wonderfully refreshing, that all these things added up to happiness, now the accordion was playing again, she measured the beat inside herself (one ... two ... one ... two) and found that it was a hesitation waltz, she waited to be asked to dance and it was Andreas who invited her, Alcmene was saying behind her, "when did you find the time to learn these dances?" but this was something that she kept to herself – one of her secret little drawers – and she liked being held more tightly now, feeling his boy's leg pressing between her own, but Haris was sitting there calmly, she saw his eyes caressing her, thought what a sweet boy; she remembered him at his house, his brothers were noisy – specially Alekos – but he always sat in a corner, looking at books, not speaking, and in the end would cuddle in his mother's arms, with her smiling and saying, "the most sensitive of them all" as if it was her youngest that she was embracing, when in fact it was the oldest.

Suddenly she heard the iron garden gate closing loudly, the metal clanged and footsteps were hurrying away, but they were outside the gate – someone was leaving – yet Antigone could see them all around her (Haris, Dimitris, Armandos, Andreas) and she wondered, who went out? Her eyes searched the darkness among the leaves but no one was lighting a cigarette, so in the end she had another lemonade and felt: how lovely. How lovely that the accordion was starting up again, she didn't know the boy who was playing, but all the girls were clustering round him and caressing him and making much of him, the boy was laughing and he began playing, and made them sway with "Komparsita", Alcmene was dancing now, albeit gracelessly, and Haris said, "your sister is like a tomboy," she looked four-square and strong and Antigone remembered how once when they'd been having a fight she'd felt her sister's hands close on her like pincers with a determination that was terrifying, and both "Komparsita" and Armandos were getting wilder, it looked as if everything was going to end in exhaustion. And she got up and said to herself, let's have a look at the garden, which certainly didn't appear very large, she stooped so as not to get tangled up in the branches, just a little further, then she arrived at the wall, a low wall – the bottom built of stone and the upper part of red brick – and then the high iron railings, which she couldn't have climbed, so instead she grasped them and looked through them into the night, a little way off she could see a small yellow hut, beside it a row of German lorries and at the end one with the large red cross on it. Then she walked along the length of the wall, reached its corner, said to herself, let's see what's on the other side, but she tripped over something, kicked some tins and felt her feet becoming wet, went a bit further and looked over at the shipyards, beyond them masts like lines drawn on the dark sky, with the stars hanging in their rigging, as if playing, a voice from the garden singing, "I have forgotten the sweetness of your lips" with the accordion accompanying it, and then suddenly she jumped as she became aware of a shadow standing there and scolding, "what do you mean by going off by yourself?" and it was Alcmene, but Antigone asked, "what are you doing here yourself?" and once more a shadow appeared behind the railings, in the street, and she couldn't contain it and said "Angel", but he froze as if he'd fallen into a ambush, threw them a quick goodnight and disappeared – "go back to the others," Alcmene ordered; and it really was a command.

And when they saw her they asked, "where did you get so dirty?" for her white sandals had become blue, at which she was bewildered, "I don't understand," she stammered, but Dimitris who seemed a bit upset took her aside, "come on," he said and took off her sandals, they stood at the garden tap and gave them a quick rinse, "thank goodness it's coming off," said Antigone, and dipped her feet into the basin below the tap, for her toes and ankles were stained blue, and she felt the cool water waking her, "where did I find that paint?" she wondered, and Dimitris said, "forget it" and ordered her to stay where she was until she was dry, to wait for him there and not speak – and she complained that everyone was ordering her about. And the only person who made her feel better was Haris, he begged her, "come and have a dance again," but she burst out laughing, "you'll tread on my toes," she said and showed him how she was barefoot, the boy looked glum, "I know I don't dance very well," he murmured, then Antigone asked, "what is your father called?" and he answered, "Elias", but he didn't live with them and they had no idea where he was (Antigone knew all this, for she'd heard her parents talking about it, so she said to herself, I'd better change the subject, for he was offended and she felt sorry for him), in the end she looked for her sandals in case they were dry by now, but no such luck – "let's go and dance," she invited him, and took him by the hand, even though her feet slipped and stumbled. For a moment Haris held her, stammered "thank you" and caressed the top of her head, her hair, whereupon she felt her face blushing fiercely and begged, dear God, don't let him notice.

But the truth was to become clear, after a while Alcmene and Haris disappeared, and Antigone was puzzled, why have they left me? Everything seemed a mystery, specially when Dimitris disappeared too, and all that remained was the accordion and Armandos murmuring, "do you like dancing like this together?" and she wondered, maybe he means the way he's squeezing me or sweating heavily, but she only smiled at him – and was racking her brain about where her brother and sister could have got to. And in the end she said, "I'll go home," perhaps they might be waiting for her there, so she said goodnight and hurried off, knew she had to go up this street until it met their own, above the avenue with the trams, beyond the lunatic asylum. And as she reached its stone wall, where the branches grew low and cast deep shadow and she caught the sweet scent of the flowering shrubs, she saw three shadows frozen against the damp stones, which suddenly came to life again and grabbed her arms and ordered, "not a word", and it was her brother's voice and she felt struck dumb, for beside him were standing Haris and Alcmene, and she asked them, "what are you doing here in the dark?" – maybe some incomprehensible naughtiness, just like the time when she was little and had gone into the cellar with Andreas and Armandos and they'd put her in between them and squeezed her like crazy.

And they really were taking a risk, for they were writing in huge letters on the wall, and she could make out that they were blue, thought to herself, now we'll get to the bottom of things, and she read "No to civil mobi" and Dimitris asked her, "are you scared?" for he could feel her hand fluttering, but "no", she whispered and he hugged her, he took her to the corner of the street and stopped there, "if you see anyone coming, whistle," but she didn't know how to whistle, she pursed her lips and blew, it sounded ridiculous and she was annoyed; so Dimitris said, "sing a song instead."

And he left her there, her spine felt icy and she was trembling, she suddenly remembered that on the upper floor lived the lunatics and huddled into the shadow as much as possible, she could see everyone without being seen, and she pursed her lips and thought I'll manage it, but once more all that came out was air and no whistle, she tried it a second time and a third time, then remembered a phrase, "the thorny garden", and wondered where she'd read it, who had said it? She wondered what the garden behind the wall was like, maybe they had sown thorns in it, however she'd never find out, for she saw that the gate was firmly shut and covered with sheets of metal, painted black, and the bell was high up, but all that was behind her. From the corner where she stood she could see in front of her a row of identical little houses, with tiny gardens or humble plants in pots – the play of the shadows created problematic shapes, a dog appeared, approaching at a crouch, she pursed her lips and whistled, once more without success, but she was determined that one day she'd manage it, the dog came up to her, it was brown and bored looking, it stopped in front of her and smelled her, she was afraid in case it might be dangerous, felt herself shrinking into the wall, but there was no room for any further retreat, and the dog stood there as if undecided, then came a little closer, it seemed to be looking her in the eyes and licking its lips, and just when she felt that she was suffocating with panic (maybe the dog had come out of the lunatic asylum, she thought), she heard whistling from further off and the sound of feet, and the others came running past her, Alcmene a couple of paces ahead with Haris and Dimitris behind her, and the dog turned fierce and barked, but they shouted to her, "run" and she realised she didn't have any choice and ran after them, she heard feet behind her catching up with her and said, it's the dog and ran faster, now they were in a narrow lane, the grass was stinging her, the nettles, or the thorny garden, but the unknown feet were getting closer and closer, spots of light were dancing in front of her eyes, the air was getting thicker choking her, she couldn't swallow, but she went on running as fast as she possibly could, until a hand grasped her, it was a man's hand and it hurt, but someone shouted to her, "jump", and the earth seemed to disappear from beneath her feet, she was flying through the air, a wail of "Mummy" escaped her, but then she landed hard on the ground and lay there motionless as if dead, and saw another body in a pale shirt flying over and landing beside her; and it ordered her in Angel's voice, "don't move" and he put his sweaty hand over her mouth and they lay there frozen.

And she had a premonition that this would be the last opportunity (it was certainly the first) they would have to be so near one another, and she was to remember later that his clothes had a different smell to them, maybe his hair too, something like freshly sawn wood, something unusual, and she thought perhaps it's from his job. And they lay there motionless and silent, then Angel cautiously moved a bit and a minute later told her, "the danger's past," for it was he who had spotted the danger and whistled, and she asked him, "where were you?" – "on the corner opposite" and thus she was sure that they were both playing in the same game, so that now what she required her friend to do was to climb out of this ditch (it was something like an overgrown trench), to have a good look around but keeping his head down, and then to reach out his bare hand to Antigone, "come on," he whispered, "there's no danger." And walking in the darkness through strange courtyards and ruined walls they came out once more onto the main thoroughfare with the trams, which was deserted and in the distance they heard the tramp of military boots – so that Angel said, "we'll go into the alley," for he knew his way round all of them and never got lost, beneath the trees and the shadows which would provide cover until they came out at the corner by her house; and her brother and sister were waiting there, asking in smothered voices, "what happened?" but Antigone didn't answer, only she confided to Alcmene – they had gone to bed and turned off the light, but hadn't gone to sleep – "I'm jealous because you're never scared," and she felt her sister caress her, and her hand had become as tender as a bird's wing, "we were all scared," she whispered. Then the light was suddenly switched on and Amalia was asking them, "but what have you been doing?" for their clothes were covered in earth and blue stains, however they made no answer, and their mother grumbled, "you never think of us," turned off the light and went out; and they heard her washing for hours.

All the next morning she said nothing, she seemed to have got through a mountain of work, but at a certain moment Antigone espied her going out into the garden where Dimitris was sitting in the shade reading, the mother went and sat beside her son and began to speak to him, and the boy remained with his head bent, she was scolding him and he was accepting it, his head increasingly bowed; however, she put out her hand and rested it on his shoulder, then got up thoughtfully – Antigone only just had time to step back, to seek a dark place to hide, in the corridor, among the hanging clothes. And she heard her mother's footsteps on the steps, she had to keep out of her way, her mother mustn't ask her, for she knew she'd tell her everything, so she smothered herself deep among the clothes, she remembered how she used to hide when she was tiny, but it was no longer possible now, for Amalia had indeed stopped in the corridor, and her daughter was afraid, she'll smell me, but she heard something like a sob, and then, "dear God, protect us" and then louder sobs, then footsteps leaving, which went into her parents' room, and then everything was plunged into silence, behind the closed door, behind the lock whose sharp click as it shut seemed to put a seal on the house.

And the girl said, I can't, I'm suffocating, and came out from among the clothes and in a little while went out into the sun, into the street which seemed to her to be pure white and unrecognisable; and she walked absent-mindedly, at one point she thought: towards the church of the Resurrection or towards Angel's house, somewhere where she could breathe again from the depths of her being, and find some relief for her tight chest. And later she was to wonder how much she had known or wanted to know – how it happened or how she found herself standing in front of the stone wall on which bright blue letters screamed at her, "No to civil mobilisation – EPON", written with a straggling, frightened tremble in them, paint spilt on the ground, and she walked past them as if mesmerised, in the end she arrived at her familiar corner, pursed her lips and then gave up – what did they do with the tins and the brushes she wondered, and arrived back at where the trams were, where she wandered as if lost, people jostled her or called her "Antigone, Antigone", and it was two of her girlfriends who came up to her and kissed her and complained, "the summer is over."

The Middle Ages – 7

They all used to dream of the horseman, they were jealous of him. He would dismount in silence, throw down at our feet the load he was carrying, withdraw into a corner and not speak. People said that he did not sleep at night, that his eyes remained wide open and staring like a statue's, "one day he'll roll from his saddle and die," insisted Christoforos, and said, "he is the man I trust above all others." The horseman listened as if dessicated so that a woman said, "anybody would think that all the blood has been sucked out of him," but still they heard not a word from him, maybe his ears were dessicated too; "let him be," they muttered, "perhaps he is a spirit, one of the damned, and he doesn't lie down at night, he doesn't feel pain," at which two or three of them drew their swords, "it is time to put it to the test," they cried, and they thought of his white horse, of which people said that it didn't sleep either. And then the horseman moved, put his weight on one hand and got up and, taking hold of the reins, left without speaking, the children grew bolder and followed him, and he walked ahead with the horse walking behind him as if hypnotised, after a bit they reached the church, chose the shadiest spot and lay down, he with his eyes wide open, his arms apart, his legs stretched out. "I admire the fact that he's always alert, one can have confidence in him," and they reminded him again how even the gods have ordained that some among their subjects should be constantly alert, but confidence is something different, he thought, it does not depend only on how much you stay awake and how much you sleep, it does not depend only on that, recollect whether Theologos ever slept, thought the other captains, but they didn't say it. And when the troubles began, there was no time for drawing conclusions, "when the tempest is raging how can you stop to think about such things?" Christoforos was to say, and panic spread, "we are destroyed and it is the end of us," they wailed, and with their horses galloping until they were out of breath they left the fields of their fathers for the last time and barricaded themselves in the castle. Since the morning ships had appeared floating on the horizon, "who are they bringing?" people asked Christoforos, and he was able to tell them, to guess, for traitors were multiplying in the city who informed him of a thousand secrets, though he could never believe them, "I am afraid of two-faced men, soothsayers, I am afraid because there are so many of them these days and they have wormed their way into our courtyards and our houses." The best way, he thought one night as he lay resting, would be to live alone, "I am thinking that we have become monks," Theologos had once said to him, but even there who could you trust? Theologos liked dark chambers, hermetically sealed cellars, which enclosed you both from without and within, and there you slept, there you awoke, and people brought you books which they had chosen, messages only from your family, "I have lived on the run" – and he meant I don't like it, it smells of mould in there. Then once more into his mind came the thought, whom can you trust? About the horseman he said he could put his hand into the fire, he has been tried and tested, whereupon friends and acquaintances fell on this and told him that he was Kokalas's man, "why has he never spoken to us, why does he avoid us?" – to which Christoforos replied, "that is exactly what reassures me." However he started asking the courier about his relatives, about where he came from and who his kindred were, and the man, almost in tears, remembered his luckless village, "I was there among the people who drove you off," he confessed, but he hadn't spoken, his father had kept him by his side, "you can hold my musket," he had advised; so the villagers were not so very peaceful then, the old men were standing at the front, unarmed, and behind them waited their sons with the muskets. And Christoforos smiled sadly, "I had guessed all that," he told him, "but it was long ago that the light fell on me" – "what light?" – "the light from God"; but who among his own people would believe it? He was doing battle with the Church and the clergy, "I too am fighting the bishop, and he has excommunicated me," he said, and did not know on whom to count, and then his courier said, "I'd like to lie down," and they separated, and he thought to himself, who else has Kokalas got huddled at his feet. If Irene were alive she would have told him, she might have woven a story out of it, a fairy tale, "I have never understood why you care and fight," he had said to her, and she had confessed that she loved them all, that is why she had never slept alone, "maybe one day you will feel for me," she complained to him, and then sought their embrace, "I feel that I belong to your body and have been torn from it, your skin has always been familiar to me, I feel it from within." In the house where they took them sat the mother, the girl and the bridegroom, once they had sat up till dawn in this chamber, it must have been the day of his betrothal; his hair was unruly, and he was constantly trying to smooth it back with his hand, for it was getting in his eyes and he couldn't dance. Their mother knew him, "how have we become opponents?" she whispered, the other two started to search out the reason, "you hid everything from the people," Christoforos told him in justification, "that is what all of us do," the other man murmured, he remembered the assembly they had held in the village, the lies, the complaints they made to him, later they carried off their booty, they took him with them and set off for the upper town. "I was expecting to be judged by the judges, by the laws," complained the first man, but Christoforos could have told him, they were scared, I tried, I called to them to come out of their houses but they all happened to be ill and sent their wives to weep – that's why there is always a solution, he remembered all the fairy tales, the good woman and the woodcutter, if we spent our time wandering alone, if we lived at sea and let ourselves drift all year long, maybe the problem would be solved, we would drown all the Kokalases, all the Farmakises out in the open sea and then we would disappear. But again they asked him, "you who are from the mountains, what do you want with the sea?", he seemed to hear them whispering in the dark, "this is the chance we've been waiting for, it's now or never," as he stood in the dark corner behind the door of the hut. And he said, "I want some comfort," if Irene had been there they would have lain down, "I am the first man who has kissed you, who has lain with you," and the woman answered "yes", not one of the others was a man, they were not whole, they did not fill her, and Christoforos held back his sobs, "I am devoured by a dreadful sickness," and he meant what drove him out of his mind. "The day before yesterday I rushed out into the street, I thought I saw her walking by," and he thought, Irene does not wear her hair in a plait, but it can only have been her, the way she drags herself along, it is she, they have exhausted her so that she is bowed, and thus he ran into the street and searched for her, but darkness and loneliness enveloped him and from somewhere a wind was blowing which froze his cheeks, his feet, but he felt the need to see her and he had to talk to her, I am weary without you, he would have told her, but in front of him there was nothing. And the wind blew again and he was chilled and turned up the low collar of his jacket, she might have gone round the corner, she might have flown away, but the most probable was that she had rotted in the earth, and he started running again as if whipped, everywhere he finds the same loneliness and darkness, walls in which windows and doors are closed, it is not impossible that she should be living in this world or in the other world, but then he withdraws once more, the next day he goes up to the graveyard, "I have become certain of the idea of death," he confessed. The greatest dream he ever had, and the most significant, was when they riddled him with bullets, he felt as if red hot nails were being hammered into his spine, that he was falling on the pavement, no longer breathing, and in his sleep he thought, now I am dead I cannot move, they will have to come and take me and adorn me for burial and say you left us in the flower of your youth, and the dead man lay there as if frozen and then he heard a carriage coming which was going to pass right over his legs, and it might crush them into fragments, yet he stayed motionless. Two days passed or two hours, and they told him, "it is time for you to get up, for us to leave," and he washed and saw that it was raining over the whole world and he had to cover such a long distance on foot; he recalled the horseman once more, he was lost in the rain, drowning, but the horseman was buoyed up on his horse and continuing onwards, seeking his village, his father, and he said, "it is divine justice," and this is the reason why he did not close his eyes, one would think he was constantly searching, afraid lest he go to sleep and his father come and recognise him, then leave again in despair. In all men there is a kind of responsibility which is called guilt, "what is it that you repent of?" – "all the people I have taken around my neck and drag with me," he whispered, there is a wife, two children, but the others told him, "a whole city is thirsting for justice, you owe it to them." And they surrounded the great house of Kokalas, "he is not blood of our blood," they cried, and they lit torches in the darkness, "he is sheltering a traitor in his house," and they murmured for whom were they being killed and weeping, and someone else shouted, "if it is possible, bring back my son to me," and then once more the mother and sister came out, "we were expecting him to grow tall like a tree, to bear flowers, and now even if they gave him to us encased in solid gold our pain would never fade." And they arrived with their flaming torches at the iron railings, took hold of the bars and shook them, "it is us the outsiders who are walled in," they said in great bitterness, this city has been reduced to a boundless prison, they looked at the ships that surrounded them, they looked at the burning villages, "they have us imprisoned here," they said. And there by the darkened house, the dumb windows, torches and sparks were amassing, and in front of them all a non-combattant clad in a sheepskin steps forward and says, "they despise us, they slam the door in our faces" – "that is not the way comrades behave to comrades," and they spoke once again of blood and of Kokalas, they say, "white dog, black dog, they're all from the same litter," he maintains his position through his wife's family, lordlings and usurers, "throw him out, the traitor," the sea surged and beat on the iron gate and foamed and caused it pain. And they cry then, "let us climb the railings and get in," yet not a single man moved forward, instead they all surged together and fell upon the gate, "there are lords in our midst who are traitors," they roared, and the tempest seemed to swell. There is a dark black line on the open sea and beyond it a row of torches flickering in the wind; and then a figure from another world seems to come out of the house, with tangled beard and hair, with the storm lamp lit, about his waist is slung a belt of cartridges, and he stands and looks at them, "who are you?" he asks, "who is your leader?" But they are pushing against the gate, and from the back, where there is no light and no end, a high voice is heard saying, "we are demanding that you give the traitor

333

up to us," and the voice remains hanging in the air, he seems not to have heard it, not to believe it, someone thinks he can detect the sound of weeping within the house, mourning, "you have embraced disaster," they shout at him, but the man stands like God, "go back to your homes," he tells them in measured and cool tones, "and anything that is suspect or criminal will be judged by those appointed to do so" – "and us, who will give our children back to us, and our houses?" a woman is heard to weep, "I have never harmed any of you, I shared my possessions with the city," he thunders, and then cries to them as if in outrage, "you must look elsewhere for those responsible, those who led you to rise up and who have kept you in misery for so many years." But they were even more enraged, he was providing them with a target here for them to hit, "he's cursing Christoforos to us, our leadership," howled two or three of them, and Christoforos himself arrived panting, someone had saddled his horse for him in haste and had said, "blood is being shed at Kokalas's house" – all the trouble and the disasters fall on me, he thought. And opening a passage between their hot, tense bodies, he arrived at the gate and stopped, he remembered I shall have to speak, to apportion, he remembered the man with the iron ring which made marriages and divorces, and he says, "I promise you justice." And then they come and unlock the door for him and the torches retreat, "we'll stay here and wait," they assure him or threaten him, his gaze catches two beardless boys, one is bending to speak to the other, they are pointing him out with their eyes, and it is as if they are saying he has vowed to take care of us, to give a good example, to set no store by riches. The day before yesterday he met a boy in the marketplace who told him, "I'd like you to read what I have written," but he merely took the paper, rolled it up and put it in his breast, that night he buried it in a corner, where he knew that he would never remember to search for it. He guessed what burden was being placed on him, remembered his mother, her words, and he stayed alert. In front of him Kokalas was walking with the lamp, it illuminated his green slippers, leaves on the bushes, the dead grass. And behind him lay the shadow of the mansion, into which in the past there had been no room for him to enter, whose door was a narrow crack.

Antigone

It was a house that she had envied for a long time, half-hidden among the pine trees, with a round tower rising at one corner which pierced the sky oddly, as if this had been the purpose of the whole mansion; and now the outside gate was wide open, the big garden suddenly accessible, and people were going in and out bearing all kinds of furniture, mostly chairs and little tables, though a few also had desks and beds, which they were hurrying out with, carrying them in pairs. The summer was by now breathing its last, October was coming to an end and everything indicated that the Germans would be departing, in the outlying neighbourhoods EPON held sway, the ELAS reserves, and – as people said – killings were happening all the time; now all the walls were covered with slogans, the blue letters large and written with greater confidence these days, the Germans no longer cared or bothered about it, and the members of the security battalions were lying low for they had to try and keep their heads on their shoulders, though every day some of these heads were rolling; and Dimitris said, "we had a boy called Brikas at school whom they've made into a hero," for he had held out for three hours in a house just below the Toumba, among the orchards, and had kept up a running gun battle with Dangoulas's men – "and did he survive?" asked Alcmene, "it's a mystery," her brother replied, "but he disappeared, they never found his body, nor did they take him," and he hadn't seemed the sort of person capable of something like this, he added, he'd always appeared to be one of the spoilt rich kids, the teacher's pet – "I remember him now," said Alcmene, "people used to say that he was a fairy," and blushed. And

Antigone remembered their own exploits, which they allowed her only to glimpse – though this had been by chance – but never told her about them, never let her listen, never made her a party to all their secrets.

Now a sea of leaves lay before her, fallen from the trees onto the paving and reaching right to the door of the mansion, for years it had been lived in by Jews, then the Germans took it over, and on the highest wall someone had nailed a huge V, bigger than any of the others in the city, visible to everyone who passed by in the street or on a tram, and no one said anything. Behind the house lay the garden, full of pomegranates and fig trees, and waist-high weeds; surrounding it was a wall, two metres high, with broken glass on the top which dated from the old days – and as the men and women ran backwards and forwards grabbing anything they could find, Antigone thought, there's nothing I can do, and thus made her way deeper into the garden, where now, right in the middle, the weeds had been exterminated leaving a circular clearing, covered with ash and charred fragments, where (they said) for weeks the Germans had been burning maps and a whole mass of documents so that the neighbours had been cursing them because of all the smoke and smuts. However, a little further off, nearer the wall, the pomegranates were still deep green, or with their leaves just turning yellow, and their fruit was swelling by now, and she went and walked under them, even though this wasn't the time for enjoying a walk, for she heard screams and cries, five Germans armed with machine-guns had dashed forward and were hitting (though only with kicks and punches) any looters they found in their path, and the looters were dropping everything in panic and running for safety, and the garden instantly emptied and the Germans laughed, then hesitated, maybe they would go to the houses further down the street which were also being plundered. So Antigone stood still among the branches, and thought this is my second escape, even though she hadn't been doing anything or taking anything. And just then a balcony door opened, it was high up among the tree tops with sky and clouds reflected in its glass panes, two men came out as though they'd been forgotten there, they had a good look all round and below them, then one said, "they've all gone," so that they could get on with the job – or the opposite – and after a minute they heaved an enormous wardrobe out onto the balcony, with mirrors from top to bottom of it, and Antigone had never seen anything so beautiful as the way that the branches and clouds were reflected in it, a peaceful landscape, then for a moment the lacy wrought iron of the balcony, and the two men seemed to be surveying the courtyard below, perhaps seeking for assistants, and she heard one of them say, "we'll need some rope," and at the garden gate figures were once more appearing – the boldest – who would be saying, "the Germans have gone," and in a little while they were standing below the balcony and talking, calculating, remembering what was still left to be taken. And just then the man on the balcony yelled, "get hold of it," for the triple-leafed wardrobe was tilting, tottering, and the others below were enraged, "are you out of your minds, you bastards," they screamed, for they only just had time to see the great mass coming down right on top of them, the men above had given it the final shove, the coup de grâce, as if having fun, which then deafened them as mirrors and wardrobe shattered on the paving, pandemonium as everyone ran blindly to save themselves. And once more Antigone was alone.

When she recounted it, it seemed incredible (Haris was with her on the verandah and he gave her a bemused look, "how did you manage not to be scared?" he murmured), but Antigone said, "you don't realise the danger" and her mother was cross with her, saying that such scrimmages are not the place for girls – by the afternoon Antigone had forgotten it, she went with Haris down to the boulevard where German lorries were roaring crazily past, "they're leaving," the boy said and both of them felt joy that they would be liberated. And he requested her, "show me the house," as if he had some secret plan of his own, and there it was in front of them, the gate gaping wide open, and she took his hand, as if he was blind, and he was squeezing hers hard, "don't be afraid," she whispered to him in embarrassment, and they advanced keeping very close to one another, they reached the garden with the pomegranate trees and she asked him, "but what are we going to steal?" – "once upon a time we used to climb over the wall at night and steal their figs," the boy told her (one night they had locked the watchman in his hut – all this was before the war – and he vowed that he'd see them hung, and thus they never set foot there again, nor ever stole again) and Antigone listened and thought, so he wasn't such a goody-goody after all, this "dandy" as people teasingly called him.

But their laughter was cut off short when they saw two Germans coming running, crossing the garden and shouting, a young sergeant, tall and bony, with curly blond hair,* and a more heavily built soldier; the sergeant drew his pistol and his eyes glittered like a cat's, they seemed to be saying here is death, and unconsciously Antigone and Haris put their hands up, the girl's thin arms, the boy's trembling shirtsleeves, and the foreigner was saying in a monotone, "steal, steal," at which Haris stammered "nein, nein kamerad," for they had learnt such words – as well as a few others – but the other man insisted, "steal, steal," for the garden was a ruin now, with bits of wood lying everywhere and broken glass trampled under foot, and Antigone felt faint, maybe she swayed, and she felt Haris support her, the man threatened them once more with his pistol, but the other whispered something to him, they looked at them, specially at Haris, and laughed, then in the end the sergeant howled "raus" and made a movement as if he would hit them; and they grasped each other's hand automatically, each finding the other's palm, and Antigone said to herself, it's as if I'd touched the electric current, a bare live wire, and the man barked "raus" at them once more, so they started walking, hesitantly at first, then increasingly rapidly, and Haris muttered, "don't turn round, they might have us in their sights," maybe they were about to hear a pistol shot (Antigone remembered the stories her father used to tell about Asia Minor, about how they would find children killed, shot in the back, and Amalia would scold him, "you'll terrify the girls" and would pack them off to bed) and thus she felt her skin was burning, she was panting even though they were walking slowly, and in the end they came out of the garden gate into the street, and without needing to agree on it both started running, the girl in front of Haris, until

---

* Even forty years later, I can never forget him; he was about twenty, with a thin, sweating face, blue-eyed, given to shouting. We stood there, Irene and I, with our hands up, I was thinking that she looked like a woman already, maybe we were facing a danger of a different kind. But I suppose he took pity on us, the way we were both trembling, and let us go.

they found themselves in a little cul de sac with fences and humble little houses and they could smell a different world, greenery. And they collapsed onto a couple of stools, where three black-clad women knew what had happened and brought jugs of water and splashed their heads and Antigone was startled to find little streams of water flowing down her cheeks and her neck onto her breast. One of the women said to her, "go on, go to the privy and pee," they had pushed Haris into a corner but the girl averted her eyes; afterwards a woman came out carrying a tin and said, "eat a spoonful of sugar" – all folk remedies – for they had been terrified, and Antigone saw that Haris was deathly pale and thought that I myself can't look much better. And when she raised her eyes she saw that they were below his house, and on the verandah was standing his mother, who was perhaps nodding (so it seemed to her), signing him to come up.

But things were not to end there, they didn't want to leave it like that, and Haris was begging, "let me take you home," which was not so very far, or not if you took the direct route; they preferred to go by a narrow street though, through the gardens, at one point water lay in a puddle which they jumped over, and they held hands again, but she sensed that Haris was uncomfortable, "we had a narrow escape," she whispered, and she meant the captain, his pistol, now they were beside the overgrown trench, where might Angel be flying, she wondered, she hadn't seen him for days, and finally they found themselves once more by the wall, the blue slogan had been obliterated, probably by the neighbours, and both of them laughed – both thinking the same thing. And just then they heard someone hissing "psst, psst" but could not tell where it was coming from, they turned round and looked at the houses, the windows, but now the voice came again from somewhere high up, "Katinitsa", it said, "Katinitsa" – and it was coming from the top of the wall, a pale boy's head was there, watching them and smiling at them and asking, "are you Katinitsa?" And Antigone shuddered, reflected that she was not called Katinitsa – and thank goodness for that – and the head spoke again, "you have red little lips like our Katinitsa," then beside the pale and fleshy head appeared his hand, holding a bright red flower, he threw it to Antigone and seemed to be crying, for the rose had fallen on the ground between them and neither of them had touched it, "Katinitsa", said the pale face once more, whereupon Haris bent and gave it to her, "take it," he said, "it would be wrong not to," but the girl held it by the very end of the stem, she dared not look at it, dared not look at the dreary building behind the wall, to the barred windows. Until she heard a howl and raised her eyes, but he was no longer there, all she was hearing was the howl of a dog, "someone pulled him back, they pushed him down," explained Haris who had watched, then "you ought to be going home," he advised.

Yet once again they took a side road, shaded by trees, Haris was saying that in two days the Germans would have left, that the resistance fighters had already got as far as the Farm School, to the Kafé Koulé and the "Kyvelia", and Antigone thought of the things that Dimitris and Alcmene said, which seemed to be the same, the same words, she suspected that they all met secretly and talked about such matters, maybe at EPON, for the walls were constantly shrieking with writing, and she asked him very timidly, "are you a member of EPON?" at which he looked at her in amazement, "of course," he answered, but at that point they both stopped as if it was painful, as if they feared where this revelation might lead – but the girl thought, he trusts me, as if in complaint against Dimitris and her sister. At last her house came into sight, from the back though, the side where the tram-driver lived, and she told the boy, "leave me here," as if they had something to hide, and he agreed, albeit with some hesitation, for a moment he took her hand, "goodbye", he whispered and both of them were bright red, Antigone said, "palms are sweaty and dirty," maybe the fingernails and the arms were too, but Haris was murmuring "goodbye", and his voice seemed drowned by his breathing.

And thus she ran to the tap, the little tap in the yard, where two bees were hovering, and rinsed her hands thoroughly, enjoying the way the water played dripping between her fingers, then raised both palms to her cheeks and held them there, as if feeling some contact with another world, as if time was slipping away like water swallowed up (but where?), until her sister awoke her once more, saying, "you should watch what company you keep," at which Antigone felt, she's jealous of me, but who is she jealous about? About everyone? – and perhaps this was the truth. And she was not taken in when Alcmene came up and put her hand on

Antigone's shoulder, stroked her, let her hand wander down her back, saying, "you have to be careful these days," just as if she was privy to hidden dangers, as if she knew all there was to be known. And then she suddenly muttered, "if the German had been going to kill you, who would have saved you?" so that Antigone wondered, how had she learnt about it?, but her sister explained, "we were in the garden next door watching," though she didn't explain who "we" were, and the younger girl begged, "don't tell Mummy," who was constantly anxious, she would look into their eyes and had a special fear for her husband, for each one of her children, she could scent that secrets were lurking all around her, that they all concealed the truth. Which now was once more to remain hidden, for Alcmene said, "no, she wouldn't understand and she'd cry," at which the younger sister remembered last summer, the smothered weeping in the corridor, the refuge sought in her bedroom, the door closed until noon when their father went in and they were both lost in talk, with the door half open, and Antigone crept up to it and saw them sitting on the bed, two bent backs, their heads on each other's shoulder and her father's arm around her mother – and she made up her mind we must never make her suffer again. However they didn't keep this promise, nor care about their mother, specially not Dimitris, nor Alcmene who was now comforting her that "in two days it will all be over", hence their mother's agony would be over too, as if replying to her sister's beseeching question.

They heard the garden gate, it was Dimitris and he was out of breath, he came up to them and said, "Alcmene, come inside," and Antigone thought: always their own secrets; they left her in the yard where the light was fading, soon it would be plunged in obscurity, and the garden with all its hiding places would be transformed, the garden where when she was little they had crouched under the rosebushes and their mother would come out and play with them, saying in a loud voice, "now where are they, where can they be?" and looking by the trees, where they certainly weren't, but never at the place where they were hiding, and Antigone would hold her breath, keep her feet tucked under her, with her white socks, her brown sandals, and Amalia would say again, "I can't find them," and it would all end in laughter and kisses, in "I caught you" and hugs, and then pleas of "again,

again" and their mother never tired of it, never wept nor was ever angry.

But now it was as if the game was torn to shreds and a phrase came inexplicably into her mind, she said to herself: we shall pass through the circle of fire and perhaps only ashes will remain, and the words seemed meaningless or incomprehensible, as if she was raving in her sleep, and she wondered, since when?, and she remembered the Germans' garden, where they burnt their maps and all that remained was a threshing floor of ashes, girls' minds have a strangeness (who had told her that?), they leap wildly from one thing to another for hours on end, they weave fact and fiction into a wreath, they say pick flowers and bedeck yourself, they say how lovely it would be to lie here, for it to be night and for me not to be afraid, for me to be surrounded by a fence like a cage made out of branches, for me to see everyone and remain invisible – and by now darkness had fallen completely, Amalia came to the window and called, "Antigone, I can't see you," and she showed herself and said, "I'm sitting in the garden," where now you could feel the chill of autumn, so that her mother advised, "don't catch cold" and came out to seek for her among the branches, the bushes, which tricked her eyes and tormented her, "I can't see you," she complained, and Antigone once more came out into the square of light that shone from the window, making the world around it lost in darkness, and Amalia admitted, "the whole of creation founders when you are scattered and I can't see you all." And in a little while they were all sitting round the table, Amalia – she alone – made the sign of the cross and they began their silent meal. Without their father, he must be out somewhere fighting to earn their daily bread, he who was the most silent of them all, full of thought or maybe reproach, "his cares weigh heavy on him," said Amalia, and he was absent from their meal, fighting.

Christos

Every time people asked him, he would say, "I'm fighting," and he meant that he was finding a way to survive, which was by no means always easy, there wasn't anything to boast about in the fact that he'd gone to a beer house – as cashier – where they raked in the money, but at least he'd get back at night with a full stomach, sometimes he'd bring a package home, delicacies of the kind that were hard to find, sweets, which his children loved, specially Antigone, and he consoled himself with the thought, "just a little bit longer", then he'd be getting back to sleepless nights and a regular job, for everyone said that a great many newspapers would be being published – and most important of all, without censorship. And Dimitris was always asking him what he had heard, although the boy had his own sources of information, their groups, the hidden proclamations, which he discovered one day in the cellar, but didn't tell Amalia in case she started crying again; only he took the boy aside (it was the same day), said to him, "let's go for a walk" and gave him a whole lot of advice. And it turned out that Alcmene was involved as well, "she's more fanatical," this he could see, and Christos begged, "be careful of your mother," then "is the little one involved too?" he asked, but Dimitris denied it – "although she knows everything," he confessed. And Christos prayed for the days to roll by and the danger to pass, because by now the killings were taking place in the streets, as near as the Fountain, and further down – and thank goodness the members of the security battalions were lying low and were slipping out of town, people said that they were all gathering at Kilkis. And he consoled himself, "I'm fighting," that his little ship had withstood the tempests, and he was proud that he'd been steering his vessel right.

But he had never imagined that he'd find himself among captains – and this was to happen. One night they summoned them (who chose them he didn't know, but there were three of them), they went to a house at Sykies, where two lonely old women lived, dressed all in black, and they took them to a room; outside there must have been a garden, for he could smell the greenery, and in a little while the door opened and in came two men wearing old suits who greeted them without expression – Christos thought, they're trying to give themselves stature – however they rapidly revealed what they were after, or what they are ordering us to do, he grumbled to himself once more. They only gave their Christian names – Aris, Frixos – and it was the second who spoke the most; that in two days the resistance fighters would be entering the city, and EAM was planning to bring out a newspaper, and, most important: before the Germans left. The printing press was all arranged, but they needed journalists, and Christos asked, "but why us?", to which Frixos replied, "I have asked around and found out about you," which must have been meant as praise, in the end Frixos took off his glasses and rubbed his eyes thoroughly – he must be a teacher or a lawyer, Christos reckoned – his colleagues remained silent, only they ended with an "all right" and Frixos left, they could work out the details with the other man. And everything was sorted out fine, they would shut themselves up in a basement the next day, and from then on "the organisation will be responsible for everything" – and Aris got up, "don't leave for another quarter of an hour," he advised, and said goodnight; as he was going out Christos noticed that his back pocket had a bulge in it, and he thought, naturally he's armed, then a little before they left the black-clad women offered them ouzo and bread and feta cheese, "it's all we had," they said in excuse, but only one of the three men had a drink and then they left, one by one. And Christos saw shadows standing on the street corners, one raised his hand to his hat, as if saluting, and as he walked on he felt that they were protecting him – when he reached the back of the Governor's Mansion he saw one of the shadows approaching him, "from now on, comrade, you'll have to look out for yourself." And indeed he proved to be the last shadow.

Except that he felt that from there onwards there was no danger, only dark little narrow streets, which unravelled or descended, which passed through the square with the plane tree, at which point he remembered that the "Black Tree" was somewhere round here, and a little further along Amalia's little house, and said to himself, "there it is," however it had grown dilapidated, the paintwork was faded, and there was not a single light, it might have collapsed, he thought – and he took the lane to the right, seeming to recall the old labyrinth, where he needed to recognise the signs in order to know how to find his way out, the tree with a crooked trunk, the window of the hat shop, a house with pale blue windows, and then the Acheiropoietos, Egnatia Street, which now he hurried down and caught the first tram he found – standing on the open platform at the back since there were no seats. And the tram-driver said, "it's cooled off," scents from the sea were blowing in the night breeze, a whole world of flowering seaweed, and Christos thought about the following day, first of all he would have to reassure his wife, to keep it all secret from his children, at least for a couple of days, and he thought that maybe they'd have to sleep alone at night, and lie listening to the creakings of the house in the dark, or to footsteps in the street. And by the time he reached his own neighbourhood it was already late, he said to himself better not make a target of myself in the main road, and thus took a little alley, he seemed to be traversing courtyards, between shrubs and cheap climbing plants, with a multitude of shadows of which most were motionless; only one seemed different, it seemed to bear the shape of a man who was seeking to conceal himself, to lose himself among the leaves and branches. And Christos stood there in two minds, he had a strange feeling, as if he could smell the shadow, recognised it, and the other man felt the same for he spoke, said "good evening Mr. Christos", in a whisper though, and he recognised the naughty boy (Angel I believe he's called, he thought), who was wearing something rather unusual, a trilby which covered his eyes and made him look like someone at a masked ball, and a red handkerchief round his neck which showed through his open jacket. And he asked in embarrassment, "have you gone mad?" (it would be funny if his own Dimitris also had a red handkerchief), but the youth begged him to speak in a whisper, he had a strange expression as if he was playing his role with some difficulty – so Christos asked him, "why are you hiding?" and the other replied trustingly, "they're having a secret meeting upstairs"; it was a grand two-storey house, between its closed shutters light could be seen, passing through red curtains, "I don't understand," said Christos – "officers and merchants, the bourgeoisie", explained Angel. And it was lucky the darkness was like a thick veil, for his eyes smiled ironically, he thought, just look what I've stumbled into, and shivered, but he bade the boy goodnight and came out into his own street, only a bit further and he'd be at his own front door, he reflected, I'll have to get dressed up too, and act a part, on the following day he would either have to be invisible or else a workman.

But Amalia didn't laugh at all, her face clouded over, she told him that it wasn't fun and games, but in the end she got out an old jacket of his and some worn-out trousers, the cap that he used to wear every time he set off to work in the vineyard, and she wrapped them all up and hid them, so that the children wouldn't see them and start asking questions – "where are they now?" he asked, and she answered that only Antigone was at home, reading. But before he could even begin to imagine in what darkness Dimitris and Alcmene might be keeping watch, Amalia murmured, "may God watch over us," and he felt all her bitterness, he would not have been surprised if she had started crying, yet he said nothing to her until she said, "every day people are found killed" – "they're from the other side," he answered, and felt this conversation had been going on forever, that both of them were eaten up with the fear "suppose that ...", even during these final hours. And just at that moment the door opened and Dimitris and Alcmene came in, their colour high as if they'd been running, out of breath, but neither of them bore any trace of a red handkerchief, they said, "we went out for a walk," and Christos asked, "sprinting?" and they all laughed, even Amalia. And their mother set the table for their simple meal, Antigone came out of her room with her eyes reddened – maybe from reading – and they ate in silence, each tormented by his own thoughts, and each chewed his own portion thoroughly and insistently, in mouth or in mind, stubbornly grinding it fine and stubbornly remaining silent, so much so that Amalia complained that she couldn't stand the deathly hush and their thoughtful faces.

And they told them that they had to keep quiet, not to attract attention, and they went down into the basement as they'd agreed, one of them every quarter of an hour, where five printers were already waiting – four who were known to them and the fifth a slip of a boy who was constantly sneezing – two tables were awaiting them with paper and pencils, and they fell to work without speaking, for there were many things to be finished, however Christos thought, I can smell the hot metal and the ink, and they awoke hopes in him, optimism, that he was returning once more to a well-known much loved land, something that he'd never felt when he'd gone to visit his mother and father, in their fields and vineyards, and the old people grumbled, "you've forgotten us," his father was bent now, as if he'd been broken in two somewhere in the region of his stomach, and his mother had undergone a transformation by wrinkles, she had shrunk into a tiny little woman, except that she still maintained her voice and her way of reproaching and grumbling. But all those matters were out of sight now, as if they had donned pale garments of invisibility, for now the only things on which the light shone were the sheets of paper, the proclamations, an announcement signed by Bakirtzis and Markos, and in the background the cases of type, the silhouettes of bent figures, and a constant play of metallic sounds, which Christos remembered, the type being set piece by piece into the chase, an irritatingly dry cough from somewhere, answered by a sneeze from the boy. And the hours merged into one another, they must have lost all sense of time, for at one point two strangers came down the stairs and found themselves in the dark, however they said, "it's night," which might have meant that they ought to be finishing, and Christos got out his handkerchief and wiped his face, the printers were scurrying backwards and forwards, and they had indeed set four pages which were waiting laid out in a row on the marble, one man took the sponge, moistened it and then dampened the pages with it, and one of the strange men was again impatient, "get a move on," he ordered from the shadows; at which the master printer seemed irritated, "we're ready," he answered and sat down, maybe because his legs wouldn't hold him up any more, and just then four boys came down into the basement, took each set of pages and carried them up between them, as they were heavy. They took them all like this and

Christos asked, "where are they taking them?" but no one answered him; the printers said, "we'll have a wash and then we'll be off."

And when they got out into the street it was indeed night, they left as they had arrived, one by one, every quarter of an hour, Christos was the third to go and rejoiced at the coolness, he stopped in the street behind St. Sophia and instantly felt that he was not alone, as if someone was following him, he thought, I'd better not turn round, but the thought was in vain, for a man came up and walked alongside him, "don't be frightened, comrade," he muttered, Christos turned and saw that it was one of the men from the printing press, one of those who had stood at the side and given orders, not one of the printers, "do you remember me?" the man asked, and Christos stared at him, no he didn't recognise him with a moustache, and his hat was hiding his face, but his eyes were shining, he must have been over fifty, and he laughed as if they were joking, "you have greetings from Euripides," he said – at which Christos thought, that's why they chose me, but they had already reached Tsimiski Street – and the other man muttered, "I have to leave you," and gave him his hand, smiled and left, and as Christos watched him move away he felt like calling, Elias, for it was his voice that brought him back into Christos's mind, and his look which always had something playful in it, as if he was laughing at you. So many emotions, he complained, coming one on top of each other, and he rubbed his hands together, as if they were deadened and numb, and he wondered, so am I a coward? And unexpectedly, automatically, he took the cap off his head and threw it into a corner, and he felt a little breeze coming from the direction of the sea.

By the time he reached home it was blowing hard, and there, at his door, two figures stood, it was Dimitris and Haris talking together, and all his son said was "are you back, Dad?", as if he was worried or had not expected him; in the little garden her shadow stirred, he thought, she's waiting for me, and his Amalia came running – "are you back?" she asked, and he smiled in the midst of all this warmth, and he took her and they went up the steps together, their two or three steps, inside he could hear the girls singing, "don't torment me ...", then he stopped short as if remembering, asked Haris, "what news from your father?" but the youth answered, "we don't know," meaning his mother and his brothers, and Christos told him, "tomorrow we'll come and see you" and felt an ineffable peace, as if he had done a good deed. And his wife was bewildered, "but what's got into you?", for their visits to Dorothea had ceased months, years ago, if it wasn't for the fact that they saw her sons they would have forgotten each other, only once they'd run into one another when out for a walk, at the New Helvetia park, she was walking with her youngest son, she seemed paler than ever, said, "how did we lose touch with each other?" and through the words was heard a different complaint, and she wouldn't let go of their hands, she's still delicate, thought Christos, she has slender lily-like fingers, without rings or bracelets now, and in the end she said goodbye and they moved off, and in the evening they talked a lot about Elias and his lonely wife.

And Christos requested, "bring me something to eat, and let me lie down," as if what he was saying was: alone; and this indeed is what happened, in a little while the songs were hushed, everyone settled down, they turned off the lights and he realised he was sinking exhausted, with an inexplicable numbness in his legs, so that he said to himself, let me bend them in case it brings some relief, but no, not even like this, so he stretched them out, and in the end begged, let me fall asleep, for darkness reigned and a benign silence; except that in a little while everything began to shine and he wondered where from? It seemed in a way to be shining from beneath him and he did indeed lean over to see what it was, oh God, a whole lot of candles which are burning just under their bed but only there none beyond it and Christos panicked he said they'll set fire to us he screamed he felt that he was howling and that the candles were lighting everything then he says I'll blow them out so we'll escape, and he leaps up in panic and it is night and smells like rain, and he feels with his hand beside him but finds only the coolness of an unoccupied pillow, he smells it, thinks it is Amalia's scent, gropes in the darkness on the empty mattress, nightmares were suffocating me, he thinks, and he seeks to find some calm, I must let myself relax, and he lies on his back, arms and legs spread wide, just like the way he first learnt to keep his balance in the sea, no matter how much the waves were swelling, which got into his ears, his nose, and tickled him. Thus he drifts once more into a world which he cannot see, which is probably taking on incomprehensible shapes, branches perhaps and spiders, which are continuously mutating and flashing on and off – until he hears someone talking animatedly, it is a man shouting, "wake him up" and at that moment he feels that he is being prodded, but by a woman's hand which feels for him and cares for him, which is begging, "don't be frightened." And over the bed his brother is bending, upset, he says, "Mother has died," he is crying, and Christos feels his insides turn over – and no one understands at all when he whispers, "the candles" and leans over and raises the linen sheet to look under the bed.

The cart was waiting for them outside, they got into it in a hurry and set off, Amalia looked at him in silence, and Christos felt that if she spoke she would say, but where are you going? It was his own mother though, he couldn't refuse. And as they were moving along fast towards the market, towards Vardari, his brother told him about it (he looked rough and unshaven, like wood that has been dried for a long time in the sun), that their mother had fallen while she was doing the washing, had turned white as a sheet and had frozen there, and had only whispered, "I can't" and then nothing more, "when?" asked Christos, and the other answered, "when it was ending," when twilight was coming. And in the night he had harnessed the cart and set off fast, "they could have killed you," said Christos, and indeed the guerrillas were everywhere, and people from the other side too; now they had come out among the orchards, they took the dirt tracks, thinking the vines and the bushes will conceal us, the Germans' cars were passing at speed on the asphalt road, all heading out from the city, towards the north, and his brother said, "they're leaving continuously," at one point they heard rifle shots and then a mortar, "we'll fill in the craters," laughed Christos – and the other man gave the horse a lash with the whip.

The sun was fully up by now, but they felt a coolness down their spines, the cart was jolting over all the potholes and bumps in the track, at last they came out into a wider road and Christos recognised where they were; there were two age-old oak trees and a stream with a stone bridge over it, which for years had borne the words "Arianoutsou Novelties", and it was about half an hour away from their own land, maybe three quarters of an hour. But he was to recount later that "we didn't calculate right" for as his brother lashed the horse again and the beast made another spurt forward, they heard a thundering and then something like whistling and Christos said, "they're shooting at us," and indeed there were three men with carabines, they raised their weapons and stopped them, said "get down" and they were not joking, no matter how much the younger man explained that they were on their way to bury their mother, that they were brothers, then one of the men turned – he must have been in command – and had a good look at Christos and asked him, "who are you?" – "a journalist and a comrade," he replied, remembering yesterday, the armed man thought for a moment, and finally decided, "your brother can go on with the cart, but you will stay for us to check your identity" – "my mother has died, we're on our way to bury her," Christos said again, he felt that he was pleading and was annoyed, but the other man raised his eyebrows, "it's an order," he said, "you are neither going into nor coming out of the village" – "listen, comrade," Christos tried again, "ask General Bakirtzis about me," but the other man remained distrustful, "I don't know him," and once more his eyebrows were raised, "our captain is Homer," he stated – "take us to him," said Christos, "he's away at a distant village, we can't go and find him." All five of them stood in the middle of the road with the cart beside them, and his brother then said, "all right, I'll go alone to the village and I'll fetch my family here so they can tell you," to which the other man said, "go and don't come back, we'll sort things out with your brother" and Christos realised that they were in an impasse, "you go," he aquiesced, "so at least one of us can be there to carry her coffin," and before his eyes passed the image of Amalia, standing there on the steps as they left, somewhere her bitterness had taken root again, she was whispering to him that she was right.

And when his brother had left, the guerrillas told him, "follow us," they left the road and walked through the vineyards and unsown fields, a little way off they could see a coppice, and Christos thought: their lair, but they were getting further and further from the village, from any chance of seeing his mother and praying by her body – and he began to cry. Then one of the men said, "have a cigarette" and offered him a broken, badly rolled one; he took it and they lit it for him with a flint and wick –

by the time he had smoked it they had entered the coppice, it was a green and shady world, in places a tangle of low-growing plants, which all smelled like paradise, and they sat down on the ground and rested, they said, "sit down and we'll get to the bottom of it." And there was no other way but to sit down and to ponder, to fear the worst, that they might kill him.

Angela

And as they were going down the stairs and he was saying, "these are evil days" and until they reached the door and he embraced her – and he was crying, "I suffocate at home" – and even when they went out into the courtyard of the three-storey house and kissed, and all the shadows and fragrances of the garden enveloped them, until in the end they realised that they were not alone, but that a man was watching them from across the road (Yannis laughed in annoyance and said, "these days the bastards are wearing red handkerchiefs), Angela was thinking, this resembles happiness, and whispered, "you are the lost angel." In the evening the same people had all gathered again in someone's house (they seemed to be a group of close friends and the men talked together in low voices while the women sat in the next door room and chatted about their own matters, gossiped), they were being entertained at the home of the retired colonel and his wife, a fat woman whose hair was getting comically thin, and in the end they got their small wireless out of the lavatory – out of the cistern – and desperately tried to listen to the news broadcast, but all that came out was the crackling of static and behind it a voice that kept fading, so they strained their ears to try and hear what it was saying. And Angela heard them declare again, "we must defend ourselves against the Communists," which was all they ever talked about at every meeting, and she felt that somewhere in the air an invisible cord was floating, which would come and strangle them – for every time they left one of these evening parties Yannis would reveal everything that had been said, or at least the most terrifying bits, since it was all about people being butchered or strung up and she wondered who was doing it – the poor? Her old acquaintances from the refugee settlement? Or those poor devils who used to frequent the tavern, which had been closed for more than a week now, since Vassilis had gone off to Athens with his musicians? And Yannis would answer her as if he could read her mind, as if he could look through her doubtful eyes and penetrate her very brain, "they're all one and the same, they want to seize everything, to strip you bare," and perhaps he was remembering the old business with his workers, in '35, in '36. And Angela would disagree, "I come from the ranks of the poor myself," and perhaps she meant I have never seized anything, neither from you nor from anyone else.

Moreover she knew that this three-storey house was not quite unfamiliar to her, a little further on was the place where Michalis had his club, further up was where the other Yannis used to grovel, and right next door (and she could see the light this very minute) was the mansion of her "uncle" Elias, all these things hurt like invisible glass splinters that have entered your blood stream and are injuring your innermost parts, from time to time they seek a way out and she would feel that her neck was burning, behind her ear, or even further down, in her armpit, at her ribs. And perhaps, if they had discussed such things, she would have confessed that she longed for all that, the old days, for now nothing seemed certain and instead all they could do was to doubt and wait and hope for better days, and think time is on our side, we are young. But now margins were narrowing, everything was channeled into a straight path, shadows and evasions no longer possible, there was no corner left to hide in or to cry in or to say perhaps here where I am standing might be a hatch through which I could descend and run and then come out by the sea, where perfect emptiness would await me, then I would be able to breathe freely and let myself go, and make plans for the better, and hope that somewhere the better really is awaiting me. But she did not dare to speak, she couldn't cry to him you are shining like a candle, only candles come to an end, you can tell by the smell that they are dying, she couldn't say this, she was afraid of him, and perhaps (she suspected) this might be wrong, for he enfolded her in his embrace once more and said, "don't be afraid, I'm here to look after you," perhaps neither understood what they were crying for, each one separate from the other, no matter how closely their arms encircled each other's back – for he could not see her face (she felt his hair on her cheek, his scent so familiar to her), her eyes were staring out into the darkness, unfaltering, unblinking, and what they saw was branches and leaves, lacy wrought-iron railings, a little way off the shadow with the red handkerchief ever present, and even further still a tiled roof, which she calculated coldly must be the Bulgarian's house (and was he still alive or had he died?), around it his roses and his pine trees, which were blocking out the night sky, robbing her of the stars, or part of them.

And she asked him, "what have I got left for them to steal" – the reds, that is – for she was still living in her poor attic, which he too knew well (familiar now with all its corners, its whisperings, the sounds of the night), in spite of the fact that he would often say to her, "whatever is mine is yours," and one night when they were drunk and rolled off her bed onto the floor, he cried out, "I want you to chew every bit of me," and he seemed to be wanting to cry and choke, to feel his sorrows (or his guilt) pulsing within him, to be saying, "I want you to devour me so that I find some peace," and she too had a wildness within her and bit him just above his nipple, so that he cried out but said in satisfaction, "yes, like that," and then lay still, on his back, and Angela heard the darkness speaking and saying, "take a knife, kill me" – she remained mute, in the end felt sorry for him, caressed him, said, "I don't like you to feel pain," and took him, totally vulnerable, in her arms, kissed him, rocking him gently as if her lost child, the only one of the three to have been killed, had come to life again. And as her gaze played over the railings, the trailing stems of plants, the solitary yellowing leaves, she thought each person is familiar with his own wounds, heals them the only way he knows, and feels no disgust at kissing them or washing them.

Suddenly they heard the steps creak once more, the others were coming down, and Yannis whispered to her, "hide within me," and he himself was smothered against a tree, and indeed a man came out, he must have been the officer of the gendarmerie, however he didn't look round at all, simply hurried off down the lane, and for a short time they could hear his footsteps crunching on the earth – then nothing. Except that the other shadow, the shape with the red handkerchief, emerged from his hiding place and moved off fast in the direction which the policeman had taken. And Angela noticed that Yannis's expression had clouded over, he seemed deeply troubled, as if he had a problem that was tormenting him, and after a moment he suddenly commanded, "let's go," hands were no longer linked, embraces put aside, they walked on as two separate figures, and covered quite a distance without speaking until, once again suddenly, he said, "will you marry me?", like a patient with a high temperature, so that Angela stammered, "but when? How?" to which he most unexpectedly replied, "tomorrow, at five o'clock, in a little church," and she looked at him thunderstruck, but he continued walking as if annoyed, terrified, his eyes looking straight ahead, his head held high and firm. He had always been quite incomprehensible, he terrified her, he seemed like something that changed shape, sometimes a child and sometimes a monster, as if his reason was disturbed, one night she had wept and had accused him, "it isn't possible," she had lamented "to be rained on and dissolved and not feel pain," and he had asked, "what do you mean?" – "everything," she had cried – and his only reply was the warning, "don't frighten me." And every time, every time they went through a crisis, she felt that they were divesting themselves of bloodied garments and then bathing; and she longed for clothes of a different kind, clean and cool.

And she became aware of light shining, they'd come out into the main street, and Angela thought it leads further and further away from youth, so that unconsciously her hand reached out and found his in the darkness, she thought how icy his fingers were, and begged as if lost, "let's go to the sea," just as if their only salvation lay there – but he appeared not to be listening to her, not to understand, and thus their fingers let go and they walked on in silence. At one point they met three young men, who seemed to be in a hurry and running, so once more they were alone and when they reached the church, the Resurrection, he asked, "aren't you going to answer me?" as if this was the only thing that had been tormenting him. Then, a few steps further on, where a dark little alley opened off the street, said, "let me grant your wish," and after a couple more steps she could smell the sea, even though it was hidden behind the reed beds; before they went any further, though, they saw a little church on the right, Yannis whispered, "it's the church of the Saviour" and the woman asked in bewilderment, "how do you know?" – "once upon a time they used to bring me here to take Communion," and as Angela looked at him without speaking, "they might have had my wedding here," he murmured. And she cast in her mind to find out where his wound was hurting him, what was making him bleed or who was biting her, for his pain seemed ever growing and blossoming, he was like a plant which in the evening you leave verdant green and in the morning you find covered in white, so that you wonder where it had been hiding all that blossom.

In the end she said, "it's the only relief," as they sat on a parapet and she plunged her feet into the water, shivering at its chill, and he said, "you'll freeze" – it was the end of October – with the sea black and threatening, like some indistinct wild beast, from whose jaws you couldn't escape, which you couldn't see, but could only catch the mutter of a thousand voices. And Yannis said, "they are not going to leave us alone," for two young men were standing there watching them, they seemed to be saying something or thinking; and Angela said, "it's as if I've been through all this before," mainly the sense of terror, like when she was washing at home and felt eyes watching her through the cracks, at which Yannis would tease her and say, "they must have wings," because her attic was high up in the sky and unapproachable, "it's as if I've lived it all before," she repeated. And they would have begun to move off and to escape, but Yannis stood still and said, "I want it now, here, in front of them," quietly and calmly, and her terror was overflowing, specially since his eyes were burning, he might fall down and roll on the ground, as she had once seen someone do, and people had slipped a knife into his mouth and forced his teeth apart, "he's moonstruck," they said, and for two nights she hadn't been able to get to sleep; and she made as if to move off, but he caught hold of her hand, "I can't bear us not to," he hissed, "now, here in front of them."

And she made up her mind that their only safety lay in flight, and she told him, "they may kill us," or something even worse might happen, for her childhood fears had risen once more, memories of cellars before the war, of Eugenios's anxiety and precautions, and in a moment she felt that she was running alone, that she must seem foolish to him, at which she turned and saw him standing as if abandoned, his light-coloured suit standing out against the background of the nocturnal beach as if he was something washed up by the darkness, or its prey. And Angela realised that he must be choking in bitterness, in uncertainty perhaps, and she stretched out her hand, but he remained standing there like a statue, so she walked back to him, said, "come, come on," she would have cried, "I love you" but that she knew other people were following them, listening; and indeed a shutter opened and a white head appeared, speaking in a woman's voice, it said, "get away, my daughter" – so she was not the only one who was frightened, she quickened her pace, stood before him and begged, "come, my Yannis," he looked into her eyes, gazing straight into her pupils, as if entering searchingly into her grief and saying: it is honest, and he took her in his arms and they left as if bewitched, for one was whispering, "I am sorry, I am your slave" and the other was taking his hands and kissing them, remembering how once he had moved her by saying, "your tears are precious, don't fritter them away on my hands" – oh God.

And now their fingers are entwining, each enters ever more deeply into the other, as if they could not be bound close enough, they feel may our skin, our blood become one, "take me," he says, like a lost child wandering and scared, "only your body can purge me of my sins," and it is not by any means their first time, "you are my sole wife," he assures her, though they have left the little church far behind them now, behind them the boundless coolness of the sea and its scent, behind them too the young men who had terrified them, who perhaps were themselves frightened, who might have preferred to hatch whatever plans they were making alone and unseen. And he enfolded her once again with his plea, "take me, marry me, my sweetheart" which no longer seemed so unbelievable, and perhaps not so difficult for them to achieve, and she agreed, "when?" she asked and doubted, and Yannis insisted, "tomorrow" – their hands once more wove together as if confessing: we are agreed, and maybe it was already today, for it must have been past midnight, the chilly darkness penetrated them, so that he in turn shivered; and he concluded, "it might be going to rain" for white clouds were sailing across the sky, and Angela answered, "it's as if we've gone crazy,". for she had no fear of the rain, only of their being alone out in the streets, in times of danger. And a drop fell on her and startled her, it cooled her cheek, just below her eye, then another drop fell on her eyelashes, then another and another, and they increased their pace, trying to walk under trees or balconies, but in vain, for within a minute her hair was sopping wet, she felt her dress clinging to her back like a second skin, and she wondered – what does he feel?

And by the time the raindrops started to become fewer they had reached Faliro, the darkness still thick, and they heard the growl of a car, "it will be the Germans," they said in terror, but an ancient taxi appeared, from the back window someone shouted, "are you mad, going on foot like that?", and they saw a white-haired man, though he didn't do them the favour of stopping, and Angela said, "we're fit to be tied up." And so they scuttled into an alley and began making their way up the road, and Yannis said, "don't turn round and look behind you or to either side," and shadows were indeed appearing and concealing themselves again, they were taking care to remain in the darkness yet could see everything; and Yannis explained to her, "if they catch you looking at them, it's the end" – at which she then felt an iciness envelop her, penetrating the very pores of her backbone (and perhaps even deeper) and finally, panting, they arrived at a plane tree which Angela had seen before, and Yannis said, "a couple more steps and we're there." But out from behind the tree stepped a man with a rifle, which he pointed and rested the barrel against Yannis's neck, "halt," he ordered as if angry, "you are in the free zone" and simultaneously two boys emerged from the darkness and said, "you are in the ELAS sector," and Yannis said, "at last," and explained to them, "at last we have been liberated" – but the man asked, "where are you going?" and he meant what are you doing out in the perilous night, but Yannis didn't lose his composure, "just a couple of steps further," at which the man turned to the boys, the barrel of his rifle still against Yannis's neck, just below his cheek, making it bulge oddly as if there was an abscess within, "are they neighbours?" he asked them, looking Yannis and Angela over, and Angela thought, we are completely mad, now they'll discover everything, where we are coming from, what we were talking about, but she heard someone say, "I know them, they live in the same courtyard as us," it was one of the boys speaking, he was about sixteen and a complete stranger.

They let them pass, and they went into the yard with the two-storey house, everyone sleeping, or perhaps crouching in silent fear, went up to the room at the top, it smelled of stale closed space, like garments that have been put away in a chest, and they lay down in their clothes, exhausted, but Angela was choking with hysteria, a scream was thrashing in her brain, struggling to get out and to spread through the room and the darkness, but in the end all that came out was a muffled crying, just imperceptible moans, which he buried in his breast, in his clothes – and all the time he was saying, "I'm sorry," until Angela stopped hearing him and felt that she was falling from a sky which was without end, which seemed a monochrome lit by a single source of light, and she could not have said when it too faded, along with the smell of Yannis, his tobacco, his cologne or his sweat.

Antigone

It must have rained during the night for the earth smelled damp, she felt the breath of the foliage caressing her; and when she went outside she saw that the sun was playing hide-and-seek with the clouds and in the end hid itself – the asphalt and the earth seemed wet. And her mother was weeping, "it's all nothing but blackness" for her father was away, he had not returned from the village, and Dimitris and Alcmene were out somewhere – "I know where they're going," said Amalia, "but who can stop them?" for she felt that they were flying from her nest (and had been for some time), and thus she cuddled Antigone, "you're my little one," she whispered, "don't leave me or I'll die" – and her daughter did not answer. She felt her sixteen years, her body crammed suffocatingly into her old clothes so that she begged Alcmene, "let me wear some of yours" but in vain, until the buttons of her blouse popped off, over her bosom, and she wept, "I'm becoming an object of ridicule"; she was ashamed when she felt down growing on her cheeks just under her ears and on her arms and legs, like Alcmene had.

The curtains stirred and the cool freshness caressed her, the doors and windows were open, and through them came voices from the neighbourhood, for a moment it sounded as if people were bursting out laughing, some people were clapping. And Amalia got up and closed the window, she said, "I can't bear it, my head is buzzing," but Antigone stayed silent, for she knew it was in her interest not to upset her mother, she preferred that everything should unfold slyly or secretly, as if they'd fallen asleep in the windowless room where voices and letters didn't penetrate, it was a world which wouldn't injure you but which instead would give peace, perhaps security for a short time, and thus she would find the opportunity to slip off and wander through the streets, where exciting things were happening which she didn't want to miss. For indeed as soon as she turned into Martiou Street she could sense the agitation, people were talking in loud voices and seemed to be waiting for something; she went down the main avenue, but there – strangely – everything seemed dead, only a few men were crossing the road, who then disappeared into alleys or courtyards, perhaps people were watching from behind the trees, from behind the shutters they certainly were.

She looked all round her as if lost, as if afraid or ashamed, as if she'd found herself naked in the street or acting indecently; she searched to see whether she could find anyone she knew, she would have been glad of Haris or Andreas, even one of the girls from school – but not one of them was in sight. So she sought a hiding place for herself too, she found the lane beside the "Zachariades" school, always shadowed by the arching acacias and mulberries, and she felt a silence as if a veil had fallen over the place or a glass pane had descended which blotted out all sounds save one, heavy footsteps on the cobbles, like a machine approaching, and her own feet were taking her nearer, and then she'd reached them and was passing – luckily. And thus she saw that soldiers were going by, one behind the other in single file, with their weapons under their arms, heavily laden, sullen-faced, and another file on the other side of the street was leaving too, another machine of boots which simply advanced without looking to either side. And Antigone said to herself I'm not frightened, for she felt that the only thing the soldiers cared about was leaving, so she continued on her way without thinking, came out of her hiding place and back into the main avenue, stood under the pine trees and watched them from closer, two files, one on either side of the road, and it was certain that they were leaving, she felt like laughing or shouting, it's over, but she stayed stock still until they were over too, they were passing and reaching the corner, the head of the file must be at the church of the Resurrection by now, or maybe Salamis, for the sound of their boots was fading and the voices of the neighbourhood heard once more, and a different kind of people were surging from the other direction, from the Depot, young boys and men who were shouting and climbing up the lampposts, smashing the German signs, throwing their flags down and trampling on them, and in the background a Greek flag was being unfurled. And the girl wondered, aren't they afraid? that the two files of foreign soldiers were only a couple of streets ahead of them, maybe they might come back and unsling their rifles, on a balcony opposite she noticed a couple, like her father and her mother, thought Antigone, who were making signs to her, the woman more insistently, as if they were scolding her or telling her to go, and now the young men with the flag had caught up with her, one of them climbed a lamppost, he had an axe and was smashing things, arches with slogans on them were falling to the ground, a V on a wrought-iron gate – and none of her friends was in sight.

And just then a rifle shot rang out, everyone seemed to freeze, only for a second though, then people were screaming, Antigone looked up at the balcony again, but now the couple had disappeared, the doors were shut, their glass panes reflecting the pine trees, maybe I'd better go, she thought, but now the spot that resembled a crossroads was inundated by crowds of people, all of whom seemed to be shouting their own slogans, and in their midst was a man wearing khaki breeches and boots, he had a grey jacket and seemed to be trying to make people listen to him, he was raising his arms and shouting, but his voice was drowned by the roar of the crowd, in the end he cupped his hands in front of his mouth, he cried, "comrades", whereupon a few people turned and looked at him, then once more "comrades", and he pointed up the road, as if he wanted to tell them where to go, however only four or five people followed him, and two of them indeed returned and gesticulated, and Antigone felt that again incomprehensible things were taking place, like Angel's and Dimitris's secrets or like Alcmene who would disappear and then reappear again inexplicably. In the end the crowd moved away, still smashing signs and shouting, then once more they stopped and watched, maybe they had seen the tail-end of the Germans, who were leaving and luckily not coming back. It must have been midday, though the sun was not to be seen, only grey sky; and so Antigone made her way back to her own familiar haunts, she could see their house from a little way off, but there was no one standing at the door, or at the windows either, so she proceeded with greater ease.

As soon as she went into the courtyard she heard someone hammering nails into something, it must have been at the back of the house, on the side where the wash-house was, and Antigone advanced quietly to the corner, stood and listened, then she bent down and saw Dimitris, who was having some trouble nailing a lath onto a piece of wood, his forehead was dripping with sweat, in the end he hammered harder, then checked to see whether it was securely fixed, and, turning round, became aware of Antigone, "where've you been?" he asked, "Mother was wanting you," and the girl said, "out, I was looking for you" – "I was here," he replied, putting the piece of wood to one side, putting his tools away in their bag, careful as always, he said, "Father still isn't back" as if he was blaming him, which Antigone didn't like, "what are you making?" she asked, to which he answered, "you'll see," as if it wasn't possible to explain it to her, but I would have understood, she thought; and she left him and went inside, "where have you been?" scolded her mother, who seemed to be thinking of something and in a bad mood, the girl made for her room, and sitting at the table she found Alcmene, she had a piece of white cardboard and green paint, she had written LONG LIVE EPO, and Antigone thought there's an N missing, "give it to me and I'll finish it," she begged, but Alcmene refused, "no, it wouldn't do" – then added in justification, "it would be in different writing." And the younger girl thought, I'm better off by myself, where she could arrange everything the way she liked, in the secret little drawers that she would always keep no matter how much she grew up; this she knew.

And thus she went out into the streets by herself again, at one point a cloud loomed overhead and heavy drops of rain came splashing down, at which everyone was taken by surprise and ran to shelter under eaves or balconies, and then once they'd found a place of safety laughed, but in a short while the rain ceased suddenly; Antigone found herself in the same place as that morning, above her was the couple's balcony, and she heard people say, "they're coming," and everyone ran in that direction, jumping over puddles here and there, but very soon they stopped, clearing the road for the resistance fighters to pass, and Antigone said, "I can't see" from behind everyone's backs, so she climbed onto a ledge, holding onto the railings. They were only a few and they walked wearily, one or two were wearing khaki but the others looked oddly assorted, with jackets or trousers that were falling down, most of them bare-headed, with their weapons on their shoulders or slung across their backs; only the one in front had a cap, like a pre-war officer's cap, and they were carrying the flag which hung down wetly, applause was heard, two of the guerrillas raised their eyes and looked puzzled, but at that moment a man pushed forward from out of the crowd – he had grey hair and looked like a worker – and went up and kissed the flag, then shook as if he was crying; and everyone applauded again.

The sun had come out, strangely yellow, Antigone was gazing at the raindrops shining on leaves and branches, it all looked like a painting in which very shortly only nature would be left, for the resistance fighters were continuing, without speaking, as if broken by too much pain, and the crowd followed behind them. And Antigone came down from her ledge and followed them more slowly; the sun was now shining like summer and wandering among the leaves, she felt a hand grasp her arm and saw Dimitris, who was holding his sign, and Antigone had an idea, said, "wait here a minute," and climbed onto another wall which was covered with plants and a whole mass of tiny yellow flowers, she picked some and wove them into a garland, she had rapidly made a rough-and-ready little wreath and said, "it's like the first of May," and she crowned his placard with it, "now it's more complete," and she laughed, and Dimitris caressed her, someone shouted, "the reception is going to be in Harilaou" and they agreed, "shall we go?" – "let's go," so they hurried up the road panting, Dimitris holding his placard high and Antigone a little way behind him admiring her wreath. By the time they passed the tram shunting "scissors" they were sweating and out of breath, but from ahead they could hear a dull roar, "there must be thousands of people there," said Dimitris, on they went past the little park and Antigone begged, "can we stop for a moment," for stars seemed to be leaping from her eyes and floating in the air in front of her; they stopped only for a couple of minutes though and then began to walk again, and the noise and the longing were swelling. Now they saw a barrier of backs, both men's and women's, who were shouting and singing, above their heads the red strips of banners – they ran for the last ten metres and pushed their way in among backs and arms then stopped, and they saw a river of people, mostly boys and young men, who were singing and raising their clenched fists into the air, and one after the other came the banners – red cloth with yellow writing – and Antigone read words like rule of the people or honour to the Communist Party or freedom, and she couldn't see a single Greek flag, and then they heard cheers and whistles, and they were coming on horseback, wearing khaki uniforms, their weapons slung over their backs, one of them with a bright green wreath round his neck, and Dimitris said, "that's Brikas," a trifle plump and smiling, and everyone applauded and the brother and sister waved their placard; then the human river suddenly stopped and a youth whom they didn't know said, "comrade, will you give us your placard?" and put out his hand for it, Dimitris turned and looked at the girl as if asking her, but Antigone shrugged her shoulders, and the strange hand had already taken hold of the wood, "give it to us," he said, "we need it," and when Dimitris let go they removed the wreath and put it on the head of a girl standing next to them, at which she shouted, "death to fascism", and the river had started flowing once more, Antigone for a few moments watched her wreath on the head that was getting confused with all the other heads, they went on being able to distinguish Dimitris's placard for longer, until it too became lost among the red banners, among the raised clenched fists.

The sun was now beginning to set, the light had become golden, with the trees, washed clean by the rainstorm, a vivid green; they set off back in silence, they made their way down the wide road, Martiou Street, which was full of houses with wild gardens in front of them, Dimitris suddenly stopped, gave a good look round and slipped his hand between the bars of a gate where a rosebush was flowering, he picked two beautiful roses, but then said "run" as they heard a window opening, in a couple of minutes they were already some distance away, and Dimitris gave her the flowers, "take them," he said, "they smell sweet," and thus Antigone laughed again and pressed them to her breast, "oh not soppiness", he reprimanded her, "I can't stand it," at which Antigone felt herself blushing to the roots of her hair. They were now a little way above their own neighbourhood – "do you remember the Jews?" her brother asked; they were alongside a vast, fenced off plot of land, on which stood the hovels of wretchedness all in a row, "they've had it, poor souls," Dimitris spoke again, and at last they turned into a narrow green lane, barely wide enough for two people to walk side by side, it smelled of roasting onions and Antigone held her nose, then Dimitris squinted in fun and stuck out his tongue absurdly. They came out of the lane laughing fit to burst, the two roses decorating them, and began to run, only one more road and they'd be home, but then once more they saw people applauding and cheering, and more resistance fighters were passing in a line, humble and weary, few and silent; suddenly Antigone realised that someone was making signs at her, it was a plump and unshaven man, only his eyes were shining, which were fixed on her, and he nodded again that he wanted to speak to her, Antigone went and stared at him, but he asked her, "are you from round here?" and the girl nodded, "then take this, go to the red house, tell them we'll be sleeping at the Migos primary school" and he put a note into her hand, "run," he ordered and seemed to laugh, his mouth had a strange smell, something like rusty metal, and Antigone felt disgusted, she set off at a run – except that for a second she turned and looked for Dimitris, but couldn't find him.

Twilight had fallen by now, and she felt the cold stinging her, the way she was taking was nothing but mud and puddles, Antigone jumped over them and ran though, some fear told her that she must get her mission accomplished, for she might get into trouble if she neglected it or delayed – and thus she ran panting up the steps, lights were on everywhere upstairs but the ground floor was dark and deserted. She found the front door half open, inside seemed to be a deathly hush that was terrifying, she knocked and knocked again hesitantly, thought that they must have forgotten the lights on by mistake or that everyone must have left in a hurry, she knocked again louder, and now seemed to hear hinges creaking, a door somewhere, she pushed it open and went into the living room, it seemed deserted, only in one corner there was an unmade camp bed, and a chair with a cup and a spoon on it, Antigone pushed another door and stopped short: at a wooden desk sat Angel and above him stood her sister, at which sight Antigone was speechless, recalling old images, the nocturnal garden and the running at night, in the end the boy asked her, "how did you find us?" and he was bright red – she put out her hand to him with the note, "they'll be at the Migos school," she stammered, she realised that a large lamp had been turned on and lowered her gaze, as if the light hurt her. And silence fell and she felt that her body was being tightly squeezed – or that she looked ridiculous – and said, "I'll be off" and left them, however she heard footsteps running down the stairs and they were not only her own, then she heard someone calling "Antigone" and quickened her pace in the dark, she felt that she was floundering in the puddles – but who cared? And then she heard someone calling her again, it was Angel panting, "why don't you listen to me?" he complained, and he was just a few steps behind her, then caught up with her, grabbed her with one hand, which wasn't like before, she felt his hand hard and rough on her, maybe used to grabbing things these days, for now he fumbled at his waist, got out a little piece of glittering metal and shoved it clumsily in his pocket, and Antigone suspected that he wanted to impress her, that maybe it was a fake. "What do you want?" she asked, and the boy said, "to walk you home since it's dark," and they walked along without speaking, searching their thoughts, until they stood at a corner (their house could be seen from here) and the boy said, "did you recognise the captain?" and she answered "no" – "he's Elias, the dandy's father," and then she remembered his eyes, for she hadn't see them for years, which had been mocking her since then or filling her with wonder at his skills.

From where she stood she could see two shadows at the door of their house and started forward joyfully, "it's Father," she cried, and attempted to run, but she was encircled by his arms, "stay," he begged, "just for half a minute," she bent backwards, though, from her waist up, for his trembling was becoming terrifying, he was struggling to find her neck with his lips, "just one, just one," he beseeched her – and she let him. She said, "let me go now, Alcmene will be waiting for you," and the boy stroked her hands, smiled at her, though he seemed to have tears in his eyes, "it's you, only you," he murmured, and the girl said "tomorrow" – which she couldn't have explained. The darkness had become thicker, and thus Antigone slipped away, and began tidying herself, her hair, her blouse; before getting to their own door she passed the Tsimonis's door, where the mother was sitting motionless in the shadow, she looked at Antigone and said, "take care, my girl," people said that she'd been telling everyone to "take care" since the time she'd lost her elder son, but Antigone bent down and hurried past her, went into their courtyard and tidied herself again, and at last opened the door and saw them all looking at her as if in question (Alcmene was already there, and she wondered, how did she manage it?), and then she fell on Christos and hugged him, feeling that she had found a refuge. Before they went to sleep, in their room, Alcmene spoke, "he's a wild creature," she whispered to her, and Antigone remembered how he used to climb trees and balance on their high walls, how she herself had been afraid of him, "yes," she agreed, "he's like a little animal," and after that they were silent. In the morning they awoke to drums and bugles.

Angel

And he wondered what on earth had got into them to be singing at night, and yelling, which could be something that happened in a dream, but he said to himself, I didn't have any dreams, and the music was playing, in the end he opened his eyes and everything was light, the window and the walls, his white shirt, then his hands and the sheets, the ceiling and the round glass lightshade, he said, "it would be much better if they were all extinguished" and tried desperately to go to sleep again. However, the songs went on, and then a voice was saying, "get up, it's nearly midday," it is Grandmother he thought, and with his eyes closed he could see her black-clad body, her shrivelled face and her wrinkles, of which there were getting to be more and more, "get up, so that we can air the room," she said again, and just then he smelled the street, the leaves, the sky – and he remembered how her son used to say, "you drive us crazy with your bee in the bonnet about ventilation and water," for she insisted that they get themselves under the tap and wash off all the odours, all the sweat of the night, and Angel felt the tyranny, but said nothing.

He had his own method of resistance or escape; he would watch to see when she was absorbed in housework, or her garden, and then would get dressed in a flash and be off – thus in a little while he had hastily put on his clothes, stuffed the red handkerchief into his pocket, and slipped out, except that, before he got round the corner, he heard them calling, "come back and eat something," he pretended not to hear however, took the familiar little road and felt alone. As he walked here he was enveloped in shadows, a goldfinch suddenly warbled and then once more he heard the songs, a drum beating, someone trying out a bugle maladroitly – he came out into a road that they often took, on a wall were painted a hammer and sickle, and a little bit further on was a group of people with flags who were shouting, one of them was pasting a picture to the wall, which showed a worker and a resistance fighter trampling the enemy, the German flag, and with the words EAM-ELAS-EPON written on it in beautiful letters. Then he got the red handkerchief out of his pocket, tied it round his neck with a bow and approached them, they were all boys that he knew (although he knew the names of only two of them), and among them was Haris the dandy, he said "hallo" and the others greeted him too, they were going down to parade on the quay, only Angel wasn't going to go with them, perhaps he had something different in mind, some secret hope or expectation, so he went off and left them to it.

And in a little while he was on a tram, standing on the platform with his head out, so that the wind blew on him and ruffled his hair, which got in his eyes and made him think it's like a game, as if houses trees lampposts men are rushing past back towards the years of his childhood, they laugh at him, he mocks them, so that in the end he jumped off suddenly while the tram was going fast (at the most dangerous point, before the White Tower, where the tram-drivers pick up speed) and walked among the trees, whose moisture he could feel making him damp, and then further on started to follow the tramlines again, until he arrived at the "Dionysia", where he saw that they were changing the photographs, they'd found an ancient French film and for a second he stood and watched. Above him people were coming down the road, everywhere he could see placards and Greek flags, from time to time armed men passed, some dressed in ill-assorted uniforms, green Italian tunics, or civilian jackets – but in their midst he saw a dark red skirt which seemed to be shouting, waving its arms exaggeratedly, and so he looked at the face, her hair was falling onto her shoulders, hiding her cheeks, but her eyes were familiar and her arms still seemed to be calling him, and he shouted, "Bettina" and ran forwards, for it really was the lost little Jewish girl, and they hugged each other right in the middle of the street, just as if they'd been lovers in the past, and the girl was laughing, acting as if neither her mind nor her body was quite under control. However, after a few minutes she calmed down and explained that she'd been living shut up in an attic for more than a year, without ever once coming out, neither by day nor by night, she had to wash in the dark, eat whenever she could, never spoke, never laughed, never even could allow herself to feel upset, "but where were you?" asked Angel, and she told him, "I only discovered yesterday" when they took her out into a large garden, through the gate could be seen the city below, behind the walls the castle, "they'd taken me there at night," she added (a few hours before they were rounded up), "and the others?" asked the boy, at which Bettina remained silent, "maybe they've been in hiding somewhere else," he comforted her, "maybe", she said, and her eyes filled with tears; and after a bit she told him more of her own story, how it was an old couple who had hidden her, they must have been paid a fortune for it, but the old woman had been very sweet, had looked after her and caressed her, "all the same, it was like a prison," she murmured.

And he was wondering what she would do now when she interrupted his thoughts and said, "tell me about our house," but she'd see for herself thought the boy, for strangers lived there now, they had wrecked the place, they'd come from some village, taken the house over and turned it into a ruin, and Myrsine was always saying, "what filth", for they'd set up a brazier in the drawing room, and burnt whatever they could lay hands on in the middle of the parquet, and the walls were blackened with smoke and the corners of the ceiling full of cobwebs, "you'll see for yourself," he muttered, remembering the white steps, the doormat, the multicoloured flowers in pots – now the people living there had taken up the marble and smashed it, they used to see two boys chopping wood, their axes crashing down on anything that lay in the way, and Myrsine often said, "you'd think they had a grudge against everything." "I'll come one of these days," promised Bettina, but first she had to look for her own people, any relatives left, for she'd be afraid all by herself, and Angel said, "we'll protect you," and he meant his own people – at the organisation, at home – and they said goodbye; the girl set off down the road, maybe she was longing for the coolness of the sea, the sense of wide open space, and the boy followed her with his eyes as long as he could, her slender body, taller now, her shapely legs, her hair, and he thought, poor little thing, maybe you're all on your own now, he suddenly stretched out his arm though there was no way she'd be able to see it, he wanted to ask her where he could find her, felt that he would look ridiculous and drew back.

And in a little while he heard a sound coming from the direction of the sea, at first vague but gradually growing louder, it seemed to be pouring into all the streets and alleys and coming up towards the city, it was the sound of drums and shouting, and Angel remembered about the parade, maybe he ought to be there among them, yet he didn't feel like it. All the same, better not miss it he said to himself, and so he started walking down, he passed the church, the old school, and he could see them clearly, in the end he arrived on the waterfront where the pavement on both sides of the road was inundated with a crowd who were clapping, having a good time; and between them like a river flowed the other crowd, young men with flags and banners, red and blue, red with the hammer and sickle, but English flags as well, and here and there the American one, excited faces, all mouths and eyes, but older men too, with placards and badges, most of them red and some green, and also old women, dressed all in black, from the populace, the mothers of those who'd been killed, carrying wreaths and white handkerchiefs with which they kept wiping their eyes. And at that point Angel climbed up high, he wanted to survey the whole scene, he found an iron lamppost that suited him, and from there he saluted them, was gladdened by them, the never-ending river, which made him dizzy, as if they were motionless and he floating on the stream, or flying; from amidst the crowd a face was suddenly smiling at him, and he recognised it, it was Haris, the boys from the neighbourhood with their banner, and behind them a row of girls like ancient *kores*, dressed in white and blue, and Angel felt that they were playing, acting like babies – but where were Dimitris and Alcmene or Antigone?

It was already past midday when the parade began to come to an end, bathed in the glare of sunlight, and Angel found himself with Haris and the others in a narrow lane, all of them sweating and excited, talking non-stop in loud voices, they said, "let's go back together," but the crowd was streaming off in all directions, some making their way up the road, some towards the White

Tower or even further – the older people were waiting for trams, though when these arrived they were already full to bursting, with people crammed on the steps or hanging on behind, so didn't even stop. And they decided, "let's walk" for the noon hour was sweet and the roads in this part of town asphalted – and thus they set off, singing and talking, one boy letting the flag play in the wind, flapping and furling, and the sight seemed beautiful to them; and it was even more lovely in the park, beneath the trees, among the flowers and sweet scents. And without being aware of it, they went chatting on past Faliro, a little way further lay the bridge over the dry watercourse, someone proposed that they go down to the sea, some of the others said yes (and started going down the watercourse), but others felt that it was late and maybe complaints would be waiting for them at home – but the rest begged "only for a couple of minutes", and the sea lay like glass, with milky lines on it, and other streaks of grey or pale blue, they picked up flat pebbles and started playing ducks and drakes, making the stones skim over the surface, counting "one, two, three ..." and only the flag bearer and Angel didn't play – for there was no tree or post or little wall for them to lean the pole on, and they didn't want to get the flag dirty.

Then Haris said, "time to be going," even if they didn't have watches, it must be afternoon by now, for they found the shops shut and everyone back in their own homes, when they reached their familiar haunts, the well-known lanes, the trees that they recognised, behind the church of the Resurrection. Where over in a corner they heard voices, people shouting, "traitor, battalion rat", there was a whole crowd of men, only three women, and in their midst a terrified figure, dessicated, middle-aged, he must have been in pain for he was grimacing, he was saying all the time, "you're mistaken," then someone punched him in the face and he collapsed on the ground, and they were pushing him, "battalion rat, murderer," they screamed, as if they were stoking their passion, their grudge, and Angel muttered, "I used to know him," the man worked as a barber and had been an EON leader, but he was afraid to get involved, Haris held him back and told him, "it's too late," and they moved away – and then turned round for a moment, they saw that the people had got hold of the man by the armpits and he was staggering, his nose running and his hair awry – Angel was to remember later that the barber had suddenly fixed his gaze on him, staring at him bewildered, as if thinking I know him, maybe there might be some wild hope, but the other people took him away, and in the end only eight or nine remained, all angry and gesticulating or talking in loud voices.

Angel had reached his own street, he saw one of their windows was half open, it was the room where Myrsine usually sat with her daughters, drinking their coffee and watching the world go by and chatting. The flag was in front, the boy carrying it now had the pole resting more comfortably on his shoulder, and the others were walking in twos and threes; the dandy and Angel were at the rear, and the first boy said, "they have to pay for it," as if they were continuing a conversation about the episode they'd witnessed, but Angel thought about it, he said, "we are liberated now," he meant everything is finished, let's forget it, but "everything is not finished", Haris corrected him, with an air as if he was devising something, an expression that didn't suit his face or his habitual tranquillity, so that Angel was puzzled, "I don't understand," he said, "we've got to set Papandreou aside," the other boy answered, as if it was his own job and duty to do so, but who would put him aside, and was the dandy one of them?* But they didn't continue this conversation, for the other boy looked as though he'd let something slip out by mistake, as if he'd revealed secrets (but whose?), so Angel said, "'bye" and walked away, for he felt like a stranger and thought my own house is familiar, where he found his grandmother talking to her plants, weeding them and talking away, she asked him, "where've you been?" and punished him with "now you'll have to eat your beans cold", but he smiled and thought, I'll give her a surprise, "I saw Bettina," he announced and his grandmother was struck dumb, "she was saved, people hid her," he added and went inside.

And he suspected that others might be hiding a lot from him,

---

* One night Paris and I were sitting on the grass talking, exhausted from running around and demonstrations. He told me, "we'll have to get rid of Papandrea" which is what he'd heard his father say, who had taken to the mountains and become a guerrilla; I asked him, "what has he done wrong?" and Paris laughed, "you don't know anything." Two days later the troubles broke out in Athens, the December events.

he was tormented by what Haris had said, thought that some people are "we" and everyone else is left out in the cold – and for sure everything must have been set in motion by captain Elias, thought Angel, who had gone off to join the resistance, they knew more up there in the mountains, and more secret things too, and he gulped down his food and went out again, this time he wasn't wearing the handkerchief round his neck. It was a good time to find them and ask them, and indeed Antigone and Dimitris were sitting in their garden and seemed to be quarrelling, but they stopped when they saw him, the girl smiled at him and he remembered their "tomorrow" of yesterday, there was a languor in her eyes, but Angel asked, "where's Alcmene?" – inside, helping their mother. Then he took Dimitris aside and asked him about Haris, how much he knew, to which Dimitris replied, "his father's got him comfortably placed," what did all this mean, though? He turned and looked at Antigone who was watching them obstinately, feeling left out, do you suppose they all know more than me? thought Angel in fury, he thought to himself that they always left him out in the cold, sought him when they had need of him, how nice... his suspicion maddened him, he felt like a cat that has put out its claws but is powerless, and he grabbed Dimitris's hand clumsily, "tell me everything you know," he said as if it was an order, but the other boy smiled at him, seemed to be saying what's got into him? – "I don't have any secrets from you," he replied, and at that moment Alcmene came out, he cried, "at last" which they didn't understand, above them a gap showed in the grey sky, like a darn, a fragment of washed out blue, "but what are you staring at up there?" the girl asked him, and he could have wept, I don't have enough air, I'm suffocating, and she said, "you've gone pale," went in, brought him some water, but Amalia had come out now, "what's the matter?" she asked anxiously, and the boy said "nothing", and left, but he was thinking, what remains to me now? and he meant what comfort or security – somewhere he could hear chanting, "power to the people, not the king" in a hoarse voice, it was coming from somewhere at the back, behind Dimitris's house, from among the trees or the little cottage, and he thought again, where now? Behind him he heard running footsteps, he turned and saw Alcmene, "wait, boy, can't you," she said, and he felt that she cared about him, she was carrying a folded newspaper, "what's up?" the boy asked, "shall we go to the offices?" she asked, to the red house, "there'll be people there," he whispered, as if confessing to her that he couldn't face them.

They had almost reached his grandmother's house, approaching it from the back, and he shouted, "I've got it," for they were standing in front of the wall and behind it lay his "own" forest, he said, "come on" and took her hand, "where are you taking me, wild animal?" she teased, but they went along round the wall, found his own secret little entrance and crept in, "the nettles are stinging me," she complained, but something else of his own was stinging him, they pushed their way in deep, and everything was green and damp, and "come on," Angel enticed her, and was climbing the tree like a cat, "come on," said the indescribable boy once again, and reached out his hand to her, but she was afraid she wouldn't be able to fly and would fall injured to the ground, "no further," she begged, but now he didn't understand her language, and she thought, he's become a little animal once more, he was like a little ape which clambers upwards, which shows you its bottom and the soles of its feet, and he was like a maniac, for he wouldn't stop but went up and up into the topmost branches, so that now nothing was to be seen but leaves, and something hiding among them which laughed from time to time, or barked at her, whereupon Alcmene said to herself, an animal that laughs like a human is the most terrifying thing of all, and a moment later he was pelting her with leaves and twigs and bits of bark from his tree. And from right up there he called her, "come," though he didn't really hope that she would, so he slipped back down to her side, he was sweating and panting, and she said, "your trousers have got dirty" and began to brush him down, but felt that he drew back as soon as she touched his legs, "don't act shy with me," she laughed, supposedly she was the older of the two (a lie), from his forehead a thread ran, it was sweat and dust, it ran down his cheek and disappeared into his collar like some strange ornament, "tsch", she said, "you careless boy" and put out her hand and wiped it off, and the boy felt what her fingers were like, and the palm of her hand, and he grabbed it and kissed it, like a maniac once more, "calm down," she begged and was excited, they both remembered the old business between them but neither said anything, though suddenly he felt like asking her, what on earth has become of Armandos.

But just then they heard voices, the sound of the dry grass being trampled, and they saw a group of little boys holding wooden swords, at which point Angel led Alcmene after him and they hid behind a tree trunk, "sssh", he said to her and held her close, the little boys had stopped in a clearing, one of them seemed to be the leader, "I'll be d'Artagnan and you can be the Three Musketeers," but there were two boys left over whose swords hung between their legs, and Angel felt great longing as he held her arms, her hair smelled of water, they crossed swords, wood hitting wood, her body had relaxed, he felt its weight, and Angel sensed an agreement, that they had come to an unspoken understanding, for as long as the game lasted – but the leader spoilt it for them, he cried, "I won" and they stopped playing, disappeared along with their swords, twilight had now settled under the trees, and she withdrew from him, she seemed ill at ease, "let's go to the offices," but the boy held her back, "stay a little longer," he beseeched her, then she embraced him and he felt her, "I'd like to too, but we can't," he felt her downiness, her clothes, then his leg between her legs, she whispered once more, "we can't," as if these were the only words left to her, and they stopped, looked at each other, considered each other, and stayed like that, as if something had been ceded, and the girl felt that it was almost over, he asked her strangely, "why Alcmene?" but she looked at him in bewilderment, "why did they call you Alcmene?" he clarified, but she just shrugged her shoulders, "they could have called you Maria or Evangelia," he said and they both laughed, then the boy became bolder, his hands were grasping her feverishly, he said, "oh God" and his knees sagged, she was scared and wiped the sweat from him, "what is it?" for Angel was moving against her, suddenly he stopped and was fumbling with his buttons, "don't," she cried, "are you out of your mind?", but he turned away, "don't budge," he ordered, "watch out I don't soil you" and she felt him shudder, she stayed motionless and terrified, and Angel bent over and sighed, "forgive me," he asked humbly.

When they came out dusk had fallen, birds were crying in the sky above them, flying in flocks, making a great racket as they went to roost, and Angel said, "maybe bats will come out," carnivorous flying mice, maybe snakes, lizards and scorpions. But they had escaped surely, for now they were out on the road, and the girl begged, "let's go to the offices" as if they were a refuge, and Angel felt some change had taken place, that she was behaving with sweetness and tenderness, for their hands were constantly meeting. In the red house they found only two youths who had already turned on the lights, and thus they sat in a corner and relaxed and read "The Voice of the People" which Alcmene had been carrying since the afternoon. And she told him that her father was working once again, that everything would be easier, smoother, now that her mother had stopped sighing and grieving.

Yannis

The way the margins were closing in, Yannis and Angela decided, "there's no other solution left to us" and they prepared to get married, for the girl was quite far gone and in a little while would begin to show; and she wept to him one night, "the other one would have been months old by now" and he remained silent, but he let his fingers speak for him, which twined and played in her hair, then moved downwards to her back, and she shivered, you devil, thought Angela, who often feared that they had cast a child of stone into the sea, who was watching them with its eyes always wide open. And Yannis insisted that "there's no other solution left to us", he felt that time was running out now, no matter how worried he was by the rumours that were all around them, or by the threatening shouts at demonstrations, the clenched fists and the hopeless eyes, no matter how he remembered the words of a friend, a wealthy merchant, regular member of their group, who had said sagaciously, "give them an inch and they'll take an ell," and then had laughed and had turned dark purple – and unbearable, murmured Angela. Just yesterday he had found his sister terrified and barricaded into her drawing room, it was quite clear she'd been crying, she said, "two men came and stood below the window, they said, 'in a short while we'll be up there and you'll be down here in the street'" and then started singing those songs of theirs; Yannis reassured her, "they were probably drunk, just riff-raff," but later he advised her, "don't open the door to anyone." But this wasn't possible, she had to go out to go shopping, to get some air, and Yannis said, "as little as possible then, only when it's strictly necessary."

And Angela insisted that "I don't want anything", and she meant pomp and ceremony (she had learned to make do with little), all she wanted was a name for her child, his father, although in fact he was constantly with her, "we are bound to one another," he'd assure her and laugh, and he wasn't going to open the factory again until things had cleared up; he would go every morning, inspect the massive padlocks, check his office and the machinery, make sure that "it's all right for today", and then would burrow his way back into her attic, into her mattress, whose smell was now familiar to him, whose every sagging spot he knew, and how he could just reach out his hand and switch off the lamp. That old house hummed with sounds, the drunkard's shouts, sometimes his daughters' conversations, the elder girl would say, "I'm knitting gloves for the resistance fighters, the struggle requires sacrifices," one day she ran into Yannis at the door and he felt her eyes boring into him, her dress was stretched taut over her body, it was yellow with grey checks, and he thought, how the wicked fellow's standing up* – but that very evening he told Angela, "I'll buy everything new for you, you can give all your old things away," and didn't want to continue, as if something was paining him.

The next day at noon he was walking in the park with Nikos, their well-known officer of the gendarmerie, who said, "things are going to get nasty now," that in the afternoon they were expecting the ships to arrive, the English, and Yannis said, "well that will be some comfort," but the other man was unresponsive, "what have you heard?" asked Yannis, for he must see people, surely someone must have told him something, but the other man wouldn't open his mouth or his heart, and only advised, "be careful." They walked on past the Electricity Works, which were hung with red banners (the officer smiled sardonically), and went a bit further

---

* In '62 when I met her, she was married to an officer of the gendarmerie, people said of the Security Police. He used to curse her and beat her, and had not given her any children. One day she told me about her youth, how she had been in love with a member of EPON who had been snatched from her and exiled to Macronissos and never returned. "When he's asleep in bed, blind drunk, I pinch money from him and go and give it to beggars" – and this was how she relieved her feelings.

down, through little streets which seemed peaceful, with their old houses and courtyards, their bushy trees giving off a green fragrance, past a humble café frequented by old fishermen, then a little low wall and beyond it the expanse of the sea, which had a slightly angry look to it and smelled of seaweed. And they stopped there to breathe the fresh air, as if they needed it, and Nikos put out his hand and pointed into the distance, past the point of Karabournou, where they could just make out two ships, long and narrow dark vessels which almost seemed to be hanging in the air, two lines against a grey background, and in a little while, as time passed and they got nearer, they became four and larger; beside them was a pill-box, one of those constructed by the Germans, circular, stone-built, with a single slit facing out to sea, at the back a low door, and the whole thing surrounded by barbed wire – which had been useless to them. And Yannis scrambled up onto it, said, "from here we'll be able to get a better view," for they were surely English (maybe they are our own, thought the gendarmerie officer) and thus they fixed their eyes on the distance, on the ships that were approaching and were now acquiring rigging and canons, they were becoming paler in colour and their flags could be seen, all of them English, which was a relief to Yannis so that he said, "they've come," except that suddenly something was bothering his eye, "what the hell is it," he muttered, he felt that something wanted to get into his eye; and indeed it was a fly resting at the corner of his eye, a maybug, he flapped his hand at it in irritation and brushed it away and felt relieved, but his eye itched, he rubbed it and it was crying, and then he felt the fly settle on his jaw, flapped his hand again, and both men laughed.

After a while they realised that the ships had stopped, two of them were warships and the other two transport ships, and they had hove to as if considering or calculating, and before long they had put down boats, so that Yannis wondered, can they perhaps see us? The boats were being rowed towards the shore; behind Nikos and Yannis a few other people had gathered now, mostly men but also a few children, who were all watching the sea – and barely speaking. And everyone also avoided saying anything when they saw two young men running along waving red flags with uncompromising determination, and continued to avoid comment when the boats had come closer and they could distinguish the soldiers in khaki, the sailors, who were examining the crowd on the shore, surely the hammers and sickles too, and thus turned and made for a landing a bit further along, perhaps in the basin of the docks or maybe by the White Tower, and then someone said, "they can't be English," not with such weary, almost pale, faces, "maybe they're French," someone else offered, and so they shouted, "eh, dis donc" at them, but the boats were moving away, in spite of the fact that they had reached the little wall, by the pill-box, about five metres away, and the bystanders could see them all quite clearly, their expressions preoccupied as if impatient, when will we land and be able to get some rest? And at that point the red banners also left, running back towards the city, maybe they'd be set up on the jetty and wave in the breeze.

And Yannis said, "I know him from somewhere" about the young man with the flag; and then they too set off towards the White Tower to see whether they'd be in time for the reception – or trouble – and suddenly they heard a fanfare, coming from the direction of the military headquarters, and Yannis said, "what a laugh," for down from the old site of the Fair, in the shade of the trees which was like a sort of twilight, a platoon of soldiers with bugles and drums was advancing, and in front of them rode a mounted officer, it could have been a coincidence, but Yannis and Nikos moved on as if in a hurry, with the scent of the sea permanently in their nostrils.

In the end it was all a waste of effort, maybe the boats returned to the ships or else made for the port, which was the most probable, at any rate the two friends stayed at the White Tower and looked this way and that in vain, suddenly a gendarme came up and spoke quietly to the officer, at which Yannis pretended to be gazing without interest at the nearby mansions, and after a moment the man saluted and left. There was a wind blowing from the sea, but they set off towards the waterfront, where the waves were now breaking, lead-coloured and foaming, the ships out on the water had been transformed into black masses, visible only because of their lights, and Nikos said, "I'll have to be leaving you." However just at that moment they heard someone crying, "Nikos, Nikos" from the opposite pavement, and saw a sailor waving at them, and beside him stood a young lad, "now, if he was carrying a red flag..." said Nikos, for these days the unexpected was constantly happening, and in the end he said, "Fotis" to the old sailor and embraced him, he'd arrived in the morning but had only just been able to come ashore, he was on his way to see his mother, "but don't you remember Angel?" he asked, and Nikos muttered, "yes, I can see him" and they were puzzled, in the end "I'll come and see you," said Fotis, and they set off up the road to catch the tram. The two friends looked at each other and laughed at the same time, "are you thinking what I'm thinking?" asked Nikos, and Yannis racked his memory, in which Fotis's son arose from somewhere, or a shape that resembled him, it was a razor-sharp splinter of glass and it wounded him somewhere in the region of his neck, but then it slipped away again before he could catch it, and he wondered, how did he have enough time?

"Well, anyway," he dropped the subject; and he announced to Nikos, "we're getting married," at which the other man laughed, but all he said was "so you've made up your mind?" and they shook their heads, each for his own reason, and an uncomfortable silence fell, but then Nikos laughed again and said, "I'll have to leave you" – what could the gendarme have whispered to him? – but before he left he offered Yannis his hand, "whatever happens I'm beside you," he assured him, and Yannis thought, he's exaggerating, just like everything he heard said at their meetings, in the drawing rooms where they foretold terrible things and felt, "we'll have to crush the proletariat." But Yannis had his doubts about this, he favoured the crafty approach, believed in money, thought that in the end the poor would back down, they'd be obliged to, and all that would be left would be empty phrases. It was evening now and lights were going on, he took the narrow road by the Cathedral, crossed the tramlines carefully and then went up towards St. Sophia, somewhere nearby were floodlights and open windows, on the balcony four flags were waving, our own and the Allies', a sign said EAM in huge letters, now two men were standing at one of the brilliantly lit windows, talking and gesticulating, he took the road to the right, preferring the narrow streets where no voices or slogans were to be heard, in this little world people seemed to live as they had always done, the humble houses and shops maintaining their habitual anonymity, he stopped suddenly on a corner, he knew they were waiting for him,

Angela and his sister, he stood there undecided and weary, felt that he'd been walking for hours, fixed his gaze on a street light, as if it was some inexplicable magnet, "I am all on my own," wept Ergini, and seemed to be expecting some kind of fatal blow, which indeed was inevitable now that Yannis had decided both for himself and for her, but he reflected, I'll always hurt someone, as if it had been thus ordained in his destiny – and his alone.

And he preferred the road that went to Angela's house, whatever I do I'll cause her sorrow, he thought, and he meant his sister; Angela's stairs were plunged in semi-darkness, but he knew each detail of them, he reached her door and knocked, grasped the doorknob and pushed, he sensed he was alone in a deserted, empty house, and wondered, "where could she have gone?" without telling him – he stood for a couple of minutes in the dark, himself seeming like part of the darkness, then went back down the stairs slowly and feared that his steps were thunderously loud, he came out into the narrow street and sucked the air into his lungs, it had the smell of trees, of old walls, and everything round him filled him with a strange sadness, he felt that everything was old and moribund, a world whose foundations were being eaten away, which might collapse, as he had seen happen to a house in his own neighbourhood which gradually dissolved into dust and broken planks and debris. He went very slowly down the road, came out a little before the Kamara and went in the direction of his family house; night had fallen completely by now, from somewhere he heard singing, from the old tavern by the Hippodrome, inside there was very little light and he saw various old men sitting and drinking, a blurred picture like a lithograph, finally he arrived at his door, saw light in the drawing room, but a familiar voice said, "Yannis". It was Angela standing concealed at the corner, one with the night, who spoke to him and said, "stay here a bit," perhaps to warm her hands and her icy fingers, because he could indeed feel that they were frozen.

But, he thought, it wasn't inexplicable, not so much the fact that the weather had turned cold, as that Angela revealed to him, "I was inside and we were talking," and he understood immediately who, he felt he was hearing a deep crimson voice, just when he least expected it, which was terrifying him like a vulnerable child, in a world which he had not had time to prepare for – or to recognise – and he asked her, "why?" as if his throat was blocked and only one word could get out. And her fingers froze even more, they became like wood, like clothes pegs, and she whispered, "I'm sorry." And they might have ended there, with Yannis running into the drawing room, saying now or never, but they walked on together once more, passed the familiar corners, went up her stairs. Beneath the first door shone a bar of light, but they heard nothing, and he concluded, "the younger daughter will be by herself," whom he liked, the way she looked at him pleasantly, she would surely be knitting or embroidering, for she never sang or played with the other children, she sat in the corner and watched, as if frightened and timid, once he had caught her crying, had asked, "who's been bothering you?" but she replied, "nothing", as if her eyes were streaming without reason.

When they arrived at the top of the stairs their footsteps were still echoing behind them, as if the staircase was holding them, preserving them in its wood, in its silence, and she said, "it's lucky you came," on another occasion this might have sounded different to him; now they turned on the anaemic lamp, a flood of shadows lying all about it, encircling them, pressing against them, and they burrow beneath her blankets with their clothes thrown onto her chair. And then he smells a scent, the blankets now tangled up with their feet, their armpits, and Yannis plunges his head into the darkness, the scent was spreading but could be identified, what can be smelled there is an ointment with which I am familiar, he concluded, and he felt, I might be infected and it might rot on me, maybe a monster is hatching within her, something like a rat perhaps which would come out without any eyes, or it might be a glutinous mass, like when you open a shellfish and smell it, and you see a faceless being, a little animal with no features, no limbs or eyes; this terrifies him so that he emerges from the dark bed with the feeling that he is arising from the waters, and the pale lamp awaits him, which reminds him of a familiar icon, which weeps and tells him, "you are quickening inside me" and they embrace, then he repents, "everything was begotten from my own blood," his own seed; and he slips between her legs once more, then deeper, from whence arise languor and sighing. Outside a gutter can be heard, running with water, singing – and then nothing.

The Middle Ages – 8

And when the three bodies were found, headless and naked and half burnt, they began to speak of the curse of God on disunity, it was never discovered to whom they belonged and they said that the citizens should be counted, that every household should declare faithfully whether all their souls were alive, whether they had members who were journeying somewhere and since when. The soldiers scurried from neighbourhood to neighbourhood, and schoolboys and priests were mobilised, in the end they decided to enlist the bakers, every soul was required to go alone to buy his own bread, but they still were unable to achieve any result, at night hundreds of people would come in from the outlying villages, they would pay something to the watchmen and hurry through the dark lanes, they'd huddle into the houses of relatives, bringing their animals and their best possessions with them, and the streets began to resemble pastures. The first man to stumble on the corpses was a much put-upon workman, people knew he was simple and made fun of him, he worked from dawn, arose while it was still dark and he was terrified and ran screaming, howling, as if his tongue had been cut out, he was like a dog, like a lamb, like an animal of which the only thing that functioned was his arms, which pointed and growled, and once managed to wail, "they're butchering us," whereupon various soldiers and citizens emerged and, still pointing ahead, he guided them, they went down into a ditch, got entangled in the bushes, then stopped speechless, enraged, "whose work is this?" they stuttered, who could the unfortunate souls be, one with his tufted chest, the second lying on his belly with his arms burnt, and the other, the boy, such things are not the work of our people, they thought, it might be a family who had been burned out, some rivalry, a vendetta, then at the brink of the ditch the women appeared, dragging their children at their feet, at which the men turned in horror, blocked their path and their view, "go back to your homes," they ordered, but one man had a wiser thought, he ran off, passing between the women, disappeared, then reappeared again and threw a rag rug over the bodies, and then tongues were loosened, the workman speaking more than anyone else, his timorous spirit gaining courage and recounting it, how he had stumbled and fallen before he'd had time to see them, had felt flesh icy and damp, he remembered how in his youth he had been a meat porter, oxen and sheep, he could tell how the slaughtermen killed them, how they skinned them, but he realised that people weren't listening to him, they were thinking whom they should inform, and one man pulled the others into a corner, they left the workman on the side, they were whispering something, one of them turned and looked all round, "only Christoforos would be able to find out the truth of it, the guilty person," but they continued to look around them, they were saying that they should see to their burial, but who would ordain where and when? People said that when two days had passed he went up the steps of the Cathedral and spoke with the bishop for two hours, and that as he came out with his brow clouded he stumbled on two priests and blasphemed, at night they knew they would find him at the hut. "Anyone more thoroughly killed than that boy I have never seen, anyone more dead, more empty, I lay down powerless on the floor until I felt her tears running down my legs, and only then did my feelings awaken once more, and I say this is her flesh, this her arm her throat, and I open my legs wider and feel as if her womanly nature is entering my body, her world of moisture penetrating into my belly and from there to my breast her arms binding me kissing me and then that our lips awaken the taste the smell and that I say, I want to kiss the part where it hurt where she bore me which every night brings me back to life and then she will tell me that we wounded our feelings our life and we lie like marble that is forgotten in the earth," there is always something that makes him remember, he imagines that somewhere within him a bleeding wound must be hidden, like a branch broken off green, whose sap flows heedlessly and forms knots like loathsome spots. Man should forget, should not feel pain, should not drag himself time and time again over the same things, if only he could pass from cold to hot, from joy to sorrow and from there to freedom from cares and to songs, for this he could envy Argyris, who comes and sits and talks to him, "each thing that happens drowns the previous one, sorrows kill each other," he says, but now who could tell what he should command, he might call the other leaders together, to decide what should be done with the three headless men, and his mother used to say, "you must devise rightly, otherwise sly men will kill you, they will set traps for you," and would weep. Then he would close his eyes, for he could not bear to see the moisture in hers, "I am afraid to see her weep," he would confide, he could not bear sobs which it was not possible for him to extinguish, and once more he would confide in her, "a wild beast like a giant arose before me, I think that I am running and that I shall be broken on a cloud of darkness, an impenetrable mass which resembles a hundred-armed beast or a blind bear," and he always remembered how, when he was a baby, an immense cat had come one night and stood at the window and watched him, it might have been a person or a dream, but he begged that the door be barred and all the windows carefully fastened, for there are men and some animals which may leap, which can reach high and tear you to shreds. Well, it was necessary now to find the murderers, or to lose the bodies, and here it is Theologos who gives him the idea, "it is not in our interest to dig too deep," he says, "either we must make them disappear or our people must go round the neighbourhoods and say that it is all a pack of lies, that the three bodies were never found, or, best of all, we should throw responsibility onto the rich people, kindle the populace to start shouting once again," and, after pausing for a minute, he told him hesitantly, "the solution might lie there, in an enraged crowd and in three dead bodies" – "and in more dead bodies?" Christoforos complained, but saw that the other man was looking at him ironically, "let the poor find an outlet for their anger and hunger to explode," ended Theologos. And he thought once more of the unborn child and of the child he had seen hunted and pierced, there is pain under a magnifying lens when you see a drop of blood emerge, you may not think of death or hurt, yet the fact is that it flows and weakens you, that your whole life is running out through your hands, as if your power is gradually being stolen from you and you know it, you hope that your possessions and your resistance may be limitless. Sometimes all these things nudge him towards beginning to believe in magic, the stars and the zodiac, for if he knew which was the proper stone for him and which the metal, he might perhaps have had to accept the ring, which might have been of silver, of lead, or bear some mystic design, these people draw another kind of power from spirits, you might imagine that those who dwell on the other side are their familiars and advise them, except that perhaps they too might have the same agonising doubt, whether those in whom they may put their trust are two people or one. And his mother used to say to him "in no one" and he despaired, it is not possible for one sole man to be responsible for all these agonies, these slaughters, the leaders ought to stand by him or Irene to be by his side now, for then he would have a place to lean on, to run to, while if he comes out from his hut at this very minute, he will fall into a sea of unknown heads, nor will their hands be visible, nor what they bear in them, when will it come to pass that he will cease feeling them to be strangers? "Many times I wonder what you are feeling" – "I feel a pain that is mostly without name, I care for them without knowing them individually one by one," and again they asked him, what is there for him to gain from this pain, but he remained silent, he feared lest they should shout at him as they had on the night when he had run to Kokalas (who will give us back our children?), the fathers of the headless men may perhaps be somewhere close at hand, but the sisters of the hungry are certainly at hand, those whose homes and livelihood were burned to ashes and who for three days and three nights ran like frayed threads floating in the air, "I used to wonder why kings hung heavy jewels of metal on their breast, why they are given the orb and the sceptre to hold, I suppose men want to weigh them down with responsibilities," for it is not easy to govern and give orders, to say let five thousand men be killed today, the victory which we shall snatch will restore them to us in solid gold. He remembered how Pharmakis had trembled and grown pale; another five steps and he would have been saved, he would have tried to climb the wall, up the ivy, to see the greenest of gardens, which he used to admire from the little attic window, as if he had never before in his life seen such a thing, and he dragged himself on his belly, no sense of smell or hearing or taste left, only nails that clawed the earth and knees that worked in hopelessness, aware that all his remaining strength resided now in them, and he shivered and remembered the garden, the three trees that grew tall and straight, and then the little water channels for the plants and around the closed room, he had remained there shut up for two days and nights, and heard the crowd threatening him, then Kokalas's sister had appeared, motioned him to follow her, and at one point he had groped and felt the stones and stopped and turned to lie on his back in order to breathe, and the thought awoke in him that it would be preferable to enter the earth before the sun came up, everything should be finished before dawn, and once more he took a deep breath, maybe this was all that was left to him now, the fact that he had succeeded in dragging himself a little way and breathing, in saying "I have set out to depart, I have achieved it, I have escaped from them and their dogs, their torches," and he filled his chest once more, said "oh God, I am in thy hands, do thou succour me," then he put his hands on the ground, now I shall attempt to rise, he thought, he understood automatically that he was standing upright, he could see neither his arms nor his legs, merely felt his body obey him, make a series of movements and find the wall, and sit unprotected on the top of it, and there at his feet, three metres below, on the grass and among the bushes, he can make out a row of shadows, men resting on their weapons, and they seem to be saying, we have been waiting for you for three hours now, at which a mysterious whistle arouses them, they raise their eyes and kill him. "So here is where my end was ordained," he whispered, he had a bitter wish to speak, which earth would receive him, which torn garments, and for a moment he hesitated whether he should let himself fall back into the garden from which he had been expelled, or fall forward weeping at the feet of the shadows who awaited him, who were more distinguishable now and who were turning into tired men, some with beards and hair, some faceless and young, clad in sheepskins or wrapped in blankets, boys who yesterday might have been with his own, who were able to go over to the other side, and who would recognise him now, who might betray him. It must have been a day without clouds, in a little while the sun would emerge from its hiding place, people would run from all corners of the city to see him, to see him lying there unable to jump up and catch hold of them and tell them apart, "that's him," they would say, they would stand a little way off from him in hesitation, maybe someone would summon up a little courage, would put out his foot and kick his leg, and then the others would all fall on him in a frenzy and hit him and tear his clothes and make a mockery of him, and they would increasingly be daring more fearful things, they would be saying that the diseased fountain in the dry land must refresh them all, in the end the water would flow and dry up, and their lips would be as burning as before, they would say that which burns us has not been extinguished, "what is Christoforos doing that he does not take care for the fountains, every last drop has run dry, both of wine and of revenge." And then a shot rang out, he must have thought that the garden was rent in twain, that the morning breeze was wounded, that he would fall. But these are stories which make you bleed, thought Christoforos, how he had been sitting a few paces away and how he was talking with Kokalas; in the end the sun came out and they heard the shot, the other man said, "now go," that all had been paid for, and that the bodies had been left unburied.

Christos

Every day there was danger and to spare, they said, "it's not possible, the killings will come here too," for people were being shot in the streets in Athens, they learnt about it from the newspapers and the loudspeakers, which talked about "the race that has never been enslaved", they showed photographs of the bloodshed, where young girls dressed in black knelt in the streets holding banners with slogans in huge letters, then the bullets rained down and killed them, and the next day there were more girls in black in the photographs; and Christos said, "there will be slaughter between us." In the morning when he left home they had stopped all trams and cars, the main street was blocked by the demonstration, mostly women, but some men and children too, who were shaking their fists and shouting, "English out, down with the thugs of the right," and people were watching them from their shops, from behind the glass and the closed windows, and Christos caught sight of the neighbour, the tram-driver's wife, a shrivelled and sickly woman, shouting and shouting like a madwoman, suddenly their eyes met, she seemed to come alive, called "come on, Christos," and she meant into their midst, she was inviting him with her outstretched arm, but he shook his head, no, and smiled, for goodness sake, he was thinking, how come so much familiarity? However, "I've got to get to work," he called – then was annoyed with himself and regretted it, he didn't need to justify himself, he thought. And at that moment he heard the vehicle, it was an English lorry, opening a path through the crowd, but fists were being shaken, some people banged on the sides of the lorry with their hands; it continued on its way though, in the back they could see five soldiers sitting, who seemed worried and doubtful, since what met their gaze was a sea of threatening fists, through which the lorry passed, and it was a case of the foreigners being up there and the people alone and on foot, before too long a stone hit the wing of the lorry, with a clang that made everyone freeze, but the engine roared and the lorry continued even faster, so that of necessity people moved out of the way, when Christos saw another stone making an arc through the air and missing its target, "we fight each other," he said to himself, but increased his pace with his mind made up to catch up with them, any day now it will come here too, he thought.

For he had unintentionally overheard Alcmene and Dimitris one day, and the girl had been saying with passion, "it's time to crush them now" and he felt, I don't recognise her voice, it's as if she's put some lump of iron in her throat which distorts it, Dimitris was gentle and hesitant, "I don't like people getting killed," he was saying to her – "but they're our own side, our brothers," Alcmene insisted – "and the others, what are they then?" the boy reflected – "are you worrying about traitors and right-wing army thugs? Have you forgotten how they were killing us in the streets?" – but the boy didn't answer; "are you afraid of them?" Alcmene asked as if slapping his face, whereupon he said, "something doesn't convince me, I'm afraid of all the people who are shouting and raising their fists, scared of what they'll do tomorrow if the others win, you know where they've all got the" – but at this moment the door opened, Amalia came in, and then closed it again loudly, the conversation ceased and Christos grumbled, "you're not careful," but the mother didn't understand, she had her own things to think of, her own way. It must have been that same evening at the newspaper that Nikos came up to him, a short man with curly hair, who'd spent years in exile on the island of Anaphi – now he had a position and gave instruction – he said, "do you want to come to a course of lessons?" and Christos asked, "what sort of lessons?" – the Party was organising them, they'd be talking about politics and the press, "I'll come," agreed Christos, but then asked, "what's happening in Athens?" – "we're fighting," said the other man and stopped short there.

And people were running through the streets, the poor, members of the youth organization with their loudspeakers, with their armbands and flags, but Christos could see other people too – mostly in shops, in houses – who watched with displeasure, they seemed to be saying, how long till all this is over?, for at any moment their breath might be cut off short, they might gasp and fall. Now he was hurrying, he'd passed the front of the demonstration and was searching for a tram or a taxi, in vain, – he said to himself, I'll go up to Hirsh, in case the trams are running up there, the little streets seemed emptier now, here and there were slogans on walls, about the "battle of Athens", the right-wing thugs, the wretched Scobie, he could see courtyards with trees, he could feel the humidity and thought the watercourses will be full now, which ran down from the Toumba and emptied into the sea. So far he had followed about ten lessons, there won't be many more of them, he reflected, people were saying that the English were dropping troops into Athens and attacking with planes, and our own people from Africa were fighting – "there you are, we're killing each other," said Amalia to him, and her heart trembled, "we were waiting for the Germans to leave so that we could have some peace," she complained, one evening they had a fight with Alcmene and Christos raised his hand to the girl (he reflected that it was the first time he'd done it), "Holy Virgin, look what I gave birth to," wept the mother; and they lay awake that night, disturbed and frightened, listening to doors or footsteps. When he reached Hirsh he stopped and stood still, he seemed to hear shouts that were fading away, he looked into the distance, he saw a mass of banners, they must be having a demonstration here too, he could make out bright red flags waving, he saw the tramcars all halted in a row, heard the faint glow of songs, anthems, decided, "I'll have to go on foot," and thus turned once more into the narrow streets, some familiar and some not, he passed courtyards and the gullies where winter torrents flow, and in the end arrived near the Fair, where the old shanties were, he crossed the last watercourse and could see the park. But the shouts seemed now to be pursuing him, he turned and looked towards the main avenue, in the distance the crowd could be seen, it resembled a wall that was approaching, a wall decorated with flags and slogans, he increased his pace as if he was afraid, as if they really were pursuing him and he was trying to escape, he plunged in among the trees and bushes, felt chilled, he was panting, he realised, but he did not stop – not even when he reached the Tower, or further on the "Elysia"; and the shouts were almost out of earshot.

Things were certainly getting nasty; yesterday they recounted how three of their own side had gone and knocked on the doors of the "Independent", they brought documents out and showed them round, saying, "everything belongs to the people now," that they would take the printing machinery, "we are confiscating them on behalf of the people," they shouted, at which point the teacher came to the window – he was worn down now, people muttered that he wouldn't live long – and cried, "aren't you ashamed?" for among them he could see one or two of his own former employees; in the end men from the civil guard arrived, two of them with their pistols in their belts, they went in and talked to the teacher, then came out again looking sour, said something to the three men, gave them some advice, and thus they all left together. He told Nikos about it at the newspaper, and the man was furious, "riff-raff," he snarled, "they've wormed their way into our ranks simply in order to grab things," and he telephoned somewhere, "they are damaging our cause," he was shouting feverishly – he may have a Party place, thought Christos, but he's also got a good brain and experience, and after a bit he came up to him and murmured, "not everything can be perfect," to which Christos answered, "that's for sure." Now he was getting near the Cathedral, but he saw another crowd, people blocking the streets and lanes, they had surrounded a mansion – on the corner – and were yelling, "English out," for the English wanted to attack them here too; he could see their angry faces, their clenched fists constantly raised, their banners. A window opened suddenly, a young girl looked out, she was terrifed by what she saw and closed the window again; but their shouts were intensifying, as if they were waiting for something, as if expecting something, Christos stood and watched, from behind him more people were arriving, those who had set out from the Depot, from the Toumba, from Harilaou, their cries thunderous, the crowd swelling, raging.

Then the window opened once more and a man in a khaki tunic appeared, his head bare, his hair curly, the shouts and the roar of the crowd surged louder, some people clapped, whistles were heard, and the man stood there and surveyed them, he seemed to be sizing up the situation, as if what lay before him was a stormy sea and he was wondering, shall I dive? In the end he spread his arms wide as if saying be quiet, a group were shouting slogans, demanding that the English be booted out, he spread his arms again more tensely, moved them up and down, ordering the people to stop, from opposite Christos said, "it's Euripides," he hadn't seen him for years, he looked old and tired, in photographs he seemed different, more laughing and sure of himself, now he kept moving his arms, for the people refused to be silent, "comrades," he cried to them, "comrades, listen to me" and he spread his arms, he needed to appear cool; the noise ceased suddenly, and "comrades," he began again. He spoke to them simply and calmly, asked them to go back to their homes, told them that the leadership was alert night and day, he had a deep voice which was convincing, suddenly Christos heard people crying "Markos" at which cheers and whistles broke out, Euripides ended with "our people will win" and cheers resounded again, then he saluted them and stepped back inside.* The crowd remained undecided, thinking perhaps of what it wanted, of what it had been promised, a light rain began to fall, Christos predicted, "that was it," he raised his eyes to the grey heavens, felt the rain wetting his face, cooling him, at the edges of the crowd people were beginning to leave, some up the road, others towards the sea; the main body of the crowd remained where it was, some people began to sing, as if showing their last, desperate weapon, then they moved off towards the market, and he thought, who is leading them? The nucleus of the crowd had all the flags and banners, which now seemed to have amassed together, to be bleeding like a wound – it must have been midday already, and he thought to himself, I'm late.

Now the earth was bound to the clouds by threads of water, he felt that his clothes and his head were soaking, he tried to find

---

* Forty years passed. I was talking to Clio N. on the subject of a book about her uncle and godfather – who was no other than the red major. In December '44 (she told me) they used to find his ashtray overflowing with cigarette butts every morning; he was trying desperately to avoid a clash with the English in Thessaloniki. He would spend hours in the bathroom relaxing under the shower. That was when they heard him sing.

awnings to protect him as he walked, at one point he stopped in front of a shop window – it was a book shop – he had got out his handkerchief and was mopping his hair, and he saw a young man within who was looking at him, smiling at him, he thought to himself I know him, but from where? for the reflections of light on the glass tricked his eyes; and Haris came to the door, he said "hallo" and explained that he worked there, Elias will have found him a comfortable berth, thought Christos, for they sold Party books and magazines and newspapers, and he asked, "how is your father? – your mother?", they were all fine, Christos put out his hand, into it fell two or three drops, "the rain has stopped," he murmured, and made as if to set off again, then remembered the "goodbyes". And now he was making his way in the drizzle and worrying about his clothes, in Aristotelous Street he saw a group from the demonstration, their flags hanging wetly down, they were discussing something heatedly, a fair-haired boy was speaking passionately, another boy with glasses was disagreeing, "we have to finish it off now," he insisted, a third boy was trying to get them to compromise, though he too was speaking in irritation, and in the end Christos said to himself once more, "I'm late." He entered a road leading towards the shore, then turned right, all along lay old two- and three-storeyed houses, perhaps they had belonged to the Jews before the war (he never usually passed through these quarters), he found the outside door wide open, went in and up the wooden staircase, all across was stretched a bright red cloth, "workers of the world, unite", which is what also used to be printed on their newspaper, right at the top of the front page, in the offices he asked for Nikos, who was sitting writing in a little room right at the back, Christos thought, this must once have been the maidservant's room, the lamp was lit on the desk and a sheet of newspaper had been placed over it to concentrate the light, outside it was still cloudy, with a few raindrops falling against the window panes from time to time, he found only one chair on which he sat down, he watched the other man continue writing, "half a second and I'll be done," he said, excusing himself.

And in a little while they were out in the street, Christos asked, "where are we going?" at which the other man stopped, he seemed to have forgotten to mention it, "oh, but I'm unforgivable," he murmured, then said in confidential tones, "they are waiting at headquarters," but "who?" asked Christos, puzzled, to which the other man replied, "Markos and Euripides will be there," he must have remembered him; the sun had come out now and it was like a surprise, everything suddenly lit up unexpectedly, they found an old taxi, arrived at headquarters, the guard saluted Nikos as if they knew each other, they went up the stairs and waited a bit, there were other people there and Christos saw the three youths, the fair-haired one who'd been silent, the one with glasses disagreeing, and the third reconciling them – in Aristotelous Street with the banners – they were now standing in silence, except that from time to time the fair-haired boy leant towards the other one and whispered something to him, and the other nodded "yes", as if he had got tired of disagreeing, the fair boy was holding a piece of paper carefully, it was folded and uncreased. Then the door opened and everyone turned towards it, and Christos thought, how the years have passed, for Euripides was standing there and he looked heavy, in the morning when he'd been addressing them he'd already looked tired, now he seemed to smile at them though, and Nikos went forward, with Christos behind him, but the general looked at him and said, "fellow warrior", so they must have told him who would be coming, maybe he'd even asked for him. They went in and sat down, he behind his desk and the two of them on chairs in front of it; everything around had an air of grandeur, "I've got a photograph from our time in Asia Minor, the two of us together" and the general seemed to be day-dreaming, "I've got a copy of it too," said Christos and they both smiled, all the same we didn't come here to talk about the past, he thought. And now he looked at the man more closely, his fair hair was beginning to go grey and he wore it combed straight backwards, he folded his arms on the desk, asked, "is the plan ready?" – Nikos got out his papers and handed them to him, "if the captain could see it," he asked, Euripides remained impassive, "he'll see it," he murmured, for he had already begun to read, he seemed to be going through it carefully and slowly, as if studying each sentence, and in the end said "yes" and put it by – and just then the door opened and a sunburnt man in a peaked cap came in, he appeared to be younger and more supple, "come in, Markos," said the general, and he stood and looked at them, he nodded to Nikos in imperceptible greeting, Christos remained stubbornly silent, I don't understand why I'm here, he was thinking.

The captain sat down by the desk and crossed his legs, Euripides gave him Nikos's paper, "read it," he said, "it's about how the press and information services will be organised," Markos took the sheet of paper but did not read it, "it has the right views," said Euripides and looked from Nikos to the captain, Markos thought a moment then asked, "does it come under our area of responsibility?" – at which Nikos said, "I'd like you to look at it first" and – stumbling for an instant – added: "comrade captain," the other man gave a sly smile, "others can judge it better," he insisted. All the same he unfolded the sheet and read, for a moment his mouth seemed to tighten, he raised his hand and played with his moustache, read on frowning, raised his eyes and looked at Nikos, as if sizing him up, "you're better at writing features," he commented, folded the sheet of paper, then opened it once more, and started reading from the beginning again, outside bugles were playing, it was well past midday, "no", decided the captain, "it doesn't follow the Party line" and Christos saw that his colleague was outraged and that Euripides remained grave, only Markos seemed to be smiling, he said, "it's not our job, send it to the central committee" then folded it up again and laid it on the desk.* Someone knocked on the door and an officer came in, "the Englishmen are outside," he announced, at which Euripides rose, said, "if you will excuse me" and handed Nikos back his paper, "you could rewrite it," he said, "and we could look at it again"; both of them had got to their feet and were saying goodbye, Markos asked Christos, "what's your name, comrade?", and he felt himself blush and was annoyed, what on earth's the matter with me every time? (he thought), but he said his name and the captain laughed and said, "I don't know you," and the manner in which he said it was perfectly simple. The Englishmen had come

---

* From the account of Manolis A. A little after the December events, Siantos and Zevgos had come to Thessaloniki. A committee of students went and handed them a political manifesto. Siantos was enthusiastic about the views expressed in it. Zevgos then read it, said, "it's wrong from beginning to end," and the students left in silence.

in by now, with the interpreter beside them, where do I know him from? thought Christos, and then remembered, he was called Mouratoglou, he worked in a bank or something like that.

They went down the stairs without exchanging a word, outside it was still sunny though less clear, "you got an idea," said Nikos, and he seemed to feel bitter or hard done by, and Christos made no answer, "they can never agree on anything," the other man explained, "I don't understand why you took me along" – "Euripides asked me to," said Nikos – "I still don't understand," he said – "leave it be, I'll tell you in the evening," and the other man was off. A tram was passing and he ran, only just caught hold of it, and waved from the platform at the back, he looked like a rag blowing in the wind, grey. Christos walked on down the road and thought about the visit, for a moment he felt that he was talking aloud, "where are we going?" he said and shook his head, he saw a man coming up the street and looking at him, maybe he thinks I'm raving, and Christos felt ashamed. When he reached their neighbourhood the sun was setting and Amalia was waiting for him in the street, she can't get used to it, he thought in sympathy for her, and he meant his work, all its ugly aspects.

Angel

It was like something out of a fairy story, the way everyone from the old days was gathered together again, a little older – or a little wiser, as Myrsine said – sitting in the same room, looking out on the familiar lane, the lunatic asylum with its high wall. And Angel wondered about Eleni, how she'd found them, how she had scented that his father was back in Salonica, a bit tougher now, wearier, with less hair but still with the same moustache à la Fairbanks, telling them tales of the cruel sea, how one night they sank off Malta and he had clung on to a rope, tossed in the waves for about ten hours, and in the end all the bones in his arm had been broken, he'd spent a month in hospital, and had met a certain Gladys there, the soft-hearted nurse – but at this point his grandmother coughed suddenly, said "let byegones be byegones" and laughed meaningfully, and Fotis got into conversation with Eleni, who kept telling him, "it's your fault," whereupon Angel felt nauseated, he said, fuck you, though he said it silently to himself, and went out.

Someone told him that they'd be leaving any minute now, people were whispering about an incomprehensible agreement, saying that supposedly the guerrillas would pack up whatever few possessions they had and leave town, would go towards Verria or even further, and they warned him that he ought to leave too, for anyone who stayed would be in danger. "But from whom?" asked Angel, for he could see the English, the amicos, getting drunk and beating each other up (one day a man cried, "don't tell me that these are the people who drove the Germans out"), one evening as he was going home and everything was pitch black, an Indian suddenly came up to him, he was dark-skinned and thin, he showed him a tin of food and begged, "the girl, the girl", Angel thought of hitting him, but he just said, "no girl" and left; and when he went into the house he saw only his grandmother and Niki, suppose the "girl" might be his aunt, he grabbed a knife from the kitchen and rushed out into the street, but couldn't find either the Indian or anyone else, he sat on their steps and swore, then suddenly heard slippers approaching, and Myrsine said, "have you gone quite crazy?", she took the knife from his hand, said once more, "Lord, forgive us our sins" and left him. But after a little while Niki came out and said, "come and eat," his grandmother had prepared something for him.

And the next day or the one after that he announced that he was leaving, Fotis gave him a lecture, "you're hare-brained," but he wouldn't listen, so in the end his father said, "sit down and I'll tell you a story" – about how they had shut him up behind barbed wire in the desert and they languished in the searing heat and the thirst, because people wanted to bring the movement to its knees, "we had the same ideas as you," no matter that Fotis might seem cunning, a man who'd known a thousand waves (and a thousand cabarets and gaming tables, thought Angel), in the end his father said, "they've got the means and they know what to do with them, look at Athens, how they've patched things up," and in his eyes sat a bitter shadow, Angel pondered his father's words, suspected that they'd prove true, however he said, "but what can I do? It's an order," at which Fotis laughed and answered, "in a month your leaders will be banished" – and the "your" bothered Angel, he seemed to be saying I'm not on your side, but in that case why had he been put behind barbed wire in the desert? He was weighing up all these things later, after he'd left home and was standing near where Christos lived, under a tree, waiting; the joke was that he might be the only one about to leave, he meant of their group, for neither Dimitris nor Haris was going, and he felt hard done by, always when they need me, he thought, he could have asked Alcmene, but didn't see her. And he stood there under the tree, feeling more and more spiteful, and he kicked at stones and pebbles and earth.

He didn't forget the story with Eleni, he couldn't stand her, he remembered all that old business, specially his grandmother's laments, the fight in her yard, his father left penniless, he felt, I don't understand where she popped up from, and suspected that only someone in their own family could have sent her a message, he suddenly remembered how his grandmother had taken him to her house, back then when they'd arrested Stratis and shut him up in the camp, and the whole family weeping, but now he complained to himself, "their sick laughter hurts me," it was like a marsh in which you don't know where to tread, or whether it mightn't be better to remain quite still on a spot where you're not sinking, where you are secure. He saw a final pebble and kicked it, felt uncomfortable, jumped up and grasped a branch, stripped off a lash, thrashed the leaves and beat the air for no good reason; no one was even poking their nose out of Dimitris's house, their mother had swallowed them all up, he thought in mockery, who was always weeping and persuasive, his own father only talked or beat him (in the old days), he said, "better serve as a cook on board ship than walk for a week in the salty desert without being given a drop of water," the English are devils, he concluded – and now he could hear a bird singing, and he hit the branches with his lash, heard the beat of its wings and regretted it, what had that bird ever done to me? he reflected, further off he saw two soldiers, they were enemies, the ones who'd come to drive them out, he said to himself, what a pity I don't have the handkerchief, the red silk scarf, he came out from under the tree as if saying, here I am, but felt foolish, for the soldiers left without even noticing him.

And he wondered who are our side and who the others? And he remembered once more his father pronouncing, "if they don't have any need of you, they won't give you a single morsel to eat" and he said "the parties" – "then what were you doing mixed up in the movement?" – "I always liked adventure" and he laughed. But he was a liar though, always frivolous, as his son considered now, and he went back in his mind over all the past; an actor through and through (he thought), what can you expect? Not a single one of the boys and girls he was friendly with could be seen, he could have discussed it with Alcmene – one evening as they lay in the grass she had sworn, "I care for you" and had kept caressing him; but where was she now? thought Angel stubbornly, now when he needed her. And they didn't even have the red house any more, the English had come three days ago and turned them out, they brought their own desks, their own beds – and girls were going in and out all day long; I'll go home, he thought, in disappointment, yet again had second thoughts.

He went in by the kitchen, treading lightly like a cat, he felt that the house seemed empty, yet from somewhere he heard whispering, he went further in, to the little passage outside the bathroom, all round him white doors, all of them closed, only one ajar, it was the door leading to the sitting room, now and again it creaked as if moving in the draught; Angel stood quite still, absorbed in his father's whisper, which soon became a low-voiced conversation, he was going on and on about his plans as if struggling to persuade someone (who?) – he'd lived a long time in Alexandria, knew it inside out, knew what the people there liked, he said, "a club like ours would make a fortune," and Angel thought, you're quite incorrigible, and he remembered their rows in Beirut, the selling of everything, the woman whispered something to him (that bitch is back again, spat the boy) and then Fotis's monologue, persistent, it sounded like a rasp filing iron, and when he stopped she must have been grumbling, and he reacted, getting angry in the end and saying in a loud voice, "I can't talk to you if you're going to measure every word I say," to which Eleni replied, "I've been through a lot" – "it was your own arse that was itching you," said Fotis crudely, then the sound of chairs being pulled back, maybe they'd realised they didn't suit each other, Angel slipped into the garden, came out by the collapsed wall, went round the house keeping an eye on everything, came in again by the garden gate, but now saw his grandmother on the verandah, she smiled and put her finger to her lips (sssh!) and Angel suspected that she'd been acting as guard to them, for he could see their heads between the little curtains, his father must be speaking again; his grandmother had arranged it, everything, right from the beginning. Who knows what she was planning, or what she hoped for.

And the next day he heard shouts in the afternoon, Myrsine was prodding him again, for Angel had fallen asleep, she said, "hurry, Bettina" and the boy wondered, but why me? However, he got dressed and went outside, the shouting was continuing, the strangers had emerged from the door of her house and were saying, "we don't know you," the girl seemed to be saying something in reply, to be gesturing, but he couldn't hear her words, after a moment the women came down the steps, they seemed to be enraged, "and our houses that were burnt down, who's going to give them back to us?" they were screaming – and Bettina took a step backwards, she seemed pale and frightened, she was looking around her for help, maybe from her old neighbours, but no one had even stuck his nose out of his house except for Angel, who came and stood beside her, he said, "she owns the house," and the women gave him a piercing look and finally said, "and here's the bridegroom." But just then an old man came out of the house, "get back inside," he shouted at them, and his voice was dry as wood, he stood in front of the girl, "what is it you're wanting, my daughter?" he asked, and the way he said it made them calm down, then he added, "we had our own houses once, but they wrecked them for us," what could Bettina say in answer to this? "They're poor wretches," admitted Angel; but the old man spoke again, "we could empty a room for you to come and live in," but the girl whispered, "no" in terror and made a move backwards, at which he shrugged, by now all the neighbours had gathered, but they were hanging back at the side in indecision, the old man cast a look around, "would to God we could leave," he shouted at them, "that I could go back to my own fields, my own prosperity" – and Angel felt a change in his voice as though the wood had cracked. Somebody said, "poor wretches", they had children, wives, they struggled to get bread to feed them – and later Bettina said, "but where shall I live?", they invited her into the sitting room and offered her food and drink, other people came in from the surrounding houses and kept questioning her, specially about her family, but "I don't know," she answered, and in the end burst into tears, "would you like to stay here for a few days?" suggested Myrsine, but it wasn't a solution; she said goodbye and left. Outside stood the old man, smoking and watching, as if their talk had been interrupted, as if he was waiting to speak to her, but Bettina set off down the road and disappeared – for a bit.

The following morning Fotis was due to depart, for his leave was over, he promised, "I'll come back soon" and said to his son, "remember what I told you" and Angel gave him a searching look. And in two days' time he himself received word, he took his old knapsack, two changes of clothes and his shaving kit, bade them "goodbye" and left them; and the house seemed empty, as Myrsine lamented.

Angela

Overhead was the shadow of a lovely cloud, but Angela was looking at the sea and dreaming, she felt, I am high up and I can breathe, except that now in front of her stretched the sea, and she missed the trees, the old houses and Beauty's garden – she had just married Yannis and they had found this house on the beach, which seemed cut off from everything. For the only thing she had brought with her from the attic was her old lamp, she had called the motherless girls and given them all her other possessions, their father had come – completely sober – and had loaded everything onto his back, whistling all the while, and in the end she had locked her door and left. They could have moved into Yannis's family home, the house was spacious, but he said "no" as if the idea hurt him and he wanted to put an end to the discussion; Angela felt that everything about her marriage had been a little like this, as if they had an illness which they would have to get over, it had taken place in a tiny little church, with the castle looming above them, around them a few friends and his sister, whose face looked as white as a blank sheet of paper, an icy cheek that kissed her, in a manner that meant this is our first and last embrace – and she understood Yannis's sharp "no".

And thus they lived alone, in a little bird's nest on a rock, over the sea – where she stayed and brooded, while he left for the factory, which he was struggling to open again and he had his own stormy seas to navigate, the workers who were constantly shouting, though there were still one or two people of his own whom they feared (Pavlakis had died some time ago), but mainly the fact that the market was moribund, the merchants would gather and discuss matters grimly, they'd say, "things can't help but pick up a bit," now that ELAS had left, its members withdrawing to the villages, and the army held sway. One day she ran into Vassilis, he had closed his tavern ingloriously, yet one more time, he complained, "we missed you," as if it had been her who had brought them good luck, when she had not even invited him to her marriage, he smiled and they kissed one another, "I'm leaving for Athens to try my luck," he told her, and there was something weary in his eyes; and Angela thought, it was I who cut myself off, it was as if she'd gone to live in another country, and she smiled and thought this was my fate, which a great many women would have envied her for, because now she counted as a lady, with her lovely house and all their acquaintances among the fine world, whom, however, they saw less and less frequently. Behind the house she could hear children shouting, but it seemed as if it came from another city, the neighbouring one, which Angela knew only from its sounds, she said, "I don't go out and I don't talk to anyone, and people will think I'm stuck-up" – and she and Yannis laughed, remembering the past, each in his or her own mind.

But Angela said, "you never can put anything behind you" when they received a letter from Constantinople, which at the beginning puzzled them, for they were confused by all the rubber stamps on it and the date, but in the end Yannis said, "it's her handwriting" and it was addressed to the factory, in a battered envelope, which made him declare, "they must have been through a lot." For indeed they'd left Vienna months ago, and had wandered and been in peril and in the end had found themselves on a ship bound for Turkey, where they were subjected to interrogations, since by now Germany was at its last gasp, and they needed all their wits about them – and with a thousand difficulties they had succeeded in being allowed to go to Constantinople where there was a large Greek population, and at the side of the letter Euthalia wrote that she no longer had any jewellery; and Yannis said, "the Turks will have stripped them bare" – and at the bottom of the letter was written "till we meet again" and greetings from her husband. And Angela had a choking feeling in her larynx, she asked, "when did she write the letter?", and it was a month ago, maybe more, whereupon she calculated mentally and said, "perhaps we'll be seeing them any day now," he ruled it out though, saying "the roads are still closed," but she asked, "till when?" and they both fell silent, Yannis went into another room and she heard water gushing from a tap and at the end a sound as if he was sighing.

When dusk fell they embraced, they had a comfortable divan and the stove gave sweet warmth, she enjoyed the scent of soap which clung to his hands especially, to his palms that warmed her breast, "we must be careful now," she reminded him, for the birth was getting near, "we might go out somewhere," he murmured, but she leant more heavily on his bosom, meaning I like it better here, they looked through the glass doors into the darkness and imagined the sea, which might be beating against the little wall below them, drenching them with its salt spray. Suddenly out of the blue he asked her, "do you remember Eugenios?" and she replied, "I remember it all," as if she was saying it grieves me or pains me, and after a moment he spoke again, "maybe they'll come to us," so it *is* preoccupying him, the woman thought, and she recalled the day when Euthalia had come to her with their father's letter, it had seemed like a knife wounding them, in those days when everything between them had still seemed uncertain, a sharp knife both for her and for him, and most of all for any hope that they might be together. Yet now everything had worked out, which was something his sister couldn't know, she wouldn't be aware of the way things had ended and their marriage – from outside came a sound like a window banging in the wind, but he said, "it's not one of ours," and she felt him stir in her arms. And she fell into thought once more (they were not speaking, hence Yannis must be tormenting himself) and then they were standing with Elias she thought she saw the basement the forest where invisible hands and speech described the threat like the touch of nothing like a suspicion they came out in the end with countless difficulties and now it was daylight and there was a river of sand on which they were walking and slipping into it Elias said hold onto me but he was being pulled down to the depths a voice was heard then nothing neither his footsteps nor any trace of smells clothes but only a tiny little hole she put her hand in it disappeared she pulled it out and it was bloody as if it was being cut off and it hurt and she began to cry, but she felt someone cuddling her and kissing her, "you got terrified in your sleep again," he chided her, for a moment or two her mind and pulse were numbed, but then she felt that the blood was flowing in her veins, that his hands were on her breast, that he was called Yannis and that they lived in a house above the waves.

And on the sixth day after that, someone rang their doorbell, Angela opened the door and a tired woman was standing there, in a narrow grey coat, her hair fair, and she smiled at her expectantly as if asking, so do you recognise me? And then she said, "it's me" and they embraced; Angela felt as if she was bringing the bitter chill in with her, for it was a windy and dreary day. However, inside the fire was burning, and they both sat on the divan, Euthalia said, "we've just arrived" – they had gone to the family house and her husband had remained there, "I wanted to see Yannis" and she laughed, but he must be at the factory, "I didn't find him there," said Euthalia; and both were puzzled. And Angela was considering that it was indeed inexplicable, with the enigmatic woman smiling and probing, now she had warmed up and was making herself comfortable, she said, "we love him" as if she had found what they had in common – or what divided them? – she was fidgeting with her fingers and her wedding ring, and in the end revealed her passion, "how much will you be able to understand him?" by which she meant stand at his side as an equal; and Angela remembered the elder sister, her chilly marble kiss, the fact that she had not come a single time to visit them at their house. And she merely replied, "we love each other," and this remained her sole comfort and support, for "he is difficult and indecipherable", Euthalia insisted again, and Angela was to think later that it all seemed worked out from the beginning, as if they were acting on a stage, and Yannis was concealed somewhere behind the curtains, directing them by signs.

And at noon, as soon as he came in, she asked, "did you see her?" and he replied "yes" – "when?" – "just now as I was coming home" – "how did you know?" she asked slyly and Yannis stopped and looked at her, he was bright red and smiling, he reminded her of a naughty child, or even more of the boy at Eugenios's house, in those days when you imagined he was playing, but then he drew blood, which was somehow sullied as if by bits of wood, rags, fallen leaves or spotted light, and so Angela left the room, murmuring, she would have liked to cry to him, they are polluting us, but she knew of their love, their secrets; they ate their lunch in almost total silence. In the afternoon he left her alone and she suspected that he had gone running to his two sisters, but this was natural, she accepted it, they're his own blood after all, he hasn't seen her for so many years, maybe he should help them, for they would have need of him now, both of his advice and of his purse – he returned as soon as night fell and seemed to bring a cloud with him, he sat alone in the kitchen thinking, so that she called, "Yannis, come, I've been waiting for you" and she saw him standing at the door, somehow hunched, "come," Angela begged him, and indicated that there was room for him at her side, but he stood in front of her, he had a glass of brandy in his hand, "I'll have to take him back again to work with me," he muttered, and this infuriated him, and Angela said, "what did you expect?" – "he's cringing, I can't stand him," complained Yannis, but he was family, what else could he do? And then there was another matter too, as her husband revealed to her – they had rights and were claiming them. And she said, "let them have money, but they shan't have your soul."

What she was trying to do was to feel her way towards some understanding of things, for they were to prove complicated and occupied Yannis all morning and all afternoon, they were setting up the business again from scratch, he told her, and she sat alone – she was heavier now for her time was drawing near – chewing over everything in her mind and her heart and she concluded that he was hard pressed, for he would come home heavily in the evening and collapse, two or three times he had fallen asleep in his armchair, just as he was when he came in, in his clothes, and she would rouse him and mother him, and Yannis would keep saying, "forgive me". And early one evening he brought her with him, they were laden with documents and files and she said, "we'll have some peace and quiet here," as if Angela wasn't something that bothered her; Euthalia was looking better these days, with her hair done, wearing make-up, elegant, but as thin as ever, and they said, "we'll sit in the drawing room" so that nothing would be in their way. And Angela offered, "I'll make you some tea, something to warm you up" but they thanked her and refused, whereupon she withdrew into her own corner, thought, I'll look out of the window, from which she could see Mount Olympus sketched in the twilight across the grey sea, and not another thing; only out at sea, far out in the middle of it, a little light seemed to be playing, as if it was a star being extinguished by the waves, maybe it was some boat pitching on the water. But the world outside had disappeared, had shrunk until it all fitted into this room, under their table lamp which shone with a restful blue light. No sound came from the drawing room and Angela felt alone, like in her old attic, where she would shut herself up with her thoughts or her jobs, now she had left off doing the housework, from time to time a poor woman would come and clean for her, she'd eat at midday and then leave, and she always took something with her in her bag, for Angela remembered her own past sufferings and felt sorry for her. Another hour passed and there was a sweetness in her cushions, a lethargy in which everything floated in the pale blue light, a world in which there were no sounds except at one point (when?) the click of the lock as a door closed.

So everything in the room awoke once more, she saw that the drawing room door was open, she went and looked but it was empty, though thick with smoke and the ashtray full of butts, and just then she heard their front door closing too; she ran to the back, to the little window in the kitchen, she saw a pitch dark lane over which the branches of trees hung low in places. She seemed to hear footsteps in the night, cried "Yannis" but in vain, for she seemed to see two shadows walking, and they appeared to be arm in arm, "Yannis," she cried again, but then closed the window, went back to her divan, gripped herself, her heart stopped then started again, "oh God, don't let it come before its time," she said, for her belly seemed to be pressing on her throat. And she thought, I'll stay awake and wait for him, but she didn't have to wait long, she heard the door open and saw him come into the room quietly; "why aren't you asleep?" he asked, but "where have you been?" she said in answer, there must have been something aggressive and abrupt in her tone, and she spoke again in complaint, "you left me," but Euthalia didn't dare go home alone at night, "I accompanied her back to her house," he murmured – "her husband could have come for her," Angela could not keep quiet even though she could feel that she was doing harm, "I don't want him under my feet, I can't stand him," said Yannis and got undressed, "I'm sleepy," he complained and stretched sharply.

But the next day when she awoke Angela did not find him beside her, all he had left was the scent of his hair on the pillow, some slight warmth from his body between the sheets, in the half light the clock showed a little past eight, and she wondered where has he gone off to? And at once some devil got into her blood, she went to the kitchen and found everything untouched, so he hadn't even had breakfast, for a moment only she hesitated, then got dressed, put on her coat, concealed her hair with a scarf and went out into the street. The morning chill was biting, but she smelt something like leaves and seaweed, she set off up the road, towards the main avenue, thought I'll take a tram, but as they went by saw that they were full and she would be squashed, in the distance she could see the park, she felt a longing desire for it, she walked heavily but steadily, a little further and she would reach the trees, the sun played between the clouds, over the wires and branches, she entered the park and breathed more freely, thought I'll sit on a bench and get my breath back, there was no one about and she felt tranquil wrapped in her coat, where am I going? what am I going to do? and she felt terror, maybe she would make herself ridiculous. But she got up again and walked on, a little further and she would reach his family house (but why?), yet she did not turn back, did not repent – now she could see their house, she had never dared think of it as her own, she didn't want it, she stopped to get her breath again, behind it was a humble grocer's shop, she could tell by the smells that came from it, an old man came out and threw a bucketful of water into the street, said "excuse me" to Angela, but she was looking at the door of the house in agony, for now it was opening – what a coincidence – and Yannis came out and stood there and behind him was Euthalia wearing a housecoat, she seemed to be adjusting his overcoat, his collar, brushing him down, which might have meant, they don't look after you at home, an upstairs window opened, a head looked out (the elder sister), he said something, in the end he kissed her and left, and she stood there and waved to him, then the elder one said something again, she closed the window noisily, and just then Angela took a step forward, her eyes met Euthalia's who was smiling all the time, and in the end she turned and fled.

She must have been mad though, all around her the world was darkening, somewhere she found railings and grasped them, she felt that her hands were swelling in size, perhaps they were turning into a monster's hands as she saw a tree bearing down on her saying, "have you gone mad, Angela?" and it seemed like the elder one who looked as white as a sheet, and then another voice, angry with her, was saying, "you were spying on us," at which point everything round her filled with gesticulations and signs, but then in the end an unknown little old woman came, she had a handkerchief and wiped her face, "keep back so she can breathe," she said, and mopped her face again, someone brought a glass, "drink this," and it was the grocer, "we've been made to look ridiculous," she heard Euthalia say, and she opened her eyes, gazed at her persistently, within her arose a feeling of spite, if I wanted I could make everything quite clear, and indeed she was beginning to see more clearly, and she heard her own voice emerge from her ears, "never set foot in my house again" and it was as if she was ripping the other woman's clothes, shattering a thousand panes of glass, "don't ever set foot there again," she was hard as iron once more, she watched them draw back in confusion, and the old woman was mopping her brow once more, "don't, my daughter, you mustn't," she whispered, "don't, because of what you carry in your womb"; it might have been the scene of a crime, with smashed jars, memories, messages, where a tap would be dripping until the whole place filled up with water and people would spread an embroidered sheet over them, perhaps it might look like a cross, or perhaps an orange wreath, which would give off a wholly novel scent, like some unknown root which people would boil and would tell her drink this and you will be cured. And afterwards everything was a green-painted room, and sitting on the chairs at the side were her Yannis and a nurse, and above her a light bulb swathed in green paper, like a relief, she closed her eyes and made an effort, she said, here are my arms, my thighs, finally here is my belly – and she was reassured. And she opened her eyes again, "Yannis," she said, quietly, at which he came to her side, and the nurse too, who put her hand on her brow, and Angela felt its coolness, "calm," whispered Yannis, he put his hand on hers and stroked it, they remained without speaking for a little while, the nurse went out for a moment then came back in, now another man came in too, I know him from somewhere, thought Angela, the way he bent over her and looked deep into her eyes, took her wrist and counted, said "fine" and smiled again, then left the room, taking Yannis with him.

She gave birth a month later, as they had expected, normally, they had a daughter, and Angela wept, "who knows what she will have to go through" for she felt that this world belonged to men, her life, her experiences, everything she saw around her told her so. But their house by the sea was suddenly filled, as if people had entered through the windows, as if sounds had multiplied and they liked it – Yannis said so, "now we are a quorum," he declared, in spite of the fact that Euthalia and her husband had left, had gone to Athens to seek a better life, this is what he told her – this is what they had decided. And Angela wondered, "how much will he have given them, or promised them?" and sighed to herself for a while, until Yannis returned with his arms full and put them at her feet and in their baby's cradle; and she forgot everything, and sang to them.

Antigone

Some of them had already returned, they had slipped in through the darkness and were kissing their families; all the others were waiting for daybreak. Their father had got back early, "I asked them if I could leave," he meant at the newspaper, outside sleet was falling, they gathered around the stove which their mother only lit in the afternoon, it gave a sweetness to the house which enveloped them, "I don't understand," Alcmene was saying, "how can they surrender all their weapons and sneak back like thieves" and Christos was looking at her as if searching behind her eyes to find what she was thinking, in the end he murmured, "our eyes are going to see a lot of things," then added, "you must be careful," and his gaze was still on Alcmene; Dimitris was examining his hands, perhaps he had managed to bury his thoughts deeper, and Amalia said, "that's how much good the Germans leaving did us," at that point Dimitris left the room, "they didn't estimate something right" and it was their father speaking again, he appeared to be worried and thoughtful, "but it's totally unjust," Alcmene burst out, and she seemed to be burning with emotion, perhaps before long she would be in tears, "unjust or stupid", said their father, and as everyone looked at him, "or incompetent", he added. Dimitris came in again, but still sat in silence, Christos smiled, "we've done our duty," he told them, "and you may as well remember, if you don't work no one's going to give you a scrap to eat, not even a cuckold," he stopped. Then, almost as if he wanted to amuse them, "let me tell you the story of what happened when they caught me at the village, when we were going for our mother's funeral."

When they reached the coppice, Christos thought, what stupidity, for he could see that they didn't have any plan but were only holding him because they had the power and wanted to show it, at one point the older man asked him, "what news from the city?" and Christos told how the Germans were leaving, the neighbourhoods breathing again, and all the other news about the resistance, he delicately said how he'd been selected for the underground newspaper, but the other man seemed not to be listening, all he talked about was the suffering the villages had undergone, "you lot in the city haven't been through anything in comparison," and Christos said, "maybe that's so" in order not to risk making him angry and lessen his chances of getting away, so he only asked, "who are we waiting for?" by which he meant who would decide his fate, and they admitted, "no one", then the older man said he was going to have a look around, for gangs were roaming about, "from your Salonica", he added, and disappeared for a while, the other two remained, Christos eyed them, they eyed him, time passed, they would be burying her now, he thought, but just then they heard the creaking of wheels and then hooves, they grabbed their weapons and barricaded themselves behind the trees, for a moment there was quiet, then someone was calling, "which way, old man?" and it was his father dressed in his best, in his black suit and white shirt he looked as out of place as a spelling mistake among the oaks and armed men, he walked in fearlessly, said, "the funeral's in an hour" and he was already by Christos's side, "well, what are you doing sitting there?" he scolded, and at that moment the other man arrived back, and "what's up?" he asked, then his father drew a piece of paper from his pocket and gave it to him, he said, "I've come to fetch him, comrade," the other man read it and scowled, said to his father, "do you remember me?" to which the reply was "I remember you" – and thus they left; later on though, as they were bouncing along in the cart, "how could I remember him," said his father, "I've given food and water to so many of them," and in the end they buried his mother, with the sound of shots in the background.

In the morning Antigone and Alcmene ran over to Angel's house, the sun and the clouds played above them, Myrsine was sweeping the steps, they stood and watched her, then Alcmene asked, "has Angel got back?" but his grandmother didn't answer, so the girls stood there and exchanged undecided glances, then went and sat on a little wall opposite, in the end Myrsine came and asked, "who are you?" and Alcmene said, "friends" – "and is this how you go and wake up boys?" she scolded, whereupon the girls were overjoyed, "so he is back," they cried, and Myrsine replied, "quiet", something must have got her worried, maybe her grandson himself, and so they left, but Alcmene said, "we'll be at home, tell him." And when they got home they stayed out in the garden, Antigone said, "it's chilly" but the earth and leaves smelled fresh and thus they chose to sit in a corner where the sun played on them, "maybe we'll get tired of waiting for him," but Alcmene would not get tired, certainly she would have a lot to ask him, "what do you suppose he's like now?" she wondered. But he hadn't changed noticeably, maybe he held himself back a little, maybe he was acting a little, but he still spoke with his eyes closed, he still pretended to smile as if mocking them, and in the end he murmured, "what's happened to us," for somewhere near Vardari boys and girls had gathered on a street corner, they couldn't have been our lot, he thought, their eyes and mouths were full of sarcasm, Angel and his group were walking along with their heads down, they saw a girl coming up to them and he didn't have time to react, she shouted, "welcome to the heroes" and slapped his face, he just stood there dumbfounded and stared at her, and Alcmene said, "I should have been there" – a little further on they boarded a tram, they reached Hirsh, and then continued on foot through all the little streets they knew so well, it was dusk now, they felt more secure, one by one they turned into their own homes, Antigone felt that she was de trop and went in, when she looked out of the window, though, she could no longer see them in the little garden.

Two days later the schools opened, Antigone was back at her desk and the girl sitting next to her asked, "are you in the organisation?" – she'd always been a graceless girl, and now seemed even more farouche – Antigone replied, "no" and saw the other girl look puzzled, she said, "but your sister is" and Antigone preferred not to answer, she might have said, but she's older, she likes being with boys, but she thought of Angel and of the blue letter. She felt that everything was somehow different, the teachers, the air, the songs that they hummed; lessons passed slowly – only the physics teacher made them get on with it, as if she lived in another world. During the breaks they gathered in little groups, she saw that her neighbour was always in the middle holding forth, the following week they had pronounced their verdict, they had their own information, they said that the French teacher and the literature teacher were fascists, all the others seemed to be on their own side, one of them indeed came straight out with it, saying that it was the kings, the blue-blooded, who had destroyed Greece, and the girls' eyes shone, they applauded, whispered, "Kalantzis is a brick." Every day at noon she left alone, she would seek the loneliest road, would sit on a wall beneath green foliage and would ponder – the things she had heard and the things that she wanted to happen to her. One day she met Andreas, he said, "how come we seem to have lost sight of each other?", he shaved his upper lip now, his hair was neatly combed with waves in it, he's a handsome boy, she thought, but she answered him in monosyllables, rather as if she was shy, he appeared slightly supercilious, maybe old for his age, that's the way all boys are, thought Antigone, perhaps they're timid and are hiding it.

Only one of them was impetuous, as was shown before too long, and Christos said, "he always causes problems" and upset their household. For they learned that Angel had been arrested, they were holding him at the police station, they were accusing him, and Alcmene wept, "it's impossible," for they were holding him for the killing of Veroglou, some people said that he himself had killed him, others that he had guided the executioners, and Amalia and Antigone looked at one another but did not speak, as if each was afraid of the other. One night their father came home upset, he said, "it's that damn boy's own fault," and explained to them that from what people were saying at the newspaper, Angel had once boasted in the old days that he served in an organisation with secret missions, surveillances, punishments, maybe popular security – or even worse – and right-minded people had grassed on him; however, he asked Nikos, his colleague, who knew the people at the top of the Party, Christos begged him, "find out" – all this during the past few days – and the man reassured him, "it all looks like a put-up job, the boy you're talking about is completely innocent," and after a moment added, "they didn't trust him, thought he was flighty" and Christos said that they weren't in the least mistaken. But none of this reassured them, Amalia scolded her children, "why do you want to be friends with him?" and looked specially at Alcmene, but Dimitris got worked up, shouted, "they're doing him an injustice," and he didn't mean by arresting him or maybe beating him up to make him speak, "he used to give information about the Germans, the shipyards," and Christos went pale, "who did he give it to?", he had long suspected it and didn't really need the answer, "to me", the boy was almost in tears, and Alcmene said, "and to me" – but Antigone remained on one side, standing, feeling that all those nights, all the running and the slogans on walls were closing in around her. For a moment she thought she saw her mother crying, she seemed to be beseeching her.

But their father held out his hands, as if ordering them all to be quiet, then he put them on the table and clasped them, he appeared to be thinking and to be reaching some decision; and indeed he said, "we need to think about it in cold blood" and his eyes looked hard, "I know he's your friend and comrade – and that you're upset," he began, but ill-advised actions wouldn't help, because now everything had become dangerous, they didn't have a single friend left or a single door to knock on, at the newspaper his own people were being persecuted and Euripides had resigned from the army, people said he spent his time shut up in a villa, towards Aretsou, he didn't know anyone among the new people (for the time being), so they themselves were in danger, "you too, and you," he ended, looking at Dimitris, at Alcmene, who were both pale, although the sister's eyes seemed to be flashing, "it's wrong, and it's cowardly," she told them, she looked at them one by one, as if it was their fault, but Christos asked her, "what would we be able to do?" in a tone that implied the answer: nothing; and Alcmene ran to her room, they heard her door slam as if the whole house was shaking. Amalia ran after her, she seemed to be saying something, and Antigone understood that she was cursing again, "that damn boy", their friend.

And at that very moment she got the same feeling that she got when she stood on a high rock and dived into the sea, a whistling of the air for a couple of seconds; she went over to the table, sat down, and said, "I saw the people who killed him, it wasn't

Angel," she felt that the whole kitchen had turned a bright, searing red, that her father had unclasped his hands, and his cold bloodedness with them, and was asking agitatedly, "what are you talking about?" She took a deep breath and told him all about it, how she had been sitting in the garden that morning, the two young men standing behind the railings, the thundering of the bullets, how the men left and then began to run; "and I wasn't the only one who saw them," she added, "they ran straight into the Tsimonis woman." They were all silent for a moment, then her father asked, "does anyone else know this?" and Antigone said, "Mummy" – though she was thinking, maybe the whole tribe of the neighbour's family knew about it as well, who had now devised a new ploy, they were working hard to get her a pension as the mother of a son executed by the Germans. And her father murmured, "I see," then, as if he'd made a decision, "don't say anything to your sister" and he was specially requesting this of Dimitris, who was looking at him steadily, and they both promised, "we won't," and their father reassured them, "just for tonight and tomorrow", he was going to ask, take action, and Antigone, as if excusing herself, said, "I've spoken the truth."

All night she heard the gasping, but why's she weeping for him? she wondered, for her sister seemed in despair, and she put her fingers somewhere between the pillow and the sheet and felt a lovely coolness, as if she was bathing her sweating hands; in her sleep she heard their bedroom door creak, saw a grey crack which was widening, a white garment, the shape of her mother's head, and then nothing. In the morning when she went to school she felt distracted, said to herself, if only I didn't have to go, she caught sight of Alcmene and her friends, they seemed to be talking quietly, only at one moment her eyes met her sister's, and her sister acted as if she didn't know her. In the end they stood in line for the morning prayer, above them the wind was blowing in the pine trees, if only I could stay here, she thought, and heard her fellow pupil "... and on earth", and then they were all crossing themselves, "through the blessing of ...", and the younger ones were going up the stairs, the second form behind them, and suddenly sobs and cries were heard, it came from behind Antigone, a girl was in tears and the others around her were calling out, the physics mistress and Kalantzis went down, said, "what's going on? Quiet," and everyone was standing in a circle around the girl who looked deathly pale and was crying, Antigone thought, she's from the other section, in the end the teachers reached her and something was said, the men left and the physics mistress put her arm round the girl and led her away; at which point Antigone noticed that her legs were red with blood, but just then Kalantzis called, "silence", they began mounting the stairs again and going to their classrooms and talking, some girls were laughing, others were telling them off, saying "it's nothing to laugh about," acting wise.

That same evening Christos said, "we won't be risking anything," he would go with Antigone to the police – at some point he must have had a talk with the Tsimonis woman, and later complained that she'd refused, "don't get me mixed up with the police," she'd begged, they already had unsettled scores – but Amalia didn't agree, "they'll have us all shot," she said, but her children reassured her that since they'd be telling the truth there wasn't anything to fear. In the morning both of them put on their good clothes, her father instructed her, "talk politely, only tell them what you saw, nothing else," and he said it again in the street, and again while they were going up the steps of the police station, an old mansion, in which the lights were on and the whole place smelled of wet wood and uniforms, Christos went up and asked for the police officer, they told him, "you'll have to wait," on the old wooden bench, in the hall – and at the beginning they sat in silence, but then Christos leaned towards her, in spite of the fact that they were the only people there, and said, "only what you saw, not any opinions," and Antigone assented, and wondered, why did he keep saying the same things? Suddenly they realised that they were being called, but it wasn't the police officer, they saw a short, stout warrant officer, his hair combed straight back, a mole by his mouth, and Antigone wondered, where do I know him from? He asked, "what do you want with the officer?" and Christos replied, "we'd like to speak to him personally" – "is he a friend of yours?" said ironically, and her father replied, "no" but that it had to do with an important case – "tell it to me," he suggested, and Antigone could see that her father was hesitant, at the desk opposite a sergeant of the gendarmerie was sitting writing, from time to time he raised his eyes and looked at them, then went back to searching among his papers. Thus her father bent down and spoke into the warrant officer's ear, who looked up and fixed his gaze on Antigone, a voice inside was telling her to go, but she took a deep breath for some relief and at the next moment the fat man was asking her, "is Angel a friend of yours?" – "I know him," she said – "what sort were the two others?" – and again she answered, then dried up – "if you saw them again, would you recognise them?" – she thought for a bit and answered "yes" – recalling to mind the two young men, the way they looked as they were leaving, smiling.

And in a minute they gave an order and two boys were brought in, they stood there as if scared, maltreated, one seemed familiar to Antigone, he must live in the Kaminikia direction, he had a high forehead and a funny nose, he must be called Kimon, Byron, maybe Simon; the other was a complete stranger – "well?" the warrant officer asked her – and she said, "well what?" – "were these the two that killed him?" and she answered "no" with certainty, and the two young men left the room immediately, someone must have been directing them with signs, "you can go," the warrant officer ordered them, but Christos had something else to say, "the police officer?" he asked, "aren't we going to see him?" however, the other man put on a sour expression and said as if cursing, "don't confuse matters further," which sounded like a threat; her father took her by the arm, "let's go," he whispered, in a manner that made it sound as if she was wounded and he supporting her. As they were passing through the door, though, the warrant officer called, "just a minute", and they both turned round doubtfully, "aren't you a journalist?" he asked sternly, using the second person singular, and Christos answered "yes" – "on which paper?" he asked again – "none right now," stammered Christos – "I know, I know," said the other man, and Antigone wondered why her father had told a lie. They went out and he was angry, "see what you got us into," he complained.

Three days later someone rang their doorbell, towards evening, and it was Angel with Myrsine, the grandmother said, "we've come to thank you," and she'd brought a jar of preserved cherries, "for your daughter to eat and enjoy the sweetness", and she kept on thanking them and making wishes for their health and happiness – and Christos said proudly, "we only did our duty." They stayed a short time and then said goodnight and left, the boy pensive, oppressed, he barely spoke to them, said goodbye as if he was ashamed, and Amalia said, "I feel like throwing it away," and she meant the jar of preserves, but the girls kept it, said, "we like it." Spring had well and truly arrived, outside nature smelled sweet, specially when a light rain began to fall, and the leaves and the earth breathed.

Yannis

A torrential downpour set in then, for spring had come, and Yannis said, "we'll be cut off" and laughed; they were alone in the factory, the boss and the girl, and they watched the yard slowly flooding, and the raindrops were making bubbles, at which he declared, "if the rain makes bubbles it means it's going to last a long time" – and he smiled at her again, for he could see that she was upset. She had come two weeks earlier, she was the elder of the drunkard's two girls, she had gone first to Angela and begged – their father didn't have a job, they'd pick him up from the gutter, and when they'd got him lying down he would scream like a madman, that cockroaches and vipers were getting him, he'd hit out with his hands at his face and the bedclothes, sweating and thrashing, but in vain, until he was exhausted, he would fall into a stupor though still groaning, and the girls would say, "thank goodness", for when he was awake he'd kiss them and cry, beg them, "forgive me", but two days later it would be the same again if not worse.

Yannis agreed, "I'll take her on, though she doesn't know anything," that is to say about the work or the factory, and Angela said, "I've never forgotten my own troubles" and she was always tearful these days, her eyes red, she'd put on weight and one day heard someone say, "she's beginning to show her age" – they hadn't noticed her as she sat in the corner, at some friends' house. In the end Yannis promised, "I'll take her on," she wasn't a baby, she must have reached twenty, she was called Mary, she had the rounded, firm body of women of the popular class, and Yannis wondered, "does she live on air?" For their penury was now extreme; one night their father didn't even come home (Mary had told Angela about it, with a long face), they had nearly gone out of their minds, he might have fallen into the sea in his drunkenness, or been run over by a tram – "but don't you have any relative who could help you deal with him?", to which the girl said, "we do," her father had a brother who was a doctor, but their aunt had closed her door to him once and for all, crying, "that drunkard makes a laughing stock of us," and one day she had sent the girls away, saying to the doctor, "you go, if you want," and she seemed to be meaning, to the riff-raff and ordure. And the following day someone came to find them, a gendarme came and they were called to the police station where they had him shut up like a wild beast behind bars, they said he'd smashed up a tram, that he'd started the trouble, as he was sitting there drunk he'd bent down and groped a woman's leg, she screamed and her husband grabbed him, took hold of him by the collar, swearing at him, but a second later he was lying on the floor three metres away, two or three other passengers joined in but he knocked their teeth out, and before they managed to overpower him he'd wrecked and smashed everything; now he was in the cells begging, "forgive me" in a constant whisper. And they called his brother the doctor, who paid and got him out, said to the girls, "don't whatever you do let your aunt hear of this" and left looking sour.

And now Mary decided, "I'm leaving," even though the rain was still pouring down, he wanted to stop her though, "you must be mad" – "no," said she, "I wasn't born yesterday," and the pupils of her eyes flashed sparks, and thus she ran out into the yard and into the rain, and she looked like a green rag blown in the wind amidst the curtains of water, he saw her plump legs jumping wildly through the puddles, until she came up against the iron gate and seemed glued to the railings, the whole place now filled with the din of the heavens venting their wrath, everything dammed in by greyness, and thus the green rag was coming back, opened the door, came in shivering, "I'll die out there," moaned Mary, dripping and panting and shaking herself like a wet dog. And without warning he began to laugh, it was a laugh that came from deep down within him, as if he'd seen something funny, and he laughed and laughed and couldn't stop, at which she fell on him and hit him, "it's all your fault," she said as if hissing at him, but Yannis grabbed her by the wrists, "be good," he reprimanded and went on holding her, at which she got mad, "let go of me," she made as if to bite him, and her face was like rain; in the end she got away and moved to the far corner, where she stood trembling, her wet dress was glued to her body and she was freezing. Yannis laughed again, for another reason now, his eyes inflamed, however he went into his office and searched, found a worker's overall somewhere, went back and threw it at her, "take your wet things off," he said, then left her alone, went outside and stood under the eaves, feeling the mist of the rain on his face, saying to himself I'll cool off, and the whole world was a darkness without end.

And the next day he noticed a red mark, a little pinhead, purplish red, just below his nipple, and he thought how strange, it couldn't be from a finger nail, he considered, and hid it as best as possible under his vest, watched the way it didn't fade for days, it must be something different, he thought; he cast back in his mind over the embraces as he slept with Angela, over the struggle with Mary, her carelessness, and came to the conclusion that something else must have caused it, perhaps it was like one of those whitlows that people get on their hands, or perhaps a mole – but as he examined the mark into his mind came Mary, like a wet animal with shining shoulders and thighs. No explanations had taken place, yet they avoided one another, he'd catch sight of her by chance from a distance, as she worked or ate her food alone, deep in thought; and he said, "she's becoming antisocial," when Angela asked after her from time to time, always in a neutral tone – even if the girl was fully ripe. On the afternoon of the downpour she had left alone as soon as she was dry, by then the rain had lightened to a drizzle, and after a while he locked up, to set off back home to his wife, yet behind him he saw a humble little house – the same one that he had visited with Pavlakis on the day the Germans entered the city – two women with their skirts up round their waists were baling out bucketfuls of water, they'd been flooded, one of them turned round and saw him, "come and lend a hand, boss," she called, and both of them cackled with laughter. So he went nearer, they still had a lot of baling to do, for there was a pool of water in their main room, the woman was young (she must have been new) and the other like a child, with plump white legs, she was perspiring and her hair was falling into her eyes; and the older of the two said, "stand back so we don't splash you," but he didn't move, stood there and stared at them, specially at the younger one who blushed but was laughing, "come another time and we'll make coffee for you," the older one teased, and he asked, "how come you don't have any man to help you?" – "where would we find a man like that?" she laughed, and the other girl laughed too, as if copying her, but just then in the half-light of the room a soldier's silhouette was sketched, the older girl said, "it's her cousin," then called to him, "hey, Voulis, go and get some air till we've finished," and Voulis did indeed go out, said "'bye" and moved away slowly, he was shortish, bushy-haired, listless. And Yannis said, "if I had my workers here I'd get the place cleaned up for you," though the girls didn't answer, they seemed to be saying something between themselves and laughing, but their hands continued their task, in the end the older girl took a broom and swept out the last drops of water, and they stopped and looked at him, "can we do anything for you?" asked the older one, but the younger girl aswered her gleefully, "he had the girl in there" and they both laughed once more; and so Yannis set off to leave, and it was already dusk.

He reached the square and gazed round at everything, thought of getting on a tram but then said to himself I'd rather walk, and he jumped over the puddles and mud, the wet cobbles smelled good, and the weeds that grew along the edges and survived being trodden on, he reached the "Pantheon" cinema, with photographs outside of James Cagney on horseback, then killing the gangster, and in the other window was a poster of an ancient adventure, I saw it in my youth, he thought, and he felt like laughing; from the tobacco factories next door arose an aroma, someone ran past, jostled him, he didn't even have time to swear, "the rabble are on the up and up," the people in his circle would have said, but had it perhaps always been like this? He stood and looked around him, two woman passed by, one caught his eye, but in a moment they had moved away, and then he decided: back, he felt within him the sort of devilry he'd had when young, he crossed the square as if in a hurry and before long arrived once more in their lane, in front of the girls' little hovel, through the cracks he could see light shining and he knocked – except he wondered: why so gently? –

and the door opened, it was the older girl in her dressing gown, she said, "come in" and smiled as if she'd been expecting him, "are you alone?" he asked, but no, in the next room the younger one and her cousin had gone to bed, and the devil came to life and he said, "you lied to me" and laughed, but she took him by the hand, into a dark little corridor, I remember it, thought Yannis, and the woman then told him, "look through the crack" in the planks, where there was enough dim light for him to make out their naked bodies, the girl was sitting on top of him, her hair streaming down her naked back, a dark mole on her bottom – and only a murmur to be heard. And the older one asked him, "do you get a kick out of watching?" but he pushed her down onto her couch.

And when they had finished and were lying on their backs, he said – "children are callous," and he confessed to her something that had happened long ago, how an Armenian couple had lived in their neighbourhood, whom they were always tormenting, and how one night they had spied on them through the shutters and seen the couple disporting themselves naked, the woman on top of the man, moving as if intoxicated, and then his friend had pounded on the shutters with his fist, and they had seen the couple leap up in alarm and fumble for their clothes, "that was a sin," the girl reproved him, "that's why you still like watching," but Yannis protested, "no, it was just chance" – at which point she stood up stark naked, "I'm thirsty," she said and poured some water from the jug, and he noticed that her buttocks were sagging and she had two creases in her belly, but then she came and fell on him again, she had a smell of sweat which he liked; "again", she whispered to him, as if begging.

It must have been nearly midnight when he left, the woman came out with him as far as the street, for a moment she told him, "I enjoyed it" and embraced him, but Yannis felt a sense of horror and pulled away from her, and thus she went back into her house. The roads were dry now and deserted, a wind was blowing that chilled his brow, he felt that a scent was emanating from him, opened the collar of his shirt in puzzlement, put his face down, found that the smell was like oleanders, something like her sheets, like her armpits – and he breathed it in. All the same, he thought that he'd better be careful, as soon as he let himself into the dark house he went straight to the bathroom, washed his chest and his hands, his armpits, yet still felt that a faint scent clung to his vest, like the memory of a garden; and then he went and lay down beside Angela who was asleep, on the ceiling light from the street was reflected, creating strange shapes, like some ungainly little animal, sometimes shrinking and sometimes growing, a Mickey Mouse made out of dark and light, for a moment he thought he heard military boots running on the cobbles, but then there was nothing. Except that at dawn Angela gave him a shove, "where were you?" she asked, whereupon he laughed, supposedly naturally, "I went to the cinema," he answered – "what got into you to go at midnight?", and he said, "I was upset and I wanted to take my mind off things, I went and saw a western," which was somewhere he knew she wouldn't have wanted to follow him, and his Angela murmured, "curious", but then she went into the other room and after a second Yannis heard water running, and the clatter of cups and spoons, "I'd like some coffee," he called out, from the kitchen came the smell of spirit burning and simultaneously their baby started crying, he thought, the poor woman won't know what to do first, and he hurried into the kitchen, "leave it, I'll keep an eye on it," she looked put out, and in the end he drank his coffee and left – and as he was kissing her goodbye he saw her white neck and put his lips there as well.

And he was thinking that a man could be a whore too, it would depend on where he slept and why, perhaps he himself was a male prostitute – a tormenting thought that reminded him of his youth, although his adolescence might in fact have been less tainted than he was today, perhaps with more excuses. And thus he went into his office and shut the door, after a little while his old acolyte the gravedigger came in, said, "morning, boss", but Yannis told him to leave with a movement of his hand, or maybe even more by something in his eyes, and he heard the other man mutter, "you've got something needling you" was what he was saying, after which Yannis went and locked the door, I have to get my mind under control, he was thinking, but even more so the pulses of his blood, which were swamping his reason, and he felt a faintness – an excess. He must have stayed there with the door locked for an hour or so, then unlocked it and emerged, got involved with machinery and workers, someone showed him a machine part that he was chiselling, he said, "we'll have to fix it" and was servile, Yannis put his hand on the man's shoulder and said, "all right", thinking to himself at the same time, what's the matter with me? By which he meant why did I lock myself in, I have started straining at gnats, he said and was cross with himself. He went out into the yard and saw the puddles, a yellowish sun was shining, he called a worker, "spread some earth in the yard," he ordered, he reached the iron gate, went out, looked over at the hovel, all its windows and the door closed, who knows when prostitutes get any sleep, he thought, then went back inside, made his way among the machines, watched to see how well adjusted the bars were, how regular and faultless their various motions – and thus all other images faded from his eyes, from his mind.

Somewhere among everything was a yellow scarf on a head which was moving around, like a coloured balloon among uniform people, now appearing and now disappearing, but gradually beginning to bother him, like a piece of grit or an insect in his eye, and in the end he said it must be Mary – as indeed it was – but without eyes, without a mouth, just a yellow scarf over her hair, whereupon Yannis made his way round, as if he had a purpose of his own, and after a bit came up behind her, behind her firm back, her buttocks, her plump legs, and she seemed to sense his presence as if by his scent, for she turned and looked at him, said, "good morning" and moved away, she became once more a headscarf that was bobbing, disappearing, reappearing somewhere where you didn't expect it, like a pointless game of hide-and-seek, but one that might prove to be a well surrounded by strange plants, whose green and yellow and other colours might conceal the darkness, the true depth. And Yannis decided, I must not fall in, and he carried on avoiding her.

Angel

He could have told them, "it's my lost paradise," for everything was becoming more difficult now (more dangerous), like one night when he saw Myrsine waiting for him at the end of the street, like a shadow among the trees, wrapped in her worn shawl, and she caught him by the arm and said, "there are people lying in wait for you," three men on the pavement opposite their house, smoking or murmuring, "and how do you know that it's me they're watching for?" asked Angel, but "I can sense it, I know it" was all his grandmother would say in reply, which seemed convincingly mysterious. And he wondered, where can I go and hide? and the only place left was the walled plot, the tall trees, his old hiding places, where now the wall had tumbled down in a few places (various people used to go at night and steal corner stones and other building material) and he slipped round unnoticed, concealed by the many shadows, and thus found himself at the back of the house, made his way through into the enclosure and clambered up into the leaves and branches, and stayed there like a roosting bird. He might have fallen asleep during the night, maybe fallen off and been killed, but after some time he saw the light being switched on in their kitchen and the door left open; this must be a signal, he thought, Myrsine's conspiracy – and he climbed down slowly and carefully, keeping an eye constantly on the lights and the door, and in a moment slipped into the house and his grandmother told him, "they've gone," though everyone had been muttering because he'd caused trouble. Only his uncle cursed the right-wing thugs, remembering all he'd been through doing forced labour, after Nikos, their friendly gendarme officer, had got him out of the camp and they'd sent him to Stavros, to the sands, where they'd dug trenches down near the sea with Asiatic guards standing over them – short, thickset men with shaven heads whom the Germans had brought from Russia, mercenary Tatar bastards, who would flick their knives in their fingers as if they were toys, then throw them and transfix whatever they'd aimed at, and then split their sides laughing. However, Myrsine used to say, "when are you going to forget all that?"

And then one day at noon the whole city was in an uproar, people said, "they're killing our leaders," someone had shot one of the leaders in the head, and the next day they read about it in the papers, the killer looked young, a former member of ELAS, who stated, "they took my wife," at which he was asked, "Zevgos did?" – "the whole leadership is responsible," he answered, so perhaps others were in danger, and people muttered, "what sort of men have they got us mixed up with?", hired killers maybe. And Angel decided, "I'll leave," go to another town where he would be unknown and maybe they wouldn't be lying in wait for him, however his uncle saw it differently, "wherever you go there will be young royalists," he said, and Angel knew it himself, "one or two of them were with us," he said, they'd written slogans on walls together, "you collected some trash," grumbled his uncle, that was what happened with me, thought Angel – but which people were better? All the ones who went into hiding and changed sides? He remembered Dimitris, who one day had confided, "maybe it was all a mistake" and had seemed to be full of thought, to be doubting and wavering, one evening they'd made their walk to "Faros", with Alcmene silent beside them, and Dimitris said, "they made mistakes and we're paying for them," and at that very moment they heard cries and running feet, so that they hurried too, they saw a knot of people, all with their backs to them, and in the middle was the trouble; a gendarme – they knew him – had grabbed some youth and was hitting him, on the ground proclamations lay strewn about, they were trampling on them, ripping them, but not one of the bystanders went forward, they simply watched the struggle, the boy trying to get away, and then a girl's voice was heard, "shame", she cried, and everyone turned round and looked at Alcmene, her face heated and her eyes full of amazement, perhaps at her own boldness, and Dimitris said, "come away" and in the end caught her by the arm and dragged her off, Angel followed, three paces behind them, and he listened to the brother and sister arguing, the girl's voice like broken music.

There's nothing else for it but to leave, he kept thinking, only once more his uncle gave him advice, asked him, "what will you eat?", for at home he always had a plate of food and clean clothes, tireless Myrsine taking care of him, "I'll get a job," he said – "but where? who do you know who'd give you a job?" Their own people might help him maybe – "don't count on it," said his disillusioned uncle, "they're all on the run, got their own heartaches"; but when had Angel ever listened to anyone? Maybe he could get on all right in Athens, they had a sister there, but once more the family judged that this wasn't very likely, for she'd married a difficult man – "and the bastard is a royalist," thus spoke his uncle and Myrsine snivelled, "we've become split into a thousand pieces," for strange things were happening, people said that in a young man's pocket they'd found a piece of paper with names on it, maybe of those who'd been proscribed, and among the other names was the boy's father, the boy got beaten black and blue – by the police and by his own father, people said – and then one day he disappeared, they said he'd been sent to France to study. "Hey, don't tell me you've killed anyone?" his uncle asked him laughing, for he was well aware that Angel was rather craven, but a little while later the nephew said, "when they arrested me and had me in the cells, there was a boy there called Byron, they were asking him about a list of names and beating him," and his uncle looked at him in terror without speaking, "he's abroad now," Angel added, and he seemed to be saying, I don't understand.

And he talked about it with Alcmene, who advised him, "keep cool," which might have meant, "don't be afraid," and she was holding his hand and gazing into his eyes, and Angel embraced her and kissed her hair and told her, "you fill me," and around them everything was dark and lonely, "we are together," she was giving him moral support, and she felt his sweating hands, his legs entwined and pressed together, in the end they lay on the grass and above them glided a star-bespangled vault, which neither spoke to them nor had any scent. And Angel whispered to her, "you smell lovely," and as he bent towards her neck they could hear a cricket, and then voices which they couldn't tell where they came from, which were coming closer and closer, and Alcmene said, "maybe it's dangerous" to be lying in this lonely spot at such an hour of the night, but Angel held her round her waist, "don't move," he warned her, for two dark figures could be seen now, one of them with a military cap and epaulettes, the other bare-headed, whose white shirt was soon plainly visible, who was talking and saying, "I saw them, there were two of them and they were searching for something," and Angel wondered, who did he think we were? And so they lay low, motionless, and waited, with Alcmene's heart beating wildly in her breast. And Angel called, "are you out of your mind?" for as soon as the strangers had passed she leapt up and began running, with the boy behind her, unable to do otherwise, and in a little while the two men as well, who were shouting. Then it felt as if his feet were flying, that he couldn't control them, all around little lights shone for a moment then were extinguished as the men pursued them, everything seemed to have become dark red, then after a moment it looked green, the air tasted different, as if drenched in sulphur; and as they reached a corner – towards salvation maybe or some hiding place – the night was rent by the pistol shot, which was maybe a gesture of hopelessness on the part of their pursuer – the last.

And he wondered where she might be in agony, for Angel had slipped into an unknown courtyard, and was frozen there, thinking, don't let them hear me or smell me, he felt that he was lying on manure, leaves of some sort were caressing his bare hands, but he stayed there motionless for a long time, until it was almost midnight and he saw a light go on in the background, as if a house and its door had come to life once more, and two female figures were standing there talking, one said, "goodnight" and the other, "sleep well," "it will pass," said the first, but received no answer; in the end the light went out and everything was quiet.* And

---

* As we ran like madmen through the darkness, I thought I could feel the gendarme officer's breath in my ears, a little bit further on and my familiar territory began, a hole in a wall with a curious looking fig tree above it. I heard the shot and was startled, perhaps the bullet whistled past my head, or perhaps I just thought so. I pushed my way into the wall gasping

Angel plucked up the courage to emerge, and wondered about Alcmene, he began to search for her through the narrow streets, the open ground, now I am alone and out of danger, he thought, and after a while, let me call her, he called, "Alcmene" but no one answered, so he decided to go to her house, he could pass by outside and listen, it wasn't very far away. And before long he was standing beneath the darkened windows, through the half-open shutters he could see a white blouse, a hand throwing a bit of paper out, then darkness, not even the sound of a single breath, Angel went a little way down the street to find some light, and he read, "tomorrow at ten o'clock at the secondary school", and he thought to himself now they can see me, they can hear my footsteps, so he raised his arm and waved, maybe she would see him saying goodnight to her, further off two dogs were barking as if having an argument, time to go home, he thought. On their little balcony he saw his grandmother, she was in her nightdress and scolded him, "where have you been, you little devil?" she asked, maybe remembering the breathlessness, the shadows that had lain in wait on more than one night, with Angel always slipping out cunningly, "but till when?" grumbled his grandmother.

Until ten o'clock arrived he made a couple of tours round the secondary school, he liked the old pine trees, in which birds lived, the place smelled of resin and their freshness was like a caress, once upon a time they had climbed the railings, watched the girls doing gymnastics, the supervisor ran with a hose and wet them, and they left, laughing at the naughtiness. And when Alcmene came she said, "let's go towards the New Helvetia park and the dry watercourse" and they set off through the streets of little houses, he asked her how she'd got away the night before when they were being chased, about the pistol shot, "I never stopped running," she answered, "they must have stayed there searching for you," and Angel told her how he had escaped, one day he might not be so lucky, and he wondered, why me? They had reached the hill now, they saw a hole in a rock and Alcmene

---

for breath and fell on my back; I could hear his footsteps for ages, then in the end nothing. The summer of '45, running breathless in Filellinon Street, with Dinos, whom we lost two years later from tuberculosis, the last victim of the Areti line.

remembered, "when we were children, people used to say that a saint was hidden in here, all the women of the neighbourhood used to gather and wait for him to come out and speak to them, and bless them" – and they laughed, "I could hide in here too," he said, "but you're not exactly a saint," she answered, and they held hands, their fingers tightly interwoven, they went downhill now where the grass was baked dry and they could find nowhere to sit down in the burning landscape, a little way off they saw a placid tree, said, "there isn't anything else for us" and in a little while they had settled down at its roots, resting their backs against the trunk, and were looking around without speaking, "what are you thinking of?" asked the girl, and he whispered, "we'll have to disappear, at least for a while," he picked up a stone and banged it on the ground, and she said, "but what's the matter with you?" and when she picked up the stone, by her foot, she saw a small lizard that he had crushed, "I hate them," he told her – "and where are you thinking of going?" she asked, and he shrugged his shoulders, "maybe to Kavalla or to Serres" – "do you have friends there? Relatives?" – and he said "no". She put her hand on his shoulder, he felt her fingers caressing it, then he put out his own hand and brought her down to lie on his breast, where her lips touched his flesh, "I am not leaving you," she whispered, and she didn't mean that she would keep him back in Thessaloniki, for "take me with you," she begged, and he felt then that it would be difficult, that his responsibility would be greater – and he said, "what will your people say?" It was like a cloud that had suddenly appeared, spoiling their love and their earthly paradise.

But two nights later they found themselves together, it was in a little lane in the Ladadika quarter, the boy was lugging a suitcase, in which they'd both put their clothes, the girl a large bag – they had packed them the day before, beneath Myrsine's feet, in the cellar, into which Alcmene had crept with a bundle of clothes which she'd managed to fit with his in the suitcase, their hands were shaking and they didn't speak, when they'd finished Angel came out, checked that no one was in sight and signed her to leave, she seemed incredibly pale and was sweating. Now in the lane there were other people waiting as well, most of them older and tired, one man was sitting in a corner and coughing, he seemed to be accusing them and the two of them stayed silent, there were so many things that could have terrified them, specially the fact that their families would go crazy. At last two headlights appeared in the darkness and the bus arrived, a prehistoric rattletrap into which they climbed and sat right at the back, they paid their fares and kept gazing out of the windows anxiously, as though they were expecting someone – when the bus started they felt relief, their nostrils filled with smoke, which rapidly got into their throats too and burned them, until they had left the city and smelled the scent of nocturnal orchards and fields. From time to time they saw trembling lights, but mostly the world through which they were moving consisted only of darkness, the gasping of the engine, various indistinguishable voices of the night, and finally an old peasant in the seat in front of them who turned round and asked, "where are you heading for?" to which Alcmene answered, "Kavalla, it's where our aunt and uncle live," and the old man advised, "be careful," suddenly the bus jolted violently, the old man swore and said, "old mines", in the darkness they could see him raise a bottle to his mouth and drink, and the atmosphere filled with the smell of eau de vie, "it does me good," he murmured and smiled. Then he seemed to be mumbling to himself, or to the night, and then nothing – the bus was continuously jolting, so frequently that in the end the passengers stopped being startled, Angel felt the weight of Alcmene against him and wrapped his arm around her, she said, "people will see" and was upset, however they were in the back seats, all around them the night was dark and full of strange ghosts, bushy trees or rocks, for everything was transformed by the darkness into fairy tale shapes, and the passengers resembled bulky objects turned to stone in their seats, "they'll all be asleep," Angel whispered to her, and now he felt her against him, his nostrils scented her girlish sweat, from her hair, from her neck, maybe from where he held her, impregnating his palm, and he thought that they had become one body, which before long lost all sense of where it was or where it was going.

And they were woken by the chill of dawn, all around them a grey-green beautiful world was unfolding, changing, becoming the faintest of pinks, until the first rays of the sun appeared and pursued them through leaves and outcrops, into gullies which for a time swallowed the sunbeams, until in the distance the white houses of a village could be made out, behind trees and vegetable gardens; then the old man woke up and said, "here we are, this is where I get off" and used the palm of his hand to smooth down first his sparse hair and then his moustache, as if it mattered that he should look presentable. The engine was labouring painfully, and once more smoke was catching their throats, the driver said, "fuck" and a woman sitting just behind him reprimanded him, to which he answered, "why don't you all get out and walk then?" and lapsed into silence, but after a moment the bus jumped forward again as if kicked, and then again – and in the end it groaned and came to a halt, from the engine poured white smoke, and someone shouted, "get out, or we'll be roasted like rats." And immediately everyone was jostling and pushing for the single exit, bundles and suitcases were being thrown out of the windows, and the smoke wasn't abating but rather was getting thicker. Angel and Alcmene stayed till last, as if they didn't feel the danger, didn't believe it, and their inexperience showed, for the smoke billowed wildly and the driver ran to where he had spotted a water trough for animals nearby, he filled a can with water and brought it back anxiously, all in vain though, for flames were coming from the engine and screams from the crowd, who pulled Angel down the steps – just in time. And the bus went up in flames instantly, despite the driver desperately throwing water on it, despite all the women crossing themselves. And they saw three men in uniform approaching from the village, with villagers, both men and women, behind them, some of whom stopped and cut branches from the trees, but the flames were growing, and the driver was running in despair to the trough again, he couldn't accept it, didn't stop, kept on throwing water on the bus, until in the end he sat down on the ground and wailed, his head in his hands, nothing but a shaking body.

And when the gendarmes arrived they could see there was nothing more to be done, the villagers stood there, their branches useless, one of them said, "we must put it out, so it doesn't set fire to us" for their fields lay alongside, but they considered it unnecessary now, for all that remained was the burnt-out metal skeleton, with a few small flames still burning within it, but all the same some braver souls among the men entered – and a woman with them – and extinguished them. The driver couldn't be comforted however and was not in the mood to answer when the gendarmes questioned him; so they turned their attention to the passengers, and specially one of them, who looked strange, curious, with a khaki uniform and stars, but with a cap which must once have been brown and had a cross at the front of it, and the old man said, "we don't know anything about it, it's no good asking us," and he meant about engines and fires, but the other man asked, "where are you from, Grandad?" as if annoyed with him, and the old man replied, "from my village", at which laughter was heard and the policeman showed a flash of anger, "clever, aren't you," he muttered, and came a step closer, his face looked sour, "are you from Moustheni?" he asked, but the old man simply said "no" without adding anything else, whereupon the other gendarme spoke, "your papers, your identity cards", he demanded. But it turned out that most of the passengers didn't have any papers on them, at this point Angel took her hand, felt her fingers gripping his, we're in bad trouble, they were telling him, except that a woman was crying, "why don't you leave us in peace with all the trouble we've had" and she pointed at their belongings strewn on the ground, then other people took courage and said, "we were expecting some help from you," but the man with the brownish cap looked at them fiercely, and behind his back the villagers seemed to be making signs at them, as if warning them, don't make him angry, and in the end the gendarmes decided, "we'll go to the village and look into it." And thus everyone loaded themselves with whatever they still possessed and set off towards it, the three policemen in front and all the others after them – although when they arrived at the village their number had lessened, for the old man hung back, went up to Angel and advised him, "when we get to the trees, slip away quietly," and as the young man seemed hesitant, said, "go down, towards the reed beds, and from there straight ahead, it's not much further" and he meant to Kavalla, for they were young and their legs were strong. And Angel didn't ask why, for the old man anticipated him and said, "he's one of Anton Tsaous's men, the bastard," maybe he meant that he might kill them – for people were telling of fearful and terrible happenings.

And thus they disappeared into the trees, and then into grass and bushes, and it was a gentle world filled only with birdsong and cawing, and from somewhere the sound of barking, and they continued onwards until they were hidden among the reeds and the earth was damp underfoot, and Alcmene said, "do you think you're going in the right direction?", but the boy had the suitcase on his shoulders and was out of breath, replied, "don't talk," and they walked for two hours, and when they stopped and looked around them they saw that they'd left the village far behind, and before them a gorge was opening, thick with oaks and all manner of trees. They sat down on the rocks and wiped the sweat off their brows, somewhere a thread of water was running quietly, and before long they were lying exhausted in the shade. They reached out their fingers to the cooling water, lay there motionless, at peace.

The Middle Ages – 9

They warned him, whichever camp you choose, naked blades, naked hopes will be waiting, beings who have forgotten how to hear or see, who preserve only instincts, a hand that never ceases to strike out at what is in front of it, to ensure for them some kind of survival, to make possible the next blow – or their certainty that they are continuing to exist. And she would dream that their time of feminine summer had been when they barred the gates, took refuge in the cellars and embraced, "I shall always remember the damp ground, in those days when we longed for obliteration," longed, that is, for the earth slowly to swallow them, so that all that would remain would be the clothes, the shoes, that they had discarded, as they lay in aphrodisiac closeness, and she moaned, "this may be our last time," for the city was full of shadows now, they had brought in the mercenaries, princes and admirals, the place surrounded by dogs and horsemen, in their full armour they seemed faceless, they could have been relatives in disguise who, they too, were placing their fingers together and making the sign of the cross, "like my wife and children", Christoforos remembered, at which she complained, "you are unable to forget them," and she gave him a handkerchief with a scarlet 'A' embroidered on it, "for you to wipe your brow", and she meant to wipe the anguish from it. "There are times when I feel that I am in disguise," he raved to her, remembering how he had looked in the windows and seen a ghost, a martial bandolier, stars, and had thought it must be some other face reflected in the panes, not my own image with its curly hair, sunburnt face, sweating brow, behind him life was unwinding, men and women who had foregone uniforms and cross-bands, I have got left behind, he feared, one night he made his way along their familiar road, the heavens alone were shining, all by themselves, and they sent a breeze which brought nothing but ease, which guided him by the scent of the earth and the trees, he said to himself in the fourth alley from now lies our house, he could trust its door, the familiar plants in the garden, the vine which decorated their wall and grew up to the roof, surrounded their window at the back, where a faint light was now burning – and he considered, "she will not be embroidering now"; knotted red thread and gold and a thousand colours, which recalled icons and chalices, the old glass-fronted cabinet where she kept her treasures from girlhood, a swan from Persia made of porcelain and silver, pebbles collected (so they said) from the Nile, combs from Venice and Saragossa, of which he wept, "they are only for fine ladies" and she looked at him and said not a word, yet kept them spotlessly bright, and with them two exquisitely embroidered cloths, perhaps her consolation for having no other wealth – or perhaps her refuge. And when he entered, like a stranger to the house, they were still all in their place, and he felt a faintness, said to her, "Despina, my Lady" and fell at her feet, he could have sworn to her I am not acting, and she asked him, "are you ill?", and indeed he was all one wound, bloodying whatever he touched, and his lady said, "come and wash, and cleanse yourself" lest he contaminate them, for she was listening as he told of his sorrows, how all men were now cursing him, how perhaps they would cast him out like a leper, but she took the sponge, some perfume of her in each drop of water, and she rubbed him gently, for a moment he seemed to sigh, his eyelids peacefully closed now, drifting, "this might be our last time," while she delighted in his pale, vulnerable body, in every mark upon it, the moles that she knew so well, the scar at his ear covered by his unshorn locks. And suddenly he sensed breathing, beyond his own or her fragrant breath, and instinctively put out his hand for his knife, but she reassured him, "it is your children," she said, two boys who were standing on the threshold like archangels, serious, silent, all eyes and knitted brows, and thus he sank back into the water, said, "if I could only stay like this forever, if I could only sink into the sweetest sleep" – yet he was afraid lest they accuse him, "you ran away and hid," they could not forgive him for what others had done, he would have to play the heroic hunted leader, while they would all be sitting comfortably on their seats – or in their armchairs – and looking at him coldly and judging him, "he should have done thus" or "in this he did not act correctly," as if they were playing in some popular tragedy, and the archangels still stood there, watching as his lady Despina enveloped him in the white sheet, supported him, made up the bed for him to lie down, and his unshaven face shone, somewhat drawn yet peaceful, and thus they extinguished the lights, he thought maybe the end has come – that dead hour – which happens just before dawn. He got dressed and put on his armour, stood like a statue in the night, listening to the sounds of the house, then closed the door behind him, he felt a welcome freshness, and he began to walk down the road; yet he turned and looked back at the house, which was now a rectangular shadow, and only one small patch of whiteness visible, which could have been her nightgown or a curtain, then in a moment the well-known oak tree rose before him and that other world had faded from sight, as he feared, "forever". And he remembered his mother lying bedridden, she had said, "bend down so that I can tell you something" and he had stooped, he had the feeling that she was disintegrating, her hand becoming smaller, her face, and she said to him, "I am dying" but he said "no", with pain in every pore of his body, she said, "I can see my grave yawning," and pointed below her bed – and the very next day they had buried her. The vegetation around was withered, and he thought of yet another nightmare, a grey world without eyes, maybe with a scar, perhaps dating from that day, like gardens that have been scorched by the frost, which you pass through, and grieve for, and leave, you say to yourself I can neither recognise nor feel for this creation, and it seems to reject you, to slam a door that is the only door, and you are left on the ground with a white mass, at first small and insignificant, which is rolling towards you as if blown by some creeping breeze or as if it is some animal, some unknown creature, for it seems to be growing, to be taking shape, to be a white mole, and then it unfurls and flutters, it is like a blood-stained cloth or discarded piece of gauze from a hospital, and as the day grew lighter Christoforos went after it, trampled on it wildly to destroy it, as it wrapped itself around his foot, round his ankle, a sullied piece of gauze which Christoforos kicked out at in disgust, he thought it is infecting me, and he meant inside himself, thus he shook his foot around which it was twisting, in the hope that the breeze would help, and finally he was free of it and breathed again, he found a grey wall and leaned against it, closed his eyes and said, "my God", for he could not bear all the silent yellow wounds, and suddenly he seemed to see the white mass rolling and spinning, as if he exerted some strange attraction on it, and he set off and left, and before long saw other people, they seemed to be running in panic, the crowd getting denser, hiding him. And then suddenly everyone withdrew and what was left was an empty square, with him sweating and exhausted and almost gasping for breath, in the middle, under the sun which perhaps was death, his eyes reddened and his memory wounded, and he thought there is no place to hide here, and felt the eyes of the crowd piercing him, all of them had withdrawn to the sides in bitterness, preferring the doorways and colonnades which gave them shade, sheltered them. And it is now or never, they said, but he had not a breath of courage or desire left, he wished neither to run nor to stand still, he thought I must find some solution in which to take refuge, raised his eyes but then closed them, for the sunlight stabbed them, his eyelids trembled in the bright light, his cheeks, his lips were burning, and then he was to remember once more that those bodies shall lie in the square of a great city, the which is named Sodom and Egypt, where the lord was crucified and the peoples of all nations and all tribes and all tongues shall see Christoforos standing among the corpses and saying, their empty eyes have killed me, they have done it on purpose and abandoned me, and then a voice from the crowd cried, "we choke in bereavement and penury, who will give us our father, our livelihood?" and he thought, but it is impossible for it to be me, perhaps I should not give myself up, if any voice remained within me I should cry to them that whosoever is not found inscribed in the book of life shall be cast into the lake of fire. And then he saw them coming from the opposite corner of the road, men in armour, and Christoforos made up his mind I must remain steady on my feet, the people shall not see me sway and fall to the ground defeated, and thus he rested his knife upon the granite stone and watched as they ran towards him anxiously, and at the final moment came the shining idea of being set free, of casting away all fear and clinging, and he shouted, "alone as I am, what do you expect me to do?", at which those threatening him froze, glancing all around as if they could not believe that the people had rejected him – how had it happened? with what had they paid him? And then he cried again – like a old bugle that has been muted – "since you let them defeat us, what do you expect?" and stood there in the middle of the square, still utterly alone, the place seemed boundless to him, and he himself but a mere dead branch no longer of any use, the only thing that seemed near at hand was the lane which could take him to the harbour, where he could board the boat that would be waiting, and disappear onto the seas; but now the armed men were running, he raised his knife and waved it at them, "I am throwing it," he said "at your feet and I am bowing my head," and for a moment he imagined that behind him his own people were moving, it was an illusion, he felt his head weighing ever heavier on him and he bowed his neck and waited, he knew, they would take his arms, perhaps bind him, and he made up his mind to it: the end has come, it was written in my fate that I should drain this cup, this poison.

Angel

And when the sun fell, they said we ought to be moving, for they could not stay and live out among the wild animals, and they felt that they'd be safer deep in the stony gorge with its thick vegetation, and as they made their way into it, in silence, sometimes walking, sometimes crawling, they seemed for a moment to glimpse lights, like lanterns hanging among the foliage, and after a bit the smell of animals and habitation. And Angel said, "it's our second night," by which he meant their second night away from their homes, in a place where the unseen dogs heard howling were strangers, and they crept into the shelter of a ruined hut, and burrowed into the familiar warmth of each other's body, said of the people who might have been pursuing them, "they must have forgotten about us by now," for the numberless bushes, trees and rocks could enclose two bodies which soon became one and were filled with unhoped for comfort. Only he said as if talking to himself, "my father abducted my mother too" – "I know," said the girl, and perhaps something close to his ear was laughing, so that he said stubbornly, "Mary herself was Jewish" – and a deep silence fell, with only her fingers speaking to his hair, then to his cheek, his lips, his throat; and they lulled him to sleep.

It must have been still dark when he awoke, although he could see her arm radiant against their dark clothes, he thought that the moon must be shining, its light penetrating through some opening or crack, it could be a sign, strange things might be happening in the dark, they might perhaps have entered a creation where trees and grass would hang in the sky, clouds grow from the ground, where they might both be walking together in the starry firmament and she might be saying, I cannot bear it, I feel dizzy. But all he could hear was a sigh, he strained his ears and in the other world, outside their stone shell, unrecognisable beings were whispering, till they too were lost in the darkness, and in the end he felt terror as someone prodded him, and to his amazement, with the dawn light bathing them, he discovered that outside their door lay a landscape which might not have been of this world, for what he saw was an unutterable chilliness, a field of bronze-green, with gravestones buried among the grass and bushes, and he called out, "we've been sleeping in a graveyard," it was like a cry of despair, and Alcmene jumped up, "you scared me," she complained.

And in a little while it was a dull day, with clouds piled one on the other, and they set off to leave, making a detour around the little town which they could see in the distance beyond the end of the gorge, they said, "it would be better to avoid meeting anyone," dangerous encounters, and thus made their way uphill, where trees and bushes would conceal them. And, rested as they were, they scrambled up without difficulty, Angel carrying the suitcase, until they were far above the village, they could see its roofs, a few men with their animals, women shaking out the bedclothes – and then in a while not even that, for they had reached the summit, and below them on the other side stretched the plain, with little groups of trees and coppices scattered here and there, like a painting. Then raindrops came to meet them, but they said, "there isn't any shelter," and thus continued walking and got wet, felt themselves becoming heavier, on the hillside they saw a shepherd in his cape, a dark figure in the open landscape who they felt was staring at them and wondering, he raised his arm and pointed, and when they looked in the direction that he was indicating, with his finger unnaturally extended, they could make out a hut surrounded by a ring of stones, and they ran to it and huddled into it in relief. Angel looked at her, though, and saw how she was dripping, her hair was running with water which dripped onto her back and her breasts, he felt the chill between his own shoulders and thought, I must look like that too, and when he put his hand up found that his head was drenched – and the rain sang all around. And it was a monotonous song in the midst of grey nature.

And he begged, "let's throw off our clothes which smell of damp," there is a different charm in the body stripped of all superfluities, but she said, "you must be mad" for it was broad daylight and the shepherd was standing there in his position, like some eccentric rock in the rain, which was lessening now, so that he glistened in the sudden sunlight, at which Angel decided, "we should be on our way" for he had not forgotten Kavalla, their destination, where they were hoping for something, even if elusive; and in a little while he had taken off his shirt, was clad in sunlight, and he said, "I have got nothing to hide or to fear," when suddenly heavy rain started falling again unexpectedly, and he laughed as it fell on him, saying it would dry and leave patterns and marks on his bare limbs, but the girl panicked and moaned, "I'll get ill," for they were running now on a treeless plateau and their feet were sinking into the mud, in the distance they had spied a stone building and had been struggling to reach it for what seemed ages, in the end they could make out its broken windows, its door hanging from the hinges, and thought, only a little further now, and Alcmene was in a sorry state, ready to cry perhaps or to collapse in a heap, but they were only a few brief strides away, jumped over a little wall and cried, "we made it" – whereupon the rain stopped in an instant and the sun shone on them totally unexpectedly. They pushed open the door, which almost collapsed, saw a mass of rusty metal, some rotten planks, for the roof leaked in a hundred places, and they took a deep breath even if the whole place did smell of mould.

And in a little while she had put on his clothes and spread hers to dry in the sun, and the boy said, "it would have been better to stay," and she asked him, "where?" – she noticed his eyelashes quiver, his usual manner (she recognised it) and Angel said, "at home" – "that's all far behind us now," perhaps what the girl meant was that she couldn't bear to go back, regardless of what she felt, of whatever frightened her, and a silence followed, which might have implied that they had agreed, either out of necessity or willingly. And now she opened her bag, got out a packet wrapped in paper, their bread, their cheese and a couple of pieces of fruit, which they both wolfed down and suddenly smiled, the girl went out and collected her clothes, said to him, "go outside a bit and change" and thus Angel went out into the lonely landscape, with the sun right overhead, and he scanned the distance, searching perhaps for orchards and trees from which they could eat their fill, and he remembered the childhood years when they'd stolen fruit, both ripe and unripe, and had been chased by all the orchard owners and neighbours; he returned to their stone shelter, Alcmene was standing fully clothed in the doorway, "people could have seen you," she scolded, she had combed her hair and tidied herself, she said, "I feel rested" and smiled, and they gathered their belongings together and set off.

They preferred to take narrow paths, through the fields, at one point she asked him, "are you sure?" and he said all they had to do was head east, and before long they were sweating in the scorching heat, but they continued on their way, the suitcase now being shifted from one hand to the other more and more frequently, though within him a settled obstinacy was insisting you are going to get there, you can do it, but now they were deep in the midst of vineyards and the girl said, "I long for some" so the boy stopped, crawled in among the vines, harvested the finest grapes, he suddenly heard a voice crying, "hey...", they picked up their things and walked on, saw a low wall a little way off, so that Angel said, "just as far as there," thinking that they needed to rest, that his arms were trembling, their breathing too, they continued walking in silence, and she wondered, what is he thinking of? for in his mind seemed to be some regrets, some fear, the unknown that lay ahead – but behind them they heard wheels and hooves, turned and saw a cart approaching, in it a man wearing a wide-brimmed straw hat, and a woman following on foot behind; they stepped back to make way for them. And the people gave them a good look as they passed, then the cart halted a little further on and the man asked, "where are you from?" Angel thought in terror, they've recognised us, for he could see that Alcmene didn't look at all like a village girl, bright red and sweating as she was, and the boy said, "we're from Kavalla," but the people went on staring as if they were asking other things too, specially the man – the woman was rummaging in the cart, but she would surely have observed them too, "we went to the village for a bit," continued Angel, "on foot?" mocked the man, but he whipped his horse and they moved off again, the woman walking with her eyes on the ground, not even turning to look at them, and they felt they could hear the man laughing, "let them get ahead a bit," Angel advised her, and he seemed to want to swear.

At the little wall they felt calmer; it must have been part of an extremely old ruin, it had grass of its own seeded between the stones, but it offered a blessed shade, and the boy laughed, said, "who would have expected it?" without explaining what he was referring to, they were eating the grapes in mellow mood, in the end Alcmene asked, "do you suppose it's a long way off?" but he had never been there before either, "we'll go on till it gets dark," he said but without assuring her that they would have arrived by then. After a while the plain ended, and the orchards, and they found themselves going uphill among trees, with the sun full on their backs, and thus they rapidly became tired, at one point he stumbled and swore, and the girl said, "let's sit down," and once more they lay side by side beneath a pine tree, and at their feet spread the lowlands, all green and gold and brown, a world divided into rectangular shapes, Angel pointed and said, "look how far we've walked," trees and hillsides fading into the distance behind them, their refuge of the past night, and then, as if it was final, "let's get together the money for our tickets and go back," he whispered, the girl looked at him askance, maybe thinking what a coward, but his fear was, they seem to have us surrounded; and he remembered his uncle, his father, they'd been through a lot and must know something, he was sure of it. He picked up a stone from the ground and hurled it as far as he could, without any reason, then finally picked up their suitcase abruptly and said, "let's go."

The sun was setting now and becoming sweeter, they climbed a little way up, out of breath, heard the growl of a car's engine, the boy said, "we're reaching the road," and he was quite right, for a moment later they were stepping onto the asphalt, walking along with a tail wind. And as they felt the road begin to descend they said, "we've got there," for they could indeed see the first lights shining through the trees, and then, as dusk fell, the sea appeared, the open water, a little bit further, then the port came into view, and after it the city, flowing down from the heights, spreading onto the shore – as the road twisted and turned they lost sight of it, then saw it again, around them the pine trees were getting thicker, and Alcmene said, "we have to make it," they held hands once more, after so many hours, felt close to one another again, and the girl suddenly said, "I feel like running," for she didn't have the suitcase to carry, she doesn't feel the responsibility, reflected Angel. And she began to caper around him and laugh, something must be wrong with her, thought the boy, it's not like the Alcmene I know who almost never laughs, but they continued on their way, increasingly downhill, the trees darkening all around as if what encompassed them was a black nature descending from the sky, now they could make out quite clearly the first lights of the city, which seemed to call them like guiding lights, and as the road turned a corner they found themselves among the first humble houses, "now I feel safe," he said to her, for they would not be obliged to live out among the wild beasts, above them the stars embroidered the cloths of heaven, the girl said, "we don't know anyone, anything," but Angel reflected that it was summer, "we can sleep in the open air," he reassured her – for it was something he'd done before.

Then they heard water flowing, longed to refresh themselves, to wash, for they were covered with a combination of dust and sweat, they saw a fountain flowing ceaselessly, "it's Turkish," he said, marble all around and in front the basin at which she stooped and threw water on her face, her bare arms, her neck, grunting slightly from time to time, as if saying how lovely, and in the end she kicked off her sandals, stood in the basin and washed all the way up her thighs, then put out her hand to Angel, wanting to share the pleasure. Carts were passing by, and every so often cars, their headlights illuminating them for a moment then dying away, the boy said, "let's get finished," filled his cupped hands with water and splashed his face, enjoying the coldness of the water which indeed he liked so much that he filled his hands a second time and savoured the pleasure, felt her hands on his arms as if she was saying, come and let me help you for I care for you, and in the end they emerged clean and refreshed, except that the boy seemed to be scanning all around, perhaps searching for a place where they could nest for the night, in the distance they could hear barking, "if we knocked on someone's door?" suggested Alcmene, and he agreed that this might be a solution.

But just then they were bathed in a light so bright that it was painful, two glaring headlamps of a car, it seemed to have them in its sights and came to a halt, whereupon Angel quailed, "it's an army car," he muttered, and he felt Alcmene hiding behind him, "it's blinding us," she said and then was silent, but two men jumped out of the car, ran towards them snarling, some incomprehensible curses it must have been, but they had no time to react, no time to think even, for one of the men shouted, "I've caught you," and the boy wondered, where do I know him from? The darkness was getting thicker, full of shadows that were constantly changing, and the man insisted, "you're not giving me the slip now," as if he'd vowed it – and Angel felt something hurting his stomach, looked down and saw a pistol prodding right into him, he felt a pain in the veins in his neck, which spread into his chest, into his burning ribs. And the man screamed in their faces, "your identity cards", but Angel was struggling to remember, and in the end when he saw the madness in his enemy's eyes he remembered the man in the brown cap, the burnt-out bus, the old man – "thought you'd got away, you little sod, didn't you," screamed the other man, and he reached out his hand towards Alcmene, at which moment Angel's mind clouded over, he felt there is nothing else left to us, like an automaton he gave the man a shove, cried, "Alcmene, run for it," and grabbed a stone in the dark, but he felt a rod of searing iron pierce his thigh and then heard the shot, yelled again, "Alcmene, run," but he felt blows raining down on his skull, as if a deep bell was tolling in his brain and splitting it, thought he saw a skirt leaping down the hill, then smelled something like earth, like grass and water embracing him and he let himself go, turned and lay on his back, losing consciousness, from somewhere he heard two sharp retorts, he thought, they are killing me, felt it in his blood, and in the end there was only a dull roar in his breast, in his guts, and it was as if all cool freshness was disappearing from the face of the earth, every last drop of it.

Christos

And Christos sighed, "what aridity", even though it was nearly midnight, he was gathering up his last papers, saw the ink stains on his palm and felt upset; beside him Nikos was sitting and writing feverishly, everyone else had slipped off, he could hear the printers in the hall beyond, talking or coughing, someone said, "did you get paid?" – Christos wrote another headline, is it perhaps too strong? he wondered, but he could have answered, how can I keep cool? For Amalia was weeping constantly, begging him, "do something," for the earth couldn't have opened and swallowed up their daughter, and that "damned boy" too, they must be hiding somewhere together, and maybe sleeping together, the other side lived a life of debauchery these days, people said – and laughed – that their offices and clubs "were full of condoms". Earlier on Christos had asked Nikos, "have you discovered anything?" for it was only through Nikos that any light might be shed on the matter, the other was writing away furiously though, and only shook his head, from somewhere a wireless could be heard now, a melancholy saxophone weeping, Christos found that his eyes hurt when he closed them, they felt metallic as if perhaps they might make a noise when he opened and shut them. Behind the glass panes two shadows were bending, appeared to be talking, gesticulating, maybe they were saying we are keeping watch over you – or we are watching you, for the times had become dangerous, specially at night, one day they had received threatening letters; and Amalia sobbed, "find some other job," this was before the trouble with Alcmene happened, her crazy disappearance, and the mother said, "it's all your fault for being so lenient," and indeed he used to boast, "I've never raised my hand to them."

But the whole place became empty and grew larger they were living in a grey hall and they were talking he and Alcmene and Amalia and they were laying their daughter on a bed and then she opened her collar and showed them where her wound was tormenting her and begged them kiss it for me and at that moment his dead mother came in and said everyone get out and they obeyed her and left them alone together and they disappeared but blows were heard as if the world was crumbling; beside him Nikos continued to write, Christos said, "oh God" and realised that it had been a nightmare, "my hair is getting as long as a mane," he said, at which the other man asked, "what on earth's the matter with you?", then he thought to himself that it had all happened during a moment's sleep, that long hair meant disaster, and said, "we're getting as superstitious as a bunch of old women," so that Nikos stopped, pencil in hand, and stared at him without speaking, "I'm confused," admitted Christos under the other man's gaze, and it was as if he was apologising for faintheartedness, for the other man could ask, "do you know everything I've been through?" and remember how he had spat blood when the Germans were kicking him, "it was near your own neighbourhood," he'd told him in the past, in the cells, in a Gestapo prison a bit beyond Salamis, and Christos whispered, "maybe I'll take a little walk outside" and felt hemmed in by guilt, however the other man reassured him that "you're not the only one".

Outside there were fewer people about, from time to time footsteps could be heard on the pavement, they hurried along and faded from earshot, and Christos reflected, so much the better, he'd be worrying if they stopped at their door; then the telephone rang in the night, Nikos picked up the receiver, said, "hallo, I can't hear you" and waited, complained again to whoever it was, "I can't hear a thing" and hung up. But a moment later it rang again, he was holding the receiver and listening carefully, as if the person at the other end was speaking in an incomprehensible language, he only asked, "Kavalla?" and frowned as if in concentration, replied in occasional monosyllables, at one point noted something on a bit of paper, which he then folded and put in his pocket, Christos asked, "is it serious?" but received no reply, the other man merely shook his head as if to say, leave me be, an expression on his face as if he was being reprimanded, until the phone call ended – whereupon he went out and didn't seem to be coming back. From within Christos could hear the pages being printed – he knew all the sounds and all the different jobs and could fit them together in his mind, like a sort of calendar of the hours of the night, so that he said to himself, "twenty more minutes" before they'd be locking up and leaving, no matter how much he was tormented by the worry, the knowledge that his wife would be waiting in agony and would question him, and he'd tell her "still nothing" and put out his hand to caress her, to calm all her nightmares which slipped in among their furniture and their bedclothes and kept bursting out all round them. Now from the other room were coming the final sounds, and just then the door opened and the youngest printer came out, his hair combed, washed and clean, like a new man, thought Christos, then Nikos reappeared, "we're finished for tonight" and he sighed, seemed to be deep in thought, however he gathered up his pens, his papers, and seemed to be being unusually slow about it, he asked Christos, "are you going home now?" to which the other man nodded, "Amalia will be waiting for you," he was sure of this, and an uneasy silence fell, at the end of which he said out of the blue, "Alcmene is in Kavalla" and stopped, for her father had gone pale, he may have stammered "how?" – "take the bus and go," he urged, then a moment later, "as soon as it's dawn," and he put the piece of paper into Christos's hand, "go there," he told him. Christos unfolded it and read it, what was written on it was "the municipal hospital" – and his feet crumpled under him.

"Leave at dawn if you can," Nikos advised him, and the father said, "would you tell Amalia?" but the other man answered "no", he'd find it hard, he might not know perhaps what he ought to hide from her; and Christos paused at this idea, realised that he was himself reluctant to ask, for although doubts were choking him he was also afraid to resolve them, preferred to lull them. He felt that the light was growing mercilessly bright, which would mean: your hesitation and your terror show; he begged Nikos, "you'd be helping me out ..." and there was a deathly silence which seemed to be piercing him through and through, he said to himself, maybe blood is welling up beneath my clothes, for he felt sopping wet. Finally the other man said, "you'll have to face it" and maybe found him pitiful, for they had been through years of bloodshed – a lifetime – and ought by now to be able to stand it, however he added, "all right, I'll tell her that you've been sent off on a job," and the father bowed his head, in token that he could not disagree, could not ask for anything more. The night was far advanced now, the printers had all left, only two watchmen remained, the road spread empty before them when they came out, with two lights shining a little way off, a café that stayed open all night; and Christos decided, "I'll go and sit there a while, till dawn" – but the other man was setting off to go to Amalia, it was some way away and there were no taxis in sight, he said, "maybe I'll pick one up a bit further down" and they separated. As he left Nikos counselled, "stay cool, show your strength, your courage" – and the father was to think the same thing throughout the whole drive, tormenting himself for not having asked, for not having dared ask, instead of which he was weaving his own versions, which were indeed worrying, but only up to a certain point, only as far as the blood coursing within him could stand, he was trying desperately to calm the panic-ridden pulse that throbbed within him, he looked at the trees, the cornfields, felt that they were so peaceful as they jumped into view, so ill-assorted with tragedies as they spread green before him or were linked to the sun that gave them life; he tried to guess how she would behave, what pain she might be feeling, what excuses she would make or how she would explode into outrage – he set up scenarios in his mind, probable dialogues, but everything always came out tailored to his own measure, to what his own courage could stand.

It all turned out to be useless though, all his plans had to be forgotten, like some dark fraying, tangled skein. For as soon as he entered the hospital – the old building – he knew that he was wrong, that it wasn't going to be anything easy, as he saw the white walls and the row of closed doors, the corridor that continued for a bit and then turned a corner, where from somewhere the smell of onions wafted, it seemed to him that nothing could ever have a happy ending in a place like this, nurses and men in white coats walked past him unconcerned, an old woman in a dirty nightdress with one eye bandaged, behind him someone snivelling in a chair, with a young man telling him off, saying, "if you won't eat it serves you right," and ahead lay an empty space, like a prohibited zone, in which Christos listened to the clock ticking and realised that his journey had taken a whole day, for the sun was almost down now and the first lights were beng switched on, particularly at the end of the corridor, the place which they'd indicated, "go there," when he'd said his name and had noticed them freeze at the sound of it.

He went into a well-lit room, saw only a desk, a man, he must have been about sixty, fat and heavy; he looked up and said "yes?" and Christos said his name, as if saying it all, and the other man closed his eyes, as if wishing, if only I hadn't seen you but murmured, "I'm sorry," the place seemed to be full of a dull buzzing, "we did everything we could," he continued, but Christos interrupted him, "I don't understand," he cried, so that the other man was frightened, "didn't they tell you?" he asked, making as if to rise from his chair, "what has happened, for goodness sake?" – and it was Christos's voice that came out unrecognisable, "we did all that we could," he heard again, the words seemed to be pronouncing a sentence and choked him, it wasn't possible, he caught hold of the other man's hands, "I beg of you," he whispered, yet at the same time admitted to himself that he had known it right from the start, from the time Nikos had been speaking on the telephone, he had felt it in his very innermost being, no matter how much his body had been deceived, no matter how much he had deceived his own mind and tried to lull it, he felt that his true self was the self that had had the nightmare, that had imagined his daughter with a wound in her breast; he asked with some effort, "was she shot?" – and the other man replied, "by two bullets" – "but where did they hit her?" and the doctor said with some difficulty, "in the heart", he felt arms holding him and guiding him, maybe taking him away, they sat him on a chair, "there was nothing else we could do" – and it was no comfort, his other self emerged and said, "I see, thank you," a strange politeness.

And in a moment they were saying, "you fainted" and he saw two or three people in the room, he felt that his temples were wet, just behind his ears, some nurse was smiling at him, she had a curious mole on her cheek, she came up to him and made him lie down, she smelled of the cologne they used, "I want to see her," he begged, outside the room it was pitch dark with only a single lamp hanging curiously, "yes, you will have to identify her," and indeed there lay Alcmene's body, white as marble, he felt his back breaking and they helped him stand upright, suddenly he put out his hand and felt her breast, a black dark red swelling that he didn't recognise, and from it ran a line of blood, congealed now, it was something that did not look fitting on her white skin, he turned to the other people and said, "I am expecting my dead mother," and was aware that they exchanged glances, someone asked, "is she your daughter?", Christos said, "certainly", they removed him by force, at one point he heard them say, "the mother?" and he replied, "she's dead," they were supporting him under his armpits, taking him away. And then in a little while they were all back in the office, he observed them one by one and sensed dead, happy faces, faces that had undergone some curious change, so that although their features were the same yet they formed other, distorted people, they seemed to give off a dull sound, he suspected that they were faking their own breathing. And he thought the same thing later, when he went to the police – "the security department" – and they were trying to fob him off with some story that supposedly Alcmene had got into trouble with her own side, that they'd come to blows among themselves – the policeman said, "she must have been raped" – but Christos asked him, "have you caught anyone?" and they answered, "only one" who was telling them lies, recounting imaginary persecutions – "someone who talks with his eyes shut?" – the policeman laughed, "he hasn't opened them yet," he said ambiguously, and Christos felt as if something was clutching his throat, he smelt the police smell and was sickened, wished they would open a window; "can I see him?" he murmured, but it was forbidden "until the interrogation has been completed".

At the hotel he found a newspaper, consisting of just two pages, he scanned it in vain for any report, so he searched until he found the editorial office, hidden away in a shop in a narrow lane; two men were in the office sorting out their notes, everything around them poor and ancient, he greeted them and added, "I'm a colleague," one of the men went into the next room and came back with a chair, "help me," he begged, explaining who he was and what he wanted from them. But he could see that they tensed suddenly, the elder of the two who had a yellowish complexion and was unshaven said, "we feel for you, but it would be better not to try and find out," as if there were someone eavesdropping in the next room, at which Christos was angered, "they killed my child," he howled, and an icy silence fell, specially at the sound of his voice breaking; in the end the other man asked, "what is it that you want?" – Christos could have given ten different answers, but felt that there was only one which would move them, "the truth", he said.

And it was to prove that he was asking the hardest thing of all, for they spoke to him of mysteries and fabrications, with the two main figures of the tragedy missing, of rumours that there'd been a robbery the same night, that they'd set fire to a car, people said that they'd quarrelled among themselves over sharing out their spoils, but Christos said, "absolute rubbish" and that he knew his daughter very well – at which the old man spoke, said, "maybe you don't," but the father insisted that Alcmene would never have stolen, then the other man hit home with, "did you know where she was?" – meaning that perhaps there might be other things the father didn't know, and the question had something dirty about it, like a grave accusation. However the younger of the two took pity on him, "we're living through evil times," he said, "and there may be worse to come," and then, as if giving advice, murmured, "you won't get to the bottom of it, nor find justice either." And Christos knew full well that, no matter how much rage boiled in his veins, in the end he would be obliged to agree, to compromise, and he felt reduced to an unbelievable poverty in which all he could do was howl or wail, he said, "goodnight, thank you", left, and was blaming himself – what politeness! – he took a deep breath in the hope that this might perhaps relieve the tightness in his chest, which felt as if some unsurmountable discomfort had been trapped in it for hours, he walked down the cobbled lane, saw a brightly lit square, was trying to find the road that led to the hospital, and behind him a man was approaching; Christos turned and had another look at him, the man was a gendarme. He felt a kind of panic, asked, "which way is the hospital?" – but the other replied, "I'll see you back to your hotel," which meant I know who you are, what you want, and Christos searched through the images in his brain, recalling them, a black background with white figures against it, when had he first noticed the gendarme, was it when he emerged from the newspaper offices or earlier?

He went on racking his memory until late at night, when he was back at his mean hotel, in his old room, and had turned off the light, he opened the shutters and gazed out; however the room looked not onto the street but onto the courtyard, with the sea shining beyond it, he could see a caique being loaded, in the dark he heard footsteps, he felt a pain in his jaw, running from one side to the other, lay down on his back and explored his pulse, his premonitions, by now Amalia and the others would know it all, they would probably be out of their minds with grief, maybe they were cursing him as well, on the ceiling dwelt a world that was hard to decipher, it seemed to be telling him I cannot help you, you will have to manage alone, that the only thing left for him to do was to return home with his daughter, the very thought of which was torment; after some time he thought, I have shed no tears, as if noting some uselessness, the beginning of a collapse. As soon as he could see the dawn through the shutters he got dressed to go to the hospital.

Yannis

But nature was suddenly shining and the rain continued to refresh him, he remembered the saying, "when rain and sun together tarry, time for poor folk to marry" and laughed, for one day he had been startled by Angela with the news that Mary was getting married, and it all seemed rather sudden, so that he said, "I don't in the least understand it," for indeed it had all happened furtively and dangerously, "she's at an advanced stage of pregnancy," she whispered to him, as if it were her own fault. And Yannis said, "when did she manage that?", he felt deceived or foolish, realised that she'd been avoiding him – and now understood why – the sun was hiding once more and a chill penetrated him, odd for the season, he felt the raindrops begin to fall more heavily, in a little while they were slapping him and he ran, and he thought, I can feel my heart, inside him, telling him that he could not remain an eternal boy or youth forever – in the end he heard his own voice saying, "she's getting married," and the sun was shining once more and the colours of the rainbow were all around.

He returned to the factory and fell deep into the armchair in his office, he heard the clang of metal, was aware of the smell of wet clothes, from his shoulders, his lapels, he didn't regret not having sought shelter, specially not now, when he felt the need to make his brain the slave of absurd thoughts. He thought, I can play games, that this stroke of the machine makes the spool turn, and the next one passes the thread into the loom, he thought, I remember the coloured blocks I used to have, red and yellow and blue and green, triangular and rectangular, which could be fitted together and create a bird, except that his mother would scold and say, "the eye ought to be yellow" every time that he got the blocks muddled up and made the legs blue and the eye red, it resembled some weird kind of bird; he said to himself again, "when did she manage it?" and then unlocked the top drawer of his desk, took out a green file, brand new, and assessed, this is a problem, they would have to work shifts in order to meet the pressure for production, Angela would say, "why did you get so involved?", but he didn't feel that it was simply because of ambition that any day now he would be deciding to expand, perhaps to import new machinery, to take on new workers, or that his heart was leaping more than he cared to say.

And Nikos was constantly telling him, "now's your chance," and introduced him to useful people, he'd received a huge order, and was fulfilling it, for blankets for the police force – outside the sky had darkened once more, but he couldn't hear the rain because of the sound of the machinery clattering continuously. In some way he rather liked this clatter, he opened his door, went out onto the factory floor where they were working, reckoned that it was no longer big enough, was aware that people, metal machinery and yarn were all crammed together, there was a flash of lightning, but the fact that the machines made an ear-piercing din didn't in the least bother him, he watched the workers bending over their tasks, three girls wearing head scarves. He counted the days the job would take, whose number actually he knew by heart and it was this that was worrying him – the heavens must be thundering, he thought of all the unanticipated things that can occur every day, all life long, Angela had proposed, "we could be best man and matron of honour for them" and he had replied, "you do it, because she trusts you," somewhere he noticed a shaven nape, the man must have a tuft of hair on his forehead, he plunged in among the machinery, one or two people greeted him with a smile, and he felt they were sucking up to him, he moved on a bit, now he got a side view of the shaved nape and the tuft, thought I remember him from somewhere, but only faintly, as if something had happened to confuse him – he went back to his office, where the telephone was ringing.

But at midday he was cross with her, "don't bother me with things like that," he told her, then after a moment, feeling sorry as he saw her disappointment, "I've got a lot of worries on my mind," he explained. And that same night he woke up, hearing coughing and choking, and it was their baby crying, he went and took her in his arms, thought, but what do baby clothes smell of? something like soap all mixed up with the scent of trees, the tiny person opened her eyes, closed them again, without realising what he was doing he rocked her to and fro, lulled her, he heard the sound of bare feet on the floor, Angela said, "what on earth are you doing?" as if rebuking him, she took the baby and tucked her up in her cot, he said, "I don't get time for everything" then smiled, he knew she was thinking something different, in the end he lay on his back in the dark, begging, "if I could only sink into a sweet sleep," as if seeking refuge, he felt her hand tracing him, touching his belly then further down, it was slipping into the flies of his pyjamas, whereupon quite without reason Eugenios appeared and said, "the icy ring" with his mouth looking unnaturally large Angela said, "she had a miscarriage" and old women were coming in with basins taking blood-stained towels and leaving and Eugenios was watching them he got up with difficulty and held his arms in front of him as if he was in pain or afraid he would drip and make the place dirty in the end a knife was quivering in front of Yannis as if all by itself, he was still lying on his back and breathing hard, he thought I slept, but he had not enjoyed the sleep, beside him Angela lay paralysed, so was she still breathing? he put out his hand and touched her breast, felt it rise and fall, said, "some nonsense ..." and heard his own words, which might have been some kind of raving.

He went to the kitchen, stood there in the dark and soundless night, his hands touched the little tiles, whose surface was smooth and cool, he opened the windows onto the darkness, smelt damp earth and leaves, looked up, the heavens were crystal clear and spangled with stars, like tiny flowers on a pure black field. He stood there rooted to the spot, until he heard the sound of bare feet walking down the road, a man carrying wicker baskets was coming along, a little further down lay the beach, he could hear the reeds rustling, Angela used to say, "I go and sit there with the baby," as if they were bathing and enjoying the feeling of being clean. After some time the darkness began to be diluted, he could make out the mass of the mountains, the upper city looked lilac and grey and from far off he could hear a tram; he thought, I'll lie down for a bit, he felt his wife's body warm beside him, her bare legs between which he placed his hand, living flesh asleep and scented, he begged once more, "let me fall into a sweet sleep," a paradise from which machinery and cares would have disappeared, where all would be black trees and tranquillity, maybe not even any sounds at all.

However, what he was fated to hear were screams and cries, a hysterical voice which alarmed them; I know that voice, thought Yannis, who knew it best in his very blood and sinews, and indeed Mary was standing on their doorstep, she seemed demented, was screaming, "they killed him" – and more screeches followed, a wounded tigress perhaps with flashing eyes, she caught hold of Angela's arms, cried, "didn't I tell you?" as if accusing her that they hadn't been in time, she was not weeping, wouldn't be caressed, in the end, with a great deal of trouble, they sat her down on the sofa, Yannis said as if annoyed, "just tell us plainly what's happened" and she fixed her feverish eyes on him. She said, "they came and took him" and Yannis asked, "from where?" – "from my room", the girl said, as if giving him a slap, from between her legs more likely, thought Yannis, but "when?" he asked – "just before dawn" – and the others had been asleep, her father adrift on a sea of alcohol, her younger sister in another little room, "now she's quivering and moaning," said Mary, becoming softer. Yannis promised that he'd go and find out, in case they really had killed him, but anyway Nikos was a friend and had some power – Angela said, "tell him that they were due to get married in two weeks," he nodded, "that I was going to be matron of honour," and she turned to Mary, "stay here a bit until you are calmer," but the other woman shrieked, "what about my little sister?" – people said she thrashed in her sleep, that she raved, once she had walked in her sleep and called, "Father, stop, a tram's coming" and then had fallen to the floor in convulsions, the doctor, their uncle, had tightened his lips and said, "send her to the country" – but where? With what money?

He walked up the road, made his way along, swearing out loud, there wasn't any tram or bus that would serve him, quite apart from the fact that he was due at the factory, the accountants would be waiting for him, he knew where he would find Nikos, at a three-storey house above Evzonon Street, suddenly he was out of breath, realised it, said to himself, why on earth am I hurrying? and then added out loud, "the little tart". And later the policeman was teasing him, "at least you mounted her too, I suppose?" and laughed, at which Yannis was strangely offended, though he forced himself to joke, "Angela would rip me to pieces," he said – and as he was going down the stairs he remembered it, the scoundrel didn't give me any promise. Things couldn't have been simple, this he sensed as soon as he arrived at the Security Police, for gendarmes and secret agents were scurrying about, they were pushing three old men into a little room, one of them was huddled in his dressing gown and sneezing, and while he was talking to Nikos (the telephone kept ringing and interrupting them) a gendarme sergeant came into his office, said, "could I have a word with you?" and he was very pale, "you could," replied Nikos, at which the man bent down to whisper in his ear, "you can speak freely," and the man hesitated a moment, then spoke with difficulty, "I'd like to ask you to let the obstetrician go" – "you must have a screw loose," Nikos told him, "he's not dangerous, I can guarantee it" and the sergeant seemed to be stuttering, Nikos and Yannis remained silent, I'd much rather not be here listening, thought the latter, "one night I dragged him over to my house against his will, and he saved my wife and baby, he wouldn't take a penny for it," and Nikos told him, "go" – and Yannis wondered, what will come of all that?*

* One morning, just before the junta fell, I was sitting at "Totti's". At the table next to me three old-age pensioners were drinking their coffee; they used to meet there every morning and chat. And the most decrepit of them said: "did you know Hadzidakis, the doctor? One day they dragged him off to the police station, along with some others, and he was trembling with cold. I remembered one night when I'd called him out for my wife, he wouldn't come, because those were dangerous times – people would get you out of your house and kill you. I wept and begged him, and in the end he came with me and saved my wife and child. He wouldn't take a penny, and instead he gave me medicines. A real gentleman, I'm telling you." The man next to him asked, "did he see you were a gendarme?" – "yes, and he called me poor bugger." They turned and saw me listening. They laughed. The one who'd been telling the story said, "those were difficult times." After a little while he paid and left. One of the remaining two said, "he goes on and on telling that story, as if it tormented him." At which the other man laughed, "it might be because he feels guilty" – and they both fell silent.

But he couldn't convince Angela, "what kind of friends are you?" she criticised them, "if I'd gone by myself, I would have managed," but her husband told her, "you don't understand." Over the next few days they lost sight of Mary, he had his own worries about the extra shifts, one night he fell out of bed, bruised his shoulder, his buttocks, and in the morning came to a decision, he called the most senior skilled workers together and asked who'd be willing to work a night shift, "I'll pay double rates," he promised, "and food" – the men looked at him slyly, pretended to smile, pretended to clear their throats, enjoying the sense of having him in the palm of their hands, "well?" he asked, getting angry, but they shrugged their shoulders unwillingly, "the others?" they murmured, "what about the others?" He got up, left them, went outside, then he said, "fuck your mothers," which they wouldn't have heard, then went back in among the machines through the side door, the first person he spotted was the man with the shaved neck, he felt sure that he knew him. And as the machinery thundered and hammered away he shouted loudly, "just a moment", took a hammer and banged on the metal, "just a moment", he shouted again, and realised that they were looking at him. He got up onto a crate and raised his arms, crossed them then opened them wide again, the way people do when they want to stop an oncoming car, "just a moment", he cried again, and felt his voice resounding through his ribs, his spine, his skull, for the machines had been switched off and had come to a halt, and they were staring at him, all faces, eyes, mouths.

That same evening they got to work; Yannis arrived first and was smiling, which might have meant, I've got my own way, at nine o'clock the machines were set in motion, at one point he heard laughter, a good sign, he said to himself, by now it must have been dark outside and calm, but inside metal clattered and reflected the light, the two oldest workers were missing, they weren't up to it, thought Yannis. When it was almost midnight he went out, over to the square to a grill-house that stayed open all night, "is it ready?" he asked, and they loaded a large tray with packets, sent a boy with him to carry the bottles; when he arrived back at the factory he set it all out on two tables (everything had been prepared earlier), he said, "will two of the women come and help me," for he was offering them grilled meat and pudding, he opened the beer for them and their eyes shone as if the lights had got brighter, he said, "one hour's break for food and rest", and a few people even clapped. However, at one point the singer came up to him, gave him a diabolic smile and said, "I remember another feast, before the war," but Yannis hissed, "get out of here before I wring your neck" – "very well, but you're a crafty one," he was enjoying it, for he could read him like a book, knew that his master was feeling like a king. And later he was to sink into his throne, he fell asleep in the armchair in his office, and outside the machines were clattering away.

Antigone

And when she opened her eyes it was snowing; Antigone read this from the ceiling, which was shining brightly, and she thought, something has happened, got up and went to the window, and through the shutters she saw that the world had turned white. At that moment the door opened and her mother was standing there, saying, "it's settling," and indeed when they pushed the shutters back and looked out the whole of creation was glittering; Christmas and the New Year had come and gone, but the house remained dumb, like a house of sickness. Then her mother said, "don't go barefoot," and began to make the bed, to busy herself, "get dressed and come to the kitchen," she said, where the fire was lit and breakfast waiting. Dimitris was already there, chewing his food, he asked her, "are you coming with me?" – he must have got chilled through and was hoarse, but where? – Antigone answered, "we agreed on it," as if it was being done as a favour to her. The one who remained silent was their mother – washing up quietly and absently; one day she had said to their father, "you won't be feeling any pain now" and then broke off, it was like an accusation, the fact that they had lost their Alcmene.

They got dressed in warm clothes and went out, but at the beginning said nothing to one another – Dimitris was going to the university to submit his application forms for the entrance exams. The previous night they'd had a row, his father asking, "do you insist?" – and him having made up his mind, "yes, I want to be a physicist," Christos wanted him to be a doctor or an agronomist, otherwise, he warned, "all you'll be doing is emptying your own head to fill other people's." As they walked up past the YMCA, the ice seemed to them to be shining, maybe the climate was changing and the universe would freeze over; and Dimitris advised her, "tread firmly," and behind them they left footprints in the snow. They passed the Fair and the high school, which was set on the top of a mound, with its hanging white garden, and soon arrived at the railings that surrounded the courtyard, with bushes and trees pure white behind them. "When I last saw it, there were flowers," "when was that?" he asked her – and she remembered it was at the time of the parade, and Antigone had found herself with two other girls in front of the University, "I was scared because they were all singing resistance songs," the boys with their excited faces, the girls shouting. And Antigone wept within herself, seared by the memory of Alcmene – the night their father brought her home dead, the whole neighbourhood had been stricken by the wailing, the keening, she remembers that the night was warm and the street filled with people, girls and boys that she didn't know came and left flowers on the steps and then withdrew, and the women were left talking in hushed voices – and the Tsimonis woman with them, all in black, grieving for her own sorrows – but nothing could console Amalia, nor could she forgive.

The brother and sister went up the steps and for a moment he held her arm to stop her slipping; the building was mansion-like, with high ceilings, and in the centre of it a quadrangle, now covered with snow. Dimitris said, "I'm going upstairs, wait for me here," for crowds of people were going up and down the stairs; others had formed circles and were conversing, Antigone looked out of the window, close to her stood a group of boys who were talking excitedly, she noticed a tall fair-haired boy whose glasses, as he got annoyed, kept slipping off sideways, he would straighten them and continue to argue heatedly, gradually the group had swollen to about a dozen, "don't you talk to me about slaughter," someone was saying, Antigone moved closer and listened, "you tell us about the gangs, about Sourlas," the tall boy shouted, but the other then said, "not so loud, my friend". For a little while their voices were lowered, but only for a little while, Antigone went even nearer and felt she was almost touching them, and she liked this feeling; now she could see them better, could see that the tall boy only had two others taking his part, most of the rest were just listening in silence, and others seemed to be right-wing, they were accusing Velouchiotis, Zachariades, one of them said that Svolos was a fool, and at this voices were raised, but the tall boy outdid them all, he showed an impressive mental agility, so might he be studying Physics or Law? the girl smiled to herself sadly. Suddenly Antigone caught sight of Dimitris, who was standing on the other side of the group listening, he seemed to her to be taking no part, looked rather pale, their eyes met and he came round to her side, whispered, "I couldn't find you," for she was shorter than anyone else. They left, went down the road, below them the sea lay grey, as if sinking into the icy cold.

And then, without any kind of prologue, Dimitris muttered, "we were betrayed" and there was a furrow on his brow; Antigone stared at him dumbly, she had a premonition that her brother's bitter thoughts had been gathering, gathering and throbbing like an abscess, which had now burst, so that he was speaking, saying as if talking to himself, "I'm afraid that we've been made pitiable fools of, I'm afraid that they're playing with us like puppets, people are holding the strings who neither know how to manipulate them nor are able to; that boy in there who was shouting may prove to be the big victim, even if what happened to our sister doesn't happen to him" – and his voice broke as if he was choking – "he may suffer even worse things than what happened to our Alcmene. And he stopped there as if he didn't have enough air; and Antigone put out her hand, it was purple with cold but was the only bit of her capable of speaking, and she put it to his forehead, stroked it, however he drew back from her touch and spoke again, from deeper within himself, "who are all the people who define us – and who defines them? Who are the people who supposedly sign bits of paper that say do this or that, what are they expecting? From where?" He took her hand as if holding her back (or holding himself back, as Antigone feared, for she heard a sob behind his anguish), "you stay out of it," he told her – but what had got into him?

She remembered Amalia's complaint to their father, "if you'd given her advice, she would have been saved," she told him; he listened and said nothing, but on his face was an expression of hopelessness which meant: everything is my fault, so be it, I shall endure it. One morning he left at dawn (never mind that he hadn't got home till three in the morning) and Amalia said, "let him go," and he slammed the door and left, and Dimitris stood in the kitchen sullenly, reproving his mother with his eyes; at midday when she got back from school, Christos was in the cellar going through old papers. From the house behind theirs they could hear a gramophone, someone who sounded drunk crying "in an English flag, if I die" – they were constantly seeing the gendarmes coming round to pay him a visit, one night his wife had been shaking and screeching, as if she was being ripped asunder or something else, and Amalia closed their shutters, "it's possible," she murmured, "with them, it's perfectly possible ..." And her father said, "what were they doing in Kavalla?" but she answered, "did you notice their faces?"

And Antigone thought that the faces did indeed look sad and ugly, as they were crammed into the tram and she was hanging on to her brother's arm; Dimitris was looking elsewhere, and seemed to be deep in thought, perhaps about what he had said, perhaps he was repenting of having said it. She was looking around in the dim light of the tram and talking to herself, saying, I'm trying desperately hard to find a face that looks happy, for everyone seemed to her to be pale and ill-humoured, two women with their hair a mess, a boy who hadn't shaved, maybe it's just my own idea, she thought, maybe my eyesight has been infected, she looked at an old woman with a mole in the corner of her eye, her nose curiously and unpleasantly red, and just then she began to cough, as if she was doing it on purpose in order to bring tears to her eyes. Suddenly she squeezed Dimitris's hand, and he turned and looked at her, his eyes questioning her – "have you noticed all the faces around us?", but he looked at her in surprise, "I don't know what you're talking about," he murmured, their thoughts were not in step. The tram was jolting up and down and the crowd of passengers becoming fewer, her field of vision was now wider, she could observe other faces, some illuminated by the windows; and "they are all ugly," she insisted. She couldn't explain it, just as she couldn't explain how she'd play with names that would come into her head, Eutychia, Eugenia, Eudocia, Eudoxia, then Theodosia, Theopisti and Theoni, Anemone and Anthi, and she would take refuge in their garden, where she could name all the flowers and play with them, when spring came and they flourished, first a whole mass of wild flowers, then the poppies and the little yellow flowers which sprang up like a heaven-sent gift, and then much later her father's flowers, her mother's, when they too took refuge in the garden and occupied themselves with its various jobs, setting aside their thoughts and their sorrows for a while – specially her mother, whose brows were always knitted now, like when she counted the stitches as she embroidered.

But things were not to work out as they expected or wished, for in the season when the flowers were coming into bloom and the lilac was making them drowsy with its scent, they learned that it is all nothing but failure, in particular the fact that Dimitris had not passed his exams; he had wasted two evenings at the cinema forgetting everything, although on the third night he was deep in his books once more, he confided to Antigone, "it's like trying on my old clothes and finding that they still fit and feeling that they smell of me." Yet it wasn't only this, their disappointment was not to end here, for the trees had all been in a hurry to flower but in March they had frost again, which seemed to be telling the lilies to forget the feast of the Annunciation, and all their seedlings turned black overnight, the garden was garbed in mourning, and above them the blossom on the trees, whichever ones had been too reckless, gave up the ghost. However, one evening Amalia went out into the garden in obstinate determination, she took her hoe and set to work in the semi-darkness, at one point they heard her say, as if talking to someone, "only nettles and weeds remain in this garden," she went on working for hours, as if it was some kind of obligation, until Dimitris went and brought her in – their father had already left for work – and as he did so he saw that their little garden was now bare earth, dark and freshly turned, giving off the scent of bruised roots, with only their old rosebush remaining at one side, and the heap of weeds. And her determination did not end there, for Amalia was up at dawn (by which time her husband had come home and gone to bed), digging and planting out seedlings, until the sun was shining in the sky and her children awoke; she washed and wiped her hands and sat down, saying, "in a month's time we'll have our garden again," and indeed in due season the stocks and pansies and carnations were flowering with a fragrance that consoled, that gave sweetness to the labour.

And just when they thought things had calmed down, someone

rang their doorbell as Christos was getting dressed to leave for work; on the doorstep stood Haris, who said, "may we come in?" and then entered with his father, whose scanty hair had now turned white but whose eyes shone just as brightly, whose expression was just the same (a lifetime of plotting, thought Christos), they went into the inner room and closed the shutters, for good or for bad, and the mother was grim-faced as she remembered. Her children stood at the side and talked quietly with Haris, and it seemed to Antigone that his eyes had grown even larger, so that they illuminated his pale face; and Elias said, "we were so sorry to hear about your daughter" – perhaps he couldn't remember her name – but added, "my Haris has had to pay for it too, he wasn't given a place at the University," Christos and Amalia looked at one another, but the other man got a little block out of his pocket and began to flick through it as if looking for something, suddenly he stopped and murmured to Dimitris, "they didn't take you either," at which Dimitris gave a smile full of meaning and said, "I could only answer one question" then was silent – but Elias had found what he was looking for, tore a leaf off the block and handed it to Christos, "it's the collection," he told him, "in aid of those who are being persecuted," whereupon the woman unexpectedly stepped into the middle of things, she picked up the coupon and gave a good look at the hammer and sickle stamped on it, she blinked as if her eyes were itching, then put it back on the table in front of their visitor, "don't get us mixed up in it," she said, "for fear we have to pay the price a second time," and the atmosphere in the room froze. Elias smiled uneasily, his lower lip seemed to be sagging somehow, "very well", he said in annoyance and looked at Christos; the coupon remained lying on the table unpaid for. And it went on lying there later, as their visitor got up, buttoned his overcoat and gave a forced smile (the egoist, thought Christos), saying incomprehensibly, "don't regret it" and then, "perhaps we shan't be meeting again; I leave for Olympus in an hour." And he disappeared into the night with Haris.*

---

* At the beginning of '46 H. took the entrance exams for medical school again. Again he failed them. The same thing happened once more in the autumn of the same year. His mother used to say, "they fail him because of his father, to get their revenge." Perhaps this was some kind of consolation

That night, though, Antigone struggled in terror, she felt that voices were coming in through the window describing how his hair rose and fell as the wind blew a dream in which surges of colour were transformed they pointed to a tall unshaven boy who was complaining that the birds of the night loved him that they flew behind him and the young man lost his glasses and rubbed his eyes which were red and he said the Furies the fairies and a voice was coming through the window again and weeping and saying, "my daughter", and the voice was followed by a quiet murmur, which seemed to be coming from the walls and the floors, as if it wished to persuade or console, but in a moment wails broke out, a door was heard closing – as time passed everything became quiet once more, as if a whole series of intervening doors had been closed, one after the other. Now the girl felt as if erased memories were dripping, from the ancient tap which they would turn off determinedly with all their strength, full of despair, so that everything could be over and done with, she thought perhaps we are crawling over sleeping ground, but she felt lost, without a body, without hands, only memory functioning, and ears and eyes, and in the end not even these.

The next morning her mother did not get up at all and at midday they called a doctor. They said, "now it's our turn," took off their shoes to walk quietly, spoke in whispers, Antigone took over all the necessary housework. Their father would leave in the evening for work; and one night the daughter got under their bedclothes and hugged her mother tightly and it was beautiful, Amalia said only, "ah my daughter, my daughter", as if she feared to open the floodgates to other words. And they both slept peacefully, in their memory the scent of the little lamp before the icon, which was flickering out.

---

for her. All the same, it is not impossible that her son simply did not answer the examination questions very well. Later, much later, it was discovered that both he and his younger brother had a mania for gambling at cards.

Angela

When she awoke it was dawn, fine weather was coming in from the sea, a Mediterranean breeze with a hint of salt to it; beside Angela Yannis lay curled up, cool when she touched his arm, his neck, and then kissed his cheek. His was a body whose feel was familiar, she knew the marks on it and the touch of it, she could find peace in his scent on the pillow, now that he slept more calmly, now that he no longer suddenly jumped up or cried out, as he had done two months ago, when he had reached the point of going through two whole nights without so much as closing his eyes, but only sat and smoked one cigarette after the other, a permanent anxious glowing tip, – and anxious-making for her too, who remained silent as she watched him in the dark, until he became aware of her and said, "the nyktalopic woman", as if he was talking to her in a foreign language. It was near the delivery date for the order, the machines were "going full blast" as he told her, he would disappear for days and nights at a time – and one day at noon she saw a bite mark on his shoulder, just below his neck.

And she would complain, "it is certainly bad for both of us," but he said, "you are mad," for the order was a big one and so were his profits. However her reasoning was different, what they had was enough for her and she remembered her beginnings, "I'm a queen now," she would say with pride, but Yannis was building palaces of another kind, sometimes he seemed to be dreaming that he was running, one night as he had his arm round her he whispered, "I wish my father was alive," and there seemed to be a certain bitterness in his breath, and into Angela's mind came images from her youth, the lost days with Eugenios, that night when she had seen him for the first time, and all the longings that were to follow in the darkened house, all the things she had been through with her employer and her young Yannis, then the way he disappeared, the tears, or his sister with that terrible letter, wandering around with it in a state of hysteria or love; the fact that he was on the run and despised, maybe on the brink of utter disaster, through pride or despair. Angela now felt it all again, to comfort him she said, "you beat them all," but as they walked in the darkness she could sense that he had his own secret longings, hidden and dark and battened down, perhaps he still held wild ideas which he kept prisoner within him, so that he wished for his father again. And indeed this was so; for as he embraced her – and they were lying on their backs – he was thinking out loud, saying, "in three years' time we may need a new factory," for the way ahead was opening up now, Nikos told him, "it's an opportunity" (one night he said to Angela, "I've got your friend's husband out," then was silent for a minute, finally wagged his finger at her, "all the same, tell him to keep quiet and be good," then another pause, "and her too, the hysterical woman," he added – for Mary would attack gendarmes and kick them), "now is the great opportunity," he exhorted Yannis, and Angela wondered, but what is afoot, for she knew how he was reckoning and calculating. Yannis was plunged into his own thoughts however, intoxicating shapes floated around him, he suddenly gripped her arm, "maybe one day this place won't be big enough to hold me," and when she then turned and looked at him Angela was left speechless, for he seemed to be shining all over – "is it something that burns you so much?" she asked, and Yannis closed his eyes, perhaps with a certain disturbance in his breast, for there was a long silence, and she turned and leaned against him, kissed him, "I wish that all your dreams may come true," maybe he dreamed of one day standing before his father, hoping for a smile or a caress, some sign of approval or recognition.

Except that she didn't always feel like this, especially not on nights when she slept alone, listening to all the passing footsteps, counting them, loving them and in the end losing them, when they were not his steps, when she didn't hear them on their stairs, coming up and slowly approaching her, when he would stand in the dark and find her by her smell. He might have some different sensitivity, she thought, he might be afraid that I suspect him, for I know his scents, his lusts, or when all the hairs on his body stand on end and he goes wild over my bare arms and my backbone, an unknown strange animal – in a moment of bitterness she asked him, "do you hear the stars?" and took him by surprise. With the passage of time her perceptions had been finely honed, she could see through his closed eyes or the hollow of his armpit, where possibly traces of some unfamiliar sweat resided, one night she said to him, "you smell of cooking," and indeed his hair smelled of charcoal smoke, he said, "I went and had a drink in a tavern," which might have been half the truth, the other half being that he had been lying in another bed somewhere, for she wove together other thoughts, dates, his touch in particular, which seemed to resemble a different garden, hostile or dangerous, a place where she loathed the seaweed in the shallows, always walked in fear keeping her eyes on the sea bed, lest she get trapped somewhere or bitten, which might mean death or disfigurement, her leg or her whole body turning black, full of pustules and ulcers.

But she didn't always feel like this – and luckily; for one afternoon, in September, he said, "get dressed, I'm going to take you both for an outing" – Angela and her baby – and the taxi was already there waiting for them, they sat in the back seat and lowered the windows, to feel the wind as they set off towards the country, past the Depot, past Votsis's, and Angela asked, "where are you taking us?" but he merely smiled mysteriously, now all around them were pine trees and a sharp breeze, but they passed them too, and she said, "there's the Peran Club," projecting into the sea from the dry land; in the old days couples used to come here to have a swim away from prying eyes and would then emerge and eat fish – however, "I don't remember us ever coming here," he said, and they were both silent. The driver asked, "which way now?" and then stopped; and Yannis got out of the taxi and scanned their surroundings, as if reconnoitering, Angela was playing with the child, who was chuckling, in the end Yannis said, "we have to go back a bit, I made a mistake," and they turned back towards the pine wood, they were further from the sea now, its scent was weaker and the smell of the trees much more noticeable. Suddenly Yannis said, "stop," two lorries were coming from the other direction, he got out again, examined the landscape, a new reconnaissance, a dirt track full of potholes wound away through the fields, Yannis pointed to it and said, "turn in here," which was easier said than done, for the driver grumbled, "it's impossible," the track was narrow, only carts could get along it, whose wheels had ploughed deep furrows for as far as the eye could see, "how'd we be able to get out afterwards?" he muttered, and Angela, listening but said nothing, wondered where he was taking them. But just at that moment a man came into sight walking down the hill, he raised his hand, hallo, he appeared to be thickset and red-faced under a wide-brimmed straw hat which hid his eyes, "Stavros, hallo", called Yannis and went towards him, and the other answered, "welcome, Captain", which was rather incomprehensible – finally Yannis came back and took Angela by the hand, "your lady?" asked Stavros, and the way he laughed spoke of the healthiness of people who live in close contact with the soil. The taxi would wait for them there; and they set off on foot, Angela and the child in front, with the two men behind them, talking – she could hear Stavros whose voice sounded like the creaking of a piece of wood, and he kept on saying, "well ... well".

After a bit they left the track, fields lay all about them, here and there the greenness of a tree, and in the distance a hedge of thick foliage; the child ran ahead happily, a small pink figure like a little flag rippling amidst the world of nature, and the adults smiled. In the end Yannis and Stavros stopped, as if they'd found the place, and began to point, to measure and to talk – the woman took a deep breath, as if it had been years since she'd breathed like this, enjoying the sense of space, the colours, the low hills rising to the east, everywhere a carpet of green and yellow and brown, in the other direction a glimpse of the sparkling sea, in the distance the hand of Karabournou, now dipped in ink and pointing towards Mount Olympus and its snows. Yannis asked her, "do you like it here?" and she replied, "it reminds me of my homeland," the lonely places where she used to wander, everything now becoming confused in her memory and strangely beautiful; then once more he and Stavros started measuring, "it's one hectare," the man told him, and Yannis nodded in agreement.

When the shadows were growing longer they set off to leave, hearing all about them the voices of nature, warblings and croakings and somewhere a stake being hammered into the ground. They got into the waiting taxi, "goodbye, Captain", said Stavros, doffing his hat to Angela and taking her hand, she felt as if she was touching the bark of a tree, his hair was white and close cropped except for a lock left longer in the front, he said, "goodnight and happy waking tomorrow", his eyes were full of youth.

And as they lay in bed at night, the woman asked him, "what are you cooking up?" to which he might have replied an empire, yet remained silent and plunged in thought (secretive, Angela complained to herself, with many other instances of it stored in her memory) – in the end he asked, "will you understand me?" and she answered, "yes" innocently. And his plan was simple, great ("all great plans are simple," he concluded) – he would build a new factory, yes, in that field which he had bought "for next to nothing", he would import new, more modern, machinery, but first and foremost it would be entirely his own, none of it belonging to co-heirs who might one day cause trouble. "With what money, though?" she grumbled; and he had this all planned too, he'd have a lot of money left over from the orders he was currently completing, he might perhaps manage to get a loan – "we'll see," he concluded. And Angela thought that what lay in store for her was more raving in his sleep, more falling out of bed and groaning perhaps, but all the same she knew that it was all perfectly inevitable, for she could hear the woodworm gnawing away inside him, well and truly installed in his innermost parts, sending a light to his eyes, as he whispered to her, "I could," perhaps he meant become a king or a lord, perhaps the head of a dynasty, whose image he was seeing painted in the darkness, or upon the curtain which was gently stirring and changing shades – "I like giving birth to things," he said finally.

At dawn she felt him shaking, she foresaw that he'd be hurrying out, and wondered, how can I keep up with him? For the path before him might hide all sorts of encounters, people who might catch her by surprise, who might perhaps bite his neck and his arms, maybe his belly – most dangerous of all – she put her hand on his spine, to listen, something inside her was laughing, yet she would not withdraw her palm, which was detecting mysterious pulses, as if something of her own was coming and going, telling her that everything is not unknown, it is simply a question of getting used to it, recognising it, like the footsteps that always pass below their house at the same time of day, or a bird that always crows at dawn, always announces that in a little while the sun will be shining and visions will be laid to rest, that the curtain will be simply a piece of material and this body will be Yannis's eyes looking at her, his arm encircling her, his leg pushing between her own legs, so that their flesh, their pulses, seem to continue the conversation. And she suddenly told him, "I liked it," and, as his eyes questioned her, added, "I liked going there" and Yannis whispered, "yes, it's a beautiful place, fresh air" – "I don't just mean that" and she caressed him, she wanted to say many things, kissed him, "I like what you want, even if it scares me"; she felt sympathy for his ambition, felt sorry for it too, perhaps she should be warming it, now that he was slipping into her arms, cuddled in her embrace like a small child. If people saw him like this they would take him for weak, yet she thought, he is dangerous to everyone, at some point – when it best suited him – he would fight them off with his claws, a little animal that would unexpectedly grow larger, which would feel like a wild beast, in the sunlit morning.

And they said it really is late, for someone was ringing their bell downstairs, Yannis asked, "who could it be?", they weren't dressed yet, the scent of the night still clinging to them; she hid under the white blanket and Yannis threw on a dressing gown. Angela heard a man's voice and her husband talking in low tones, footsteps in the drawing room, then a door closing, it must have been the door of his study – and she reflected, it seems to be someone he knows. Time went by and she heard nothing else from within, only at one point her daughter cried, standing there barefoot and half-naked, a little person with her own language which could simply demand; Angela went and picked her up, and at that moment heard the door opposite open, she only just had time to slip further into the room and saw Nikos in uniform coming out behind her, with Yannis following him and saying, "I was expecting it." And when the other man had gone, he stood at the door with an expression that said, where to begin telling you, with Angela all agog to hear – "he's asking for Ergini," he said, but she didn't grasp his meaning and stared at him, "Ergini, my eldest sister, he wants to marry her"; and Angela said, "that explains everything," by which she meant the way he was always helpful and never refused to do them favours. "But what on earth made him come at daybreak?" – one more dark casket – yet there was an explanation for everything; "he was sitting up with her all night long, discussing it" and they both burst out laughing, Angela asked, "doesn't it bother you?" but instantly a suspicion flashed through her mind, "you knew about it," she said, to which Yannis made no reply. Always secretive about his own affairs, she complained to herself, and a feeling of contrariness flooded the space between her ears, she too could bite, "there's your new partner," she shot at him, but his expression soured, "absolutely not", he hissed at her, "not in my own business" – and he was the wild beast, who had got his claws well and truly out, who was displaying them deliberately.

Christos

But a season of fear arrived, when the wisest thing, people would advise you, was to lie low, no matter that Christos said, "we lost the light from our lives" by which he meant what worse could happen to us, and he felt that Amalia's voice echoed round him, or her wailing, for she was continually running off to the Evangelistria Cemetery, she would wash the gravestone and place flowers on it, and at night she would start from her sleep; one night she suddenly hit him out of the blue, the outburst of a nightmare, she was still attacking him when she woke up, as if the rage in her blood was something she couldn't control, he spread his arms in despair, as if saying, I can't help it, yet deep within him he sympathised, understood, felt guilty, even though she would cry to him, "you only pretend to." All this was at the beginning, when he was patient with her, spoke kindly to her with self-control, kept saying, "I am beside you," tried not to hurt her any further, knowing her soul was bleeding – when the first rains of autumn began to fall and they had to think of winter her behaviour changed and she was silent, and Christos developed a sixth sense which told him that an embittered gaze was seeking desperately to penetrate to his very core, every time that he sensed she was standing behind him or sitting in a corner, taking care of them all.

However, everything around them had changed now, and Christos warned, "be careful," his words were directed not so much at Dimitris (one day he put on his boy scout uniform, a rank holder, and laughed) as at his young daughter, who was always disappearing or hiding, who looked at them with blank eyes, stuffed books under her mattress, and Amalia would shout at her, "concentrate on your school work." One day at noon they received a thick envelope, carefully tied up with twine, they searched in vain to find the sender's name on it, and came to the conclusion that it couldn't be anything that boded well; they opened it slowly and carefully in case it was a booby trap, and when they emptied out the contents – a ribbon, a little handkerchief, and sheets of paper with writing on them – Christos took a ruler and turned them all over, as if they were red hot and would burn him, whereupon Amalia screamed, "have you gone mad?" and grabbed the ruler from him, threw it aside, laid her hands upon the ribbon, the handkerchief, as if in a trance, and wept, "they're hers, you've forgotten her," so that all of them fell silent. Only after a couple of seconds the father stammered, "how could I have recognised them?" and she responded in anger, "what did you expect? Some of her hair or one of her fingers?" – and a sob was suffocating Christos, making his jaws tremble, he struggled to hide it, to choke it back, but in vain, and he was afraid lest he set her off again. After a while the mother froze, and like a grey stone speaking pronounced, "only one person could have sent them, could have had them," the lost sender whom the earth had swallowed up, of whom they'd been thinking that he might have flown to heaven, yet whom they had avoided either mentioning or cursing.

And storms and tempests were now loosed, passions, screams, errors, they lived through unpredictable times with Amalia, when she would go out and work in the garden at night, one day at noon Christos noticed that she was trying on old clothes, one of which must have been a girl's dress, he laughed and murmured, "what are you doing?" but she looked at him quite blankly, as if she didn't even see him. And her oddness went on and on, she washed her wedding dress and ironed it, opened old trunks where she kept her children's baby clothes, unfolded them, looked at them, arranged them, once they heard her crying, saying, "it's my life" – and Christos thought, how much further can this go? One night she got out her photographs, which she kept in a box, examined them one by one, then began to shuffle them together, he asked her, "why, though?" but received no answer – as if she saw no reason to explain or hadn't heard him; the following day at noon, however, Christos got out the box and searched through it, as if some answer might lie hidden within it. At the beginning he found nothing, then he noticed that the photographs told the story of their life year by year, maybe this was a way for her of re-living it, an attempt to put things back in order, to set their life on an even basis once more, for she did indeed feel that everything had been overturned, that dissolution threatened. And the great hope, behind everything, was that Amalia would become calmer, that she would come back to the present, accept it, admit that, in some ways at least, the family is making progress, Dimitris has got a place at the Department of Chemistry and Antigone is preparing for her university entrance exams, our dad has found a comfortable job at the "Independent" and no longer gasps in his sleep, anyway, all the mourning weighs heavy on us, constricts us; once at dawn he enfolded her in his arms and spoke to her, but the woman said, "you're a man, you think differently and deceive yourself, you like consoling yourself" and it was as if she was making an accusation, for a moment she looked at him searchingly, how much had she hurt him? – "you work all night," she added, "you'd do better to get some sleep now, some peace."

But this was just a word; every night at the newspaper people were muttering about fearful, terrible things, the worst of all being that the guerrilla movement was growing, civil war yet once again where brother would kill brother. One night they came down and set fire to Litohoro and set up ambushes in the streets – he concealed it all as best he could from Amalia, but in the end he took Dimitris aside and spoke to him, "your mother mustn't be upset," he begged, "you're a man now, you understand me," the boy listened in silence, "be careful of yourself – and of your little sister," he added, it upset him that Dimitris didn't say anything, could it mean that he felt disapproval of his father? "These are evil times, don't forget what we've been through, what heavy burden we've had to bear," but his son still remained silent, maybe he wanted to speak but the subjects of their thoughts were ill assorted, they looked at each other again, "why don't you say anything?" challenged Christos, and the boy said, "they've killed the University stone dead," a year ago the corridors and quadrangle had been buzzing with discussion, now all was dumb, the corridors deserted. Dimitris seemed to be balancing on the fence, uncertain of what he would choose, where he would lean; he asked, "Father, which side are you on?"

He could have told him, everyone knows; he would never vote for the king, had abstained from voting at the last elections, "they killed Alcmene," he said, as if he needed to find support for his position. However, "we have to be careful," he added, and noticed that his son was frowning, but what does he expect? he thought – someone has to keep cool, someone has to lay himself open to the charge that he didn't dare, and who else if not the head of the family? It was something anyway that he worked nights in order to secure a livelihood for them – and went begging for them when it was necessary – something that he had gone hungry in the evening during the Occupation so that he could give them an extra mouthful; he felt bitter, "who recognises all that?" he asked, at which Dimitris was puzzled and said, "all what?" but Christos blocked these thoughts out, "take care," he simply advised. At the paper he would often listen as each man ran over the things that could be held against them; two of their own colleagues were without work because they had gone to appropriate the printing machinery – it was said that the old teacher, who now lived permanently bedridden, under the shadow of death, had given orders that these men should never set foot in the place again, and thus all their begging was in vain (and even their tears too), people told Christos, "you got off lightly," by which they meant that he had worked for the reds, the lessons for journalists given by the "Achtida", maybe also the business with Alcmene.

"Don't delude yourself, from now on we shall all have to drain the bitter cup," Mr. Aristos told him; he had aged and his skin had a sickly colour to it, every so often he would disappear into the lavatory and when he re-emerged his face would be wet, he'd be mopping himself, always with the same motion, with that white handkerchief of his which seemed boundless, he would sit for hours lost to the world, his pen poised in mid-air, a ghost of his past glories, his cuffs worn and his collars not matching his shirts. "I've heard that Euripides has committed suicide," he announced, totally out of the blue, "when? who told you?" – but the old man put his finger to his lips, "they're keeping it hushed up," he whispered, "but I knew that you knew him, had meetings with him, and that's why I'm trusting you with it" – something was burning on Christos's skin, something that was rising and swelling, suddenly his eyes seemed to be on fire, his elderly colleague had returned to sit at his desk, his pen was writing something, rising from the paper then stabbing it once more, as if he was only writing full stops or acute accents, and nothing else. Christos thought for a bit, hesitated, then went and bent over Mr. Aristos, "are you certain?" he asked – for Euripides was far away, on some remote barren island, and no one ever heard any news of him; the other man replied, "I'll tell you when we leave," which might have been some kind of reprieve, but no, "it's been confirmed," he added.

When they came out it was not yet dawn, the chill of the May night caressed them, above them stretched a starry expanse and round about them fragrance, three gendarmes stood at the bus stop and greeted them, Christos said, "they know us inside out." Right now, though, he didn't even care, "are you certain?" – and the other man said "yes". A host of questions sprang to his lips, however for each one of them there was an answer, no matter how much these answers involved meaningful shakes of the head or an emphatic tone of voice in the right places: yes, he'd received a bullet in the heart, yes, he'd been alone, though only for an hour, yes, the Communists knew of it (and the news had come from them), no, they didn't believe it was suicide, said that he had been "disposed of" by some foreign individuals, yes, he had disagreed with the second guerrilla movement, yes, they knew about it at the "Independent" and were keeping quiet about it, they'd been in contact with the Security Police ("from his bed", snorted Christos, "that old crock's been playing safe all his life"), who had advised them, "don't be in any haste over it." They got into the first tram as day was breaking, Aristos laughed meaningfully, "they say he had relations with the English" and it had the air of a question, maybe he meant you knew him, but the other man denied it, "it's out of the question." Through the open window came cooling air, but Aristos drew away from it, "I'm sensitive to draughts," he said and coughed.

When Christos was alone once more, he walked slowly and pondered, over Hortiatis the sky was lightening, he heard a single bird whose voice sounded like weeping, he reached his house and stood outside it, leaned inexplicably on the wall for support, all round him he saw a world deprived of shadows, in the end he tiptoed in, took off his clothes and lay down without making a sound – as if he was seeking quiet in which to think his thoughts and make his soul comfortable with the dead, whose number seemed to be ever increasing. Behind his closed eyelids a black vault expanded, against which pale sparks darted, beside him Amalia was stirring, but the man decided not to come out of the sphere, nor to break into it, outside he could hear the creaking of a cart, a horse's steps on the crushed stone suface of the road, up in front it bore Euripides, but he looked old, from the war in Asia Minor, he thought they got him too, he became aware of a grey cat licking herself at his feet she was as small as a rat so he flapped his hand to scare her away but she jumped up and grabbed it and hung on persistently he flapped his hand again but without effect he could feel her teeth piercing his flesh and he kept on flapping and flapping his hand until he heard a loud noise, "what is it?" Amalia was alarmed, and at the same moment he felt a sharp pain in his hand where he had hit it hard on the bedside table, "what is it?" asked his wife, and he said, "nothing, go back to sleep."

He tried desperately to get back to sleep but in vain; gradually he began to hear the morning sounds as daily life awoke once more in the street and in the house, doors opening and closing, water running, utensils, then a little later street vendors crying their wares, a girl laughing and singing "wherever you go ...", someone was hammering a sheet of metal, "... the blue sky" – he could see through the shutters that the sun was shining, but his eyes were sore from sleeplessness, he closed them again and felt relief and sighed. He got dressed and went out in a hurry, saying, "I'll be back soon" when he saw Amalia looking at him doubtfully, bought the morning papers and searched through them, not a word about Euripides, he thought to himself, maybe they want to forget him, he arrived at the main avenue and stopped, he felt a river within him, but thought, where does it lead? There was a hint of the smell of the sea, it would relieve him to sit beside it, in the little café, on a cane chair, to be gradually drenched by the salty air, a hope that would drug his anguish, the numbness that had started in his arms and was spreading frighteningly to his chest and to the base of his neck; he cleared his throat out of some instinct, it might relieve his breathing. A tram stopped in front of him, he jumped onto it, his mind was tricked by the images that changed and flashed past, shops and houses, lampposts, trees, two women who were laughing, their faces bright red, shops again, flowering courtyards, a convoy of military vehicles, at one moment, like a spelling mistake, a horse wandering by itself, with nothing on its back but only a scar on its hind leg, then the park and the Tower, the "Elysia" which announced, "Ali Baba and the Forty Thieves" in gold and green letters.

He jumped off the tram and walked, he could still catch the scent of the sea – some particularity of the day, he reflected – he searched for the mansion at the corner, in spite of the fact that he knew perfectly well where it was, and wondered, what should I do? But just then a girl came running by, crying as she ran, waving a newspaper in her hand, and Christos thought, where do I know her from? but she had passed him in an instant, she went into the mansion and disappeared, and he hurried in after her as if he was being pushed; he saw the marble staircase winding upwards, heard the girlish footsteps going up, a door upstairs opened and through it came wails and sobs, a man's voice saying, "it's over" and the sound of the door closing.* And Christos thought, I'd better go and, without realising how he'd got there, found himself once more in the main street, he felt that he'd suffered a blow to the centre of his brain, that only half of it or part of it was still functioning, and not the cleverest or the coolest part, but he walked to the tram stop, saw a midday paper, a photograph of Euripides, a headline confirmed it all, he saw the printed man in the peaked cap with the expression that he knew so well, both stern and laughing at the same time, and something in him kept on and on saying like a cracked gramophone record,

---

* In 1984 I was in that very same house, with the same girl, who was now a grown woman and who used to recall the general often, who bothers about finding out the truth, a vindication of Euripides. She has recorded a conversation that she had with a lady, the general's one and only (perhaps) love. The tape says in a deep, coquettish voice, "he was a brave man, a brave man" – somewhere an echo said, "my brave man". Apart from all the documentation, the evidence, she confirmed that Euripides played an honourable game, with his cards open, when he went to the Middle East, but also later, when he returned once more to Greek soil. He played with his cards open – and thus he lost the game or was cheated, in a lonely village, in St. Keryko. Later she recounted how they lived in Cairo, with the Venizelos and Tsouderos families, and she was once more the woman who had moved in high circles at crucial moments – and was proud of it.

they got him, they got him, they got him. He bought a newspaper and folded it without being aware of what he was doing, then stuffed it into his pocket; when he got back home he shouted, "they got him," threw the paper down onto the table, as if to say, here, but Amalia gazed at him without speaking, and in the end said as if in censure, "you forget our own troubles."

Angel

He lay huddled up and without appetite, he was saying, "let me not remember," for memory was painful, the hospital was a solution, maybe even his salvation, except that one day a captain came and prodded him all over, his belly, his ribs, then raised his eyebrows; "what are you taking all those medicines for?" he scolded, "they're no use to you at all," which might have been the truth, for now he had recovered from all his ailments and was dreading the following day, and the one after that, the two years during which he would have to go on being tormented. As his uncle used to tell him, "the army isn't fun and games," you didn't need to draw too much attention to yourself, "specially not you", stressed Stratis, for, as they had heard, Macronissos lay in wait for them, it was where they sent everyone who belonged to the Left, "just stay quiet in your own corner and don't get mixed up in anything," he remembered this advice; except that it didn't seem so easy to follow, specially not the first days at the camp, where they had them running night and day, their heads cropped, loaded with their equipment, a sight to cry over, where their sergeant was a dark-skinned little pint-sized man who roared at them, "you fuckers, you'd better forget all about your homes and your girlfriends" and made them run until they were well nigh bursting and collapsed. The young men from villages could have done without any further exhaustion, but they thought more of their homes, one of them burst into tears one night – and Angel said, "what have I got to forget?" since he didn't have a mother, nor did he live with his father.

He sat by himself in a corner, trying to feel that he still had arms and legs, but the straps and the webbing were cutting into him, he thought, I keep everything spick and span, even when they were drenched in the Thracian rain or trudging through the mud and getting filthy. They had sent him to a camp not far from Alexandroupolis, where the earth was fat and rich, a little way off lay a world of trees and birds, and occasionally a woman's skirt glimpsed through the mists that rose off the verdant land. Even when he ate he never spoke, often he went to bed without eating and would sigh, for his ribs and his back hurt; all the same, at dawn he was strong, loaded his equipment on his back, took his weapon and ran. Until one day his legs wouldn't help him, they felt as if they had weights on them, increasingly a torment, and then he crumpled to the ground as he ran, in his memory remained the impact of his body on some gravelled road, the way his shoulder scraped on the rough surface, the sound of his gun being dragged along; he tried to get up but collapsed once more, the sergeant screamed at him, "you soft little bastard, I'll kill you," the others slowed down and two or three of them stopped, but the sergeant shouted in fury, "keep running, you wankers" and went on blowing his whistle, as if from it would come some magic power that would get him onto his feet.

He remembered how they had taken hold of him from under the armpits and got him to his feet, tried to support him, to tidy him up, for his weapon and helmet had got out of place, and his flask, and it proved impossible to set them right, or his trousers either which had got twisted so that the crotch was bothering him; he remembered that the sky had suddenly darkened and it was about to rain, that in front of his face was the sergeant's mouth screaming, that he could smell something like garlic on his breath, and then that the blood seemed to be rising within him and spewing from his mouth, that he bathed the sergeant's face and shoulders with a yellow gruel and perhaps blood, at which someone was cursing fuck your mother, fuck your Christ, fuck your whole family – and that was the end. When next he was able to hear or to feel anything he was in a white world, white ceiling, walls, sheets, and in a little while a middle-aged woman in a white coat was telling him, "don't move" and was pouring into him a pure white liquid with the consistency of mud, telling him, "you're delicate" with a heavy accent. However, she straightened his bedclothes and then embraced him, though without meaning to, and put her hand on his forehead; he enjoyed it and floated off and heard only a buzzing sound, as if bees were lulling him to sleep – but then they disappeared, the days and nights all ran together, he could not tell how many had passed, the nurse said look at my thighs but they were crippled and twisted around his legs she seemed to be wearing make-up and beautiful and he lay with her and she showed him a hole like a wound but in the wrong place on the upper part of her buttock which was pure white and she said here is where you must put it and he felt soaking wet.

They kept him there for thirty days, they fed him and watered him and, in the end, he got two weeks' leave. As he was leaving for Thessaloniki, the others said, "you've had a lucky escape," that somewhere they'd found his name, on a register, the captain called him and swore at him, "when you get back we'll settle accounts," he threatened, he was wearing an ancient cap and his tunic was always unbuttoned, he looked at Angel with the eyes of a wild cat, "we sent you to hospital and got you cured," he muttered; what he probably meant was we'd have done better to leave you to die in a ditch. When he got his leave order he breathed again, he walked to the station slowly, because he had plenty of time; he was thinking that his pockets were empty, his only supplies a piece of army bread, some cheese and a tin of meat – at the bottom of his kit bag were his pills, which he was always forgetting to take. The air was strangely damp, the sun could sometimes be glimpsed here and there but it looked yellow and sickly, and in the afternoon it disappeared for good, the ground was damp even though it hadn't rained, he crossed a playing field overgrown with weeds, enjoyed trampling on them and crushing them, in the distance he saw two trees whose leaves were rose-pink, like paintings, he remembered once again that he was penniless and swore.

By the time he was sitting in the train he seemed calmer, maybe feeling reassured that he'd found a place of refuge, that he wouldn't be standing in some corner waiting for them to come and get him; possibly the fact that he was on his way home had something to do with it, to his grandmother Myrsine, who must certainly have been missing him, for a few days they would pamper him, they'd surely give him a bit of money, for he was a man now and they'd understand his needs. And he felt even calmer when other people got in and sat near him, an old couple and a woman with a child, they filled the place with baskets and bundles, a smell of henhouses wafted to his nostrils – and just as the train was jolting and beginning to move, a soldier came in, a soldier with his weapon and all his equipment and his baggage, red in the face and covered in sweat. Before long they were all enveloped in semi-darkness and Angel kept staring out of the window at the plain which was gradually disappearing, the trees which were turning the deepest of blacks, an occasional hut here and there which you felt would sink into the water, as if all these things were merely the peelings left over as nature collapsed; in the end there was nothing but inky black chaos in which dark masses could only be guessed at. An anaemic light bulb was turned on, under which everyone's face was dyed pallid – consisting of shadows mostly – their noses, their cheeks and chins.

Gradually bodies and mouths relaxed and the soldier freed himself of his weapon, unbuttoned, "you, mate, where are you heading?" – Angel answered, "on leave", and the old woman then started investigating her nosebag, she pulled out a package wrapped in a handkerchief, unknotted it carefully and got out half a loaf of bread, cheese and olives and two onions, which she cut up and offered round, and she was serious about it as if performing some ritual; however Angel refused, he pointed to indicate he had something wrong with his stomach, and she didn't insist, the woman also said "no" and smiled, the soldier accepted though and began chewing. The old man ate slowly and in silence, maybe he had problems with his teeth or didn't have any, Angel remembered Myrsine, he watched the old woman who kept on giving food to her husband, pushing him as if she was forcing him to eat, while he closed his eyes and shook his head, but she continued the same way until she persuaded him, and then the scene was repeated, as if they were acting in a pantomime – "Grandad, your old woman loves you," said the other woman laughing, but the old woman looked at her and scowled, and Myrsine was fanning Angel again, something suggested to him that women stay stronger and can withstand more. The whole world had shrunk to this single ill-lit carriage, they almost forgot that it was speeding along, except that at one point the soldier said, "we'll be leaving the plain any minute now and starting the climb into the mountains," and Angel wondered how he could see, he looked like a peasant, like a hunting dog, "the guerrillas may have set an ambush for us," he was speaking again, but the old woman said, "don't go looking for trouble," and he gave a meaningful smile, with a spark in his eye as if he was proud that he knew of such things and maybe disregarded them – "and you, mate, what do you think?" – but Angel wouldn't be drawn, "I've been in hospital for a month," he answered; the other people gave him a good look and were silent. Later the old woman searched in her bag, offered him an egg, and advised, "you need to eat well and get your strength back."

The train had apparently lulled them all to sleep, with its swaying and the rhythm of its wheels; and when Angel became conscious once more and sighed he saw that he was alone with the old couple, the man said, "you slept a long time," and indeed the world of nature outside was now lit, mainly by an orange line like a rent in the clouds, "the others all got off at Serres" – so Salonica must be not far off, they might be there before noon. The old people began to eat once more and the same old comedy was acted out, he refusing yet always being persuaded – and Angel thought, they might have been doing this all their lives. Outside the world was grey green, the trees hanging in the rain, at rare intervals a cart could be seen, the people in it hunched, nothing but backbones, hoping for a bit of sun. However, they found the sun somewhere else – Angel and the other passengers in the train – for at midday the sky cleared and the greenery shone strangely, further off lay the mountains, and elsewhere houses; he felt that he recognised this plain, a secret voice told him that he had walked it then, in '45, when they had abandoned Salonica and had wandered from village to village and from city to city, and would gather together and talk loudly or sing, to avoid falling into defeatism or despair.

But now it was a different season, Angel smelt a different scent, which in the end he decided was of trains and factories, for they were passing through Harmankioi, then after a bit between humble little houses and orchards, garages and old railway carriages burnt and disintegrating. The old couple tied up their nosebags and buttoned their coats, "where are you going to?" asked

Angel, feeling that he ought to help them, but the old man said, "our children will be meeting us" and indeed they were standing there, laughing and waving, a rosy-red girl with her husband beside her. The old woman told him, "mind and get your strength back," as Angel watched them get down onto the platform and they were running and kissing them. And in a way he did follow her advice, or else this was the way it was fated to be, since Angel didn't leave the house at all for six days, but lay the whole time in a darkened room, begging Myrsine not to open the windows at all and the door as little as possible, and ruminating on his own thoughts, his fears, that the people in the world outside might be hostile or certainly unpleasant, and he was unmoved by either Stratis's sarcasms or Myrsine's pleadings or his cousin's company. And it was only on one evening – he was due to leave the next day at noon – that he attempted a walk in the neighbourhood, round the enclosure with the ancient trees, and then a little further, along a road that caused him pain, that had remained a bleeding wound, for so many months now, the road that he knew so well, mainly knew where it ended, which trees offered the deepest shade, which doorways could conceal him. And indeed he stood in a shade that was deep and bound and rooted, and he comforted himself with the thought, I am in disguise and unrecognisable, with greedy insistent eyes that suddenly were full of longing and were stinging, as the figure of a woman emerged from the darkness, out of that particular door, and was approaching where he was – and he thought, I'll climb up the tree, into the dense foliage, and he neither breathed nor spoke even when the woman came unhesitatingly and stood in front of him, Amalia like an apparition in black, who spoke and said, "get out of here, devil," but Angel put out his hands, begged, "don't be angry," and he was burning, "I'm sorry," he stammered, "I'm sorry, Mother," but the woman raised her hand and slapped him and cried, "never let me set eyes on you again." And as he left, whipped and beaten, he imagined that another figure, also female, was coming hesitantly towards him.

And as he watched the familiar landmarks disappearing, one after the other, he considered that this second journey would be worse, specially because he remembered the captain, and his threats, knew that a time of trial was once more at hand, they might put him aboard a ship for Macronissos, and he'd asked and had learned about the punishment block there, where anything at all could happen, even to the point of madness; and every so often the previous night's episode stung him, he remembered Amalia's burning feverishness, her face that had looked utterly hard, her hand that had left a vivid imprint on his memory, more from the unexpectedness of the action than from the pain. And he sat there trapped between a painful memory and the web of tomorrow's terrors – or, at best, those of the day after tomorrow – and thus noticed nothing around him, couldn't even listen properly, for once more there were people around him talking, laughing and eating, one of them was telling stories about the first war, and a woman said, "let's just concentrate on getting back to our fields, and forget all that past history." And after a while everything was once more sucked into darkness, except for the Furies who were tormenting Angel, squeezing his chest and destroying his ability to think, leaving only the torments to survive, and he begged, let me go to sleep and escape from them, and he huddled up in his seat, in the semi-darkness, focusing his mind on the rhythm of the train, which now could be heard more clearly as gradually the conversations around him died down. And this rhythmic beating of wheels and rails might be an antidote, a drug against insomnia, like the little rhymes which Myrsine used to teach him when he was a small child, little rhymes about saints and crosses, which would drive away the terrors of the thunder or the black man, which insisted that "Jesus Christ conquers all ...", even if outside there was a wall of darkness, made of some malleable material through which the train passed, something fluid which parted to let them through, then closed again behind them.

Suddenly (was he asleep? was he awake?) sound died or his ears were blocked, and then came a deafening noise, as if a pit was yawning between his ears and behind his palate, and at the same time someone was giving Angel a hard shove, as if he'd been caught by a wave which was casting him up, in the end he realised that people were hitting him on the chest, wildly – from the background came shouts and repeated machine-gun fire. The train seemed dead, and shots rang out once more, now almost between their ears – most people had fallen face down on the floor, a voice told him, "keep away from the window," however this was to prove pointless, for the doors opened and two men rushed into the carriage shouting, "everyone out," one was shooting over their heads and riddling the ceiling with bullets, "get out," they ordered again, "the train is going to be blown up"; and everyone then surged towards the door and poured out. Angel was one of the last to leave, but when he stepped down onto the ground he started, realised that the ground was icy cold and he was barefoot, that at some point he must have taken off his boots – without being aware of it – and he had to go back and get them, but an armed man grabbed hold of him and shoved him away, "where are you off to, you bold fellow?" he shouted, and threatened him with his gun, and Angel recognised that he was stumbling, maybe he had put his hands up, for certain he was going to be tormented yet again. However he had no time to act or think, for all the passengers were huddled together and surrounded, a girl was crying hysterically and pulling at him, while he himself was trying not to crumple up, to preserve some air in his lungs and keep breathing.

Very soon they had been divided into two groups, and it was discovered that quite a few soldiers had been travelling on the train, and two men with stars, Angel felt that people were talking to him, "let's tell them that we were unfit for active service," and he turned and looked round, beside him was a short little man, white as a sheet, "I'm afraid they might be going to cut us down," he muttered – and Angel thought to himself that the man couldn't be from these parts; then they were divided again, officers to one side, soldiers to another. The train was standing there, on the brink of a small ravine, the bridge blown up; the place was treeless, you could make out only bushes, further off the black mass of a hill, in front of him a broad slope. They stood there trembling, only the voices of the armed men could be heard, until in the end a man on horseback came up and said like a slap, "what are you waiting for?" which meant that they had to move, to leave – the soldiers went in front, behind them a few young men in civilian clothes and all around them armed men, just as if they were driving a flock of sheep. Angel was frightened, they may be going to butcher us a little further off, his feet hurt so much that he realised he would very soon be collapsing, for the ground further up was impassable – for him – as it was covered by scrub oak and other prickly bushes; and it didn't take much longer before the worst happened and Angel tottered and found himself embracing scrub and thorns, whose scratches hurt his face and he moaned. And it was no comfort when he was grasped under the armpits and pulled up, and someone hissed in his ear, "get a move on," and then, "you're making trouble, mate," as they realised that such obstacles were not in their interest.

However, no amount of begging did them any good, and in the end he fell on his knees and gave in, "kill me," he said and bowed his head, but an armed man came up beside him, grabbed him by his collar and pulled him up, mocked, "Queen Frederica's little lap-dog", but it was a woman's voice, low, she got hold of him, almost dragged him, and Angel felt her body – later he was to say that he smelt it – and felt shamed. They walked on for a bit (or were dragged) and suddenly she stopped, the young man felt a shadow over them and could smell the horse, which whinnied but passed them, the armed woman sat down, he standing like a bent tree, then she pulled off her boots, "take these, damn you," she said and gave them to him. The young man screamed "no" though, and felt like crying, at the insult, but the woman was not going to wait, was not allowed to, she threw them down at his feet and ordered, "get on with it" but she gazed at him as if examining him, "I'm wearing my thick socks, they'll protect me," she explained. They walked until dawn, with the woman behind him; and before daylight came, before anyone could see them, they made their way into a wood and went to roost, Angel dumb and speechless, the others looking at him and smiling, as if they had definitely got away with their lives. And then they fell asleep and slept like the dead.

You walk along the street, you see familiar windows, you remember. The little house where Christos used to live with his three children is still there, except that two more storeys have been added to it and it has turned into an abortion of a building. Of the whole family the only one still alive is Dimitris, who works for a newspaper, is up at night and remembers his father, all his torments. Antigone now walks in heaven. A little bit further down, like an immortal ruin, lies the tall house that once belonged to Elias, his family now also gone. The "dandy" and one of his brothers hijacked a plane and disappeared, their mother is plunged deep into old age and (as people say) loss of memory. Angel and I telephone each other from time to time; he went through a lot, in the mountains and later in penal servitude, in Albania, in Serbia; he is now a family man, an accountant, he still suffers from his liver, he is an enthusiastic football fan. Angela and Yannis no longer exist, but they have left behind them a whole kingdom, with colonies and descendants. However the fate of all these characters could one day form another book, perhaps one that might decode them, where words like "preoccupation" or "compromise", "peeling back", "redemption", "wandering" might leave deep traces, like stones thrown with force into the mud, making wounds in it.

TRANSLATOR'S NOTE

The following is a very brief – and necessarily highly simplified – summary of the main political events that form the background to this novel.

Following the crushing defeat of the Greek Army in Asia Minor in August 1922, the Treaty of Lausanne stipulated an obligatory exchange of populations between Greece and Turkey, with a resulting influx of approximately one and a half million Greek refugees from Anatolia into Greece.

During the years that followed, the antagonism between Royalists and Venizelists (Republicans) was intense; the army remained an active participant on the political scene and a series of military coups took place, including – in March 1935 – an attempted revolution (promptly suppressed) by a part of the army still strongly Republican.

In May 1936 a general strike in Thessaloniki was suppressed with great brutality. On the 4th of August 1936, the Prime Minister and former General Ioannis Metaxas proclaimed martial law and suspended the constitution. With the support of the Crown a dictatorship effectively took over the country, employing the classic totalitarian mechanisms of control: censorship of the press, the suppression of the trade union movement, a paramilitary youth organization (EON), and so on.

On October 28th 1940 Mussolini issued an ultimatum to Greece and, without waiting for an answer to it, ordered Italian troops to cross from Albania into Greece. By the end of the year the Greeks had succeeded in forcing the Italians to retreat well back into Albanian territory.

In April 1941 the Germans attacked Greece from Yugoslavia and Bulgaria; by May the whole country was occupied. The National Liberation Front (EAM) was created by collaboration of the Communist Party with other smaller democratic parties in order to resist the German Occupation; under its auspices a People's Liberation Army (ELAS – whose resistance activities were at this point supported by Britain) came into being. The authority of EAM-ELAS was unchallenged throughout most of the countryside which, by 1943, they largely controlled. The influence of other resistance organizations was more local. By this time the King had set up a government-in-exile in Egypt; in April 1944 George Papandreou assumed its premiership. During the German Occupation well-armed groups of collaborators formed "Security Battalions".

As in the other countries of occupied Europe, so in Greece too the Germans deported the Jewish population to concentration camps. The Jewish community that flourished in Thessaloniki before the war was reduced to a small fraction of its former size.

In October 1944 the Germans evacuated Athens and a few days later a British Expeditionary Force under General Scobie entered the city. Later in the year negotiations between EAM (no longer supported by Britain) and Papandreou regarding the transfer of power from the guerrillas to the central government broke down. When a mass demonstration was held in Athens on 3 December 1944 firing broke out and scores of unarmed men and women were killed or injured. More died the following day, 4 December, when EAM called a general strike and mass rally whose demonstrators were attacked by an ultra right-wing organization. Scobie declared martial law. An armed struggle broke out in Athens between ELAS on the one hand and the British forces together with the Greek brigade from the Middle East on the other. In February 1945 an agreement was signed at Varkiza between EAM, the British and the government of Nicholas Plastiras (the new Prime Minister) by which, among other things, all the guerrilla units were to be disbanded and ELAS was to surrender its arms. Several Communist ELAS groups refused to accept this agreement and, as persecution from the extreme right began once more to make itself felt, took to the mountains again. Right-wing extremists, many of whom had been armed by the Germans and had collaborated with them, allied themselves with the security forces. Between 1946 and 1949 Greece was riven by a bloody civil war.

NIKOS BAKOLAS

Nikos Bakolas was born in Thessaloniki in 1927. He studied mathematics at Thessaloniki University, and also English. He worked for many years as a journalist and theatre critic and was twice Artistic Director of the State Theatre of Northern Greece (1980-1982 and 1990-1993), as well as being the Manager of the State Television ET-3 (Thessaloniki) for a short period. He is a member of numerous Greek artistic societies and institutions.

Crossroads, published in Greek under the title of *The Great Square* in 1987, won the Greek National Book Award. Nikos Bakolas's other works include *Don't Cry, Sweetheart* (1958), *The Garden of the Princes* (1966), *Military Marches* (1972), *Mortal Sleep* (1974), *Mythology* (1977, winner of the Plotin Award), *Trespass* (1990), *The Head* (1994), *The Hurting Journey* (1995), and *The Endless Writ of Blood* (1996, one of the Greek nominations for the "Aristeion" European Literary Prize).

He has translated into Greek novels by Faulkner (*The Sound and the Fury, A Rose for Emily*), Scott Fitzgerald (*The Great Gatsby*) and Henry James (*The Turn of the Screw*). Several of his own novels and short stories have been published in English, German, French, Dutch and Swedish translations.

CAROLINE HARBOURI

Caroline Harbouri was born in London and educated at Cambridge University, where she studied English and French. Since 1970 she has made her home in Athens.

LIST OF TITLES IN
THE "MODERN GREEK WRITERS" SERIES

PETROS ABATZOGLOU   *What does Mrs. Freeman want*
   Novel.   Translated by Kay Cicellis

ARIS ALEXANDROU   *Mission Box*
   Novel.   Translated by Robert Crist

NIKOS BAKOLAS   *Crossroads*
   Novel.   Translated by Caroline Harbouri

SOTIRIS DIMITRIOU   *Woof, Woof, Dear Lord*
   Short Stories.   Translated by Leo Marshall

MARO DOUKA   *Fool's Gold*
   Novel.   Translated by Roderick Beaton

EUGENIA FAKINOU   *Astradeni*
   Novel.   Translated by H. E. Criton

ANDREAS FRANGHIAS   *The Courtyard*
   Novel.   Translated by Martin McKinsey

COSTIS GIMOSOULIS   *Her Night on Red*
   Novel.   Translated by Philip Ramp

MARIOS HAKKAS *Heroes' Shrine for Sale or the Elegant Toilet*
Short Stories. Translated by Amy Mims

GIORGOS HEIMONAS *The Builders*
Novel.   Translated by Robert Crist

YORGOS IOANNOU *Good Friday Vigil*
Short Stories.   Translated by Peter Mackridge and Jackie Willcox

YORGOS IOANNOU *Refugee Capital*
Thessaloniki Chronicles.   Translated by Fred A. Reed

IAKOVOS KAMBANELLIS *Mauthausen*
Chronicle.   Translated by Gail Holst-Warhaft

NIKOS KOKANTZIS *Gioconda*
Novel.   Translated by the author

ALEXANDROS KOTZIAS *Jaguar*
Novel.   Translated by H.E. Criton

MENIS KOUMANDAREAS *Koula*
Novel.   Translated by Kay Cicellis

MARGARITA LIBERAKI *Three Summers*
Novel.   Translated by Karen Van Dyck

GIORGOS MANIOTIS *Two Thrillers*
Translated by Nicholas Kostis

CHRISTOFOROS MILIONIS *Kalamás and Achéron*
Short Stories.   Translated by Marjorie Chambers

COSTOULA MITROPOULOU *The Old Curiosity Shop on Tsimiski Street*
Novel.   Translated by Elly Petrides

KOSTAS MOURSELAS   *Red Dyed Hair*
Novel.   Translated by Fred A. Reed

ARISTOTELIS NIKOLAIDIS   *Vanishing-point*
Novel.   Translated by John Leatham

ALEXIS PANSELINOS   *Betsy Lost*
Novel.   Translated by Caroline Harbouri

NIKOS-GABRIEL PENTZIKIS   *Mother Salonika*
Translated by Leo Marshall

SPYROS PLASKOVITIS   *The Façade Lady of Corfu*
Novel.   Translated by Amy Mims

VANGELIS RAPTOPOULOS   *The Cicadas*
Novel.   Translated by Fred A. Reed

YANNIS RITSOS   *Iconostasis of Anonymous Saints*
Novel (?)   Translated by Amy Mims

ARIS SFAKIANAKIS   *The Emptiness Beyond*
Novel.   Translated by Caroline Harbouri

DIDO SOTIRIOU   *Farewell Anatolia*
Novel.   Translated by Fred A. Reed

STRATIS TSIRKAS   *Drifting Cities*
A Trilogy.   Translated by Kay Cicellis

ALKI ZEI   *Achilles' fiancée*
Novel.   Translated by Gail Holst-Warhaft